Book 1

The Gateway Series

# Brittany Dixon

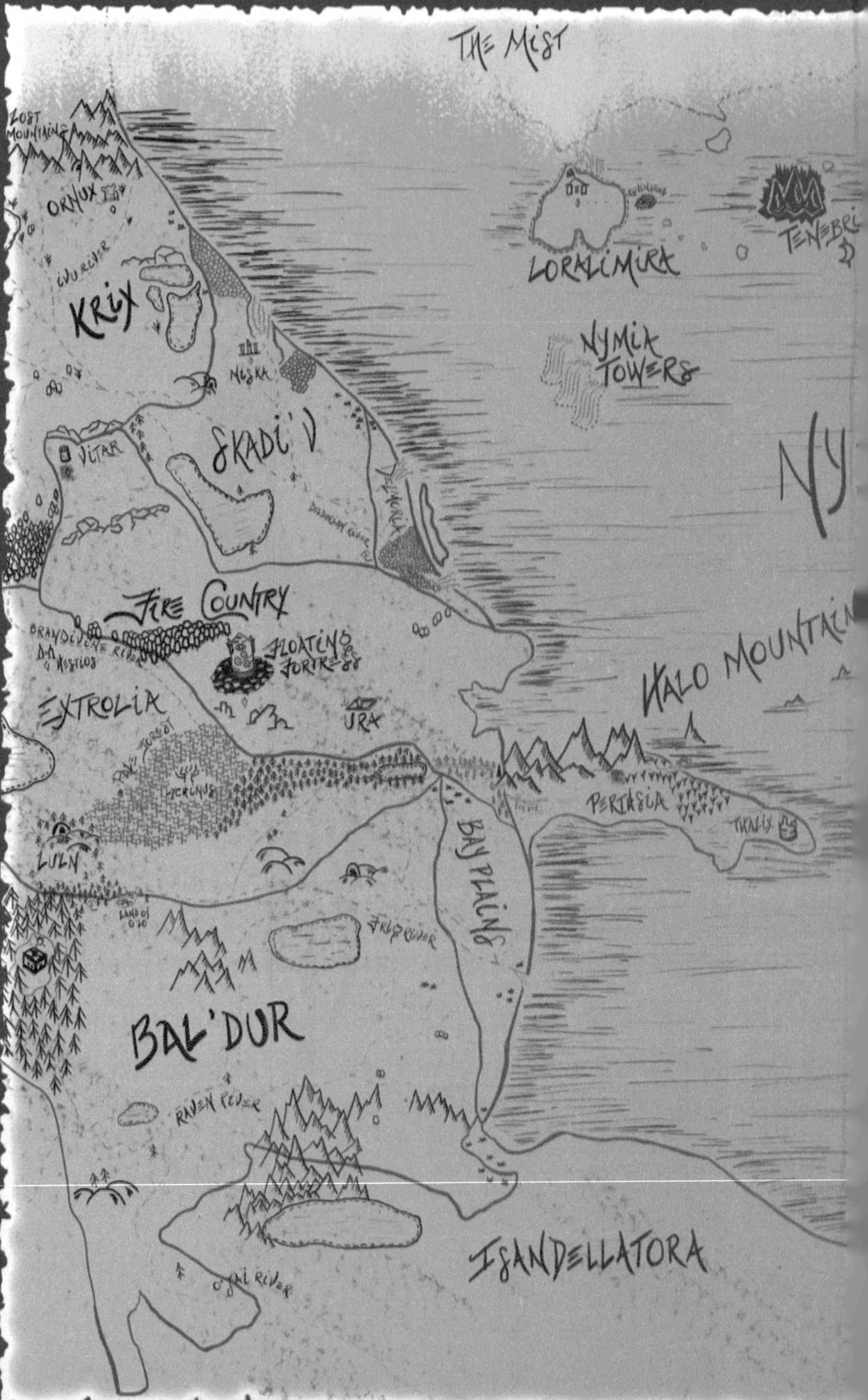
THE MIST
LOST MOUNTAINS
ORNUX
KRIX
NESKA
LORALIMIRA
TENEBRI
NYMIA TOWERS
SKADI'V
VITAR
NY
FIRE COUNTRY
FLOATING FORTRESS
EXTROLIA
URA
KALO MOUNTAIN
PERTASIA
LULN
BAY PLAINS
BAL'DUR
RAVEN RIVER
ISANDELLATORA

# Atlastova

N

W      =

S

AQELWENA

KEELN LEIT

A'REU TALIK

IDRAZOK

JUELCO

JE VEIN

## "THE MIDLANDS"

| | |
|---|---|
| M mountains | Immortal Realm border |
| lakes | giants |
| Cave | rivers |
| hills | trees |
| rocks | swamp |
| MR faery tree | antro-dwarf town |
| IR faery tree | Waterfall |
| Mora's Sanctuary | gorge |
| | Ekklips' symbol |

# ⊹Prononunications⊱

## *Ethnicities:*

Glodians: GLOW-dē-an-s
Cau'o'tas: kaw-OH-tas
Piquonese: pē-kwon-eeze
Xyrons: ZIE-rons
Coutarian: coo-TAR-ee-an

## *Locations:*

Atlastova: at-las-TOH-vah
Bal'dur: ball doo-er
Extrolia: ex-troll-EE-ah
Borgoria: bor-GOR-ee-ah
Lychinus: LIE-see-noos
Lucynith: lew-sign-nēth
Vitar: vē-tar
Deldurian: del-DOO-ri-an
Demurian: de-MAW-rē-an
Loralimira: lorah-ly-mērah
Nymian: neh-ME-an

Nymia: neh-my-AH
Tenebris: ten-EH-breh-s
Qailuena: KEH-lew-en-ah
Hestios: hes-TEE-ōs
Niska: nēs-kah
Ornux: ORN-uh-x

# ⊹ Pronunications ⊹

## Names:

Meridan: meh-REH-duhn
Nephani: NEH-fan-ee
Dresden: drehz-DEN
Glodians: GLOW-dē-an-s
Marwen: mar-when
Bogheim: bog-HEE-m
Cau'o'tas: kaw-OH-tas
Piquonese: pē-kwon-eeze
Virtoc: VEER-tok
Veridian: VER-eh-dee-in
Guilderon: g-EEL-dur-on
Xyrons: ZIE-rons
Coutarian: coo-TAR-ee-an
Alidyah: AH-lē-dē-ah
Didac: DIE-dak
Draelia: dray-lē-ah
Ura-Ca: OO-ra-kah
Ca-Dul: Cah-DOOL
Dierdan: dē-AIR-din
Gornya: GORN-ye-ah
Solienne: SOL-ee-in
Hepshig: Heh-p-sh-ēg
Esos: EE-sohs
Aiy'Anna: EYE ah-na
Yaw'Ren: YAH reen

# ⊁Pronunications⊱

### *Words & Phrases:*

*i'mun luex* (my light): EE moon lew
*i'mun dai* (my precious): EE moon day
*Cuthos* (The Keeper): COOth-Ōs
*Dundi fra* (Take flight)*: doon-dē frah*
*Athon'mi* (Welcome): Ā-thōn mee
*cun'ta* (loose female): COON ta
*Av'mycav* (Good tidings): ahv my-cahv
*val resurgimus* (I will prevail)*: VAL rā-sur-geh-muh-s*
*O'thensh' t'* (Reveal your intentions): Ō tehn-sh t
*linas'ta* (my innocent): leh-nah-s tah
*Antro incolenthium* (cavern dwellers): an-tro in-cowl-en-thee-um
*O'curem y'teruo* (We will meet again)*: Ō coo-rim Ē tour-ee-oh*
*Linthel ro, cartileron, fraethlin* (Oh Spirits, release, friends)*: len-TĒL roh, car-THĒL-air-on, fray-th-LĒ-n*

# Table of Contents

Thank you to those who have trudged with me on my 14-year journey to create the first glance into Mora's world. I dedicate this series to my strong family, my spirited childlings, and my dearest friends. But most of all, to the little girl who was so captivated by the fantasy stories filling her imagination, she spilt the images into words with such ferocity, it would put the Falls of Loralimira to shame. It is truly a magical adventure to open the gateway into the world of Atlastova to *All*.

### The Keeper

She dreamt it again last night. This time, the cold metal kissed the nape of her neck. She could feel the hard, rhythmic beating of her heart while her blood rushed like fire through her veins, her sweat undulating toward her breasts as she took deep, meditative breaths. *Is this it?* She sighed deeply, *Please purge me of my sins and forgive me of my relentless attempts to carry this burden alone. I am no hero. I am no sorceress. I am no savior. I am merely Mora, daughter of Meridan. For thousands of centuries, Creaturality has yearned to possess the knowledge I hold, while millions have died to capture a glimpse of the mystery behind my eyes. I fear I have nothing left. Greed, denial, and temptation have betrayed my trustful nature. I am alone in my quest until the day my mind is released from this prison of flesh.*

# *Beyond the Curtain*

 "Mora!" her mother cried from outside of the bathhouse.

Mora opened her eyes. The first rays of sun seeped through the closed, wooden shutters of the small opening across her bedroom. It was morning.

"Mora!" her mother yelled again in a rigid tone, hinting at a strained, yet calm, sincerity.

Throwing the covers to one side, the icy, thick air stung her unadjusted skin, sending a wave of tiny bumps down her body. She pulled herself out of the warm, hay coverlet, grabbed her tunic, and scrambled to pull it tightly over her shift. Before she rushed out of the door, she threw a wool shawl over her shoulders, crossed the ends around her upper body, and tied it in the back. The ground nipped at her feet as she scrambled over the cold, stone floors, following the distant light to the back doorway leading out to the bathhouse.

In silent haste, she reached the threshold. Stopping short, she glanced nervously at her mother. Not settled more than three footfalls away, was a distinctly strange serpent. The scales were immensely dark, appearing indigo as the light danced over the cylindrical backside. Flush against its scaly skin were wings like a bat, but longer and more narrow. Her mother stood stone still as if entranced with horror. There was an overwhelming fear in her eyes. Afraid any sudden movement would cause the serpent to snap, releasing a furious energy of venom directly toward her mother, she hesitated to utter a word.

Then, she watched in horror as her mother shifted quickly, causing the serpent to release a vile substance close to her feet. It was a warning. Eyeing her mother, she saw a slight nod in return. Stealthily, Mora released the curtain of the doorway to conceal her actions and reached cautiously for her bow and arrow centered above on the head of the door. Once again, opening the curtain ever so slightly, so as to not alarm the serpent, she aimed the arrow at the large reptilian head. Taking a few deep breaths to calm her nerves, she mentally prepared to shoot. However, suddenly, the serpent raised its head and turned in her direction. She froze as its piercing eyes coaxed her own, locking their gazes. She could not look away, frozen in a vulnerable, icy stare. Never wavering, the onyx eyes stilled her breathing as a growing weightiness delved inside her soul, searching for something deeply hidden. Feeling horribly exposed, she watched its eyes begin to transition, radiating an intensity which burned brighter through blood red slits. After a moment, with their gazes locked, she started to sense it was...*laughing*?

Although she attempted to avert her eyes, the gaze held firm. She was its captive while a helpless sensation melted over her flesh. However, a sudden, desperate burst of denial raged in her mind. Severing the bond, she furiously released the arrow, sending it flying directly at her target. As if the serpent knew, it had already slithered away, the black, iridescent scales reflecting like flashes of lightning into the dark, wild forest. Her arrow was left grounded in the dirt where the serpent had once been.

Mora looked at her mother. "Are you all right?" she asked worriedly, her chest heaving fiercely, as though the weight of a boulder had been lifted. She dare not move past the threshold. Her feet were solidly attached to the floor.

Her mother turned warily toward the forest, her tone hinting at both fear and sadness, "We must leave."

"Leave?" Mora was horribly overwhelmed with the emotion of fear, the sudden suggestion felt completely illogical. Shuddering, all she could think about was the imprint left by the serpent's eyes in her mind. The image would be eternally burned as a warning, an omen. She shuddered. Gazing into the forest beyond, she breathed deeply and asked, "Why must we scurry like small mice into a dark corner? Serpents feed off mice. The chase will only entice its thirst to devour the fleeing prey."

## *The Keeper*

Meridan turned toward her daughter, an apparent darkness growing inside her light green eyes. "I fear this is no normal predator. It is an omen."

As she languidly proceeded back to her small, personal area in their stonewalled dwelling, Mora thought back on her life. She was educated solely by her mother, Meridan, who taught her to read and write. She possessed manuscripts and books from far-off places she only could dream about, conjuring an insatiable longing in her heart for adventure. How her mother came to possess them was beyond her comprehension. When asked, she merely waved a hand in dismissal.

On warm days, they would walk along the forest edge, discussing the current study topic of the day, many of which coaxed Mora to inquire more questions about the surrounding forest and the creatures who dwelled within. Her mother would answer through elaborate descriptions of experienced knowledge; knowledge Mora yearned for desperately, and experience she could only encounter in dreams. She taught her to track animals; explaining what parts were good to eat and how the other parts could be used for making tools or clothing. She mastered the bow and arrow on large stags at the forest edge, feasting in celebration the following night. Her mother would train her on the complexities of sword fighting, disarming her on countless occasions, and even drawing blood. It was during the aftermath when she would teach her the ways of doctoring various wounds, including rubbing itchy leaves upon her skin and letting them fester with irritation before concocting balms and ointments to treat the rashes. Then, when the sun disappeared over the surrounding trees, her mother would teach her the constellations and navigation techniques; explaining how one can always find their way if they look to the celestial bodies.

On cold days, they would sit together by the fire in the cottage, baring the door from the bone chilling air with a shield of layered wood her mother had tied together with animal hair. She would teach Mora how to read and make medicinal remedies from accessible plants and left over animal parts. It was during these quiet times she quickly learned to sharpen a blade and start a fire using the smallest of rocks.

She always had the faintest feelings throughout her life she was being trained and molded for an unknown task. Although, every time she inquired, her mother would simply respond she wanted Mora to be prepared for what may come lest she ever not be around. That created knots in her stomach, especially as a small childling. She remembered thinking she could never live without her mother. She believed her mother possessed an immortal quality, a sentient feeling she never would abandon her only daughter.

Then, Mora distinctly remembered one evening, when she was young, a tale her mother told her about a brave warrior. He had been a male of great stature and wealth who was given the daunting task of destroying the most fiercest of beings known to creaturals, The Faceless One. The Faceless One was a monster of extreme manipulation, which would transform into the desire that would weaken you the most.

One day, as the brave warrior was camping, closing in on where he believed The Faceless One could be found, he saw a beautiful female walking through the woods. Being a bold male, he followed the female, yelling out to her despite her indifference to his obvious presence. She took no heed to his calls and kept walking until she reached the edge of a pool of water, bent down, and took a sip with cupped hands. She proceeded to remove her garments, step into the water, and walk gracefully until it pooled around her waist. Cautiously, he crept up behind her, staying hidden in the shadows as he watched her bathe in the moonlight. Being a warrior of great stature, he felt confident she would do as he commanded if he were to reveal himself. However, as he walked closer to the edge of the water, a growing anxiety commenced to stir and vibrate in the pit of his stomach. As if sensing his presence, she turned her head and smiled timidly, neither in modesty, nor humility, but in seduction. He was entranced in her beauty and slowly placed the weapons from around his garments on the ground, transfixed deeply in her beautiful dark eyes which contrasted fiercely with the smooth, crystal skin and radiant gold hair. He removed his breeches and tunic, setting them on a rock at the edge of the water. Slowly, he stepped into the pool, embraced her warm body, and felt the heat rising through his skin as he kissed her lips, the swell of his malehood on the brink of pain.

When his fellowship awoke the next morning, eager to start their journey, the warrior was nowhere to be found around the camp. The company searched for half a day until one discovered his body, face down on the edge of the pool, with bloodied water lapping against his exposed flesh. They quickly retrieved his body, turned him over onto his back, and were horror struck at the gruesome sight, for the warrior's face was no more. This once strong, great being had fallen victim to the clutches of The Faceless One.

Of course, Mora knew her mother told her the stories to frighten her from journeying outside of the parameters around the dwelling when she was a childling. For the past five and twenty name days, it felt as though they lived on the far side of the world. Many years she believed if she walked across the forest wall, she would fall off into the void that contained the stars. However, deep in her heart, she knew there was more beyond the bubble they inhabited, the books and maps told her of foreign names and distant stories she could only imagine in her limited exposure. A small flame of desire burned inside her core like the first, brightest star in the evening sky, and she hoped to one day discover what called to her outside of the sanctuary.

One day, she asked if they could walk through the forest a short distance to see what lay beyond. Although the answer was always the same, '*You are not ready. The time has not come*', it did not discourage her from inquiring to the brink of annoyance. Despite the respect she held for her mother, Mora felt secluded and irritated at the way she kept her aloft of their *purpose* for being amongst the dreadfully cold trees as if they were hiding from something or *someone*. She sighed heavily. Her mother was her only companion, and through it all, she loved and admired her for her strength and determination to fulfill the elusive duty.

A voice broke through her memories.

"It is time. I cannot tell you where, but it must be fast and it must be quietly."

Absently, she stared at her mother in confusion. Meridan had never been impulsive. Mora had always been frustrated by her lack of imagination and spontaneity. A solemnity overcame her when they communicated about the lands outside their own; and a potential scolding if she were to ever venture alone toward the forest wall. On multiple occasions, she even felt the dwelling a prison. She believed deep inside the solitude was a punishment for an unsettled past her mother would never dare speak aloud. Ultimately, she could never have left her mother alone.

Therefore, the only escape she possessed was her mind – her imagination and her dreams.

Mora could remember as a childling, waking in the middle of the night to hear her mother exchanging words with someone in the dark, the voice unnaturally neither male nor female, babbling about "him" and "the coveted". She would silently climb out of her bed, cross the cold floor to the cracked opening in the door, and peer at her mother on her knees beside the bed, absent of any other, conversing with the darkness. Other nights, she would hear her mother screaming, yelling at a shadow in the night. However, when Mora would run to her side, she realized sleep was her only foe. She would grab a flask of cold water and splash it upon her mother's scalding skin. Awaking with a gasp, Meridan would slap her in the face and order her to return to her room.

Therefore, in the present moment, she merely fixated a serious gaze at her mother and gawked. "I'm not going anywhere until you tell me what the connection is between the serpent and our departure!"

She was furious, and as though trying to convince her own insecurity, she screamed to herself, *My mother has no right to hide anything further from me!* The increasing frustration boiled beneath the surface of her skin, her chest constricted, and tears welled in her eyes.

Then, throwing her hands in the air, she yelled aloud, "I have endured your secrets my entire life without questioning why you have kept me here like a prisoner…" before sputtering to a halt. At that moment, she knew she had gone too far.

Meridan turned an icy glare toward Mora, fury in her eyes, the veins in her throat pulsing as she vehemently spat, "A prisoner? How dare you speak to me like that! You have no godsdamn idea what my motives are and always have been. I have been protecting you through my slowly failing body, a sacrifice I made the moment your birth became inevitable. The reason you live is because I allowed it, raising you to complete a task I was sworn so many years ago."

As she spoke, her very being appeared to grow in stature, overshadowing Mora's self, blocking out the sun.

"You foolish *chavèin*, go wash and prepare to leave."

Mora's cheeks felt flushed. It was the most information her mother had ever revealed. As her mind cleared from the shock, she saw a massive shift from the intimidating, unrecognizable form, to the subtle, mild mannered female she knew.

Meridan turned her back on Mora and spoke no more.

Defeated, Mora timidly walked back toward the curtained doorway. As she approached, there was a brief gust of cold wind that rustled her hair and took her breath away. Glancing at the spot her arrow had landed, she watched the rising sun shadows shift through the canopy of trees. Hauntingly, she thought she heard a whisper from the depths of her mind say, *My love, we will meet again.*

She shuddered and quickly stepped past the curtain.

# The Messenger

The fire had gone out and the smoke was billowing, entangling itself in the low-lying fog. There was no light save for the silvery sliver of the moon, the pinpoints of stars, and the tiny glowing embers that were slowly fading with the cold air. The wind started softly blowing through the leaves and the chill stung her ears, but from a distance she heard her name, *Mora*, whispered softly. Then again. The sound of her name was sweet, making her feel warm, a spark conjured through the bleakness of her growing despair since departing the sanctuary, the only home she had ever known. Curiously, the voice seemed familiar, and yet it did not sound as if it were coming from the surrounding trees, air, or ground. It appeared as though it called from the stars, the moon, or the wind. She breathed deeper. Feeling the sweat trickling down her face, she wiped her cheeks and stood up. Suddenly, she panicked, realizing she was naked and exposed to the surrounding forest. A sense of modesty swept over her flesh while tiny bumps rippled down her skin. Attempting to cover herself, she glanced around desperately and saw no one. Her body began to shake with nervous vulnerability, and try as she may to call for help, she could not speak.

The voice, neither male nor female, came again, *Mora, do you know me?*

As Mora stood there, fog commenced to rise and embrace her nakedness. She tried to speak again. Nothing but a faint whimper resonated from her throat. The fog swirled faster, creating a tunnel of warmth. Within the swirls came a multitude of vivid hues, as if watching the sunrise and sunset simultaneously. In the colors, there were tiny, sparkling lights, brilliant enough to mirror stars, stolen from their homes in the blackest of night behind. With a magnitude of unfathomable distinction, great billowing clouds moved in elaborate droves across the sky above the whirlwind like tumbling fabric, blowing playfully upon the lines on a windy day. The fog gyrated with a force of passion, causing her heart to flutter higher than any eye could see. The sensation was sensuous, yet powerful, and it made her whole body soar as though she sat with her arms outstretched upon the wings of a giant bird.

She closed her eyes. When she opened them, she was once again lying on her back, wrapped beside her mother, the smoke from the fire dwindling and mingling into the low lying fog. The brilliant hues were gone, her body stiff with chill and hard ground. Unable to return to sleep, she quietly removed the blanket and gently pushed it underneath the form of her mother. Through the impenetrable darkness, amongst the distant trees, a night bird echoed in the most hauntingly fragile of noises. She pulled her woolen cloak closer around her shoulders, tucked her knees to her chest, and sat facing the edge of the wickedly dark forest, seeking the memory of the day's journey from her sleepless mind.

They left their sanctuary shortly after her mother scolded her for her ignorance. Packing in utter silence, Meridan filled a knapsack full of food and supplies while Mora prepared two of their best leather satchels with an extra tunic and warm cloaks for the both of them. They had lived off the bare essentials her entire life. She was used to living on scarcity and felt this venture would be no different. Within her leather bootstrap, she tucked the sharpest of their knives, the hilt made of antler and carved intricately with protection runes. Over her shoulder was her quiver and bow, an invaluably crafted weapon her mother had gifted her on her eighteenth name day. Finally, she trudged toward the door, the weight of realization causing her mind to feel heavy, her skin to prickle, and her knees to weaken. She looked out of the old stone walls with a flooding sense of guilt. For all the time she dreamt of leaving, she never imagined she would not be able see her home again, touch it again, or smell the aromas associated with her life in the dwelling, ever again. She had an overwhelming feeling, once she stepped over the threshold, everything would disappear.

*This feels dreadful.*

They followed a small trail through the forest and into a vast, unfamiliar terrain. Grass extended infinitely in hills of green and gold with sporadic clusters of rocks looming in the midst of the outstretched land. Mora held her hand to shield her eyes from the glaring sun as she beheld gigantic, brooding mountains with white peaks in the distance. She had only seen drawings of mountains from the manuscripts her mother kept close to her sleeping chamber. However, standing at the edge of the tree line, they appeared more threatening, intimidating, and mysterious.

Briefly peering behind at the thick, dark forest they emerged, she felt a sense of urgency to run back to the safety of the stone walls. Her arm hairs stood on end as the life she had known before was slowly disappearing. If she cried, her mother would see her as a coward, a childling running to the safety of the familiar, the innocent. She would never allow herself to be caught in that precarious situation knowing her mother's tendency to lack sympathy in the matter. Shamefully, in order to avoid eye contact, she stuck close behind Meridan's brisk walk, never venturing to either side. Taking a moment to glance around, the forest's edge seemed to stretch forever in both directions, neither feeling inviting, nor tempting, to follow. However, they had trekked north of her homestead according to the placement of the sun, following the inhospitable trails in the liminal space between the borders of the tree line and the rolling hills of grass.

Barely a day's journey along the forest edge, Mora felt as if they had walked for days. The bright orb of the sun moved from one side of the sky to the other, changing the shadowing of the trees and fluctuating the temperatures from dusk to dawn. It was a sight she had seen all her life, but only through the canopy of the tree guardians above her roof. Presently, it was the expansion of the sky which awed her very nature, as the grandeur of the sun's impact was even more brilliant when stretched across the majestic ranges of stone outcroppings and glistening upon the expansive grasses. Although her observable experience amongst the sanctuary was limited to the change from day to night, it was obvious the light had begun to bow to the dark earlier.

*The leaves are beginning to turn as well.* She smiled.

It was her most favorite moment in the wheel of time, as everything began to drastically change its appearance before lulling to sleep, hibernating from the frigid onset of winter's embrace. The smell of the air ripened and became crisp as the wind changed directions and carried pockets of coolness, cutting through the summer's heat. The mornings were layered with blankets of frost, while evening was full of floating hues of saffron, marigold, citrine, and emerald dancing and glistening in the failing light. It was a harbinger of the harshness and solitude to come, but a time of abundant beauty and ethereal appreciation.

She knew if they were still in the comfort of their sanctuary, with autumn on the cusp, they would have busily begun collecting the harvest and properly preparing it for storing. Although they would work from dawn to dusk, she endured the grueling tasks with little complaint because it meant they would be able to relish the darkest season inside their stone walls without much hostility from the wild winds and frozen dirt. The reward for their progress came when her mother would light the fires, signaling the beginning of relaxation and hearty sustenance for the evening.

She wiped a tear from her cheek.

When the light began fading, Meridan slowed down. She sent Mora to find some kindling to start a fire. Being on the edge of the forest, small sticks were accessible, but by the time she wandered back to the camp, her mother had already built a fire amidst four large rocks, canopied by tree branches for protection from the growing bite of the night's wind. The air and landscape felt strangely different from the sanctuary. From the way the wind blew, she feared it may be sooner, than later, that everything would commence to turn inward; and all, but the evergreen trees, would become dormant.

Stumbling on an extruding branch, she dropped the sticks at the foot of a large stone and stared into the fire. The flames danced in the fading light, shining miniature figures onto the nearest stones. Curiously, the figures appeared to be alive, their movements fluid and coaxing as the sparks of embers provided rhythmic popping sounds. A loud *crack* of the fire made Mora jump back from the mesmerizing figures and toward the edge of the overcropping rocks. It was dark, save for the luminous shine of the waning moon, but an eerie sensation pimpled across her skin, standing the hairs on the back of her neck on end. While the waxing and waning moon had only been visible on certain nights through the forest roof, she could always observe the multitudes of tiny lights stuck in the black abyss on a cloudless night. Even as a childling, it made her realize the vastness of All and her finite experience. Currently, the wealth of possibility outside her own safe haven was terrifying and caused her heart to beat faster as she peered into the dark, brooding future that awaited her next step.

Mora came back into the presence of her body. There was no sound save for the quiet howl of the bitter wind. The magic of a potential dream was lost, the last memory of her home waning like the moon. She could feel her flesh taut around her bones, her beating heart against her chest, and her breath straining in her throat. It was a feeling of panic unlike she had ever felt before. Her mind raced, trying to grasp the sensational elements of the surrounding night, every sense vividly apparent. The stark black became laced with outlines of ephemeral shadows as her eyes adjusted. The air was thick and stifling within her nose, causing it to run freely. The ground was uncomfortable underneath, hard and lumpy. No matter how she shifted, the irritations dug deeper against her bones. The dry, parched taste in her mouth was unpleasant and made it hard to swallow. Hearing her mother shift next to her, the call of an owl and the rustle of wings escalated the pumping of her heart to the point it was the only thing she could hear anymore. Uncomfortably, she laid onto her back and glanced toward the stars. Yet, curiously, there was nothing but an impenetrable black slate.

Unexpectedly, she saw a speck of light falling toward her, softly, delicately. Mora watched it, as if waiting for a feather to float down from a wing or a leaf to fall from its branch. Once again sitting up, she held out her hand as it neared. It fell sweetly onto the middle of her palm. It was cold to the touch. However, it sparkled brilliantly before melting into a tiny light illuminating inside her flesh. She peered back toward the blank sky as more started to dimly show through the emptiness, appearing as though the stars were falling eloquently from the void. Slowly, she stood, pulled her cloak tightly around her shoulders, and walked away from the nearly deceased fire. In dainty droves, they began to land all around her feet, on her skin, and in her hair, encompassing her in an ethereal light.

*It is like snow, but where is the light coming from?*

*You are ready,* a voice resonated from behind.

Startled, Mora twirled around on her heel so fast she stumbled back on a small, jagged rock. Landing hard on the cold, wet ground, she gasped as the rock pierced the side of her thigh. Horrifyingly, she realized her vulnerability to whatever enemy had approached. Squinting through the dark, her eyes watered from the approaching fog. No more than ten paces from the tip of her foot, appeared a subtle glowing apparition cloaked in majestic violet, face concealed by the hood of the fabric. Through her anguish, she clumsily rose to her feet, the piercing wound in her thigh throbbing. She could feel the warmth of the blood running down her leg.

*If this is my death*, she thought, *it is a pathetically foolish way to die.* She felt like a bleeding animal awaiting the slaughter without a chance to fight for freedom, no weapon in hand.

*You need no weapon. I am not Death.*

Mora straightened up and stared at the otherworldly being, stunned at the clarity of her thoughts, but startled it seemed to read her mind. As she stared, she noticed how gracefully tall the ethereal figure stood. Amazingly, it appeared to be floating. Feeling she was owed at least a shred of dignity despite her humiliating fall, she gathered her courage and asked, "Who are you?"

*Some refer to me as The Messenger, a herald. Others, The Guardian.*

She examined the apparition closer. The voice did not sound as if it was spoken from the being, but from the hollows of her mind. This time, Mora formed the question in her head, as to read the depth of The Messenger's communication. *Do you have a name?*

*You may call me Nephani.*

It made no gesture, nor movement, toward her direction. Realizing the light specks had stopped falling, she felt the bitter wind begin to blow harder. The biting cold had made the blood clot on her wound; it was no longer warm, but ice against her freezing flesh. She formed another thought, *What are you and what do you want of me?*

*It has been bestowed upon me the task to watch over you, to guide you without predilection. It is your time, there are no others. You are the* only.

The stillness became impenetrable and she felt as though the being, Nephani, and herself, were the only two elements within a bubble of halted time. Slowly, the wind ceased completely and the faint glow of Nephani became more visible around them.

"The only what?" Mora chattered. Her mind raced to the experience with the serpent and the way his black eyes seemed to be searching for something within her mind, the way she felt he laughed mockingly at her as she stood there, bow and arrow in hand.

*Nay. That is The Dark One. The ruler of night, darkness, and shadows.* Nephani paused, unclasping the armholes of the cloak.

Curiously, Mora saw nothing but bright light, no trace of a hand, no distinguishable fingers. Within the light appeared a beautifully carved, white box. She stepped closer with caution, entranced by its beauty. No larger than her own palm, the box looked as if it were made of a pure, white bone. Living a simple life, she had never laid eyes on such a luxurious item. All of her possessions were handmade by the availability of goods provided by the edge of the forest and were transient. Intricately hand-carved on the top of the box was a tree. This tree was a full tree, with each leaf individually carved onto the branches and no bigger than a speck of dirt. They were painted with what hinted of gold. Comparatively, the filigreed roots of the tree spanned from side to side, each inlaid with what also appeared like thin, golden lines. In each of the four corners was a symbol. The bottom two were entangled within the roots, while the upper two were intwined with the branches. She had seen a similar tree element in a manuscript once.

The top left symbol appeared to be a detailed knot. The fluent line wove in and out of each other, having neither a beginning, nor an end. The top right symbol was a sun eclipsed by a full moon. The five rays displayed the only visible inclination of its radiance, stretching beyond the seal of night. The bottom left symbol was a triskelion of interconnected leaves. The leaves met in the middle, sharing one point without separation from the curves of the pattern. On the bottom right corner there was an intricate relief of a skeleton key. The head of the key contained three rungs, reading from right to left, each contained one of the three symbols, the knot, the eclipse, and the triskelion leaves. All of the elements had a small string of gold braiding the shaft of the key, forming a solid base. Circumventing the sides of the box, written in gold relief, was an inscription in a language Mora was not familiar. Fixating her gaze on the masterpiece, she felt it daunting to look away.

*Mora, daughter of Meridan, you are The Keeper, the keybearer.*

At the sound of her name, her gaze broke and she took a few anxious steps back, attentively searching for rocks with her heels, but keeping her eyes locked on Nephani. "The Keeper? The Keeper of *what?*" Her mind raced frantically.

*That I cannot tell you at this time. It would be dangerous if you were to know without knowing yourself. To have access to the Truth would make it more vulnerable for your enemies to seek out. Nay. You will find out in time, and when the time comes, you will make a choice. The choice will be of your free will. As of this time, you have a journey, Mora. It will neither be easy, nor without consequence, but the future of All lies within you.*

The box opened on its own accord. Lying within, was the skeleton key from the outside of the box. The key was attached to a chain. The chain was made of tiny, gold, interlocking metal leaves. *Wear this key around your neck. Take heed, for it is sacred. In the wrong hands, the fate of All would pose disastrous.*

In only a blink, Nephani was gone. There was no light and no box, but around Mora's neck lay the chain; and, as if made out of the weight of a feather, appeared the key, tucked between her breasts. Lifting the chain eye level, she squinted through the darkness. The stars had reappeared, along with the sliver of moon, but she could only see a barely visible sheen along the black outline. Although the chain appeared delicate, it was deceptively sturdy, because no matter how hard she tugged, the chain would not give way. She stood in the dark feeling completely helpless, turning over the current events in her mind: the sparkling snow, the rock, the voice, the apparition...*the key*.

In frustration, she screamed out, "What does this all mean!"

As if awakening from a dream, she was answered through the growing consciousness of a sharp wind rustling through the trees and the familiar night bird faintly cawing through the dark. She suddenly felt the searing pain in her thigh and, to her astonishment, real snow began falling intermittently around. Glancing upward, she saw the subtle outline of gray, flat clouds slowly commencing to blanket the sky.

Shocked, she pulled her cloak tighter and wiggled her toes. *How can this be? It's still too early for snow.*

Mora lightly pressed back through the snow on the tips of her toes. The ground started to feel like a river of black ice. She had not been prepared for ice. It was searing the bottom of her feet, much like fire would if it could freeze. Desperately, she attempted to keep her mind off her feet; and although her thigh burned, it didn't distract her from all the unanswered questions that flooded her mind alongside the unexpected presence of the illuminated, formless being, Nephani. She posed thoughts in her mind, trying to reach out to a thread of communication. *Nothing.* Tired and aching to feel the warmth of a wool blanket and a fire, she willed herself to continue despite the increasing numbness.

*How and when did I walk this far from the fire?*

Mora turned a familiar bend around the rocks to see her mother sitting next to the glow of a freshly lit fire. The light illuminated her face with a spectrum of oranges, yellows, and white, but accentuated the harsh lines beneath her eyes and around her mouth. Her mother suddenly appeared old and frail, not the immortalized figure she once knew. Hastily sitting across from her mother, she held out her feet and hands to the warmth as the flood of heat seared painfully on her frozen flesh before it began to find a satisfying relief. They sat in lingering silence, both staring into the sparkling embers. Every unspoken thought weighed on the heavy air and was building with the annoyingly overwhelming stillness of the night.

Finally, Meridan whispered, "Where did you go?"

This was the last question Mora expected to be asked. "I was awakened by a dream and sleep would not befall me. Therefore, I proceeded to walk."

"What did you see?"

"I'm not sure." Mora delved deep into her mother's stoic eyes for a sign she was hiding an answer or a glimpse of understanding. Finally, she inquired, "Do you know what I saw?"

Meridan wrapped the shawl closer around her shoulders and handed Mora a flask. "Nay, the mind is a world of its own. You choose who you allow to see what you see, to not see what you do not want them to see; to know what you know, to choose what you do not want them to know. Stumbling into the realm of answers you are not prepared for will lead to a door you may never be able to close."

She stood up, strangely appearing taller than normal, her shadow creeping to the forest's edge. Coughing a little after tasting the bittersweet contents of the flask, Mora peered at her mother's silhouette and asked weakly, "Am I to be left in the dark, to wander aimlessly without direction until my last breath?" The pulsing pain was searing in her thigh again.

"We all wander aimlessly through the dark and ought to embrace it as a vital part of our beings. It is a harmony All must accept. Just as the night cedes to day and day cedes to night through the continual dance of All, we each are required to find the benefit of both within our true beings. Through what means, one may never know. Light can illuminate the darkest corners of the soul as easy as dark can extinguish the brightest light, if allowed. Have faith my love, you are never alone. However, be leery of the magical energies at work, they wane and wax like the moon." As if summoning the clouds to briefly part, Meridan turned away to savor the waning smile of moonlight.

Mora watched her mother in awe. *She is majestic.*

Another long stretch of silence followed. However, a faint, haunting laughter gradually penetrated the silence, sending a chill down her spine. Feeling an uncomfortable dread fester in her stomach, she watched to see if her mother heard the same, but the features remained frozen, eyes closed, face subtly illuminated in the moonlight. Finally, Mora became too tired to sit up any longer. Therefore, she sighed and laid down in front of the fire, watching the flames dance their wild, savage dance; sing their cackling tune; and taunt her reality until her eyes became heavy and she drifted into an empty, dreamless slumber.

# Abandonment

At the first subtle light of day, Mora awoke to a world of white. Her eyes started adjusting to the sparkling lights bouncing off the snow. Still startled and confused about the snow, she tried to recreate the memory of the night before, but her head was throbbing with an intense pain. Rubbing her forehead and temples, she attempted to lift her head. It was then she realized she had been lying on a rock the whole night. Begrudgingly, she slowly and achingly sat up. A searing twinge struck her left thigh. Cursing out loud, she pulled her wool cloak higher to expose the wound. To her amazement, the wound had been neatly washed and carefully sewn. It felt warm, but nothing appeared to be festering around the exposed skin. She reached down and picked up some fresh snow, gritted her teeth, and placed it on her wound. *Damn!* she huffed, feeling lightheaded. Her heart fluttered, her stomach rolled, and her head started swimming from the pain. Managing to reach for the excess wool at the bottom of her cloak, she tore off a long strip and tied it tightly around the wound.

After a few moments of closing her eyes and taking deep breaths, she opened her eyes and focused on the surrounding terrain. The snow had fallen deeper around the rocks, reaching mid-way. Straining against the reflections of sun off the ground, a flashback of the previous night appeared in her head. She remembered sitting across from her mother, her features waring on the abnormally fragile, sunken face. During the conversation, her mother had handed her a flask. *That must be why I slept so heavily.* The brilliance of the last fire had dwindled to charred, crumbling wood, creating a nasty sludge as it had melted into a watery mess and mixed itself within the black soot. She looked beyond the fire, but could not recognize the land under the fresh coat of snow. It had been lush and green merely the day before. Oddly, the trees appeared more barren and the rocks lacked their previous night's grandeur. There was no sound save for the slight hiss of the wind. Bewilderment was an understatement, it felt like an entirely different world.

Realizing she was alone, she listened for a sound of returning footsteps or clanking of the morning pot, but the world stood still. "Mother!" she called out with what energy had been left from her heavy night's sleep.

There was no answer.

She called again, "Mother!", but the stillness won.

*Where would she have wandered off to in such an unexpected snow? And after tending to my leg?* A curious feeling ran through her bones and she scrunched her nose. *Although, to my recollection, I mentioned nothing about my wound in our conversation.*

She slowly stood, relieving pressure from her left leg by concentrating more on the right. The snow was deeper than she surmised and rose halfway between her ankle and knee. Hobbling over to the soot left by the fire, she picked up a stick and commenced to jab it through the sludge. *It will be impossible to build another fire in the mess. I will have to look for a drier spot further under the hanging rocks.* Peering around for any sign of movement, she limped away from the rock quarry, still searching for footprints. However, the snow appeared as though someone pulled a fresh blanket over the ground. Any tracks would have been long forgotten.

Suddenly, a distance away from where she stood, Mora heard a cry of pain. The deep reverberation echoed fiercely through the silence, bouncing in a cacophony off the solid surfaces of stone and tree. Attempting to pinpoint the direction of the cry, she decided it was coming from further down the edge of the forest. Listening closely, she slowly limped through the snow, being exceptionally cautious of her surroundings. As the wind began to increase, she pulled her cloak higher on her chin as tears from the blisteringly icy wind slid down her face. As bright as the sun was when she awoke, the sky was steadily becoming a dull mixture of gray and neutral blues with very little light currently showing through the clouds.

A crashing sound, and a heavy flapping of wings, shook the air. Another cry of pain echoed in the bleakness. Trudging quicker, blistering bits of falling ice began hitting her skin like needles. Wrapping every part of her face, save for her eyes, Mora finally came upon a grove of trees that shielded her body from the daunting wind and ice. Moving the stiff branches from side to side, she climbed over logs as she advanced in the direction of the cry.

"Mother!" she cried out.

There was no reply.

Suddenly, the sound of brush being crushed by a larger creature than herself made her jump. Through the trees, she could see something running in the opposite direction that made her heart race. With her heart pounding violently against her chest, she ducked swiftly under the nearest brush, hoping whatever it was running had not seen her arrive. Waiting until all she could hear was the rustle of evergreen needles and bare branches from the wind, she stood up and continued hobbling. After several large, agonizing steps, she happened upon a clearing, the trees making a ring around a thick sheet of ice. However, the ice had been cracked, and lying on the opposite end was a large body.

Glancing up, she thought, *To create a crack in the ice, the unfortunate creatural must have fallen from high in the trees.*

Cautiously stepping around the edge of the clearing, she watched the body carefully as she advanced. Grabbing a nearby small branch, she guarded herself in case the form moved, knowing it would merely be used as a distraction in an attempt to run away and not as a weapon. Because it was clearly not her mother, she analyzed what lay before her eyes. She supposed the creatural had the body of a male being, although she had never seen a male in person. His body was twisted and turned in an awkward manner. On his back was a pair of grand, white wings with a hint of blood stained streaks from where they connected to his back. His hair was a beautiful gold color, but it too, had blots of blood matting the curly strands of hair together on his forehead. Glancing around his chest, which had been exposed ever-so-slightly from his cloak, she noticed he was still breathing.

### The Keeper

Taking her branch, Mora poked his stomach area and a little on his hands. There was no sudden impulse in response to the jab. Lifting his cloak away from the ground, just enough to see beneath, she saw a saber fallen to his side. She picked up the weapon and held it at eye level. It possessed an unusually large hand guard of pure silver. Inlaid in the silver hilt read the name, *Aloria*. The one-sided blade was slightly curved, but not terribly thick. Feeling it was not the most impressive weapon in size, especially for such a large male, she deduced it must have originally been made for a female, since it possessed a delicate design and weight.

Glancing around at the tops of the trees, the ever-increasing, ominous, light gray and purple clouds silhouetted the branches. She surveyed the forest. Out of the depths, she heard another terrifying cry. The cry sounded neither in pain, nor sadness, but in anger. Horrified that whatever thing did this to the male being might come back for its prey, she frantically peered around for a plan to remove them both from the broken ice.

Quickly, she flung off her cloak and placed it on the snow next to the body. Expecting more resistance, she rolled the male onto his chest. *He's more lightweight than I expected*, she thought. Gruffly, she took a deep breath and began to drag him back toward the camp, aware that her wound was throbbing even more violently with the added force. A snowy mixture was beginning to fall heavily from the sky once again. However, to her advantage, the icy snow made it easier to drag the cloak across the ground. Even though his weight did not compare to the visible size of his body, it still became harder as she neared the destination. Breathing heavily, she paused underneath a decently large, overhanging rock, and then drug the body toward a rough patch of dry and crunchy leaves. To her chagrin, there was still no trace of her mother. Using the leaves to stuff underneath a woolen blanket she retrieved from one of the satchels for comfort against the extremely hard and bumpy ground, she rolled the body onto the pile. He made a groaning sound that made her stiffen.

After several moments, not realizing she was holding her breath while waiting to see if he would awaken, she released a long sigh. Wrapping her cloak back around her shoulders, she peered beneath the outcrop. Deciding to wander the perimeter to find useful kindling before the ground was covered in fresh snow, she briefly glanced reluctantly at the body before trudging beyond the rocks. *I must build a fire.*

As she gathered some small sticks not too far from the hanging rocks, Mora looked again for a trace of footprints or broken twigs. *Nothing.* The snow had picked up furiously, leaving a fresh new layer of powder lying between her vision and any evidence that may help her solve the whereabouts of her mother. Sullenly, she walked to the rear of the rock clearing where the ground hadn't been touched by snow with a handful of twigs to supplement a decently lasting fire.

Feeling the familiar twinge of pain in her thigh coming back from the night before, she peered beneath her tunic to see fresh blood beginning to soak through the bandage. *Gods,* she cursed loudly in her mind. Knowing there was nothing she could do until she built a fire because her hands were freezing, she occupied her mind with the pleasing image of roaring flames despite the menacing laceration burning through her endeavors. Finally, sparks spit from the kindling and she moved to sit on a hard rock across from the barely breathing body of the winged male. Lifting her leg onto the rock, she surveyed the wound. The stitching had unraveled itself. *It is most likely a direct result from the strain of moving the body,* she thought annoyingly to herself.

Grudgingly, Mora removed Meridan's needle and thread from her abandoned satchel. She glanced from the needle, to her laceration, and groaned. Rummaging once more, she found a small bottle her mother had concocted for the journey. Knowing not what it was fermented from, she knew her mother used it for wounds; and she also knew it was safe to drink. She had seen her mother take a swig before placing the stopper on the transparent bottle multiple times when she thought Mora was not around. The liquid itself was also transparent. Unstopping the bottle, she inspected her laceration once more. Desperate, she held the bottle to her lips and swallowed a mouthful. Her stomach lurched in disagreement, but she held it in, shuddering in disgust.

Then, through gritted teeth, she poured the liquid on the open wound. She nearly passed out with the searing pain. As it bubbled and sizzled, the warm liquid felt as though it were eating her flesh. No longer able to hold in her emotions, she wailed loudly. Above, inconspicuous birds fluttered, frightened from their perches. Her chest heaved in and out, almost bursting with the heavy pounding of her heart. Quickly, she took another few gulps of the burning liquid. Thankfully, the liquid begun to settle and she could feel her senses numbing. Dousing the needle with the clear liquid after holding it over the flames, she decided the extra sterilization would be beneficial. Warily, she laced the thread through the needle. Tying it securely, she stuck the needle in her cloak as she proceeded to dislodge the remaining thread from her flesh. Wincing, she shuddered as the last bit slid out. Finally, taking a large breath, she began to sew her laceration tightly. The resulting effort was painless and bloody, but the experience odd. She could sense the needle and thread running through her skin, yet she could feel nothing.

Once Mora had completed the sewing, she took another swig of the transparent, burning liquid before setting it securely back into the satchel. Taking a deep breath of relief, she patted the wound with her cloak and wrapped a new bandage around her thigh. Peering toward the battered and bruised body, a sense of pity sparked the need to clean his wounds. Therefore, stepping lightly to his side, she pulled back the cloak and surveyed his skin. His lip had been badly cut, but not deep enough for stitching. His nose appeared broken, however, she would not attempt to set it without his permission. *Hopefully, he will awaken soon, or else his nose will permanently mend itself in that awkward distortion.*

She continued searching for other wounds, but found none that required stitching, merely cleaning. Finding herself enamored with his peculiar physique, she flushed and recovered his exposed flesh.

*He is abnormally warm to the touch, but that may be a result from the trauma of the fall.*

Before gathering snow, she decided to wrap his arms tightly in the cloak in fear he may flail if awakened. Then, she began to work steadily. Her extremities were still numb, but she felt unstoppable and untouchable. *Both,* she thought smirkingly to herself, *may be the burning liquid.* To her surprise, his body only twitched as she cleaned the wound on his lip with the snow. Otherwise, he remained comatose.

By the time she was finished, Mora was exhausted and could feel the effects of the medicinal liquid wearing off. Satisfied with her work, she stumbled over to the rock where she had left the satchel. A hope her mother would return to find her capable of taking care of herself made her strangely giddy. However, it directly subsided at the menacing thought that her mother had not returned from wherever she had ventured. This feeling left her overly anxious and sad, with a hint of anger and resentment. Settling herself down sloppily on a leaf-padded blanket, she dozed off quickly.

# A Placid Introduction

Slightly shaking and nerved from the subsiding concoction, Mora sat up by the small, dying plot of embers. She pushed the few strands of matted hair away from her face. *How long have I been asleep?* She glanced at the body wrapped in the blanket across from where she sat. *The slumber must have been brief.* However, she suddenly wanted to scream, the urge rising in her very soul, yet her mouth would not open.

She was alone.

*Alone.*

The word repeated relentlessly in her mind. Feeling restless, she decided to take a walk, the urge pulling her toward the mouth of the rock cropping. Surveying the embers being consumed once again by the melting snow, she figured there would be no use attempting to build another in its place. Briefly glancing at the unconscious, winged male, she thought, *If he is still here when I return, I hope it will be an amiable encounter.*

Commencing to trudge lamely through the deep snow beyond the camp, she concluded it was late afternoon despite the absence of sun. Luckily, the snow stopped sometime during her brief slumber. As she ventured further into the forest, she felt the sharp air pierce her extremities. She had not been prepared for this type of weather since the kiss of winter was at least two full moons away. She listened after every breath and heard nothing save for a few ravens interrupting the silence from their disguised roost on the tops of the trees. Frustrated, tired, cold, and hungry, she eventually perched on a nearby tree trunk. Fear and hopelessness lurched deep in her stomach.

She had never experienced this vast amount of snow. Very little dusted the inside of the sanctuary each winter, the majority gathering in the surrounding forest. To her, it always felt like a spell or enchantment kept everything beyond the borders of their home. *That is...until the serpent.* Shuddering, her stomach settled enough to continue walking, searching. Eventually, she gave up on distancing herself any further from where she left her effects. Because the snow was rapidly becoming increasingly thick, the points of familiarity she created while walking was blending in with the icy surroundings. The cold was bone deep. A drier spot desperately needed to be located soon to build another fire or else she might freeze to death.

Realizing she would need to move a stone to reveal the ground underneath, Mora gathered a branch, the thickest she could find, and walked to the nearest stone cluster. After attempting to push a medium-sized stone away, she decided it would be too heavy to move on her own. Clearing the snow from around the stone with her numb fingers, she dug a small hole under the rock, slightly big enough to fit the bottom of the branch. Placing a smaller rock under the end of the branch, she tested the leverage by pushing down on it. The branch felt it could handle the pressure. Then, with all her might, she pushed down on the top of the branch, struggling against the force of the small stone penetrating into the thick wood. Harder and harder she pushed with all her energy, jumping to apply all her weight. Suddenly, she felt the stone give way a fraction, despite the menacing result of the splintered branch. She shrugged and started searching for another branch.

Another nudge of the stone, the second branch broke.

Again and again.

Finally, after exhaustion settled deep in her bones, and slightly light-headed, the stone moved, and rolled down beside her feet. Under the stone proved to be home to a few multi-legged crawlers trying to stay warm, but they scattered into the dirt or under the nearby stones after being exposed to the frigid air. She patted the dirt evenly and trudged along the edge of the forest to find dry sticks she could use to light the fire.

After a distance, something caught her eye beyond the large rocks to her right. Amazed, she saw an immensely tall tree with branches that fell eloquently around its trunk like a thick cloak. Its branches were not adorned with leaves, but thin, dirt-colored needles. Looking closer, there were copious amount of thin sticks on one branch alone, creating the overwhelming appearance of solidity. She pushed back one of the branches. Inside, the tree was curiously spacious and bare. The enormous trunk twisted from within the ground, spiraling high up to the middle of the tree, when it started sprouting out the soft, cloak-like arms. It was warm and the ground was dry. Despite her efforts with the rock, she peculiarly felt drawn to the tree, and was confident it would be a perfect spot to settle for the oncoming night.

Walking around the tree trunk curiously, she studied each twist and turn in the wood. To the touch, it felt like a light, softer material, foreign to her fingers, and appeared as though linen had been wrapped softly, but tautly, around itself. In each strand of the wood there was a subtle, metallic glow. As she pressed her hand to the wood, it seemed as though the trunk was breathing, that there was life inside. A pulse ran through her fingertips and a tingle trickled through her veins. Moving closer, she tried peering inside the cracks of the twisted bark, but disappointedly saw nothing past the subtle illumination except a dark interior.

Turning, she walked to the softly swaying branches. The straw-like leaves appeared infinite in number on each individual limb. Every strand was intricately woven with the same precision as the trunk. Mora gathered a handful of needles, only to be greeted with a multitude of rows beneath. Looking unsettlingly sharp on the end, at the touch of the point, it seemed able to pierce any unsuspecting prey. Attempting this theory, she softly touched the end of the strand. Slowly, tiny drops of blood congregated on the tip of her finger before languidly dripping onto the ground. In awe, she continued to make her rounds about the tree.

She thought to herself, *how was I able to enter in the first place without being pierced?*

On closer inspection, to her surprise, on the tree floor were little wooden piles of burnt sticks no bigger than her palm. Strangely, it appeared as though small fires had been lit underneath this majestic, natural canopy. Mora could not comprehend the possibility of inhabitants within the tree itself, much less the possibility of fires amongst the warmth

**43**

of the branches. With apprehension, she walked to the edge of the tree and began to carefully sift through the layers. Outside, the world was covered in a sheet of white ice, while floods of new, white powder had once again commenced pouring from the gray skies. Her mind started to wonder about the unconscious, winged male at the camp, but an intense fatigue abruptly plagued her body. Sensing the stinging of the cold and the darkness falling, she subconsciously yearned for the warmth inside the tree. As though a string were tied to her waist, she felt pulled back into the sensual warmth of the curtain.

Once again inside, she felt dizzy, her mind suddenly feeling like a thick blanket of fog was slowly numbing her thoughts and extremities. The haze was similar to the effects of the medicinal liquid she had drank before mending her wound. She swayed to a low, melodic hum that hung in the air. The tree commenced to radiate brighter, the intensity not unpleasant. Entranced, she undressed herself, leaving on only one of the linen shifts she had recently added to wear under her woolen frock for extra warmth. Unbraiding her unkempt, damp hair, she laid down on a lovely bare spot of grass. The last fleeting thought in her mind before she closed her eyes was of wonderment at what kind of special magic bequeath this natural palace.

When Mora opened her eyes, she felt the whole world needed adjusting. Everything blurred together. No longer feeling she was in the safe haven of the beautifully warm tree, she sat up slowly. To her amazement, she was overlooking a vast terrain of stars dancing amongst planetary dust clouds. Adjusting her position, she stood carefully, nervous of the surrounding void. Rubbing her eyes as she swept past the mystical blue glow of the twisted tree trunk, she placed her palm on the severely faint outline of the tree needles. Parting the strands, her eyes were met with a twinkling, intangible wall of stars. Panic set in as she stepped to what felt like the edge of an oblivion. *This must be a dream.*

Training her eyes, she could decipher a vague, black path stretching away from where she stood, lined with pinpoints of lights as if beckoning her to travel amongst the formation of the stars. Then, to her amazement, she peered upward and noticed a grotesquely shaped cloud in the process of warping itself around another of a different color. Among consumption, the massive area became a sensational reflection of radiant blues, pristine violet, and luminous teal. Floating amidst the clouds were clusters of small, black circles, orbiting around in a sensual gesture before becoming one with the clouds. Hearing a subtle rumble, Mora glanced behind and saw another gargantuan, oddly shaped cloud billowing around a smaller, horse-head cloud. The horse-head was rearing up in a defiant gesture, looking to escape its prison amongst the yellow-green array of smokey matter. Chains of bright stars clustered together to gate the poor, magnificent creature.

To her bottom left, there was a spectacular arrangement of bright reds and oranges rippling from its torrential center. The ring that was emitting from the core was a powerful force of rage and emotion. Suddenly, an explosion of light radiated from the top right. The surrounding light began to rapidly diminish as it was being sucked inside the ominous darkness. She took a deep breath. Deep inside, all the transcendental sights provoked a lure of mystery into where the light disappeared.

"Breathtaking, isn't it?"

Startled, Mora jumped around, twirling on her heel. The voice seemed to resonate from the inside of the tree. Hugging close to the side of the branches, she desperately hoped they would not allow her to fall into the abyss of floating stars.

"Ah, we meet again, and yet it pains me you do not recognize my voice," rumbled the deep, sensual voice.

Frightened, she barked, "Who are you? Show yourself!" She could not muster the courage to move any further from the unyielding fear of vulnerability. However, the sharp tips of the needles stung her flesh, causing her to wince each time she moved.

An alluring figure stepped through the curtain of stars opposite where she was standing, clad in a stark, black tunic wrapped with a silver buckled belt at the middle, and black breeches. His boots were laced to mid-shin and He did not appear to possess any weaponry. His hair was of the darkest onyx and reflected indigo in the subtle blue glow of the tree trunk. His eyes were the most captivating of all and mirrored the shadows of the night sky. Butterflies danced her stomach when He smiled. It was shockingly pleasant and warm. Familiarity tugged at the deepest corner of her mind as He spoke gently.

"It is I, Solora. There is no need of panic. Your blood pressure is rising and your neck pulses in fright. I am no enemy to you, as you are no enemy to me. Come, sit with me, and talk." Sitting down, He gestured to a spot on the grassy floor next to Him, just above the horse-head constellation.

Watching Him suspiciously, and after careful thought, Mora realized the formations were moving around the tree slowly. From where she stood, it appeared as though the land she inhabited was invisible and nothing but the tree and the sky existed. Cautiously, she sat down on the grass in front of the dark eyed intruder. His complexion was light, paler than her own, but nonetheless, it was a beautiful sight to behold. A subtle glow illuminated upon His flesh and she felt surprisingly comfortable. He had no noticeable lines, nor wrinkles, around His pristinely shaped cheekbones. He was tall, for even sitting He towered a head and a half above.

She looked Him in the eye and inquired, "Who are you and how did you find me?"

"I am always with you, Solora, for eternity." He smiled nonchalantly. "Ever since you traveled from your safe haven, I know when you sleep and when you rise. I know when you feel sad, or when you feel alone. As for my presence, when you laid down to slumber tonight, you felt alone, and so I am here. I yearn to make you feel needed."

Again, His roguish grin curved delicately, but it never revealed His teeth, nor reached His eyes. Despite her previous assumption, she felt her stomach begin to turn uncomfortably in knots in awe of His apparent, supernatural beauty. This was the first time in her life she met another being face to face beside her mother. *Or is He a figment of my imagination?* she questioned.

Deciding it was good to gather information, but to not get too close, she inched back a little. "I don't recall ever seeing you before, and yet you address me as if I'm an old friend. My name is not Solora." Mora tucked her loose hair behind her ears and glanced nervously in His direction.

46

*The Keeper*

"Oh, aye, we have met on occasion. The blood which flows through your body is of my creation." He reached for her hand and started caressing it with His thumb like her mother did when she was afraid to sleep as a childling. "Your True name is Solora."

Unsettling heat rushed through her veins until she could feel it in her face. "I don't understand. Blood? Creation? Don't…" she attempted to jerk her hand away abruptly, but His grip tightened, "don't…touch me!" Shaken, she felt helpless and scared. Her mother would never approve of such behavior.

"Of course you don't," He glared, "your *mother* deprived you a multitude of information." His voice never changed inflection as she continued to struggle from His grip. "Meridan was never actually worthy of such a task."

Upon hearing her mother's given name, she fought harder. "What do you know of my mother?" she screamed. The heat running through her was becoming unbearable, but her skin felt oddly thick and cold. His grip was suffocating her hand. Not allowing herself to cry, she felt her tears taunting their emergence. "You are hurting my hand. Leave me be!" Harshly, she struggled against His grip. Suddenly, she felt a release of tension that sent her falling back on to the floor of the tree.

Within seconds, the darkly clad male was on top of her; she could feel the weight of His body bearing down on her thin shift. Frightened, she yelled, "Remove yourself from me!" It was useless, His weight was impossible to budge. She looked desperately into His eyes of black ice, pleading with any inkling of mercy.

Holding the weight of His own body with His arms, a coy smile formed upon His face. "Please don't make this harder on yourself than you have already accomplished. I mean you no harm, my Light."

Mora managed to free one hand beneath His body. A panic rose and she started sweating, tears fighting harder as they welled in her eyes. She moved the matted hair on her face aside. "I don't understand," she panted again under the exasperated weight of His body, powerless against His advances. He replied with an acidic sweetness that did not sit well on her tongue.

"Ah, my Sun! Your body is my prized creation, and the most valuable. You are merely a product of negotiation, a possession by birth right, and the key to my desires. I am your Maker! You will abide by my doing." The heat behind His eyes became intense, like fire roaring, passionate and destructive.

However, seeing the unwavering fear in her eyes, His mind settled with realization. Subtly, He cleared His throat, "My apologies, my Light, a loss of temper will never resolve or dissolve an issue. Let us start again?"

This time, His eyes met her own with the vehemence of the night sky, dark and filled with unknown desire. A familiar ease tugged in her mind again and a wave of peace settled over her body.

He grinned sweetly. "Aye, there we are. I must say, you have beautiful eyes. They are the color of leaves after a spring storm, lusciously dark green and full of vitality."

A glaze surfaced on her eyes and she smiled shyly. "Thank you," she said giddily.

"Fear not, Solora, force is not my motive." He felt the tension completely subside. "There you go, my love." Sighing, He continued to hold Himself against her body. "Allow me to explain. Your body and soul are mine entirely, and you must allow me to access each individually. We can rule All together, my Light."

As His hands caressed her skin, sending tiny bumps down her arms, He sensed an awakening in the depths of her stomach. "Your body was never yours to possess. It has always been a product of my power, a feat Life believed He was only able to fashion." His hands cupped her breasts and she sighed. "Presently, as you lay before me, whatever you think, I will hear; whatever you devise, I will know; whatever you feel, I will feel too. Do you understand me?"

Mora nodded gullibly, feeling His hot breath on her face. Then, a voice appeared in her mind, *Don't give up Mora, you are stronger than you know.*

He let out a low, droll rumble of amusement, kissed her cheek, and moved down to brush His lips against her neck. "Ah, the sweet scent of innocence. How I do love thee." Dastardly, He took a deep breath, whispering, "Your strength will never match my own because I am in physical form of my own design, but you are Chaos, caged in flesh because of me." Vowing, He added, "If you betray me, I will lullingly, but undoubtedly, devour every part of you."

**48**

His sudden change of speaking made her flesh prickle and inflame. He kissed her neck as her body temperature started rising. She could feel tension fluctuating between their bodies as He pushed against her harder. The heat of the canopied trees began to unnervingly feel like fire against her skin. Sweat rolled down behind her ears and onto the back of her neck. She could feel His heavy breath swallowing the silence between them, as if He was taking in each rise and fall of her chest. Each sound intensified in her mind. Slowly, He moved her arms above her head, grasping His hands around her wrists. A sense of alertness, and realization of this being's intentions, made her body writhe beneath the pressure. Her mind was no longer entranced as she began to struggle free of His harsh grip.

"Oh, Solora, the millennia I waited to feel you in my grasp, the sacrifices I have made, the lives I have willingly destroyed to find your whereabouts!" Fire suddenly appeared deep within His pitch eyes. "Your mother may have been able to shield you from me for the past five and twenty years, but it is only a droplet of water compared to the vast ocean of time I will spend possessing your mind, body, and soul."

*Help me!* she silently cried out, warm tears streaming down her face onto the soft turf beneath.

Like a predator in the midst of conquering its prey, she felt His chest heaving up and down like an animal, the power radiating within His deep voice.

"It was only a matter of time before your mind started to call to me, desperate for my presence, despite Meridan's pathetic pleas. Feeble magic!" As He spoke each of the last words, the rage inside Him burned through His violent tone and the friction between their skin began to scorch her wrists.

Writhing in pain and agony, Mora screamed. Closing her eyes tightly, she felt her body split open, surging from the concealed corners of her mind, all the way down to tips of her toes.

# *Loralei*

"Me not so sure brother dearest. Me thinks it look like a skinny troll with less pimply buggers popping out of them here's skin!"

Beneath her eyelids, Mora could hear little voices murmuring and felt little pressure points riding the intervals of her heaving chest. *Are those footsteps?*

"Oh come off it, will ya?! A troll? That ther's a' oversized dwarf, that is! Sure got some hilly skins it does. Me can barely get me balance to look over into that side of its face. I suppose it gots some kind of mutations going on," another voice chimed in to argue.

She barely opened her eyes as she began to feel little pricks from beneath her breasts. Unsure if her previous encounter was a dream or reality, she felt slightly sick and tried focusing on the sight above her for a moment, noticing the familiar glow radiating from the inside of the trunk. However, there was something different about the trunk of the tree. The cracks between the twists were a bit wider than when she touched them last. Emerging from the cracks were tiny little heads and bodies. Unsure of what she was seeing, she groaned. Finally, she looked down at the figures on her chest still arguing over whether her breasts were unfortunate mutations of a battlefield mishap, a sickness of the skin, or she was merely born an uglier creatural than the rest of her 'brotherly clan of trolls, or possibly oversized dwarfs'.

They were small figures, about the size of two hand lengths. Each was grotesquely thin and adorned with plant-life vining around their waist for clothing. In the light of the tree, their skin appeared light green with curious brown inscriptions scrolled across their chest, back, arms, and legs. Protruding from their back were beautifully intricate wings, with designs that could rival snowflakes. Each wing was unlike its partner, as if both were plucked from two separate makers and placed oddly onto the thin, wiry back of the strange figures. Their faces were similar to her own, save for the over-sized eyes, causing their fully formed nose and mouth to look slightly disproportionate. Each had two variant eye colors to correlate with their two different wings. The enlarged irises were surrounded by a thin halo of color. One eye was gold, the other was opal. By their lack of considerable garb, Mora assumed they must be male. While both adorned long, white, braided hair, the slightly ganglier figure donned a plait of various sized, individual braids. However, made from the vines they wore around their waist, a woven band stretched across their forehead and intermingled into the white strands, tucked behind long and pointed ears.

"Excuse me?" Mora finally asked as she propped herself on her elbows. The figures began to loose their balance and fluttered their wings.

"It speaks!" they squealed in unison as they hovered above where they had been standing on her chest. Their big eyes were even bigger with astonishment and, with no defense save for their ability to fly away, they did not seem the least bit frightened.

"I would gladly appreciate if you could cease poking around on my body. I'm not a troll, nor a dwarf, and I do not have mutations. I am a creatural," she thought for a second, "I am a female creatural, that is." She glanced around the tree. All the abnormally sized eyes were staring at her in curiosity.

The two figures who had been poking at her looked from where they had been standing, to her face, and back at each other several times, gawking all the while.

*Obviously, their intelligence is even less than their stature.*

"A creatural? A *female* creatural?" Their stunned faces suddenly burst out in spurts of laughter. Each surrounding squeaky, high voice from the tree trunk joined in with their amusement.

Mora moved off her elbows into a straighter sitting position as the laughter continued. She remained annoyed until one of the figures from the tree emerged and everything went silent. It appeared to be of a similar stature to the other two. However, it donned a deep, auburn-hued hair, opposed to the white of most around. The physique appeared to be female. She was more rounded around the middle and chest area, and had gold bands encircling each arm from the wrist to above the elbow, ankles to knees, and around the neck. The inscriptions on her body were white instead of brown.

She smiled pleasantly. "Apologies, you will have to forgive them as they lack in proper etiquette. We do not receive a multitude of guests amongst our kind. We have never *actually* seen a creatural such as yourself before, much less a female one." Her complexion was pristine and her large, heterochromatic eyes were kind.

"Where am I?" Mora warily stood. While they no longer burned, she could still feel the mysterious male's seductive grasp ingrained on her wrists. Inspecting them, she noticed a faint, red band fading into her skin.

The small, winged female tilted her head and replied in a lyrical voice, "My *Eroth*, you are in a Faery Tree."

She pointed toward the twisted tree trunk, its awkward deformations currently obvious from the previous closed state Mora had encountered on arrival.

"They are difficult to find and certainly not accessible to the naked eye from *most* beings other than faeries." Peering at Mora suspiciously through squinted eyes, she added, "Which makes us curious *how* and *why* you are here."

Mora shrugged. Honestly, how she arrived beneath the Faery Tree was becoming hazier and more confusing as time passed. She didn't even know how long she had been away from the camp. Wondering if the winged male she had drug to the outcropping had awoken yet, she attempted to piece together the details. "I think I was searching for fire wood, but everything was so damp and cold. I was hoping to find a small batch of sticks to ignite before dark. There had been a break in the snow and before I realized, I saw an abnormally gigantic, looming tree amongst the sheet of white."

The laughter had ceased when the female faery began conversing with Mora, but as she looked around to the other big eyes, a nervousness churned in her stomach. Hoarsely, she continued, "The branches were so strangely thick, like a curtain, I decided I would find dry bramble for my fire. The warmth was such a refreshing change from the outside. Unbeknownst to me, the longer I stayed, the more my senses became intoxicated. I had little inclination there was any sort of habitation in the beautifully intricate twists of the trunk. I am truly sorry for the intrusion."

"Thank you for your kind words. Faery Trees have been around for thousands of generations. With over one hundred different species of faeries, our fey ancestry has continuously tried to hide our existence from threatening creaturals such as your kind. We do not see much of our sister species, they are scarce in this country, save for the invisible clan, and we do not see them nearly as much as we would like."

A giggle came from the two male faeries. The female faery glanced annoyingly in their direction and back to Mora, whispering, "We shall not count our losses if their absence should become more consistent."

Mora glanced at them. Their stunned expressions appeared to be faintly hurt by the comment.

Then, the faery continued, "Five Faery Trees have been burnt by Dark Ones, beings who search and destroy all that has potential for good and light." She paused, contemplating. "Not mortal beings that is, for Faery Trees are not visible to mortals unless under extenuating circumstances. At least, that has always been in the creed."

Her face became sullen as if pained by a distant memory.

Shaking her head slowly, she peered innocently at Mora. "This is why it has baffled us all how you came to be present in our tree. You cannot be fully mortal; and for your kind, you have an incredible essence surrounding you with great potential. Whether it be for light or dark, that is not for me to determine. Who are you?"

"My birth name is Mora, daughter of Meridan. I left my home with my mother only days ago," she choked back the stifling wedge that had lodged in her throat at the thought of her mother, "that is, before she vanished. I know not where I am, nor where I am going." There was a silence, all eyes were focused on her very stance. The anxiety began to seep into her core once again. Her skin was clammy, perspiring, and bordering on cold, despite the intense warmth.

"Mora."

The faery spoke it deliberately, but there was an abruptly unnerving still at the mention of her name. After a small interlude of silence, Mora heard the she-faery's voice, yet, it was not spoken aloud.

*Aye, we have heard a great deal about your presence in the forest.*
Her eyes were gravely set on Mora's own.
*Come.*

On that command, the tree trunk twisted open to reveal a brilliant wafting mixture of oranges and raspberries, intertwined with the comforting scent of fresh grass and lilies. Mora tried to focus on where the trunk opened, but the light was so intense it burned her eyes to look directly at the source. Feeling the tiny pressure of faery hands on the small of her back, she held her arms at length and allowed them to lead her blindly. However, once she stepped inside the trunk, the blinding light slowly subsided. As her eyes adjusted, she noticed it looked similar to the inside of the tree she had emerged from, but as she pulled back the curtain of soft, hanging branches, the world revealed a breathtaking scene of color, flooding together in droves of various flowers and foliage. The bees and butterflies were swarming in the air, diving and fluttering thirstily from petal to petal. Her head swam with the drunkenness of the overwhelming aromas. Taking a deep breath, a smile lightened her face as she had never seen anything so abundantly splendid.

She continued to follow the she-faery to a small patch of flowers near a trickling stream. Observing the rainbow-hued water, she watched as faeries basked in the warmth of the sun from atop their delicate flower petals, while others floated down the stream on soft leaves. A clump of pink, green, and blue moss covered rocks formed a winding staircase onto a plateau. In the middle of the plateau, surrounded by thick, fluffy, pink moss, sat an intricately vine-woven throne with the tiniest flowers decorating the back. The faery settled herself on a seat layered with flower petals and sat patiently, motioning Mora to sit below. Utter fascination could not describe how this world made her feel. She gawked at everything around the forest, circling several times before finally taking a seat next to the stream. The twinkling of the lights, the cool breeze, the bright colors, and the unrelenting harmony of each life present was drowning her in ecstasy.

Glancing down into the stream, Mora could see clear to the bottom despite the faint colors glistening atop the surface in the sunlight. The multitude of river rocks were a vast array of smooth neutrals.

Reflective fish scales swam hurriedly past her view. The faeries lounging on the leaves goggled in her direction as they floated under her gaze. However, it was not the ethereal community of nature which sparked her curiosity, it was her own reflection. She rarely had an opportunity to see her reflection throughout her life. If she had, it was muddled, normally by raindrops or dirt. Because there were no reflective surfaces in the dwelling, she had never seen herself clearly. Through the trickling water of the stream, she could see every feature of her face. Startled, she never knew how much she resembled her mother. Her dark, auburn hair was a tangled, curly mess rolling down her shoulders. Quickly braiding it, she smoothed it roughly and pushed the loose, curly ends away from the deep, green eyes staring back at her beneath long, black lashes. The iris color reminded her of the evergreen trees at dusk. Her slightly sloping nose mirrored the simple shape of her mother's nose, but her full lips were a pale pink. Her face was soft, her jawline smooth, not sharp.

Once again, she hopelessly tried to mat the loose hairs into parts of her braid and behind her ears. Although fascination resonated through her bones, she pulled her eyes away from her reflection and inquired, "Where are we?"

"You are in one of the nine surviving Faery Trees. They are parallel realms, roaming side by side with the dismal realms of Mortal and Immortal creaturals. Each Faery Realm is connected. I am Loralei, one of the nine, living, fey queens. I brought you here under complete discretion, for faery magic does not allow the dark magic to be present within your mind. However, we must be quick, for the Faery Lands are not to be occupied by non-fey for long. Unfortunately, the intoxication of our lands will eventually drive you mad, leading you to a demise you will inflict upon yourself."

Mora stared at Loralei. The smells were intoxicating, but her head was not filled with such nonsense. *If I were to become belligerent, surely I will feel the onset of the effects filling my mind.* She consciously set her sights on Loralei, hoping she would notice her staunch attempt to ignore the rapacious temptations of the surrounding Faery Lands.

Loralei smirked. "You are strong Mora, but you still are non-fey. Now, what is it that you seek?"

Knowing she must guard her mind more fiercely, she pushed all outside thoughts aside and cleared her throat, "I seek answers to my mother's whereabouts and…" she thought for a moment, gathering all the questions she sought in her mind, "…why I experience otherworldly dreams as if I were physically a part of another world?"

Closing her eyes, sounds started becoming even more clear: the buzzing of the bees; the chirping of birds; the rustling of the leaves; the constant trickle of the stream; the sighs of faeries basking in the sun; and the flutter of each tiny wing. All the sounds kept echoing incessantly into her ears, making it hard to concentrate on the inquiries. "Who is Nephani? And why does time seem to stand still whenever I am face to face with it?"

Loralei sighed.

A sound of pity twisted tenderness trickled out with the sigh and, suddenly, the weight of Mora's whole being pressed on her shoulders. She had created a disconcertedness amongst the faeries; a feeling of fear that she could not explain. Even though silence encompassed her surroundings, she thought she could hear the steady beating of tiny hearts. Shaking her head, she knew there was no fathomable way to hear the fey heartbeats. *Remain calm, Mora,* she repeated to herself.

It felt like everything was listening closely, the flowers, foliage, and fey, too afraid to move, save for the occasional flutter of wings. Slowly, in the back of her mind, she felt her world start to swim faster. She could feel the wave of emotions roaring into a sea of jumbled thought. The intoxication was beginning. Squeezing her mind shut, she desperately attempted to bar the sensation. She knew she only had to allow the flood gates to open and all would tear through, along with the feeling it would destroy everything in its path.

Mora's thoughts were interrupted by Loralei's empathetic voice.

"I cannot give you all answers you seek. I can tell you that your mind is you and not you at the same time. In a way, it's a separate entity that you control alternately. The flood of emotion you are currently feeling pressed against your skull is not the anxiety or intoxication of the Faery Lands, but the overwhelming darkness that is trying to feed on the information you are about to retain." She fluttered closer to Mora, placing a small hand on her own.

"Throughout time, beings big and small, mortal and immortal, have fought for two things - ultimate knowledge and ultimate power.

### The Keeper

However, in this fight, you also define your passions, your motivations, your being as a whole in All, and whether you worship a loving deity, a morose deity, or none at all. This determines your loyalties. My ancestors have always imagined themselves as beings of light and good. That does not mean our nature is completely pure and just. We, like any, have our severe faults, some to the detriment and demise of the fey. Yet, we serve the Light. For millennia, this Being was a kind one, loving and fair. Many knew the Being by several names: Solora, the Sun Goddess…"

Mora's head raised abruptly at the mention of the name Solora. The dark clad male had called her such. Fully invested, she listened intently as she fought the creeping intoxication of her mind.

Loralei continued, "…Light-Bringer, Enlightenment, the Radiant One, The Keeper, keybearer, amongst others. Regrettably, darkness has hidden the light, and the absence has been detrimental to all beings."

A subtle rumble echoed, but Mora dismissed it, curious at what Loralei was saying. *The Keeper…keybearer…* A desperate search for answers tore at her core like hungry wolven in the night. However, she noticed a tinge of concern flash in Loralei's eyes and the pitch in her voice was lower the more the rumbling appeared.

"There was a time of Primal Beings, the highest-immortal predecessors of creation, who lived harmoniously amongst All. The Trinitas were the Superior Beings, providing life and sustenance into each and every, consistently."

Loralei glanced nervously behind her as if she was relaying a secret and the ears of the trees would give them away.

"But even through happiness and purity, only one drop of taint, the size of a mustard seed, can alter the whole entity. Jealously and greed lashed out fervently amongst the gods. Dark felt it His turn to create sole life and walk amidst creation in reverence and exultation. He wanted to be praised by All…" she trailed off.

A louder rumble in the distance made her jerk her head in the direction of the thunder. A frightening hush befell the land. "He is here."

# Hospitality

His eyes opened to the darkness of a wide, rocky ledge. Grotesquely long, thin icicles hung a short distance from where he lay. He rubbed his eyes harshly as they adjusted to his surroundings. With a skull splitting headache, his whole body ached with a searing pain when he attempted to sit up. Finally able to prop himself on an elbow, he stroked a hand through his curly, golden hair. An agonizing torment caused him to convulse. His nose was broken. With a sick feeling, he encompassed his nose with his fingers and swiftly forced the structure in line. Another convulsion shook his body, and he rolled over, purging what little was in his stomach.

Sore and sick, he laid on his side, glancing down to see his body wrapped in a woolen blanket, firmly pulled around to ensure warmth. To his right, he saw small remnants of a fire, the embers glowing softly with tiny sparks dancing against the darkness. He could see hints of snowflakes wander into the flames every now and then, making a sizzling noise as they hit the kindling. Surveying his surroundings, he saw a satchel close to where he was lying. Attempting to reach his long arm toward the sack, he retracted as pain seared again through his limbs. *Fuck*, he groaned through gritted teeth. Disgruntled, he decided he should sit erect quickly before his body thought about the pain.

Successfully, and loudly, he sat up. Night birds fluttered, startled, atop the outside branches. Sickness lurched in his stomach once more, but he managed to hold it back. Wiping his mouth with the back of his hand, he reached again for the sack. Grabbing the handle, he pulled it to his lap.

Inside, he found a few pieces of frozen bread and a piece of cold, but succulent, fruit. Not knowing where the owner was, he assumed, from the kindness of the blanket, whomever it was, was not a threat to his safety and would gladly share their meal. He began to stuff fruit in his mouth and rummage through the rest. He pulled out a transparent bottle of clear liquid. Popping the cork, he balked as his nose was met with a strong sensation. However, desperate, he put it to his lips and drank. A fiery, bitter liquid burned his throat as he choked back the fruit he consumed. *Gods!* Despite the throbbing pain in his head, he laid back down. Weariness tugged behind his eyes as he stared into the dark. He fought the temptation of sleep, but his eyes closed gently, sending him back into a deep slumber.

# Dancing into Darkness

The sky started turning ominous in nature. Mora stared up at the canopy of contrasting treetops, her mind entranced by the events occurring at the moment. As if a forbidden force pulled her to her feet, she stood up and lifted her arms toward the darkening sky. The wind started to violently gust around the trees, which appeared to wither in fright, wailing desperately through the air. In her mind, mirroring the encroaching storm, a black cloud approached, billowing over each of her own thoughts, hindering and consuming her own will power.

Suddenly, she felt a tug on her ear. She turned to see Loralei, terror-struck, fluttering in a crouched position.

*Please*, Loralei whispered without words and pointed toward the opening in the curtained tree.

Grasping on a thread of light, Mora realized what had happened at that moment. Her mind had opened, the gateway flooded into the world of purity and light. Without her realization, she let the unknown open a destructive portal of opportunity into the Faery Realm. Becoming clammy and cold again, she shuddered against the wind. She nodded guiltily toward Loralei. Like molasses draining from a pot, she slowly picked up her feet, one by one, from their place in the dirt. Against the gale she walked, feeling it fervently push at her linen, her hair, and her skin, as if each one would rip away, leaving her bones to decay on the fragile ground.

*It does not want me to leave.*

## The Keeper

She could not feel more ashamed as she trudged closer to the opening. Her heavy heart felt it betrayed the trust of beings she could not afford to sever an alliance. Glancing back at the catastrophe behind her, all she could see was the faery queen, holding her stance on the rock, radiating a glow so immense it blinded her eyes for a moment. The darkness fought back, violently ripping its way through the light with long, sharp claws. When she forcefully stumbled through the opening, she reached for her mind's voice, *I'm sorry.*

Her body hit the icy, hard ground of snow. Aware of the tragedy that had just befallen the Faery Land because of her presence, she spat out a lump of snow that had lodged in her mouth, noticing a barely visible taint of blood. She swallowed. She could taste the tangy, metallic sensation of warm blood mixed in her saliva as it ran down her throat. She had bit her tongue during the fall.

Ashamed of her unintentional ruthlessness, she stood up, shivering. Dressed in only her shift, she could sense the omnipotence of the surrounding darkness luring its sly prowl from a distance, dissecting her weaknesses through her already present fear. She needed to seek shelter right away, but her feet could barely move. Desperately trying to acquaint herself with her surroundings to become aware of the territory from her earlier journey, she panicked because she could hardly see the hand in front of her own eyes. She stopped as her eyes adjusted to the environment a few steps away. Shadows started jumping out of every corner, opaque figures lunging from all directions in the darkness.

*Are they laughing at me?* The cold air tightened her jaw, helpless to scream out into the distance.

*Can anyone hear me?* Mora desperately called out in her mind. *I need help, I need shelter, I need...my mother.* A tear rolled down her cheek and froze under her chin. She screamed into the void. She was alone, deserted, trapped in a world she began to despise. Slithering down beside a cluster of rocks, she pleaded the snow would stop for the night. The shift was piercing her skin with its wetness, soaking deeply against her flesh, the woolen gown and boots lost with the Faery Tree. She felt like she was dying. *I will not last until morning.*

Out of the void came a low humming. It was a familiar tune, but one her mind could not place in her current state of desolation.

## The Keeper

*Dance with me,* a sensual voice commanded out of the darkness, *I always love dancing. It is like flying without wings. Take my hand, dance with me.*

She looked up to see the clouds part and stars appear, brightly shining like jewels beset an indigo cloak. Then, while vehemently shivering, she saw a darker silhouette come into view against the sky. It was hard to focus because she couldn't feel her face, her eyes were almost swollen shut from the ice, and touching the source would be impossible because her fingertips and toes were numb. Licking the ice covering her lips, she could feel the freeze give way under the small amount of warmth provided by her tongue.

*If I reach out, will you warm me? Will you keep me from dying?* Mora pleaded in her mind, her voice stuck inside her frozen body. She felt the presence slowly fading away at the request as her heart beat slower. Moving her head slightly toward the dark shadow obstructing the brilliant stars, she painstakingly raised her arm toward the sky, yearning to touch whatever, or whomever, was out there. Against all odds, something grasped onto her hand and pulled her close, covering her with a woolen cloak before cradling her between large, warm arms. Before everything went black, she nuzzled deep against the chest of her savior and caught the faint smell of honey and a heavy, woodsy smoke.

*You didn't trust me. You didn't open your mind to my presence. Why? I offered you a hand, and you reached to the wrong shadow. All you had to do was close your eyes, my love. I would have given you the sun, the stars, and placed you against the most brilliant of fires, if you would have merely given in to the darkness. Solora, my Light, don't abandon me. Seek my presence in each dream, behind each eyelid, and deep within your mind's eye. Surrender yourself to me and I will give you all you desire. You were born for a world unseen, a divine realm that churns deep within your soul. Let me show you, I will guide you on your quest, instilling passion and power into your very body and mind. Come, be my muse.*

*If you didn't take me, who did?*

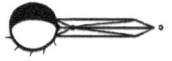

## The Keeper

The darkness faded away behind Mora's eyelids to reveal a warmer, lighter glow. Fluttering her heavy lashes, the brightness burned and the world was blurry. She could not make out shapes, the edges were fading back and forth against the glare of her surroundings. She could smell sweet, smokey meat and honey. As her mouth watered for sustenance and yearned for water, she fingered the soft animal hide coverlet that kept her body cool in spite of the stifling heat. Shifting slightly, her stomach rumbled fiercely.

*Where am I?*

Slowly, the world came back into view. Feeding the smell, she saw a puff of smoke billowing graceful tendrils into the air. Above her loomed a thatched roof. It was a mixture of large, thick, greenish-brown bramble leaves and thin, brown leaves. Where the log beams reached toward the center of the roof, there was an oculus releasing the smoke. The five, thick beams were smoothed and stripped of excess bark and knots. The big, bramble leaves were positioned in a sloping manner from the oculus, with the thinner leaves filling the space between them. Connecting the branches and the bramble to the beams were evenly-spaced, twisted ropes, made from three, leather strings. Various clothing hung from three of the five corners, along with satchels, tools, a cloak, and two pairs of leather boots. Nearest Mora, hung a deep blue, dyed, belted, linen apron-frock with two, silver, oval brooches fastened to the straps.

She slowly rose to her elbows while attempting to keep her head from forcefully pounding behind her eyes. Her body felt distressed from the heated air pushing out the cold from her previously frozen limbs. Panning around the room, she searched for a sign of where, or with whom, she had been rescued. Once again, hunger groaned in her stomach so roughly it was painful. She followed the smoke trail to see the source of the delicious aroma.

*When is the last time I ate?*

Suddenly feeling horribly faint, she pushed the strands of curls away from her eyes. To her surprise, there was a female sitting at a spit while methodically turning meat slowly amidst the lapping flames. She was extremely old, her skin awfully leathery with tired eyes. Her bronze flesh was so taut around her face, she wondered how it had not split or sunken into her skull. The firelight danced off her skeletal features. Her hair was pulled back behind her ears in multiple thin braids that fell well below her waist. It was a pure silver, the brilliance mimicked the glow of the moon at night and contrasted with her skin. Even though she was sitting, her back was visibly hunched and crooked. She wore a forest green, ankle length, wool tunic, covered by a heavy, fur lined, brown vest, and tied around the waist with a leather belted rope. Her boots were a thick hide with visible fur peeking out of the top. The old female had been watching her the entire time with glazed, melancholic, light gray eyes.

Mora sat up fully, grunting while she stretched her back and arms away from the hay she had been laying. Without realizing, the covers she was wearing slipped below her breasts and fell to her waist. Modesty befell her impulses and she burned with an embarrassment, causing her skin to sear with warmth and flush a bright pink from head to toe. Immediately jerking the covers back over her breasts, she stared wide-eyed at the old female, the glazed eyes still never wavering. Frantically, she searched around the hut for any sign of her clothing while she held the blanket around her body, but she could see nothing of familiarity.

Then, her eyes landed on the old female again. Curiosity sparked. *Did she just smirk at me? Or is the light playing tricks on me?*

Tediously, the hag continued to spin the meat spit without a word. Finally frustrated, Mora attempted to speak. Trying to coax the words from her harshly dry mouth, she saw the hag slowly reach her other hand toward a rope right above her head. Following the rope, she saw it was attached to a small bell, about the size of her fist. Before she could object, the old female pulled it three times. She followed the rope back down to the tanned face in time to see her crooked, weathered mouth pine upward into a terribly strange grin.

*She did smile before.*

A nervous twinge vibrated the hairs on the back of her neck as she heard noises starting to stir near the outside door of the hut. Whisperings and giggles filled the air, followed by the sound of horses grunting back and forth with each other. Momentarily, heavy footsteps lingered outside the door before a hand suddenly shoved away the thick cloth draped in the doorway.

Stomping inside the hut, a deep voice boomed, "Well, what might we have here? The sun is rising bright and strong, and ye, m' dear, have slept three days long!" A jolly chuckle echoed around the hut. "Oh, how I do love a good phrase."

The male who walked into the hut was large and burly, dressed in animal skins with a long, thick, black beard attached wirily to his square jaw. A familiar scent of honey and woodsy smoke filled her nose. His smile reached all the way to his warm, amber eyes, the color of liquid honey, and was quite pleasant. His mannerisms were not intimidating in relation to his looming stature.

"So, tell me little dove, from whence you came to be in our lands without a cloak on yer back for warmth, or thick boots on yer feet?"

His accent was foreign to her own, with various inflections on the end of his words. He grabbed a meekly sized chair from the corner, and from the way he plopped down, Mora thought it would snap like a twig beneath a boot. Then, shock soaked in and her senses heightened. She realized he had said three days. Choking on the words, she stuttered, "Three days? I have been sleeping for three *full* days?" Mind racing, she frantically glanced around the room. Hoarsely, she added, "And what land do you speak? I was not aware of any change of lands when I was released from the...uh...er...," she stumbled silently over the words to say. She did not know if she should bring awareness of her previous whereabouts in the Faery Tree.

"Three days now, for certain! Ol' Nema here has been making sure ye don't slip into the lands of the dead while watching over and mending ye frozen extremities. Ye were like an ice cube when I found ye. Brought ye back to camp and me wife's made sure to remove yer garb and wrap ye in the warmest animal skins we own." He smiled proudly at the revealed accomplishments. "Ye in the middle of the Bitter Winds belt, in the Land of G'lo."

Leaning back in the awfully small chair, he crossed his ankles, pulled a pipe out of his vest pocket, and stuffed a mossy textured clump into a hole on the top end before lighting the grass. He sucked in the smoke aggressively before releasing it back into the air in front of him and sighed happily.

Curiously watching the threads of smoke slither through the air toward the oculus, Mora scrunched her nose as the bitter scent stung her nostrils. While eyeing the light through the oculus, she replied, "I know not where that is, I have never heard of the Land of G'lo."

### The Keeper

The heady aroma made her mind a little fuzzy. Running a nervous hand down her braid, she thought hard about her mother's maps. Then, with sudden realization, she glanced down at the blanket covering her *naked* body. Urgently, she clasped around her neck, feeling the light metal chain dangling between her breasts, and let her shoulders drop in exasperation. Not wanting to make any sudden movements, her wide-eyes stared in his direction uncomfortably.

Seeing that he was completely oblivious, she cleared her throat and said, "If you could be so kind as to bring me my clothing, or at least a linen, I would be most appreciative. I'm quite...*uncomfortable*." She could feel the heat rising on her skin and was sure she was turning pink all over her body.

Slapping his brawny hands on his knees, he clicked his tongue. "Certainly!" his voice boomed amusingly, a warm smile reaching to his glowing amber eyes again. He walked over to the thick curtain, pulled it aside, and shouted, "Adeline! This lass needs her clothin'!" Walking back over to the too-small chair shaking his head, he chuckled, "How delightful, another jaunty phrase!"

His grin could not get any bigger, but his jolliness was, in a way, a bit disturbing to Mora. Her mother had never shown happiness that much, but when she did, it was brief and mild. Unable to bring her memories to the forefront of her mind in fear she may begin crying, she continued to hug the blankets closer around her body like a small childling. Turning toward the old hag, Nema, she was met with the same glazed, continuous stare. No emotional expression shown upon her face.

The big male turned his head to Mora's gaze. "Don't worry 'bout ol' Nema! She is blind as a bat, and mute for as many years as I have known her." He stood once again from the chair as it creaked horribly. Walking over to Nema, he patted her on the shoulder of the arm not turning the spit. The grin lessened across his face in deep thought. "M' wife says that she used to speak great tales, beyond the wildest forest, to the most terrifying seas. I don't know if I believe 'em, young'ns tales, I call 'em. All for their imagination, make 'em grow up dreamin' of far off fantastical lands of magic and other worlds unlike our own." He took another big inhale of smoke from his pipe, breathed, and returned the eye touching smile to his face. "No matter what, although she may be blind, she can hear better than a gods forsaken hound in a busy forest. She is the reason we found ye!"

He bent down and pulled a piece of meat from the spit, stuffing it into his beard covered mouth, juices dripping down the coarse, black hair. Licking his large, thick fingers, he roared, "Good ol' Nema! That meat will suffice the tastes of any overgrown male!"

Again, his jolliness grew more disturbingly jovial each time he opened his big mouth to speak. Lifting an eyebrow, Mora asked confusedly, "Found me? What do you mean, 'that's how she found me'?"

A chill met her body as a tall, thin, dark skinned, black haired female entered the hut through the curtain. Her silent entrance amazed Mora after the precocious sounds babbling from the overgrown species stuffing his mouth. Adeline, he had called her, was carrying a stack of neatly folded clothing. Her eyes caught Mora's own. They were piercing; a brilliant dark blue color, like the sky at the peak of nightfall. They were kind, rivaling her pleasant smile. Unlike the male, her smile did not reach all the way to her eyes, but calmly pushed her cheeks higher on her unweathered skin. However, on her face, there was a large scar stretching from her left ear, through her cheek, across her mouth, and stopped on the bottom of her chin. It was not grotesquely obvious, but if it were not for the scar, her face would have been flawless. Despite the scar, she was still exceptionally beautiful and possessed an otherworldly essence. Dangling, dainty, silver chains hung from her ears, the right attached to a delicate ring in her right nostril. Across her forehead, she wore a headband of bright blue, interwoven through a shower of curly, black hair. Her robe mimicked the headband, accentuating her bosom. Around her slim waist was a wide, leather belt, hugging her midsection tightly.

Mora felt a rush of insecurity, but Adeline smiled and gently handed her the clothing.

Turning to the burly male, she politely said, "Dresden, please leave this female to dress herself."

Pipe in his mouth, he smiled and winked at Mora before leaving the hut.

*He took his leave without a word.* This left her shocked.

The female's accent was not of her partner's, Dresden. She had a small inflection in her voice, causing her words to appear not as fluent and blended. Turning back to Mora, she held out her hand and gestured for her to begin dressing. Gracious, she half smiled in acknowledgment as she turned around to remove the blanket. She recognized her linen shift and hose, but she did not recognize the woolen, full-length frock. It was a fine burgundy hue with a brown, woven belt. *This must be Adeline's. I can't accept such a fine piece of clothing.*

Holding the garment toward Adeline, her eyes turned down and she said humbly, "I can't accept such a lovely piece of clothing."

Adeline placed a hand on Mora's wrist. A warm sensation radiated from her core. "Not to worry, I insist. Please, allow me to help you, Mora."

Mora jolted her head up so hard, she felt a crack in her neck. "How do you know my name?" she demanded. Though none of the events she had experienced recently had made any sense to her, the shock still made her hands shake. She met the female's sharp, blue gaze. Sympathy pulsed in Adeline's eyes.

"Please, do not be alarmed. I..." she paused, "we...mean you no harm."

This was a phrase Mora had come to know well, and highly distrusted. However, Adeline's disposition did not alarm her at all. An ancient sadness echoed in her eyes, a time and place foreign to her young existence.

Adeline held up Mora's shift. It smelled of honeysuckle. "I have seen your presence in the stars. I have spoken with the trees of your wanderings." She bowed her head. "My kin are sky readers, nature wanderers. I am a guest in the Land of G'Lo, a gift of alliance for our clans."

A loneliness loomed in her gaze, but her sincerity did not waver.

"Dresden is a kind-hearted partner, a wonderful soul, but I miss my own, and the only way to feel close is to reach toward the stars. Nema is my great-grandmother, an old soul of six hundred and thirty name days. She came with me to this strange land when I was merely fourteen name days. Before she became mute, she taught me the way of the stars and the trees. Now, she only communicates through symbols." Placing her soft hands on Mora's shoulders, she looked her straight in the eyes. "I apologize. I have frightened you."

Mora realized her shift was still in her hand, stretched in the

**68**

process of pulling it over her head, and the other pieces had been set down while Adeline was talking. She was in awe of Adeline's words. The way she spoke was enchanting, like a calm, serene lullaby. Slowly pulling her linen over her shoulders, her mind raced through the confusion centered around how her life had been turned upside down in only a few days.

Then, her mind started racing. *Wait. Dresden said I have been asleep for three days. How long have I been away from the camp? Is my mother worried? Is she still alive? What has happened to the winged male I rescued from the fall?* Fitting the long frock over her linen, she securely fastened the beautifully decorated brooches and tied the thin, woven belt around her waist. It was still warm in the hut, but her body's anxiousness had subsided a bit. It was replaced with a longing for home, overwhelming her chest and threatening the unwanted tears to surface. She bit down on the inside of her cheek.

Sitting carefully down on the hay bed, she picked up the hose and pulled them up to her knees, one at a time. Flinching at her memories, she remembered her boots had been left under the Faery Tree with her frock. They had been the only pair of boots she currently owned, getting very little wear at home. Stifling another choke of tears, she ran her hand nervously down her disheveled braid. Finally, straightening her shoulders, and comfortable in the clothing, she looked toward Adeline and cleared her throat.

"Nay, I apologize. I am unfamiliar with the vast amount of recognition I am receiving through my journey." She peered at Nema under her lashes and was taken aback when she saw her glazed, light gray eyes staring piercingly back. Hesitantly, she continued, "I greatly appreciate the hospitality, and I am surely indebted to you and your kin."

Adeline smiled and pushed some of her thick, curly hair behind her shoulders. Mora caught a glimpse of a symbol, located directly beneath her right ear, on the side of her neck. It was a small, crescent moon with what appeared to be a sword through the bottom point. A seven-pointed star connected the hilt of the sword to the top point of the crescent.

Adeline noticed Mora's curiosity. "You are intrigued by the symbol." Grinning, she ushered her toward a chair near Nema. She pulled up the wooden chair Dresden had been sitting on earlier, making a three-point arrangement around the fire pit. "It is the symbol of my faith. I am

*69*

from the lineage of the Cau'o'tas." She began to stir the fire diligently with a flat iron as the sparks danced off the metal and the flames reincarnated.

Mora stared into the fire while she listened to the faint hiss of the whistling embers as Adeline began speaking.

"Long ago, the Cau'o'tas were the warriors of the Tree Isle and the readers of the skies. The Tree Isle is in the northeast, across the sea. For centuries, the Glodians were a sister clan. If there was unrest, our clans fought in peace, side by side, staking our enemies abroad and seeking continued harmony with our allies. We have always looked to the stars for answers, the correct path, and the rise of potentially dangerous alliances. That is when we saw a prophecy."

Mora shifted uncomfortably in her chair as she began to hear a small rumble of thunder in the distance. *It's starting again*, she thought to herself nervously. *Has He found me? Is there danger amidst?* Attempting to shut the low droll from her mind, she wanted answers, she wanted to know what in the gods she was doing here, and why she was now suddenly alone in the world, without her mother, her mentor, her only personal contact for five and twenty years. Another faint, monotonous drum of thunder echoed outside. *If Adeline can hear it, she is not showing a hint of alarm.* Staring desperately at Adeline, she watched her deep blue eyes swim with an intensity that mirrored the heat of the flames.

Adeline continued, "Through the revelation, eight hundred years ago, an argument arose between the Land of G'Lo and the Tree Isle. There had risen a blunder in the battle to the south. Through this tryst, a vast number of the Glodians turned and made an alliance with an enemy in a desperate turn of favor for what seemed like a hopeless battle. The enemy took the opportunity to discover a weakness with their opponents and commissioned the traitors to assassinate the commander of the Cau'o'tas. Through fear, the traitors agreed and infringed upon their allegiances, successfully killing the commander of the Cau'o'tas - the sister of the Glodian chief.

"It is said, desperate and enraged at the turn of events, and seeking revenge upon the traitors and their new allies, the Glodian chief made a deal with Death. If Death would allow her to win the battle, she would sacrifice her own daughter to Him. Death accepted her offer and allowed the chief to conjure a spell to wake all the dead soldiers under her command." Adeline paused briefly. "However, thinking Death's attention was distracted, she covertly sent her most entrusted nursemaid to warn her family of her unspeakable pact with Death. She hoped it would give them the opportunity to flee for safety before her return."

Upon the mention of Death, the thunder resonated louder, becoming more frequent in its faultless argument with the lightning. It was the first time Mora watched Adeline's strong eyes show a faint flash of nervousness. However, the story beguiled her and she yearned to hear more, despite the rumble of thunder vibrating her core. A familiar clammy sensation started on her neck and ran down her body, causing the hairs to stand on end and her body to feel cold against the heat of the fire. As the rumbling became louder and the light around the hut began to darken, Adeline's face eerily illuminated with the orange glow of the fire. An intensity grew in her slightly quivering voice.

"You cannot fool Death, for Death wants, and will take, what He is promised. Upon her victory, the chief rode back to her homeland to find her family slaughtered by a band of renegades. She cried out in angst to Death, but Death would not hear her plea. As punishment for defying the pact with Him, the chief would live a ghastly existence for all eternity.

"Within a few days, the chief suffered a horrible accident. She lost both her legs from the knee down and was struck blind from fever. She tried countless times to take her own life, getting grotesquely creative with each of her attempts." Adeline shuddered. "But Death neither allowed her to heal, nor die, for it had become a game He would gladly play for retribution."

Lightning flashed, lighting the entire room briefly with an surreal glow. The scar on Adeline's face appeared deeper than Mora remembered. *Is the light tricking my eyes?* She blinked. The scar on her face appeared to be subtly glowing, intensifying gradually. *I must still be weary.* She shifted uncomfortably.

Adeline lowered her voice to a whisper, the scar like a streak of lightning across her bronze flesh. "When the Cau'o'tas received word of this monstrous deed, they turned their backs on the Glodians for centuries, refusing any relation with the damned. Mine and my sisters' marriages helped mend some broken pieces. And while the Cau'o'tas still mourned their commander, they looked once more to the stars for further guidance.

It was then they stumbled upon the prophecy. For hundreds of years, the prophecy was not clear, it contained holes, gaps of significant magnitude... until last night."

She glared hard into Mora's eyes, as if probing for answers, the scar glowing brightly against the darkened room. Mora realized the fire was now merely a subtle glow of embers. She glanced at Nema, a quiet figure with a nasty, toothless grin, her hazy eyes glaring. Surprised, she noticed a similar scar along the leathery cheek she had not noticed previously because it had been turned away from her view. The scar cut through her hair, over her left ear and down, stopping at her jawline. It too, was glowing like a streak of lightning. She slowly turned her gaze back to Adeline. Both females were frozen like stone statues. Dread and fear filled the pit of her stomach, and the silence made her want to escape, to run, and never look back. Before she decided to bolt, a horrendous clap of thunder broke the silence, making her nearly hurdle from her chair. However, feeling stuck to her chair by fear, Mora swallowed and whispered, "Where am I?"

This time, it was not Adeline who spoke, but the raspy voice of Nema, "*I'mun dai*, you are in the Realm of Immortals."

# Rejuvenation

At the first light of dawn, he stirred. With his outstretched arms, he blindly felt around for a cloak to pull over his exposed flesh. The immensely cold wind was hitting his face like needles. When he did not locate what he was looking for, he opened his eyes slightly, trying to adjust to the excruciating bright light. Tears from straining ran down his cheeks, nearly freezing mid-stream from the cold. Suddenly aware, he realized it wasn't just his face that was abnormally cold, it was his flesh, taut from overexposure to the rapidly dropping temperature. He was stiff, and could not feel his feet. This was exceptionally hard to believe considering his higher body temperature. He was rarely cold.

As his eyes adjusted to the light, he looked down to see he had apparently kicked off the blanket during the night, exposing his flesh to a thick layer of newly fallen snow. Attempting to move his wings, he slowly pulled his body onto his elbows, propping high enough to survey his surroundings. To his surprise, the snow had taken its toll on the encompassing vegetation. The flowering plants were buried, leaving nothing but the utmost stems exposed in a dangerously lethal position amongst the snow. It appeared as though the snow had thorns protruding from its icy layers. Many smaller trees were uncomfortably bent over, the weight from the ice heavy atop the branches and the sinews of the trunks stretched to the point of breakage. Cautiously, he rose to his feet and attempted to wiggle his toes into his boots, an effort sorely constricted by the lack of feeling.

## The Keeper

Once he was finally able to step around the spot he had lain, he looked around the forgotten camp. The fire pit had been long covered by the snow, no longer easily seen, save for the tainted sludge from the burnt embers. He kicked it around with his boots, stirring up the icy slush that had accumulated under his body. There was no sun. He could not remember the last time he saw the sun. *Have I been asleep for a day? A week? A month?* Whomever had placed the blanket around his body had long been absent from the camp.

He began to take a couple of steps around the clearing, his wings heavier with the ice dangling between the feathers. He attempted to shake the shards out. However, the wind was so cold, it would not thaw enough to loosen. Sluggishly, he scanned the clearing beyond the camp for any hope of dry wood to ignite another fire. Nothing appeared viable in the bleakness of wind and swirling flakes. The current hit his face again, forcefully ruffling his wings. The direction had changed. This space was no longer useful for keeping warm and dry. Feeling defeated, he decided to search for another area to brace against the growing storm.

*It's not time for the onset of winter. I wonder what has caused the disturbance in the weather.*

Gathering and consolidating the supplies lying around the once inhabited area, he hoped whomever was here had abandoned the clearing - no matter how awful he felt for the unfortunate soul enduring this blizzard without their belongings. Slowly, he trudged to an overhanging rock formation to the far north side. Satisfied it provided enough protection from the wind, he began to dig the snow out from beneath the furthest protruding rock. The ground was hard and brittle beneath his fingers as he scrambled around in the stiff dirt. Creating a medium sized hole, about five hand lengths wide, he stopped and gazed around the overhang. Listening intently, he shuttered as the wind howled violently in the entrance. Unaware of how long the direction of the wind would stay current, he knew this could not be a long term option for shelter.

*Once the snow lightens and the wind calms, I will continue my journey,* he paused, thinking, unable to recall every detail of that said journey, *whatever that had been.*

Sitting down on one of the drier rocks near the hole he dug, he reluctantly sighed as he peered over his shoulder to one of his wings. He

74

had attempted such a deed only a few times before; and while he did not want to rely on his wings to save him, he was desperate. Taking a big breath, he winced as he plucked a small, frozen feather from his left wing. The feather shimmered with a hint of gold and silver, accentuated even more with the ice. He cupped the feather between his large hands, feeling the ice slowly melting through his fingers. Hesitantly, he studied the feather. His wings had been a heavy burden, more than a blessing, throughout his life. However, knowing the potential consequences of using such extreme measures to complete even the most menial task was enough to make him leery. The result could be an insatiable hunger for more power, an unquenchable thirst to continue the surge of energy, an irreparable desire to tear each and every feather from his wings until he had mutilated himself beyond repair. The thought of it churned his stomach. He sighed, loathing how he was relying on his affliction at a time of weakness.

He held the feather caged in his hands and brought them close to his mouth. Through a small hole between his thumbs, he pressed his lips against his skin and blew softly. It only took a moment, but he could feel the warmth building against his flesh and saw light seeping from between his fingers. He opened his palms. A spark popped, light illuminated his face, and a tendril of seductive smoke languidly slithered into his nostrils. He began to feel the animalistic awakening of energy and saw the subtle glow of his eyes reflecting off his skin. Immediately lowering his hands, but with a wry grin of temptation coaxing his desires, he placed the feather into the freshly dug hole. Watching the flame grow larger, melting the snow around the dirt, he held his hands out to the flame. Although the lingering scent incessantly taunted him to indulge more, he took a deep breath and concentrated on the warmth. The steady increase of heat made the ice melt away from his skin, and he could feel the life fueling into the rest of his body. He turned his wings toward the flames. Feeling the thaw of ice slide down his back, he lifted his arms into the air and stretched. Shuddering, the sensation could only be compared to the euphoric surge of sexual release. After a moment, the rejuvenation of life completely soaked into the depths of his hollow bones.

# Amidst the Storm

A blinding light barreled through the oculus, crackling in the middle of Mora, Adeline, and Nema, followed by a ferocious *boom!* which violently shook the hut. There was a smell of scorched ground and smoke that made Mora's eyes sting. She could hear the rush of footsteps, both creatural and animal outside the doorway. The chaotic sound of frightened horses and dogs sent tiny bumps along her skin. A nasty growl howled close to the curtain. She could feel the hairs rising all over her body as she sat shaking in her chair, still too frightened to move. Eyes darting around the hut, she noticed Nema rocking back and forth in her chair chanting in a language she was not familiar, and Adeline, her eyes glazed over as if in a trance. Willing a sense to move, she pulled her body free from the chair and frantically fell to Adeline's feet. She clutched her cold, stiff hands.

Desperately seeking for awareness in the deep blue eyes, the lightning scar almost too bright for her to see her face, she shook her violently and yelled, "Adeline! Adeline! What is going on! Release yourself from this terror struck state and speak to me!"

Another flash of lightning struck through the oculus, landing only a couple hand lengths from Mora's leg. She bucked. Suddenly, she could feel Adeline's hands grasp harshly onto her wrists. Holding tightly, her fingernails dug fiercely into her skin. Drops of blood dripped onto the scorched dirt below, hissing. A shriek radiated from her throat. "Adeline! What the gods are you doing to me! Release me!"

## The Keeper

She relentlessly tried to shake off Adeline's hands, wriggling her whole body to get free, but the entranced female dug harder. Another loud crash of thunder shook the hut, nearly knocking her off her feet.

"Solora," a low, sensual voice projected from Adeline's mouth. It was not her own. It was a familiar sound, one Mora had recently come to know.

"Look upon me," the voice commanded authoritatively. "Cease your struggle, for your strength is no match for my own."

Knowing to fight the situation would be fruitless, Mora acquiesced. Continuing to shake with anxiety, she spoke brashly, "Leave these creaturals be, it is I you seek." Pleading with her eyes, she knew He could see her face while Adeline's possessed hands were still wrapped tautly around her wrists.

A deep, gruff laugh echoed through the hut. "These are not mere creaturals you are in the presence of! You are in the Realm of Immortals. They are not innocent, defenseless, *mortal* swine herders! They are killers, each after their own continued immortality. An eternal damnation to attempt a normalcy of sort, while still declaring their individual superiority over each other and their ultimate dominance over the Mortal Realm."

"Immortals? To die would be impossible!"

"So much to learn foolish *dali*! There are weapons created and wielded to extinguish immortality. While the task is more difficult than a mortal, it can be done. Not to mention, higher immortals can slaughter those equal or lower than themselves," a seductive grin flashed on Adeline's face, "for their own pleasure."

Mora winced. "Are you not immortal?" A warm trickle of new blood started to run down her wrists, hissing as it hit the dirt.

"Tis so. But unlike this weak species of immortality, I *am* Immortality," the voice paused only to draw a grimace across Adeline's sweet face. "I go by many names my love, but in the end, the last name they cry is..." a growl resonated deep in her throat, "...Death."

A rage roared within her mind. No longer caging herself behind the bars of fear, between gritted teeth, she snarled, "If you are Death, show yourself to me instead of using a pawn to relay your foolish game."

Adeline's hands began to release her wrists. Mora could feel the long fingernails exiting her flesh, causing a nauseated feeling in her stomach to lurch. Her hands fell hard against her side. More fresh, warm blood trickled down into her palms. Lightheaded, she glanced up at Adeline. The smooth lines of her face started to wince in pain, the glowing scar fading quickly, and her body commencing to twitch. She scrambled to her feet and slowly backed away. Adeline clutched her head and let out a high pitched scream. As if removing a spoon from honey, a shape took form, parting from Adeline's body. It was a dark, smokey shape, emerging from her skin. She could see the pain on Adeline's face as she reached a desperate hand out in agony. However, she felt helpless and unable to bring comfort to her writhing body. As the last of the smoke emerged, Adeline's convulsing form fell back in the chair behind her, slumped over, and hung motionless.

The dark, smokey figure walked languidly toward Mora. She backed up until her spine was flush against the wall. From the bottom to the top, the shape of the bewitching male in the Faery Tree materialized. Her throat tightened. He was naked, exposing a beautiful pale color of flesh with a hint of shimmer upon His taut, muscular physique. Her cheeks began to flush. Attempting to look no further than His chiseled hips, she imagined His body was an exquisite example of the perfect physical form. Quite taller than herself, she looked up as the sharp jawline grinned slyly. His hair fell loosely over His forehead, the hint of indigo apparent in the black strands. She could almost see her reflection in the brilliant onyx eyes. Under both elbows, there were three, thick, black rings surrounding His forearms, spanning from the thickest, which was closest to the elbow, to the thinnest, which was only slightly thinner than the previous two.

*It* is *Him.*

He lifted His head in response. The grin grew wider across His face, reaching His eyes, and grandly exposing pure white teeth.

At that moment, Mora realized her mistake in summoning Him here. In fear, there was no escape. She thought about all her past transgressions, especially her mother. A desperate yearning surged through her body. She closed her eyes as the burning sensation of tears amassed beneath the surface. *I will not be broken. I will not be weak.* Startled, she felt soft fingers brush her hair over and behind her ear. She slowly opened her eyes.

Standing only a hand's length away from her body pressed against the wall, He spoke gently, "Did you miss me, my love? I can only assume that is why you wanted to see me here, amongst this forsaken land, to gaze upon the flesh in which you desperately long to touch. Don't fear me."

His gaze caught Mora by surprise. As much as she tried to look away, His eyes were uncontrollably fixed.

His lips lifted on one side in a half grin. Caressing His thumb softly across her cheek, He inquired gently, "Why do you shy from me? My lack of Creatural intuition hinders my empathy toward your shyness. Are you ashamed for my nakedness? I will gladly clothe my flesh if you would feel more comfortable approaching me."

Taking a step back, similar to how He materialized, the black garb He wore under the Faery Tree appeared from bottom to top, clothing Him with an incomparable radiance. Subtly, she could still see His pristine chest peeking through the top slit of the tunic. Each and every bone in her body started to waiver under the pressure of her skin. Nervous He could sense her emotions, she attempted to wipe her mind of the crippling fear she had sensed was slowly becoming a beacon, signaling her weakness. Swallowing what could only be described using the physical qualities of a brick, she held her head high in defiance.

"I do not *fear* you. I know not what or who you are, except for your proclamation that you are ultimately Death itself. How must I know with whom I am speaking if I have never had death reveal itself to me before?"

Mora knew it was a juvenile response, one she miserably feared He would see through immediately. However, the truth was she had never thought about the *experience* or the *concept* of death before in terms of anything but the sustenance she acquired around the clearing of her sanctuary. Even then, it was not something her mother spoke about in relationship to the concept of their own beings. The only time she had seen a description of the death of a being like herself was in one of the books she would read when her mother wasn't around. *How can He be Death?*

He shook His head in a pathetic condolence. "I need not explain myself to you. For deep in your heart, you know it to be true. If not sooner, than you will later." Steadily, He began to walk toward her despite her obvious stiffening of stance. "If it weren't for you, I wouldn't be here in this godsdamned land. I do not need to extend my courtesies amongst the brutalities of your naivety to only believe what you see and not what you feel. My rightful place is amongst All. Therefore, Solora, why make my vengeance all the more difficult?"

Skewing her face, she muttered, "Vengeance? For what...or whom?"

He placed His hand against the wall behind her and leaned closer.

She could feel His breath, His aura, caress her flesh. His lips grazed her ear, the warmth affecting her senses. A slow, steady heat bloomed inside her core, building an indecent awareness of her extremities.

He deeply mumbled into her ear, "Are you *that* foolish as to think you could hide from me for so long?"

She sensed the passion behind the words. "I know not of what you speak," she replied, trying to hold her voice steady. A tremble vibrated through her and she whispered, "I am merely a chance happening within this Realm of Immortals. I know not why I am here, nor how I stumbled upon this place."

"If that were not shit from the gods directly." He grabbed her waist with His other hand, held her face to face, and pressed His hips into her own. "You are here for one purpose and one purpose only. There is nothing you can hide from me. I know when you lie." He brushed His lips against her own, tasting the sultry sweetness of her innocence beading like dew at dawn. He licked her bottom lip and purred, "Now tell me, why do you keep running?"

Mora stared Him directly in the eyes. There was only one thing she desperately wanted to know and she knew it had to do with His unexpected appearance in her life. She would not back down. She swallowed and snarled, "I care to know what happened to my mother."

He loosened His grip on her waist and pulled back His head as He snickered. "Your mother?" He replied dully. Capturing her gaze with His onyx eyes, He contemplated the statement before saying, "Your mother was nothing but a vessel. Unfortunately, she neglected to tell you who you are and why you are required to oblige to your Maker's demands."

Slightly pushing Mora back against the wall of the hut, He pressed Himself against her body again. With a presence that was both commanding and seductive, His hand grasped softly around her chin and pulled her eyes up to His own. Darkly, He murmured, "The whore thought she could hide you from me."

His mouth turned into a grimacing line and the intensity of His mood hatched a heaviness around the hut.

"I underestimated her desperation for protection. I was too blinded with desire to feel her wavering loyalty." Thunder rumbled outside, echoing His deeply chested voice. "I do not appreciate subordination."

An anger rose in Mora until her face was burning with a rage she had never experienced. She tried to wriggle free, pulling her arms above her waist in an attempt to release herself. "Never call my mother a whore!" She spit into His face.

Wiping the saliva off in His callous manner, He forcibly lifted her arms over her head, caustically responding, "Because of your so-called-mother, you have become an insolent pain in my side! You know not what you want and deliberately disobey in an attempt to earn a chance to live life the way you compensate as *freedom*. You know nothing of the world beyond the shit ridden boundaries Meridan attempted to conjure. Don't worry," lifting His eyebrows as a sinister smile swept across His face, "your mother struggled just so when I gave her a choice."

"It fucking kept you away for a quarter of a century!" The malice of His grin continued to awaken an emblazoned rage in her mind. *I will kill Him!*

Still ferociously wriggling, she bowed her back, attempting to put space between His body and hers, despite how tightly He held her wrists. Glancing quickly to each side as she arched, she noticed a few sharp-tipped metal objects hanging on the wall about an arm's length away. *They are not knives, but they will do*, she considered. She turned back to see the seductive grin appear once more.

"I can feel your rage, and every ounce of it only strengthens my very purpose. You think you can kill me that easily? Show me Solora, what would you care to make of your situation?"

He leaned down toward her ear, and as His grip loosened slightly, she snapped. All at once, her anger burst in a wave of strength, pulsating from her core. First, she managed to slip a hand free from His grasp and grabbed the nearest sharp object she could reach off the wall. Then, with all the power she could muster, she made contact with His ribs, twisting for added pain. Finally, as she forcefully ripped it out, a black smoke burst from His side, tainting her fingers as He drew back in shock for only a moment. It was enough for her to struggle free of His grasp.

"You bitch!" He roared as she shoved a chair between them.

A sadistic laughter pierced her ears. Lightning flashed through the oculus, nearly missing the left side of her body. Panicking, Mora glanced in His direction as His body began to become transparent and billowy, like the smoke from which He manifested earlier. Hastily, she turned to run. A loud *boom!* of thunder rattled the hut, making her loose her footing and nearly fall to the dirt. Catching herself, she looked toward the doorway. A desperate, hopeless feeling rushed in as she saw Him materialize into His physical form, blocking her from the door.

A deep growl resonated from His throat, "You cannot escape me! I am everywhere and everything. You cannot hide from your purpose. I am the shadow, the darkest and most concealed corners of All. I will have you for the rest of eternity!"

Mora threw the metal object like an axe toward His form and He ducked. However, as she straightened to locate another object for a weapon, she froze. His entire body became engulfed in flames, screeching in anger. Frantically, she whipped around to see Nema standing at an unbelievable stance, tall and strong. Her body didn't look frail and old anymore. Her arms were outstretched and she was muttering a chant in the unfamiliar language she had heard earlier. There was an ancient hum radiating from her presence, causing Mora to cower in reverence.

All of a sudden, Nema caught her gaze. Penetrating her stare with glowing, light gray eyes, she commanded, "Run, young one, run!"

Frightened and without question, Mora dodged the burning body stumbling aimlessly around the hut as it clutched its head. She pushed aside the curtain and ran with all her might toward the village edge. Briefly pausing to look around, she realized darkness was quickly settling all around, making it harder to see. *But it is not night,* her memory whispered. She strained her eyes to her sublime surroundings. The dark appeared to be a result from the menacing thunderclouds billowing overhead. The wild wind was whipping her hair around her face, making it even more difficult to decide where to run next. It was strong and blowing through the trees ferociously, lashing the branches around in a violent dance. Bright flashes of lightning were sporadically lighting up the land, but only for a few moments, and then her surroundings would disappear.

Her chest began to heave, her breathing shallow. The feeling of danger was crawling up her skin, but she knew not what to do, nor where to go. Briefly glancing back at the hut, the screams tore through the thick air and echoed on the wind. Fire bursted from the oculus. Correlating with His fury, the storm intensified, raging through the air with an unleashed vengeance. Deep inside her mind, a feeling of sympathy ignited, an unwanted need to go back to His aid and to surrender herself to His will. She fought the urge vehemently. Knowing it was another ploy to coax her to Him, she shook her head and screamed.

Through her screams, a hand grasped her arm and hissed, "This way!"

Swiftly, Mora was being pulled against her will toward the silhouetted outline of the trees. Every few pauses, the lightning crashed and she saw the brief outline of a large body leading her further in to the forest. The sympathetic feeling inside her mind grew into a formidable yearn to turn back to Him. It felt like He was attempting to reel her back with an invisible, unbreakable thread.

Faintly, she thought she heard Him whisper in the wind, *Solora.*

Suddenly, a searing pain exploded in her face. Mora whelped as a branch smashed into her nose. Grasping her face in agony, she could feel a warmth running down to her lips and tasted the metallic bitterness seep into her mouth. Tears swelled in her eyes and cascaded down her face, mixing their saltiness with the gut-wrenching taste of blood. She wanted to scream, but the pain of her nose was excruciating, and her chest was tightening as she gasped through her mouth for breath. She stumbled across a fallen tree, twisting her ankle in a hole. Blind to her surroundings, a heavy grunt sounded beside her as she was lifted into heavily muscled arms.

Her head rolled back as the pain threatened to tear open her skull. Rain drops were beginning to fall across her face, further obscuring her sight. She closed her eyes. Somewhere deep inside her mind, another type of hurt emerged. Instantly, she knew it was the pain *He* was feeling. The pain wasn't a physical pain, it was full of sadness and loss. The rain drops were *His* tears. Raining harder, there was no longer a feeling of terror radiating inside her chest, but a feeling of guilt. She reached further into her mind and realized she could see the outline of the world through her eyelids. She could feel each surface the rain fell upon, taste the tears on her tongue, and hear the thrumming of vibrations in the various rain soaked textures. She felt connected to everything.

*Solora, return. Allow me to show you the truth, and help reveal the secrets that have been bestowed upon your mind. Let me help you carry the weight of your Knowledge. Together, we can sustain the order of All!*

The words were whispered with love, mixed with an emotion so intense, it bordered on insanity. Mora was beginning to realize His pull over her emotions. He was controlling how she was feeling, stronger in this world than she had ever felt before. Desperately, she was trying to block His plea from her mind. Because, despite the feeling of profound love, there was a horrible darkness that followed, looming in the shadows. Forcing herself to open her eyes, she recognized her captor. *It is Dresden.* She smiled and lulled back into an empty void amongst the scent of heavy smoke and honey.

A flash of lightning lit up an enormous tree ahead of Dresden's path. He trudged swiftly on the wet terrain, knowing if he didn't make it to the tree, he couldn't help Mora. *I'm doing this for Adeline*, he repeated to himself to encourage his trek further. If he didn't, he knew he would run back to her in the hut, but that's not what she made him promise. A bolt of lightning struck a tree in front of him as he dodged out of the way, nearly tripping over a cluster of rocks. The thunder clapped louder and the wind shoved him violently, attempting to throw him off course.

"Stay with me!" he yelled as Mora's head rolled back.

Panting, he leapt over another fallen tree, catching himself before he stumbled into a hole. The mud thickened under his boots. He had another feeling this was an attempt to slow him down. However, he never gave up without a fight, and he was not willing to fail this time. He gritted his teeth and took longer strides. Finally reaching the trunk, he banged a big fist hard against the base, roaring through the thick wood. An answer from the opposite side retaliated and a latch snapped from inside. Dresden brutally pushed the hidden door wide open before waiting for the other body to move out of the way. Storming in forcefully, he turned around and flung his body against the door, closing it quickly with Mora in his arms.

The pain of Mora's nose started making her head swim, wakening her from the dreamless void. Flickering her eyes open, she attempted to focus on her surroundings, but still felt lightheaded. A familiar nauseated feeling caused her to lurch to the side, dry heaving because she had had nothing in her stomach for...*days?* Wiping the spit from her mouth with the back of her hand, she looked down to see she was drenched from head to toe with rain and blood.

"Lay still, m' dear. Let me look at yer face," a husky female's voice echoed from across the room.

Heavy, but steady footsteps, shuffled closer as she squinted at the back of a large bodied female. Steam was rising from the pot she was stirring, and there was a severe grumble in Mora's stomach when the smell reached her nose.

"There, there, yer look positively shaken. Yer also skin and bones!" The big female made a *tsking* sound as she brought over a small, steaming bowl and laid it next to the bed. "Yer nose is broken, my dear. I'm going to set it back into place before I help yer sit up."

The voice was kind. Although Mora couldn't focus clearly on her face, she did not feel alarmed.

"Here, bite down on this." She placed a piece of flat bread between Mora's teeth, settled her hands on each side of her nose, and quickly moved her hands, causing the nose to make a *pop!* sound.

A whimper escaped Mora's mouth between her clenched teeth. However, once she tasted the bite of flat bread on her tongue, her hunger took over as a welcomed distraction. She groaned and carefully chewed the bread. It tasted of sweet honey and had a satisfying crunch on the outer shell, followed by a center that melted in her mouth. Once swallowed, she took another couple large bites before she devoured the entire piece.

"She's starving!" the large female yelped. "Here love, let me help yer sit up and drink this broth."

With her large arms, she effortlessly swept Mora to a sitting position, pushed pillows behind the small of her back, and blew the steam from the bowl. Holding the liquid to her lips, the heat and scent of the broth caused her to grab the female's big hands and ravage the bowl, not stopping until the last drop was consumed. It tasted of seasoned vegetables, similar to what her mother cooked for her when she didn't feel well. She handed Mora another few pieces of flat bread, which was hastily consumed in large, rapid bites.

Taking a deep breath, Mora was finally able to see the face clearly. She resembled Dresden, rivaling him in her stature and square jawline - minus the burly, dark beard. Her eyes were also a liquid amber, bright and jolly. Her smile was pleasant and, while her teeth were stained with browns and yellows, it reached all the way to her eyes. Reaching in her pocket, she pulled out a brown clump of grass, but instead of putting it in a pipe like Dresden had, she placed it in the side of her cheek.

Seeing Mora's curiosity, she cleared her throat, "It's an herb, made from the roots of fungi located around the forest. Unlike Dresden, I prefer to taste the raw, natural root instead of inhaling it. Same herb, different effects." She winked at her and lowered her voice, "He can't handle the full experience it creates."

"Fuck off wench," Dresden mumbled from a leaning, appropriately sized chair on the other side of the room, his head against the wall, eyes closed, and his pipe hanging from his lips. "Don't fill her head with yer nonsensical judgments."

Mora looked back at the large female who was now turning at the hip toward Dresden.

"Yer nearly got her killed ye fucking oaf!" She threw a nearby plate. It crashed into the wall next to his head and shattered.

He covered his head from the shards as his chair fell forward onto the front legs with a loud cracking sound. "What would ye have me do? She was standin' there, frozen, lookin' back at the hut. I could see in her eyes that He was enticin' her back to Him! Therefore, I jerked her from the trance. Figured if she ran, it would take her mind off the bastard. Anyway, I promised Adeline I would." Dresden grunted. "I didn't mean for her to run into the branch," he paused, "although, if it weren't for the damn branch, I may not have been able to make it here with her at all!"

Clearly not convinced, she walked over to a small table and picked up a bottle of brown liquid, another of clear liquid, and a small, green pouch with a black drawstring. Still eyeing Dresden slyly, she sat in front of Mora and grinned.

"Sit still, my dear. Yer have a lot of journey ahead of ye very soon." She sighed heavily. "Yer cannot stay here. He will be comin' for ye."

Handing Mora the bottle of brown liquid, she made a motion and commanded, "Drink," before she pulled out a white cloth, a needle and thread, and some brown powder from the small, green pouch. "I'm sorry young 'un, but this may sting a little. Ye have a nasty gash across your eyebrow that needs to be tended soon before it festers. I will work quickly."

Mora heard Dresden guffaw in his chair. Reaching her fingers her eyebrow to feel what she was referring to, the oversized hand gently swiped them away and resumed the tedious work of threading the needle with her own, obese fingers. Obediently removing the cork from the bottle, she held it to the entrance of her lips and threw back her head as the burning sensation scorched her throat. She coughed, wiping her mouth with the back of her hand. The large female snickered. She knew this liquid would have the same head swimming effect as her mother's healing liquid. On numerous occasions, thinking Mora was not watching, she had taken several swigs while also pouring it on her open wounds.

"Thank you," she managed to sputter.

"She speaks!" The husky, yet slightly feminine voice, slapped her knee, smiled, and chortled, "Now hold still."

Mora allowed her to work on her face. A searing pain burned when she poured the clear liquid over her left eyebrow, nose, and lips while catching it with the white cloth. Gently blotting it from her cheeks, she motioned Mora to drink again while she cleaned the wounds. Grabbing her chest, Mora cringed as the liquid slithered like a fire down her throat, the warmth rapidly spreading under her skin.

Before the heavy hands began sewing, she assured Mora, "This serum will allow ye not to bruise much under your skin while easing the pain and numbing the area I'm about to stitch. It will also allow yer nose to heal quicker and not continue radiating the throbbing pain throughout yer skull."

Mora nodded like a helpless childling, took another swig, which was much easier this time, and braced for the needle. Closing her eyes gently, she could feel the thick fingers pinching the tender flesh a little and feeling around for the correct place to begin. As the needle poked through her skin, she thought she would faint. While the pain wasn't excruciating, the feeling of a needle lacing that closely to her eye made her queasy and lightheaded. *Or maybe that's the liquid.*

She braced herself for each pull and tug of thread until she heard the snip. *It's done.*

Opening one of her eyes carefully, she watched the overly large, but gentle hands, pour more clear liquid onto another white cloth and sterilize the wound again.

Applying a small dab of the brown powder over the newly stitched area, she placed her larger hands on Mora's shoulders. "There," with a satisfyingly toothy grin, she bellowed, "all done!"

Mora smiled sweetly, realizing the room was starting to feel dreamy. She tried to adjust her eyes, but an intoxicating sensation took over her body and mind. Looking down at her hands, she felt like she could float away. She felt happy and care free. She giggled with delight.

"That is a good lass. Drink more." She encouraged Mora to take another swig. Turning toward Dresden, she tossed a pillow at his back. "Dresden, go prepare the way through the back door and be quick about it."

Dresden glanced back at Mora, smiled, and headed into a smaller room toward the back of the tree.

Mora could feel an excitement restoring into her limbs. A butterfly danced in her eyes and copious amounts of flowers commenced to bloom on the floor at her feet. Like her youth in the little garden next to her home, the colors were bright and luscious. She wanted to desperately reach out and touch a nearby butterfly, slowly tickle its wings, and feel it dance across her hand. However, disappointment quickly replaced her curious excitement as her brooches were unfastened and the beautiful dark blue frock Adeline had given her was cautiously tugged over her face, causing her wet hair to slap against her cheeks. Sulking, an uncomfortable jerk shook her limbs, raising her hands above her head to remove the soaked garb. Then, her dirty flesh was cleaned and patted dry with fresh rags.

Curious, Mora lifted the unstitched eyebrow. "What happened to Adeline? And Nema?"

Once the large female placed a fresh linen shift and a mossy green, shin-length frock back on Mora's nakedness, she sighed, "They will be fine." She brushed through her hair quickly, but carefully, before braiding it securely down her back. "Dresden will check on their state once ye are safely away from this Realm." Handing her a pair of leather boots, she added, "These are the boots Adeline was going to gift ye before He showed up. She will not mind me personally giving them to ye."

Hardly able to feel her fingers, Mora fumbled with the laces. Stubbornly, she tried to lace them again. Finally frustrated, she howled and slurred, "Godsdamn forsaken laces!" If the company was irritated with her, she could not sense it. A familiar pang of need nestled into her stomach. *Mother*. Tears welled in her eyes and she sniffled.

Lifting Mora's chin, the other female furrowed her thick, strong brow with a look of pity. "Now, now, m' dear, it is well. The intoxication is necessary to fog yer mind. Ye will return to yer cognitive state when ye reach the other side." She finished lacing the boots, despite Mora's ticklish squirming.

"It's not that," Mora turned her saddened gaze down at her hands in her lap. "He said He killed my mother." She didn't know if the tears were falling freer because of the brown, burning liquid, or if she was horribly upset. However, she had felt like she was going to find her mother and all would be well, that she would no longer feel alone. "I'm scared."

Muscled arms pulled Mora into a tight embrace, holding her for only a moment before the oversized hands rested on her cheeks. "Ye will succeed. Ye are stronger and more powerful than ye realize." Then, her amber eyes glowed brighter and she whispered, "Find the winged one with eyes the radiant hue of violets after a summer rain."

Mora didn't know what to think. *Winged?* A faint memory tugged deep in her mind, vaguely hinting at something she should remember. She stared into the big, deep-set eyes, tilted her head, and asked, "What is your name?"

Motherly, full lips kissed her forehead and said, "Marwen, eldest sister of Dresden, the big, bloody oaf."

She grinned so wide, her eyes lit up again with the warm amber glow. "Marwen," a taste of sweet honey and lavender coated her tongue as she spoke the name. "Thank you, Marwen. I hope our paths will cross again."

Marwen smiled. "It is not likely, my young one."

The reply baffled Mora. It was as if Marwen sensed something she couldn't quite place. The wind commenced to wail terribly outside of the door, branches scrapping like fingernails against the wood.

With a jerk, Marwen's head turned toward the door. She whispered darkly, "He's here."

Swiftly, she whisked Mora toward the back of the room through the small, open door lit only by a faint candle hanging behind the doorway. "Is it ready?" she asked hastily to Dresden. "We must send her through before He realizes she is gone. The spirits are just enough to cloud her mind so He will not sense her thoughts."

When Dresden turned toward them, Mora giggled at his furry beard, drenched like a small animal and smelling sour from the wetness of drink.

"Aye, it is nearly done. I have gathered the twigs an' leaves around the doorframe and placed dirt in a semicircle in front of the doorway. All she will need to do is stand on her own within the dirt." He grabbed Mora's arm as she stumbled over to where he was pointing.

Feeling like she was floating on a cloud, she groaned, "Ouch, you have quite a strong arm Lord Big Bossy Black Beard!" She giggled again and sighed, "Why do I have to stand here alone? I demand a chair to lean on, so I can straighten out my eyes." Stumbling again, she caught herself on the wall. A pout appeared.

As Dresden turned to grab a chair, Marwen hissed at him, "Just leave her there ye big oaf! We have no time for folly. I must concentrate." She grabbed the candle and started chanting around the semi-circle.

Mora, realizing she was still holding the bottle of brown liquid, took another swig of the drink, swaying in her semi-circle. She listened to the howling wind, heard the torrential beating of the rain, and felt the crash of thunder vibrate beneath her feet as it intertwined with the chanting.

"He is getting angry." Mora raised her eyebrows, almost lurching because of the sudden pain above her left eye. However, she still managed to snicker and pester along, slurring at the end of her words, "He wants to talk to me, but He is saying He is going to kill you both for your disloyal-neth." She hiccuped. "Tampering with His posse-sthion."

Dresden's eyes widened and he rubbed his beard nervously. Without warning, Mora saw a growing bright line of light forming from the ground, up the wall, and into the shape of an eloquent doorway, converging at the top. In the middle, there was a beautiful flower. It was shaped like an upside down tulip, pouring out a golden liquid. The golden liquid ran back down the wall, into roots like little thin labyrinths, intricately woven in each other. She was standing in front of the door, too fascinated to move. Upon a loud crack from the other room, the light door flew open, revealing a sunny, snow-covered land. The reflection of the sun made the ground look like twinkling lights.

*It's cold, but inviting,* she thought through the haze as she shielded her eyes. Stumbling to the entrance, she cautiously peeked inside before actually stepping onto the crunchy, frosty ground with her thick, leather boots. Once she was through the door, she glanced nervously back to Marwen.

She tilted her head curiously. *Where is Dresden?*

She could see Marwen holding her hands high, eyes shut, and chanting. She wanted to run back to her desperately. Marwen was caring, thoughtful, and strong. The longing festered deeper, pulling her back toward the doorway. Anxiously, she turned to stumble back. However, to her horror, a dark figure arose. She froze in her tracks. As He lumbered closer behind Marwen, Mora could see His eyes of black ice manifesting, full of malice.

Mora screamed to Marwen, reaching a hand toward the full figure, but a voice inside her head shouted, '*Run, my young one!*' An invisible force harshly pushed her away from the opening as a black sword stabbed through Marwen's back, the end protruding from her abdomen.

Her liquid, amber eyes opened wide in agonizing shock. She raised her arms even higher and screamed the word, "*obl'i'terious!*"

The doorway disappeared.

# A Valuable Gambit

He woke to the low light of the morning. The clouds donned a soft gray coverage, but snow no longer fell outside the overhanging rock. He stretched and sat up. Fastening the cloak around his neck, he looked down. There was nothing left of the flames. *That's odd. It should still be burning.* Begrudgingly, he rose to his feet. Stumbling a little, he could feel his head swimming slightly, sloshing around inside his skull like water. His eyes attempted to adjust as he managed to wipe the crustiness away from his eyelashes. He surveyed the empty forest, squinting his eyes for any visible movement. The land lay still, hushed by the effects of early snowfall.

He was hungry, but had eaten the rest of the contents in the borrowed knapsack the night before. Begrudgingly, he decided to search for sustenance. He bent down to gather his saber. He had tried hard to remember how he had come to be at the fireside of the clearing and his wounds cleaned. However, the last thing he could recollect is being perched upon a high branch, when an object hit him bluntly in the side of the head. It was fast and it was hard. After that, he woke up at the clearing, bruised from the rendezvous, but covered with a blanket. He reached behind his head, only a small lump remained. Glancing back at his wings, the blood had soaked from his back, to the base of the wing. He needed to clean himself off, but the land was covered in sheets of ice. *Water will be difficult to find right now.*

Frustrated, he knelt into a deep pile of broken ice at the entrance of the rock overcrop. His chest muscles tightened and the ice melted through the knees of his breeches. As he rubbed his face vigorously with the snow, a tingling sensation made his whole body shiver. *I have never seen this much snow.* Reaching behind his back, he rubbed the base of his wings thoroughly, but gently, with the melting chunks. *They still hurt like a damn fire scorching my skin.* Finally, he was able to clear enough of the taint of blood from his wings that the only traces were tinges of light red.

The familiar rumble of hunger resumed to taunt him incessantly. His stomach was uncomfortably empty and he felt faint. Sheathing his saber, he consolidated the available contents of the cloth satchels into the one containing a couple sharp knives and some twine. *Extra supplies will come in handy*, he thought. Leaving the overcrop, he wandered further into the forest, marking spots along the way so he could find his way back if his venture proved fruitless.

During his trudging, he thought long and hard about what had happened to him, and what had led him so far away from his own land. Desperate, he began to recollect his most recent memory. The last viable impression was leaving the gates of Borgoria. *Am I on a quest?*, he thought anxiously to himself. Frustrated, he stuck his hands beneath his cloak. Feeling his arm scrape against the corner of a piece of parchment peeking out of an herb bag hanging on his belt, he pulled it out. When he opened the parchment, there were symbols, a description, and a name, *Solora*. He paused abruptly as the familiarness of the name sang in his mind. He clenched his teeth. While intensely centered on trying to figure out the correlation, his concentration was interrupted by a slight movement darting from the corner of his eye. The small, distinctive form ran past, contrasting starkly against the white snow. Quickly, he pulled out one of the knives and slung it forcefully in the direction, hitting the animal square in the throat.

Walking heavily over to the prey, he snickered to himself, *While I am no hunter, apparently my confused mind does not discriminate against my ability to catch food, if forced.* He smirked, wiped the knife in the snow, and picked up the lifeless form by the long ears. *A rabbit. That will do.*

Wanting to calm his insatiable hunger, he found a drier patch of dirt under a well canopied tree nearby. He moved around some slushy snow with his boots. The ground was manageable. He gathered a few nearby sticks, pulled out the flint and stone from the satchel, and began to attempt to light a fire against the slowly increasing wind. While the branches gave a sparse shield, he maneuvered closer with his body to block any residual breeze with his wings. Finally, there was a spark. Settling his frame comfortably between the wind and the flame, he began gutting and tearing the unwanted innards from the rabbit. Satisfied with the unsavory work, he mounted the remains onto a long stick from the tree. Turning it around in the burning twigs, he watched the remaining fur sizzle and burn away until exposing the meaty flesh. As he sat languidly watching the dancing flames, he began to feel exhausted yet again. *My body is still not recovered.* The air was biting. It was unusual for him to feel the effects of cold, but this air was different, something had changed to create this discordant feeling in his core. It made him nervous and leery.

Because there was not much heat, the rabbit took three times as long to cook. Hungrily, his stomach rumbled, echoing low threats of destruction if he neglected to feed it any longer. Assuredly though, after an overextended amount of cooking time, the rabbit was reasonably edible. He smelled the delicious meat closely before he tore into the flesh. Normally, he was slightly choosier at what he consumed, but he did not know the lands around this forest. A strange thought intruded his mind, *There is an unsettling scarcity of meat available in the wooded area. I wonder what has caused the disruption.* This strengthened the feelings of uncertainty.

As he finished his meal, he felt sufficient and ready to return to the overcrop, determined to remember the sole purpose of his journey and what led to his sudden wakening amongst the stones. Making sure the parchment was tucked snugly again in the herb bag, he covered the flames with snow, stood up, and turned around.

Out of sheer horror, he eyed a grotesque, abnormally large figure leering in his direction several trees away. He grimaced as he saw the one, red eye staring at him, his left sewn shut with a disgustingly deep scar torn into his flesh. His heart skipped a beat in his chest and his skin became clammy as the memory of its horrible eye flashed into his mind. The memory of the figure standing over him, beating him in the face relentlessly with his awfully overgrown left hand, while his right, which was no more than a round, metallic rod, held him securely to the ground, surfaced in his mind. The nostrils were nothing more than two holes where a nose should have protruded. This gave the face a nasty, reptilian-like appearance. He could see a number of pointedly sharp teeth salivating out of the sides of its mouth when it grimaced.

"We meet again," it ruthlessly guffawed.

The figure stepped forward as he took a couple of steps back. It possessed mangled, black wings that reminded him of an oversized bat. Bulbously protruding from its skin, sharply angled rivers of veins beat rhythmically. It wore no cloak, nor tunic, over its upper body and had barely enough cloth to cover the horrendously bulging legs. Disgustingly, it only had two bony toes and three skeletal fingers on each limb. Weaving in and out of the skin on its bald head was a copper band, clean through its eyebrows. The skin was callused, scarred in ritualistic form.

A fleeting memory appeared again. The monster had used its brute strength to crack his wings before he passed out. *That is why they burn like fire.* Bile rose in his throat, threatening to lurch into the pristine, white snow.

"I will finish what I started before the fucking little female showed up." It beat its fists together primitively.

Another memory emerged at the mention of 'female', but he could not grasp it. He pulled out his saber, praying to whatever deity will listen to his plea. Unaware he had been hunched over, he rose from the cowering position and stood tall in front of the ugly form. "Who sent you?" he demanded.

It laughed maniacally. "I don't work for anyone! I merely smelt the fear and loathing on your skin - the puny soul covered in your pathetic flesh and bone. For me, it is a game, and the quicker you give in, the less painful it will be." It twisted its mouth and snarled, "However, I feed off resistance. It fuels my tortuous methods for foul play."

They began to dance around each other, one with a saber, the other with a metal rod. Hunched over at the ready, he taunted the monster, "Yet, you were scared off by a female? Nay, you have been commissioned, or else you would have moved on to another unsuspecting victim by now."

It growled and then snickered, "What say you are right? It won't matter when you are dead. I would kill the commander if I was paid in advance." It glanced through its one visible eye directly at its prey, a nastily salivating sound coming from its mouth. "I work ultimately for

*The Keeper*

Death, and He will gladly ransom any soul for pleasure."

It swung gruffly at him, barely missing his chest. He jumped back toward the tree, darted around the trunk, and sunk down low against a bank. A nasty gurgle from its mouth made him gag. It guffawed again and stomped toward the bank. Silently, it stood there for a moment. When he peeked over the edge, the figure had disappeared. He listened motionlessly. Suddenly, he was pulled over the bank by the back of the neck and thrown onto his back. This knocked the air from his lungs. A foot bared down heavily on his chest, the metallic rod pointing at his throat. Panting for breath, with all his might, he pushed its foot from his chest as the end of the sharp rod nipped his skin, burrowing into the ground where his shoulder had lain.

Immediately rising to his feet, he pierced his saber into the scarred side. Unfortunately, its skin was too rough for deep penetration. It merely fell to the ground as black liquid seeped through the shallow puncture wound. In desperation, he searched for a soft spot around the body, avidly blocking the blows as it kicked his limbs violently. It veered its good hand, crashing into his knee. He stumbled back as it scrambled awkwardly to its feet. This time, it got close enough to knock him stoutly in the head. Shaking the pain away, he dodged its metallic rod, ducking quickly, making the form loose its balance.

As the monster hit the ground, he hastily gathered himself, securing a hold of his weapon. He raised his saber high into the air before bringing it down with brute force on the mangled wrist. The saber cut through half of its flesh before stopping. It was a clean slice, but not enough. It bellowed in fury. Enraged, and not detoured, it pushed itself to its feet. Holding its nearly severed hand in the air, it charged into him with all its strength, knocking his breath from his chest again, and sent him flying through the air onto a large rock. Gasping and choking for breath, he rolled to the ground.

Hazily, he looked up to see the menacing form soaring through the air before it landed directly onto his leg with a *crunch*. He writhed in pain. His saber was knocked from his hand and flew out of arm's reach. Struggling against the weight of the monster, he continued to reach out for a weapon, any weapon. Barely able to wriggle his hand into his satchel for a knife, he moaned as his leg was slowly being contorted further into an

*96*

unconventional direction as it burrowed its leg further into his bone.

*Godsdamnit!* Pain seared through his body.

Groaning as it continued to dig further into his leg, he glanced hopelessly in the hideous eye. It was on fire, completely void of mercy, and ready to crush him completely, breaking every bone before it considered killing him fully. Finally, his fingers gripped the hilt of a knife. He roared at one last desperate attempt to defend himself with the knife until a booming voice commanded, "Enough!"

Both froze, searching around fervently for the source of the disturbance.

Suddenly, the figure stumbled quickly to its feet, bowing as it sputtered, "My Liege."

He staggered to his feet, resisting the urge to run despite the unyielding pain shooting through his leg. He looked in the direction of the monster, its breath pummeling from apparent nervousness and perspiring from...*fear?* A figure walked from behind the shadows of the trees dressed in a black, linen shirt, breeches, and knee-length, laced, leather boots. A severely dark, heavy cloak rustled in the wind at His back in the growing breeze. A thick twilight of hair fell seductively onto the forehead, almost hiding the pair of fiercely, pitch-rimmed, onyx eyes.

The being was an extraordinary specimen, unlike he had ever witnessed in his own lands. The figure was tall, poised, and pale skinned with stark, dark features. Curiously, there appeared an essence of immortal superiority about the presence, one that should never be challenged, nor ignored.

With hands behind the cloak and a half grin upturned with contempt, He commanded the monster, "Leave him be."

Mumbling at His direction, it moved hesitantly. "I was commissioned to kill him by another of his kind."

"Ah, but I will pay you three times as much to keep him alive." The dark garbed figure smiled. "He will become a valuable gambit."

He swallowed hard. An uncomfortable tension knotted in his stomach. *My kind? Who, in the bloody name of the gods does it speak?* Glancing at the beautiful stranger, he shuffled his feet uncomfortably. *I neither know who the dark male is, nor what He refers to as a 'gambit', but I have the terrible feeling that His game is a murderous game, full of destruction.* Desperately, he glanced at his saber through the corner of his eye.

"I would not even consider such a terribly foolish move." He stepped closer, clicking a tongue. "You will have to become much smarter if you want to survive this life. For once you are dead, your soul will stand no chance at being saved by any such weapon."

He swept his eyes back toward the overwhelming figure, noting He was only a couple footfalls away from where he stood. "Who are you?" he finally inquired.

"Who am I?" The onyx eyes were amused. "It is heartbreaking to be asked such a question." Shrugging, He replied callously, "I am your Savior."

The dark stare penetrated his soul, holding him captive. His heart began to beat alarmingly fast in his chest, threatening to burst from his flesh at any moment, strewing his red blood across the pristine, white snow.

Without loosing eye contact, the deep voice commanded of the hideous figure, "Now, come with me you fucking maggot, I will need your assistance on much more pressing matters at hand. I am in a bind with the Faery Realm and need assistance with the asinine immortals that will follow."

Breaking the glare with a slight gesture of hand, it followed the haunting figure back into the darkness of the surrounding forest, disappearing in the blink of an eye as though they stepped through the veil. He shook his head at the impossibility, for he could not sense an entrance into the Realm of Immortals from where he stood.

Left standing in the sun's fading light, he stared blankly into the untamed forest, confused by the previous events, and what the dark figure meant by him becoming a valuable gambit. A sharp, cold tingle shivered down his spine and into his nearly crushed leg. Suddenly, the pain ceased. *What the bloody curse of the gods?* He shook his leg. Then, as if emerging from a dream, he remembered his purpose and why he was far away from his home. *I am seeking a female. A female who is the ultimate embodiment of Light.* A bone shaking clap of thunder startled him from his thoughts.

# *Bog*

With the ceasing of the portal, Mora's mind cleared and she stared blankly where the door had been. Heavily panting, her eyes focused on the forest beyond. The ground was covered in thick snow, reflecting the sporadic patches of sunlight through the foliage like flickers of daylight stars. Frantically, she was trying to recreate the events in which, only moments before, took place, but her stomach lurched at the thought of the blood accumulating on Marwen's apron from the piercing sword. In an attempt to move, she sat down, legs crossed, hands outstretched, palms face down in the snow. Feeling the connection to the land made her senses mellow and her breathing even. She cleared her mind and commenced to calm her body. However, in a wicked flash beneath her eyelids, she saw His beautiful, flawless face in the shadows, the starless eyes seducing her thoughts. *He awakens my deepest desires, yet frightens the shit out of my whole being.* Resonating like a sensuously dark melody, she felt as though she could not live without Him; and although she feared Him, she wanted to feel His caress upon her flesh, hear His deep, euphonic voice inside her mind.

A spark filled her head. Mora opened her eyes. *Enough of this nonsense. I need to move, to find out where I am, and to free my mind of His presence.* Her legs were sore as she pulled herself off the ground, but the pounding in her head made her stumble. She reached up to her face, feeling the sensitivity of her nose and the pulsating of her eyebrow. A flashback occurred. *I was running through a forest. A branch crashed into my face. I couldn't see.* Walking over to the trickling creek, she gazed into the crystal clear water. Her face was swollen, and there was a deep purple and green mix of color surrounding the left eyebrow and her eye. Another flashback jolted in her head - *Dresden was pulling me along the pathway toward the hollowed tree in the forest.*

At the side of the creek, she sat on her knees, closed her eyes, and lifted her head toward the sky. Drops of sunlight kissed her cheeks and the cold wind caressed her hair. She listened to the serenity of the trickling water, touched her inner most thoughts, and silently whispered, *what do I do now?*

To her surprise, a neutral voice replied, *Follow the water.*

It was not His voice, but another familiar voice from the night in the snow...*Nephani.*

Mora opened her eyes and contemplated both directions of the stream. *How do I know which way to follow?* At that moment, a floating leaf caught her attention, whisked away by the water to her left. *I must follow the leaf.* The weight of Marwen's death and the loss of her mother tugged violently on her mind, but she splashed the cold water on her face, let the shock of the frigid liquid settle on her flesh, and rose once again to her feet. The snow had soaked her knees and she could feel the heavy leather of the boots drag her feet as she took each step. Determined to not feel helpless, she embarked down the creek.

Curious splashes followed her advance. Small wisps of transparent fish jumped, to and fro, in her peripheral. A faint smile graced her lips. The snow was not as deep as she remembered before she appeared in the Realm of Immortals. She squeezed her hands over her head, tugging at her braid. Bits and pieces jostled around her mind - winged male, the Faery Tree, His eyes, Loralei, Adeline, Dresden, Marwen. She sighed. *Dresden saved my life, and because of me, I don't know if he is still alive. However, time has begun to bleed together and continues to not make sense.* Her heart hurt so fiercely she felt it would burst from her chest. She could certainly feel it throbbing in the wounds on her face. She didn't know how long she had been away from home, but she knew her life had forever changed. *I am alone.* A silent scream roared in her mind.

Continually following the stream's edge, she began to crunch upon a ground of light frost and dried leaves. *The snow is melting quickly here, but why? Winter's frozen touch has kissed the lands prematurely, but its retreating as suddenly.* Glancing nervously around, the trees were not familiar, but she could feel a strange peace surround her mind. She took a deep breath and decided to enjoy the moment of solace after the events of the past few days. The cold air felt good in her lungs. *I don't know what or from whom I am running, but I will fight to experience the freedom and answers I deserve.* She closed her eyes and listened to the slow trickle of the water. The silence of the forest was loud. Curiously, no living entity, save the transparent fish, moved around. Briefly, she paused to watch the fish play. However, while it was a happy event to watch, a sadness encroached, reminding her of the euphoric Faery Realm, the floating faery leaves, and the eventuality of Loralei's fear.

Guiltily, she looked up high in the trees, watching rays of sunshine faintly falling through the mixture of bare and evergreen branches. The sun was slowly setting. Soaking in the evening beauty of the golden forest, a serenity haunted the air. She was abnormally calm, but that may have been the effects of the waning spirits she received from Marwen. *Marwen.* Her heart skipped a beat at the memory of Marwan's scream as the black sword pierced her abdomen. His onyx eyes were startlingly captivating as they absorbed Mora's soul. The smirk upon His beautiful face made her shiver.

The nauseating effects of the brown liquid had all but completely worn off at the disappearance of the door. However, she could still feel the subtle remnants percolating around in her mind. Her stomach grumbled violently. *I must find something of substance soon, or I feel I may start eating my own arm.* She yearned for the delicious flat bread and broth.

As the sky began to transition from a brilliant array of pinks and oranges into dark purples and blues, Mora started feeling a significant drop in temperature. Shivering, she surveyed the trees and down the stream, attempting to find a sheltered area to huddle for the incoming nightfall. Satisfied with the appearance of a cluster of thick trees some distance away, she decided to try and grab one of the transparent fish that had been following her down the creek before she walked any further. However, as she crouched down to the edge of the water, she froze. Leaning her head to the side, she thought she heard a murmur in the wind. Immediately pulling her hood over her head, she quietly skulked toward the nearest tree. To her frustration, it was growing darker quickly and became harder to focus on where the voice was mumbling. She paused and listened carefully. The voice was lower, resonating with a slight sense of conviction and, she thought, *possibly fear.* Strangely, it sounded like it was arguing with itself, for there was no other voice present.

Straining her eyes despite the excruciating pain on her eyebrow, she lurked closer to another tree. Taking a deep breath, she peeked around the trunk and saw a figure wandering around the woods picking up sticks and murmuring lowly. She watched intently. A memory tugged at the corner of her mind. She could see the white outline of grand wings and the half-clothed body of a...*male?* A wave of shock shook her awareness. *It's the winged being I saved from the snow. He's alive!*

Not wanting to startle him, as the result could be utterly devastating for both of them, she decided to stay a good distance away until the opportune moment. As night threatened to engulf them both, Mora decided she should try to carefully catch his attention. Cautiously, she made a low-lying bird sound. He jerked, frantically glancing around at the skies. *He is very skittish. I must be careful.* He turned toward her direction. Standing, his towering, muscular physique was intimidating to her own small frame. She could see his features more clearly than when she found him blood-stained. He had a kind, smooth face and his nose had nearly healed completely. His hair was cut short with beautiful, light golden curls, glistening almost silver, sweeping across his forehead. However, it was his eyes that made her catch her breath. His eyes were a striking violet. Contorting her face, Marwen's intense, liquid amber eyes penetrated her mind and the distant echo of her voice whispered, *Find the winged one with eyes the radiant hue of violets after a summer rain.*

"Who goes there?" he proclaimed loudly, squinting his eyes in the direction of the sound. Since there had not been much life, save for the occasional rabbit and grotesque goon with the one red eye, the sudden appearance of another living sound made him suspicious. *I haven't heard any birds recently.*

Mora continued to observe him from behind the tree. He wore no tunic, his chest exposed to the cold, but he wore a cloak, slitted in the back to accommodate his majestic wings. The black breeches were multi-pocketed and were tucked inside sturdy, leather boots laced to below his knee. From what she could see, his exposed skin appeared to be covered in

**The Keeper**

a soft, golden, sheer fabric. It shimmered. The large, white wings were a solid color corrupted by one black streak across the inside of his right wing. *I've never seen anything like him.*

An impulse of courage persuaded her to speak clearly, "I mean you know harm." Slowly revealing herself from behind the tree, she carefully made sure not to make any sudden, alarming movements. Looking toward the ground instead of directly at him, she spoke lowly, "I found you unconscious upon the ice a few days ago. You had been mauled, with blood soaking your wings and face. I did not want to leave you lying there in the snow. Therefore, I dragged you back to my camp. I left to find a drier area, believing if you were there by my return, well..." she trailed off not knowing exactly what she had expected herself to say. *So many things have occurred since that day.*

Barely raising her gaze, she saw his eyes squint against the oncoming night. He appeared to be thinking very hard about something.

With eyebrows crossed, he tilted his head sullenly, trying to remember her face through the darkening sky. Finally, a realization dawned and he responded sincerely, "I am grateful for your kindness. I owe you my wellbeing and am indebted to your sympathies. My name is Bog."

A momentary stretch of silence ensued between them. His deep violet eyes penetrated her very soul. Eventually, she grew tired and broke the silence, "Thank you, Bog, but there is no need for indebtedness. I'm sure anyone would have been as sympathetic." Mora looked around cautiously and sighed in defeat, "Although, I know not what kind of world it is anymore." She shuddered at the thought. Nodding absently, he walked toward a nearby part of the creek she had been following and sat down on a rock.

Placing his hands in the water to wash his face, Bog glanced in her direction curiously. "Where have you been?"

She tilted her head, scrunched her nose, and shrugged. "I'm not quite sure how to answer that." Kicking a rock from beneath her foot, she added quietly, "I'm not quite sure myself."

Not completely convinced, he nodded and drank a handful of clear water. He shook the water off his hands, stood back up, and listened to the surrounding trees for any other sounds before moving.

Watching him pick up the pile of wood he had been collecting, he walked over to the cluster of trees Mora had previously thought about inhabiting for the night. Thankful she had not settled in the trees before hearing him muttering to himself, she timidly inquired, "If you don't mind me asking, what are you?"

Clearly startled by her question, Bog shook his head in confusion. With a note of obvious pity, he replied, "What am I? Am I that different from you that you must see me as some ill-weathered creatural with wings?"

Mortified, she felt she had deeply offended him, and was not sure what to say. She stuttered, "Nay, I humbly apologize. I did not mean to offend you. It is just that I am not familiar with the lands. I have known no other creatural or being growing up save for my mother. As of late, it seems I have been the object of some otherwise supernatural being's claim to have been 'waiting on me' for some time. I have not only observed these abnormalities in my own reality, but also in my dreams, some pleasant, but others horrid." She began to feel unusually warm and stammered, "I have only recently discovered my own mother has been possibly... extinguished." She averted her tear welling eyes from Bog, hoping he did not sense her hurt.

After another long pause of silence, Mora heaved a big breath. She could feel his eyes, big and bold on her, closer than he was only moments before. Realizing he was significantly taller than she previously thought, a small bud of fear bloomed. Forcing herself to resist eye contact, she suddenly felt a large hand softly touch her arm. Through her sleeve, she could feel the spark of warmth in his touch and could smell a hint of lavender and bergamot. Reluctantly meeting his eyes, his pleasant smile made her feel safe. She released the tension that had built uncomfortably in her shoulders like taut knots on a rope.

Feeling her energy become less tense, Bog whispered, "Calm down. I mean no harm in my own defensive inquisition. It has been an entirely rough fortnight for me and it seems I have stumbled upon the purpose for my quest, despite the wicked circumstance under which you found me in the snow."

His violet eyes illuminated with a kindness unlike Mora had ever seen. She grinned back timidly. Gesturing to a nearby rock, she sat down as Bog cleared his throat.

## The Keeper

"Let me begin again. I am Bog. I am Borgorian. It is not that my kind are so different from yours, I am in part physically the same as any male you will know, but I also possess attributes from that of birds."

She could feel her eyes squint awkwardly despite her best effort as she swallowed the word, "Bird?"

Lighting a fire quickly, he turned back to Mora, smiled, and sat down. "It is awkward, but nonetheless, it is truth. Long ago, part of my ancestors roamed the lands far from here in…" he searched for the words, "…what would be considered the dominant erect race, or *Creatural*, the fallible idea of immortal and mortal beings possessing a higher intelligence and superiority in survival than other living entity."

He waved his hand in dismissal. "Anyway, they scoured for food, both animal and bird, living like savages. They were a violent race, bloodied and relentless. Until one day, the tribe stumbled upon a winged female, naked in a clearing not far from the camp. She was beautiful beyond imagination and her skin sparkled in the sunlight. The tribe felt the prize would please their chief, for they believed her a gift from the gods. Bound by her hands and feet, they drug her to the camp and presented her to their staunchly brutal leader. The chief, overtaken by her beauty, had his own wife put to death by drowning in order to claim this captive being. Disgusted, she cursed his ruthless ferocity and vowed to take her own life if he were to touch her in any way. He merely laughed at her spite and chained her in his tent."

Mora noticed how Bog fidgeted nervously with his hands in the intensifying firelight. *For such an intimidating being, he seems to be gentle and docile.* His deep, violet eyes glowed intensely as he spoke.

Bog looked at her and wondered briefly if she was actually interested in his story, but seeing as she made no notion to question him further, he continued, "The chief, overwhelmed by his good fortune, feasted and drank the night away with his followers, cursing and fighting amongst an orgy of foul smelling stenches and bodily discharges. Many whored themselves to the chief, hoping to be his sole wench for the evening.

"Alone in the chief's tent, the exquisite captive was chained in a life-sized bird cage, naked and cold. Tears fell heavily down her eyes as she listened to the males howling outside the tent, comparing the size of their malehood and who could drink the most without vomiting, as well as females, screaming and choking. Feeling defeated, she merely hung her head low, awaiting the coming of the chief."

Seeing her skeptically scrunch her eyebrows, Bog paused and smirked, "You may ask how legend knows of her tears of abandonment and disgust, but amongst the tribe, the chief had seven daughters and ten sons, eight of which were born of his drowned wife. When the ethereal captive was brought to the chief, his eldest son looked upon her with both infatuation and sympathy, for he possessed his mother's heart. Upon the chief's command to drown his wife, his son's mother, in silence, for he could not condone the chief's command, vowed vengeance on his mother's unjust death. While the chief and his tribe indulged in their own waste, he proceeded to his father's tent and watched the prisoner in silence.

"This son was quite a specimen. The brawn he had inherited from his father's side, with skin of a light olive color and hair of deep auburn. However, his heart and his empathy were rooted deeply in the blood of his mother, as well as his eyes of forest green and a significant height that surpassed his own father's. There was none like the son in his tribe. None like him in his kin. He was uniquely shaped and hated by his father. Within the shadows he stood, gazing upon the female, delicate and fragile, with sheer skin that sparkled. Her hair was a pristine silver, and her eyes a deep violet. He watched her full lips quiver as they whispered words in a language unknown to his ears. He was entranced.

"Slowly, he walked from the shadows, revealing himself in the dim fire light. She gasped and crouched further into the back of the cage. He placed his finger over his lips and fixed a look of warning should someone hear them. Because she was no ordinary creatural, she sensed the purity of his soul, the innocence of his intentions, and the rising nervous body temperature he was emitting into the air, causing him to sweat on his brow." Bog rubbed his hand through his metallic hair and half grinned.

Mora noticed a small, but very deep dimple appear on his cheek. She listened intently.

"Further details on their escape together were told to me throughout my youth in various interpretations, but there was always a constant. While the female escaped unscathed, the son was slashed across the face. This left him with only one good eye and a scar running diagonally from forehead to chin. The chief was furious and declared war against any descendants of each tribe, remaining enemies for eternity."

He shrugged casually. "Tales have introduced the captivating being as Aloria, mother of the skies, my grandmother. Legend has it that Aloria was a Divine messenger, a pure white dove, with the ability to transform into a creatural figure and walk amongst the lands in search of compassion and innocence, but only in accordance with Their bidding. On the day she was discovered by the tribe, she had been attacked by the Vulture of the skies, causing a wing to become damaged. Because birds were food for the tribe, she felt her only chance of survival was to be discovered in creatural form. However, she could not transform her wings.

"After her capture, Aloria tried to change back into her complete bird form in the tent, but try as she may, it was hopeless. She believed He had forsaken her, left her to be tormented because she had become creatural without His consent. It was in her forlorn state she saw the chief's son, Borheim, step out of the shadows. She immediately knew her pleas had been answered, but her punishment of abandonment from His graces was to walk the land as an erect being and never again soar through the skies. She humbly accepted the reprimand as she watched Borheim fight bravely against his tribe to rescue her from their terrors. In her mind, both had been exiled, only to create a new beginning. Because Aloria and Borheim were faithful to the Trinitas throughout their fight, their descendants were granted wings to remain protectors of the skies."

Mora shifted herself on the rigid rock, it was the second mention of the existence of another race she had ever heard. Her mother had kept so much from her as she was growing up. *Why?*

Bog continued, "I suppose this is where my ancestors, my predecessors, and my descendants have and will rejoice. I am a Borgorian."

When he smiled, Mora sensed his friendship could be vital. However, this time, his smile did not reach his eyes, nor show the dimple. A sense of hesitancy tugged in his voice, an uncertainty hinting of past, unhealed wounds.

He cleared his throat, "Therefore, you see, Mora..." and stuttered to an abrupt stop, eyes wide. *I fucked up*, his voice repeated on high alert inside his head, but there was nothing he could do to take it back. The horror on her face showed the damage had already been done.

She jerked her head at the mention of the name she had not given Bog. His face was petrified, stunned in dumbness. "How do you know my name!" she yelled.

She projected an intensity that penetrated to his very core. Trying to interject, he stammered at how to appease the unwanted revelation.

She jolted up in front of him and commanded as hard as she could muster, "Speak!"

Hesitantly, he flinched at her aggression. Finally, he gathered his thoughts and motioned her to calm down. "Do not speak loudly. There are ears all around the forest, the trees and streams talk. The wind knows all." He stood, looked worriedly at the darkened forest, and then down into her anger twisted face. He stamped out the fire, held onto to her arm, and whispered, "Follow me."

Jerking her arm over her head in a circular motion to shake free from his sudden grasp, she took a heavy step away from his looming figure. "Why should I?" she sputtered ostentatiously. Despite her previous feeling toward Bog, this had drawn a severe line between them.

Not wanting to waste anymore time on her stubbornness, he turned his vivid, violet eyes to lock her gaze severely. A flicker of pity briefly flashed between them, and he instantly knew he must be truthful, no matter how hard it would be for her to hear. Therefore, he sighed heavily and glanced toward the horizon before he quietly responded, "Because, you have no where else to go."

# Cuthos

Realizing the depth of truth in his statement, Mora reluctantly, but obediently, tread heavily behind Bog. She didn't necessarily follow because she was incapable of finding her own way, but deep down, despite her anger, his companionship made her feel less alone. In a way, she was told to seek his company, it was Marwen's last demand. As gut-wrenched as Marwen's death made her feel, she couldn't help hoping someday she would avenge her death and Bog would aid her in that quest. But first, she needed to seek answers as to who she was and why she was plucked from her obscure existence into a world of unknown perils and existential threats.

Through the night, they walked in silence over frosted terrain. The entire world felt frozen. All hints of life - sound, movement, breath - appeared nonexistent, like they were walking through a relentless void, a strange shift in time and space. For the first time, she felt like she would sincerely go mad. Quickening her gait, she stayed as close to Bog's warmth as she could without touching or interrupting his footsteps. She could sense his aggravation, but felt no remorse. *It is not the first time something or someone has known my name without it rolling off my tongue.* Looking at the ground, she wondered how far she had traveled from the first night away from home. *I don't even know where I have traveled. It feels like I have ventured the world, or worlds, and I'm no closer to knowing answers than when I began.* Slipping on a bit of ice, she caught herself before she fell to her knees. *The weather is certainly strange. One day it is green with the hint of color change, and the next it is snowing heavily and freezing.* She adjusted her hood once again, blending into the thick night air and blocking the frigid breeze from her ears.

Folding her arms at her chest, she was thankful Marwen had given her such a warm, thick frock. She smirked. *The first chance I get, I'm going to find some breeches to wear underneath.* Truthfully, she wasn't entirely convinced why she should not escape to a secluded dwelling to live like a hermit for the rest of her days, however numbered they were currently. *If they are numbered,* she sighed. *Possibly, I am already dead and this is a sorry excuse for a relaxing afterlife. Surely I froze to death the last night I spoke with my mother. It is the only logical reason I have been experiencing this damned chaos of events since.*

Being lost in his own thoughts, Bog tried not to fault Mora for being defensive. While he couldn't relate to her situation, he needed her trust. Glancing back with amusement, he smiled smugly. "We are nearly there. Don't be such a sullen golp."

Startled by his voice, she cut her eyes in his general direction. "Golp? What the gods is a golp?"

"Serious? You know nothing of golps?" He began to bellow with laughter, but then calmed himself and glanced around cautiously.

She sneered. *A stupid laugh, if you ask me.* Mora retorted angrily, "Brilliant, make me feel like a fool, you winged brute."

Sensing how upset she was, his playfulness subsided. "My apologies. Let us not start on name calling." He took a deep breath.

*Gods, he is beginning another one of his long, descriptive answers.* Annoyed, she braced herself.

"A golp is a pitiful mutant, who, like a goblin, has a sour fixture upon its face constantly. They are low-life buggers who serve the households of the Borgorians. Mangy little nuggets. A bit bigger than a goblin, they pack a tough bark. But a pull of the ear, or a kick of the ass, and they shut their nonsense and go about their business. However, not without turning their beady, black eyes toward you and muttering some shitty quip about you under their breath before they walk away." Pausing briefly, he added, "Similar to your nasty retort."

Startled, Mora ran into him and embarrassingly backed up, apologizing beneath her breath. She heard him chuckle. Relieved it was not

*The Keeper*

as long as his previous description of his lineage, she realized, whether or not Bog knew her name, he was harmless. *And a bit awkward.* There was nothing very intimidating about him save for his stature. Wondering why he was so far away from his lands, the fact he knew her name made her think their meeting was not entirely happenstance. *His clan either highly trusts him, or thinks him a fool, believing he will fail miserably and return unsuccessful...if he returns at all.* Regretfully, she assumed the latter.

Rummaging on the ground, he picked up an arm length branch and lit the end. Shining it on a large hillside draped with ivy, he motioned to Mora. "Here we go."

"Climbing?" she guffawed, "In the dark?"

"Nay, in here." He pulled back the ivy to reveal a small opening within the moss covered rock. "After you." He gestured, slightly bowing at the waist.

Horror lurched and she took a couple steps back. "You must be mad! I refuse be coaxed in there first. How do I know this is not a hidden trap to put me back into the Realm of Immortals and hand me over to Him again?" Scowling at Bog's face, she saw a quick dark shadow pass over his eyes and his smile faded instantly. Realizing she had said too much, she turned to run away. With quick reflexes and an underestimated strength, he wrapped his arm around her waist tightly and pulled her through the ivy. Kicking and writhing with all her strength, she screamed, "Release me!" but to no avail. His grip was secure and determined.

Once inside, Mora could feel the draftiness of the cold rock engulf her being. Because of her hood, she couldn't see anything in front of her eyes. The movement was terribly uncomfortable over his shoulder, but most of all, she was mortified she was lifted and carried like a sack of potatoes. Finally, the grip on her waist released. When he returned her to her feet, she threw back her hood furiously with every intention of fighting her way around him reverberating through her bones. However, hearing a rock being rolled, she whipped around in time to see the stars through the ivy disappear. It was pitch black, the previous flame apparently becoming snuffed in the struggle. Her breathing became shallow as a growing fear beat heavily against her chest. In the corner of her eye, she saw a spark. Then, another flame engulfed a charred cloth at the end of the thick stick.

The dim light danced onto Bog's sullen, heavily shadowed face.

## The Keeper

"Follow," he commanded stoically.

Knowing she could not escape easily, she trailed behind him closely through a damp corridor, deeper into the rock. The air was becoming stifling and tight in her nostrils. His body took up most of the tunnel, his wings almost scrapping the ceiling. She could see small streams of water leaking down the tight rock walls. After what seemed an eternity, they entered a spontaneously spacious room barely illuminated by the small torch Bog was carrying.

"Sit," he instructed without hesitation and pointed his torch down to a deteriorated, wooden table with two, dingy chairs.

Carefully, she sat down on one of the chairs. It creaked under her weight. Leaving her alone in the dark corner, Bog walked further into the room where he commenced to light an area on the rock wall. When the flame touched what appeared to be a trough, it slid rapidly around the entire perimeter of the room until it roared to life in a triangular fire pit in the middle of the chamber. His form was silhouetted against the bright light radiating from the fire. Sparks spat and sizzled. Smoke began to billow through three large holes carved deeply in the domed, stone ceiling. The cavern felt empty, as if it hadn't been occupied for centuries. It smelled musty and old. Dirt covered the entire floor. There were no other furnishings save the decaying table and chairs. *I wonder who dwelled here before and why has it been abandoned.*

Bog stood in the firelight, his back to Mora as his mind raced through all the possibilities of what had happened since he got knocked unconscious. Copious memories had begun to resurface, but it had been like trying to put together a puzzle without all the pieces. *Have I already failed?* A flood of disappointment lurked through his mind. *She's here, and that means He hasn't taken her away. What stopped Him?* A shadow crossed over his eyes as a cold shiver shot violently down his spine, causing his wings to tremble. *I cannot fail.*

Walking back to where Mora sat, he secured the end of his makeshift torch into a hole burrowed in the side of the table before sitting across from her on the other chair. He rubbed his hands over his face and through his hair.

The silence grew weary. His eyebrows were furrowed in stern contemplation, making his previously cheerful disposition feel like a distant memory. Mora began to become irritated and restless.

Noticing the increasing agitation of energies, Bog leaned forward, placed his elbows on his knees, and clasped his hands together under his chin. Gathering his thoughts, he looked her directly in the eyes. "This is far worse than I expected. I apologize I was not able to reach you sooner. You see, from what I have been able to recollect, I was ambushed from a tree above the ice from whence you found me. I had been watching you and your mother since you abandoned your home."

She winced, willing to speak, but he held up his hand.

"Please, let me finish." He moved nervously on his chair. "I had never expected you would stumble upon the Realm of Immortals. At least," he paused, "not this soon. Bal'dur is not known for its highly significant links to the veil."

She grimaced, settling at the scornful retaliation on his face. "Bal'dur?"

"The land we tread is referred to as Bal'dur. See," he retrieved a map and pointed, "Bal'dur. The Luln Mountains are on the border of the lands called Extrolia." Leaning back, he continued, "Anyway, I merely believed, in my naivety, your dreams would continue to baffle and befuddle your mind, not that you would physically be introduced to the Other side. Therefore, I am going to ask you a few questions. Please try to answer to the best of your knowledge, but do not elaborate any further than necessary. Agreed?"

She nodded impatiently.

"Are you experiencing abnormal dreams?"

"First, tell me where we are." Mora looked around at the dust-covered rock walls again.

*She's so damn stubborn.* He groaned frustratedly. "You didn't even *try* to answer my first question." Then, realizing she was not going to let it go from the fixed look of annoyance of her face, he explained, "We are beneath the mountain of Luln. Honestly, it's more like an oversized hill. But, it has long been abandoned by the Luln Dwellen Dwarves since the elves on the outskirts of Lychinus moved further south. I occupied the dwelling for several moons while I continued to search for you. That is a longer tale than we have time for at the moment."

*That's the first.* Mora sensed the pity in his eyes again, assuming it was in response to her innocence and lack of knowledge beyond her own bubble. She fumbled with her braid, attempting to avoid eye contact.

Bog glared at Mora. Clearing his throat, he persisted, "To proceed with my question. Are you experiencing abnormal dreams?"

"Aye."

There was silence.

He gazed at her impatiently.

"Pardon? You told me not to elaborate if not necessary. I felt it was not necessary to elaborate on the question." She shrugged.

He rolled his eyes. Annoyed, he leaned back and covered his face with hands.

Sensing the silent scream of frustration, she took a deep breath. "Aye. I've had several throughout my life, however, recently, they have been highly abnormal, unlike I have ever dreamt. They feel like pure out-of-body experiences, as if real life is not real anymore, but this intermingling of time and space, full of parallels and contradictions."

Returning his chair to the ground with a large *thunk!*, he placed his elbows back on his knees and inquired, "Do they revolve around a certain thing or being?"

"In the distant past, they always involved the darkness and shadows, but never any tangible concept. Lately, my dreams have evolved. Sometimes, it is a brooding figure. He mostly appears in a creatural form. A male of rare beauty, but with a hauntingly dark, ancient allure. He is the taste of sweetness and bitterness alike. He talks to me like a lover, but looks down on me like a possession." She scrunched her face. "Others? I speak to one without gender who has acted as though a guide."

Noting to come back to the other being, he persisted, "And can He touch you?"

"Aye, passionately." Mora could feel her cheeks flush. *I hope he can't see my face clearly.*

"He was present in the Realm of Immortals?"

Slowly, she nodded as if revealing too much information would prove to be dangerous. "Both times He came with the thunder. The Queen..."

Bog interrupted, "*Both* times? The *Queen*?"

*Shit. I have said too much already.* Knowing he would continue to pry until she broke, she nodded. "In the Faery Tree, the Faery Queen, Loralei, said I opened my mind too much. The flood gates burst wide and it allowed Him to see through my eyes. He spoke through me, as if I summoned Him. Then, in the Realm of Immortals, He appeared through the female, Adeline, before materializing inside the hut. If it weren't for Nema, Dresden, and…" she sniffed, wiping a tear from her eye, "… Marwen, I would not have escaped." *Gods, I'm spilling over.*

*Godsdamnit.* He became silent once again. An uneasiness settled. Then, the gravity in his voice weighed down, "Mora, you are not *mortal.* And by now, you suspect that, do you not?"

Shuffling her feet through the dirt, she closed her eyes tight as tears leaked down her cheeks. Every ounce of her being felt like it could fall to the floor and shatter into a million pieces. Gruffly, she responded, "It has been suggested."

"Do you know who you are?"

Throwing her hands up, with a hint of defensiveness, she responded snidely, "After further research, I assume I am merely a vessel for folly, a puppet on a string, a thorn in every one's side. Wherever I am, *whatever I am*, someone is always going to get hurt, or die."

Bog sighed. From beneath the table he pulled out a dusty book, tattered from years of use. "For the time being, and from what I have studied about Atlastova, I fear the least you know, the better. But I feel that more lives than previously counted upon, hang in the balance. You need to realize the magnitude of the situation and embrace your purpose. I cannot provide all the answers, and neither can this book, but it will tell you of a prophecy and a secret revealed to devour the lands and the skies, conquering *All* through Chaos and Death."

"Atlastova?"

"Atlastova is a part of All, the land upon which we tread, and the combination of the physical realms."

Still confused, Mora sneezed when he placed the book in front of her, disturbing the top layers of dust on the table. She pulled it closer. It was sturdy, with a faded brown, leather cover, bound loosely at the spine with black, leather strings. Blowing the dust from the cover, a single word appeared, burned deep upon the skin in scripted gold filigree.

*Cuthos,* she read silently.

# A Prophecy

The word pounded through Mora's head like the sound of tanning an animal hide taut across the skinning poles outside her home. Her mother would strike it violently after pulling the fur off and removing the excess pieces, revealing the fleshy color of the animal's skin underneath. The sound was deep and rhythmic, resonating through the flesh and vibrating the poles with its harsh tone. She used to be frightened of the sound, running into her mother's skirts before she was trained in the process after her tenth name day. Still, the sound was unpleasant, as the word *cuthos* taunted her memories with the same, harsh resonation.

She glanced at Bog, coaxing his assurance what she was about to read would not be painful, unpleasant, or potentially deadly. He nodded in return, pressuring her gaze to look at the cover once more before opening the leather bound front. She caressed the pages, certain they were a physical representation of a time long gone, one passed through generations of knowledge seekers. *Is this what ancient feels like?* The book smelled archaic, filling her nose with the various scents of lingering dust, spice, and moisture. Inside the cover, there was a page with the inscription: *Scyentiav n'est avmans avsh clavs'm ment'm; knowledge is no lover to the closed mind.* She thought back to the many times she had to translate *Lenith*, the primitive language of a bygone era, attempting to interpret the stolen books of her mother's private library in the excruciatingly fading light of her bedside table. Some nights, she would listen to her mother's screams and hear her speak the old tongue. It was exquisite, yet haunting.

The words slowly began taking form, one by one, as she read them in her mind: *Knowledge is no lover to the closed mind*, she repeated. *Curious. A blatant statement, surprisingly accurate in its common sense.* She turned the page. Midway down the page was a symbol. It was a tree, yet its roots were intricately overlapping each other, with no beginning, nor an end. The trunk was the only dull line, for the tree top wove a similar pattern, yet the lines were simpler and more delicate than the roots. Underneath, the words inscribed: *Yn pryncip'o er't Trinit's*. Realization dawned on her memories as the cacophony of sounds echoed through her mind. *This is the carving on the box Nephani showed me!* She placed her hand upon her chest, the hard outline of the key was nestled between her bosom.

As she read silently, Mora began hearing the voice of Bog taking over.

"In the beginning was the Trinitas, whom created All. Although the land was without form, void, and full of darkness, the Spirits loomed over the essence of potential. Light commanded, *Let there be light! Bring forth the sun, shallow waters, and ground to tread. Emerge elements of essence, fortitude, and desire.* And thus appeared the light, water, and dirt, followed by willpower and energy. Next, Dark demanded, *Let there be darkness! Bring forth the moon to rule in the sun's absence, stars to guide, and stone to forge. Emerge elements of depth, hope, and dreams.* And thus darkness appeared, followed by rest and harmony. Finally, Life proclaimed, *Let there be life! Bring forth the beasts and Creaturals of day and night, supple land, fresh air, and clean waters; plants of large and small, living amongst the deepest caverns to the highest of mountains; and the unyielding soul, a unison of light and dark, existential equality, cognitive balance, and a palpable pleasure for a higher purpose.* He led out of the ground every living entity and walked amongst the Realm of Immortals. Then, He instilled His plan within an entity most dear to His Being, one that would align with His ultimate purpose…" he paused briefly, torn between the brevity of the concepts and the actual circumstance that followed, "…and fundamental secrets. The Keeper and its image produced."

The abrupt silence of words made her question how much he

believed of what he spoke. However, the simple fact he was able to recite word for word made her suspect he had read it more times than he would admit. As she read further, the words started to jumble together, her eyes began to feel weak and her stomach gurgled for sustenance. A recollection festered in her mind and she spoke cautiously, "Loralei, the Faery Queen, spoke of the Trinitas."

Apprehensively glancing at Bog, her voice cracked, "This is all very overwhelming, and I am not sure I understand it completely." She began to thumb through the rest of the book. However, strangely, the majority of pages were blank. "And why are these pages blank? Is it not complete? There is a beginning and yet no end?" Methodically, she shut the book and slid it across the dirty table, staring dumbly at Bog to weigh his reaction.

His comforting glance of pity assured her she had not grasped the importance this book held. He carefully slid it back to her and turned it to the last page she had read. "Mora, the prophecy. You have not read the prophecy. There is no end because the prophecy has not been fulfilled. The pages are not filled with falsehoods, nor predictions on the potential outlook of All. They are written as the prophecy comes to life, whether or not the prophecy is fulfilled through the most hypothetical outcome, has yet to be determined. Creaturals are fallible, but this was written by one of the oldest clan of star readers, the Cau'o'tas."

Another cacophony of sounds echoed through her memories, and this time, it was in the subtle voice of Adeline. Then, the commencing drown of thunder and Nema's chanting made her grasp her ears and shake her head violently. "Stop!" Mora screamed. When she opened her eyes, Bog's stare met her with confusion.

He pointed with his long finger at the book and murmured, "Look at the last paragraph of the last written page and read it aloud."

*Whether he realizes how undeniably foolish he is making me feel, or he is receiving pleasure for his apparent vast knowledge and my lack thereof, it is motivating him to be a complete ass,* Mora grumbled to herself. Either way, she hesitantly turned to the last written page and read,

> *Betrayal tempts to acquire Ultimate Knowledge. An exile occurs to spawn Chaos.*

### The Keeper

*From the hour of birth, the vanity of Their doctrine succumbs to a choice made. Therefore, a form shall rise from ash and quell iniquity. It will, by the end, be of quintessential knowledge in the perfection of All, allowing a union between the Realms of Mortality and Immortality. Alas, closing The Gateway at the Tree of Ember and Blood from taint and corruption will ever be sealed. Ultimate balance will alter the chthonic, shifting an unprecedented canon to be birthed.*

She attempted to reread the paragraph slowly in her mind before grunting in frustration. "I am not sure I comprehend the meaning. Knowledge, I assume, had taken form as Chaos, then there is a bit about unions, a tree, balance..." she fought the words to describe the rest of what she read, but she laughed nervously and glanced up to see the twist of unpleasantry fixed on Bog's face.

"It is not something to be read lightly." He settled himself further back in his chair, the squeaking making him abnormally self-conscious and less confident in his approach to explain the passage, but he continued. "*Cuthos*, or The Keeper, was one of the Trinitas, the three powerful deities, the Creators who flourished in the Divine Realm. Life entrusted the secrets of life to The Keeper, also known as Light, or The Keybearer. This was one of the most sacred tasks. However, jealousy ensued, and a choice was made. When Light chose Dark, Chaos was unleashed. You see, superior knowledge without The Keeper is dangerous," he shrugged, "and some say that Dark was the original betrayer. Life knew Dark wanted access to His secrets, but could not vanquish both His counterparts completely because they are all comprised of the same. However, He made a sacrifice to secure Dark from returning by creating a new duality, Death, binding Him to the physical world. Thus, mortality was created.

"Dark swore ultimate revenge. Using ancient, sacramental magic, some say in the form of necromancy, The Keeper was then reincarnated in a creatural form with the intention to rise up against All, take siege, and construct a world in the image of Death and Chaos. Alas, through Life's intervention, The Keeper, or Light, is meant to become a weapon against the original betrayer and join forces with both the Mortal and Immortal Realms, relinquishing Dark's growing control and sealing Ultimate Knowledge away from Chaos for eternity."

Bog, consciously proud of his description, placed his feet on the table and folded his hands behind his head. Mora cleared her throat, "Obviously, your interpretation is not analyzed from the mere description given in this book, but from years of research of other resources." She could sense the air of ego expand as if she had inadvertently graced him with a compliment.

"Well," he shrugged his shoulders, "I can't take all the merit. It was a compilation of suggestions taken from other spoken and written sources. I have been told the prophecy all my life, but never knew exactly what it meant. Naturally, I searched for answers. I am a scholar at heart." He stared mockingly in her direction. "However, of course, this is only a prophecy, a perfection of ideals, not a set foretelling of the future."

"From other *oh-so-knowledgable* sources, I am assuming." She hunched at the possibility of an underlying falsehood.

"Well, I did need to clarify details," he coughed, "but that is neither important, nor relevant! The vital piece of information is the prophecy and this is why I am here."

She guffawed so loud, she realized it startled him, "You are mad! You are suggesting *I* am Light? That *I* am the embodiment of this superior, ultimate knowledge, that was Chaos, and then spawned into a creatural form by Dark? And possibly having the ability to *defy* Him in the end to establish *order* throughout All?" Exasperatingly, she jumped out of her chair, knocking it to the ground, and started pacing.

Holding up a finger, he retorted, "Actually, correction, you would be the one who is currently, *out of your mind*. If you think back on everything you have experienced throughout your lifetime, and more so, *recently*, have you no inclination you are no ordinary *female*?"

He rose to his feet as well. Stopping her mid-pace, he grabbed her shoulders and crouched a bit to hold her gaze. He could feel the energy pulsing between their touch and see skepticism warring in her vivid, forest green eyes. "You think that every *normal, mortal* creatural has visited the

## The Keeper

Realm of Immortals? A Faery Tree? Did you not realize that when you close your eyes, you could fundamentally reappear in another *world*?" he questioned.

She shrugged him off and began pacing again, fist clinched.

By this time, he was highly frustrated. *I didn't think convincing her would be this difficult. She doesn't trust me,* his shoulders shrank, ... *but, then again, why should she? After everything she has been through leading up to this moment has made her more jaded and skeptical.* Watching her pace a few more times, he decided he needed to earn her trust more, but they didn't have a lot of time available before He would attempt to grasp hold of her mind once again. Therefore, he needed to move efficiently.

Sweeping a hand through his curly hair, trying to not feel defeated, he spoke softly, "I understand your mind is clouded by your own acquired being of rationality, judgments, and emotions. But, can you see a shred of truth in my words? I need you to understand that I'm *not* your enemy. I'm not the epitome of a warrior, but I..." he sorely stumbled on the words, "...can fight, and I will help you along the way the best I can. I need you to trust me."

She paused, tears threatening to emerge again. Not wanting to meet his gaze yet, she felt his sincerity. He no longer seemed like the idiot bird-being she had imagined before. She could see he was strong-willed and possibly a...*friend?* However, she could also sense a deeper strain of emotions in him capable of torment. *He's my only hope right now.*

Regaining her composure, she said unabashedly, "My apologies. If, and I only say *if,* you are correct, and I am this embodiment, how do you suppose I control it, trigger it, or even conquer it?" Slowing down her tone, she hoped to create a less tense atmosphere. The thick, balmy air was already becoming too stifling. Fanning herself with her hand, she loosened the ties at her neck, joggling the chain carelessly. Realizing its exposure, before she could cover it, she saw a hint of curiosity in his gaze.

Looking away quickly, he wondered what was on the end of the chain. Knowing it was inappropriate to inquire at this time, Bog began to breathe slower and his shoulders became more relaxed. "That I cannot tell you. I am merely a possible defender. I will take you to where you need to go and to whom you need to speak, but I do not guarantee secure protection. Again, I do not pride myself a fighter. I'm a...,"

"...a scholar," Mora intervened and waved her hand in dismissal. "I know, you said as much. If *I* know not where to go, how will you lead me?" Placing her hands on her hips, the perspiration became overwhelmingly thick on her forehead and neck, making her gasp a little harder for air. *Why is the air suddenly becoming too much to bear?*

"I will take you to my land. There, we will seek the answers from one of the oldest Immortals." He knelt in front of a small chest against the wall, opened it, and pulled out some breeches, handing them to Mora.

Gawking at him as if he could read her earlier thoughts about breeches, she turned the thick pair over in her hands.

"I suggest you shorten the frock."

Peering down at her dress, she absently nodded and unlaced her boots to pull on the breeches. "How did you acquire..."

"Don't ask questions you are not ready to hear," he replied without looking in her direction. He gathered the rest of the chest's contents and slung the satchel over his shoulder. "But it is a treacherous, long journey. We must leave now. We can never stay in one place for too long. He will find you."

Raising an eyebrow at his elusive answer as to where he acquired female breeches, she used her knife he had packed from the clearing to cut the hem of her frock right above her knees. Tucking the excess fabric in the extra satchel procured by Bog, she inquired, "Can you at least inform me who *He* is?"

Finally, he gazed at Mora and muttered sorrowfully, "*He* is the Creator of your physical being." With the last word, the flames rippled out.

# The Undead Dead

The forest was treacherous. Bog had forewarned, once they exited the backside of Luln Mountain into the trees, there would be only one viable path, and it would be through the Pale Forest. He told her the forest did not willingly allow visitors to escape its terrible branches and marshy floors. The forest reeked with death. Every step felt as though she was going to sink beneath the dirt colored slush and vanish forever, no one to hear her cries, no one to save her from its malicious grasp. Like before, it was uncomfortably quiet. She glanced at Bog, his face appeared pained and sullen. She could still see where some of the blood had stained his feathers a pinkish tint. They were rippling in the wind, bringing attention to the one, taunting, black spot on the inside right. They hadn't spoken terribly much since the previous night inside Luln Mountain, but had departed hastily once the fires had abruptly ceased. It had created an energy of fear in him and she began to feel he was daunted by the task he had taken upon himself.

*I am grateful for his company, despite my speculation about this whole prophecy nonsense.*

Attempting to keep up with his long strides, she warily scanned the forest as they walked deeper. When the silence got too overbearing, she asked, "How do you know which direction to go?"

"I watch the skies." He turned his head slightly, a sly grin exposing his dimple. Then, nervously, he rubbed the back of his neck.

## The Keeper

She squinted her eyes, barely able to see through the treetops. "But you can't see anything in the sky. It's mostly covered with the canopy of the forest, and beyond that are sheets of gray clouds."

"I see things you can't because I am trained to see them. My mind comprehends my surroundings through a connection of previous experiences." He adjusted his straps. "I don't just look at things from the outside, I look at them from the inside." Smiling, he added quietly, "I was also not sheltered in a sanctuary for my entire life."

*That damn dimpled half smile.* She grinned. "Fuck you," she jested comfortably. "I'm not exactly sure what that means, but if you really do know where you are leading, the only thing I can do is trust you." She glanced back at the direction they had come, her doubled footsteps keeping in line with Bog's own single stride.

He stopped in his tracks. *She trusts me*, his chest fluttered. Then, he looked at her wide-eyed. "You really have no idea who you are? Your mother never said anything about why you lived in the sanctuary without any contact to another living entity, or really anything, other than her? Why you were never allowed to travel outside its borders? Never taught to ask questions or demand answers?"

Mora, finally a few steps ahead, stopped and looked back inquisitively. "Should I?"

Shaking his head in disappointment, he gasped, "It would make my purpose, and everyone else who is relying on you, mean more. You do not understand how long we have been waiting for you to reveal yourself, along with the uncertainty we have had to endure."

Frustrated, she lifted her arms and let them fall dramatically. "Pardon me for being so damn aloof! I was dragged out into the middle of nowhere, with a mother who I can only assume is dead, and I am walking through a forbidden forest with a large bird-being, who cannot even fly, claiming I'm some dark spawn of great power who is supposed to fix this gods-forsaken existence because I used to be an exiled superior deity!"

She heaved knowing her words were probably too harsh and irrational, but she did not want to be blamed for Bog's problems. Her voice became even higher as she continued, "I have also been given a key to some godsdamn place with no clue where or how to get there. I've been having strange, nonsensical dreams, and I am communicating with beings that utter riddles about how 'the less I know, the better' and then get hurt or die!" Spittle ran down her chin. She wiped it off with the back of her hand while days of pent up tears started pouring down her face. Exhausted, hurt, and overwhelmed emotions projected a violent surge through her body and she began shaking. Falling to her knees, she threw her hands over her head to stop the agonizing frustration.

Shocked, Bog rushed over and crouched in front of her petite figure. He didn't know exactly how to comfort her current state. He prodded the air around her with his hands, not exactly sure what would be acceptable. Thoughts fogged his mind. *She's been shielded from pain her entire life, but how do I help her find the strength she needs? And...did she just mention a key?*

Not wanting to exacerbate her current state of distress, he held his tongue about the key, suspecting it was what hung from the chain she was concealing beneath the neckline of her frock. Finally, he took a deep breath and placed his hands on her shoulders. "Look, I know you're overwhelmed. A lot has happened over a short amount of time that...that you should have been prepared for as you were growing up. I don't necessarily fault your mother for her choice to hide you from Him, but that does not serve your wellbeing and has...um...frankly...placed you in more danger." He lifted her chin, locked eyes, and spoke carefully, "She knew she couldn't outrun Him forever."

A deep pain resonated in her green eyes. He could see it clearly through the red puffiness and splotches covering her face. *The red makes her green eyes appear much brighter.* He wiped his thumb across her cheek as an odd spark pricked his finger. Thinking it a result of the wool, he shrugged it off. A tug of compassion made it hard to swallow. He didn't have many friends in his youth, he spent the majority of his days studying and rummaging through the library for old texts. He got used to being alone. *My seclusion was by choice.* A protectiveness filled his heart. *But I don't want her to get hurt.*

Mora's head fell against his chest. If he didn't know what to do with his hands before, he certainly had no idea at the present. Affection was something that had become foreign to him as the years passed. Finally, he put his arms softly around her back as she let out a steady cry, and waited.

Suddenly, a sound pricked his ears. He whispered, "Mora, hold your voice down," he urged, "please?"

Appalled, she pulled back and looked at his face. Wiping her eyes, she stuttered, "Out of all the heartless..." she trailed off when she noticed the horror twisted in his face.

Out of nowhere, there was a low, droll chanting. Scurrying to their feet, she frantically whipped her head around. She couldn't see where the chanting was coming. Unaware of the source, she felt the wind began to stir through her hair. The growing breeze made the chanting appear like it was resonating from all directions in her mind. It was haunting and cold.

Not realizing Bog had moved, she turned at the sound of a *psst!*

"Over here," he hissed and gestured his hand over to a fallen tree.

Climbing quickly over the trunk, she peered slightly over the edge as the chanting came closer and whispered, "What are we hiding from?"

He pointed in the direction of the chanting. Even though she could hear the haunting song swirling around her, she strained her eyes in the general direction. She couldn't see anything but the wind rustling through the leaves on the trees. Her heart beat loudly in her ears. Faintly, after squinting at the snow, she could see parts of the snow-ladened ground pressing into footstep-like shapes, one after another in a straight line. Her skin began to prickle. The chanting escalated to an excruciatingly depressing moan.

Terrified, she looked at Bog. He was watching intently, appearing to be studying the beings she couldn't see. She tried again to concentrate on the forest, opening her mind like she did the night she had spoken to Nephani. However, at that moment, the chanting stopped, and there was an eerie silence that consumed the forest.

"What is that?" whispered a voice on the wind.

"I feel it too," replied another gruffly.

Bog turned his eyes at Mora, horror struck. *Shit.*

"It's coming from over there," another raspy voice chimed in.

Not wanting to look toward Bog, Mora's heart beat faster. She could hear the quickened crunching of snow underneath the heavy footsteps getting closer. Aware of her thoughts, like a piece of twine vibrating, she realized it was pulling the beings toward the tree trunk.

All of a sudden, something struck her on the back of the head and everything went blank.

The steady thudding of pain engulfed her skull. Opening her eyes, everything appeared extremely bright. She began slowly focusing on the icy ground. *Why is everything upside-down?* Then, as white feathers tickled her face, she had the startling realization she was being carried.

"Put me down!" she shrieked.

Bog stopped. "Oh, you're awake. My apologies. I had to think quickly before they found you." He placed her down on the cold, icy snow, catching her before she slipped.

"What happened?" She dusted off the little down of feathers that were stuck to her frock.

"You opened your mind. They sensed your connection to the Dark One and knew you had to be close." He stood straight, peering around the forest.

"Who are 'they'?" She plopped down on a tree stump and rubbed the back of her head. It ached severely.

"Skulkins," he said casually, "the undead dead,"

"How can you be 'undead' and entirely 'dead'?"

"Skulkins were mortal creaturals in life who sold their souls to the Dark One for an exchange. The Dark One would promise them the request on the account they would be loyal to Him for eternity, leading them to believe they would be immortal. However, they would eventually die an extremely painful death and be forced to absently skulk the lands in their foul state, fulfilling any deed, or request, instilled in them by the Dark One. They have no escape." He handed her a small flask of water.

Not realizing how thirsty she was, she upturned the flask until it ran dry. "Why could I hear them and not see them?" She stood up and handed him the empty container.

Bog looked disgruntled into the flask before stowing it away in a satchel. "Because they have no visible flesh. And you have not mastered the consciousness that allows you to see things for their essence instead of their physicality. It also helps when you have accepted the concept of death. It will come in time. My first priority is to get you safely to Borgoria." He dropped one of the satchels on the ground. "Sorry about the head. The closest thing I could reach was a rock." He pulled out a few effects and handed them to Mora. "Here, some of this is yours."

"How did they not see you?" She rubbed the snow on the back of her head and placed everything into her own satchel. Deciding to change her boots when Bog handed her Meridan's extra folded pair from home, she remembered her departure from her sanctuary and inquired, "You didn't happen to come upon a bow and quiver in the clearing?" Everything had become twisted, but a pang of sadness tugged at the idea of loosing the gift from her mother.

"As you lay unconscious, I shielded you with my body, my feathers were able to blend in with the snow. When they lost the connection to your mind, they were forced to give up the search, but not before documenting the trace of the connection. This will give the Dark One a more concise idea about your potential whereabouts. Even more reason why we must get to Borgoria with greater urgency." He looked toward sky for direction. "And nay, I saw no weaponry besides the knives in the satchel, else I would have collected it. Anyway, we don't have long before nightfall. We must make haste."

She looked up too, but the only thing she could see was the canopy of the trees. Her head felt dizzy. Squinting her eyes, the naked trees of the forest appeared to tremble as she attempted to focus on them. An echo resonated in the depths of her mind, *Presently, as you lay before me, whatever you think, I will hear; whatever you devise, I will know; whatever you feel, I will feel too. Do you understand me?*

She cleared her throat, "He said He knows what I think and feel. Is that true?"

Bog paused and twisted his face in concentration. "I'm not entirely convinced He can all the time. It may be a scare tactic to make you more vulnerable. However, I know He can do more than I will ever be able to comprehend. Therefore, we must be cautious and aware." He peered over his shoulder as she started slowly stumbling toward where he stood. Lifting an eyebrow, he smirked, "Do you need me to carry you further?"

"Wipe that damn dimple off your face," she said snidely, looking at him unamused. "Nay, I'll be fine. I just need to walk a little."

## The Keeper

With a shrug of his shoulders, he threw his hood over his head, turned his back toward her, and started walking at a quicker pace than she anticipated. Hurriedly, she placed the satchel over one shoulder and trudged behind him with an overwhelming sense of solemnity. The snow had become deeper since she had been knocked unconscious; it was already past her ankles. *I wonder what he sees. All I can see is the bloody canopy.*

Thankful she had switched her boots from the heavy pair Marwen had given her, to the lightweight pair, Mora remembered when her mother had made them the year before. They felt different from the pair she lost beneath the Faery Tree and she had never seen her mother actually wear them. At the time, Meridan had neither informed her, nor discussed, what animal the leather hide was skinned. She had assumed the poor beast had made its way past the boundaries of the forest and walked straight to its death. However, after the recent events, she speculated her mother had gone looking for the beast without her knowledge in preparation for their eventual departure, an event she was starting to believe Meridan foresaw. Nevertheless, the boots were impenetrable against the deepening snow and provided extra comfort to the amount of walking.

*At least Bog had the foresight to grab the knapsacks from the camp...even though it was stealing at first.* She smiled at his back.

A hawk cried from a long distance. As dusk commenced to fall, Bog began to look for a safe place to start a fire. While he didn't get cold easily, he could see Mora was shivering beneath her hood, entangling her hands in her cloak. His mind was ablaze and alert from the Skulkins happenstance. *The last thing we need right now is to try and fight in the encroaching darkness.* However, he was also leery about what may happen during the night. The Pale Forest had been abnormally quiet. He peered behind. *She needs sleep. I can feel her exhaustion weighing heavily on our progression.*

Cautiously, they climbed over a few, fallen branches onto what appeared to be a small, frozen pond. The ice was slippery, but his boots held his balance as he helped steady Mora. Briefly glancing down, he could see strange, dark shapes floating around under the ice. *Gods, I hope those are large fish.* Hoping she didn't look down, he slowly held back the broken branches over the frozen water which eerily resembled thin, bumpy arms with long, distorted fingers. He shuddered. Finally, he noticed a very thick brush overlaying a small inlet on the side of a hill. It was nearly out of sight of the straight path they were trodding, and full of dry branches.

Crouching low under the rocks, he said quietly, "We will stay here for tonight. Gather some brush and I will go search for food. Stay as close to this place as you can." Then, he disappeared around the stone.

Wearily, Mora gathered the several dry branches she found close to the rocks. With the flint from the cloth satchel, she lit a pathetic pyramid of wood. Hoping it would not draw any attention, she shifted her body in front of the growing embers and held out her hands. It crackled fairly well, but stayed minimal. However, the warmth began to finally thaw her frozen hands as her eyes grew heavy staring into the subtle flames. The headache pounded again. Leaning sluggishly against the rock at the mouth of the small cave, she absently broke a few more twigs, tossing each individually into the pathetic fire. Her eyelids fluttered up and down. She fought against sleep with the urge to stay awake until Bog came back, but her eyes blurred heavily until the image of the flames drifted away behind her eyelids.

# An Ambiguous Illusion

Mora sat on her knees on a lusciously green, forest floor. It was neither cold, nor damp. *Where am I?* she mused to herself. The snow made a perfect circle around where she was kneeling. Within the circle, there was an array of magnificently dark flowers. Hues of deep indigoes, rich purples, dark blues, blood reds, and stark black sparkled with drops of dew and twinkled like stars upon the ground. She glanced upward toward the uncovered sky. The pinpoints of light were endless and full of radiating brilliance. The flowers reflected the stars, and vice versa. The colors of the night sky boasted of the same fluid darkness of the flowers. *It's breathtaking.*

Unable to visually reach the end of the night sky, she could feel the infinite pull of an unknown familiarity, a place of solitude amongst the infinite specks of light, rays of countless suns, and massive mists of colorful, billowy clouds bursting from the very hearts of both young and old stars. She closed her eyes. It was rejuvenating to both her emotional and physical being. However, there was a hint of sadness tugging in the back her mind as she sat there within the warm circle. It pulled enough to make a single tear fall from her eye. Without being hostile, the feeling was trying to penetrate an invisible bubble that covered, like a glass dome, the clearing in which she knelt.

Methodically calculating every minuscule detail affecting her presence within the dome, Mora opened her eyes. Holding her hands in front of her vision, hooked over her middle fingers, a sleeve of sheer cloth, lighter than air, sensually began to manifest down her arms and around her body. The bodice was pure white, with an illuminating neckline of shimmering, tiny stones. Lace accentuated her breasts, while a threaded silver filigree swirled like symmetrical vines on each side of sparkling stone buttons that stopped around her navel. The gown loosened at her hips, draping like icicles around her knees with the softest material she had ever known. Twisting at the waist, the fabric trailed behind on the forest floor, blending into the snow at the edge of the circle.

"Solora," whispered a seductive voice from outside the light.

She shielded her eyes and strained to see beyond the circle.

"Solora, come with me," the hint of intimacy whispered again.

"Who calls to me? Show yourself." Mora slowly stood, the magnificent gown pooling around her feet, searching the darkness for a sign of life.

"You must come to me," the deep voice echoed sweetly.

"It is cold outside of my ring. I do not wish to step beyond."

"Nay, my Light, I will not allow you to be cold. Come sit with me. It is warm in here."

As the alluring voice spoke, a subtle light appeared in the shadows, slithering upon the ground toward her like an illuminated serpent. Then, a door opened beneath the trees. Its warm glow was bright and inviting.

She walked languidly toward the edge of the ring and softly touched the air beyond the dome. Curious footsteps already dented the snow like a pathway to the door. Something inside her felt uneasy, but she was exceptionally mystified. Hesitantly, she placed her bare foot into the first indention. At first, she could feel nothing under her sole, no warmth, nor the freezing expectation of ice. Then, as she allowed herself to be coaxed beyond the clearing, her feet began to feel cold, nearly frozen with each step.

An accelerated desire to run back made her heart beat faster. Midway to the door, she glanced over her shoulder toward the flowers. They had withered and died, the vibrancy no longer erotically alluring. Light no longer radiated from the ground where she had stood, but had formed an abysmal black hole. The sheer, delicate fabric of ethereal light had faded from her skin. Her brief nakedness was clothed by a translucent black cape. A bodice of deep violet accentuated her breasts. Embracing her neck, an elaborately woven, black lace choker, with a thin serpent chain, arched hungrily toward her bosom. Weighing down the middle of the chain was an oval, onyx gem. A black, laced skirt, lined with indigo stones and filigreed with a detailed, metallic thread, brushed the forest floor. An eerie chill caressed her skin like the callused fingertips of a harsh lover, igniting a yearning to be warm again. Taunted by the surrounding darkness, she quickened her pace along the already laden path.

Upon reaching the warm, saffron glow, she discovered the doorway was detached from the forest itself. Peering around the corner, there was nothing but dark, menacing shadows. Nervously, Mora pushed it wider. Inside, there was a grand, circular room. A great fireplace roared in the middle of the round, stone floor. Stepping foot on the floor was like walking on black ice without the searing freeze. Shutting the door soundlessly behind, she craned her neck to gaze at the ceiling. It sung with a mural of a breathtakingly marvelous, enchanted world, floating amongst seas of billowing pink, green, and gold clouds. Amidst the mounds of delicate clouds were beings, beautiful, otherworldly creaturals and beasts of light, smiling and interacting playfully with one another. Sections of stars and spherical masses full of color twinkled and danced harmoniously together through the effervescent skies.

Feeling a magical presence, and intrigued by the ambience, her eyes marveled at the intricately carved pieces of sectioned wood lining the wall at eye level. Walking over to the closest one, she realized they were individual boxes with miniature doors and little, shiny knobs. Carefully opening the tiny door, it contained little figurines carved out of delicate crystals. Mesmerized at the detail, she gently took one out. It was a young female twirling around on her toes. Tiny, dainty wings protruded from her back. With an innocent smile, she clasped a little ball of gold above her head.

"Magnificent, is she not?"

Mora was so startled, she nearly dropped the figurine. Not realizing she had been contently saturated in the silence, the emergence of sound was highly unpleasant. Cupping the figurine between her hands, she turned on a heel toward the voice. Her heart pounded in her chest as He stood strong, dark, and brooding within the far reaching shadow of the room. Stepping closer to the fire, the brilliant flames illuminated every flawless feature. Her breath caught in her throat. His liquid onyx eyes were intense and the indigo in His hair radiated in the firelight. He was still the most majestic being she had ever seen.

"My apologies for startling you." He feigned sympathy, but could sense her arousal. "Your beauty is so alluringly captivating, I was merely overwhelmed in your fascination with the figure. I wanted to bask in the intensity of your feelings."

Not realizing she had been holding her breath, a long, drawn out wind escaped her lips. "It is you," she whispered and placed a hand against the revealing part of the bodice. She didn't know where to look because His eyes were disturbingly captivating, but they also filled her with apprehension.

"How did you come to be in my dream?" Fanning herself as drops of sweat accumulated on the back of her neck, she suddenly realized how constricting the bodice was against her ribs. *I am starting to feel faint.*

A wry smile parted His lips and He purred, "What makes you believe this is a dream?" Standing beside a chair, He held the back with one hand and gestured toward the seat. "Please, take a seat. You are feeling faint."

Mora shook her head slightly. Shrugging and moving the chair to the side, He indicated toward a small table she had not taken notice of before.

"Then, would you care for a dram?"

Walking closer toward Him, as if a force was pulling her slowly, she acquiesced.

Nonchalantly, He handed her a glass of dark amber liquid. She held it up to her nose. It smelled sweet. Barely touching it to her lips, she took a slight sip. It tasted smooth and sweet as a sensuous vibration tickled her tongue, but the sweetness melded into a faintly bitter aftertaste as it slithered down her throat.

He watched her intensely, becoming aroused by the scent of her flesh as it anxiously perspired.

Taking another sip, she asked, "What are you called?"

A brief shadow passed over His face and a rogue smirk stretched across His lips. "You may call me Ekklips."

The name pierced her mind vigorously like numerous tiny needles, resonating loudly with haunting warnings. However, she was beguiled in His mysterious and glamorous nature, unable to fully comprehend her surroundings.

"Are you a magician?" she inquired sheepishly. "It feels like magic."

"Some may see me as such. Though, I do not pride myself on the objective worldliness of my ideals; I use a much more powerful tool to go about my…business."

"But I saw you appear. I saw you kill," she stifled a cry, "Marwen. I felt your anger encompass me." Pity made her heart hurt. She leaned over the table, took a sip of the sweet, amber liquid, and placed it back down harder than she intended. A small crack climbed like lightning on the outer layer of crystal.

"It is hardly an interest to discuss." Imperturbably, He waved His hand away in dismissal of the petty topic. "I merely want to know more about your life as a childling, Solora." He stepped closer, nearly flush against her back, and placed a hand on her hip.

*Oh my gods.* She could feel Ekklips breathing on the back of her neck. Running a finger down the curve of her exposed collarbone, she shivered at the coolness of His flesh.

"Don't be afraid, Solora," He whispered sensually in her ear. Pressing Himself against her back, He slid His hand across her corseted torso and held a magnificently dark flower to her cheek, caressing the soft petals over her radiant flesh.

Mora's mind was swimming and her heart raced. Cupping the flower in her hand, she whispered, "An iris?" His hands were traipsing over her hips, then lightly slid down her breasts over the tight, violet satin. Holding the petals in her vision, she tried to focus on the indigo bloom spilling over her fingers.

"Aye, it was always one of your favorites, my Goddess." Ekklips smiled slyly. Closing His eyes, He took a satisfyingly deep breath. He held up another seductively dark flower and placed it behind her ear. "I also know you loved the sensuality of a black rose."

She felt the connection between her limbs and her mind slacken.

**The Keeper**

Carelessly, she muttered, "The drink…"

The scent of His skin and the flowers made her heady, drunk with desire and lust. Her head fell heavily onto His chest. Thoughts commenced to cloud her mind. Closing one eye, the only object she could focus on was the glass on the table. Stumbling a little, she turned around to see the burning passion consuming His midnight eyes. As she attempted to gaze into them, she thought, *they look like the darkest corner of the night sky.*

He pushed a long curl behind her shoulder and growled, "You are so magnificent, Solora. I've been waiting eons to see you clothed in the hues of the night. Let me help you become more comfortable." He unfastened the satin ribbon on her black cape. It fell seductively against her arms and onto the ground. Watching her chest heaving, He bent to kiss the visible flesh of her breasts pouring from the top of her corset. A low rumble escaped His throat. *She tastes like the stars, hot, savory, and sweet, full of energy and intense power.* His eyes traipsed over her neck and down to her hips. Leaning over again, He lightly drug His tongue against her glistening neck.

Swallowing hard, she felt the warmth rush fervently to her intimate extremities. "Please…stop. I must be going." She tried to slide away, but Ekklips' hands tightened on her hips. Her hands grasped hard onto the table behind as He pushed closer.

Effortlessly, Ekklips slid her hips onto the table. He groaned. "I do not wish to force you into my embrace." He leaned over again and kissed her jaw. Taking a deep breath, His low guttural voice rattled, "But I can smell your desire. I can taste your lust on my tongue." He moved a thumb closer to her inner thigh and whispered, "I can feel your warmth escalating."

Moving His lips toward her chin, teasing against her cheek and lips, He pressed His forehead against her own and mumbled, "You make it hard for me to resist your flesh, though. Don't be afraid my love. I want you to stay with me. Together, we can accomplish great things as we have for lifetimes before."

Mora could feel her body heat rising in excruciating intensity from her feet and into her head. The dizziness escalated. Breathlessly, she moaned, "This isn't real, it can't be. I am dreaming." Closing her eyes, she could smell the intoxicating scent of His breath as though she had just

*136*

inhaled the night sky. His lips lightly danced above hers and the electricity of His proximity escalated. The impulse to taste Him was unbearable. She reached a hand behind His neck and ran her fingers through His sultry hair.

Ekklips purred. Claiming her lips and tongue, He kissed her until He felt He would explode from the inside out. He had yearned and waited too long to feel her in His embrace. After a moment, reluctantly, He pulled away to gaze into her lustful, green eyes. "Imagine it Solora, this can be our reality if you choose." He pushed His length harder between her legs, a hand firmly holding her lower back closer to His pulsating body. The roguish grin stretched across His lips again. Caressing His fingers down her cheek, onto her jaw, He drug His thumb across her bottom lip and moaned, "Let me in Solora. I would set fire to All merely to ignite the flame in your soul. The power can be yours…"

As the spark threatened to ignite within, Mora arched her back and squeezed His arms, the dark petals crumpling onto the floor through her fingertips. His lips sensually touched hers and she yearned to feel their bodies entangled. However, as His tongue danced over her damp flesh, she heard a voice in the distance call out her name. Suddenly, as though she were being fiercely pulled by the waist with a rope toward the enchanted ceiling, she felt the desire in His hands and body slip away.

"Why?" she cried toward Ekklips.

As her fingers slid from His own, He stood slack against the table with His arms and legs crossed, the artful grin from her warming presence replaced with a scowl. He watched her float away, the petals swirling violently, ascending into the encroaching storm amongst the ceiling's changing mural.

Coldly, He mumbled, "I will find you again."

Mora awoke.

Bog shook her gently, fervently patting her cheek. *Godsdamnit Mora! You weren't supposed to fall asleep while I was gone searching for food!* He had omitted telling it was a possibility because she already had more than she had been prepared for since she left home. When he rounded the corner, he heard her talking in her sleep. Ever since she told him about the Dark One's threat of knowing her thoughts, he had feared her falling asleep without him near. He knew the more her mother's magic dissolved, the easier access He would have to her mind, especially in her dreams.

*I'm afraid she may not awaken if I'm not around to rouse her.*

He carefully helped her sit. While she appeared to be in pain, he didn't know the extent of her interaction with Him. He knew his face was skewed with an alarming concern, but it was truly how he felt. "Mora, what are you doing?"

With her big, green eyes, she peered toward him blankly. He cradled her head, waiting patiently for her to come around. Worry clutched his chest. Finally, he could feel her mind transcending slowly from a place far from her body.

Blinking her eyes, she said hoarsely, "I fell asleep. My head was pounding and the fire was warming my entire body. It was too tempting not to succumb to sleep, despite my fight to stay awake. I'm...sorry," she whimpered through the tears.

"You were talking to someone. Who?" He had no intention of frightening her with the possibility her dreams of Him were going to become more frequent if she allowed it, so he made no further inquiry about the details. *However, I won't stop her if she feels inclined to tell me.*

"Was I?" She blinked to adjust her eyes, rubbing them vigorously before continuing. "I was talking to...Ekklips." Touching her lips, the strong desire to still feel Him against her body was abnormally strong. She felt like a blood thirsty animal.

Bog's eyebrows rose. He watched her face twisting uncertainly, as if trying to remember details. Sensing her emotional ambiguity in recollecting the experience, he started to respond, but she interrupted.

Hesitantly, she stuttered, "First, I was in a circle of magnificent twilight flowers in the middle of a night-consumed forest. They were the hues of the night, breathtakingly dark with star-like dew kissing their petals. However, I heard a voice and, as I walked from beyond the circle, the flowers died miserably. I was shocked and hurt by their withering radiance, but there was a warm light amongst the trees and I walked toward it." She took a deep breath, the lingering taste of Him still lush on her tongue. "The light led to a room with no walls visible from the outside forest, but when I stepped within, I saw a circular chamber. It appeared to be a tower with a radiantly burning fire in the center. Around the edges of the room, there were small boxes containing intricately carved crystal figurines."

Bog noticed how she held her hands in front of her mesmerized face as if imagining holding one of the figurines. He shifted nervously. *This makes me incredibly uneasy.*

She continued, "Then, from out of thin air, He appeared from the shadows and began to talk to me. He poured me a drink of sweet, dark amber liquid which vibrated on my tongue. He touched me in ways I have never felt before. He said I could have the power to do whatever I wanted if I chose Him. I didn't know what to do. I could neither run, nor speak." Desperately, she tilted her eyes toward him and added sweetly, "And then, from a distance, I heard your voice, and it was as if a rope reached through an invisible layer of dreams to pull me from His midst." Lifting her hand, she opened her fingers as delicate, indigo petals fell to the ground.

He saw the growing shock on her face and pitied her naivety. *The unknown. The uncertainty. The solitude. I can sense her weariness with the overwhelming amount of details and pressures placed on her within such little time.* Shaking his head, he knew there was no time to meander on pettiness and folly. *The lands have become restless and are beginning to change. The winds are dancing in all directions, menacingly playing with the minds of the feeble and pathetic. Only those who are willing to fight will survive, not for themselves, but for Her. If only I had the strength to wield the power myself, but not even I understand the details of the unknown.*

A cold wind howled from beyond the entrance of the small cavern. He glanced down at Mora, her eyes closed once more. *Food will have to wait until the dawn.* He nestled down beside her, pulling his wing over their bodies to conceal their location. Before lifting his wing over his bright, violet eyes, he scanned the Pale Forest as a harbinger of thunder rumbled like the distant drums of battle.

# The One in the Forest

The fire was slowly dying by the time Mora opened her eyes. She vaguely remembered waking up once before, but when she drifted off the next time, she had a dreamless sleep. However, His ethereal face would always be burned into the backs of her eyelids. Adjusting her position, she suddenly realized how close Bog was lying, his breathing heavy in her ear. She was on her back, but could barely see over his broad shoulders. Slightly lifting her head, as to not disturb him, she could see the thin, visible line of dawn emerging.

Sadness encompassed her, a weighted painful feeling. *The deeper I travel with Bog, the more my life changes, the more I feel lost, and the more I feel uncertain.* The visible stars and dark indigo sky reminded her of Ekklips. *He is beautiful and seductive, but in my heart, I know He is also extremely dangerous.* She saw it in His eyes, but the more she replayed the memories, the more the heat resonated. *His...eyes. Those heavy eyes of black ice with the stars reflecting...* She could feel the low tingle between her thighs she had only felt with Him. *The way He looks at me, the way He touches my skin, the way His body pushes up against me, and the way His fingers trace every line and curve.* It was nearly impossible to resist not desiring to run into His arms.

She shook her head clear of those thoughts. *Stop, Stop! I am entering into savage territory. If I sink any further without control, there will be no hope of surviving.*

## The Keeper

She clenched her teeth and balled her fists. Intimately close to Bog, she knew she needed to calm herself. There was nothing she could do at the present time, and the pain and torture of her thoughts would overtake her mind like a plague. A sharp breath intake from Bog made her head turn cautiously, but tenderly.

*He is a comfort. Despite how close he is, I do appreciate the security. I wonder what, or whom, caused the pain behind his violet eyes. He has been hurt, damaged. He may claim to not be a warrior, but he is fighting torrentially with something...a memory?...a love?...an identity?... a...*

The thought faded when, without warning, she looked up to see little gleaming eyes peering from beyond the blackness. Her terrified heart leapt. She slowly, but harshly, reached her arm out to shake Bog.

"Bog!" she whispered forcefully through gritted teeth. "Wake up, Bog!" She shook him a little harder, keeping her eyes fixed on the potential threat.

Suddenly, multiples began to light up around their small, rock cave.

"Bog! Wake up!" In a desperate attempt, she plucked out one of his feathers.

"Bloody curse of the gods!" He sat with a jump and bumped his head on the stone above. "Godsdamnit!" he cried out while rubbing his head. "What the fuck did you do that for?"

Mora pointed over toward the eyes. "What are they?" Fearful of an eminent attack, she slowly grabbed for the knife belted to her thigh.

"Wait." He pushed the knife back, stood up, and shook off his wings. "Come to the light if you proceed to follow us through our travels."

*Is he out of his fucking mind?* She gawked at him in shock.

From out of the fading night, a small figure appeared. The being was not much taller than her knees and dressed in a black cloak and hood. The eyes were still glowing a radiant gold-green tint amidst the growing dawn. When it removed its hood, she could see his petite, pointed ears. His left ear donned a shiny, silver, metal piece which hung from the middle of the lobe, around the back of his head, and into the back of the lobe of the right ear. He was not unusually disproportional, despite his stature. Startlingly though, his flesh was perfectly radiant, a creamy ebony.

The big, gold-green eyes blinked annoyingly.

Bog spoke first, "Why have you been following us in the shadows?" He stood up straighter.

Mora breathed deep. His stature was severely gigantic compared to the being and breathtaking in the growing sunrise.

"We have been looking after the One in the forest," the miniature being replied in an oddly deep voice, peering into Mora's eyes. "We were told when she entered the Pale Forest to make sure no harm would come to her."

The authority, and a hint of overconfidence, baffled Mora. She continued to watch the interaction intently.

"Where were you at the appearance of the Skulkins? You were not there to aid." He stared boldly, demanding an answer with a tinge of annoyance in his voice.

"We were watching, as you well know." The tiny being shrugged. "But before we could act, you smashed the female in the head and covered her with your feathers," he replied with a mocking smirk, "appearing as though you had taken care of the dire circumstance."

She noticed the snide inflection in his voice.

"Hmph," Bog grunted. "Aye. I'm perfectly capable of handling the situation on my own."

Fascinated, she looked at Bog, then at the being. She cleared her throat.

"Oh aye, Mora." He pointed flippantly. "This is Guilderon. Head warrior of the Piquonese Elves. The Piquonese are the smaller race of elves this forest inhabits. They are the guardians of Lychinus, an elvish dwelling amongst the trees."

"Elves?" She stared solidly. "I thought they were myth."

"And you're traveling with a large, talking bird-brain?" Guilderon barked.

Slightly taken aback, she timidly smiled up at Bog, who was clearly not amused.

"Nevertheless," Bog cleared his throat, "why have you decided to appear to us today of all days?"

"We heard the female talking in her sleep earlier. We know the Dark One is now pursuing to grasp control of her mind." Guilderon whisked his hand in an odd gesture toward the forest and two more similar looking elves appeared, clad in black cloaks. "There are more of us who will remain in the shadows. But for now, my brothers and I will follow our orders to travel with you. This is Milderon and Don."

Mora could not help but snicker at the last of the names. However, Guilderon did not appear entertained. Apparently, neither was anyone else. Seeing the little elves brought a feeling of joy back into her soul. She did not know why, but it was as if someone were wanting her to feel better about the journey and her struggles.

"By whom?" Bog asked cautiously, squinting at Guilderon.

She could sense the hint of indignation in his words.

"I do believe you already know the answer to your inquiry. She needs no introduction to you." Guilderon peered snidely back at Bog.

"She?" Mora spoke.

"Aye." He pushed his hair back from his forehead without looking at Mora. "It is no concern of yours at the moment."

She saw his cheeks flush red. *A female?*

The last thing he needed was for Mora to be introduced to her, especially since he had hoped to avoid going through Lychinus. Clearing his throat, he finally looked at Mora and nodded toward Guilderon. "I hope you do not mind the company that we have acquired."

"Not at all. I welcome it." She forced a smile in his direction, deciding not to push the obviously sensitive circumstance any further. "How much longer until we get to the outskirts of Lychinus?"

"It is another day's journey from this point," groaned Guilderon.

"Oh my. Well, I would appreciate if you could tell me more about the reason why I need to go beyond that point." She nodded amusingly toward Bog. "He's very elusive in his conversations." Out of the corner of her eye she saw him gawking.

Guildreon cut his eyes uncomfortably at Bog, seeing his seething gaze, and cleared his throat, "That conversation will have to be left until a later time." He watched her suspiciously. "You must get ready to continue your journey." He put his hood back on, turned around, and faced the sunrise. Pulling out a small lute, he commenced playing a soothing tune.

Grudgingly, Mora reluctantly stood with the help of Bog's outstretched hand and commenced to venture in the brush behind to take care of her personal business.

Annoyingly, she peered back through the foliage. *Why do they think I can't handle a godsdamn thing?* At that very moment, the wind blew through the air and she caught her breath. Whether it was because of the previous night's dream, or she had merely been too tired, the air suddenly felt very...*odd.* The wind blew her hair awry as she turned to notice a figure beneath the trees about a hundred paces from where she stood. Recognizing the figure instantly, she breathed, *Nephani.* Slowly, she started walking toward the opposite edge of the brush.

*Good morning,* Nephani lyrically whispered when Mora approached.

Nervously, she reached toward her neck. *The key,* she thought to herself, *I have completely forgotten about it.*

*Aye, it is still there.* Nephani lifted its head of light a little more, creating a visible halo inside the hood.

Mora could see the light radiating from the absence of a tangible face. *Have I fallen asleep again?* she sighed.

*This is not a dream. You are merely in a different...space.* The light inclined. *The moment you stepped away from your companions, to the moment I leave you, is not the same interval of time.* Nephani pointed to where she emerged. *However, you are truly standing here.*

*This is all so strange.* Mora shook her head.

*I'm here because I must warn you of an impending disturbance,* Nephani intervened.

*A disturbance? What kind of disturbance?* She thought back to the dream she had the night before. *His touch...His face...*

*Aye, illuminated one. That is the disturbance. You must not allow Him to enter your mind, touch your flesh. You must close off your thoughts before He delves into a deeper connection that may allow Him to overcome you.*

Sheepishly, Mora muttered, "Whom do you speak of?", knowing very well of whom Nephani spoke. However, realizing how ridiculous the question resonated, she quickly added, "Ekklips." Shifting uncomfortably, she looked down at her feet.

*Aye. The Dark One, my light.* There was a hint of pity in its voice. *The one from the Realm of Immortals. He is capable of entering into your mind through your weaknesses, your sensualness, and your creatural needs. He will then read into them, grab hold of your subconscious, and force you to do His bidding. There can be no glory or triumphs for you, only death and an eternity of chaos if you allow yourself to be consumed by Him.*

Mora sighed, unwilling to think she should never take pleasure in His touch again.

From underneath its cloak, Nephani conjured a ball of light. *Look further into the light. You will see of what I speak.*

It was a brilliantly lit illumination, but within, Mora noticed small figures moving to and fro. Looming closer to the glowing light, a spark of lightning shot out and attached itself to her forehead. Struggling against the unwanted force, she could see nothing else but the emergence of a chaotic environment.

# The Illusive Gathering

The brightness gradually faded as the mist of a moor settled before her feet. A cacophony of sounds began to fill Mora's ears, the clanking of metal and the rough grunts of masculine beings. Like a sheer curtain drawn back, a battle arose out of the mist. Creaturals and animalistic mutants alike were fighting, bloodied by the blows to a comrades limb or the clean slice of a severed neck. *It is brutal chaos and blatantly obvious no one side knows with whom they are fighting.* Each battlement flag was shredded, torn to pieces, and strewn across the dismembered and disemboweled bodies on the muddied ground. Every beast slaughtered the first figure in sight.

It was the unyielding carnage that made her stomach lurch violently. A flash, and another veil parted to reveal a massive camp. The pathway to the camp was aligned with tall poles. As she proceeded cautiously up the mud ridden path, she noticed upon each pole, almost to the top, were corpses, flogged, sliced open from neck to groin, and surrounded by flies and carnivorous birds. Her stomach turned again at the sight, causing her to heave what little she had left. As she stood up, her body began to shake. Between each pole, she could see the sight of filthy, broken tents. Terribly ugly monsters were mingling, spitting, drinking, cursing, and fighting amongst themselves. One horrid mutant sliced the head off of another while it raped a female from behind. The female flopped into the mud, barely moving, and bleeding from every orifice. Taking the female for itself, the hideous beast grabbed her by the hair and drug her into the nearest tent where a blood curdling scream rang out. An existing knowledge she was invisible from her surroundings allowed her to proceed quicker upon the muddied path. However, she still twitched at the brutality of an unexpected fight or spontaneous scream.

The thick, slimy mud was deep and it tugged at her leather boots every time she took a step. Though, when she glanced back, noticed there were no footprints left at all. *At least I'm concealed by whatever sick and twisted illusion this is.* Turning once again toward the middle of the camp, she spied an unusually oversized tent at the end of the path. It was concealed behind a heap of overhanging, mangled, and rotted bodies. With the appearance of a ginormous hole, it was a looming, black splotch in her vision, stark against the gray background of torrential rain clouds. As if being drawn by an internal thread, she hesitantly walked toward the entrance of the tent. Two silver poles stood at the doorway, both with an identical flag at the tip. Blowing sensually in the wind was the image of a winged serpent constellation, threaded in silver against an onyx fabric with small encompassing pinpoints of silver stars. *The wind makes the serpent appear as if it is slithering through the night sky.*

Standing in the entrance, she sensed a familiarity, a feeling she had been there before. The drapes were sheer, black lace, making it easier to see there were already figures inside the tent. Reluctantly, Mora pushed aside the drapes of the doorway. Inside, there were four beings. Almost immediately, she recognized Ekklips, the dark figure of her all-consuming dreams and, despite the twinge of disgust, she knew, her desire. He was leaning over a large map in the back center of the room, His pitch black and indigo hair falling seductively over His forehead. He was dressed in the same black tunic, revealing the top part of His immaculate, shimmering, pale chest, and black breeches. He had donned a similar garb most of the time He revealed Himself, except when He had manifested naked in the Realm of Immortals. She knew her body flushed at that moment. Shaking her head, she glanced back at where He stood over the map and caught her breath. It appeared His liquid, obsidian eyes were staring straight to where she stood at the entrance. *It can't be. He can't see me.*

A voice from her right startled her from her thoughts. A fifth figure she had not seen, began walking passed her to the table. Unlike the other non-creatural mutants plotting the map at the table beside Ekklips, this figure appeared a creatural similar to herself. However, standing with his back toward her, the shadows covered the side of his face. The only distinguishable characteristics were his light, curly hair and abnormally large stature.

The low, droll voice said, "My Liege," he bowed his head, "the massacre has already commenced. Chaos has inevitably ensued."

Mora saw the nasty, tall, grotesquely shaped bodies on each side of Ekklips smile crookedly in satisfaction. Each had skin the color of the harvest moon, with large jewelry attached by a gold chain to each orifice. Both were completely naked and void of genitals. Their eyes were embedded deep within their skull with a horribly large, disfigured nose.

She balked. *The mouths are sewn shut with their own scraggly hair.*

However, it wasn't their diabolical extremities that kept her attention, but the figure in the corner nearest the fire pit. The form was lean, possessing a smaller stature than present company, save her own. Long, curly, auburn hair fell to the silver belt cinching her saturated indigo robe.

"You flatter me, Commander."

When she turned, Mora caught her breath, nearly passing out from sheer exasperation at the appearance. It was as if she was peering into the pristinely clear creek bed in the Faery Realm. Blinking rapidly, she thought, *It must be a deception of the eyes, a pure coaxing of the mind, for I cannot be there, and yet here, at the present moment!* She gawked curiously into her own forest green eyes, unsettled by their intensity.

"Solora."

Ekklips' deep, sultry voice pierced her back, making her turn suddenly in His direction.

"Aye?" their two feminine voices answered simultaneously, one heard and one not.

Oddly, Mora knew what her reflection was about to say, "Aye, my Darkness? Would you care for a drink?"

She mouthed along.

"Or, would you and your guests care for something to eat?" A wry smile grew across her lips.

## The Keeper

"Solora, my Light, bring us some spirits. My guests will need them later as they skulk through the camp." He glanced sidelong at the monsters and they began to laugh heartily through their disgusting stitching.

The vision of herself apparently found it quite amusing and partook in a sardonic smirk. The only two not laughing were Ekklips and the shadow figure. Watching an unspoken conversation between the two commanding figures in the room, the fifth nodded toward Ekklips, took his leave, and, turning away from Mora, exited through the black, lace curtains. She attempted to glimpse his face through the material, but it was too skewed.

Sickened by the very thought of the living arrangements, she watched the events unfold further. After an allotted amount of time discussing carnage tactics and loyalties, the disfigured guests dispersed from the tent, leaving her reflection alone with Ekklips. He walked silently toward the other like a predator after His prey. The thirst in His eyes was overwhelming. With arms outstretched, He grabbed her around the waist.

She giggled.

Mora rolled her eyes.

An intrusive growl emerged in Ekklips' throat as He kissed her exposed neck. His voice rumbled, "You're mine. You will always be mine."

Disgusted, but curious, she watched the scene unfold. Standing behind her, Ekklips pulled the layer of skirts around her hips as her head draped back onto His shoulder. He placed a hand around her throat, still kissing the back of her neck and exposed shoulders. His other hand caressed the sensitive flesh between her thighs. She moaned and moved her hips in rhythm with the movement of His hand. The faster His hand moved, the stronger her breath heaved and her hips swayed. Finally, removing His hand, He forcefully picked her up and carried her to the table with the map.

A growl in the back of His throat commanded, "Tell me what you want, my Light."

She mouthed as her reflection purred, "To feel you deep inside me, my Dark."

Mora swallowed. Wanting to watch, but not wanting at the same time, she could feel her chest heavy and the sweat beading on the nape of her neck. *I need to fucking leave this gods-forsaken place.* Grabbing her head, she screamed in her mind, *Nephani!* To no avail, the attempt to channel herself, her inner thoughts, was lost in a sea of ambiguity for longing and pleasure.

*Am I jealous? Do I want to be her... or me?*

Daring herself to open her eyes, she saw Him pull her skirts around her waist again and unfasten His breeches. Pushing Himself inside her, He rhythmically thrust as her back arched violently. She cried out in suspected pleasure, yearning for more. He continued as she clutched the table, seemingly floating above the surface as her flesh started to subtly glow.

Mora averted her gaze, unwilling herself to partake in such an action. However, reluctantly, part of her hungered for His touch, for Him to physically admire her beauty as He caressed her skin, penetrating deeper into her soul. Shaking her head manically, she screamed, *This is wrong!* She knew not of what fire scorched beneath her flesh, but the ache festered. Closing her eyes again, she cried out, *This is not real!*

Without warning, heat burned through her own thighs. Frightened, she opened her eyes. Immediately, she saw His hungry, black stare before her face. A yell reverberated as a sensation from her core rose violently. Arching her back, her hands gripping the side of the table, she released a pleasure she had never felt before. Her body jerked and eyes widened.

*Help!*

Tearing from His grasp, she ran from the tent as fast as she could without looking back. Her legs burned and she stumbled through the deep mud. Tears stung the corners of her eyes as rain started beating against her face. She could feel every drop like sharp needles stinging her skin. A crash of lightning made her falter, followed by the omnipotent sound of thunder beating in rhythm with her heart.

Suddenly, she stopped, nearly sliding through the mud. Ekklips had appeared from the crash of lightning. He was standing in the rain, drenched and naked. His hair was matted against His forehead, nearly covering His piercing, liquid eyes. His skin illuminated with each successive bolt of lightning. Sparks danced across His tattoos, invigorating the charge.

## The Keeper

"You cannot escape me!" His voice bellowed. "You are mine and always will be mine, no matter what foolish game you play."

She was frozen, drenched, and unable to speak.

Slowly, He started encircling her shivering body. "You think this imaginative ball of light can keep me from entering Their domain? It is I who helped create it!" He spat on the ground. "Your memories are *my* memories!"

She could feel Him close the distance between them, His lips upon her ear. Her breathing became heavier, but she did not utter a single word.

He whispered in her ear, "It is I who conversed at the right hand, equally imputing my creative details on this pathetic world. And it is I who ultimately coined Chaos from the ruins of His jealously."

He continued to walk around her, dragging His hand against her ass and hips until they were eye to eye. His face turned contemplative and serious. "We were all three equals. The beginning and the end!" Thunder vibrated the sky. "And now He is trying to sway you from me...*again*!"

Her whole body shook with frigid anxiety. Watching His eyes through the rain, she could hear the agony in His words, feel it lightly caress her flesh, and hear it burn with rage and abandonment.

"The tragedy *He* cast out upon All to reek the consequences of actions your stories and prophecies spin against me, are all products of *His* envy and inability to lessen *His* ego. They are lies, falsehoods to weave their own tangled web of fearing the shadows of the unknown! *He* aided in the rise of Chaos and, in the process, secured my increasing control over this domain, tightening my grasp over All. *His* impunity will be my rise!"

*Who is He?* Mora was confused about Ekklips' constant emphasis.

The words spat maliciously through His teeth, "He cannot take you from me! I brought you to life again and I will have my vengeance! My increasing transformation into Death has only made me stronger." The passion burned intensely in His eyes.

Then, a broad smirk appeared across His face. "You will learn soon enough. Your body, soul, and mind cannot be protected by Him forever. Life is weakening. I can feel the desolation rising. The tyrannical restrictions of Life can only be released by complete Death, even in the Realm of Immortals. I am the only true salvation now. With you, we can create a balance Life could never achieve alone. But Dark will always be my True Being. I am not your enemy!"

He pressed His lips against Mora's so passionately, she felt like she would explode. However, before she could return the desired reaction to the taste of His lips, the lightning crashed again and she was kneeling outside the illumination, her gaze broken by exasperation. Her breathing was uneven. Trembling, she stood straighter and peered into the light of Nephani.

*You see, Ekklips will not allow you to succeed easily in your quest. He seeks to use you as a weapon, the key to both His pleasure and revenge. You must take heed in your decisions and not allow Him to manipulate you into following His plan.* Nephani started to fade slowly. *There is an element. A tangible object of importance in His possession. The Dark One obtained it through manipulation. However, His connection to your mind is knotted both ways in connection to this object. Trust within your mind and you will control your own fate, Mora. You know more than you realize and are stronger than you know.*

She began to plead, "I don't understand everything. It's a puzzle, so many pieces, yet none of it makes sense!" She cried out loudly. "Please give me real answers! Not riddles! I know not where to start, nor who to trust! Please!" She tried grasping onto what was left of Nephani's cloak as it disappeared.

Hopelessly, she screamed out in frustration before collapsing to the ground. *I don't want to do this anymore.*

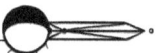

Bog glanced nervously toward the direction Mora had wandered only moments ago. *I know she is frustrated, but I am struggling to be of use to her internal fight.* Running his hand through his hair, he glanced at Guilderon.

The elf smirked at him with the lute still to his lips.

He nodded. An uneasiness resonated through his bones as thunder rolled again in the distance.

"Mora," her name echoed faintly, "Mora, my love."

At the sound of her name, Mora lifted her head steadily, tears reddening her dark green eyes and splotching her cheeks. A startlingly bright light was shining from amongst the tallest branches. From where it was coming was hard to tell, although it appeared as if the sun had broken through the growing clouds. Straining her eyes, she shielded them as the snow began to swirl around into the form of a female being. Her stomach churned because when the figure smiled, it was so like her mother's, but the form was young and beautiful.

"Mora."

The soft voice was sweet, full of love and compassion.

"Please don't be afraid. It is I," the form hovered above the snow with arms outstretched, "your mother."

"I don't understand," she responded shakily, the wind slowing down. "What do you mean?"

"I have been freed of my creatural form and allowed to breathe again in my original state of being," she came closer to Mora, "because, I have fulfilled my penance. I have been rewarded for my loyalty."

With furrowed eyebrows, Mora stuttered, "Your penance? I was your penance?" She dusted off the icy shards on her knees and moved back a couple steps.

A sweet smile appeared and whispered, "Nay, my little bird, my life in creatural form was my penance, to face the challenges as mortals would and to suffer as one, too."

Mora rubbed her eyes, shaking her head in disbelief. "Am I cursed?" The figure approached her and kissed her on the forehead. Tears threatened to return, but she fiercely thwarted the burning sensation.

"Thousands of years ago, I was tempted by a being, a magnificent being, one of the most superior of Beings. I was innocent and naive, made of pure light and love, one of the seven original Primordials. He was one of the Trinitas. The seven were of the Trinitas, and created through what was deemed as perfection.

## The Keeper

"He yearned for power, never satisfied with His position. He secretly gathered followers through whatever means possible. He prowled on weakness. He called me His muse, His possession, and He promised a utopian realm. I breathed in His words and every promise. However, I did not comprehend the increasing shadows around our Realm, our souls, and us."

Mora shifted uncomfortably.

"One day, when I was alone, I began to feel jealous, to feel the greed myself. I wanted to be the powerful one; I wanted to be the one to hold the authority. So I took it upon myself to challenge He who was desperate for power. I appeared in front of Him, demanding Him to share the power He claimed He would soon possess and vowed I would lead the followers into a battle larger than any soul ever beheld. We would undoubtedly win, for the forces of numbers would prevail.

"I underestimated my sway, for He maliciously smiled at me and spoke plainly, '*Nay, my muse. I cannot give you what you ask, for what you ask is, and always was, mine. I have deserved this more than your feeble soul can comprehend.*' Nonchalantly, He stood and walked toward me, circling me like a predator. From the nape of my neck I heard Him breathing softly, making me weak. Closing my eyes, I suddenly felt a sharp pain pierce my back. As I dropped, I turned a shaky gaze upon Him, His smile just as beautiful and malicious as it had been before. I started to feel cold. I didn't know what had happened, for there was no such thing as death where I originated. I was scared and He began to laugh hauntingly.

"As He laughed, He walked around me, callously whispering about how He had just conquered the first of the seven, and I certainly was not His last. He helped breathe life into our souls and mold us to become the primordial race of immortals. However, jealousy between the Trinitas was tainting All. Therefore, He was going to overthrow All and continue to create a race of His own using His interconnectedness with Light. He would start with the ones who would not join Him, the ones who stood firmly with the Others."

Mora's breath caught in her throat. She could only assume her mother spoke of Ekklips. However, the sheer concept that Ekklips was a god was nearly inconceivable. Despite the fact He was the most glorious being she had ever laid eyes on, she still couldn't grasp onto the postulation He was one of the most highest of Beings.

The voice of her mother continued, "He walked away from me, neither glancing back, nor caring to finish me off. I knew there was little time left before my light went out. I was scared, but I needed help. I steadied myself, taking one long step at a time until I could feel Their presence. For you see, my childling, nothing is materialistic in my realm like the one you see before you. It is merely a unity of souls, an eternity of ruling the balance of All, an interaction of love and acceptance, no need for possession.

"I reached Them through the cold, bitterness, and pain. They were aware of the circumstances. They knew who had stabbed me, but did not have patience for foul play. I told Them everything from my side. I felt it my duty before I was cast out, left to die. Forgiving as They were, this was not without punishment. I was banned into creatural form, sent to wander the land for eons.

"Eventually, the other six were cast out as well. We watched the deeds of Chaos unfold. In due time, we were forced to choose sides, for They had lost Their union of power over All." She looked Mora in the eyes and placed a cold, snowy hand onto her cheek. "I was to suffer through wars, not being allowed to die, nor be saved, until I fulfilled my penance."

Mora pinched her eyebrows together and inquired, "What do you mean...penance?"

"Before Chaos, through the growing unrest, Ekklips was forced from His divine throne. After, He fought with Life for thousands of years to return to the Divine Realm. Dark Ages flickered through time and space, until He convinced Light to join Him. Life, angry and distraught at Light's choice, made a sacrifice that ultimately exiled Dark from His ability to return to the Divine Realm and spawned mortality. Thus, Dark also became known as Death, and He swore unwavering vengeance.

"As we speak, He has been building an army of monsters, mortal and immortal, to rise against everything He created with both Life and Light. Ekklips discovered how to increase His power, to take on any form He wished, and to build a kingdom of His own design. He was beginning to become the direct balance of Life, but as Life sought His own vengeance after the sacrifice, His presence became altered. In spite of Life's unknown tactics, Ekklips needed an empyrean weapon. And that my love, began within you."

Mora gasped, "Me? What lies within me? And how am I supposed to guard something I know nothing about?" She suddenly became frantic and completely unsure of her surroundings. A dizziness sloshed around in her mind and she stumbled against the nearest tree.

"The key. The key is what will lead you to destroy all evidence and guarantee you eternal aid against the forthcoming battle of All," her mother spoke gently.

"Why me?" she pleaded as she clutched the key to her breasts.

"Because All cannot exist without the unification of Life, Light, and Dark. Even Death has an important role in preserving All, now. Dark is in existence because it dwells as the opposite of Light. Since His exile, His essence feeds off of Life's manifestation of Death. To take control over Him and restore balance, you must embrace the weapon."

"But you said the weapon was *within* me." Tears welled up in her eyes and began to stream down her face.

"This task is daunting and it will be difficult." She placed a cold hand on Mora's cheek. "There is something else, though. While I remained loyal on this land to fulfill my purpose, you, Mora, stood in Life's presence at the beginning, along with the Ekklips. After my banishment, I know not all the details that incurred during the Dark Ages, but your True Being was coaxed from Life's grasp, and it spawned Chaos."

Sputtering, "Chaos? You're saying I really was one of the *Trinitas*?" Mora started pacing through the snow. Bog's words began flooding through her mind. The information was becoming overbearing to her senses and she began to heave.

"Mora, I know it is overwhelming."

As the soft hand fell to her shoulder, she threw up her arms, turned, and yelled, "You don't! You left me! I've been thrown into a world I know nothing...and I reiterate *nothing*, about! All because I am part of your...*penance*? You still have yet to tell me about that godsdamn detail!"

The image of her mother sighed. "Because I was lonely and began to feel forsaken by Them during my penance, I summoned Ekklips to help me find a way to die, to rid my spirit of the flesh I had been tortured with for so long. He agreed to help if I would, under every circumstance, allow Him to use my flesh and bone as a vessel for His plans. Reluctantly, I agreed out of desperation.

"I stayed the night in one of His fortresses. It was a dark, lifeless, cold place, full of grotesquely shaped mutants and mangled beasts. During the night, I awoke with horror, only to see a sheer, blue figure floating above my body, a hand's length between us. It was ghostly, haunting. I asked what it wanted, for it did not resemble the Dark One. I asked again, but no answer. Without warning, I felt a ghastly stabbing pain through my naval. I glanced down and saw a sheer, glowing blue dagger protruding from my skin. It pushed harder into my flesh as I writhed in pain.

"Screaming, I awoke again in terror. Immediately, I lifted my gown and peered at my naval to see my flesh perfectly intact. I sighed in exhaustion and quickly ran from the tower. As I ran, I could hear a seductively deep laughter surrounding me. I frantically glanced back, but there was no one there.

"It was not until two, full moons later I found that I was with new life. How I became with new life, I could only assume it was the stabbing pain from the ghostly figure which had been implanted in me in the tower of the Dark One's fortress. I realized I was now the vessel we had agreed upon. Frightened by my choice, and in desperation, I cried out to Life and received an answer. I would be given the solitude and power to raise the childling neutrally, allowing you a free will. However, I would not be released until I was deemed worthy.

"I spent my days concocting spells and barriers to keep Ekklips from discovering where I was hiding you. After I gave birth, I had nightmare encounters with Him through my dreams. He would torture me, His darkness clawing for access to our location. I fought back with the best of my ability, much to my own cognitive detriment. I spent countless nights crying out to Life for answers, but all was moot, for He had become silent to my pleas. I thought I could not climb high enough for mercy.

"You see, I was becoming numb to my salvation. I was already the vessel for the Dark One. I had made my choice. Our threads were knotted, but while I raised you..." Meridan tucked Mora's curl behind her ear, "...I did not feel ultimate remorse for my actions, despite limiting my communication to Life. Finally, one night, a stag came to me. It spoke sincerely about my ultimate deceit and how I must come to control my mind once more, or my soul would eternally cease to exist. It alluded to

*The Keeper*

Ekklips' ultimate plot to possess Light and the possibility that the childling, you, my love, are the reincarnation of Light, born of Dark, Death, and Chaos. You are Ekklips' attempt to release your True Being once again; for in the form of Chaos, He could not grasp the knowledge Life had hidden within the depths of your mind. Therefore, at that moment, I knew not how, but I must not emotionally attach myself to you until you became mature enough to choose your own path. I was to only be your teacher, your mentor. And while I had my suspicions, it was not until the day the serpent broke through the barrier, I realized it was an omen my protective magic was weakening."

Tugging on her braid, Mora struggled with the idea of her existence as the snowy hand stroked her cheek.

"And this is why I must leave you. I am no longer a pawn in Their game; I am now a spirit of eternal solitude. I have taught you everything I learned in the Mortal and Immortal Realms. If you can see it within yourself, you will be able to prevail, but you cannot do it alone. You must seek help from those who are the guardians of the truest form of the Trinitas. There are countless followers and you will be provided for along your journey if you're willing to accept it. But you will need to seek counsel within the most concealed parts of your mind, isolated from Ekklips. Remember Mora, you are never alone."

With that, her mother's spirit was gone. She fell to her knees, angst and grief swelling deep within her soul. A detrimental fear of abandonment settled in her stomach. *How much more can I take?* Bigger tears strained sadly down her cheeks, the ghostly feeling of her mother's hand still present. She brushed them away with the back of her hand and sniffed. Squeezing her eyes shut, she screamed at the top of her lungs and fell forward.

A flash of lightning illuminated the surrounding trees, followed by a slow, loud rumble of thunder which vibrated the ground beneath her palms. Digging her fists into the snow, she clenched her jaw and embraced for the oncoming storm, her green eyes blazing brightly.

# From Above

Mora braced against a tree trunk, dropped the fistfuls of snow, and buried her face in her hands. She could feel the burn from the chill of the ice in every extremity of her body. Although her head was pounding, she could faintly hear foot steps running toward her through the thick snow.

"Mora! Mora! Are you all right? What bloody happened?" Bog shook her shoulders and removed her hands away from her face. Trying to see if she were visibly hurt, he noticed a lingering flicker of luminescent green in her eyes before it faded away.

The warmth of his hands stung, but comforted her fingers. She replied gloomily, "I am fine. Weary, but fine." The front temple of her head started pinching as well. Impulsively, she felt around her neck for the key, sighing with relief when she brushed against it.

"What happened?" he repeated again as Guilderon and the other Piquonese Elves appeared throughout the woods around them.

She cut her eyes at him and quietly said, "Nephani." She knew he would understand by that one name. However, she dared not speak of the encounter with her mother. *It is a completely different burden on my shoulders.*

*Damn.* Angry he wasn't more mindful of the possibility of an encounter, he stuttered, "Oh, certainly. You can inform me about it later. First, you need to get warm. Come back to the fire while we pack to leave." He wrapped her shaking body in his cloak and placed his hand at the small of her back, holding her against his side as they walked to the fire.

Thankful for his warmth, and the fact he didn't carry her, she clung tightly to his cloak as he guided her over to the place she had departed in what felt an eternity ago. The journey through time and space spared no little detail in torturing her mind to the fullest. She could barely comprehend the details and scenes from Nephani's illumination. From low and deep inside, there was a burning feeling she had to leave quickly, but knew not where to start.

Ekklips' haunting words, *They are lies; falsehoods to weave their own tangled web of fearing the shadows of the unknown*, were filled with a subtle desperation. While the claim, *I am the only true salvation now... Dark will always be my True Being. I am not your enemy*, felt like He was trying to not only convince her, but Himself, it was the truth.

*What is the truth?* She sighed.

Pulling an extra frock out of her satchel, she modestly walked behind a bush, kicked out a hidden, nosy Piquonese elf, and quickly undressed, placing the non-soaked material over her cold, wet body. Glancing down, she realized it had been her mother's garment. It was a plain, mossy color with wide arms and a laced slit at the collar. Because her mother had been a tad bit taller than herself, it fell to her ankles. She tore part of the hem off and stuffed it inside her satchel. *The extra cloth will be beneficial at some point.* Tightening her leather belt around her waist, she slipped on a hand-sized leather pouch with a flask. She laced the strings at her chest tighter so she couldn't feel the bitter wind against her skin and trudged silently back to the fire. She placed her wet frock in the knapsack—noting she must take it out to dry the next time they stopped... *or else it will ruin and I won't have anything else to wear.* She tried to hand Bog his cloak.

He waved his hand absently. "Nay, you keep it for the time being. I do not get as cold as you do and it's better against the wind than the one you have."

She tilted her head and frowned slightly.

He smiled.

When she saw his dimple appear, she knew he was sincere. Shrugging, she said, "I have been wanting to ask you how you don't ever appear cold."

He smirked and cut his eyes toward Mora. "There is a difference in appearing cold and being cold."

Unamused, she threw a stick in his general direction.

Overplaying his dodging of the stick, he chortled, "Oi, there is no need for violence." He handed her a piece of meat he had skewered while she was gone earlier. Then, he shrugged. "I do not know the actual history."

"That's the first," she mused tauntingly, rolling her eyes.

"Someone is certainly in a shitty mood." He bit off a piece of the meat, chewed it quickly, and licked his fingers. When he finished, he cleared his throat. "Despite our similarities to the birds of the sky, speculation is, since Aloria is of divinity, a messenger of Life, He graced her with the ability to withstand all changes in temperature she may have experienced during her time by His side. But I don't really know if that's true or a tale the elders like to tell us when we were borglings. I don't get really cold, but I can feel the cold." He glanced at her face, glowing by the firelight. "If that makes sense."

She contemplated on what he said, but then her head snapped back at him and she sputtered, "You said Aloria *is* of divinity." Her eyes widened. "Does that mean she is still alive?"

Choking on a piece of meat, he beat his chest before he replied, "Uh, aye. We *are* immortal beings. That is, unless our lives are ended by an equal or stronger immortal. And..." he swallowed, "because she is one of the oldest, there is none who would dare challenge her everlasting superiority."

"Can I meet her?" Upon her words, she thought she saw a moment of panic flash vibrantly inside his violet eyes. Although, the way it disappeared quickly, she thought it might have been an illumination from the sporadic peek of the sun through the matted clouds.

"First, let me get you to Borgoria safely before you make... arrangements." He averted his eyes from her eager stare. He felt very uncomfortable referencing home and the possibility of who may be waiting his return. *I'm afraid she won't be as eager to arrive if she only knew.* Averting his eyes, he cleared his throat again before taking a swig of water. "We must depart."

## The Keeper

Disappointed, Mora wondered further what he was holding back. Instead of continuing on the sensitive subject, she helped him cover the fire with snow and threw her satchel over her shoulder. Watching him shake off his wings, she noticed a sullenness had filled his eyes. *He is harboring relentless secrets and I want to know why.* However, before she could apologize, her thoughts were interrupted by a small movement over the rocks. Guildreon's head appeared, lute in hand.

"Get along with it. You two are slower than me drunk, great-uncle Hilderon."

Groaning from the slight, persistent pounding in her head, she commenced to follow the elf. They headed north. The sun was beginning to break through the splotchy clouds and branches of the Pale Forest. This was a welcomed sensation after the previous snow. Vaguely, Mora could see a slow spread of vibrant colors from the sky across the twinkling ice crystals, the icicles in the trees, and the snow lain forest floor. Unfortunately, the snow was harder this morning, like walking on rough ice. Her feet tread heavily, breaking pieces into circular shapes. Keeping her eye intently on Bog's bare back in front of her, she took big strides to stay in the middle of the pack. *Despite the smaller stature of the elves, they are quite quick on their feet, nearly at my heels.* She quickened her pace.

Noticing the growing intensity of Bog's mood and gait, a tension had built so taut it could be cut clean with a knife. A cloud had fallen upon his mood following her morning inquiry about Aloria. Out of courtesy, she decided not to attempt to make conversation. *However, it may also be my nervous perception of this world around me, considering my state of unrest since this morning.*

He lead the company further into the bramble of thorns. *How the curse of the gods am I going to explain Mora when I get home? They think I've been idiotic since the beginning and she thinks I'm full of shit most of the time.* He cut the thorns violently with his saber.

As if in response to his frustration, the wind whispered to him softly, *We are the wind guardians of The Keeper. We are the communications between the Land Dwellers and the Beyond. Continue your journey brave one, but beware of the prodigal return.*

It wasn't the first time during his journey the wind had spoken to him, but it was the first time it spoke directly of a warning. Not entirely

*The Keeper*

comforted, he glanced over his shoulder. He could barely decipher her face under her hood, but he knew he must continue to make her trust his intentions. Slowing his pace, he stepped in line with her own and spoke low, "How are you holding up?"

Shocked at his presence, she caught his eyes from under her hood. "I'm doing fine. These elves are abnormally quick paced. I'm having a hard time keeping ahead of their advances."

He smirked.

She tripped and Bog caught her arm. "Thanks," she sighed. After a moment, she said quietly, "I'm curious."

His eyebrow arched. "Aye? About what?"

"I want to know who, or what, attacked you, and how you came to find me?"

The question sent a shiver down his spine. He rubbed a hand through his hair and on the back of his neck, leering behind at the elves. "I had the fortunate chance to locate your presence with the help of the wind on my journey south." He grimaced, knowing it sounded frivolously far fetched. "When I was attacked, it was an unfortunate occurrence I had not anticipated. After realizing I had miraculously not been captured, I tried to recall the details of my fall and my journey's purpose. It took several days, but I realized I had come to be where I was observing all along." Whacking at the brush absentmindedly, he continued, "Your mother's spirit was also very…" nervously looking at Mora, he muttered, "…strong."

Stopping abruptly, she gawked, "What do you mean my mother's spirit was also very *strong*?"

He grabbed her arm, tugging her forward. Lowering his voice, he replied, "Don't be angry, Mora. Before you came into this world, concepts were formed by a multitude of immortal scholars, shaman, elders from various regions, nations, and tribes. The primal question, hovering above all the various speculations and theories, was: 'Is this All?'. Mortals fear Death more than immortals, and therefore, have created a multitude of their own beliefs about All. Many of which have divided and destroyed nations beyond reason. However, most immortals live significantly longer than mortals. They, *we*, have the ability to focus less on dividing the concept of All, and condense it to that sole question. The majority of mortals are completely ignorant to the Realm of Immortals, parallel with their own.

*163*

However, immortals can easily live a multitude of lifetimes in their expansion and have vastly penetrated their presence into the Mortal Realm."

He placed his hand on the small of her back and leaned closer. "There are greater things at work, whether they benefit Natura or seek to destroy it, a struggle for ultimate power is evolving each moment. In the scheme of things, knowledge is becoming an obsolete concept to the masses of creaturals. Once the struggle for power was forced by the feud between Life and Dark, a new hand was dealt and Meridan became a vessel, entrapping Chaos and birthing the reincarnation essence of Light."

Feeling the warmth of his breath on her cheek heated her chest. Then, remembering what her mother's spirit said, she questioned, "A vessel? And what of Light?"

Her mother had never discussed anything before her birth directly to Mora. Any revelation from her mother's lips were from the encounter with her spirit. However, thinking back to the days of her youth, she felt pieces falling steadily into place. A flood of emotion poured in her mind - the lonely nights she stayed up scared, clutching her knees because her mother would scream uncontrollably; the incomprehensible conversations her mother would seemingly have by herself, with no answer; the emotional detachment Mora grew up encompassed by; and the lessons that accommodated everything from hand to hand combat, to the theology and philosophies of a world Meridan had never allowed her to physically explore. However, she never prepared her for the vast population difference outside their dwelling. Despite the books and maps her mother had acquired, she still felt she knew nothing of the truths that lay beyond the sanctuary, the hardships she had and would face, nor the unnerving reason for her very existence. Her thoughts snapped back to the present moment at the sound of Bog's voice.

"Some beings became vessels. They will serve their purpose, for good or bad, and then they are relinquished of their task through the releasing of their spirit, or..." he grunted, "...soul. There is an unknown factor, a trigger to obey their Creator, or Creators. Most of the time, it is the mortals which are made vessels."

He shrugged his shoulders. "Through the kind of information scholars have been able to acquire, they believe there were three, immortal,

*The Keeper*

female vessels commissioned by Dark. We know not if all were from the Primordial status, but your mother was given the most important of tasks. The others are yet to reveal their purpose." His face scrunched. "Though, I think your mother's task was allowed out of pure desperation for a release from an eternal life of misery. As for Light, we don't know exactly how her...uh, *your* True Being was transformed into Chaos, but it happened during the divine reckoning."

She contemplated his words. *Was the reflection in the chamber at the camp the embodiment of Chaos? I'm not sure that makes sense because I would not have been myself before my birth...would I?* Shaking her head, she persisted, "And these 'others', they may or may not be departed as of yet if their purpose has not been fulfilled?"

"We know there were seven Primordial Beings, all an initial type of male and/or female essence. After all were banished, only the one, female Being, that we are aware, was eventually used as a vessel. This assumption is made on the basis females can handle more power mentally and emotionally. Also, because Meridan was one of the original immortals, the connection to your essence would be closer to the source, regardless of her exile. The male counterparts are unknown. For the other vessels' purpose, we know it must come soon because Meridan's magic weakened and your physical presence revealed. Of whom else knows of this information is beyond my reckoning. And, obviously, this is purely speculative, interpreted by a profound amount of scholars since the inception of the star reader's prophecy. However, because you have free will, a by-product of having a creatural birth, all will fall in accordance to your course of action since it is you Dark wants. But, you will shape your own outcome. Which direction you choose will depend on whether the existing Primordials will become your protectors, or weapons to destroy you. Predetermined and inevitable fate is nonsense. Therefore, choose your way with caution...for there will be many." He stopped to think. "Preferably in accordance with the salvation of All, if you will be so kind." He smirked.

Mora returned a slight smile. *The damned dimple of sincerity.* Suddenly uncomfortable at his words, she thought, *I know not why he seems so cautious about iterating the need for me to choose life rather than death; as if I am capable of any unnecessary evil on living, or non-living,*

*165*

*beings.* She continued to tread solemnly at his pace. "The laws of destiny, do they exist in the Realm of Immortals?"

"Nay, they exist nowhere. And certainly immortals need no predetermined path. Again, it is in their capacity to create multiple paths throughout their lives without much consequence to themselves. Although, if their lives are to be cut short of eternity, it is only by the hands of a more ancient or equally matched immortal, and not outside their laws of *vitali.* Otherwise, they are murderers and shall be punished by Him." He added quickly, "Not that Him. Mortals are governed by Death, immortals are governed by Life. Now," he looked back to make sure the elves were out of earshot, "about the key."

Before Mora could gawk at him, unexpectedly, a hum vibrated next to her ear. She turned rapidly, watching an arrow barely miss Guilderon's right shoulder and penetrate the ground. Bog pulled her arm fiercely and they frantically dove behind a couple of nearby trees. Another arrow hummed, this time, striking a Piquonese elf in the back.

She inhaled sharply.

The elves scrambled, jumping inside hollow, fallen trees and into the crevasses of a nearby quarry. Numbers began to dwindle as the arrows continued to fly.

Immediately, Bog hissed a command, "Get lower!"

Slowly, so as not to attract attention, she knelt closer to the ground. She could feel the wet snow soaking through to her knees. Staying close to his body, they slithered like legless serpents over the bramble, pushing their way to a gigantic, fallen tree.

He mustered himself together and peered from over the log. He cursed and pointed ahead to a dense, shadowy area of the Pale Forest. His eyes skipped over the branches, from bottom to top, hoping to catch a glimpse of something moving.

She surveyed the surroundings, too. At first, she couldn't see anything but the endless horizon of dense, dead trees. However, she caught sight of movement above one of the taller trees. Catching her breath, she squeaked, "There!"

Numerous black figures were sporadically sitting on branches further back in the receding forest. They were only noticeable with the slightest of movements, such as when they reached into their quivers.

## The Keeper

Bog mouthed a word.

*What?* she mouthed back.

He did it again. This time it appeared as though the word was '*Hawkends*'.

All of a sudden, she saw small forms dart across her line of vision. *It is Guilderon, Milderon, and Don!* They moved terribly fast, it was hard to catch a glimpse of their faces. She saw them running to the opposing sides of the forest from where they were concealed. The hostile figures began jumping from branch to branch, hastily following the little elves. The leaps were graceful and skilled. For a moment, she was entranced before she felt Bog jerk her arm harshly. Almost falling over, she scrambled after him as he ran fast, opposite the elves.

Panting, she looked back. "But we can't leave them alone!"

"They wanted you to run, that is why they are leading them away!"

The brush was beating at her face and a flashback of the night in the Land of G'lo sparked her memory, flooding with the emotions she had been feeling.

"Bog, stop!" She was heaving. She paused, wheezing until her chest felt like it was going to beat from her ribcage.

"Mora, we can't stop now!" As he reached back to take her arm, an arrow hit his shoulder. "Godsdamnit!" He clutched his shoulder and fell to his knees.

She jerked around to see a black figure jumping toward them on the branches above, quick and stealthily. Frantically, she scanned for something to shelter them. Ahead, she spotted bramble, full of thick, twisted, slender trees. "Quickly!" She grabbed him by his waist and they stumbled through the wet, slippery snow to the branched shelter.

Looking over her shoulder, the figure was gaining. Another arrow flew past their heads. Tripping over the protruding roots and rocks of the forest floor, she gathered her strength and shoved Bog into the brush. Helping his deceivingly light frame stumble further inside, she searched around for the most concealed part of the treed cave.

When Bog let go of her support, he plopped down against the tree, blood running down his arm. Looking around for something to help remove the arrow, she froze. Before she could object, Mora gawked as he

*167*

mustered enough grunt to pull the arrow swiftly from him shoulder. He managed to toss it out of sight before grasping the wound in pain. Biting on his lip hard enough for blood to also trickle from his mouth, she pulled out a ripped cloth from the knapsack and helped him tie it tightly around the wound to subdue the bleeding. As she touched his skin, she could feel the strong, rapidly increasing beat of his heart.

He kept his eyes closed, attempting to pace his quickened breathing. "Thanks," he whispered.

Reluctant to leave him, she crouched lower, watching over her shoulder for the threatening, winged beast. "I'm so sorry, Bog. I shouldn't have stopped." Trying to hold the tears back, she could see the hurt in his bloodshot, violet eyes.

He smiled and wiped away the tear beneath her eye with his thumb. "Don't. Take this. I'll be fine." Holding his shoulder as he tried to remain calm through the pain, he handed her his saber. "Go find help. Stay low, and I will join you shortly."

Before she could retort, a shadow appeared over the thick brush.

His eyes widened. "Fuck," he mumbled. Quickly, he jerked her against him and wrapped his wings around them both.

It peered inside. Mora could vaguely see the hideous, merciless stare through Bog's wings. Its feet were birdlike and they clung onto a fallen branch with razor sharp claws. Its body was slender and covered with feathers, while the neck was long and scaly. Its beak was deathly sharp and the large, glass eyes were like orbs of black ice. The wings were not nearly as impressive as Bog's; they were wilted, black, and jagged. Its presence reeked of Death.

Holding their breath, the Hawkend snarled and moved on. Bog grunted as he removed his wings, groaning at the agony shooting through his shoulder.

Waiting for a brief moment, Mora crouched stealthily through the bramble toward the thinning branches. She attempted to steady her hand, but the saber shook unsteadily. The pulsing beat of her heart increased in both her ears and against her chest. Briefly glancing back at Bog, she saw him strain a nod. Turning back around, she proceeded to peek outside the brush and survey the whitewashed area.

The sunlight was barely noticeable through the trees. *Curse the*

*The Keeper*

*gods. It must be getting close to sunset.* Emerging step by step, saber at the ready in one hand, knife in the other, she inspected the treetops. Unnervingly silent, the only sound was the slight crunch beneath her boots. Staying low like Bog suggested, she continued watching for any sign of danger. The air hung with a putrid scent. Scrunching her nose, she held her arm to her face to block the heavy smell.

Without warning, she felt a piercing pain clutch onto her shoulders. Turning her head side to side, she could see claws digging into her flesh, the intense pressure from the talons breaking her skin. Her feet felt weightless as she was lifted off the ground. Struggling, she struck her knife wildly at the nearest exposed limb. Finally, she made contact. With a horrifying screech, the grip on her shoulders loosened and she fell heavily to the ground. Dropping hard upon an icy patch of snow, the saber jolted from her hand and the wind was knocked from her chest. She desperately inhaled the cold air as her lungs shook with force.

Horrified, her eyes focused in time to see the beast turn back angrily. She crawled quickly on her elbows toward the saber. As she desperately reached out for the weapon, it grabbed her ankle and tossed her into a tree, knocking the breath from her lungs again. Rolling onto her stomach, whimpering from the impact, she opened her eyes. The nasty, mangled form had touched down on the ground several footfalls away, reaching for its bow and retrieving an arrow from its quiver.

Twisting her face in disgust, she watched the disfigured arms closely. Bulging veins twined around its arms, protruding from the end like vines. Instead of a hand, the veins twisted into a wrist-like connection with three, grotesquely jointed appendages maneuvering its clutch on the bow. Long black claws jutted out of the tips.

It lifted the point toward her head as she pulled herself to a kneeling position on the ground in front of the tree. From the corner of her eye, she could see Bog's saber glistening in one of the last rays of sunshine.

*If I could just reach it before it releases the arrow…*

*Don't touch it,* a cruel voice hissed.

Apprehensively, Mora peered into the black orbed eyes. *Its mouth didn't move.*

*I will release the arrow into your fucking head if you dare. If it were not that He wants you alive, you would already be bleeding from each arrow I pierce into your flesh.*

It took a few steps closer until the arrow point was nearly touching her forehead. She could sense the tip of the arrow hovering above her flesh.

*Turn around, cunt.*

Gradually standing with her hands up, she turned around.

It grabbed her hands and tied them tightly together. *Back on your knees where you belong.*

She knelt down, chin upon her chest.

A wind started to beat down on her as she realized it was beginning to fly again. It clutched onto her shoulders with the painfully familiar, piercing grasp. She winced as she was lifted a second time into the air.

*Gods, help me.*

Bog watched Mora disappear through the bramble, the pain in his shoulder excruciating. The arrowhead was poisoned by Death and he could feel it burning through his veins. He needed to get help before it reached his heart. Pulling himself to a kneeling position, he reached around and plucked a white feather from his wing. With his shaking hands, he held the feather up to his mouth and blew slightly. The feather caught on fire and crackled to black dust in his palm.

He blinked. His eyes were becoming blurry as he fought against the poison.

All of a sudden, Mora screamed from outside.

Without hesitation, as if her voice ignited his senses, he closed one of his nostrils and hovered his nose near the palm of his hand. Taking a deep inhale, the charred feather disappeared. Lifting his chin, his violet eyes flared open with an iridescent glow.

## The Keeper

Mora barely opened her eyes as the Hawkend turned past a tree. Before she could take another breath, out of nowhere, something large knocked hard against them both. Falling to the ground once more, she scrambled around to see Bog on the opposite side of the ground. Both he and the Hawkend struggled to their feet. She could see his shoulder profusely bleeding through the makeshift bandage. However, it wasn't his shoulder that caught her attention as he peered in her direction.

*His eyes are bloody glowing!*

The Hawkend made a run for an off-centered Bog, knocking him off his feet. Violently, it started to thrash him in the face with its three, veined-fingered fists.

Still struggling against the loss of blood and the immense pain from his wound, Bog blocked the next hit and flung his body to the side, catching the Hawkend off guard. He could see Mora out of the corner of his eye.

"Run!" he barked without looking in her direction. Grabbing the scaly neck with one hand, he hammered his other fist against the disgustingly mangled face. Ferociously, it attempted to grab his wrist in retaliation, writhing vigorously from beneath his weight.

Startled into consciousness, Mora rose to her feet, hands still strapped behind her back. Rapidly taking notice of where she stood, she ran back behind the tree. Searching frantically, she finally saw Bog's saber, buried halfway in the dirt-colored snow where she had dropped it. Struggling, she sat down on the ground and pulled her bonded wrists below her backside and around her feet. Grasping the hilt of the saber, she secured it between her boots and rubbed the rope aggressively against the blade. After a moment, they snapped and she grabbed the hilt, scrambling back onto her feet.

Bog howled as the Hawkend slammed its sharp claws into his ribs. Barely letting go of its neck, the disfigured appendage shoved him onto the ground. He squinted down at his side. Blood was trickling slowly from three puncture marks. *Curse the gods!* Throwing his body against the force of the Hawkend's form, he managed to escape, roll, and stumble onto his feet.

Panting loudly, the Hawkend smirked. Letting out a low grumble, it said silently, *I can taste the poison from the arrow in your blood. Your feather dust won't save you. You won't last much longer, violet eyes.*

He wiped the sweat off of his upper lip, shaking his head. "Neither will you shithead," he growled. With a deep shout, he barreled toward the Hawkend and slammed his entire weight against it, pinning it to the tree behind. Forcefully, he beat the ugly face, a sudden surge of adrenaline willing him more strength.

The Hawkend laughed maniacally, blood trickling from its mouth.

Peering from behind the tree, Mora saw Bog holding the bloodied body against the trunk, flailing his fists angrily as black features floated onto the red and pink snow. However, she gasped when she saw his shoulder still freely bleeding and the new puncture marks in his side. He flinched every time its claws grazed his skin.

Running quickly along the inside of the small, encompassing trees, saber in hand, she decided to try and give Bog his weapon until she noticed the Hawkend's bow and quiver had fallen on the ground several paces away. *If there is one thing I can thank my mother for, it is how to defend myself with various weaponry.* She grinned. *And this was always my favorite.*

At full speed, she propelled herself toward the bow and quiver, scooped them up with one motion, and nocked the arrow. Holding it tightly, she aimed between Bog's shoulder blades and shrieked, "Move, Bog!"

Shocked, but obediently, he bent down, dropping his grip on the Hawkend as she released the arrow. He could feel the wind above his head vibrate as the arrow penetrated deep into the beast's chest.

It belched a horrifying squawk.

The arrow had impaled its body all the way through to the bark. It glared disturbingly at Mora. Blood dripped faster from its mouth. As it started to cackle, it began to pull its body further onto the shaft of the arrow. *You cunt. I should have killed you when I had the chance. Fuck His orders.*

Enraged, and heavily disgusted, she strung another arrow, releasing it at a closer distance.

It grunted. However, the arrow only deterred the Hawkend briefly before it continued advancing, the slick sound of organs and tearing flesh sliding over the shafts.

### The Keeper

She stepped closer and released another.

It gurgled more blood.

Finally, she came face to face with the malicious stare of black eyes, bow taut and arrow pointed straight at its forehead as it had done to her earlier. She grimaced and spat, "Your mistake."

He snickered, choked on blood, and whispered in her mind, *You are damned, cuthos.*

*As are you.* She released the arrow.

# The Dire Rescue

Bog stumbled to his feet behind Mora, barely able to focus on the mangled body of the Hawkend splayed against the tree trunk, arrows jutting out from its chest and head. Black blood oozed from its body, face, and mouth, sullying the icy floor beneath. He could feel the effects wearing off, the rush of energy leaving his body. *I bloody hate when it wears off.* Placing a palm against his forehead, he steadied himself against a large rock. *I've got to get the poison out before it takes over my heart.* Reaching around his shoulder, he untied the blood soaked cloth and tossed it on the ground.

Standing in front of the dead Hawkend, Mora turned around when she heard a faint thump on the ground. The raw, animalistic high she had merely experienced from the overwhelmingly strange headiness of killing something, had distracted her briefly from her surroundings. Noticing the blood soaked cloth on the ground, her head cleared and she rushed over to Bog. She tossed the quiver over her shoulder and knelt down in front of him, placing her hand on his neck. "Bog," she whispered, "look at me Bog." His pulse was alarmingly fast.

He removed his palm from his forehead, managing a grin. "Nice shot."

She could see an iridescent glow flickering in the violet rim. Worried, she pushed the hair away from his eyes and wiped her hands down his face. "We must take care of your wound immediately. It's bleeding profusely."

## The Keeper

He shook his head, trying to focus his eyes. "It's not the blood that's the problem, Mora. The arrows are poisoned. I've got to extract the poison."

She blinked back tears and coughed, "What? Poison? How?" Quickly, she tore another scrap from her cloak and wrapped it tightly around the wound. "You're immortal!" Reaching for his body, she braced herself under his armpit.

He was rapidly loosing blood. However, the thought of the one nearby being he knew could assist in saving his life was someone he never wanted to lay eyes on again. He groaned. His vision was becoming hazy and rimmed in black. Grimacing, he managed to sputter, "Guilderon... Death poison."

Nodding absently, worried on how she would locate the little elf after they ran away to distract the Hawkends, Mora surveyed the surrounding forest. "Aye, we must find Guilderon." Swallowing, she choked back more tears and whimpered, "He will know what to do."

As she supported his weight, they trudged back in the direction they had seen Guilderon run, calling out to him periodically. Every so often, her hand slipped around from the slickness covering his body, making the trek even slower.

"We mustn't be too loud," he struggled to say, "I guarantee there will be others to come." He flopped his chin against his chest, his mind becoming more clouded with every effort to walk erect.

They continued to bustle through the twisted trees of the Pale Forest, the trunks appearing even more skeletal as they progressed. Mora kept a sharp eye out for movement, dismissing the rapidly approaching dusk out of sheer determination. Struggling against the pressing weight of Bog's body as they traveled further, despite his deceiving lighter weight, she could sense his grip weakening. However, a mix of stubbornness and terror drove her further. *I can't let him die.* Stopping to adjust the position, she heard the faint sound of water trickling.

Whipping her head around, she whispered, "There is a stream nearby. Walk this way." She followed the sound of the running water until they came upon the tiny trickle of a stream, not completely frozen in the icy snow, but barely eroded into the ground. "Sit right here," she said as she bent over to help him lower next to a small tree trunk. "Gently," she added.

When he settled onto the ground, she hurriedly traipsed over to the water and scooped it into an empty flask that had been hanging on her belt. She brought the water back, held it to his lips, and let him attempt to drink. When it started running over the sides of his mouth, she ran back to the stream, refilled it, and dropped to her knees beside his slouching body once again. Placing a hand on his shoulder, she strained, "This may hurt a bit." She drizzled the frigidly cold water over the cloth wrapped shoulder.

Bog gasped and groaned, but he did not have the energy to move away.

"My apologies." She wiped the dried blood from around his skin until she could see the amount of scratches and puncture wounds he had accumulated from the Hawkend. "I'll be right back, Bog. I promise."

He nodded faintly.

She felt his exhaustion. Gathering her flask, she darted back through the trees. The ground crunched harsher beneath her feet from the ice and the temperature of the forest was dropping significantly. Pulling her hood around her face against the growing wind, she heard a whisper. Caught off guard, she glanced around cautiously. With nothing suspicious in sight, she continued to squint in the failing light for any sign of Guilderon.

Another whisper in the wind said wistfully, *Mora.* Then faded away.

Startled, she felt her heart beating faster. Shaking her head vigorously, she assured herself, *there is nothing.* Feeling hopeless, she hurriedly circled back around in the direction of where she left Bog.

The wind whispered again, *Mora.*

Tugging nervously on her braid, she briefly looked over her shoulder, tripped on a jutting root, and fell to the ground. In front of her face, small booted feet stood strong. Peering up with discretion, she saw the silhouette of Guilderon.

"Guilderon!" she huffed as she pulled herself to her feet and dusted off the ice shards.

A small smile left Guilderon's face as soon as it appeared. "I thought the Hawkend might have captured you." He looked around and said abruptly, "Where is the Borgorian?"

"He is injured. A Hawkend arrow struck him in the shoulder. I left him to rest by the stream as I searched for something to medicate his wound." She yelped desperately, "He said it's Death poison Guilderon!" Cocking her head to the side, she added, "Where are Milderon and Don?"

"Godsdamnit." He pulled on his beard. "Make haste! You must retrieve the Borgorian and follow me! They can hold their own!"

"Where can we go?" she asked desperately.

"You will know soon enough." He motioned for her to move. "Now! They will smell the blood and come back for him. He should have never been fucking left alone with a wound. The poison of the Hawkend arrow is from Death. It has probably already started to set in," he glanced nervously through the trees, "but it *cannot* be allowed to reach his heart."

*Nay!* Anxious, she sprinted through the trees, retracing her footsteps back to the small stream. Relief flooded her senses when she noticed Bog's large form still slumped over by the tree. Dropping to her knees in front of him, she shook him lightly. "Bog! Bog! I found Guilderon! We must be on our way."

*His breathing is too shallow.*

His head flopped back and forth as he fought to control his muscles. He moaned. Gasping through breaths and barely audible, he grumbled, "Horn."

She scrunched her nose. "I don't understand, but we must leave!" Once again, she struggled to help him to his feet, throwing his arm over her shoulder.

"Aye!" Guilderon appeared, his eyes lit with fear. "Quickly! I can sense the darkness calling for more."

Her stomach dropped. "Bog, you must move! I can't leave you!"

He attempted to take a step and stumbled over the stream, jerking Mora to the side. He mumbled something loosely.

"The loss of blood has made him weak and delirious!" she yelled toward Guilderon, who was already hastily walking away to survey the treetops. She helped Bog stand up straight. Placing her arm tightly around his waist, she grabbed a hold of his belt. Gripping strong, she screamed at Guilderon again, "Which way do we go?"

"North! Follow the stream!" he beckoned, pointing as he began to hurry back in the direction of Mora. An unusual presence made the hairs on his neck stand on end. A wisp of air blew and he glanced over his shoulder. A barely visible outline caught his attention, crouching in the trees at an unsafe distance. However, it made no sudden movement toward them. *It doesn't look like the silhouette of a Hawkend.* Suddenly, manifesting behind the form, was another silhouette. He gasped, because it was clearly the impression of a creatural being. Increasing his pace, he darted off down the path of the stream. For good measure, he peered once more over his shoulder. Both figure and creatural had disappeared.

By the time they had travelled a ways down stream, Mora was undeniably carrying Bog's full weight on her shoulder. Gasping for air against the cold restriction of the settling night, she panted, "Guilderon, I must stop for a moment."

He cautiously looked around the barely visible forest, the trees radiating an eerie glow. He gruffly replied, "A moment."

She gently helped Bog prop onto a small stone jutting from an outcrop bank nearby. Inspecting the wound, she noticed it was beginning to fester. Digging into the belt at her pouch, she wished they still had their satchels. Unfortunately, she couldn't remember when she lost hers because everything had happened so rapidly, it was becoming a blur in her mind. *Bloody Hawkends.* Relief warmed her skin as she pulled out some of the herbal concoction her mother had made before they left. She had placed a small amount in her pouch in case of emergency. *This is a gods forsaken emergency.*

"Do you have anything to sterilize the wound?" she asked Guilderon pitifully.

Rolling his eyes, he reluctantly dug around his belt pouch, popped the cork off of a small, leather flask, took a giant swig, and handed it to Mora. Wiping his bearded chin, he grunted, "Bloody bird-being owes me."

"I'm sure he'll be more inclined once he heals," she replied sardonically.

"Hurry. I have no time for female snark."

Rolling her eyes, she squeezed the blood-soaked material into the bitterly cold water of the stream and wiped the rest of the blood off of the wound before tossing it on the ground.

Bog groaned.

She grimaced. "You think that's bad? Prepare yourself."

# The Keeper

Slowly, she began pouring the contents of Guilderon's flask over the wound. It sizzled violently. Unprepared for the reaction, she covered her ears as he let out a horrifyingly loud yell. This was the first time she had seen the violet of his eyes since the beginning of the stream.

Wincing, she handed the flask back to Guilderon, who eyed the inside gloomily. "My apologies," she muttered insincerely. She stuffed a wad of herbs into the hole, careful not to touch the wound, and wrapped it tightly with another torn scrap of her frock. *I'm not going to have anymore scraps if we can't find help soon.*

Impatiently, Guilderon barked, "Are you finished?"

Bog grunted a word inaudibly.

"What?"

"H…or…n," he slurred.

She glanced nervously at Guilderon. "He said that earlier. What does he mean?" She thought she saw a mix of fear and frustration flash through Guilderon's eyes.

Hastily coming back to, he shook his head, "Nothing. Come."

She knelt down and helped Bog to his feet. Her shoulders were aching terribly. Supporting his waist, she struggled along the stream. Finally, she asked, "Where are we going?" as she adjusted his arm around her shoulder.

Nervously surveying the trees, Guilderon responded, "To the only safety in this gods forbidden forest."

She had noticed his growing discomfort of the Pale Forest as soon as they had started following the stream. Trying to listen for any familiar sounds of night, the faint trickle of water was the only noise she could hear. Nothing living could be heard beside the heavy breathing of Bog at her ear. His body was becoming extremely warm against her own and he was dragging his feet, creating a tugging sensation every time she tried to walk forward.

*The fever has set in.*

Panic rose in her chest. "Guilderon! A fever!" Fear resonated through her voice, "He's going to die!" All of a sudden, she heard a distant scream reverberate through the trees.

Guilderon whipped his head around and barked, "We're all going to die if you don't let me think!" Anxiously, he took a deep breath before retrieving a small horn from his belt.

Her eyes widened with anger and she spat, "Is that the fucking horn Bog's been muttering about?"

"You better plead to the spirits they deem this a godsdamn emergency by *their* standards!" he furiously retaliated.

Placing the white, curved, bone horn to his lips, he blew hard. The instrument created a surprisingly monstrous noise. He paused and listened. The forest was quiet. Setting the horn against his lips again, he blew harder. This time, the note was a smoother, baritone sound. He waited.

From beyond the furthest sight of trees, came a faint echo, followed by a cry. This was not the same sound that reverberated only moments before Guilderon blew the horn, but a throaty, morose noise. Mora could feel a vibration under her feet, followed by a circling movement through the tops of the trees. Without warning, a great wind whipped through her hair. If it was not for Bog's extra weight against her side, it would have knocked her down. Shielding her eyes, she saw a gigantic winged creature. It possessed the body of a stag, with its mighty wings stretching double the length of its body, tip to tip. Trailing behind, it rustled a plumage of brilliant greens, blues, and violets, mirroring the sheen of the wings. A majestic pair of white antlers stood tall above its head. On its back sat an elf resembling Guilderon, except his eyes were more gold than green, and his beard was neatly cut flush against his chin, not scraggly. Large, brass pieces of metal protruded from both of his earlobes.

"The Horn of the Bark is not meant to be used foolishly, you belligerent ass!" the elf spoke harshly, a heat lighting up the gold sections of his eyes. "Why do you summon the Xyrons?"

Guilderon lifted his chin defiantly. "I do not misuse the privileges I have been bestowed, but we seek your immediate aid in a matter of life and death." He gestured to Mora and Bog with a slight of his head. "This Borgorian traveler is dying, and you know *she* will be angry if he does."

Mora heard the emphasis again. *I wonder who* she *is*.

Guilderon lowered his voice and added, "*They* are here. I saw it with me own eyes."

The elf suddenly glanced up to examine the trees behind Mora, Bog, and Guilderon. The winged stag began to step restlessly.

"Very well," a sense of urgency resonated in the elf's voice. *"Hythola!"* At the command, the winged stag knelt down on its front legs. "Bring him quickly."

Mora, surprised by the change of events, staggered over to the side of the creature and helped position Bog's body over the midsection of the unusually large saddle in front of the elf. With precision and haste, he tied a leather rope around Bog, holding his wings down.

*"Dundi fra!"* he commanded as the winged stag stood up, reared on its haunches, and took off at great speed through the trees.

She was fascinated by its agility. However, a sudden crack behind her startled her from her gaze. A brilliant burst of flames exploded through a tree footfalls away, knocking both her and Guilderon to the ground. Scrambling to their feet, Guilderon grabbed one of the lit branches while he barked at her to run. A huge rumble of thunder drowned out his voice. Without glancing back, she darted after the elf, surprisingly quick, over roots and rocks. The Pale Forest commenced to tremble under her feet, shaking the trees...*alive?* Branches violently reached for her cloak and frock as she dodged each advance. A sharp point of a branch cut into her cheek. Wiping away the warm blood, a root almost knocked her to knees. Stumbling, barely able to see the lashing trees further than the extent of Guilderon's torch, she felt like her feet were on fire.

"How much further?" she screamed.

Without turning his head, he yelled back, "Close!"

A root reached out to catch her ankle. As she jumped over the root, a razor sharp pain sliced against her calf, right above her boot. Falling to her knees, she rolled across the quaking, forest floor. Roots began wrapping around her wrists as she thrashed.

"Guilderon!" Mora cried as loud as she could muster, her eyes wide as she spied a branch leaning toward her face.

An eruption of flames ignited the branch. She shielded her eyes. A terrible screeching sound burst from the forest. Another flame caught her attention as she felt the tension on her wrists loosen. She rolled to the side as the roots cracked like whips on fire. Struggling to her feet, despite the searing pain in her leg, she saw Guilderon setting fire to the surrounding trees. Running once again, she briefly glanced over her shoulder. To her astonishment, the Pale Forest was rapidly disappearing, falling into a black abyss. Fighting for breath, she could sense a strong force attempting to grab her maliciously and pull her into the darkness. The feeling was strong, but her will to survive was stronger. She needed to resist, to run faster, to fight harder.

All of a sudden, Guilderon caught her hand, jerking her in another direction. They leapt over a small stream. From the corner of her eye, she saw him throw the torch over his head, hold up his arm, and place his palm flat against the air in front of his slight form.

His voice boomed, *"Linthel ro, cartileron, fraethlin!"*

Suddenly, she felt a change in the air.

Guilderon let go of her hand and wrestled to a complete stop, barreling over to catch his breath. "Bloody curse of the gods." He fished another small flask out of his pouch, popped the cork off the top, and chugged the liquid inside, taking huge gulps. His face scrunched and he coughed.

Gawking, heavily panting, and struggling to coax the words from her throat, she managed to mutter, "You had *more* the entire time?"

"Never leave without a backup, lass." He tauntingly offered the flask to Mora.

Obviously not thinking she would acquiesce, she snatched the flask from him and took a big swig. The liquid hit her throat like a wave of fire, shocking her senses clear. Shaking her head, she tossed it back.

He snarled and finished off the flask.

She started to make a snide retort before a firefly zipped in front of view causing her to whip her head to the side. Her face illuminated in the glowing light of a magnificently grandiose tree surrounded by luminescent toadstools and fireflies.

"Oh, my bloody gods," she murmured, gawking awestruck at the sight in front of her eyes.

# Lychinus

Mora gasped as a tiny, delicate wisp floated in front of her face, transitioning through various hues. Another colorful wisp floated freely passed it. Little elves were running around a wide open space, trying to catch the wisps, giggling every time one slipped from their fingertips. A multitude of swirling pathways of illuminated stones were lit around the mountainous tree. Large fungi provided steps, accentuating the sections of bark as both breathtakingly intricate decorations and woven accessibility to the intertwining branches.

Entranced, she stood to her feet and made a full turn to take in its beauty, briefly looking behind from whence they came. She held out her hand, palm exposed, and pressed against the space at eye level. Her fingers brushed a thick sheet of air. A cobweb of milky strands tussled around her hand. Beyond the veil, she could see the Pale Forest standing once again, no longer falling into the black abyss. *Strange. Is it all an illusion?* Squinting, her stomach flipped when she saw a dark, tall shadow lurk passed a moonlit area of the forest floor. She knew instantly why Guilderon had severely quickened the pace. However, it was not Ekklips' eminent threat disturbing the forest at this moment, it was another foreboding, elusive element.

Vaguely hearing the droll chanting, she mouthed, *Skulkins.* She remembered how Bog had knocked her out from the invisible beings because they sensed her opening her mind.

*Bog.*

Placing her hand to her chest, Mora sighed and turned to Guilderon. "Where have they taken Bog? And what was the creature that transported him?"

"The Xyrons are the warriors of Lychinus, the elvish tree of light." He motioned toward the massive trunk. "The winged stags are called Peryians. The horn summons the protectors in times of grave danger. They secure the power of the elves given by the elders. They will not take kindly to the circumstances tonight." He turned and grumbled, "I could have made it with him."

She scoffed and ignored the last idiotic comment. "The circumstances were grave." She continued to survey Lychinus. "Am I in the Realm of Immortals? Loralei said there were nine Faery Trees that connected both worlds."

Guilderon guffawed, "Faeries are always trying to command ultimate superiority in connecting both worlds." His lip upturned on the side. "There are other ways to access the Realm of Immortals, much to the fae's chagrin."

Clearing his throat, he continued, "However, nay, you are not in the Realm of Immortals. You still stand in the same forest as you see when you look over your shoulder. Lychinus parallels the Mortal Realm, you just need to know how to command the curtain. It is the heart of all the elvish lands in the west, nestled in the country the mortals refer to as Extrolia. All come far and wide to speak with the *Disio*, elvish for authority. She is the eye of the land, a prophetess of the elements."

"The elements?" she replied with a curious inflection.

"Aye, the naturalizing of the physical body within space and time. She reads your essence in relationship to your surroundings. How do the plants react to your presence? How does the rain run off your skin? How deep does the grass succumb to the weight of your body? And so on. Glimpses of foresight will emerge and your soul will become intertwined with what purpose you serve in accordance to the elements." He commenced to walk toward the massive tree. "She isn't a seer, but an elemental reader."

She was still unsure what Guilderon meant by the *elements,* but she followed. Then, the question emerged again. This time, she spoke it aloud, "Who is *she*?"

# The Keeper

"Our Queen. Be respectful."

He didn't glance back toward Mora, he had no interest in answering any more questions. He had completed his task of bringing her to Lychinus. *I need a damn drink.* He had to deliver her first to the Queen before he could be released from his duties. *Hopefully, with no more questions.*

Not satisfied by his response, Mora huffed annoyingly, but followed him along the gorgeous, swirling pathway, despite her frustration. As they progressed, she observed his small figure stepping heavily through the grass. Interestingly, every time his foot stepped, a hint of green light would appear and then dissipate. Curious, she watched as other elves walked along the ground, each had a color: green, purple, blue, orange, but there appeared no particular pattern. Peering down at her own footsteps, patches of sparkling gold appeared and disappeared as she stepped lightly. *I wonder what each color represents?*

Unable to comprehend the gigantic size of the tree, she watched it grow more incomprehensibly massive with each step closer. *The entire world is breathtaking.* When she saw Guilderon start to ascend the large mushroom steps, the green light no longer appeared at every footfall. However, the mushrooms gave off their own faint, mesmerizing glow. To keep from falling off the edge, the mushroom rim angled gracefully, creating half a bowl shape. The height of the steps were easily ascendable, but she noticed the slight jump Guilderon had to take as he approached each angle.

She smiled. The tree had a calming effect on her mind. Studying the bark as she stepped, she noticed it shooting tiny, faint, pulsating streaks of light into the mushrooms where they were connected. Guilderon placed a hand on the trunk to steady himself, and the same green light that appeared on the grass melted into the surface. It dissipated slowly downward and joined the rest of the pulsating streaks. Pausing, she placed her hand against the soft, patchy wood. She watched as the twinkling, gold light sparked and illuminated into the tree. Excited, she placed her other hand against the bark. The gold light grew significantly, sending a multitude of wispy streaks downward and into the mushroom, creating a strikingly luminous step. She lifted her hands off the tree. However, the gold, sparkling light did not disappear. Instead, all the other faint light from the bark began to crackle like little lightning bolts and attach themselves to her palms. Each one mingled with the gold light around her fingers and she could feel a tingling sensation as the lights soaked into her skin. *It doesn't hurt.*

Suddenly, Guilderon pushed a hand against her arm and stared annoyingly at her, mumbling sternly, "Don't touch the tree." Turning on his heel, he began high-stepping once again up the mushrooms.

Confused, and slightly disappointed, Mora climbed higher and higher around the massive trunk. Peering nervously over the edge of a mushroom, her stomach flipped when she noticed how far they had climbed around the tree. The light of the mushroom steps radiated so bright from above, there appeared to be no ground. This made her head swim. Then, glancing up, branches started to veer off in different directions, intertwining elaborately. Each branch accommodated a variety of rounded, one-room huts, lit sporadically like twinkling stars. Squinting at the closest branch, she noticed a multitude of movement. Bustling along each branch like ants, were what appeared to be small-bodied elves, carrying lanterns of flickering fireflies. *I wonder if they are all Piquonese Elves like Guilderon?* She suddenly felt very tiny in relation to this world of floating light.

Finally, they came upon a balcony. A hollowed doorway was carved through the thick trunk covered by dainty, flowering vines. Mora followed Guilderon through the doorway, lifting the vines gently, feeling the fragility beneath her fingertips. Stepping inside a room within the trunk, a warm glow greeted her presence. Luminous mushrooms grew out of the wooden walls in the shape of lanterned sconces, while slender windows of delicate, colored glass and meticulously intricate designs were placed intermittently between each mushroom light. While no two were identical, every design was abstractly carved behind the glass from the trunk into distorted swirls and star shapes; each possessing an ethereal movement when light kissed the panes. The floor donned the ancient circles of the mountainous tree. However, an elaborately delicate tree inlaid with gold and labyrinthine branches was painted over the circles. Little stones of diamond and sapphire were embedded in the floor, sparkling like stars.

She inhaled. *It's even more breathtaking than the outside of the tree.* Gazing around the room, the air emitted an exquisite essence.

Guilderon walked to the middle of the chamber and knelt down on one knee. He placed his palms onto the gold bark of the painted tree and the green light rippled through the tree circles. He stood up and waited.

From the far side of the room, a curtain of white lilies hung sensually to the floor. A hand emerged on the right side of the curtain and the flowers were pushed back to reveal a young female. Her shoulder length hair was raven black and her eyes were as gold as the morning sun. Gracefully laced through her hair was a ring of gold with fine, sparkling strands glistening in the subtle scone light. Tucked behind her ears were two strands of braided hair which hung gently to her hips, swaying as she stepped. Her ears were softly pointed and her smile was kind. Diaphanously draped over her curved body was a burgundy, silk dress, cinched just below her breasts with an intricately woven, gold belt. Her arms were exposed by finger-length holes cut into the tight sleeves. Each hole was connected by gold rings, the last of which graced her middle fingers. Voluptuous wings rustled on her back. They were not the pure white of Bog's own glorious appendages, but a mixture of mild browns and grays. She was half a head taller than Mora.

With an air of authority, she walked over to Guilderon, gracefully kneeled down, took him by the hands, and bowed her head. He did the same.

*A harmonious gesture*, Mora thought.

Rising delicately, the female looked at Mora.

Gesturing politely, she proceeded over to where the graceful being and Guilderon stood. Offering her hand, she took Mora's own in her grasp and placed her other hand on top.

"*Athon' mi*," she spoke sweetly, "Welcome. We have been expecting you. Lorelei said you were young."

Stunned, Mora replied, "I am five and twenty." Peering around the room, she enthusiastically inquired, "Lorelei? Is she here?"

With subtle amusement, she replied, "Not at the present. I am Katheryn."

*Oh my, she is magnificent.* Mora felt very plain in Katheryn's presence. Anxiously, she asked, "Where is Bog?" A subtle, unpleasant flicker of disappointment flashed and she saw Katheryn's eyes twinge.

Recovering quickly, Katheryn smiled and replied, "Your friend will be fine. He is resting. His wound would have been fatal, if it had not been for your determination." She gestured to the curtain. "Would you care to join me in the garden chamber?"

Guilderon took his leave, stepping quite hastily out of sight.

Feeling uneasy, Mora slightly nodded her head and followed Katheryn to the flower curtain. As she pulled the flowers apart gently, she stepped onto a large, open platform with vine railings. Night blooming flowers she had never seen before radiantly sprouted amidst the dark green leaves. Like the previous room, but smaller, luminescent mushroom sconces lined the perimeter of the platform. Looking up, there was no ceiling. It was open to the brilliantly twinkling lights moving amongst the massive tangle of branches.

*Do I hear rain?* She surveyed the platform.

The trickling sound of water echoed from a three-tiered fountain in the middle of the platform. It appeared the entire fountain was carved from a brilliantly deep shade of jade. On the bottom tier, there was a wondrously carved statue of three, little, whimsical Piquonese Elves, each one sitting atop the shoulders of the previous. Upon their faces were smiles spread ear to ear. The top elf held a large basin of water, tipped a little to one side to allow a steady dribble onto the outstretched palms of the other two.

The slightly elevated, middle tier feeding water into the bottom, contained another statue. The simplicity was divine. It was a meticulously carved female, her flowing tunic draped, frozen in time, over her sensual form. Her feet were bare and her hair flowed gracefully down to her buttocks in curled locks. Intertwined with the undulating texture upon her head was a crown of flowers, similar to the night blooming foliage on the vine railing. Grand wings protruded from her back and the expression on her face was pure elation. She cupped her hands in front to allow the water to run off her stone fingers.

On the highest tier of the fountain, there was a tree. The tree reached high, the branches outstretching over all three tiers. The magnificent tree mirrored the image of the gold tree painted on the floor of the previous chamber. The twinkling lights from the live branches beyond the fountain reminded her of the embedded stars. Water droplets dripped from the jade stone leaves as though it were raining on the other statues. In its entirety, the piece of art left her speechless.

Katheryn traipsed to a simple, wrought iron chair on the left side of the platform near the railing. It was oddly plain compared to the grandeur of the fountain.

She gestured to Mora and said sweetly, "Please, take a seat on the edge of the fountain. I think you will find it most surprisingly comfortable."

Although the uneasiness was still persistently tugging in the depths of her mind, she replied, "Thank you."

"Tell me, Mora," Katheryn spoke softly, "why do you feel you have been brought here to Lychinus?"

Slightly taken aback, Mora cautiously replied, "I'm not entirely certain." She shifted uncomfortably. "However, I do seek answers about my relationship to this world, both in the Mortal and Immortal Realms. So much has happened since I left home that has baffled me to the point of near madness."

"Aye." Katheryn waved her hand.

Mora whipped her head around. Uncertain how long there had been another body in the room, she saw a small, female elf standing in the back of the platform. She immediately, but gracefully, brought a pure crystal tray over to Katheryn. Picking up a crystal glass decanter filled with crimson liquid, the elf poured it carefully into two, crystal chalices. Bowing to Katheryn as she held the tray steady, Katheryn picked up a chalice. Then, the elf proceeded to do the same for Mora. Mora thanked her with a nod of her head. Pressing her lips gently against the cool rim, she could smell the subtle aroma of sinful fruit and sweet wood. When she sipped the crimson liquid, her insides began humming a haunting, bittersweet melody. Notes of cherry and blackberry thrummed against her taste buds. She took another large, more satisfying sip, letting the liquid dance upon her tongue before swallowing.

All the while, Katheryn had proceeded to talk, "'Tis a question in all cognitive recognition of one's inferiority to control the ordinance of life. This sobriety is hardly justified through bouts of over-confidence, but rather small acts of faith the journey is only but a stepping stone to a more satisfying acceptance. Treading upon the stones will allow you to find the answers you seek while gathering the necessary tools for revelation. Your purpose can only be uncovered by a realization of your true, spiritual self, reaching a higher cognitive level than your physical body. Some may call this religion, some call it spirituality, and some will never reach out past their physical bodies, but whatever you want to refer to it as, there are comprehensive nuances in every level of thinking. Each grows deeper in every natural fiber you possess. You, my dear, possess a strong, spiritual nuance. Stronger than myself. My sight cannot tell me what will happen within your future, but I know what has happened in your past."

With that, Mora perked up, intently focused on Katheryn's eyes. "My past?" She stared blankly. "What do you mean, *my past*? I have memories already of my past." She narrowed her gaze and asked skeptically, "What would you be able to tell me that I do not already know?"

Katheryn smiled. "You know what you have experienced at the time, you know not what details lie within your experiences that have shaped who you are in the present." She held up her hands. "Place your palms against mine, I will allow you to see."

Mora sipped her drink once more before she set it down on the fountain's edge. Leaning closer to Katheryn's chair, she lifted her hands with hesitation and placed them against Katheryn's unnaturally smooth, pale skin. As their palms touched, she felt a pull behind her naval and her mind went tumbling through a vortex of swirling color. Before she felt too nauseous, she landed in a patch of grass. In front of her stood an achingly nostalgic sight, the three roomed shelter that kept her safe and warm for five and twenty years. *Home.* It looked as painfully beautiful as she remembered in the brilliant sunlight. She restrained a welling tear blurring her vision and swallowed the lump in her throat.

Suddenly, her heart leapt at the sound of her mother's voice.

"Mora!" Meridan cried. "Mora! Come here my firefly!"

Mora placed a hand on her mouth as she started to run up the walkway.

"Mora! Where are you?" her mother's voice echoed again.

Mora burst through the front door in time to see her mother walk steadily into what was once her bedroom. A memory manifested from deep within her mind. *Under the bed.* At the same moment she moved through the doorway, she saw a little head pop out from beneath the frame.

"Here I am Mummy!"

She cried as she watched her younger self giggle wildly.

Meridan crouched down by the bedside, a slight grin flashing briefly. "Come out firefly. You must start on your reading." Her mother stood up and dusted off her hands.

The little body slithered from under the bed and stood next to her mother. "Mummy, I don't want to read right now. It always makes you sad when I read."

She watched a sudden sadness fill her Meridan's eyes as she whispered, "You must *i'mun luex*. It is your duty."

As her mother spoke, the childling skipped across the room and sat in the small, rocking chair she had built for her on her third name day. Meridan pulled a familiar, square, leather bound, dark blue book from a dusty shelf and place it in the little Mora's lap.

"Read and do not get up until I give you permission."

Kicking her legs up and down, little Mora bit her lip until her mother was out of sight, then opened the book and began to read, "In the beginning, All was created. Life…"

Mora quietly walked into the room her mother occupied and knelt down beside the shadow, the well known scent of sage filling her nostrils. Tears started watering in her mother's eyes, spilling over as she blinked. Ritualistically, she watched Meridan pull up her sleeves and pick up a small, sharp knife off of the table. Panicked, she attempted to remove the knife from Meridan's hand, but as she reached closer to the blade, her hand hit a barrier of air. She could not move any further toward her mother, no matter how hard she pushed. Helpless, she realized she had never seen her mother's arms. They had always been covered by the sleeves of her linens, even when she worked in the garden. To her horror, abreast the flesh, were distorted scars, both raised and sunken. Symbols, sigils, and words covered every piece of flesh. Fixated, she watched as her mother placed the blade tip to her skin and commenced to cut into an already mangled area. Tears ran down her cheeks and fell onto the barrier, sizzling when they hit. She could vividly remember the stifled sobs of her mother from the other room where she innocently sat, reading in the rocking chair.

The squeaky voice lowered and staggered, listening to what was emerging from the next room. "Mummy, you are crying again."

Mora saw her mother perk her head toward the room, wiping away the tears from her cheeks. "Keep reading love, all is well. They are not sorrowful tears."

The little voice paused and then proceeded to read again, "Then Dark..."

Meridan began to whittle once more. Mora scooted closer, attempting to read what she was writing: *misericorthiav.* She mouthed, *mercy.*

"Aye, but what is it the little one reads?" a voice suddenly appeared behind her shoulder.

She jerked her head to see Katheryn calmly standing behind her, her hands interlaced in front. As tears ran down her cheek, she peered back at her mother, listening to the drops of blood hit the floor. Standing next to Meridan, she turned to walk slowly to the room, in which, as a wee one, she had spent many long lengths of time reading the same book. She could recite every last word:

*...And then the stars called out, to whom do we serve? For we are infinite to the naked eye, our vastness is beyond the count of the furthest corner of All, and will not bow to the coveting hand of darkness attempting to diminish each pinpoint of light beneath its merciless grip. Nay. We do not radiate under the jowls of emptiness. Our power to live and die, only to be born again, lies within the unseen force fueling our very core and churning the ability to resonate an energy so spectacular, the darkness itself shivers in awe of our grandeur. It is only when we focus our energy inward, becoming inflated with our brilliances, do we implode from the capacity of our own foolish deeds and allure as much commodity into our path of destruction. This, in turn, forces our demise into the darkness, leaving an emptiness and ultimately seducing all within its path into the void. We provide balance. We are the stars. We serve Light...*

## The Keeper

Mora wanted to listen no more. "I don't want to be here anymore. Let me out," she pleaded desperately to Katheryn.

The pain of her mother's tears and her own small voice, oblivious to the actions of her mother, tore at her heart, leaving her broken. She had the feeling the pieces may never make a whole again. She peered down at her own forearms and examined the light tan hue of her flesh. She was the physical match to her mother, only younger and not as tall. However, the closer she examined, she realized the birthmark she had had all her life, was beginning to darken. It was a thumbprint size discoloration located on the bottom inside of her wrist in the shape of a crescent moon. She studied it harder.

Then, moving closer to her mother, the arm bloodied from the tortuous carving knife, she examined Meridan's wrist. In the same area of her own birthmark, underneath the streaks of blood, she saw a shape. Although the shape was not a birthmark but a raised scar, it had a distinguishable characteristic which separated it from the other hideous scars on her flesh. She glanced from her birthmark, to her mother's scar, and back again. Curious, she leaned closer to the scar and noticed it was the same crescent moon shape.

Stunned, she immediately glanced toward the direction of Katheryn before falling back onto the hard, stone floor in horror at seeing a looming, cloaked figure standing in her place. She gasped.

"Salve, Mora."

# Desperation

 *Agonizing. Blistering. Desperate.* Savage emotions ran from his head to his toes. Opening his eyes a little each moment, Bog attempted to take in his surroundings.

*Where am I?*

He was lying on a bed of grass, covered with sage. Blinking roughly, he focused on his translucent confinement. Lifting his body onto his elbows, he saw a bubble of glass surrounding the grassy area in which he lay. Intricately etched tree roots twisted in decoration around the glass. The tree roots were thin and sparkled of silver in the moonlight. The sound of trickling water echoed in his ears while the sweet smell of patchouli and orange filled his nostrils. Still weary, he shook his head. A twinge of recognition filled his body. Sitting up stiffly, he grabbed his head from the explosive dizziness. Pain also seared through his shoulder. He glanced down to see white, willow leaves hugging his flesh.

Suddenly, realization punched deep in his core. *Shit!* Cursing wildly, he tore himself from the grass bed, the willow leaves dropping to the ground, and frantically searched for a door.

He could feel the anxiety setting fire to his skin and sear throughout his whole body. He began to pound the glass dome hard. This captured the attention of a tiny, alarmed elf. He hit the glass harder. A shocked expression was clear upon the elf's face as he quickly ran from the room.

"Stop! Come back! Let me out!" Bog yelled through the glass. He hit the surface harder with more consistency. Using his good shoulder, he reared back and rammed the glass multiple times in the same spot. Finally hearing the structure start to give way, he took one, long step back and flung his entire body through the encasement. Glass shattered to the floor.

Taking a brief moment to survey his location in Lychinus, he realized he must have been in the infirmary, but did not know exactly where it was in relationship to *her* quarters. Grabbing the nearest lantern, he sprinted wildly down the narrow pathway made of soft, flat mushroom caps to another branch. Frantically searching side to side for another way to the trunk of the mountainous tree, he stumbled along a path made of fungi stepping stones. Each mushroom glowed a brilliant silver as he ran. Leaping without hesitation on to a lift made of thin vines, he began pulling rapidly on the adjacent vine. Elevating higher into the branches, he spied a less congested pathway leading toward the trunk. Wobbling under his weight, the lift tilted to the side as he reached the branch. Steadying the swaying vines, he leapt out of the lift onto a short, mushroom platform. Hastily, he adjusted his footing and jumped the rest of the way onto the sturdy branch.

Breathing heavily, he continued sprinting across the bridge. Many startled Piquonese Elves cursed and made rude gestures after his advance. He didn't have time to apologize to all of them, but he tried to excuse himself as often as he could. As he approached an intersection of busy branches, two elves halting his progression.

"Pardon me," he said abruptly, but politely. He could see the trunk was very close.

"No one may enter the tree of the Queen without prior permission," one of the elves proceeded lightly.

Panting, he replied frantically, "I am in desperate need to see the *Queen.*"

The elder elf squinted and held his lantern up to Bog's form. The light started from his waist, which was barely eye-level to the elf, and proceeded upward until the light reached his face. The elder elf's eyes widened and he jumped back, startled. "The bloody bird being has awoken!"

The younger elf took a step back, but kept a keen eye on Bog. "Bird being? He looks like no bloody *bird* to me."

The elder elf huffed at the younger and walloped him upside the head with his hand. "Don't you see, you imbecile? He has those huge bloody wings that glisten in the moonlight. Obviously, he is part bird."

The younger elf rubbed his head sourly and mumbled, "He just looks like a damn creatural male to me," he studied Bog up and down, "and a bloody big one at that!" He paused and thought a moment. "However, the wings kind of make him look a bit ridiculous. And I seen more hair on my mum than he has on his whole body!"

In his frustration, Bog aggressively grabbed each elf by the front of the tunic, in spite of the burning in his shoulder, and held them at eye-level. "I beseech you again," he spoke through gritted teeth, "I am searching for company with the *Queen*. Who, if you haven't noticed with your imbecilic skills of observation, has *wings*!"

Shivering, the elves retracted as he placed them back on their feet. In a desperate hurry, the elves immediately ran down the pathway. He could hear the elder say, "To the Dark One's prick with your mum's hair!"

He sighed, rotated his bothersome shoulder, and glanced around. The pathway continued to ascend in front of him to the trunk, but he didn't know how far up the Queen's meeting room was in relation to the top of the tree. Shrugging, he gathered up his strength once again and darted up the pathway.

Periodically glancing over his shoulder for any unwelcome company, a darkness crept along the path around his steps. He could smell a foul stench permeate his nostrils. He wiped the sweat from his brow. *Curse of the gods, something isn't right.*

Finally, he reached the top of the pathway. Panting with sheer exhaustion, he studied the mushroom steps, balconies, and branches emerging from the pulsating trunk. He leapt across to a neighboring branch and pulled himself up, scrunching his face in agony. A light caught his eyes at the same time he recognized the faint sound of rain echoing through the night. *I know that sound.* Wildly searching for the three-tiered fountain, trying to sift through the multitude of fireflies amongst the branches, he saw the point of lights he'd been hoping. The surrounding mushrooms of the platform were flickering madly in a circular fashion, distinguishing them from the surrounding fireflies. *Why are they flashing?* Squinting, he could barely make out the image of two females, one with grayish brown wings and the other with long, dark auburn, braided hair. Black smoke was whirling around their forms violently.

*Mora. She can't.*

He became overwhelmed with desperation. Taking a step toward the ledge, he calculated his options. Out of sheer hysteria, coupled with the blasted pain of his shoulder, he backed up on the pathway and seized a running leap off the ledge.

Tears streamed from his eyes as the night air stung, forcing him to close them periodically. When he opened them again, he saw the absence of a reachable ledge. Painfully, he forced his wings to extend. The bloody wound opened again. He yelped in affliction as his wings caught the air and abruptly jerked him upward for a brief moment. The moment was just enough to give him the ability to harshly grasp onto the protruding ledge of a wooden balcony. He gripped tightly to the beams of wood, but they began to crack and give underneath the weight of his body. *I'm no fucking Piquonese Elf.* He cringed and pulled harder, attempting to anchor himself on a protruding mushroom closer to the trunk of the tree. The beam under his right hand gave way and fell below his feet, crashing against the branches beneath him and into the darkness below. Dangling helplessly by one hand, he could feel the wound on his left shoulder tearing further across his flesh.

Grimacing and grunting, he inhaled and grasped onto the next beam with his free hand. A cracking sound filled the air. He maneuvered his hands around, closer to the trunk of the tree. Swinging a leg up, he braced one foot on a mushroom and another against the trunk. Another crack. Without hesitation, he heaved his upper body up the vine railing of the balcony, pushing hard with his feet until he was straddled from the mushroom to the edge of the balcony. Finally, he climbed quickly over the railing, dodging the hole made by the missing wood beams. A fleeting thought that *someone should fix that soon* deterred him for only a moment. Immediately turning around, he ran as fast as he could the rest of the way to the platform. *I hope I'm not too late.* He could feel the fresh blood from his newly open wound trickling down his chest, mixing with the distressing stench of sweat. *Godsdamn Hawkend.*

### The Keeper

The hooded figure stood still as Mora cautiously lowered her arms and rose to her feet.

*Have I been deceived?* She looked curiously at the hooded figure's silhouette. She did not feel fearful it was Ekklips. *It cannot be Him, for He doesn't hide His desires.*

She tilted her head to the side and walked nervously toward the figure. It did not recoil at her advance. A familiar scent of lavender and honey, the sweet aroma her mother placed in her hair, warmed her nostrils. She inhaled deeply. It coaxed her closer. Cautiously, she stepped, sweat menacingly running down the back of her neck. In the darkness of the corner, with a face concealed by a hood, the figure loomed motionlessly. Finally, only a couple footfalls away in front, cloaked arms lifted gracefully, pulling back the thick material of the hood.

Startled, she lunged backward at the sight of her own face. Everything was familiar, the lightly tanned skin and the dark, auburn hair falling over her shoulders in a braid as random, loose curls feathered beyond the patterned knots, as well as the stoic expression of sadness she was feeling for her young self and her mother. Everything was mirrored, except the eyes. The figure's eyes were the same piercing gold as Katheryn, not her own forest green. Standing eye to eye, she saw her reflection clearly.

*This is not the first encounter I've had with my own reflection.* She thought back to the experience with Ekklips in Nephani's illusion. *But that felt like a memory.*

"What do you want of me?" she broke the silence with the simplest of questions flooding her head.

The figure stared contemplatively in her eyes, a radiant gold hungrily pulsating. "I want what everyone else wants...to know who you *are*." She reached up nonchalantly to touch a loose hair falling in front of Mora's shoulder. "I stand in almost perfect form of yourself and I can normally sense the essence of a soul by this point. However, you are rejecting my presence, you are rejecting the connection." Katheryn blinked her eyes, smiling sardonically. Tilting her head, she persisted, "Why are you resisting my presence, Mora?"

Mora thought she could see a spark of rage fighting against the fires within Katheryn's mind. "I am merely Mora, daughter of Meridan."

## The Keeper

Averting her eyes, she whispered, "I am nothing more."

Suddenly, she felt a hand grab her chin and pull it forward. "Who are you!" Katheryn raised her voice harshly, a merciless tenacity seething in her tone.

Mora shrank in horror; though, not because of Katheryn's presence. Without warning, a shadowy figure rose unnoticed from behind her reflection. It towered above her manipulating disguise and raised its arms. She faltered back, feeling helpless.

A sudden wind whipped around Katheryn as she screamed maniacally, "I command you, Mora, daughter of Meridan, tell me what you are! You are not of this world. Inform me, *deceiver*, of your knowledge outside of this realm! Your forces are violently rejecting me!"

Shielding her face from desperation, she cried, "I am Mora! Daughter of Meridan! Leave me be!"

Katheryn wailed and lunged toward Mora, her face cracking into a multitude of broken shards of light.

Terrified, Mora watched the long, shadowy arms emerge from the stoned wall. Screaming against the overwhelming screech of Katheryn in her ears, she knew not what to think. The horror of another unforeseen being was beating her senses like a violent sea, thrashing around her body, and torrentially bruising her internally. Squinting her eyes, she noticed the whirling, black vortex encompassing their bodies. The shadowy figure behind Katheryn was still advancing out of the wall. In a moment, it outstretched its arms and wrapped a golden vine around her neck like a noose.

Katheryn gasped, eyes wide open. Panicked, she grasped firmly onto the vine around her neck and struggled to pull it from her skin. "Help," she choked, knowing her effort would be hopeless.

Bog knew Katheryn. He had known of her intentions. He had to release Mora from her grasp. His chest, shoulder, and feet burned fiercely, but he ran faster.

## The Keeper

Reaching the interior meeting room, he could vaguely see the two females at the opposite end through the hanging vines and whirling, black smoke. A jolt of anger ripped through his core. He saw Mora on her knees, eyes glazed over with hands over her ears, cowering in the presence of Katheryn. Katheryn hovered above the floor, her hair whipping wildly around her face, her eyes a molten glow of gold. A silent scream radiated between them as their bodies appeared frozen in another space and time.

He knew Katheryn well enough to know her guise. The Queen of the Elves in the Middle Lands of Atlastova. The Silver Lady of the Pale Forest. She ruled the trees of the Piquonese Elves; yet, she was not an elf. All whispered in her wake of her gentility, but quickness to reprimand. Her fault laid in her overwhelming thirst for power in both the Immortal and Mortal Realms of the Middle Lands. He suspected she would not stop there. He had been entranced by her glorious beauty and hospitality on his travels south. Had she not suspected the purpose of his journey previously, he may have savored the sweetness of her company. However, she lured him into her dwelling and seduced her way into his mind. It was answers she had wanted and provided whatever means necessary to obtain them.

A darkness filled his thoughts, *She will not rest until she is satisfied.*

Agonizingly, he had fought to continue his journey south, but with the assumption she would seek answers through whatever force necessary on his journey back. Whether for self purpose, or from the sheer horror of failure, he made up his mind to journey northwest on his way back to Borgoria, but she had already sent her spies into the Pale Forest.

Silently, he stepped across the room to the vine doorway. Gently, he pushed through the foliage, immediately noticing the Piquonese Elf cowering next to the flickering mushrooms. He knew she wouldn't be a threat to him, especially after witnessing the way the elven guards had retreated earlier. Quietly, he stepped behind the hovering figure of Katheryn. At his stature, he towered over both females. From the corner of his eyes his saw a glistening vine hanging over the balcony. *Possibly to pull up objects from below without leaving the luxury of the single chair.* Shrugging, he reeled in the vine, tying the end into a loop.

Peering at Mora's glazed expression of horror and pain, anger throbbed in his skin. The black smoke began to swirl menacingly around him as he crouched closer behind Katheryn. *She is too invested in answers to feel my presence.* Pushing against the wind, he willed himself further into the torrential, violent whirl. Within arms length, he forced the vine around Katheryn's neck, tugging it tightly as her power whipped ferociously in his grip. He held the rope secure as he pulled her body against his own. Once he felt her weaken, he flung his arms around her waist and bounded forcefully from the black smoke with her tight in his clutches.

A momentous crack of sound and a flash of silver light exploded in front of Mora's eyes. Then, the entire world around her succumbed to an array of sparkling lights, floating in front of her eyes like fireflies. Gradually, her vision began to focus on where she was kneeling. Tears were streaming pitifully down her face and an anger raged inside her stomach, making her heave.

*What the fuck just happened?* was all she could think as she heaved again.

Blinking the tears back, she wiped her face irritatingly hard. Adjusting once again to her surroundings, she saw the cowered body of Katheryn miserably staring in her direction. Then, a brooding figure approached her and reached out a gentle hand.

*Bog,* she breathed silently.

Bloodied from the wound, his chest was panting severely, but his violet eyes were fiercely radiating. He leaned over, gesturing his outstretched arm to her again. Flushed, she grasped his hand, feeling the satisfying warmth of his skin. Shivering from the previous events, he drew her close against his body as she shook. She could hear the vicious pounding of his heart against her temple. She knew not what had simply happened, but she appreciated his embrace.

Bog smiled.

# The Sleeping Dragon

"We need to go," Bog commanded Mora with an authority beyond his friendly inclination. Peering concernedly at her as she lifted her head in his arms, he felt a twinge of pity for the poor creatural crouching next to him, but that was not his concern at the moment. He steadied her again and whispered, "We will go amidst the treetops."

Mora's bleary eyes gazed up at him with confusion and sorrow.

Leaving Katheryn on the platform, he led her past the fountain, further on the fungus pathway, and up toward the canopy of the tree. He had insisted she get some air, but he wanted to take her as far from Katheryn as he could in present time. She was shaking terribly. He wanted to scoop her in his arms and carry her the rest of the way.

*She would hate me for that,* he thought as a slight smile upturned on his face.

He brushed the thick leaves aside, revealing the vast, night sky. On the top of the canopy, he helped her sit down and watched as she brought her knees to her chest, hugging them tightly. He pitied her for what she had just experienced, but it wasn't pity making him cautious. He could feel another emotion knocking against his caged chest he had erected so long ago. He pushed his curly hair from his eyes, crossed his arms, and looked up at the untainted sky. Tonight was unusually magnificent. The autumn sky never ceased to amaze him despite the shortening days. There weren't many autumn, nor winter, days in Borgoria, and it very rarely got cold. However, images from his youth emerged, the ones that made his heart ache. His mother would travel south during the winter months so he could frolic and play around in the snow.

Tears threatened as he imagined his mother's smile. *Fuck.* Rubbing a hand across his face, he composed himself.

The moon was waning as of tonight, but its luminosity was not faltering. Withering in a wave of emotions, Mora felt the events of the night were a puzzle in which missed an important amount of pieces. She gripped her legs, squeezing them harshly to her body, pain searing from her breasts. She screamed silently in angst. *How could I have allowed myself to become so vulnerable?* She had given her guard up too easily in the presence of another female.

To her surprise, she felt a cloak fall around her shoulders. Immediately looking up, she saw Bog, a small grin trying to ease the tension. He casually sat next to her and said nothing. In her peripheral, she could see him gazing the stars. With a bloodied shoulder and no cloak, he looked like she felt. Finally, she mustered the courage to say, "Thank you."

He did not respond, merely nodded his head in acknowledgment.

As they sat in silence, all she could hear was his heavy breathing. Occasionally, he would raise an arm and point to a shooting star. It was peaceful and pleasant after the most recent events. Gazing back up, she saw a shower of stars falling from the sky. A short gasp of amazement faltered from her lips. They illuminated the darkness like glowing raindrops, freely falling to the horizon, soaking it with radiance. As they fell, they hit the cusp of the land with a tiny burst of light, causing the mountains to the east to emit a luminescent glow.

*What is beyond the lands?*

Only the full moon prior, she had never travelled further than the edge of the woods surrounding her dwelling. Only a handful of times did she remember catching a star shoot across the night sky. *Why do the stars fall from the sky?*

However, the aching memory echoed in her heads though in reply ...*And then the stars called out, to whom do we serve? For we are infinite to the naked eye, our vastness is beyond the count of the furthest corner of All...We are the stars. We serve the Light.* She shuddered as a voice broke through her trance.

*The Keeper*

"It was of no consequence. I did what I must."

He sounded deeply saddened. "Bog, your wound." She reached her hand toward his shoulder.

He shrugged her hand away. It was more forcefully than he meant for it to be, but a mixture of emotions were tormenting his thoughts and he wasn't thinking clearly. "It's fine," he replied glumly.

Mora rose onto her knees to better look at Bog. He sat with one leg outstretched and the other bent, facing toward the majestic sky. His good arm lay causally over the bent knee, while the arm containing the wound hung at his side. She could feel his resistance to talk, but she was curious, "How did you know where I was?"

"I didn't," he replied quickly, finally looking in her direction, "it was a fool's luck." Attempting to smile felt foolish and fake, but he tried.

She had never felt him so jaded. In the short time she had known him, he had mostly been annoyingly uplifting, but cautious. His contemplative gaze returned to the skies. Aggravated, she remembered the passage again in her head. Deciding to inquire his opinion, she asked, "Who do you think the stars serve?"

His breathing slowed from the hurried pace it had been fluttering only moments before. It was not a question he had expected to hear. In a sullen tone, he replied, "Why do you ask?"

"With an infinite number of beauty as far as the naked eye can venture, one can only speculate whether something as grand and majestic as the stars could ever worship anything but themselves." She flashed a taunting look in his direction, hoping for a semblance of rebuttal from the statement.

"I agree."

Disappointed, she sighed. She accepted his mind was elsewhere, somewhere beyond the realm of intimate conversation and emotional response. Finally defeated from the weight of persistent silence growing cataclysmically, she stood up and began to walk in the direction of the descending pathway in search of a place to find a distraction.

Aware of her frustration, but not wanting her to think he was upset with her because of the events that had transpired since the Hawkend incident, he cleared his throat, "But it is not the stars themselves who birth their own being from the darkness, only to die again, dispersing the energies into the great unknown. Is it not Light, Dark, and Life that have formed together to create All? While each star becomes possessed by an enormous surge of force creating its very own existence, does it not also live in the presence of consuming darkness, feeding its light off the dark matter in which surrounds it?"

He sighed. "And when it dies, does it not again dissipate into the darkness, awaiting its reincarnation into the light? And while, possibly, the ones in which feed solely into the darkness inwardly implode from their own weight of shortcomings, bringing with it all its surrounding elements. However, is there not redemption? Therefore, if all this is deemed as truth, are we not all made of the same essence as the stars?"

He upturned his eyes to her, a slight catch of breath as he noticed how serene her form looked against the backdrop of the stars. Even after the torture she had been through only moments prior, the chaos of small curls fluttering in the night breeze, the mess of scratches and dirt upon her face, and the sleep making her eyes heavy, brought a protectiveness to defend her through whatever means possible he could endure. She was strong, but she was stubborn.

As silence fell once again, Mora smiled crookedly at the menacing, barely visible dimple. "I see your mood has not wreaked havoc on your mind. Good night, Bog." She descended the pathway in pursuit of a familiar face.

After a while, he heard a muffled sigh from behind. Although he knew who was making their presence known by the subtle change in energy, he closed his eyes in frustration.

"You have become too attached."

It was not that he desired to engage in conversation, but she had pushed him to his limits. Annoyed, he turned around at the mocking inflection in her voice. "How dare you speak to me in that nonchalant tone after what you have done."

"How dare I?" Katheryn snickered as she stepped onto the canopy and commenced to smooth her dress. A provoking tone echoed in her voice as she said, "I saved your life. You forget your place here, Bog, son of Gornya. I am Queen of these lands. You are a guest in my house."

He snickered, "A guest? Is that how you treat your 'guests'? Imprisoned in a glass bubble, guarded by godsdamned miniature elves!

You used me to get inside my mind and now you pursue Mora!" He shot to his feet quickly, his rage far too gone to restrain at this point. Feeling his blood boiling, he clenched his fists. It was a side of him he despised, yet it hid deep inside him, waiting...

...*like a sleeping dragon,* his father's voice echoed.

Katheryn flashed a livid glance toward Bog. "I use what I want to get what I need!" Her golden eyes began to illuminate and spark fiercely. She twisted her hands at her sides, attempting to calm herself down. Finally, she sighed, "And besides, you insult my sentry. They do their best. And they are the most funny, little creaturals." Attempting to change the tide, she smiled sweetly.

He grimaced, grunted, and turned away from her presence. Breathing deeply, he locked away his anger.

"I dare say, you are quite intimidating when you are radiating this heat." She sashayed toward Bog, inclined her head, and watched his fixed gaze upon the stars. She placed her arms sensually upon his chest. "Of course, your companion does not know *this* side of you." She smiled slyly. "I did gather that from her thoughts. She does think the world of your... friendship," placing her finger up to her lip, she added, "Much like that of a *sibling,* I suppose."

His shoulder's shrunk at her words. Still averting his gaze, he said solemnly, "Apologies. It is not an appropriate behavior in the presence of...females." Then, lowering his gaze to her golden eyes, he quipped disdainfully, "And while you are completely void of my respect and title of lady, I will honor you in your house."

Only slightly taken aback from the comment, she walked around him, her fingers traipsing across the ripples of his flesh. "Ah, you are quite taken with the youth. Obviously, it is an unexpected grievance to the purpose of your journey." Pausing in front of him once again, with a malicious frown, she whispered, "But I have seen her heart. She does not return the same gut-wrenching emotion. Tell me Bog, do you plan to fulfill your promise, or does it lie as empty as a jar full of air?"

Spitefully, he pushed her away. He didn't want her touch, nor did he need her deceitful tongue. Silver rings of light faded away from where her hands had touched his skin. He gritted his teeth. "I will not let you overtake me again. Besides, you insult the element of air."

## The Keeper

Perturbed by his quip, but feigning innocence, she pouted. "I never meant the young one harm."

He sensed the lack of complete sincerity.

"She wouldn't let me entirely in. I know she is an old soul, despite her very young life. I could taste the ancient history of creaturals upon my tongue, mortal and immortal alike. It was a mixture of wood, dirt, and salt." She peered up. Standing on her toes, she lowered her voice and hissed, "But do you really feel like she is who *you* think she is?"

Turning away from her gaze, he said harshly, "I know I am right." He briefly glanced down upon her face and then turned his eyes to the stars. Sliding his hands absently into his pockets, he kicked at the leaf under his boot and cleared his throat, "Because I know if I am wrong, I am leading her to a death no one deserves."

Turning back toward Katheryn, he knew he couldn't continue without her support. In spite of their past, he needed her to aid his journey with Mora. Shuffling, he stuttered, "This is why I came to you at the beginning. We need your alliance. It is essential we have as many supporters throughout this task, or you know what will befall each race upon the lands."

She shot him a defiant, golden glance. Gliding gracefully across the canopy, she held her chin at a scornful angle. "And what if I refuse?"

Anger grasped him on a deep level. He stomped over to her and grabbed her arm forcefully, turning her toward his face. "Then *He* will be back for you and all your bloody lands. He will demand each kneel to His command, whether you oppose Him or not!" He pushed her from his grasp and sighed darkly, "but who knows, you may prefer the kneeling."

Shaken, but still poised, she closed her eyes and smoothed her hair.

He watched her silently. She was a beautiful creatural, one whose beauty will never fade with time. However, he knew her cunningness and sharpness of tongue. She was a natural born ruler, devious and power hungry. Her alliance, if true to the cause, would account for a potential stronghold against an opposition fiercer than any venomously fatal blow.

She looked at him coldly. "Even if I had spoken sincerity about refusal, you have scolded me as if an elfling, threatening me with unforeseen circumstances."

## The Keeper

Reluctantly, he sighed. "The circumstances are foreseen. And there is a very real, fatal danger in taking the wrong path, both for the creaturals and animals of the Mortal and Immortal Realms. Balance has been challenged, the seal has been broken, and life has steadily become obsolete and dangerous. We no longer have a choice."

Katheryn smirked. "We always have choices. Whether it is to live or die, it still is a choice. One cannot rely on another to awaken their soul's purpose. Our kind, our immortality, will never eternally fade. Do not fear the beyond my winged one, it is only a doorway for the soul's journey," her grin widened, "lest you forget your choice so readily."

Bog half smiled, but emptiness filled his eyes. He turned and stepped toward the mushrooms he had almost wanted to carry Mora upon a shadow's length before. Stopping, and without turning to Katheryn, he spoke sternly, "It is not dying I fear. It is Death himself." He picked up the cloak Mora had dropped before descending beneath the canopy.

*I know who you think she is,* he heard the soft voice reiterate silently behind him as he descended the pathway.

His mind was racing, full of regret and grief. The undulating need for clarity made him stop and peer back toward the canopy where Katheryn stood. Before his journey south, he knew the circumstances. An alliance was set in blood with the Lucyniah Woodland Nymph Queen of Lychinus years ago for peace with the Borgorians, and he needed it to remain strong. However, many murmured of a darkness invading the hearts of several nymph clans, leading them toward Ekklips' cause.

Katheryn's words echoed in his mind, *Lest you forget your choice so readily.*

He shook his head maliciously as the memory resurfaced.

Bog had been traveling for many moons, and the borders of Lychinus were opened upon his arrival, as if he had been expected. His feet were weary and his heart was heavy from his journey. Soon upon his arrival, *she* greeted him and he was led to her dwelling amongst the mountainous tree. He was wrought with hunger and thirst.

### The Keeper

"Bog, son of Gornya, I welcome you to my humble land."

He could barely focus upon her face. However, when his eyes became adjusted to the light, he could see her beauty radiating. Her gold eyes pierced his flesh and her dark hair fell to her shoulders with tucked braids falling below her breasts.

Melodiously, she spoke, "I can feel you are famished. Please, sit, and I will have my elves bring you sustenance and water." Her hand guided him passed an intricately carved fountain which sounded of rain, to another chamber with a comfortable swinging chair made of silk.

After indulging himself in various meats and deliciously succulent fruit, his mind gradually cleared. He glanced around the chamber at the massive, woven columns, topped by scrolls and dainty decoration. Everything he saw contrasted with the dark hair of Katheryn. He focused his gaze in her direction. "I thank you for your hospitality."

"All is well. I rarely receive such intriguing guests." She smiled wryly. She poured a couple of crystal chalices with red wine, stood up, and gracefully walked over to where he was sitting. Offering him a glass, she sat down next to him on the silk and placed her hand over his own. "Tell me Bog, what is it you are seeking."

A strangeness pulsated through his body. He quickly stood up, nearly spilling his wine, and took his hand away from her grasp. Rubbing the back of his neck as he took a large gulp of infused blackberry and cherry, he nervously peered at Katheryn. When he started to speak, it came out as a stutter, "I, well, I…am searching for a friend," he cleared his throat, "that…uh, well, went missing a while ago, and," he took another swig, "well, I," his eyes darted uncomfortably around the room, "knew you would be hospitable on my journey. You had been spoken highly of your, er," he grazed a hand through his hair, "well, your…hospitality."

Terribly embarrassed, he walked to the edge of the chamber and peered out over the tree. The lights were flickering in the breeze and he could see the bustle of little elves on every branch. *Idiot*, he thought. Turning back toward Katheryn, he muttered, "My apologies, I am not feeling well. Could you show me to a place I can rest for the night? I will leave at dawn."

Her movements were almost lyrical. She stood up and smiled sweetly at him, gesturing to the right of the doorway. "I always accommodate my guests."

He pushed away from the rail and followed. The small, half-open, circular chamber on the opposite end of the branch was mesmerizing. Its grandeur was not in the size, but the interwoven lights hanging from the ceiling, containing tiny fireflies jauntily flickering on and off softly. The bed was majestic. The white sheets were made of the finest linens and stuffed with down feathers. At the outside edge was an intricately carved railing with intertwined white and silver branches. The poles were adorned with succulent, gold flowers. Walking to the outer edge of the chamber, he beheld a brilliantly diverse garden of flowers in the grand, grassy area below.

Turning toward Katheryn, he reverently bowed his head. "It is lovely, and it is more than I deserve. You spoil me, but I am humbly appreciative."

She smiled politely. "If you need anything, just ring this bell." She pointed to a palm-sized bell above the bed attached to a long vine leading outside the chamber. Then, she eloquently left him alone.

The darkening sky was surrounding the trees as he took off his boots, but left on his breeches. Settling into bed, he drifted off immediately into a dark, restless slumber. From within, his heart started racing and sweat poured down his brow. It was his recurring nightmare. Faintly, he saw his mother standing opposite his gaze. *She was the most magnificent of all the Borgorians.* He smiled at her and she smiled sweetly in return.

Then, a looming figure manifested from behind his mother. It was his father, Gornya. Bog wanted to lash out at him and grab him by the throat, but he could not move. He was stuck. When Gornya approached his mother, her face twisted in pain as bruises darkened her eyes and a trickle of blood slid down the side of her mouth. He watched helplessly in horror as she turned slowly to face Gornya. He struck her across the cheek and tore the linens from her body.

Fiercely, Bog clawed at the darkness surrounding the bodies, attempting to grasp his father. However, his fingertips never reached the figure. He swam through the blur of space around him, screaming in rage. His ears resonated with his mother's painful screams. As she fell to the ground, she wept in rivers of blood.

He shouted in terror and woke with a gasp.

## The Keeper

His chamber was dark; the fireflies asleep, the elves asleep, the tree asleep. He wiped the sweat from his face and felt a sharp pang of venomous force run through his veins. His mind was racing and he could feel the blood throbbing through where his fingertips clutched the sheets. The linens were soaked through with sweat. Violently, he threw off the covers as a welcome night chill brushed softly over his skin. He slid to the end of the bed and put his head in his hands.

A faint sound from the chamber made him whip his head to the door as the elegant figure of Katheryn appeared. His head was swimming, but when he tried to speak, a finger caressed sensually across his lips. Breathing heavily, he felt a surge of heat engulf him as she straddled his body. Pressing her breasts against his chest, she lightly touched her lips to his own. His mind raced wildly. It had been a significant length of time since he had lain with a female, a terribly long time before his journey for Mora had begun.

Katheryn's teeth gently tugged at his bottom lip. Then, she moved lower as her tongue caressed gradually down his neck in small circles. Her hips rhythmically moved across his lap.

He groaned deeply. He felt high, his mind clouding his judgment.

A passionately primal thirst raged through his mind. As a desperate urge to feel wanted overtook his movements, his large hands grasped her hips and guided them forcefully back and forth. The anger building from his nightmare, coupled with her touch, made him throb violently. He picked her up, turned, and tossed her down onto the bed. He locked his mouth with her own, his tongue sweeping across her lips before following her jawline and down her exposed neck.

She gasped and sank her fingernails into his arms, encouraging him to explore her eager body.

He rose to his knees and violently tore the sheer slip away, exposing her breasts fully. Continuing to kiss down her neck, he could taste the heat rising on her skin. Swirling his tongue over her nipples, he grasped onto her right breast with one hand as she arched her back in response.

She moaned sensually as she dug her hands through the masses of golden curls.

Rage burned deep inside as he growled and guided her hips. He slid her down to the edge of the bed, pulling her forcefully to his waist.

*The Keeper*

Hysteria settled as he unfastened his breeches. It had been too long since he had felt the touch of another, and he was so hard, it was painful. Thrusting strongly at the apex of her legs, the sudden warmth caused his skin to burn even more fiercely.

She cried out in pleasure.

Powerfully, he penetrated deep inside. A throaty moan rattled from his chest. Suddenly, his violet eyes glowed bright as an ancient, lethal passion begun to awaken in his mind. He wrapped a strong arm around her waist, picked her up, and threw her face down into the sheets. Grabbing her hips, he jerked her onto her hands and knees, vigorously thrusting his strength inside. He could feel the sweat dripping from his neck and chest, his head swirling like a tumultuously savage whirlpool.

*Godsdamn, what am I doing!* his voice scolded his conscious.

She clamped around him as she let out a breathy moan, spurring his animalistic hunger before he could think straight. He grasped onto her shoulder with one hand and yanked her up forcefully, holding her breasts, her wings against his chest. He groaned deeply as he succumbed to the pleasure of her essence.

Then, with a heaving chest, he pushed her hips to the side as he fell back onto the feather bed. The primal feeling melted away as the violet of his eyes faded to normal. Too parched to speak, he wiped off the sweat drenching his forehead with the bedsheet. The rage was starting to subside and his eyes were trying to focus. He felt drugged. Faintly, he saw Katheryn stand gracefully at the end of the bed.

She turned her head in his direction and smiled cunningly. "Thank you Bog, I now have the information I needed."

Too tired to respond, he could vaguely see her traipse out of the doorway while the menacing flicker of his eyelids bore down heavily. A cold chill raked across his flesh, no longer satisfyingly soft. Before he closed his eyes, a sudden realization sparked. *She bloody used me.*

Bog returned from his memory, a blank stare residing on his face. His departure that day, while distant and shadowy, deemed suspicious in his mind. From the moment he awoke that morning, to the moment he stepped onto the grassy courtyard, he never saw Katheryn's face. Elves helped prepare him for his continuing journey. However, before he walked through the veil into the Pale Forest, he glanced back at Lychinus to see her standing stoically upon her deck, her black hair falling ominously around her face.

A distance whisper echoed in his ear, *You won't save her*.

He shook his head, trying to joggle the memory away. Untrustworthy, ambivalent, and potentially malicious, are only a few of the words he repeated constantly in his description of Katheryn to himself. Turning from the sight of the canopy, a dark impulse overcame his mind and he balled his fists tightly. He punched the tree trunk hard enough to break the bark. A flash of red resonated and sparked from the dent. He growled, his violet eyes faintly glowing in the surrounding night. Shrugging his shoulders and cracking his neck, he finally collected himself once again, and descended the pathway of the grandiose tree.

# Lucyniah Woodland Nymphs

The back of Mora's eyelids brightened and she felt the warmth of the morning sun on her face. Exhaustion swept through her body, but she had had a dreamless slumber, a relief from the previous sleep. However, a viciously low thrumming pestered incessantly against her forehead. *What in the curse of the gods happened last night?*

Yawning, she wrapped the soft, thick blanket closer to her body and rose carefully to her feet. Shuffling across the cold, wooden boards, she peered over the railing and into the splotchy sunrise through the leaves. The hues were magnificent. She saw a brilliant mixture of oranges and yellows running together with streaks of pink and intertwining with spots of dark blue clouds. The rays of sun exploded from the horizon, reaching far overhead, pushing back the blanket of darkness with its glorious arms. The battle for daylight was won and the sun the victor. She closed her eyes and let the scent of the new day fill her nostrils. *This is what autumn should be.* She could faintly smell freshly fallen mist, a twinge of sweet, floral blooms of the reawakening land, the morning breeze, cool and crisp, and the faint smell of honey. It was a pleasant change from the unexpected onset of winter weather outside the Pale Forest.

"*Maythen*, good for all ailments, relaxes the body. The honey is from the beehive garden."

The lyrical voice startled Mora, who quickly whipped around to see Katheryn pouring two cups of hot tea from an intricately decorated, clay amphora.

Smiling slyly, she said, "It also helps the hangover sickness from the elven spirits." She subserviently lifted the tray and brought it over to Mora.

Mora scraped her menacing forehead curls from her brow and shuffled quickly back to the bed.

Kneeling at her feet, Katheryn smiled sweetly and offered her a cup. "My apologies for the events that unfolded last night. I did not act as a decent hostess to such an honored guest."

Clearly blushing, she politely responded, "I am not..." But before she could finish, Katheryn held her fingers to Mora's lips.

"May I?" Katheryn gestured to Mora's eyebrow.

Mora had completely forgotten about the stitching. Marwen had sewn it flawlessly, it had not bothered her since she stumbled out of the portal. She nodded. However, her calf hurt the most. When she lifted her leg to inspect the wound, she found it was a cauterized burn, but nothing which required stitching.

Handing Mora a wet cloth to clean the burn, Katheryn carefully cut the stitching and sighed. "I am speaking heavily. I am merely referencing your friendship with Bog. I do greatly admire his...*passion*." A faint. smug smile graced her lips before she paused to take a small sip from her tea.

*I wonder what* that *means.* Mora winced when she placed the cold, minty cloth on her burn. After last night, she had little trust in the Queen, or her intentions. She shifted uncomfortably, but held her tongue. Smelling the sweet aroma of herbs and honey, her sipped the tea. It was satisfyingly comforting, and the warmth quelled the pounding behind her eyes. Strangely, there was an ethereal calmness that settled after each sip.

"This is delicious." Mora nodded politely.

Bowing her head in acknowledgment, Katheryn gently patted a salve on her eyebrow and calf burn before she walked over to where she had lain Mora's her clothes.

## The Keeper

Mora adjusted the blanket and watched her smooth out the linens. To her surprise, they were no longer dirt-stained and tattered.

"I took the liberty of having my elves wash your clothes in the spring fountain and patch the holes. They are excellent tailors. My faeries are even handier, but they are fickle and their aura's shine a bit brighter than the elves. Last minute instructions don't boast well for their kind." Noticing Mora's paralyzed expression, she flashed a smile of pity.

"I also had my shoemaker fashion sandals for you. Leather covers the toes and woven, elven strings, made from their sacred silk garden, lace around your leg to your knees. However, when it gets cold, you can place wool underneath the laces to keep your legs warm. He is very clever and an excellent gardener." She smoothed her own gown. "The material is divine."

Picking off little bits of leftover pills of wool from the stitching, and seemingly satisfied, Katheryn turned to face Mora. Mora took another sip of the Maythen and honey. She closed her eyes as the warmth slid down her throat. It was a wonderful taste, and it made her tiny, blonde arm-hairs stand on end. Even the aroma had a taste, a sweet scent that tickled her nose.

"Thank you. I greatly appreciate your hospitality and gifts." She took another sip of the savory concoction and massaged her temples. "My memories of last night are sorely intermittent."

Katheryn giggled and sashayed over to the railing. "You apparently went looking for the loyal Guilderon." Leaning against the vines, she mischievously said, "After multiple inquires, you found him at his local watering hole. Word has it you demanded a drink from the barkeep and decided to ensue a running tally with the best. Finally, reluctant to serve you any further, Guilderon located your knight in shining armor. Elves have an astonishingly high tolerance."

Mora flushed, too embarrassed to ask who it may be, despite the vague memory of his face before she fell asleep. "Bog," she whispered, barely audible.

"Aye." Katheryn smiled pitifully and floated back to her side. With her delicate hands, she reached to grasp her cup. "He was the perfect friend. He tucked you in and left you to slumber deeply."

Mora sighed. The way Katheryn had said *friend* made her weirdly anxious. Then, she caught site of the petite, six-sided star on the bottom side of her wrist. "What does it stand for?" she inquired, desperate to change the subject.

Katheryn grinned sweetly, but it did not reach her eyes, a sign Mora believed was her way of hiding her true feelings.

"The balance between the *inner* and the *outer* for which all energy flows. I am subject to nature as nature is subject to me. It is a never-ending cycle. It is red because that is the color of energy and fervor. The energy flows in our veins and is a calling to pursue a higher-sense of self. It stimulates the heartbeat and connects with other life forces. It is a highly revered mark of my kind."

Mora's shock resonated in her voice, "Your kind?"

Katheryn rubbed the star lightly. "Aye. My kind. I am one of the few survivors of the race known as the Lucyniah Woodland Nymphs." A sparkling tear trickled down her cheek.

Mora spoke gently, "May I inquire into your burden?"

Katheryn whispered only one word, "Chaos." Abruptly, she stood, dried her tear, and smoothed her jade gown. "My apologies, I really must be returning, my elves are a pitiful lot without my guidance. Enjoy your tea." She swiftly turned on her heel and floated through the doorway.

Stunned at the impulsive exit, Mora thought deeply about her last word, *chaos. Is she referring to the action itself? Or has she referenced the concept I have been recently introduced to about Dark's Chaos?* She thought it very strange her answer had been so brief. She took another sip of the tea. It ran fiery down her throat, a refreshing feeling against the cool, morning air. It was strange. She experienced a new, pleasurable taste every time she sipped the Maythen. *It is as if it responds to my emotions.*

Glancing at her clothes, carefully laid out and pressed, the desperate urge to lay back in bed and close her eyes nearly won. However, she was curious to explore Lychinus before they continued their journey. She steadied herself with the thick blanket around her body. Standing, she shuffled her feet across the cool floor to the fresh garments. Running her fingers down the fabric, she could feel the softness in which was once hidden beneath the layers of mud and dirt. Then, she lifted the new underlinen and held it to her nose. The scent made her heart flutter. *It smells of lavender and vanilla.* Never in her life had she spent much care on her clothing.

## The Keeper

A large clay bowl sat next to the garments for washing her skin. Glancing around, she quickly shed the blanket and splashed the water all around her body, the coldness making her flesh pimple, but it was delightfully refreshing. Rubbing the soft cloth over her face and all of her exposed flesh, she made certain to take care of her most intimate areas before discarding it beneath the basin.

Then, in a horrified moment, she remembered Katheryn said Bog put her to bed. *But...I'm naked.* Her entire body flushed with a heat so intense, she began to sweat nervously. *Did he remove my clothes before he placed me in the sheets? Curse of the gods!*

Hastily, she slipped into the clean, linen shift and tugged the frock over her head, securing it with her obviously repaired, leather belt. Unfastening her hair, she drenched her locks with the leftover water and rinsed it with a soap smelling of fresh morning flowers. Fighting her poorly neglected curls, she tussled through the tangled mess with a bone comb. Dousing her face in the water once again, she braided her hair down her back. Glancing down to her clothes, to her surprise, were a pair of thin breeches. Mora's eyes widened. *Thank the gods!* She stepped into the skin tight, mud colored breeches. Feeling the soft material hugging her legs, she sighed. *They are magnificent.* Finally, she slipped on the sandals, laced them tightly around her calves, and made sure they didn't rub her burn.

She had never given much thought to her appearance, but in the company of Katheryn, it was all about an outward approval. Looking briefly in the semi-muddied water, she was satisfied with the result.

Mora picked up a navy cloak and walked to the railing on the side in which Katheryn had exited. Looking over the vines, she saw a great number of elves ascending and descending the pathways amongst the entanglement of branches. The railings were made of the same intertwining vines from the fountain platform Katheryn had taken her the previous night. A dark shadow skulked through her mind. Although she had been more concerned with Bog and the threat pursuing them, she should not have readily trusted Katheryn's intentions.

Shielding her eyes from the brightening morning light, she began to wonder where Bog was located.

### The Keeper

Bog awoke to a brilliant sunrise. The brightness pierced his eyelids, causing him to stir restlessly at the unwelcome interruption of sleep. Weariness had attacked every muscle in his body after he left Katheryn. However, it wasn't until Guilderon found him, that he realized how exhausted he had been. Carrying Mora to her quarters took another toll on his body. She had been belligerently drunk, something he blamed Guilderon for, even though he feared Mora had been highly susceptible after her encounter with Katheryn. His thoughts drifted to the previous night as he turned away from the rising sun.

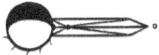

"Bogggg!" Mora screamed. "Cometh joineth us!" Her arms flung wildly over her head.

Smirking at her slur of strange -*eth* suffixes, he ducked through the doorway. "Bedtime for you, Sunshine," he replied to her rant.

She then proceeded to stick her tongue out and spat like a childling. Placing her hands on her hips, she slurred, "Noteth unlessth you carryeth me outeth!" She hiccuped and pointed a finger toward the ceiling.

Upon her words, he scooped her into his arms, much to her chagrin.

She proceeded to flop around annoyingly. "Leteth me downeth!" she barked, hiccuped, but gave up soon after, her head lolling onto his chest.

Finally, about halfway to her quarters, she started tracing small circles on his skin. She attempted to whisper, "Bog?"

"Mmm?" he grunted.

"Do you love her?" she sheepishly inquired.

His stomach turned into knots. While he knew with whom she referenced, he replied gruffly, "Who?"

As if hiding a secret, she had looked around briefly before placing a hand to her mouth, covering it at a wonky angle. "Katheryn," she slurred.

An anger arose in his chest. *I despise the damn nymph, but I can't tell Mora in Lychinus.* He settled on, "Fuck no."

She giggled. "But somethings happened betweenths you twos."

**The Keeper**

She walked her fingers up his chest and poked him on his nose with a high *boop!*. "I cans telleth by the ways yous responds to her. She's…beautiful." Her head fell back again and she groaned.

He cringed. *Not if you* knew *her.*

After the brief, yet awkward, conversation, they reached one of the empty sleeping quarters similar to the one Katheryn had allowed him to occupy upon his journey south. Gently laying her onto the white sheets, he knew he couldn't leave her soiled from head to toe. Glancing around nervously, he decided he would attempt to remove her clothing without being indecent.

First, he unlaced her boots and set them next to the bed. Next, he untied her leather belt, laying it next to her boots. Then, he tucked her into the thick blanket with her arms over her head. Carefully, he tugged gently on the fabric until it started rising. Scrunching the fabric, he finally pooled it above her breasts before he successfully pulled it over her head and arms. *The shift is soiled too.* Commencing to pull it over her head, she snorted and he retracted. Seeing she was not going to awaken, he continued to retrieve the shift. Satisfied with his efforts, he tucked the blanket once again around her naked body and smoothed her hair away from her face.

Tossing the dirty garments to the side, he turned to leave, but a hand reached out and grabbed his arm. Startled, he looked back to see Mora's forest green eyes glistening with tears.

"Stays with me," she whimpered.

"I…uh," he stuttered, "but…I…your…um…"

"Please?" she pleaded. A tiny hiccup escaped her lips.

"I…uh," he couldn't think straight, "um…sure." He sat down next to her on the bed, one leg up, the other foot firmly on the ground.

She laced her fingers through his and grinned. "Thank you," she slurred and closed her eyes.

Within moments, he felt her body jerk slightly as tiny wisps of air puffed steadily from her lips. He shifted uncomfortably and looked down at their interlaced fingers. *Shit.*

After a while, even though he thought he had only closed his eyes for a moment, Bog opened his eyes to see the sky slightly lightening through the branches. His heart fluttered. *Curse of the gods!* He looked down. Mora's head was lying sweetly on his lap, her arm wrapped around his elevated leg, while the thick blanket had exposed her breasts.

He groaned, averted his eyes, and rubbed his face. *Fuck.*

Carefully, he shifted her head to the pillow and shimmied his leg through her arm. Aching from the sleeping position, he pulled the blanket back around her neck and crept softly across the platform. Glancing back briefly, squinting through the final stretch of slumber in the retreating night, he could see she had turned over and positioned herself once again comfortably cuddling the pillow, her backside exposed. Nervously lacing his fingers behind his head, he hurried out the door.

Once he had left Mora, he could feel each muscle in his body slack and wither in exhaustion. No matter how hard he forced himself, his body would not cooperate with his mind until he succumbed to a comfortable sleeping position. However, he was overwhelmingly frustrated and nothing was satisfying. He was beyond exhausted at this point. The wound, the jump, the climb, the run, and even the confrontation with Katheryn, had been all too exasperating. He lay on his back on the makeshift palette he located on a nearby branch and watched the faint stars twinkling through the canopy of thick leaves.

Beginning to question why Mora had talked about the stars in a subservient manner last night, he wondered, *What did she see with Katheryn?* He admired Mora's spirit, but he never allowed himself to think anything more. Katheryn spoke as though she had not experienced the wrath of darkness clutching them until the last moment he had pulled her away from Mora's mind. *That is concerning.*

He knew of Katheryn's past. He had heard tales of the Lucyniah Woodland Nymphs. Powerful and overwhelmingly cunning beings, they lived in an ever-growing, authoritative state. They were the Goddesses to the Piquonese Elves, and joined alliance with the faeries to rule an expanding woodland, a space of liminality within the corrupted Pale Forest. That is, until the then-Queen of the Lucyniah Woodland Nymphs made a deal with a dark spirit. The spirit, they say, was Death himself, or, at least, His creation.

The Queen vied for power over all the woods on both sides of the veil. She would allow the spirit access to all the souls within her kingdom in exchange for the ability to rule each and every one during their life. With the agreement sealed, she reveled in subjecting stray mortals to servitude.

## The Keeper

However, during the Queen's rule, she began to notice the faults within every one of her subjects. One by one, as her sickness grew, each one who displeased her would hang until dead from the branches of Lychinus. It wasn't until one day, an unnamed mortal servant confronted her with an argument.

The mortal was believed to have said, "*If you are so displeased by your subjects, have no mercy and kill them all. Build an army comprised of solely mortals, for we are disposable. We will serve and gravel at your power. If you are in an arrangement with a dark spirit of death, the mortal souls can be reanimated to create an indestructible Army of the Dead.*"

The Queen, who was already becoming a servant of Death herself, disheveled and taken aback from the forwardness of the mortal, proposed a deal with the male. The mortal was allowed free rein of the surrounding territory, establishing any punishment he deemed fit. In turn, he would serve his time in life and death as the commander and chief of her Army of the Dead. She commanded him to take no survivors, for madness had consumed her mind. Her cognitive ability to think clearly was forfeited by her absurd commands to release the souls to the torture of the dark spirit.

Bog's studies proved the Queen's kin had been opposed to the act from the beginning. However, the Queen had forged her soul to the darkness and could never return to the light. For countless years they fought the forces of the Queen. Casualties after casualties fell at the feet of the merciless ruler and her Army of the Dead.

One day, a rebel by the name of Hagog rose in opposition from the outside forces. With only a shield made of oak and a sword made of iron, he challenged the Queen. In the midst of winter's kiss, Hagog set out for the Queen's camp with one thousand, immortal rebels at his side. Through the morning's freshly fallen snow, Hagog trudged violently toward the Queen's fortress in the midst of what is presently the Pale Forest. He was a ruthless being. Neither the darkest of dark, nor the midday sun, could hinder his cause.

By the time they had reached the camp, the Queen had summoned the dead to her aid. Skulkins and lost souls alike wiped out three-fourths of Hagog's army. It had been a brutal undertaking, but he never wavered in his pursuit of the Queen. He pushed against the unbridled chaos.

Cowardly, the Queen hid amongst her tents until the mighty

## The Keeper

Hagog forged his way through the carnage of the fight. Into her tents he went, smelling of blood and rotting flesh. The Queen was struck with terror. Thwarting Hagog at every possible movement, she fought back against the madness raging in his eyes. Her heart beat fast. Beads of sweat blotted her skin, blocking her eyes and making it harder to focus. She pushed and shoved at the furniture between them, breaking glass and clay alike. Hagog continued pursuit. The Queen struggled immensely, putting up a fantastically barbaric fight against Hagog. However, before she could reach the doorway, he grabbed her by the hair and pulled her back into the tent. Crying out to the dark spirit in which she bargained, Hagog turned her around and gazed into her eyes. The Queen automatically fell silent as she realized he mirrored her own chaotic spirit in which she had made the irreversible pact a century before.

Hagog lifted her gown roughly as the unadulterated chaos grew around the lands. The Queen was unfathomably raped of her tainted dignity and merciless brutality in the name of power, both in the literal and metaphorical sense. She screamed in terror and clawed his flesh. It only lasted a moment in the life she led, but through her agony, she was able to use what little, remaining conscience she had left to consume the both of them in an undeniable, final act of heroism. The force of the magic swallowed her essence, crushed their bones, and they both ceased to exist in the world of the living. The aftermath of the energetic release wiped out the grueling monsters of the Army of the Dead and the Pale Forest was recreated from the rotting flesh and bone. It had since, and will forevermore, surround the liminal, safe haven the ancestors had placed around Lychinus. The tree covers the ruins of the Queen's fortress.

Bog smirked. The details of the story had been orally passed from generation to generation, and most likely contained fabricated elements as most do. *Although, there are always morals left after you sift through the fanciful elaborations.* What he interpreted from the story was - *Don't make a deal with unknown spirits. They will always expect the debt to be repaid tenfold.*

The tales he had read throughout his life had to be the most amazingly enchanting stories anyone could have ever concocted. However, though he could dissect the subtle differences of elaboration, the tinge of authentication could only trickle deep enough in his skin, he eventually had to recognize a story for its underlying veracity. Most of the time, it humbled him quickly. He knew Katheryn had struggled deeply in the treacherous wrongdoings of her kin, but it did not forgive the malice and apathy she exhibited in her dealings with Mora.

He shivered with anger. *I'm afraid she may have sensed traces of who Mora* had *been...*

Although he had no sign of sympathy toward Katheryn the moment he awoke in her realm, he didn't realize she would take advantage of Mora so vigorously. Running a hand through his curly, golden hair, he finally fell asleep amidst his thoughts.

Bog awoke again, this time fully aware and grateful of the allotted sleep. A little sore from the lack of proper cushioning on the palette, he decided he would walk to the canopy. Splashing his face and skin with the refreshing, cool water left in the basin, he changed out of his soiled breeches into the ones the elves left for him folded next to the stand. *At least that is an extended kindness.*

Once he rose above the liminal, leafy world, he glanced around at the gargantuan leaves holding the canopy atop Katheryn's precious territory. They were thick and strong. Deep within the veins, as he peered closer, pulsed a shimmering liquid, running through them like the blood within his own veins. He knelt and placed his hand flush against the smooth surface, sensing a slight vibration as though he were placing his own hand to his chest to feel the very life force pumping deep. The leaves were alive with the magic of the ancestors. He placed his fingertips to his lips to relish the cold dew of dawn. A bitter aftertaste lingered on his tongue. The leaves were full of unquestionable vigor, but were becoming subject to an encroaching force that tasted like the transience of mortality. This was concerning. The natural world was evolving, and not with vitality, but a narcosis. He stretched his legs and arms. Ungracefully stumbling to his feet, he strained his eyes to glance upon the horizon. He knew where they must venture next, though he loathed the road in which they must travel - *north. We will be amidst strange lands, each diverse in*

*their own right and foul beneath the shadows. However, Borgoria lies
beyond those lands, and I have not travelled this far to give way to failure.
I am no warrior, but I am a resilient being of truth. I will prevail.*

His mind wondered to Mora. She had proven herself a skilled
fighter and a loyal companion. He admired her emotional and physical
strengths thus far. Her mind was still weak, and her reluctance to believe in
anything outside her own perspective of what she was taught was
becoming particularly annoying. However, he knew it was only a matter of
time until she realized their meeting was not by chance. He had been
searching for her for a long time, and even more recently beyond the
confines of his own library.

Before turning to proceed down the pathway, he turned to glance
toward the eastern horizon where the sun was already proud in the sky.
Vaguely, he thought he could see a dark cloud churning. He blinked and it
disappeared. Knowing it was possibly a trick of the eye, an ominous
twinge settled in his stomach as the blinding brightness of the sun rapidly
ascended back into the sky. Alarmed, his eyes reflected a violet brilliance
in the sunlight. *We must be off.*

# A Ripple

Not exactly too keen on finding Bog and listening to him possibly scold her for her behavior with Guilderon, Mora still tried to discreetly inquire into his whereabouts. However, no one was particularly helpful with information. Therefore, she decided she would descend the massive tree and explore the grassy area below where the little elves were playing the night before with the fireflies.

*If Bog wants to find me, he can make the effort.*

Taking a copious amount of care stepping on the mushrooms, she looked around thoroughly and decided she would slide her fingers along the trunk as she made her way to the bottom. Circling around on the mushroom steps playfully, she was enchanted by the delicate strings of gold trailing behind her fingers. It felt like the pulsating light of the tree was following her descent, desperately attempting to catch up and tickle her fingertips. When she stepped upon the grass, she glanced around cautiously, then placed her palms gently against the trunk. An illumination of gold surrounded her hands. The undulating strings of light from the tree began to weave around her flesh, dancing in beautiful swirls and encircling her arms. When the light reached her chest, a spark of warmth kissed her heart.

She inhaled deeply. *Good morning*, she whispered to the light and smiled.

Reluctant to leave the warmth of the tree trunk, she decided it would be better to explore before anyone stopped to question her activity. She didn't feel like making current conversation, and knew it wasn't going to be enjoyable when she did have to come face to face with their journey once more. Curiously, there were not many Piquonese Elves on the ground this morning. *I wonder if they are still waking with the morning sun. It was quite a busy place last night.* She flushed. *At least, from what I can remember.*

Placing those thoughts aside, she strolled around the tree, taking in the delicately overgrown gardens which contained a prodigious variety of flowers and foliage. Everything appeared to be frozen in the eternal transition of spring to summer. Patches of sunlight peeked through the tangle of huge branches, creating various warm spots on the grass as she walked. Occasionally, she would hop shape to shape, a nostalgic delight from her youth. The sandals were a welcome addition to her wardrobe, especially when the warmth would caress her exposed skin. However, she desperately wanted to feel the soft grass between her toes.

Peering around to make sure no one was watching, she unlaced her sandals and squished her toes into the ankle high blades, wiggling them happily and savoring the fur-like texture beneath her soles. She sighed. It was the first time she had felt warmth inside her heart since Marwen, and their time together had been too brief. She savored the essence of the forest floor, grounded the pads of her feet, and closed her eyes to listen to the awakening of the tree. Light gold patches pulsated beneath her feet and, as ridiculous as she felt imagining it, she sensed the surrounding nature of Lychinus was happy she was there.

Finally taking another deep breath, she opened her eyes and proceeded to walk around the haven, sandals in hand. The mushroom paths continued to glow faintly in the shadowy areas, while every once in a while, she thought she saw the faint ephemeral passing of a faery. The sound of delicate, playful laughter would appear and disappear with the slightest breeze. Wary about accidentally reaching through the veil between Lychinus and the Pale Forest, she kept all her senses open to a change in the air.

Hearing a familiar trickling of water and a soft pull in her mind, she stumbled upon another fountain tucked in a shady thicket away from the main hustle and bustle of Lychinus. The tangled, unkempt vines had conquered the delicate trellis archway opening to an intimate grove. Meandering to the seated ledge of the fountain, she dusted off some dead detritus littering the pink stone and sat down. Picking up a lovely indigo flower growing near the base, she held it to her nose and inhaled the sweet, dark scent. It was an abnormally sensual scent, one which sparked a memory in the depths of her mind. She wove the stem of the flower through her braid, tucked the petals behind her ear, and admired herself in the fountain's reflection. Startled, it made her eyes appear radiantly green.

*That's odd.* She cocked her head to the side and decided it must be the profound iridescent effects of Lychinus.

Running her finger along the smooth, pink stone, she peered up at the statue in the middle. The female figure smiled sweetly down at Mora and gave the impression she was offering her a small sapling she held delicately in her cupped hands. Tilting her head, she thought the water should be trickling from the sapling, but, shockingly, nothing was spilling over. *I heard the delicate percolating of water?* Studying the statue, the female resembled Katheryn in stone form. They had similar facial features, save for her lips and hair. Her lips were fuller, with a grin reaching her eyes. Similar to Katheryn, the two braids fell to her waist, but the rest was tied together, tumbling down in heaps of wild curls between the wings on her back.

*She must have been a nymph like Katheryn.*

The sun barely twinkled through the shadowed grove, only enough to shine onto the statue, exposing the cracks encompassing her body. Observing the intimate copse of tangled trees, the whole area appeared to be fading away from years, if not centuries, of neglect. *That's unfortunate to let such a gorgeous, serene place deteriorate,* she thought sadly. Placing her hand on a circular splotch of sunlight dancing upon the surface of the pink stone, its warmth made her feel safe and radiant. Similar to the strands of light in the tree, the heat pulsated through her veins. *What is this feeling I am experiencing? It is rejuvenating...a breath of fresh air.* She breathed in the cool, crisp morning, closed her eyes, and relaxed her shoulders.

Sliding her fingers across the top of the stone, she opened her eyes and leaned over to feel the water. The water glistened like a sheet of glass. Fidgeting with the pristine surface, she watched the ripples splash gently

## The Keeper

across the feet of the statue. Winter had not wrapped its icy blanket around Lychinus and it gave her an idea. Quickly, tossing her sandals to the ground and pulling her tight breeches to her knees, she carefully slid her bare feet into the water. The cold shocked her senses at first, but then the coolness was irrefutably welcomed.

Wiggling her toes, Mora sighed happily. The youthful feeling warmed her heart once again. However, as she began to wade through her thoughts, her happiness teetered on the precipice of the recent memories in which brought her to this very moment. The emotions and feelings toward her mother as she watched the vision unfold the night before brought tears to her eyes. *Katheryn obviously placed me in that particular memory to obtain information. But what?* The experience had felt almost tangible, similar to the encounter in Nephani's illumination and the realistic depths of her dreams. Although the vision had shown her a softer side, a more maternal memory she had long forgotten, she channeled the strong emotions of sadness and anger Meridan had grown to exhibit over the last twenty turns of her life. Her mother rarely showed signs of love and sensitivity towards her own feelings and it undeniably affected Mora's ability to accept anything different beyond her experience. She knew this much from dealing with the various creaturals and beings since leaving home.

Throughout Mora's life, Meridan would listen loosely to her words about the confinement of their home and how she desperately wanted to see beyond the heavy, encompassing forestry. The response was always the same, '*You are safe within this dwelling. There is nothing more of grandeur outside these forest walls that will not seize the opportunity to puncture every part of your being until you have bled out your soul, leaving you drained and weakened for Death.*'

She would wipe a tear off with the back of her hand before her mother saw and leave to gaze upon the mysterious woodlands.

At times, she would not see her mother emerge from her room again until the next day or the day after. However, Mora vividly remembered nights she would hear Meridan mumbling strange words into the empty, silent darkness. A scream may awaken her in the middle of the night, and she would get scolded for running into her mother's room to aid in her wakening. This had continued all her life, an emotionally draining

**229**

relationship full of unanswered questions and unfulfilled needs. Other times, the more the years melted away, she felt her mother a solidly, militaristic figure who hid her true feelings out of spite or sadistic punishment.

On night's Mora thought Meridan was sleeping soundly, she would secretly turn to the books she had covertly collected from her mother's possessions. They had been stashed away in the corner, covered in layers of neglect. A few were read in their entirety without her mother's knowledge. If she were caught, she would be scolded and reprimanded through whatever means Meridan thought necessary at the moment. Many times it was the thorough cleaning of the dwelling, others it was to clean the shit from the few animals they owned for sustenance and dispersing it into the gardens for fertilizer. This was a task she particularly loathed. However, it was the lashing that proved most heinous. During the act, Mora believed her mother's mind possessed, for she was determined to leave scars. The older she became, the higher the lashes; until one day, she held her arm firm and the leather wrapped around her forearm so taut, it nearly broke the skin to the bone. When she screamed in agony, she swore the trance slipped away from her mother's eyes and the look on her face appeared frightened. She received less lashing after that moment, but more grueling chores.

Wiggling her toes once again, the cool water pulled her back to the shadowy grove. Feeling a sting of sadness behind her eyes, she wiped away the only tear she allowed herself to shed for her mother. She could not let herself give way to the petty emotions of her youth anymore. She was almost upon her six and twentieth name day. The memories would fade with time, leaving both the visible and invisible scars, along with the numbness she had learned to endure.

Slowly pulling her feet out of the water, she sat on her knees and leaned over the pool. As the water eventually stopped waving, she gazed at her clear reflection again. She smiled to see a smiling face looking back at her without a hidden agenda. Clean and fresh from the weary journey to Lychinus, she solemnly wondered, *what will become of me after I leave this shady grove?*

A ripple disturbed the calm water, catching her off guard. The lapping grew and faded. *What caused the ripple?*

## The Keeper

Mora leaned further over the crystal surface. Watching closely, another ripple appeared and expanded, only to be smoothed away once more. She squinted harder at her reflection, but it was becoming faintly distorted by an undulating series of compact waves.

"A ripple starts small, but then begins to expand, consuming all within its path," a deep, seductive voice whispered from behind.

Alarmed, a chill vibrated down her spine as if a finger slid down each vertebrate. She sat erect. *I know that voice.* Hesitantly, she stood and turned around. Her stomach flipped violently and a heat radiated through her entire body. In the shadow of the thicket, Ekklips stood still, unwavering in His alluring stare.

On her heels, she leaned backward, bracing herself on the ledge of the pool. *How?* she thought silently.

The side of His mouth turned upward in a coy manner. "I am wherever you are. I am within you. You *are* because of me."

A lump still stuck in her throat as she tried to swallow. *You can't be here!* she wanted to cry out, but her voice was viciously lodged.

He shrugged casually, hands concealed in His pockets. "I am here because *you* want me here."

As He began to saunter toward her, her heart beat in such an untamed rhythm, she thought it would burst from her chest and splay all over His beautifully chiseled face. A snarky comment echoed in her mind, *He would like that too much.* Trying to rid the thought from her head, she glanced up to see Him only a hand width from her body.

His smile widened wickedly. *You know me well.*

She wanted to scream and not scream at the same time, a passionate battle of lust and hate constantly waging war in her mind.

Leaning down, His lips grazed her ear as He whispered, "Let me show you what else I would like."

Immediately, she closed her eyes tightly and waited. His breath brushed her throat before a shadow passed in front of her eyelids. From far away, a voice awakened her senses.

"Mora!"

Shakily, she reached a hand out in front, feeling for Ekklips' body. A cold chill blew up her arm as her fingers tingled with the softness of the...*veil?*

"Mora!" the voice yelled again, heavy footsteps running closer.

With great strength, she opened her eyes. Aghast, she looked straight into the barely visible veil between Lychinus and the Pale Forest. Frightened, she didn't realize it had been close to her the entire time. *I couldn't see it in the shadow of the forest. He can't come through the veil... can He?*

A faint snicker rumbled in her mind as a hand reached around her arm. Startled, she nearly screamed.

"Mora?"

Shocking her senses, the familiar voice finally calmed her mind and she turned around to see Bog standing there, heavily panting from running. An unsettling haze passed over his eyes, but his features remained unaltered. He smiled with a pleasant awkwardness.

Then, noticing his wound, she saw it had been treated with a clear, sticky substance she did not recognize and stitched up cleanly with red thread, causing it to appear as though laced with blood. Her eyebrows furrowed and she inquired, "I didn't notice that last night. It's red?"

He wiped his brow and looked down at his wound calmly. "The elves. They insisted I allow them to treat it before we leave. It opened again when I leapt off the branch last night to the balcony." He touched the strings and grumbled, "They walked away sniggering about how they didn't have anything *but* the color red. Shifty bastards."

Repositioning himself uncomfortably as he surveyed the shady orchard, he thought, *Something isn't right with this place.* Glancing at the statue on the fountain, he knew instantly it was the depiction of the first Queen of Lychinus, the mad, bloodthirsty Queen. Without taking his eyes off the cracks woven into her face, he added, "We must leave now."

She asked distractedly, "Leave? We must leave now?" Then, her mind drifted and she balked, "You *jumped* to the balcony? What the curse of the gods were you thinking?"

He snapped his eyes back at Mora, shuffled uneasily, and cleared his throat, "You."

She absently twisted her braid in her fingers.

After last night, he was having a hard time looking Mora in the eyes. The image of her breasts exposed from the fallen blanket filled his mind. He blushed. *Gods, I hope she can't see my face very well.* Nodding his head, he added, "Aye. We must be on our way."

A soft, lyrical voice responded, "So soon?"

Both Bog and Mora peered over to see the graceful figure of Katheryn approaching beneath the delicate tree limbs.

Mora caught sight of his apprehension grow into annoyance. *Curious,* she thought.

Without looking directly at Katheryn, he gruffly replied, "We must make haste at once. From upon your canopy, I have reason to fear there may be disturbances rising to the north in which will hinder our journey severely if we do not depart."

Discreetly, Katheryn glanced between Mora and Bog, and bowed her head. "If you must."

Mora intervened, "Must we go now? Your wound is still so fresh." The truth was she was scared of what may occur if she left the veil. *That is...if it can keep Him out.*

Bog glanced at her, uninterested in compromise. "I'm not bloody concerned with the damn wound. We do what we must. We leave at direct sun." He said the words more harshly to her than he desired, but Katheryn's presence made him tense. Annoyed, he turned and skulked away from the shady grove.

Mora was disgruntled. Tensely, she met Katheryn's eyes. "My apologies. He isn't usually so...flustered."

Katheryn grinned slyly. "If you say so," she replied and left the grove.

*That is odd.*

Silently, Mora walked around the pool before finally deciding she must get ready. She knew if Bog found her unprepared for their continued journey, he would be slightly irate. Before she left the copse, she glanced back and saw the veil flutter with an absent breeze as the subtle percolation of water commenced once again.

The sun was leisurely rising higher above the canopy. Bog had trudged back after informing Mora they would leave when the sun was high. Irritated Katheryn had shown up abruptly, it proved to him she, or at least her elves, were spying on them. *I wonder if Mora can sense how uncomfortable I am about us staying here any longer in Lychinus.*

He felt a spark of sympathy for her naivety. Wallowing emotions of hurt and apprehension filled his every breath. He knew she didn't know the extent of Katheryn's world and its extremities. If Katheryn delved deeper into who he knew Mora to be, she would be murderous in her retribution. He desperately wanted nothing more than to present her with the other side of Katheryn's perceived perfection, to let her see the festering maggots of deceit and impurity. *But after today, it's not going to matter. We'll be gone from the confines of the liminal, elvish bubble.*

Sighing, he had laid a number of maps and parchments out amongst the leaves. He had packed them in the chest at Luln Mountain, knowing he would be back for them, and tucked them away in his satchel once they departed for the Pale Forest. Luckily, Piquonese Elf scouts had found both their belongings amongst their trek in the forest and had brought them back to Lychinus. There had not been much damage, and no obvious signs of tampering as far as he could see, but he still felt nervous Katheryn had them searched. However, when he inquired as to whether they discovered his saber, he was met with vague answers and suspicious looks. The thought of loosing Aloria's saber greatly concerned him because it was made of a metal unlike any outside Loralimira. Regardless of its size, it was capable of administering more damage to its prey, especially if melted down. Although he was sincerely convinced the elves were not being truthful, his main concern was removing Mora from the confines of Lychinus.

Sitting down next to the biggest map of Atlastova, he squinted at the small writing. The original plan for his journey had faltered off course two days after he started on his quest. Contrabands had gathered on the outskirts of the Fire Country and he could not travel southwest on the congested roads due to the unexpected migration of travelers. Therefore, much to his chagrin, he had to sail down the coast on the border of Borgoria. This led him to traverse the eastern side of the Deldurian River. It ran parallel with the Nymian Sea. The Delmorians were known for their obsession with river gold. Outsiders were not allowed to touch the waters. Therefore, he had to stay close to the jagged rocks lining the shores, a feat not easily accomplished in a small boat.

There was only one time he laid eyes upon a Delmorian on the strip of land between the river and sea. It was a young male, charred skin, who was jumping around on large rocks jutting out amongst the crashing waves where the mouth of the river met the Nymian Sea. There was a distinct difference between the two bodies of water. He watched as the youngling crouched down on the edge of a rock and cupped his hands into the river. When he lifted his hands, Bog could see the water running through his fingers, twinkling in the sunlight. He lifted his head and gave Bog a nearly toothless grin as he clawed the air, his hands covered in a shimmer of gold dust. A crack of a stick made the youth's head twist unnervingly fast and Bog saw a primal hunger in the fiercely, red-orange eyes, a rival hue of the sunset. Barring his teeth, he darted along the viciously sharp rocks back to the Delmoria side of the river and disappeared into the thick underbrush of the Demurdorian Forest.

*Savages*, Bog thought to himself. He wanted to avoid returning to Delmoria at all costs.

He sighed, his mind coming back to the canopy from the soft tickle of the wind against his face. He enjoyed being away from the familiar, but it was different now because he was traveling with Mora. Regrettably, he hated thinking about their inevitable return to Borgoria. Least of all, he loathed being face to face with his father after knowing they probably already declared him dead. Bringing Mora was not going to make the encounter any better.

Gathering the maps and parchments spread around the thick leaves of the canopy, he was at least thankful he had brought them along after finding them in the under chambers of his home in Borgoria. After studying them for years, he still had not interpreted everything upon the torn and dusty pages. However, giving them one more glance before he rolled them tightly together and secured them with a leather rope, he squinted his eyes at the minuscule, fading print again. Each of the maps contained a series of foreign paragraphs he had only been able to interpret parts of, struggling to read them in their entirety.

*There* must *be something more to the words upon these surfaces,* he thought.

Finally, with each piece securely tucked away in his satchel, he started to descend from the canopy. Briefly searching for the ominous cloud, he deduced it must have been a trick of the eye, for he did not see it rise again into the jovial sky. The refuge he sought in the presence of the skies did not come as readily as he had hoped. It was as if the universe had manipulated the serenity of his mind on purpose.

Pausing, he shaded his eyes to the south and then toward the north. The sun was almost directly above the canopy. He felt a nervous twinge of regret thinking of the journey ahead, but the elements had now been set in motion, and he must follow through. Once they leave the haven of Lychinus, they will return to the premature winter air. *If we take the very northwestern veil into the Pale Forest, we can progress through the wood much quicker. That will take us to the southern most part of the Fire Country. Borgoria has allies there. Hopefully, the unrest has not migrated too much to the south.*

He heartedly descended the pathway around the trees. Strangely, he noticed a sudden chill following him down from the canopy. An inaudible whisper in the wind tickled his ears. The slight breeze felt like it was coaxing him to a divergent pathway. Curious, he decided to follow the breeze until he came to a cluster of tree fungi. Taking a step onto the first trumpet shaped mushroom, it illuminated silver. Each time he stepped on a mushroom, a hint of silver appeared. The whispers escalated until he reached the end of the mushroom cluster. Before him, the subtle breeze rustled a thick curtain of ivy. Inspecting the odd dwelling, he thought it looked like an overgrown turret. He took a long step onto the ledge of a balcony. Surveying the area around the branch for any onlookers, he ducked his head and stepped through the swaying ivy into a tiny, dimly lit room.

Dusting himself off, he stayed crouched from the low ceiling. The room was the size of a larger vestibule, but the ceiling was severely low. Even though the breeze continued to rustle the vines, it didn't help the old, stale smell that made the room stuffy. Through two, rectangular, vine covered windows, sunlight hit the walls in splotches and was projected from dozens of small, hanging objects. The whispers continued to echo around the elf room. As he carefully attempted to dodge through the hanging objects without hitting them with his wings, he realized a whisper would increase the closer he stepped to them. Focusing on a miniature,

The Keeper

reading table, he ducked lower and took a couple steps toward a clear jar resting on the top. Inside the jar, there was a multitude of ever-glowing fireflies. He picked it up hastily with a nervous gazing around the room.

*It's not enough damn light.* He paused. *I wonder if whomever was here will be back soon. I must be quick.*

Finally, he decided to softly push back a section of the ivy covering the window to allow enough sunlight to illuminate part of the room without looking too conspicuous. When the sunlight lit the room, he was amazed. There was a swarm of sparkling lights reflecting off the ceiling. Observing closer, they appeared to be hollow pipes hanging at various lengths. Each pipe had a different width. The one next to his head was the size of his forearm. It was not adorned with decoration, but small holes punctured in a circle at the top and bottom of the shaft. In the middle, there were four larger holes descending around the pipe. He peeked inside one of the holes about the size of his pinky finger. Inside the pipe, he could see hundreds of thin, wispy, silver strands. He lightly blew into the hole. Peering back in, he saw the strands quivering, creating a subtle whisper. He moved to the next pipe. It was smaller, about half the size of the first. The holes were not the same design as the first and varied in radii.

Amidst the sound of whispers, another caught his attention. A book's pages were rustling with the breeze, flapping back and forth until resting on a particular page. Cautiously trying to avoid hitting the pipes with his wings, he walked closer to the book stand. He squatted down at the tiny table. A series of sketches displaying the hollow pipes were drawn onto the right page of the book. Each had a brief note on the size and calculation of each hole and pipe. Some sketches were crudely drawn, others were immaculate and precise.

On the left page, there was an unfinished set of instructions, possibly steps on how the pipes worked. They were called Whisper Winds, used for the purpose of catching whispers on the winds and storing them into the silver strands of the pipe.

*Fascinating,* he thought and read on.

The pipes were created from fallen stars, crushed, and melted into a silver coating. The wispy strands were woven by a Seer Spider, a highly venomous arachnid barely visible to the naked eye. However, as he continued to read, it wasn't the process in which intrigued him the most, it

237

was the scribbled notes on the bottom of the page. It appeared to be an alphabet, a series of letters written in both the common tongue and a foreign tongue. A twinge of recognition made him gasp. Many of the letters were the same as the ones on his maps.

Without hesitation, or regret, he ripped the page from the book, rolled it roughly, and stuffed it in his satchel. He shut the book immediately and knocked around several hanging pipes as he hurriedly stepped to the door. Before exiting, Bog's ears perked up. He jerked his head toward the nearest pipe and yanked it from the ceiling. Securing it in his pocket, he stepped through the ivy onto the balcony. Surveying his surroundings, he hopped down on the mushroom cluster and darted back down the path before anyone took notice of his presence.

# The Whisper Winds

Anxious to be left alone any longer, Mora hastily exited the orchard and headed toward the room she woke that morning. Sitting on the end of the bed, she stared out at the busying branches. While she had felt a mixture of emotions since entering Lychinus, departing did not bring her comfort. It was one of the very first times she had felt solace since leaving home, and she was afraid she would not experience the warmth anymore once she stepped out of the veil. Bog clearly didn't trust Katheryn, but besides the unfortunate events in the vision, Katheryn had been hospitable enough toward Mora. *I don't trust her, but I also don't want to leave.* Another fear also haunted her mind. Even though the encounter in the grove made her uneasy and suspicious of Ekklips' inability to stay beyond the veil, she knew the moment they left the bustle of Lychinus, He would appear to her more frequently.

She shivered.

For a while, she watched the small Piquonese Elves come and go around her, naive to the dangers outside their liminal haven. Earlier, a little wee elfling, no more than five name days, came to gather water from a neighboring platform fountain. She was dressed in a miniature, green frock with a white apron around her waist. A long white ribbon held her golden hair away from her face. She had timidly smiled at Mora as she approached with a bucket in each hand. Then, prior to walking away, she curtsied. Mora smiled and bowed her head in return. Tickled, she watched the

*The Keeper*

elfling walk away carefully in a desperate attempt to keep the water from sloshing out of the sides of her buckets.

A female elf around her own age came through the doorway and offered her some bread and cheese. The similarities to the little elfling were striking with the white ribbon tying back her golden hair and the frock of green. Graciously, she accepted the food. *Such kind-hearted, hospitable beings.* She adored the natural rainbow of the Piquonese Elven race. They were all so different and kind, despite being a little brash under pressure. She smirked as she thought of Guilderon.

After eating the bread and cheese, she stood, wiped away the crumbs, and walked languidly over to the railing. After a moment of basking in the serenity of Lychinus, a shadow blocked out the sun from behind. Startled, she twisted around. Holding her hand against the increasing fluctuation of her chest, a flush of overwhelming relief melted through her entire body. Bog stood there quietly. Finally, allowing the relief to show, she greeted him with a half smile.

"My apologies, I did not mean to startle you...again," he spoke abrupt, but amiably. He still felt awkward around her, and that didn't taste good on his tongue.

"It's really fine. I merely did not expect anyone's company," she replied. "Anyone much larger than I, that is."

He smirked. "Aye. Well, are you ready to depart?"

She was dreading this conversation, but wielded her energy. "Why must we leave now? Can we not stay another night?" She sighed and turned back around to stare over the edge at the branches once more.

He ran a hand through his hair. Glancing back at the bed, the memory of her nakedness made him blush again. *Fuck.* Quickly turning his gaze back to Mora, he replied, "I knew you would feel as such."

A silent pause stretched uncomfortably between them. After a bit of time, he started to speak, but she interjected.

"I'm scared, Bog. I don't know if I can handle more of what has happened to me since I left home. This is the first place something completely horrible hasn't occurred, and..." she took his hand, "I have felt a little bit of serenity."

He squeezed her hand gently and flashed a sympathetic smile. He thought twice on trying to comfort her with tenderness. *It won't help her*

240

*find her strength.* Approaching the railing himself, he replied, "This is why I must show you something."

Confused, she followed him over to a shadowy area in the doorway of the platform where he could block the sight of her from wandering eyes. Kneeling to the ground, he unstrapped his satchel and glanced around before pulling out the pipe. Standing back up, he took great care holding it, making sure his hands did not cover the holes. After he had left the overgrown turret, he tested the pipe, confirming the suspicious whispers he heard while it was hanging from the ceiling. Concerned the elf in charge would notice one was missing, it gave him more urgency to depart Lychinus. Therefore, it was his only means to truly persuade Mora they were not safe while staying sedentary.

"What is that?" she raised an eyebrow and asked quietly.

"It is a Whisper Wind," he nervously responded. It was the closest he had physically been to her since he left her in bed this morning.

"A Whisper Wind?" She reached out to touch the pipe, but he shifted it away.

"Better I hold on to it for the time being." He stepped closer to her, so there was only a hand's length between their bodies.

Disgruntled, but curious, she kept her eyes fixed on the pipe.

He spoke low, "I took it from a tiny room I discovered..."

"You stole it?" she interrupted loudly.

He threw his hand over her mouth, but seeing her eyes flare as if she was about to bite him, he pulled it away quickly. Annoyed, he cleared his throat and hissed, "Aye, but that is entirely beside the point. Please hold down your voice. *She* has spies everywhere." Peering through the shadows, he whispered, "As I was saying, I took it from a tiny room I discovered while descending the pathway from the canopy. The reason I took it was because I heard something come from the pipe."

She furrowed her eyebrows. "You're accusing Katheryn of spying on us? And what do you mean you *heard* something?" It looked like a little instrument. The breeze could have easily created a lyrical sound.

Frustrated, he ignored her Katheryn comment and continued, "I heard a whisper resonate from within this pipe."

Confused, she stuttered, "The pipe *whispers* to you?"

Aggravated, he held the pipe by the string next to her ear and placed a finger to his lips.

*Nothing.*

She snickered. "I hear nothing. You are a fool, Bog. We will leave at morning light." Forcefully, she squeezed past him as a breeze wafted into her face.

"*O'curem y'teruo,*" a deep, sensual voice whispered. "We will meet again."

*Bog's voice is low, but not that low.* Mora turned around timidly. "What did you say to me?"

Irritated, he stared back into her eyes. "*I* said nothing to you."

She stepped back into the shadow and leaned closer to the hollow pipe.

"Solora," a gruff, lustful voice resonated from the pipe.

"What in the gods' bloody curse are you attempting to do, Bog?"

Her forest green eyes stared at him wildly in a mixture of fear and disbelief. He shrugged. "It is not me. It is the Whisper Wind. I have gathered, from the page I ripped from a book, it captures whispers from the air. The mechanism is quite impressive. You see…the string is made up of…" he halted when he saw her unamused face. Surveying the hollow pipe once more in his hand, he cleared his throat, "This voice, obviously a male since you thought it was me, do you recognize it?"

Apprehension settled on her features. Glimpsing from Bog to the hollow pipe, she remembered again how close Ekklips had gotten to her in the shady grove. At the time, she didn't realize how near she had been to the veil, but a shadow infiltrated her thoughts. *His words, 'we will meet again', I heard them the day in the tower with the enchanted ceiling.* The hauntingly radiant, black eyes made her chest flutter and her skin warm. Shaking her head free of His seductive presence, she told herself, *but He is the reason I'm standing here now without my mother. He penetrated my soul and has spoken to my mind, using alluringly arousing words to cajole me into His presence.*

Trying to catch her gaze, Bog's heavy voice broke the silence, "Mora? We must leave now and make for Borgoria. It is our only hope to find more answers."

The word *hope* reverberated in her head as a breeze caressed her skin, vibrating the Whisper Wind.

## The Keeper

"We will meet again," it purred.

Frenzied, she nodded her head at Bog. "I will follow."

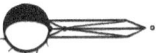

Once they stepped through the veil, the trek from Lychinus, into the Pale Forest, had began with an immediate mixture of wintry, mild winds and light snow. Holding out her palm, she watched in youthful joy as beautifully carved snowflakes fell delicately onto her heated flesh and melted.

Before leaving, Bog told her they would make it to the outskirts of the forest by night fall and the bitter temperatures would gradually warm. Relieved, but still weary from the heavy emotions she had experienced with their departure, it would be foolish to wait for Ekklips to find her sedentary. Bog had made it very clear to her after she heard the whispers. Also, he informed her, once they left the border of Lychinus, it would be too dangerous to stop before they reached the edge of the wood. He mentioned dark forces were growing steadily after their attack and they had to take every precaution to avoid staying stationary for terribly long. Persistent they should leave without announcing, he tried to encourage her to not draw unwanted attention from the Piquonese Elves...*or Katheryn.*

"I can't do that, Bog," she had replied in exasperation.

He had been frustrated with her decision. She saw it flash in his sullen, violet eyes. Although, regardless of his suggestion, Katheryn found them anyway. She had come to give her regrets about their decision to depart and wanted to offer a parting gift to Mora. She presented her with a dagger, and she graciously accepted the well-intentioned weapon. It was fine in its craftsmanship, the details severely intricate. The hilt was a thin tree trunk, the length fitting her hand perfectly. The miniature pommel was knotted in a duel-sided symbol of interwoven branches. The roots expanded as tiny guards and also faded into the smooth silver of the blade. Upon closer inspection, emerging from the roots, was an engraved figure of a serpent, its head stretching painfully close to the sharp tip.

When she noticed this, she hesitantly glimpsed at Katheryn, unsure of the meaning. The serpent reminded her of the one which convinced her mother, without hesitation, to drag Mora from their home.

Katheryn smiled in her sweetly sly manner, placed her hands on Mora's shoulders, and leaned her lips closer to her ear. "May you always know the strength of the serpent."

Bog aggressively shuffled in her peripheral. He was standing the furthest away from Katheryn. Clearing his throat with his back turned, he attempted to push the anger down and grumbled, "Mora, we must leave *now*."

They departed hastily.

Stoically watching Bog and Mora walk through the veil, Katheryn turned her golden eyes to the nearest elf and coldly commanded, "Bring me the saber."

Fortunate the Pale Forest remained unnervingly quiet, Mora trudged heavily behind Bog's keen awareness. Finally, a warm breeze hit her face as they gradually came upon the edge of the forest. The snow was thinning under her leathery soles. She was glad she wore her boots when they left Lychinus; however, she now wanted to change into the sandals Katheryn had given her this morning. It began to look green again, like the forest around her sanctuary. A twinge of sorrow tugged in her chest as she remembered a time period of ancient, longed for happiness, but it faded rapidly beneath her hardening feelings. She decided to reach for simple pleasures to help rejuvenate her soul. The closer they walked to the edge, the more she could hear water joyfully trickling in a nearby stream and birds beginning to chatter in the treetops.

The line of life was like night and day between the border of the Pale Forest and the mossy bed of green beneath her feet. The coldness was fading rapidly. Her bones were no longer being penetrated by the icy air of the forest. As she thawed, the brief, painful pricks of cold gave way to a rush of welcomed warmth. She took a deep breath. It was heavily satisfying in her lungs. Stopping to remove her thick, fur cloak, she unlaced the top of her wool frock and let it drape open over her shift.

Bog stretched his back, popped his spine, and shielded his eyes to the setting sun. The tiny bits of ice on his feathers were thawing into beads of water droplets and running down his wings. It created an illusion of glistening, melting diamonds. After rustling his wings, he shivered before walking over to a stone a few footsteps away to sit down.

Mora followed to the stone across from Bog, sighing as she felt the weight lifting from the burden of her bruised and callused feet. "Why is the contrast of weather so stark when we crossed the tree line?"

"We have reached the Territory of Abin, in the Fire Country." He gazed steadily in her direction.

She tried to reflect on the maps she had seen at home, but couldn't recall every detail of the land borders. "Who is Abin?"

"Abin is the ruler of the Coutarians and sits at the head of the Coutarian Council. He knows of everything entering and departing his country. He will already be aware of our arrival." Picking up a few, small sticks within arms length, he absently cracked them in half, creating a pile between his feet.

She felt the soft hairs on her arms rise. "Everything?"

Barely glancing at Mora, he responded mildly, "It's old magic. Nevertheless, Abin is an ally of the House of Gornya. There should be nothing to fear. However, in these uncertain times, one should always keep their guard up."

She watched him straighten his back and smirked. "You're going to tell me a story, aren't you?"

Slightly annoyed, he cleared his throat. "Long ago, the Coutarians battled the Vitarians, the giants of Vitar, in the northwest of the Fire Country. The Vitarians are a fierce clan, currently led by an assassin of unyielding power. He is called Didac. Didac was not originally of the Vitarian clan. Speculation has changed about the origins and purpose for his sudden appearance in the lands, but no one knows from whence he came, only that he challenged the head of the ruling family of Va." Standing from the stone seat, he began collecting bigger sticks from around the area, talking while he worked.

## The Keeper

"Vitarians never back down from a challenge. However, they knew not of what power Didac possessed. With the entire clan of Vitarians watching, a battle to the death took place outside the fortress walls. Legend has it, the most vital and youthful of the family of Va was the anointed warrior, Virtoc. Virtoc towered above the wretched creatural, Didac, by at least two body lengths. They commenced to dance around each other, Virtoc with a mallet, Didac seemingly unarmed. As he snarled through the side of his grotesquely shaped mouth, Didac simply snickered, staring straight through the giant's flesh with fierce, crystal blue eyes.

"Virtoc delivered the first blow, swinging his mallet with head-splitting force. However, he was countered by an invisible shield in which eventually splintered his mallet after several continual blows. Didac moved with such agility around the arena Virtoc could hardly focus on his whereabouts before striking over and over again."

Mora sat entranced with his story. *His knowledge of this world is really quite fascinating. If only he would open up more about where he came from.*

"Virtoc's frustration turned furious. He started to linger around his target, choking horribly on his breath, huffing and puffing profusely as his fury grew exponentially. Didac, not seemingly weary, continued to dance his circular motion around the giant, taunting him with his gaze and whispering words unspoken by any mortal tongue. His lean shadow appeared to loom over the giant whenever it blocked the sunlight, spreading across the multitude of onlookers."

Bog shuddered, dropping a few, large pieces of wood next to the stone. He wiped his hands off on his breeches and crouched down next to the pile of wood, angling the sticks into a pyramid. "Tongues whisper what came next was horrific to look upon. They say Didac's shadow came to life, building higher above the ground until it was larger than Virtoc. The giant became horror struck and too stunned to move. The black figure had Didac's sapphire eyes, and when it opened its mouth, the black lips would stretch from top to bottom like the bars of a cell.

"It wailed loudly, causing the giants to shake their heads in madness, trying to cover their ears. Virtoc unfroze at the sound, took out his axe, and with all his might, swung at Didac's shadow, only to be foiled by a useless slice through thin air. The shadow wailed once more, and in all its fierceness, tunneled into Virtoc's mouth, nose, and ears in the form of a black cloud. The arena hushed in complete silence. Then, aghast, Virtoc looked toward Didac, whose smirk was plastered on his ghostly face. He whispered one word and Virtoc's giant body started to implode, his ghastly screams reverberating through the arena, each giant too afraid to move." He moved nervously, pulling a piece of flint from his pocket.

"Implode?" She gawked, disgusted.

Without looking at her, he nodded his head. After a few moments, he blew on the subtly growing flames in the pyramid, his face illuminating subtly with the fire. "What happened next was unspeakable. Those who have passed the story down about the meeting between the giant and the immortal being, Didac, tell only one story, and none have ever spoken of what happened when the giant's body imploded. I still have yet to find out. However, Didac has not died, and rules the land of the Vitarians with a bloodthirsty fierceness. Many have tried to escape Vitar, but only one giant has been successful in crossing the floating sea. Virtoc's youngest brother, Veridian. You see, giants live extensively longer lives than most mortal creaturals. Veridian had endured years and years of hardship under the rule of Didac. His mother killed herself after seeing Virtoc implode and her husband dismembered. Because his father was mutilated attempting to fight back following the implosion, eight of his brothers were also executed after their attempts to escape.

"Veridian was the only brother left. When he traveled to the southern land of the Fire Country, he pleaded his life. At the mercy of Abin's greatest grandfather, he was allowed to enter the fortress on the Coutarian's terms. Since then, the Coutarians have had to fight the Vitarians only once before a disturbance tore the floating sea further apart. The heart of the Fire Country now holds its guard tightly against any outsiders who they feel would harm their kind. The further we go into the country, the more dangerous it will be to keep peace with various inhabitants. They know my kind, but they know nothing of you. This is why we must reach Abin."

Mora stared silently. The story had been horribly tragic. It made her stomach churn at the thought of Didac's wrath upon the giant race. However, before she could ask questions, she saw Bog pause and a coldness resonated in his tone.

### The Keeper

"I'll be back," he murmured gruffly and walked past the light of the fire toward the sliver of yellow on the horizon.

A chill crawled up her skin and there was a darkness hovering like a low-lying cloud around the air. She could not tell if his pain and agony was a result of the story, or if it triggered the remembrance of a memory. Either way, his naturally warm façade had drained from his presence. She watched the flames of the fire thrusting through the wood. *He's the only one I can trust though.*

Disgruntled, Bog walked away from the fire. He needed to clear his head of images beginning to surface. He could feel the bubbles of unsettling depictions he had locked away and hidden deeply in an expanding abyss through the years, banging incessantly against his memories. Crossing his arms, their entry into the Fire Country made him feel restless, unsure of the journey he had chosen for himself.

*I've been away from home so godsdamn long, I don't know how ready I am to return.*

He stared longingly into the indigo blanket falling over the last strip of light on the horizon. Perilous feats through treacherous lands, coupled with ghastly enemies, awaited their arrival. Sighing, he rubbed his face roughly. *Mora hasn't shown any more extraordinary power than any plain, young female I've run across in Borgoria. I don't know if she will be able to evolve into who I believe her to be in the end. And then...what if I'm wrong?* Angrily shaking his head, he knew he was being tempted by failure. He had known it well throughout his life. His father had never been proud of him, only allowing and encouraging the journey because he wanted to rid the House of Bog's presence. Every one had mocked his endless research, his startling revelation, and his search for the possibility of aiding the restoration of balance to All. This would require him to seek Dark as well. *Unfortunately, I haven't even been able to convince Mora. I feel utterly...alone.*

Discontented, he sat down on the grass with one arm resting on his knee. He grabbed his hair harshly between his fingers and groaned as

**248**

the image of his father reared violently in his thoughts. Gornya was a terrible father, beating him for his inability to keep up with the *other.* Bog hated the lessons he was forced to participate to become a warrior. Humiliated and mocked, it would only fuel the rage festering inside. When it came time to combat for the title of Vanquisher, Supreme Annihilator of Gornya's prized military, he had declined on the grounds he didn't want to be a pawn for his father anymore. His punishment had been severe and shuddered thinking about how painful it had been.

A silent anger bubbled under the surface of his skin. *I am nothing but a fucking waste of space to him.*

Then, he gritted his teeth as an image of his mother's smile surfaced. Her fair hair would flow magnificently in the wind as she stood on the portico of the House. He choked back the stinging sensation of tears behind his eyes. Outstretching her arms to a little Bog, he would run exuberantly to her skirts. However, as she called out his name, he would see his father enter, astute and proud, purposely blocking the pathway. He would shove him away and turn to face her distressed form. Staggering to his feet, Bog would run crying behind the bushes. Growling, Gornya would command her to see reason, attempting to convince her Bog was weak minded, unworthy of being a warrior, and would taint the Borgorian name, just like his tainted wings.

With red and swollen eyes, Bog would shakily touch his wings with his small hands. They had always, and would forever be, his greatest burden.

Solemnly, but strongly, his mother would dismiss his claims, attempting to step around his dominating figure. This would enrage Gornya, causing him to jerk her by the wrists and hit her across the face. Although Gornya was abusive, Bog never saw her cry. He found pleasure in her refusal to fight back, and many times would repeatedly strike until he drew blood. To exert his sadistic power even further, Gornya would hold her firmly by the jaw, smearing the blood with his thumb and kiss her mouth. Then, sneering in Bog's direction, he would force her toward the bedchamber.

One night, when Bog had run frightened to her chambers, he paused when he saw a thin, sliver of light shining from the doorway. Creeping silently toward the door, he peeked inside. The heavy breathing from his father echoed from the large, naked lump of flesh on the bed. His mother was sitting on her knees with her back toward the door, the silhouette of her grand wings refracting the firelight. A small, silver bowl lay in front of her knees. He watched her blow gently on a feather and place it into the bowl. A thin wisp of smoke would swirl from the burning feather as she began to mumble an enchanting slur of words Bog could never comprehend. Picking up the bowl, she inhaled deeply.

After some time, the smoke slowly burned down and sashayed passed the rustling curtains and through the open window. Peering through the dark, Bog gasped quietly at the sight of her glowing, violet eyes, swollen and rimmed with bruising. She always knew when he was around and smiled sweetly toward the door where she knew he was watching. Putting a finger to her lips, she blew a kiss in his direction and silently crept back into bed. He never realized what had made her eyes glow until many years after she died.

Anger arose in his core. Under the craze and loathing for Bog, Gornya repeatedly raped and abused his mother, many times forcing him to watch. Holding back the tears again, he wished he had been strong enough to save her, but he had merely been a borgling. As he got older, he vowed he would never show weakness in his father's presence, and he wouldn't do it when he arrived with Mora. He sought vengeance in his mother's memory, even if it included his father. Although he didn't want to revert to violence, he wanted to prove his father wrong.

*I must get Mora to Borgoria.*

He knew it was only a matter of time before Dark's sway would embrace Mora. The meaning of Life was weakening, Light was fading fast, and Dark was embracing the growing shadows, giving rise to the power of Death. The lack of balance was a clandestine, ever-expanding scourge upon the land. Immortality, once bestowed with great honor, was becoming an over-duration of cruelty and mangled wickedness. It was defiling All of the quintessential core, desecrating the harmony of Life's balance between Light and Dark. *However, if she really is who I thinks she is, it will leave her with a life-altering choice that can go horribly wrong.*

A breeze rustled the feathers on his wings. Standing, he thrust his hands into his deep pockets. His emotions had gradually consumed him ever since the day his mother died. It was the fateful day his shield fell away, leaving him exposed to the ruthless hand of his father. His slight, but present, yearning to return to Borgoria was not from the simple pleasure of watching his father growl at his successful return, but to feel surrounded by his mother's spirit, and that of her kind, once again.

He looked at the skies as a shooting star sped rapidly across the darkening, indigo sky. He knew he must return to Mora calm and collected as she would be curious to why he walked away silently. However, he had no desire to expose his deepest emotions to anyone, especially Mora. The burden was solely his to bear. Stretching, he curved his back until it popped. He wanted desperately to feel like he could protect her from harm, but inside, he knew it was a dangerous route he would try to avoid at all costs. He would not be able to control his rage if he ever allowed it to completely control his mind.

Mora saw Bog approaching from the edge of the shadows. He knelt down to the fire and added a few more twigs and sticks, poking around to make the flames grow bigger and warmer. Grabbing his satchel, he rummaged through until he found the clear liquid Guilderon had so happily refilled for them before they left the veil, claiming it was for *medicinal purposes*, while grinning slyly. He took a swig before holding it at arm's length toward where she sat. Reluctantly, she shook her head, the thought of last night still churned her stomach.

He chuckled, "I wanted to see if you would pour a bit on my wound?"

Shocked at his genuine, dimpled grin, she smirked. "Of course." Grabbing the flask, she stood and stepped closer to his shoulder. "Which way do we go from here?"

Bog cursed and winced as the cold liquid sizzled onto his skin. "We will settle here for the night, next to the fire. I'll stand guard until I know it's safe. I don't know what living things have sensed our presence around here besides Abin. Hopefully, all will remain uneventful through the night."

She dabbed the liquid running down his arm with a torn piece of cloth. "You don't need to stand guard by yourself. I know you are exhausted from the past several days, too."

Taking another large gulp before placing the cork back on the flask, he lifted his eyes toward her and jeeringly said, "It's fine. I *know* you didn't get the most restful sleep last night."

Giving him an irritated look, she guffawed, "What do you mean by that?"

A deep, soft laugh emerged from his throat. "Let's just say you were quite the center of attention last night, Sunshine." He crossed his hands behind his head and leaned back on a jutting stone, his piercing, violet eyes reflecting brightly in the fire.

*Sunshine.* She blushed.

# The Floating Fortress

The back of Mora's eyelids were becoming a bright orange with the rising sunlight. Fluttering her eyes, trying to ward off anymore sleep, she saw the feathers of Bog's grand wings lightly flapping in the wind. His body was lying no more than an arm's length away from her own, his arms crossed on his chest, and his breathing heavy.

*Some guard he is,* she thought and rolled her eyes.

However, the way he positioned his wing was similar to how he had done when they were in the Pale Forest, semi-concealing her between his body and a stone. Stretching her arms down by her side, she rolled closer to the stone before stumbling to her feet. She wanted to take care of herself before he awoke. Therefore, grabbing her knapsack, she discreetly traipsed over to a nearby tree.

Everything was so much greener as far as the eye could see. Butterflies and birds rustled and flew around, the dewy grass twinkled beneath her toes, and the air was crisp and warm. Shielding her eyes, she saw several clusters of trees and stones scattered across the sweeping field. Closer to the horizon, the stone outcrops seemed to multiply and small clouds floated, appearing black against the brilliant hues of the sunrise. Otherwise, the land was extremely flat.

Before she pulled her garments over her head, she peeked around to see Bog still lying motionless on the ground. Hastily, she untied her belt, grasped the bottom of her frock and shift, and vigorously pulled them both over her head. Deciding to leave the tight breeches on to make it easier to move quickly, she retrieved the blood red, linen tunic Katheryn had the elves bring when they cleaned her clothing. She was thankful for the extra garments, even cleaning her mother's old frock. Eyeing the length of the tunic, and already feeling it may become humid throughout the day, she rummaged through her knapsack, pulled out the dagger Katheryn had gifted her, and decided she would cut it shorter. It didn't take much force. The dagger was exceptionally sharp. Smoothing the bottom down, she pulled it over her head. Then, she looped a circle in her belt and hooked the sheath before tying it at her waist. Satisfied, she placed the dagger in its leather skin.

*It will hold for now...I hope.*

Tucking the loose curls from her re-braided hair behind her ears, she threw the extra material into her knapsack and tossed all the soiled clothes on top. Walking around the tree, she paused abruptly to see Bog sitting against a stone, nibbling on some bread. She blushed. *Gods, I hope he couldn't see me.*

He smiled widely. "Good morning, Sunshine." He gracefully pulled himself to his feet and stepped passed her while grinning widely. Leaning over as he passed, he whispered, "I like the new look."

She closed her eyes tightly in embarrassment. She knew her face was as red as her tunic. Huffing over to the stones, she sat down to lace the sandals onto her feet.

"There is bread on my satchel," he shouted from behind the tree after relieving himself. Surveying the land, he could see the area on the horizon they needed to arrive by midday. *Then, it gets fucking complicated.* He grunted, tussled a hand through his curly hair, and walked back to Mora.

Flustered, she said, "I thought you said you would stand guard?"

Lacing his boots back onto his feet, he glimpsed at her from beneath his eyelashes. "I said I would stand guard *until* I knew it was safe."

Grimacing in his direction, she pulled her sack over her shoulder and stood up again. "A bit of trivial bullshit," she murmured.

He lifted his head, grinning in his annoyingly dimpled manner, and replied, "And yet, you're still alive." Rising to his feet, he scuffed the leftover fire with his boot.

"You're so annoying when you smile like that," she retorted.

Feigning hurt, he heartily replied, "Oi, I know you don't mean that." He nudged her shoulder with his arm. "By the way," he snorted and tugged lightly on the sheath of her dagger, "I'll make you something to better hold your dagger, Sunshine."

She elbowed him in the ribs and he pretended to keel over. "You're a fucking ass." Cutting a sharp glare, she added, "And oddly in a good mood."

He shrugged. "I've got good company."

He stood achingly close to her, she could see his chest rise and fall in front of her face, feel the warmth of his skin, and smell the slight tinge of salt and sandalwood on his flesh. It was overwhelming. She could sense her cheeks getting red. Turning her head, she changed the subject. "So, why do you loathe Katheryn?"

*Damn.* Choking back the shock of her inquiry, he threw his satchel over his shoulder and moved away toward the open, flat, green field. "We should be able to make it to the horizon line you see over there," pointing over her head, "by midday."

She shrugged her shoulders and began walking in the direction he pointed. Taunting him further, she gleamed back in his direction. "Sore subject, eh?"

"I'd rather not discuss it," he replied gruffly as he followed behind. "But you sure know how to kill a good time."

Ignoring the jilt, she peered over her shoulder again and asked, "It's obvious you two were lovers, right?"

"Fuck, no!" the answer was so immediate he cursed himself. He paused. "She…she's not who you think she is."

"How would I know? The only moment she gave me the creeps is when she infiltrated my memories. Other than that, she was exceptionally kind."

He grunted. "That's more fucked up and insane enough to me."

"You still haven't answered my question." She plucked a long grass, slowed her pace, and pestered him with it.

Dodging the annoying grass with his arms, he nearly yanked it from her grip. "It's none of your damn business," he replied angrily.

"Ouch. I hit a nerve." She tossed the grass away.

His shoulders sagged. "Katheryn wants what most rulers want... power." He began feeling extremely uncomfortable. *And the last thing I want is to blatantly admit I slept with her.* However, he figured she had already come to the conclusion anyway. "She...used me for information about *you*."

Mora whipped around. "*Me?*"

He nearly ran into her petite frame. Staring down into her forest green eyes, he saw a hint of madness flicker.

"Why in the curse of the gods does she want to know more about *me?*"

Slightly annoyed by the question since he had already tirelessly attempted on a few occasions to convince her of what he believed to be her origins, he pushed a curl away from her forehead. *Gods. Why did I do that?* Nervously, he moved to the side and continued walking. "We have already established this answer. This is why I am taking you to Borgoria."

Stunned, she pirouetted and ran to Bog's side. "You're a bloody oaf when it comes to *relevant* information."

"I'm going to ignore the jab. I've told you enough of who I think you are to suffice until we arrive in Borgoria." Flustered, he started to hit the stalks of grass with his hand as he walked.

Disgruntled and unsatisfied, she changed the subject yet again. "What happened the night I found Guilderon?"

He was amused by the offhanded question and cut his eyes at Mora. "I don't think you want to *actually* know that bit of information."

"I do!" she gasped. "I didn't even know you were there."

He smirked. "I wasn't...at first."

She stopped. "What do you mean by that?"

Gesturing for her to continue walking, he replied, "Apparently, you kept screaming at the barkeep to give you more drinks. Guilderon's brothers decided it had been enough for you, and you...didn't agree."

She cut him off, "Wait. Milderon and Don are fine? Katheryn had said Guilderon was the one to summon you."

*Of course Katheryn would be the one to speak about the incident first.* He nodded. "They were there to monitor Guilderon. They didn't realize you were encouraging his...tendencies." He laughed quietly. "Therefore, they went looking for me. Luckily, I had been skulking about the branches searching for a place to sleep when I heard them yelling my name."

"Creepy," she whispered.

He lifted his hands in confusion. "I've been nearly fatally wounded by one of Death's arrows and you accuse me of being *creepy*? Damn. That is harsh. Anyway, they called me to help you to your chambers."

Reluctantly, she said, "And I went...willingly?" There was an unnerving silence before he spoke again.

"Well...uh...nay." He cut his eyes at her and replied, "I had to carry you, Sunshine."

*Sunshine*. The word echoed in her memory. However, she was too appalled to inquire about the new sentiment presently. "Carried me?"

"Yes. *Carried*," he emphasized.

A heat rose violently in her blood. "You *bloody* carried me?"

Without looking at her, he laughed and retorted, "We have already established this. Aye. *Carr-ied*."

Shaking her head, Mora gasped. The way he emphasized 'carried' made her seethe.

"If it makes you feel any better, it wasn't very long."

"That does *not* make me feel better!"

He shrugged and eyed the horizon. "We are making very good time."

She chose not to respond to his observation. Humiliated and shocked, she didn't know what else to say.

After several, long stretches of silence, Bog started, "The key..."

Without looking at him, she peered out of her peripheral. "What about the key?"

"Is is heavy?"

Thinking it was a strange question, she held the chain and placed the key in her palm. "Nay, it is actually very light," she said bouncing her hand up and down.

He cleared his throat. "That's not exactly what I meant."

Anxiously, she stopped, shielded her eyes from the sun, and looked at his figure as he turned around, blocking the light. She put her hand down. "I suppose it is burdensome. It weighs heavy on my conscience with responsibility." She tucked it back beneath her tunic, shrugged her shoulders, and started walking again. "It feels exceptionally vital, but I do not know exactly what its purpose is for."

"Nephani did not specify?" It was the first time he acknowledged her apparition aloud. The name felt strange and foreign on his tongue.

"It only alluded to its sacredness. In the wrong hands, it could be used as a weapon to destroy All."

Nodding, he furrowed his brows and contemplated on her words as they trudged further across the fields.

Once the sun stood a bit past midday, they reached the rocks Mora had seen on the horizon line. There was a low-lying haziness beginning to grow over the terrain. However, as they approached, she realized it had not been clouds she had seen floating above the horizon. They were big, flat stones. Even though the number became obscured by the growing thickness of mist, she realized they were numerous and...*floating?*

Bog trudged to her side and said, "These are the Staggering Stones. They lead to the gates of the Floating Fortress." Pointing to a vast terrain of unstable rocks, he could see the subtle, black mass of the castle looming beyond the stones.

"How are we supposed to cross them?" she inquired. Although she could not see much in front of her face, there was a low, monotonous drone of heavy movement and the occasional scrap of stone against stone. She shifted uncomfortably away from the first platform.

"With great care." He nodded toward the stones. "I have been trained to know which rocks to advance on and which will give way to the perils below." Kneeling down on the side of the cliff, he pushed an unsteady stone, knocking it against the next. They hummed in the wind. Peering over the ledge, he saw thick, slate-colored clouds covering the abyss below. An uneasy feeling pricked his skin. The clouds seemed unusually active today, moving in a slight, circular motion around the edge of the cliff as the wind had commenced to blow harder.

As a youth, he remembered seeing the vicious clouds give way to the terrifying, endless pit of black below. Occasionally, as borglings, Gornya would order his sons to accompany him during his military training. Prisoners of Borgoria would be taken to be released onto the Staggering Stones, thinking they were free. It became a sick game to the warriors, eventually making bets on how long it would take, or which stone would give way first. Eventually, all plummeted to their death.

His stomach churned at the very memories. Dreams had haunted him for years as a youth, dreams of falling and never waking, dreams of darkness and death. His mother would come to his chambers as he screamed to calm him down and wipe away his tears. His father would always be looming in the shadows beyond the doorway with a disgusted look plastered on his face. Snidely, he would eventually walk away from the door, slamming it in its wake.

Straightening back up, he quickly spoke, "We must make haste. I don't believe the weather will lighten as we move further. Something feels amiss." Holding his breath, he took a step onto the first rock. When the rock stayed still, he let out a sigh. Turning toward Mora, he held out his hand.

She hesitated, sensing he was nervous. However, the unspoken urgency in his eyes was alarming. Therefore, after a moment, she inhaled and grabbed his hand, squeezing hard. The stone was stable enough; but the idea they were standing on a stone platform which, if it gave way, could send them falling to their deaths, made her feel sick.

He could feel her pulse beating violently through her veins as he held her wrist firmly. When he started to let go of her hand, he felt her attempt to grasp onto him tighter. He gave her a reassuring squeeze and leapt to a rock diagonal from the one they were standing. His heart fluttered as another rock bumped against it, making the stone tremble beneath his feet. Finally, he gestured toward Mora. She leapt into his arms. For several more stones, accelerating the pace, he jumped and she leapt behind him, one by one.

Steadying himself, he stood and felt the wind on his face. *It has become stronger.* He could smell the hint of rain settling in the air. A small rumble of thunder echoed in the distance beneath. Sensing the subtle changes within the air, he cautiously peered through the crack of the adjoining rock. Although the haze was rapidly thickening, he could still see the length left between them and the fortress. He jumped again, kneeling against the stone. When she leapt, she landed with a jolt against his back. He supported her carefully, but watched as the clouds began to swirl at a faster pace.

## The Keeper

His heart beat hastened. "Quickly!"

He leapt again, turned, and reached out to her as the wind whipped through their hair. When she grabbed his hand, he lifted her from the stone as it fell beneath her feet. She screamed until he clutched her close to his chest. Against his exposed flesh, the heat of her body was nearly overwhelming.

"What in the curse of the gods is happening?!"

Fervently, he shook his head and yelled, "I am unsure! The winds are changing, and not for the better. I have not seen such before. We must keep moving, or be swallowed by the encroaching storm!"

Reluctant to release her fully, he kept a firm grasp on her hand as he rapidly leapt onto another stone. She kept up with his pace as they awkwardly jumped stone to stone. With wicked intent, a bolt of lightning flashed from beneath the Staggering Stones, illuminating mysterious shadows. Glancing around for assurance of their progression, he could see the outline of the Floating Fortress becoming clearer.

"We are nearly there!" he yelled back into the wind.

All of a sudden, a burst knocked Mora off her feet, her hand jerking out of Bog's grasp, and her body flung toward the edge of the stone. When she landed hard on the opposite side of the unyielding surface, it knocked the breath from her lungs. As her arms flung over her head, the back of her hand struck the adjoining rock, sending it plummeting out of sight. Immediately, their stone began to tip, causing her to slide closer to edge.

"Bog!" she screamed, desperately looking for something to grab to slow the slide.

Seizing the rising edge of the Staggering Stone with one hand, Bog attempted to stabilize the ridge, digging his fingers in fiercely. As the stone slowed down its tilt, Mora twisted her body and scrambled to reach out toward his free hand. Outstretching as far as his arms would span, he felt her fingertips scrape against his own. He immediately curled his strong fingers around hers as she gripped onto his wrist with her other hand.

The swirling clouds were visible beneath the tilt of the rock, but the terror in her eyes sent a protective surge through his being. Despite the excruciating tension in his wounded shoulder, he pulled her arm firmly. The rock began to wobble unsteadily as their bodies shifted the center of balance. With all his might, every muscle tightening and every vein pulsating, he yelled and yanked her arm, catching her against his body. She held his waist with all her strength as her breathing wildly fluctuated.

As though the wind was angry it did not prevail, it increased its violent churning. Before Bog could speak to Mora, the rock shook from the blunt force of the air whipping against the side. Without hesitation, he grabbed her by the waist and flung her screaming to the next rock. She landed hard, but scrambled up quickly before he jumped. Once his feet left the rock, it collapsed into the torrential mouth below, swallowed by the merciless abyss.

Landing in a crouched position, he yelled, "Keep close!" Sprinting forward, he started jumping frantically from rock to rock, occasionally glancing back to see Mora.

Reaching the last rock, he paused, grabbed her arm, and leapt forcefully onto a thin turf of grass in front of the Floating Fortress. Heaving, he glanced back at the Staggering Stones. The skies had turned an ominous crimson with flashes of greens and purples. The clouds below twisted maliciously, illuminated by brief streaks of angry lightning. A deep gurgle of thunder shook the ground.

"The Staggering Stones are restless," he said darkly. Turning back around, he surveyed the impending sight.

The Floating Fortress was enormous. It was purely a stone stronghold, seemingly impenetrable from every side. The gatehouse was wide, surrounded by a large, stone wall which seemingly stretched around the entire island. Falling from the rectangular hole in the bottom side of the gatehouse was a mighty wall of water, raging as it fell into the endless abyss below.

Mora carefully peered over the edge, watching the water feeding into the growing vortex of clouds. "Where does the water go? Are we at the end of the world?"

"Nay," Bog coughed. "Beneath us is a hole in the land created by a great disturbance eons ago when the Fire Country was in its prime. Apparently, it was a punishment to the ancestors. They were the predecessors to Abin's lineage. Angry, Life exiled the clan to this desolate land."

"What did they do?" she inquired.

He shrugged. "The reasons have been lost throughout time to outsiders. If Abin is amicable to you, he may be able to inform you of why. However, I know the clan had to learn how to manipulate the strong forces holding the fortress in place in order to gain access to the mainland of the Fire Country. This is how the Staggering Stones were created. They are levitating by the same, elemental magic supporting the fortress." Holding a hand above his eyes, he looked over the Staggering Stones and muttered, "However, it all appears to be growing disturbingly weaker." Aware of the fickleness of magic and the waning power it possessed, the concept it appeared to be lessening through multiple facets of its existence was highly concerning. He wondered how it would affect his own ability to perform simple magic with his feathers.

Observing the walls of the fortress, she fondled her braid nervously. "There seems to be no door." Knocking on the stone, she could feel the solidity firm beneath her knuckles.

"That is because they hide it from all trespassers, ally and enemy alike," he blatantly responded.

"How can they have enemies? Their opponents would stand no chance by crossing the Staggering Stones in the first place." She peered back at the floating sea of rocks. "And if they did make it, the army would be so staggered themselves, there would not be a proper charge. What would they do? Knock and ask to set up inside before attacking?" She snickered at the thought and glanced at Bog.

Unamused, he replied derisively, "There are other ways to cross without using the Staggering Stones. That is, if you can acquire such."

Curiously, she stared. Then, recognition dawned across her face. Her eyes lit up as she stuttered, "You mean by…flying?"

He smirked.

"Can *you* fly?" she balked.

"If I could fly right now, do you think I would have put our lives in imminent danger by crossing the Staggering Stones by foot?" He rustled his wings. "Ever since the force knocked me from the tree, my wings have been useless. It got worse with the arrow wound. I even attempted when I leapt off the balcony in Lychinus. They merely caught the wind enough to increase the distance of the jump." He touched the feathers on the bottom of the right wing. "It's really quite annoying. Not that I used them often anyway. I've always despised having them. Regardless, I would rather not have them if I can't use them."

She was speechless. It was more information he had ever given her about him personally, and it wasn't even much. "I apologize."

Taken aback, he looked sideways at her and laughed, "Why?"

"I take full responsibility for the arrow wound."

He placed a hand on her shoulder and meet her gaze. "I'm glad it was me and not you." Then, he grinned fully. "But it *definitely* was your fault."

She gasped.

This time, he dodged her elbow. "Calm down. You need to smile more, Sunshine. It suits you."

"When you make ass remarks like that, it's hard." Despite her frustration, she smirked a little.

Anxiously, he ran a hand through his hair and turned back toward the stone wall.

Standing in front of the gatehouse, Mora turned her head toward the tallest bastion on the wall of the Floating Fortress. A flash of lightning illuminated the stones in an eerie, glistening, grayish black, causing them look like they were melting. However, a figure caught her eye. There was a creatural watching them from one of the lower ledges. He was crouched with a tall bow in his hand, appearing to glow even after the lightning faded. When another crash of lightning lit his face again, she saw a stern, expressionless gaze with a distinguishable scar on the right side of his forehead, cutting through his eyebrow. His shoulder length hair was dark and wavy, glistening with specks of rain. However, his lustrous, blue eyes were the most striking feature of all, almost appearing white. With an unyielding fierceness, he stared straight into her own eyes. As though an apparition, when the sky brightened again, he was gone.

"Bog?" She hesitantly tapped his wing.

"What?" he replied feeling the stones.

She pointed to where the figure had crouched and was about to speak when a horn sounded from deep inside the fortress.

The stone started to quake and excess rock fell from the cracks in the stronghold walls. From halfway up the wall, a molten substance began to carve a thin line eloquently through the stone. It commenced to form three, large spirals, each connected by an expanding line of fire. As the flames carved its way into the center of each spiral, a heavy click followed. Within the three, conjoined points of spirals, were nine, smaller spirals as well as a master spiral in the middle. The master spiral protruded a little more every time a spiral would click. After the twelfth click, in the middle of the master spiral, a stone opened like an eyelid, revealing an eye of flames.

Bog leaned toward Mora and whispered, "The smaller spirals symbolize the generations of the Abin family. They have unusually longer lives than most mortal clans. The symbols read from right to left, starting at the very top spiral. After the current ruler has passed, the wall engraves another spiral. They all revolve around the Old One, who is said to be the father of the Fire Country and his essence preserved in the Eye. It only allows those it sees fit to enter."

Upon his description, she proceeded to gaze into the Eye. She could feel the pressure of the Eye weighing on her mind, reading her thoughts, and analyzing her soul. Flashes of thought ran through her memory at a rate she could not fully grasp. Without faltering, her heart rate increased. When the image of Nephani flashed, the Eye dropped the gaze and focused on her neck. At once, she realized the Eye had discovered the key. She quickly clenched the key, but within an instant, her hand lost all feeling and fell to her side. She knew not if the Eye had controlled her impulses, or her mind realized there was nothing to fear, but she peered desperately into the flames. After a moment of intensity, relief swept over her as the Eye darted from her to Bog. She could once again move her arm. The analysis did not last nearly as long with Bog.

He smirked at Mora.

She grimaced back.

The stone cracked open, slowly pulling back its doors with an inordinate magnitude of force. It was blinding. She could not see the other side clearly until Bog stepped in front of her and began to proceed through the doors, blocking the brightness with his wings. She followed. Placing her hand in front of her eyes to lessen the intensity of the light inside the outer bailey, she realized there was a wall of fire burning along the inside perimeter.

*I wonder why it isn't scorching hot,* she thought inquisitively.

## The Keeper

She squinted hard to see the figures lining the doorway. One particular figure stood out amongst the rest. It was the being from the bastion. His bow was slung around his shoulders and he leaned stoically against the stone steps leading to a thin room at the gate.

"Place any weapons on the ground at your feet," a voice rang out, gruff and serious.

Bog peered back at Mora, briefly nodded his head in approval, and knelt to place a couple of knives from his belt and boot on the ground.

She reached behind her back and pulled the sheathed dagger off of the loop she made in her belt. *I'm so glad it didn't fall into the clouds under the Staggering Stones.* Kneeling down, she placed it next to his knives and straightened.

With authority, the blue eyed figure watched them heavily as he walked over, knelt down, briefly inspected each weapon, and placed them in an opened chest. "They will be returned in time, when I see fit." He turned his back, proceeding toward a steep, winding path leading to the main castle. Gesturing backward, he mumbled, "Follow."

The guards picked up the chest and pushed them both in line to follow.

Inside the outer ward of the stronghold, there were vacant, adjoining, stone houses with beautiful, large windows, beaming with the brilliance of colored glass. Reflecting off the stone walls were mixtures of reds, violets, and yellows illuminating with the intensity of the flames. On many of the interconnected walls, there were elegantly carved symbols and repeating patterns of the spirals carved intermittently between diamond shapes. In the center of each spiral were lustrous stones.

*It's suspiciously vacant*, Bog thought.

After walking down a winding, dusty street, they reached another tall, stone wall. The blue eyed guard placed a long, thin piece of metal into one of the stones, turned it completely until an echo of clanking metal began to scratch inside, and then tucked the metal back into his pocket. Opening slowly, she saw the dusty street transition into an enormous, stone spiral with an intricately carved, multi-gem walkway down the center. Carved into each stone was an eye, very similar to the master Eye on the outside of the fortress. Aligning the stone pathway were elaborately sculpted statues of male and female figures in various, militaristic poses.

The veil covering the female bodies left little to the imagination and the males were completely nude.

*They are breathtaking,* Mora gawked. *They remind me of the fountain statues in Lychinus.* However, as she contemplated closer at their meticulous beauty, she noticed their eyes reflected a hauntingly extensive sadness.

With an expressionless grimace, the blue eyed guard paused in the middle of the inner ward and faced toward a gigantic, dark gray colonnade at the far end of the area. Like the outside, the stones were glistening, making the columns appear they were melting into the garnet-black, marbled floor.

A silence had overtaken their band as they closed the gate behind. Mora and Bog stood behind the blue eyed guard for several moments in anticipation. Then, abruptly, there was a click echoing throughout the inner bailey, ricocheting off each of the inner walls. Mora watched a figure emerge from a gigantic, garnet door. He was clad in a dull yellow robe with an arrow shaped, fiery red trim trailing along passed the hem. He was a thicker male, stout shoulders, with a hobble in his step. His hair was white, brighter than the snow, but balding from his forehead to his scalp. However, because his skin was grotesquely milky, it blended in with the color of his extremely fair hair. He limped across the stone steps at a surprisingly fast pace.

Flashing a curiously false grin, his unusually high voice screeched, "Remmi, it's so nice to see you."

Remmi stood like the erected statues they passed. With a gaze sharp enough to cut through the hardest metal, he positioned himself opposite the fat male.

"In all regards, Master Verquan, I cannot return the sentiment."

She noticed Master Verquan's gaze falter, revealing his true hatred for the guard called Remmi.

"Aye, well, I see you have brought us company." His eyes maneuvered to Bog and Mora with an entirely new emotion.

*Greed,* her mind whispered with an air of warning.

Thirstily, Master Verquan rubbed his knuckles and licked his lips. "Who has graced the Fire Country with their presence?" He started meandering toward Mora and Bog before Remmi stepped in front of his path. Disdainfully, he stopped and sneered, "I see you covet your... *visitors*."

"They have no business with you, nor you them. Where is she?"

Remmi sternly projected his words, standing firmly between them and the grotesquely large, Master Verquan.

"She sent me to inspect your find. If she had known you were going to be such a stubborn bastard, curiously coveting a couple of visitors, I'm sure she would have sent me with my own guards to defend her rightful property."

Immediately, Mora stepped closer and barked, "We are no one's *'property'*."

Bog rapidly grabbed her arm and pulled her next to his side.

Remmi flashed her an unnerving, austere glare.

"Oh, we have a feisty one!" He tapped all his fingers together at his chest. "How fun! I'm most positive she will find a lot of enjoyment from this one."

*His enthusiasm is disgusting.* Mora sneered.

"I'm not going to ask again," Remmi sputtered through pierced lips. "Where is she?"

Master Verquan chuckled while keeping his eyes locked on Mora, his jowls shaking like a hog's backside.

Remmi raised a hand to strike him across the face. "Tell me!"

"Enough!" a female voice reverberated around the inner ward.

Mora searched anxiously for the source of the voice with no prevail. She stood on her tiptoes next to Bog until she felt his hand on her shoulder. Shooting him a frustrated glance, she looked back toward the colonnade. Suddenly, her stomach lurched and her head felt light as a figure appeared from amongst the guards. *Adeline.*

# Pretense Amidst Pleasantries

 The female appeared to float across the stone pathway to Mora and Bog, stopping only a few steps away. She looked as tall and elegant as she did when Mora ran from her in the hut. *How can she be here in the Mortal Realm?* Her heartbeat sped to a ferocious pace.

The tall, elegant creatural smiled softly.

*Wait,* she thought, *Adeline had a scar running across her face, this female has none. Otherwise, there is an uncanny...unnerving, resemblance.*

Magnificently dressed in the same, fiery red hue of Master Verquan's trim, her waist was cinched with a bodice of metallic gold. The dress, slender and long, covered her feet and left a fairly long trail in her wake. On her elegant, elongated fingers there were magnificent, diamond rings. The same gems graced her slim neckline, accentuating her distinct collarbone. Large, gold hoops hung from her ears, while a significantly smaller one pierced her right nostril. Unlike Adeline, her black hair was straight and draped down to her waist. Gently upon her head was a band of gold. Metal lowered from the band on her forehead, pointing like an arrow, the sharp tip settled between her eyebrows. A bright ruby sparkled on the face of the arrow. Her striking eyes were the same dark blue of Adeline's. Paired with her bronzed skin, she was statuesque.

She bowed her head gently. "Welcome to the Floating Fortress. We have been expecting you, Mora, daughter of Meridan."

### The Keeper

Mora stood stunned. After a moment, and a small nudge from Bog, she found her tongue, "Thank you." She continued to stare stupidly. Stuttering, she finally asked, "Forgive me for inquiring, but have we met?"

The elegant female smiled. "Nay, youthful one." She tilted her head in curiosity, but responded pleasantly, "you may be referring to my sister, but as to that, I would certainly like to hear how you are acquainted."

Mora thought her eyes were kind, but there was something more suspicious to her demure demeanor she couldn't pinpoint.

"Come, let us walk." She held out her slender hand gently.

Mora took it without hesitation. *It is unnaturally warm.*

"Remmi, stay close behind, and Master Verquan," she tossed her hand flippantly, "you may go about your business."

Mora glanced to the side at Bog.

He stared apprehensively at the tall, elegant female, to Remmi, and then to Mora.

As if Adeline's sister could sense Bog's concern, she spoke sweetly, "You may join us Borgorian. You have safely guided this beauty along your journey, I would greatly cherish your strong presence."

Mora smiled with uncertainty at Bog, but as she did, a faint glance from Master Verquan caught her attention. A nasty grimace melted his snarky features and he trudged off to the door in which he emerged.

Adeline's sister led them passed the stark colonnade, to the side of the castle walls, and into a vibrant garden. It looked more like the wide, spacious grasslands they crossed to get to the Staggering Stones. Although the thick fog was still present, the surreal difference in weather from when they arrived at the Floating Fortress was alarming. There was no rain, nor encroaching storm. Currently, the peaceful clouds were low as the sunlight was fading from the sky, coaxing an eerie darkness to commence its shadowy embrace around the inside of the stone walls. Beyond the garden, there was a labyrinth of pomegranate trees where various, brilliant torches were shining brightly of all heights, some taller than a neighboring tree. The flames danced off the diverse, fiery foliage, illuminating them with a deep saturation of pinks, reds, bright blues, yellows, and oranges.

In the corner of her eye, she saw Bog keeping step with Remmi at the rear. Inhaling deeply, she thought, *This is a sanctuary, a section of light and beauty amongst the foreboding stone walls.*

Noticing Mora's curiosity, Adeline's sister spoke lyrically, "The torches never go out. They burn with an everlasting fire. After the exiled tribes learned to live amongst the elements, the beings chose a family to peacefully rule the Floating Fortress, making it the stronghold of all the Fire Country. The elders and bards speak of how the very first generation of Abin's family, Qu'Abin, then bargained with the Sun Goddess for an everlasting fire to burn throughout the kingdom in hopes the creaturals would live long lives of worship to the Goddess, and then the king. Every generation has diligently followed the decree with all their loyalties."

Adeline's sister grasped Mora's hand, causing her to shift slightly, tugging a little on the grip when she did. The last time she trusted another being, the touch was in order to gain access to her mind. She did not want it to happen again.

"However, what Qu'Abin did not know about his bargain was the fire from the Sun Goddess cannot be removed by mortals. Thus, in times of harsh winter, the sun fire could neither be touched, nor used to heat the castle grounds, and they were forced to light the traditional fires around the castle accordingly. Such power cannot be given to *mortals*." She led Mora to a sitting wood underneath a pomegranate tree between two torches and gestured for her to take a seat.

Amidst the chill of the night, Mora could feel the heat of the fire radiating off her skin. *Curious*, she thought, *I can feel the heat.* She watched as Remmi moved into a position in front of them, back turned toward where they were sitting, bow in hand. Bog merely moved cautiously around Remmi and leaned against the nearest tree with folded arms.

"Now, my lovely, tell me how you have come to mistaken me for my sister."

Mora slightly twitched. Remembering the night was like a bad dream. She could still feel where the branch smashed into her nose and the searing pain throbbing in her skull. Shaking her head slightly, she inquired, "How do I know you are who you say? I have seen too much dark magic arise in a very short amount of time. I cannot trust an acquaintance so easily."

Bog's wings rustled from behind.

## The Keeper

She side-eyed him and grimaced.

He pretended not to look at her, but he felt uncomfortable. *She trusted Katheryn way too easily.*

Adeline's sister smiled. "I understand. However, if I give you my word, how can you trust it either? I can only begin by informing you I can guarantee you know more about my kind than anyone I have ever met in this realm." With intensity, her dark blue eyes reflected the nearest torch. "To me, *that* is a dangerous game."

Agitated, Mora shifted and glanced at Remmi, who was still turned with his back toward them. She cleared her throat and said, "First, tell me who you are."

"I am Alidyah, daughter of the house of the Cau'o'tas, twin sister of Adeline."

A calm came over Mora. It felt refreshing. She relished the idea of having another female to share the extremity of her journey. *Bog is lovely, but he can't understand my yearning.*

She commenced to inform Alidyah about the events that happened during her unexpected venture into the Faery Realm and stumbling unknowingly into the Realm of Immortals. She spoke of Adeline's kindness and the unfortunate experience in the hut with *Him*. She could not, unfortunately, inform her of her sister's current state. She expressed how she fears His rage may have hurt, or killed, anyone in His path. This made her feel extremely responsible and remorseful. Astonishingly, Alidyah's face appeared unaltered by the despairing information of her sister. Mora was faintly alarmed at her lack of reaction. However, she continued until she spoke of her escape from the Land of Glo.

A brief silence occurred before Alidyah warily spoke, "Thank you for this information. It is certainly grave, and I feel I must send immediate word to my sister. However, I understand the discrepancy of the situation and will not put you in danger of being sought."

Mora watched her ponder for a moment. Then, Alidyah slightly upturned her lip in what she assumed was her interpretation of a comforting smile.

"I apologize, we were taught not to sympathize with the way of Natura. While my heart yearns for closure, my mind forbids it. I am one of seven links to the sacred Cau'o'tas tribe for distinguished immortal and mortal beings. It is a very high honor. My father decided long ago he wanted an eternal peace with certain strongholds throughout the paralleled worlds. Therefore, he sent me to Abin, to be wed on my thirteenth name day. I was terribly young and afraid, but Abin is a kind mortal, and he treated me respectfully. I grew to feel comfortable with my new surroundings. I...," she paused, "...came of age to understand myself."

A harrowing chill ran up Mora's spine as the wind blew from beyond the fortress walls. She could hear a slight howl and a distant rumble of thunder. Occasionally, a flash of lightning would streak across the sky, partially hidden by the ominous clouds beginning to billow. She noticed Remmi slightly turn his head toward Alidyah as she sat with her delicate hands folded on her lap.

He cleared his throat. Gruffly, he spoke, "My lady, it looks as if it may storm soon. Let us proceed inside."

Mora twisted her head to glance at him, and then back to Alidyah. *It is curious how he speaks to her, not as a superior, but as an equal.* She heard the rustle of Bog's wings again as he stirred beside the tree.

Alidyah stared blankly into the growing tensity over the walls and whispered, "Aye, I concur."

Turning back to Mora, her voice purred, "Oh, don't be alarmed my sweet, it is normal in the Fire Country to have sporadic storms. Sometimes, they dissipate as fast as they develop. The elders say it is because of the warmth and the cool bickering. The cold winds do not terry when emerging from the northwest. They, like their creaturals, do not care for the heat of the Fire Country. They constantly battle for co-existence."

Mora considered this for a moment. "You speak of the winds as though *they* have a mind of their own."

"Do not overlook the elements as though they have no personal intentions or interests of their own in the affairs of All. They are your most dire threat and yet your most strongest of allies." Standing up gracefully, she offered her hand to Mora. "Come, I will lead you to your chambers."

Bog suddenly interjected, "What of Abin? Is he not to join us tonight?"

"He is feeling ill tonight."

She spoke strangely clear and smiled in his direction.

"I'm most certain he will be optimistically awaiting to meet you tomorrow."

He grumbled inaudibly.

Mora feigned a gracious smile to Alidyah, despite how uneasy she began to feel in her presence. The growing storm beyond the wall mirrored the one she sensed faintly in her mind before she opened her thoughts in the Faery Realm. *He comes with the storm*, she thought before shaking her head in disbelief. *Nay, I'm safe within the walls of the Floating Fortress.*

Arm in arm, Mora and Alidyah walked down the side of the castle walls as Bog followed Remmi. Glimpsing back in Remmi's direction, his light blue eyes were set cold in the darkness, a mere flicker of the torches illuminating a portion of his face. He loomed in unemotional and dangerous tones. However, she was not necessarily uncomfortable with his presence, merely alert to his severity. Also, he was the only one thus far who had shown no emotional attachment to her presence.

Bog paused for only a moment to look over his shoulder. The clouds twisted strangely, and in the flash of lightning he thought he saw a black figure disappear into the trees. *Something doesn't feel right.*

They continued down the pebbled pathway until they came upon a small, black door set in one, large stone on the side of the castle. Alidyah took the sconce from the outside of the door in her hand and led them into the dark corridor. Bog had to duck as he entered the door, his wings scraping the rough ceiling. He sniffed the air. It was stuffy and wet inside.

Mora could not figure out why they had been led through the back of the castle, into what felt like the most abandoned part of the fortress. Ascending a spiral staircase was a bit more reassuring when it began to warm slightly. Alidyah proceeded through another door at the top. The adjoining corridor was wider, at least twenty paces, and there was light from illuminated sconces secured up and down the walls. They turned toward the left side and stopped in front of a double door.

When Alidyah opened the doors, Mora could smell the scent of camomile and honey emerge. A roaring fire was lit in the corner, and there were two beds separated by a stone wall which spanned half of the room. She was bewildered. Turning her eyes to Bog, she could see the relief upon his face. As they walked further into the chamber, both considered all of their surroundings a treasure to the perils of sleeping outdoors.

"I hope you both will be comfortable in here. It is our largest guest room." Alidyah stood poised by the doorway, hands crossed in front of her bodice. Before turning to depart, she paused and smiled sweetly. "And please, cook has procured his best wine," she gestured toward the fireplace, "and the grapes are locally grown."

Mora respectfully bowed her head.

Bog noticed Remmi was no where to be seen. He cocked his head. *When did he leave?* Mora's voice broke his thoughts.

"We greatly appreciate the hospitality. A warm bed is always a gift after sleeping under the elements." The longing for Lychinus tugged in her chest, but only because it didn't have the cold, stone feeling in which currently surrounded them. The suspension of the Floating Fortress over the abyss did not ease her tension either.

"Very well. I will leave you now to get your rest." She bowed her head graciously and pulled the doors shut.

"This is amazing!" Mora gestured with wide arms to Bog. "It's not Lychinus, but it will do."

"It is," he stated with suspicion.

"Why are you being such an ass?" she retorted.

He looked at her sullenly and said, "I don't have a good feeling about the place. The fat fuck acted terribly brazen earlier. And then all his flesh melted to add another chin when he didn't get his way. I could just hear him thinking of a spiteful plot against the emotionless shell called Remmi. There was certainly tension." He rubbed his hands down his face in frustration. "Then, there's Alidyah. There was something weird about the way she reacted to your story."

"I noticed it too, but let's not jump to conclusions. Alidyah was pleasant enough."

"You said the same about Katheryn," he muttered, eyeing her from the side. Seeing her annoyed look, he decided to change the subject. "I am still curious as to why Abin didn't accompany either of them."

Mora shrugged. "She said he was ill. I'm sure we will receive the opportunity tomorrow." Collecting a corner of the fresh linens into her hands, she smelled the alluring aroma of cleanliness in the sheets. "I am going to ready myself for sleep, though. I feel like I could sleep for an eternity."

Undressing herself behind the stone wall, she pulled one of the

*The Keeper*

hanging nightshirts over her head, left on her tight breeches, splashed her face with the refreshing, cool water in the basin, and crawled beneath the covers. She released a long sigh of exhaustion.

Bog wandered around the wall for a moment before he sat down on one of the larger armchairs by the fire. Lost in thought, he stared vacantly into the flames.

Watching him, she decided he was becoming upset over nothing. *He acted the same way in Lychinus...and toward Katheryn.* Turning her back to the fire, she tucked the sheets beneath her chin and closed her eyes.

Briefly peering back at her nestled in the sheets, facing away from him, he uncorked the decanter of wine and poured it into a jeweled goblet. *Oddly decadent for this moment,* he thought, examining the bronzed drinking piece. The reflective gems glistened in the firelight. He gently swirled the wine and sniffed the heady aroma. From what he could decipher, it carried lustful hints of red grapes, blackberries, and oak. However, a foreign, bitter scent followed in its wake. While not an expert on wine, he prided himself on the accumulated knowledge of the different varieties he had experienced throughout his life and extensive travels. *This scent does not tickle my memory.* Nevertheless, he was weary, and with Mora already asleep, his yearning to embrace a moment alone with his thoughts was too enticing. Therefore, still staring thoughtfully into the fire, he sipped the maroon liquid.

# Treachery in the Towers

When Mora awoke, everything was bitterly cold. There were no flames roaring in the fireplace and the windows had been opened, letting a mist of rain trickle through onto the stone floor. As she looked around the room, flashes of lightning, followed by distant rumbles of thunder, illuminated and trembled the wet stones. Save for herself, it felt as if the warmth had been sucked out of the room and was completely void of life.

"Bog?" she called out faintly, but there was no answer.

The room was empty. The castle was silent. When the lightning flashed again, she caught a glimpse of the chair Bog had been sitting in before she drifted to sleep. There was an overturned, broken goblet and a puddle of red liquid creeping toward her bed, the frigid air slowly freezing its progress. Horror-struck at the sight, she began to hear her heartbeat accelerate in her ears.

*Bog.*

Quickly, she threw off her nightshirt and pulled on the blood red tunic. Thankful she had left on her tight breeches, the savage winds bit into her flesh, sending a wave of tiny bumps all over her body. She shivered, yearning for warmth. Another flash of lightning illuminated a small chest next to the stone wall. Immediately, she recognized it from the outer bailey when Remmi had commanded them to place their weapons inside. Thrusting the top open, she grabbed Bog's knives and threw them into her knapsack. Slipping her dagger's sheath onto the makeshift loop of her belt, she securely wrapped the fur around her calves and tightly tied the laces of her sandals over the extra cushioning. Swinging Bog's satchel across one shoulder and her knapsack around the other, she tied her cloak around her neck and flipped the hood over her head.

Mora made an advance for the door until she heard a low, hissing sound of wind coming from the window. The rain was pelting harsher onto the slabbed floor. Despite how bitterly cold it already felt, the air unexpectedly became even more frigid, the accumulation of water steadily turning to black ice and crawling across the floor. The tiny cracks sounded like the hiss of a dangerous animal on the verge of striking. Hesitantly, but hastily, turning back to the door, she noticed a brief movement of shadow through the crack at the bottom.

Lowering her voice, she called out, "Bog?"

No answer.

As she shakily reached for the iron handle, the shadow disappeared. Then, the sudden sound of moving liquid sent an alarming chill up her spine as she spun around on her heel, nearly flinging her back against the door. She could feel the heavy thumping of her heartbeat in her chest and it became excruciatingly louder in her ears. Squinting, she surveyed the dark room as she discretely retrieved her dagger. Trembling and terrified, the slurping sound of liquid slid across the icy stones. Her eyes flickered madly over the floor as her breathing became burdensome.

Lightning flashed. To her horror, in front of her face, a black liquid began rising from the floor. Too stunned to move, she watched the form manifest into the figure of a faceless creatural. Backed against the door, her breathing filled the space between them with rapid, white puffs. Everything became silent, save for the slight sound of running water as the black liquid appeared to be melting and rejuvenating like a fountain. The looming figure, tall and ominous, tilted its head to the side and then back to the other. Petrified, she stood as still as a statue, hardly daring to breathe anymore.

All of a sudden, with a horrifyingly piercing scream, its mouth became a wide cage of black strings. The hairs all over her stood on end and her eyes were bulging with terror. When something deep inside her mind snapped in response to the noise, she panicked and thrust the metal tip into the liquid stomach. Her hand met a cold, wet, sticky substance.

Flinching, she jerked the dagger, slicing easily through the viscous matter. The form's upper body flopped over to the side, melted back into the lower body, and started to form itself again through the midsection. Not waiting for it to rejuvenate, she quickly fumbled for the iron handle and bolted around the door. Slamming it shut, she barreled down the opposite way they had come earlier.

Stumbling, she could hardly see the empty sconces lining the walls. The corridor was completely dark, save for the flashes of frequent lightning illuminating through small, round windows between each sconce. Briefly peering over her shoulder as she ran, all she could see was the incessant and taunting veil of emptiness. However, a terrifying scream echoed through the corridor, followed by a splashing of liquid against the slabs of stone. Her heart pounded faster in her chest as she ran harder, completely oblivious to where she would be able to hide from the hideous manifestation.

A light flashed at the end of the hall, revealing a window. Nearly slamming into the wall, she began slipping on the wet stone, fervently searching for a door handle, an exit of any kind. It was no use, there were no rooms to be opened, nor staircases to run down.

*What is the point?* she thought with hopelessness.

Another screech pierced the surrounding darkness, followed by the rushing sound of water vibrating beneath her feet. A surge of frigid air sent an ominous warning down her spine. In an act of desperation, she peered outside the window as the rain beat down on her hood. The torrential storm cloaked the darkness in sheets of water and the ground was no where to be seen. Craning her head, she saw another window above when the lightning flashed. *If I am to die tonight, I prefer falling into the abyss then surrender to that hideous monster.*

Hastily, Mora sheathed her dagger and scrambled onto the thin ledge of the window. She searched for the protruding stones on the outside wall of the fortress. Then, fueled by the adrenaline shooting through her veins, and her unwillingness to surrender, she pulled herself higher. About half way up, she heard another maliciously high scream. To her horror, she peered down to see the gut wrenching sight of the black form hanging out of the window. As it turned its repulsive, liquid head, its sealed eyes splayed open to reveal two, piercingly blue eyes. Her stomach lurched.

## The Keeper

Shaken with terror, she swiftly reached for the nearest stone. Her hand slipped. Nearly loosing control with the growing weight of her cloak and satchels, she grasped tighter with her other hand, willing her body closer to the wall. Sheer panic heated her entire flesh and her head swam with the possibility of falling into the chasm. Closing her eyes and coaxing her breathing to even, she listened. Out of the darkness, she heard the muffled screech from below and realized the monster had not followed out of the window. Relieved, but confused, she began to reach again for the stones. After a few more protruding stones, she reached the ledge of the upper window and painfully pulled herself in, tumbling hard onto the wet, unforgiving floor. Breathless and drenched, she started pacing herself through a similarly dark corridor, keeping her body close to the wall, hoping to reach a door. Despite how numb her body felt, it was still painful to run her hands against the sharp, textured wall. It tugged on her skin and created tiny cuts on her palm. Exasperated, but determined, she quickened her pace.

Suddenly, her hand hit a piece of wood. She squealed in pain, stopping abruptly. A finger long splinter ran shallowly through the base of her palm. Her stomach flipped when she saw the contrasting wood through the top layer of skin. Gagging at the thought of pulling it out, she held her breath and carefully extracted the wood. Attempting to keep her hands from shaking, her head swam in pain and disgust as a clamminess flooded her body. Finally, as the tip emerged, blood freely filled the open flesh. Catching herself on the wall, she knew she had no time to swoon. Cautiously feeling the wall for the wood once again, relief flooded her mind. *A door.*

Trembling, she felt around for the handle. Finding the lever, she immediately pushed it down and stumbled through the door. A dense draft collided with her soaked garments, sending a violent shiver all over her body. *It feels like an ice chest inside this room.*

Quietly closing the door, she fervently began to search for dry clothing and something to light a flame. Lightning flashed. A chest caught her attention at the end of a bed. Hurling herself to her knees in front of the chest, she flung open the top. Wool scratched her bloodied palm. Ripping through with disregard for whose it may be, she strewed it all on the floor and rummaged through the pile of garments. Luckily, she found a woolen tunic. Untying her cloak and belt, and throwing off the satchels, she tore her blood red linen over her head. A bitter bite of cold pelted against her exposed breasts. With ferocity, she wrestled the new tunic savagely over her drenched nakedness. It was made for a larger male, but it would suffice. Scrambling to replace her belt, she stuffed her wet cloak into the knapsack and threw them both back around her shoulders.

Peering around as the lightning flashed again, she saw a enormous fireplace in the far wall. Not having time to rummage through her personals to locate her flint, she thought, *It must have something I can use to light a flame.* Desperately, she stood, held her arms in front of her body, and proceeded to walk toward where the fireplace had been illuminated. In no more than a few steps, she tripped over a large mass on the floor, nearly loosing her footing. Kneeling, she started feeling around. As her fingertips grazed over the surface, she was horror struck. It was a body.

Discreetly, she backed away from the body. Because it had made no sound, nor advance, she cautiously toed around the stone. As she avoided the body, she accidentally kicked broken glass. *Damn,* she cursed. Continuing toward the fireplace, the temperature dropped even more and the malicious wind increased, blowing through the window as it created a hauntingly low moan. *How has the floor not become frozen?*

She attempted to calm her mind despite the sinking feeling of death and dark filling her physical and mental spaces. Fumbling around the mantle, her fingers stumbled on the hard surface of flint and a striker stone. Grabbing them down with one hand, she hurriedly scrambled along the wall to the bedside table. She felt around for a candle, her fingers searching blindly in the dark until the lightning lit the image of a candleholder. Trembling with cold more than fear, she blocked the wind with her body as she struck the flint rapidly toward the wick. Sparks crackled and fizzed.

"Come on, come on, come on...," Mora pleaded, tears beginning to stream down her face, "light the godsdamn candle!" Finally, a flame sizzled. She gasped and wiped the tears from her eyes.

With quivering hands, she dropped the flint and stone into the knapsack and held the candle at arm's length. Sweeping the candle over the stone floor, she maneuvered to the body. Hair covered most of the face, but she could see a liquid leaking from the side of his slightly exposed mouth. A faint, but pungent, smell burned her nostrils. *He's been poisoned!*

## The Keeper

Without warning, the door swung open. Nearly flying backward onto the floor, she strained her eyes against the candlelight. Light footsteps pattered across the stones as the intruder stepped closer. Because she did not hear the sound of running water or the slurping of slimy, black liquid sliding across the floor, she didn't make any sudden movements. The figure of Alidyah flitted into sight, her dark skin melding with the surrounding darkness of the doorway.

In relief, she cried out, "Oh, Alidyah! You frightened me!" Stumbling to her feet, she adjusted the straps on her shoulders.

"What are you doing here Mora?"

From the strain of her voice, she sounded worried. However, when she gazed into her dark blue eyes, they appeared to have a distinct blankness. Cautious, she said, "I awoke in my chambers alone and was attacked by a monstrous, dark substance that liquified into the form of a creatural." She stood firmly a few footsteps away, reluctant to trust the intentions of Alidyah's sudden appearance. "I...I...I ran down the corridor and...and climbed out the window. Running next to the wall in the dark, I chanced upon this room."

With only a hint of sincere surprise, Alidyah responded, "Mora, my dear! My apologies. Come with me, I will take you through the castle to the guards. We can send them after this..." her face twisted in an odd expression, "...creatural. Make haste!"

She motioned a hand toward Mora, flicking her fingertips in an odd way which made her appear as though she didn't have much control over her extremities. Wary, she took a couple steps toward the bed. In a stunned grunt, she gestured to the body and asked, "Alidyah, there is dead male in here who has seemingly been poisoned. Do you not find urgency in the matter?"

Lifting her eyebrow, she hovered her hand in a position at her side that would allow her to quickly access her dagger. Strangely, Alidyah walked languidly toward the bed with a thin, guileful grin across her lips, eyes never wavering.

"Aye, he *was* a good male. We were sadly informed of his passing earlier. He will surely be missed by some of the most foolish of loyalties."

Mora saw a slight, wicked upturn of her lips. "Loyalties? Who is he?" Trying to discreetly side step the end of the bed, she felt the heavy,

*The Keeper*

cold, unwavering gaze turn hateful.

"Why, *he* is Abin, my dear."

The horrid grin widened and Alidyah started advancing quicker. Sweating, Mora turned to run, but the door slammed shut. She nearly ran into the wood.

"I don't think you are going anywhere tonight. He will be here soon, and I will take my reward for your rapturous capture." A droll laughter filled the room.

"But I trusted you!" she screamed as Alidyah steadily approached, a madness radiating from her eyes. Frantic, she looked for a way to escape. She had to run as far as she could, run until she could no longer feel her heart beating louder than her thoughts, but there was no visible escape.

Instantly, Alidyah grabbed her by the neck. Picking her off her feet with an unnatural strength, high into the air, she spoke angrily through gritted teeth, "Give me the fucking key!"

"I won't," Mora choked. The candlestick clanked to the ground as her grip weakened. Attempting to lessen the tension around her neck, she fought against the strong hold of Alidyah's clutches.

"I will kill you for it! Don't let your defiance seal the fate of your puny, feeble body."

Mora managed to spit into her face and sputtered, "You wouldn't kill me bitch. He needs my mind and I'm the only one who can control it for Him."

Alidyah screamed manically in her face, the black strings connecting her mouth visible through the dying candlelight. She tossed her to the ground. With a forceful impact, the key revealed itself with a clink on the floor. Dragging herself to her hands and knees, she tasted the metallic warmth of blood on her lips. Smearing the blood across the arm of the tunic, she had only a moment to breathe before Alidyah grabbed her throat again, forcing her to her feet. Squeezing her throat harder, Alidyah grasped the key and held onto it tightly with her other hand. The faint smell of burning flesh filled Mora's nose and mouth as she attempted to gasp for air. Smoke swirled in front of her face as a dim light appeared through the cracks of Alidyah's fingers. Steadily glowing brighter, Alidyah's hand began to quiver violently.

Then, she screeched, "Cursed!"

## The Keeper

As Mora struggled for words, she suddenly felt a small pinch on her stomach. As Alidyah dropped both her and the key, a sharpness scratched against her shoulder as she fell to the ground. Gasping for breath, she peered up at Alidyah. When her eyes focused, she saw an arrow point jutting through her chest. Shock was plastered on her face as she glanced down, feeling around her chest with her fingertips. Black liquid trickled down her garment.

All of a sudden, Alidyah's body jolted again as another arrow head protruded through her stomach. Then, another. Scrambling to her feet and backing away cautiously, Mora watched Alidyah fall to her knees after a fourth arrow hit. To her surprise, she saw a figure emerge from the furthermost corner of shadows. It was Remmi. His bow was strung taut.

A rush of black liquid ran freely from the wounds onto the stone floor, pooling around Alidyah's knees. When she lifted her head, Mora gasped. The eyes were not Alidyah's eyes. They were a piercing, metallic blue. The dark liquid slowly oozed from her eyes and nose until the entire body had melted onto the floor. The arrows sank into the puddle.

Appalled, Mora looked at Remmi.

"Come," he commanded coldly.

She leapt over the black puddle, scooped up the candlestick, and jerked open the door.

Remmi pulled the arrows from the puddle before the liquid started to bubble and churn. He grunted. Harshly, he shut the door behind, barring it with a nearby piece of wood. "Follow, quickly."

Still in shock, Mora ran behind him and yelled, "What was that? Where is Alidyah? Where is Bog?"

"This way." He opened a door on his right, surveyed the corridor, and slipped in, shutting it directly when Mora darted through. "Watch your step," he said as he struck a loose rock against the wall and lit the torch hanging on the side of the door.

She tossed the candlestick to the side with a loud clank. Remmi shot her a nasty look before descending a staircase, spiraling deeper into the fortress. Slipping on a step, she caught herself against the wall, but he kept going. Frustrated, tired, and without answers, she continued following out of stubborn determination. Finally, they reached a doorway at the end of the steps and paused. From a distance, she could hear the familiar sound of running water. Her breath caught in her throat. *Gods, I hope it isn't coming down the staircase.*

Drawing a breath, Remmi turned right and sprinted.

The corridor was much tighter than the one upstairs. Reaching a door at the end of the hall, he cautiously cracked it open. Vaguely, she could see the courtyard. Parting the door slightly wider, he glimpsed up and down the rocky pathway, tossed the torch to the side, and motioned to continue. Discreetly, they hugged the wall of the stronghold as the rain poured in sheets and the wind whipped with malice, threatening to tear them away from the stones. The everlasting flames of the torches violently danced despite the downpour.

Another screech wailed. Her stomach dropped and she hastened her steps.

At last, they reached another vaguely familiar door. He opened it, allowed her to pass, and closed the door in silence. A grand room lay open before them. Pitch garnet-black floors made it look as though they would step into the looming abyss in which constantly threatened to swallow the Floating Fortress. Without making a sound, they crept around a large column in the corner of the room.

A small whistle sounded.

She squinted.

Remmi turned toward her, his light blue eyes appearing to glow, and whispered stoically, "Stay here." His boots clacked loudly against the marble floor as he walked out into the open room with his bow slung around his shoulders and hands raised.

She glanced around the space hesitantly. Then, at the far end, spots of bright, flaming torches appeared. In the front, the mass of flesh, Master Verquan, waddled. Approaching Remmi, she counted six guards.

"Traitor! Seize him!" Master Verquan hissed, pointing his fat finger toward Remmi's direction.

The guards charged. With the skill and power of an immaculately trained archer, Remmi whipped his bow around, arrow in hand. Firing upon the guards, he shot three consecutively down before the others advanced. Using the end of his bow, he slammed it into the ribs of an oncoming guard. Forcefully flinging it upward into his face, he gouged the end straight into the guard's right eye and pushed it through his skull. As

*The Keeper*

the guard collapsed, Remmi grabbed the guard's sword from his hand before slicing off the head of another. The last guard was the biggest. He wiped the end of his bow on the closest fallen guard's uniform before slinging it back over his shoulder. Brandishing the sword in his hand, both beings circled each other while heeding the splayed bodies. The blood blended with the floor, making the fight exceptionally unstable.

The large guard sneered at Remmi.

For the first time, she saw Remmi's lip upturn in an oddly devious grin before charging at full force.

Using the thick column, he leapt high and projected himself off the stone, sword raised above his head. A piercing clash of metal caused the guard to stagger backward. Gaining his footing, he retaliated with a blow to Remmi's head. He leaned back with such agility, she gawked. Brushing the blow off, Remmi continued to fight with overwhelming stealth and stamina.

Between the fighting, and the grueling back and forth blows, the giant guard managed to knock the bow off Remmi's shoulders. Seeing him eye it, the guard kicked it further behind. Panting, sword drawn in front of him, Remmi shrugged. Unamused, the guard sneered, blood leaking from the side of his mouth. Then, a dance of swords commenced fiercely, the metal echoing throughout the room. The guard grabbed another fallen sword and swung both in a harmonious motion. Remmi deflected each advance. Sweating profusely, the giant guard wiped his brow and angrily threw one of the swords directly at his chest. Spinning around, Remmi caught the handle and knelt with both in hand. This made the giant guard even angrier. Without hesitation, Remmi sprinted toward the giant, but unexpectedly turned, kicked off the wall, and twisted around, stabbing him deep in the back with one sword.

As the giant guard roared in pain, he slung his sword aimlessly at Remmi, catching his own forearm as he narrowly missed it being severed from the rest of his body. Blood trickled out. Both breathed heavily, staring menacingly at each other. With the sword lodged deep in his back, the giant guard faltered. In a maddeningly desperate attempt, he lunged toward Remmi. However, unaffected, Remmi pelted forward, slid under the giant's legs, and snatched his bow and a couple of fallen arrows. Gracefully, on one knee, he laced two arrows and fired them into the guard's head. The

*285*

guard fell face forward to the ground with a huge bone crunching *thunk*!

Concealed in the shadows, but too engrossed in the fight to notice, Mora suddenly felt someone grab the back of her neck. Before she could turn around, a knife appeared at her throat. A fat hand grabbed her wrist, twisting her arm grotesquely behind her back while her other arm was pinned against the wall. Struggling against the weight of such an awfully round being, she knew it was hopeless to break free of Master Verquan's grasp. Managing to wriggle a hand around both of her wrists, the fat stomach forced her beyond the shadows and on the outskirts of the massacre.

Remmi stood up unfazed, his chest heaving and his nearly white eyes daring his opponent to press him further.

"Drop the weapon," the familiar, nasty, screechy voice of Master Verquan hissed from behind her head, spittle landing on her neck.

Disgusted, she scrunched her nose.

Curving his lip, Remmi set the bow down and raised his hands. He spoke in a pleasantly calm and clear voice, "You don't want to do that."

"What are you going to do about it, bastard?" Master Verquan snarled.

"I'm not going to do a damn thing about it." He smirked.

Her eyes widened in a desperate attempt to read his meaning. *What the fuck?* she balked in her mind.

Then, an unfamiliar voice growled from behind them both, "Pitiful lard ass."

A second later, she felt the body tense, a warm splash against the back of her neck, and the grip was released. The knife clanked against the floor. A disgusting, wet thump hit the ground. She whipped around to see the ghost of the poisoned, dead male standing behind her with a knife in hand, his wine-stained, toothy grin visible in the dying torchlight.

"Thought I dead, ey?"

# A Gift of Gold

 Mora looked down at the sliced neck of Master Verquan, then back to the being whom she had seen dead upstairs.

He flashed another sly, toothy grin.

"We have no time to waste. He will be upon us soon," Remmi spoke sternly.

She gawked, too engrossed in the undead being who stood before her to pay attention to what Remmi had said. "You were not breathing and poison ran from the side of your mouth!"

He chuckled as he took hold of her arm and led her passed the dead guards into a door on the opposite wall. "Poison? An unimaginative female's weapon of choice. It was clever, but foreseeable. I *am* Abin. Details needn't be explained until later." He turned his head, glancing toward Remmi. "He is headed to the dungeons Rem, intending to use the Borgorian as bait."

"Bog!" she shouted. If anything happened to Bog, she would feel more guilt. He had put himself in too many positions for her protection, but she had not been able to repay the favor in any way. *This is what happens, creaturals get hurt or killed when I'm involved.* The thought sickened her to the core.

"Shh...hold your voice down *cun'ta*, before you get us all killed." He guided her forward. "We need to come from the back, the front will be heavily guarded."

"We can't let *him* take a hold of her," Remmi retaliated, flinging his head in her direction. "She must be kept away from the dungeons."

"Cun'ta?" Even though she knew not what it meant, she knew it could not mean anything positive. She scrunched her nose angrily. "I'm not a *cun'ta*. And if you two asses would stop talking about me as if I were not here, I would be more inclined to help."

Abin raised his eyebrow in skepticism. "As long as you can keep your damn mouth shut and stay where you're told. You already own a feisty reputation." Upturning the side of his mouth, he quipped, "I do admire a female in my tunic though."

She blushed. *Gods.*

They turned the corner of the hall and stopped a few paces from a undersized door. Remmi forced it open and, much to her chagrin, descended more stairs. This time, however, once they settled two flights, there was only one direction to go. Moving abruptly, both Remmi and Abin had to hunch over beneath the lower ceiling. Remmi stopped abruptly after several hundred paces, under what appeared to be a vent. The runoff from the rain was steadily pouring in from one side and running down the slanted floor on the opposite side, further into a hauntingly dark space. With great caution, he stood, maneuvered the vent loose, pushed it slightly away from the opening, and peered discreetly through the hole.

"It's clear," he whispered gruffly and pulled himself through the opening.

Abin gestured to Mora and bowed in a snide manner. "Cun'ta, after you."

Annoyed, she rolled her eyes and reached for the rim while Abin lifted her feet. He followed with great agility. Her drenched breeches made her shiver when the wind gusted roughly from behind. Nevertheless, she could not feel the sting as severely because of the amount of nervous energy running in her veins. Surveying her surroundings, she realized they were at the edge of the inner ward.

Remmi checked the perimeter around the vent and came back to talk with Abin. "It appears as though the guards haven't reached the area yet. We need to leave her under the vent for when they arrive. None will suspect anything if we place brush over the bars."

"You gather the brush then. We will move in from the south side. The winds are picking up," Abin groaned, "and he is getting closer."

## The Keeper

As the words were spoken, she wondered, *Who are they talking about? Surely I would know if Ekklips is close.* A fear crept slowly up her spine. *Who else can stir as much fear?*

Abin barked again at Mora, "Fuck! Are you deaf? I need you to climb back down into the hole!"

Lost in her own thoughts, she didn't realize he had been speaking. Snidely, she glared at him beneath her lashes, daring him to bark at her again. She stepped over the vent and allowed him to help her descend carefully.

"For your bloody safety, and at the risk of your actions killing your Borgorian friend, we need you to stay here until we return." He handed her a sword and placed the bars back on the rim.

Remmi covered it with brush.

Annoyed, she sat down against the wall of the tight passageway, away from the vent, and placed her knees to her chest. Examining the sword, she realized it was one of the weapons from the guards Remmi massacred. *Brilliant.* She tilted her head against the stone wall and closed her eyes. Listening to the rain pelting on the objects above her head, a rumble of thunder rattled her mind. She recreated the events as they had happened that evening, from Alidyah to the appearance of Abin. However, no matter how hard she tried, the events were a tangled web of lies and deceit, woven at the expense of their safety. *Has this been a godsdamn ruse from the very beginning? Bog had been confident the Floating Fortress would be a safe ally.* She held her knees tighter. *And who in the curse of the gods is Remmi?*

Amidst the rolling thunder, she heard footsteps and the twang of clanking metal. Gruff voices muffled through the wind and rain. Slowly standing up against the wall, she peered through the bars. Her view was obstructed by the brush, but from what she could see, two gigantic, grotesque figures were trudging closer to the brush. *They don't look like any of the guards I've seen thus far. They even surpass the giant guard Remmi slaughtered.*

A heavy, raspy voice asked drearily, "What do ya think we get out of this?"

"We better get what we asked! If we are killed, I'm coming back to haunt the son of a bitch we bargained with! I didn't bloody travel all the way here for a smile."

Both guffawed at the thought.

"What are ya going to do with it?" the other gruffly replied.

"Well, firs', I'm going to castrate the ass who stole me whore. Then, laugh about it when he writhes in pain. Ya?"

"I'm going to have as many cunts as I can take! Can ya imagine? An eternity of whores?"

The giant slapped him on the back. "Way to think with yer heads!"

Both roared with a gurgling, malicious bout of laughter.

When a horn rang out, a series of laden footsteps ran closer. "They are bringing the prisoner out into the outer bailey!"

Muffled grunts mumbled from the giants as they trudged off toward the direction of the other guards.

Her heart sank. *Bog,* she mouthed. *I can't leave Bog alone to die. Fuck Abin's warning.* Hastily, she retraced the way they had come earlier. Racing up the stairs, she opened the door slightly. Peering out into the wide, open room with the garnet-black, abysmal floor, her eyes settled on the bodies of the fallen guards. Quickly, she tiptoed and unfastened a belt from the smallest guard's waist. Thankful it didn't have as much blood on it, she fastened it over her makeshift belt. It was a little large for her waist, but she pulled it tight enough and sheathed the sword Abin had handed her in the vent. Crouching low, she decided to go into the room Master Verquan had unexpectedly emerged from earlier. Pressing her ear to the door and holding her breath, she listened silently for movement.

However, before she turned the handle, she heard another door open. Low, grumbling voices could be heard from across the floor, but not far enough to notice the massacre of guards. Quietly, she crouched low in the corner, concealed by a massive column. Squinting through the darkness, her throat tightened. There were four giants. Between two of the guards, Bog slouched low. She could not see his face. Across his back, between his neck and wings, there was a long, wooden pole. His arms were outstretched on the top of the pole and his hands were tied on each side as the giants carried the ends, bearing all of Bog's weight. They dragged him through the massive, stone doors leading to the inner bailey.

Frustration bubbled deep in her stomach and her skin was hot.

## The Keeper

Staying low and amongst the shadows, she unlatched the door and peered inside. The only source of light was a dying candle on a table at the far end of a medium-sized room. Creeping inside, she latched the door, shushing the lock as it clicked. Peering around, she saw very little furniture, as well as being oddly windowless. Bookshelves lined the perimeter of three walls. With the exception of one on the far wall, there were also no other tables, nor chairs. Many bookshelves were full of books, but some had been strewn recklessly about on the floor.

Remaining alert, she cautiously approached the table. Immediately, she noticed a piece of parchment. A candlestick was holding the top right corner down and appeared as though it had been burning for a while. There was barely a finger length left of wax. Rivers of wax had slithered and dried on the corner of the parchment. On the left side of the parchment there was a quill and ink. All over the surface there were various, black splotches, as though someone had splattered the ink in bouts of frustration. Above the top left of the parchment, was a book. The writing shimmered in the candlelight. On the top of the open page, in beautiful calligraphy, was the inscription: *The Legend of the Sun Goddess*. Intrigued, she ripped the page from the book and stuffed it in her knapsack.

A movement in the corner of her eye caught her attention. On the floor to her right, pages of an open book were rustling in front of a bookcase. *That's strange.* She peered around again. *There are no windows in here to produce a breeze.* Walking over to the book, she knelt down and looked beneath the shelf. A faint breeze caressed her face. Shocked, she stood and began removing all the books from the shelves. Then, she drug the shelf away from the wall. The stone wall appeared like all the other ones in the room, gray, cemented stone. She knocked softly on the blocks. To her surprise, it sounded hollow. *Stone doesn't make that sound.* Removing her dagger, she dug the tip deep between the stones, twisting it as she bared down on the crack. Jerking the blade out, a miniature, thin line of light glowed. The draft wafted through a little more. Gawking into the hole with one eye, a pull of excitement tugged at her mind. *It's a fake stone door!*

She tried to push against the door with all her might. Nothing happened. Rearing back, she threw her shoulder into the hollow stones. A small amount of dirt crumbled to the floor. Rubbing her shoulder, she proceeded to dig the thin, metal blade into the line of light more, forcing it all the way down to the ground. Then, she took a few steps back and sprinted, shoulder first, into the door. It opened slightly. Grunting in frustration, she rammed into it again. Finally, it opened just enough for her to squeeze her body through. However, before she attempted, she grabbed the candle from the table. Taking a deep breath, she forced herself through the tight space.

Once inside, Mora examined the backside of the false door. It was made of wood and had been camouflaged to look like stone in the library. *This passageway must have been the way Abin descended into the inner ward without being noticed.* Then a thought crossed her mind. *But it would have been easier to open. Unless...there are more secret passageways throughout the stronghold.* This made her curious to explore the fortress more, but the thought of Bog hanging unconscious between the guards stopped her from over-fantasizing the idea. *Focus.*

Stepping carefully down the tunnel, she noticed several, open doorways leading to various staircases, each with a lit sconce illuminating the bottom. Faintly ahead, she saw a glimmer of flickering light inside a room about fifty paces from where she was standing. Dagger at the ready, she moved silently to the doorway and peered inside. To her surprise, there was an inordinate amount of weaponry stowed in the room. It was a little larger than a vestibule, filled with swords, knives, spikes, maces, daggers, spears, axes, bows and arrows.

*It is a hidden arsenal!* She goggled.

"Who goes there?" a meek, hoarse voice cut through the silence.

Taken aback, she jumped around an anvil, holding her hilt tighter.

A frail, old creatural walked out from the corner of the arsenal with a cane in his hand. "Speak. For my eyesight is no longer of this world."

With a lump in her throat, she attempted to speak bravely, "I am Mora. I happened upon the passage. I apologize for the inconvenience. I will take my leave." Without turning her back, she quietly sidestepped toward the door.

The old being momentarily pondered. Shaking his head, he muttered, "Aye, they told me you were here. You seek the sun fire."

"The sun fire?" With a skewed look in her eyes, the words toppled out of her mouth, "How do you know me?"

"*Dali*, I see more than you do with your own eyes."

Hobbling further into the light, she gasped. The old being's eyes were white and clouded. His hair fell straight and scraggly down to his chin, mixing with a beard which mirrored falling water to the end of his belted tunic. A horrible hump protruded from his left shoulder blade. He stood about her height, but was missing one leg.

Gesturing a hand in her direction, the old male whispered, "He cannot die, for He *is* the manifestation of Death. You cannot escape Him. Nevertheless…"

She squinted her eyes and interrupted, "I am not sure I understand what you speak wise one. For I have been told I am the physical creation of Death Himself."

Nodding flippantly, he replied, "Your spirit is old, my childling. Older than All. He merely gave you flesh. Ultimately, you are no actual *Creatural*, merely one in form, nor are you the property of Death. However, what He did not foresee, was by taking on the power of Life, you are now woven with the laws of sentient. You have a conscious. Not like the nasty monsters He generates in His fortresses to do His bidding. We immortals are not *entirely* lack in the functionality of mortal constitution. It depends on our purpose for existence at the time. We are, though, without *ultimate* freewill as we are still bound by the laws of Life, not the laws of Death. You, my childling, are restrained by both Life and Death in your current state." He licked his lip and raised a shaky hand. "I am a Collector. My immortal purpose is protecting all that is fragile and securing relics when they are lost or stolen throughout the ages."

"Relics?" She scrunched her nose.

"Aye, there are those of us whose fundamental purpose only lies within the Mortal Realm. I was born to protect the fine line, the veil, between the Realms, and ensure no mortal may possess a power too great to wield, causing carnage in its wake. My purpose will finally be fulfilled tonight." He limped in pain to a large cupboard made of rich mahogany. The doors were intricately carved with the spiral patterns from the main gate. He opened them and reached inside.

Watching closely, Mora saw the glint of a golden bow and a quiver filled with gold tipped arrows. She gawked.

## The Keeper

He handled the bow and quiver meticulously, sliding them off a mount and laying them on the anvil. "This bow belonged to Solora, the Sun Goddess, The Keeper and keybearer. It took me eons to locate the bow after legends were told of it falling from beyond the veil on the day of Her betrayal. Each time I would get close, I would be punished by frailty and age, for no one save for a Primordial or Deity should be able to touch the Goddess' weapon. It was a sacrifice I was willing to make. I knew I would be rewarded for securing it five and twenty years ago on the Winter Solstice, the shortest night, when the prophetical babe was born and the war of All became inevitable."

She was swept from her mesmerized gaze as recognition settled. She whispered, "I was born on the Winter Solstice. You are not suggesting I am the reason for the impending war and chaos?" While not entirely stunned by the accusation since Bog had briefly informed her of a similar story, she was unsure how elaborately this story, supposedly of her, would continue to spiral. She was teetering on the precipice between skepticism and acceptance.

"You became Chaos when you betrayed Life. You are still the embodiment of Chaos, but within your mind, contained in skin and bones, your True Being is concealed, locked away until you can unleash it. Death successfully created life, but there was an vengeful intervention." He shuffled on his cane. "War is inevitable within the physical Realms, but that is not the only battlefield you will fight on."

As he handed her the bow carefully with gloved hands, she kept eye contact despite his cloudy, enigmatic eyes.

"I cannot reveal more than this, for I have very little time remaining upon the land now the weapon is in your possession. Wherever you go, many will be hurt or die to protect you. However, like myself, it is a price they are willing to pay. They believe you will restore balance to All. Do not act meek. Let your light radiate. *Remember.*" A subtle vibration resonated through the walls. "Now go, there is an evil nigh."

# Didac

When Mora accepted the bow and quiver, she felt an overwhelming sense of empowerment. A brief shiver ran down her spine. Suddenly, bright lights illuminated from the old being's eyes and fingertips. He emitted a satisfying smile as he lifted his arms above his head and subtly disappeared before her eyes in a glistening array of light. On the floor, where he had been standing, was the boot he had been wearing, along with the rest of his clothing. Shocked at his sudden disappearance, she took a couple of deep breaths and grabbed the cloak off the ground. She unfastened the borrowed belt and sword, throwing them to the side before slinging the bow and quiver over her shoulder. Without turning back, she headed for the door at a determinate pace, turned right, and continued walking down the passageway.

An acrid scent singed her nostrils and she slowed her pace. The smell was of decay, the pungent stench of physical deterioration. Her eyes watered at the intensity. Proceeding with caution, she grabbed a torch off the wall and lightly stepped into the shadows. She held the torch at arm's length as the potency increased. As she rounded the corner, she stumbled back in horror at the sight of several, compiled bodies, many of which wore the uniform of the guards. Most were decapitated, being feasted upon by the creatures of the darkest corners. However, the most disturbing factor was the head she had kicked with her boot. When the light hit the flesh, the head was faceless.

Retching, she fervently flung herself down the opposite corridor, running despite the slippery stones. A voice in her head recited the story her mother had told her about The Faceless One. *If the legend is true, then the monster is real, and it is near.* The image frightened her immensely, sending a harrowing chill through her body.

When she reached the end of the corridor, she placed an ear against the door. She figured this door led outside the fortress, but she knew not exactly where. Holding her breath, she lifted the handle, making a slight *clink!* before she pushed it open. Immediately, she recognized where it emerged. From a distance, she saw the open area where the pile of brush was placed over the vent. *The inner ward.* Cautiously, she proceeded. However, before she took another step, someone grabbed her arm and covered her mouth to prevent the scream she felt rising viciously in her throat.

Pulling her passed the door and around the corner of the wall, a low, gruff voice hissed, "What the fuck are you doing?"

Breathing heavily, she turned to see the tense face of Abin. Defiantly, she retorted, "I will not be left in a cage while Bog suffers in my place!"

Shaking his head, he muttered, "You are a wild one."

Then, she heard footsteps behind them. She turned in time to see Remmi running around the corner.

He stopped abruptly in his tracks. After a brief wave of shock at the sight of the bow and arrows, he mumbled, "He has returned."

Abin stared reluctantly at her weapon. Then, his eyes caught the glimmer of gold. "Where in the bloody curse of the gods did you find that?" he demanded, shaking her arm.

"I found a passageway, and within it, a small room filled with weaponry. An old being appeared from the shadows and said it belonged to the Sun Goddess. Then, he pulled it from a cupboard and gave it to me," she paraphrased flippantly, exempting the faceless heads she stumbled upon in the corridors. She did not understand why Abin looked so belligerent. She also could see the subtle look of consternation on Remmi's face, but then she spat, "And why is Bog still out there!"

"Because, by the time we reached the dungeons, they had taken him out," he replied coolly. His blue eyes were dangerously bright with a slight, white ring surrounding the outer edge.

## The Keeper

The clanking of metal from outside the gate made all three flinch.

Crouching, she threw the cloak over her shoulders, pulled the hood over her head, and took a defiant step toward the gate.

Abin caught her arm again and pulled her back. Exasperation echoed in his tone, "You can't just fucking walk into the open and start shooting."

"Why not? I have nothing to fear. *He* will seize me eventually." At this point, all she could think about was Bog. He had become a friend and the only constant she felt she could trust.

Remmi responded harshly, "Because it is not the time."

She huffed, but knew she was in no place to argue. Deep inside, she needed to trust their intentions before she made any rash decisions. She was a stranger in a strange land, it was dangerous to trust anyone. However, she needed to rescue Bog and escape far away from the Floating Fortress. "I *need* the sun fire from the torches."

Abin and Remmi glanced at each other and snickered.

"Why is that humorous?" she groaned.

"Even if you were able to reach the torches, it would be waste of time. You hold more than the eternal flame in your arrow tips."

"Then what are we to loose?" She balked at Abin and stayed low while she peered around the wall.

"With that sharp tongue? Our malehoods," Abin guffawed hoarsely.

Side-eyeing both of them spitefully, she muttered, "And what makes you think they're even *useful*?"

"I'd be willing to let you find out, *cun'ta*."

Unprepared for his response, Mora blushed at the thought.

Stealthily, all three crouched in the direction of the torches, hearing nothing but the soft patter of rain on the stone and an occasional rumble of thunder. Mora strained her eyes to see Bog. *Thank the gods the rain is settling*. Sneaking through the gate, concealed in the shadows of the strangely vacant dwellings, they reached the familiar area of the outer bailey. The perimeter of fire still burned as brightly, despite the earlier onset of heavy rain. Surveying the area, she caught sight of Bog and her stomach turned in knots. He was kneeling in the dirt, hands tied to the poles in the middle of the deceptively clear area. No one else was in sight.

She knew it could likely be a trap, but her impulses latched on to her tightly. Irrationally, she flung herself out of the shadows to him, running at full speed.

Abin attempted to grab her cloak and cursed her for running ahead.

She ran faster until she reached Bog, her hood falling to her shoulders. Dropping to her knees, she grasped his beaten face in her hands. His eye was swollen and his ribs were bruised. The wound that was once healing on his shoulder from the Hawkend arrow was trickling blood once again from an open slit on the side of the stitching. There were also several new lashes carved into his flesh. He groaned as she lifted his face.

"Bog," she whispered desperately, "please, look at me!"

In agony, he looked into her eyes and a tear ran down his cheek. "I'm sorry."

He had barely spoken before she realized they were suddenly surrounded. Guards were enclosing in a circular fashion. Frantically, she searched for a way out until her chest heaved at the sight of a being with piercing, blue eyes advancing from between the guards. His mid-length, dark hair was combed back with intertwining silver strands. With a pointed nose and sharp chin, the grin across his face made his teeth appear wickedly angular. She gasped. The eyes were the same as she had seen stare out the window when she scurried up the wall. They were the very same as the liquid form in Abin's chamber.

"We meet again," he mused, a dark and sinister growl vibrating from his throat.

She bravely stood in front of Bog as tall as her petite frame could stand. Although her stature was nothing compared to this being, she tilted her chin boldly. With an amusing smirk, he stepped toward her, hands behind his back, no obvious weapon visible. "Who are you?" she demanded sharply.

He glared through his sharp features and monotonously replied, "I am Didac, conqueror of the northern Fire Country and soon to be Floating Fortress."

A pain lurched in her stomach as she started to remember the tale Bog had spoken when they entered the Fire Country. The demise of the Family of Va had been unsettlingly terrifying, but the most disturbing and horrify detail in the defeat of Virtoc was something he could not vocalize. A strange voice whispered in her mind, *If his shadow rises, it could destroy each being within a blink of an eye.*

"What do you want with him?" She pointed to Bog and barked, "I know it is not him you ultimately want, it is me."

Didac flashed a smile and shrugged his shoulders. "It is true," he said in a conniving tone, "but he has become someone unfailingly dear to your heart and, fortunately for me, makes him a very enticing weapon or… bait."

She noticed he had shadows cast in each direction from the guard's torches. Upon his last word, one began to emerge from the ground. "Wait!" she shouted and halted them with her hands.

The shadows lingered.

"I will go willingly if you allow him to be left alone," she bartered.

"That is a tempting offer and surely would make my job less messy. However, no matter how small of a chance this pathetic excuse for a warrior may be, your friend is a threat to your future demise. I will prefer to take you, and kill him, both at the same time."

The shadow flanked on his right continued its ascension from the flat ground. Without realizing what she was doing, she flung aside her cloak, strung an arrow, aimed, and shot it directly at the shadow. In mid-air, the arrow burst into flames and seared right through the smokey body, setting it aflame as it passed. Its scream echoed throughout the night. Frantically, she turned, took the dagger from her belt, and cut Bog's ropes.

Didac grabbed his head and wailed, "Bitch!"

Shoving Bog to the side as a bolt of lightning struck the ground where he had been kneeling, the dirt erupted into violent sparks. Quickly, she glanced at Didac as he furiously yelled again and advanced in their direction. In a desperate attempt to move Bog to his feet, a shadowed hand grabbed her ankle. She kicked to no avail, her boot passing through the entity. Persisting, she rolled over as an arrow sliced the air above her head, striking Didac in the right shoulder. Only halted for a moment, she watched him pull the arrow from his flesh as a string of black liquid bubbled down his blue tunic. Undeterred from the wound, he advanced again. Another arrow flew swiftly, followed by three others. While Didac was distracted with the multitude of arrows protruding from his body, Mora coaxed Bog to his feet, limping to a small door at the opposite side of the bailey before he collapsed again.

Abin dodged the guards and knelt down to inspect Bog's wounds. "He will live, but we must get to the wall."

"He can barely walk!" She panicked.

"I will hold him up. You need to stay alert with the weapon." He threw Bog's arm over his shoulder, hoisted him to his feet, and started moving through the archway into a dark part of the grounds amongst a small grove of trees outside the back of the fortress.

"How will we hold Didac off?" she panted as she tried pacing herself with Abin.

Abin ignored her questions.

When she glanced back through the trees, she could see guards scrambling around the wall on the thin ledge of land running alongside the stronghold. Hastily, she picked up the pace and snarled, "I cannot see a thing!"

"Keep running!" Abin shouted from quite a distance ahead.

"My eyes are blind to the path!" she exclaimed as the silence grew deeper.

Faltering, she felt around for the fortress wall. Finally grazing her fingertips against the stone, she kept one hand out as she cautiously jogged, hoping to hear the sound of Abin and Bog in front. However, horror struck her cold in her tracks when she heard the sound of running water reverberating around the encroaching darkness. Lightning flashed in the clouds above, slightly illuminating a path out of the trees. She jerked her head around. The rain continued building again. Hurriedly, she ran faster and faster, panting for breath while the sound of rushing water echoed from ear to ear, gaining on her movements. *How is it coming from all around?* She wanted to cover her ears and scream to drown the haunting trickle of liquid penetrating her mind.

All of a sudden, the ground rumbled, causing her to stumble. She peered above her head when lightning flashed. Flying high above the trees was a grotesquely winged beast, soaring amongst the thunderous clouds with its claws outstretched. It roared a piercing screech, locked eyes with her, and dove from the sky. Opening its mouth wide, a forceful tunnel of fire burst forth. Throwing herself onto the grass next to the stone wall, she felt the searing heat erupt behind and a sharp claw graze her leg. After noticing the blood seeping down her leg, she hurdled herself to a full sprint. Another screech resounded through the night. Enormous wings beat like a deep, rhythmic drum against the menacing gusts of air.

Weighed down by the thick mud and rain, she screamed, "Abin!" at the top of her lungs.

Searching fiercely through the trees, the same voice echoed in her mind, *the sun fire*. She needed to light an arrow. Pulling one from her quiver, she shook the arrow violently. Nothing happened. She smashed it against a stone. Nothing. The sound of running water crept incessantly into her ears. Enraged, she looked up to see the frightening image of bright, blue eyes staring at her from the skies. *Curse of the gods! It's Didac!* Dashing frantically in the dark, she ran until she heard a familiar voice call her name.

"Mora!"

*Abin.*

"Where are you!" she screamed in response.

"On the wall!" the voice blared as it became clearer.

She saw a small flame burning directly in front. *A torch.* Abin had Bog propped against the wall in order to motion the flame in her direction.

Finally reaching the torch, she spoke rapidly out of breath, "He's in the sky." Then, panting, she managed to sputter, "Didac's flying."

"A dragon," Abin appeared stoic, yet enamored. Snapping out of his thoughts at the sudden outburst of a wailing roar, he glanced at Mora. "We must make it over the Staggering Stones if we are to survive." Motioning, he demanded, "Give me the satchels. You need to be able to run quickly."

"How are we supposed to do that? The rocks will be impossible to see in this darkness!" Hopelessness and fear pounded loudly against the walls of her mind as she threw Bog's satchel and her knapsack to Abin.

"Chance." Abin smirked cruelly. "Come on bird-beast, stand up and put this on. We've got to hurry."

Groaning, Bog, with the help of Abin, stumbled to his feet. He winced when Abin threw the satchel over his shoulder. *He looks like he's been drugged*, she thought.

## The Keeper

The scream from the dragon rumbled the stones. As the ground quaked, the sound of small rocks began rolling off into the abyss. Abin held the torch high.

She could only see three stones in the torchlight. She yelled through the growing winds, "How do we know which ones will hold?"

He answered derisively, "They are my stones. They will hold me until I command otherwise." He shoved an arm under Bog's armpit and steadily stepped onto the nearest rock.

Hesitantly, she followed.

Glancing back at the gathering guards on the edge of the stones, he nearly lost his footing when he saw a familiar face appear and then disappear from the crowd, the cynical smile haunting his mind. *Fuck. It can't be.* Rapidly, he turned around and continued.

One by one, they stepped on each suspended rock; and one by one they fell once her foot stepped off. "How are they being released?" she shouted. "And what about Remmi?"

"Stupid questions don't demand answers!" he yelled back. "But Remmi stayed behind to save your idiotic ass!"

Suddenly, something sent a ripple across the rock sea and silence fell. They froze in their tracks as they listened for what caused the disturbance. No more than a moment passed when she saw a black shadow looming in the skies overhead. A flash of lightning lit up the dark.

Lacing an arrow, she screamed at Abin, "Move!" Pulling back her string, she sent it slicing through the mist, bursting into flames, and piercing the dragon in the lower, right stomach.

The dragon wallowed and writhed, attempting to extinguish the flames.

"Go!" she exclaimed to Abin, but he was already heaving Bog over the next several stones.

Picking up the pace, they leapt faster across the ocean of stones. The dragon whirled around, rapidly blowing a ferocious wall of fire in front of their path. The seemingly impenetrable wall of fire lit up the rocks with belligerent intensity. Abin turned, dodging the whipping tendrils at the last moment. Mora followed ardently, leaping across before the stones released into their unknown demise. Turning to glimpse at Didac, she saw his malicious, blue eyes penetrate through her mind. Lightning crashed,

*The Keeper*

thunder shook the Staggering Stones, and the rain became a torrential downpour. Didac reared up and jostled the floating rocks violently, creating a series of gigantic ripples. The lightning bolts started hitting down, one by one, near where Abin, Bog, and Mora ran.

The dragon melted away into the distance while roaring through the blanket of rain. Mora could not see the enormous body clearly; though she knew the arrow had merely hindered his advancement and he would soon return. The great flames behind them sizzled in the rain and their path became unlit yet again. Following Abin diligently, a sudden wailing sliced through the bleak surroundings. Covering her ears, she nearly staggered on the stones. An explosion sent a shock through the air. The castle turrets erupted in violent bursts under the fiery siege of destruction. The dragon rounded rapidly. Another crash, the billowing smoke and flames no match for the curtains of rain and gusts of wind. She faltered on the slippery rocks as they gained more ground. However, the pathway started falling faster than she could run.

"We are close!" Abin yelled over his shoulder, nearly dragging Bog's slower footing across the stones.

Within moments, the rocks broke violently in between the distance of Mora and Abin, directly in front of her eyes. Stumbling to a stop, she balanced on one, suspended rock, staring straight into the belly of Didac. The ferocity of the body circled around the rest of the floating rocks, leaving the one she was standing as the only rock suspending her above the desolate chasm.

She was petrified.

Rolling across the stones from the impact, Abin hurriedly collected Bog and yelled, "Mora!"

"Run! Save Bog!" she screamed in desperation, pulling an arrow from her quiver.

As tears spilled from her eyes, she thought of how her life had become turned upside down. She didn't want to die this way, but the thought of Abin carrying Bog to safety was enough for her to feel a small pang of relief. Reacting too late to lace an arrow, the dragon form of Didac bolted through the air from beneath, overturning her rock. Without a free hand, she gripped her bow and arrow tightly and tumbled off the edge. Suddenly, falling into the abyss, the horror of her situation became insurmountable. Awaiting her death, a series of memories began to replay, rushing frantically through her mind. For only a moment, she squeezed her eyes tight in desperation, the streams of water flooding down her cheeks. In her mind, she whispered, *Will you let me die this way?* The thought was fleeting, but she knew to whom she called.

In response, an unexplained rage flared in her mind, but it wasn't directed toward Mora. She barely opened her eyes when she saw the blue eyes of Didac watching her fall. A wave of callousness forced a smirk upon her face. *He will punish you.*

A scream wailed from Didac's scaly throat as something hit her body excruciatingly hard. She felt the crack of her ribs, the impact making her nauseous. Even though the needles of rain stung her face, she attempted to focus on her surroundings. Wearily, through the increasing pain, she looked over her left shoulder to see the hardened face of Remmi, hand held securely on his bow. Following a rope with her vastly blurred gaze, she saw it was possibly connected to the massive, flying, writhing monster above.

Without warning, Remmi shoved her onto a section of cold, hard ground. She rolled over, panting. Her face was submerged in the welcomed, but uncomfortably drenched, feeling of grass. Attempting to pull herself up, she heaved as the agony in her body and lungs became too overwhelming. Her skin prickled and seared all over as if it were on fire. The rage still blared malevolently in her mind, causing her head to feel like it would split open in two. At the pinnacle of pain, she caught her breath before everything went dark.

# Imprisoned

Abin lowered Bog down beside an old tree and crouched to examine his wounds. Remmi scooped Mora's body from the grass by the cliff and carried her under the tree next to Abin and Bog. Standing straight, he trudged back over and watched the fire across the abyss deteriorate the once great stronghold.

Abin joined Remmi and muttered, "Fucking Didac."

Lifting an eyebrow, Remmi mumbled in return, "You knew it was coming."

"It doesn't make it any easier to witness."

Through squinted eyes, Bog could see the soft features of Mora's face covered in soot and blood. Managing to hoist himself against the trunk, he fought the lump in his chest. Barely able to speak, head swimming, and eyes tired, he stuttered, "Is she dead?"

Standing cross armed, Remmi turned at the sound of his voice. Shaking his head solemnly, he replied, "Nay," and bent down to place his two fingers against her neck, "but we must take her further into the woods. There is a small, Fire Country village close. It's where we evacuated most of the fortress dwellers. While they must not know about our whereabouts, Abin can collect the supplies we will need without drawing too much unwanted attention."

Before Abin helped Bog to his feet, he scooted closer to her and pushed her hair from her face. "I'm sorry," he said again, voice strained with sadness.

Remmi lifted her into his arms. With her head lacking support and her arm bobbing, Abin followed as they proceeded to find a safe spot to rest.

Bog peered over his shoulder. The Floating Fortress, which once sat amidst the mighty, nearly impenetrable Staggering Stones, was crumbling under the malevolent fire. He could see massive sections tumbling into the abyss below. A dark mass wove through the angry flames, bellowing persistent, ear-piercing screams. He shuddered at the image of the terrible shape Didac had formed and thought to himself, *He's a shape-shifter. We must be even more alert.*

Then, he thought about Didac's vivid, blue eyes. A chill ran up his spine as he discreetly glanced at Remmi, who had stopped and turned around, waiting for him to follow. Remmi's eyes, as hauntingly blue as the monster, seemed to glow in the darkness. *The comparison is uncanny,* but he immediately shook his head, ridding his mind of the speculation. *Remmi saved Mora's life.* Bog felt indebted to his heroism, yet continued to feel uneasy about his loyalties. Carefully, he slumped over to pick up her effects from the wet ground. Peering down at the golden bow and quiver, an ominous twinge simmered low in his stomach. The sudden appearance of the relic was evocative and unsettling. As they trudged across the mud and grass, he began to recall the events leading to his horrible display of vulnerability, tied in the bailey.

When they were settled in the chambers, Mora had drifted off to sleep while he sat beside the roaring fire. Disgruntled with the leery events since crossing the stones, he had decided to partake in some of the wine provided on the fireside table. After pouring the wine, he merely touched the glass to his lips before a drop hit his tongue, sending him spinning and choking onto the floor, gasping for air.

*Poison?*

Immediately, he tried to fight the urge to close his eyes, strained to pull himself across the floor, knocked the table over, and spilt the rest of the wine. *Clearly, the wine had not been meant for my lips.* Not much time after he began crawling across the floor, a figure walked into the room and began briskly whispering to another who stood right outside the doorway. However, at that moment, he lay helpless, twitching on the floor.

"What do we do now? The son of a bitch drank the wine, spilling the rest on the floor. The whore is the one lying in bed asleep!" the first voice said miserably.

"Just take him," a muffled, yet familiar, voice hissed. "When she wakes and panics about his disappearance, her mind will be too preoccupied and scared to fight. Strap him up and be quick about it! Douse the fire, I will get another guard to carry him down to the dungeons."

He rolled over, attempting to focus on the tall, lean figure of a… *female?*

Bog snapped back into the present moment. Abin gestured him to a log before proceeding to help Remmi build a fire. He glanced around nervously. He could not see Mora. *How have I been so bewildered by my memory I did not see where they placed her?*

"Where is she?" he asked frantically. "What did you do with her?"

"Relax bird beast," Abin spoke curtly, "she is amongst a mossy log in a clover bed a few footfalls to the right. She is lying quietly, comfortably, and out of sight from the fire." His face glowed in the spitting embers.

Peering through the darkness, Bog squinted his eyes to see if he could pinpoint where she lay. As his eyes adjusted, he could see a faint reflection of the light dance upon her outline. Bloodied and broken, he sighed, stood up, and limped over to her slumbering body. He blamed himself for her condition and settled next to a log. Whether she was consciously aware of her surroundings, he leaned over and kissed her on the forehead.

"I'm sorry," he whispered a third time as a faint spark hit his lips.

*Strange.* He rubbed his face vigorously. Exhausted, he folded his arms over his chest and drifted into the land of memory, recalling once more, the horrors of the previous night.

Bog awoke in a dark, damp cell, his hands bound harshly above his head. The rancid scent of mold and decay filled his nose. He was hanging from an unusually large hook secured tightly to the ceiling. His feet were barely touching the ground, resulting in his arms becoming progressively weary and numb. He groaned. With great difficulty, he tried to move his body toward the cell wall, attempting to stand on the ledge of the small, protruding stones. The effort was fruitless. His boot slipped clumsily on the damp rock.

"Help!" he cried weakly, despite being filled with a subtle anger.

"Silence!" a gruff voice replied harshly from the dimly lit entrance.

Fatigued, he retorted, "Where am I?" Straining to stand on his toes, he hoped to relieve some pressure from his arms.

There was no answer.

"Speak to me!" he pleaded hoarsely as the sensation of pinpricks trickled down his flesh.

The sound of a key clinking against the iron bars echoed in the cell. Bog heard the lifting of a cell door and the beat of heavy footfall advancing. An abnormally large individual stepped into view with a long braided beard and deep, heavyset eyes, absent of any visible white around the pupil. His nose was extremely disproportionate to the rest of the mangled features on his face. There were two small bones placed in the skin of his ear from top to bottom, and he was completely bald. In his hand, he held a rather long whip, wrapped in leather with tiny thorns protruding in between. He was rhythmically bouncing it back and forth in his palms. Bog flinched when he snapped the whip.

"Turn around bird dick," the giant commanded.

When he refused and spit in his lowered face, the guard shoved him violently into the wall. His spread wings tore his skin. The giant cracked the whip again, this time creating a thin gash across his right chest plate. He held his tongue as blood started to percolate. Another crack, and a longer gash appeared on his lower stomach. He grimaced.

## The Keeper

Gruffly, the guard spoke again, "Shut up, or I will fucking dig deeper next time." Snarling, he turned away and locked the door.

Bog's chest and stomach bleated in pain. It was hopeless to cry out for help. His mind began to ponder about Mora and if she was currently in the same amount of trouble. Regrettably, he wished to be dead. He wondered if it would have killed him if he had consumed the entire goblet of wine. The poison only scathed his lips before he realized what it contained. There had been enough to kill a desired *mortal* target in an instant.

He peered up at the ropes around his hands. Fear seeped through his thoughts. He did not want to give up hope, but the alternative looked more desirable than the cell. Wriggling his hands from side to side, he worked the rope looser. He realized he could slacken the ropes enough to fit a finger underneath a loop. Tugging as hard as he could, he finally managed to free his hands. Forcefully, he fell to the ground, his legs numb from suspension. Pausing briefly to listen if the giant heard, he scooted into the shadow of the cell. With his arms limped to his sides, the burning feeling of ceaseless needles progressed down his arms until it faded away. Cautiously, he shook his legs and staggered to his feet. Walking around the cell, he scoped out each corner for a loose stone or a blunt object. Neither could be found. *Fuck.*

Out of sheer exhaustion, he decided to sit down against the back of the cell, the darkest corner out of sight from the iron door. With the rope pulled taut between his hands, he decided to rest his arms on his knees in anticipation of the guard. Glaring at the cell doors, he contemplated the use of such a rope. Then, the image of Mora appeared in his head and his lips curled. Roughly, he reached around and plucked a feather from his wing. Blowing into his cupped hand, he inhaled deep. His violet eyes illuminated and he grinned wildly. *I will kill to see her safe.*

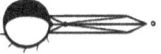

Waking up on the wet moss was not the ideal place to sleep. Bog's back was rigid from the hard ground and his wings were soaked with drops of dew. He rubbed the back of his head and glanced to where Mora had been lying. She was not there. He jumped up immediately. Looking around frantically, he saw Remmi sitting near the soot of last night's fire.

He leapt over the log, vigorously shook him, and yelled, "Where is she!"

Annoyed, Remmi batted him away. Rubbing his eyes, he spoke harshly, "We moved her last night to a more secluded area."

Bog pointed around. "More secluded than this?" He gawked blankly in utter frustration.

"Come off it you lunatic," a raspy voice appeared out of the woods.

He spun around.

Abin was trotting through the moss. "We laid her in another hollowed log, packed it with moss, and covered her body with an extra cloak. She is merely over the ridge. There has been no activity there for ages. The villagers haven't wandered through this part of the forest in many years. It's too close the Staggering Stones. They are exceptionally superstitious." Looking Bog up and down, he spat on the ground and said, "Go clean yourself up mate and be of some use to keep the fire burning."

Bog huffed. He did not trust the present company and knew not of their motives. Regardless of their help in escaping the wrath of Didac, their companionship had become a sudden inconvenience. Shrugging his shoulders, he brushed passed Abin, glancing briefly into his tattered face. Passing under the trees and over the moss in which Abin emerged, he heard one whisper, "He should be leery of his temper." Bog grunted and continued to search for Mora.

Finally, he came upon a heavy group of fallen trees. Lying still as death, Mora's face could barely be seen over the side of the tree trunk, the cloak tucked snuggly by her sides. Save for her undulating chest, he was terrified she would not awaken from sleep. However, he could see her eyes moving rapidly from beneath her lids and her lips were still moist.

*Luckily*, he thought gazing at the canopy of trees, *if it rained, she is protected by the thickness of the branches and leaves.*

Knowing there was nothing he could do for her, he sulkily twisted away from her body and, glancing toward the way he had come, decided to explore the forest. It was dark, even though he knew the day had to be around mid-morning. Listening to the sounds of the breeze rustling the branches, he found a cool spot to sit down. Picking up a red twig resting on the blue-green moss, he twirled it around in his fingers and continued his recollection of events from the previous night.

      The iron gate rang throughout the cell and Bog could hear the sound of footsteps trudging closer. Crouching further into the darkest shadow in the corner, he waited until the guard dumbly stepped into the cell. Rolling the rope around in his fists, he could feel his veins becoming more taut under the tension.

      The giant guard paused and peered at the empty space the prisoner had hung. Alarmed, he swung around to search for him in the cell. "Where are you, you piece of horse shit?" he bellowed at the back wall. Pulling out his whip, he held it at the ready as he advanced into the shadows.

      Without warning, Bog silently jumped onto the guard's back and swung the rope around his neck. He pushed the knot closer to the back of the thick rolls of flesh, pulling the excess rope tight. The guard struggled to swing the end of the whip around his body. Thorns caught his skin, but he continued holding the noose relentlessly. Choking, the guard fell to his knees, his voice unable to surface from his throat. While the guard gasped fiercely for air, Bog dragged him over to where he had been hanging earlier and strapped the long section of the rope through the iron hold. Pulling it taut, he raised the guard higher off the ground. Convulsing, the guard finally passed out from the lack of air and released a nasty stench of urine. Satisfied, he twisted the rope tighter in the loop around the guard's neck and took the keys from his belt. Quickly, and with stealth, he stepped to the iron gate and peered back and forth down the corridors. He could see no movement. Locking the cell door behind him, he turned left, took the torch from its hold, and proceeded through the cellars.

      The stone floor was covered in slimy water and there were rats running to and from the cracks in the wall. Bog could hear the increasing sound of rain echoing from the end of the corridor. After a few more strides, he came upon a source of light. There was another torch in the corner of a bend. He peered about. Seeing nothing of trouble, he continued into the hallway and advanced further. Suddenly, the sound of footfall echoed from a nearby staircase. He panicked. Running frantically back down the corridor, he turned the opposite way he came, tipped the torch over into the water, and backed into a small niche. He could feel the walls encroaching on both sides. Not able to see the hand in front of his face, he listened carefully to the gruff voices advancing on where he stood concealed.

"I hear they found her in the Great Hall, her and that *traitor*," one spoke.

"What happened?" the other gurgled.

"I know not. They sent one down to inform me to get the bird shit from the cell. All I know is they are gathering in the garth." He snickered. "We are going to have a good bonfire outside tonight."

The other joined in with more stupid laughter.

"Horgon!" a voice cried out, "Why did you extinguish the lights you ass! We can't see a fucking thing down here!"

Bog knew they were standing close and stopped breathing. Finally, they turned the way of the dungeon. Once their footsteps were faint, he crept cautiously from the niche and proceeded to the staircase.

Just as he reached the bottom, he heard a voice cry out, "Damn him!"

At the sound of running footfall, he darted up the staircase, only to be met by two more guards. Once they caught sight of him, they immediately grabbed him and threw his cheek straight into the wall, holding his wrists behind his back. His head felt weary from the collision of the stone and he could taste blood running into his mouth. He fought against the tension around his wrists, but he was severely at a disadvantage. The effects of his feather were waning after the amount of time it took waiting in the dark for the guard, Horgon, to arrive. Melting to the ground, he saw the two guards from the cell appear in the doorway.

"He murdered Horgon!" they barked.

The two who had thrown him against the wall lifted him off the wet floor and tied his hands to a large piece of wood, wrists on each end. Jerking his body around so he was facing the two who had discovered the dead guard, he was held tight while they began to punch him in the face and gut. He keeled over, lurching forward as they did. Beginning to feel helpless once again, battered and bleeding, they drug him to the corner of the wall.

Piling him against the cold, hard stone, they sputtered, "Wait 'til *he* hears. He will tear you limb from limb and leave your head for all to gaze upon. Filthy bird shit."

With a final, swift kick, Bog fell to his knees and purged, blood spewing from his mouth.

"Bog," a faint voice whispered, "Bog, awaken."

It was a pleasant sound, certainly not one to fear. However, an alert coursed through his subconscious because the voice was *not* familiar. Attempting to open his eyes, he realized he had fallen asleep against the tree.

"Bog," the voice lyrically repeated.

The world was blurry and dark. *Have I slept all day?* Lethargically rising to his feet, he rubbed his eyes.

Faintly, as his eyes adjusted to his surroundings, the forest was glowing with twilight and fireflies were dancing amongst the trees. He shuddered his wings, removing the dew collected from the low lying mist.

"*Av'mycav?*" he called out.

A small giggle echoed to his right. However, spinning on his heel, he saw nothing save a firefly. Then, he heard another giggle from behind. Again, he turned, seeing nothing but the multitude of twinkling fireflies.

"*Av'mycav?*" he repeated, "*O'thensh't'.*"

Subtly, the breeze commenced to rustle his feathers. He could feel a slight chill in the air. Twisting around repeatedly, he listened for the source of the giggle. Gradually, it started to increase, growing louder as he saw the fireflies jostling through the air. From across the clearing, the light whimsically danced in tune with the sound of the breeze through the trees, the unwavering harmony of crickets and bullfrogs, and the very own beating of his heart. Fantastically, the fireflies began to emerge as one and he beheld the sparkling formation of a female, giggling distinctively in his direction. As she sashayed toward him, her skin appeared to interweave with the fireflies, while the light created a sheer drapery down her silky, nearly translucent, skin. Her hair grew dark, grayish brown, the deepest color of the evergreen bark. Her eyes possessed a true, leaf green, and her stature was petite, no bigger than Mora. *Fragile is the term for her appearance,* he thought.

The giggling dwindled. Gazing up at his face through her glowing, green eyes, she spoke softly, "Friend. There is no need to speak the old tongue here, I will pose no threat…as of right now." She snickered, flashing an entrancing smile.

"Am I to suppose your future threat will be much more intimidating?" He gazed down at her, slightly cocking his head. "And you are?"

"Draelia," she replied sweetly, "I am a tree nymph."

"And how is it that you know my name?"

"There is not much in this land we do not know who, or what, they are." She began to circle him seductively slow.

The sheer draping of fireflies left very little to the imagination. He tried not to stare as he turned around to keep an eye on her form. "We?"

"Aye. We are the land and the land is us. We are not flesh and blood as you. Our hearts beat with the rhythm of the wind, the trees, the rocks, and the water." She fondled his wings. "Most majestic," she twinkled.

"Thanks?" He nodded reluctantly. He had never cared for his wings, yet found it interesting when Draelia touched them. "You have not answered my question, who is *we*."

She peered straight into his eyes. "We are *Natura*."

Contemplatively, he watched her walk back in front. He was intrigued by her delicate features. She wasn't like the tree nymphs who resided in the north on the outskirts of Borgoria, nor a nymph like Katheryn. Her presence was almost youthful, but her physique was distractingly mature. Finally, he cleared his throat, "I must inquire about your presence."

She sighed as she caught a little firefly in her hand. He watched it crawl around in her palm before disappearing into her skin, leaving a tiny blotch of light still lingering where it vanished. "Our Mother is worried. Life is becoming weaker each day. There are whispers of Light dwindling in the alluring shadow of the Being once known solely as Dark, but now encompasses the growing stench of Death. She has always been able to feel every heartbeat, every soul that treads upon the land, but there has been an impediment. The heartbeat at question is unrecognizable, and it is troublesome."

She stepped closer to his chest. He could feel the suppleness of the tips of her breasts against his flesh. Curious, he lifted an inquiring eyebrow.

Innocently, she glanced at him from underneath her eyelids. "However, there has been whisperings of a prophecy. For eons, we have dealt with the darkness accordingly. Our Mother does not discriminate against any one thing thriving with her resources. She finds joy in pure reliance and worship. Though, the murmurings have come to the surface, feeding on the ground like a fungus. The mycelium say to whom the heartbeat belongs is Light, her spirit Illumination, her mind Enlightenment, but her essence Chaos. She is not traveling alone, for there is an immortal, a Borgorian, who is leading her to his homeland. They have escaped the wrath of Didac with the help of Abin, once supreme ruler of the Fire Country, and a mysterious passerby with piercingly blue eyes and an unknown essence."

Placing her palms on his chest, she watched his violet eyes lighten with pleasure. Inching closer, Draelia continued, "The heartbeat in question now lays in a bed of moss, her dreaming long and undeniably dangerous. Dark seeks her with an insatiable thirst and hungers for her mind. Our Mother feels her internal struggles." Pressing her lips sensually to his own, she whispered, "I have found you, have I not?"

Solemnly, at the thought of Mora lying unconscious, he moved away from her seductively tempting touch and sat down on the nearest rock. Rubbing a hand through his hair, he adjusted his excitement before he sighed, "Sadly, I cannot help her. I have grown fond of her company and believe she is how the legends depict. However, by choice, I am no warrior. I know not what or where we must venture next. I am leading her to the only soul I know who has dwelled on this land for thousands of years. Only then, do I sense we will know what we must do."

"I know of whom you speak and it is a sorrow to inform you of a weakening heartbeat, the flesh dying, and a wavering soul."

## The Keeper

He jerked his head up as Draelia walked to a nearby tree and touched it softly. A small flash of light radiated and dimmed into the blood red bark. "That cannot be!" he spoke abruptly. "If you truly knew of whom I speak then you would know she surpasses the typical immortality and possesses the characteristics of an insurmountable superiority!"

She turned to lure at him, shaking her head slightly. "There is so much more to living than just the utter fleeting of flesh and bone. The spirit lives on. Even after death, your soul feeds All. In return, you are able to know life amongst other entities. The decomposition of the body nourishes future generations and reincarnations, a true gift from our Mother's treaty with Life...and Death."

As she languidly stepped closer to Bog, she held out her hand. He guffawed, not knowing what she was referencing. Death was a creation of Life's sacrifice, there would have been no compromise. "Then why is Death a concept? And what of the souls and bodies He is collecting for His own personal gain?"

"Do not judge another's ideals because they do not adhere to your own personal morale...," she flashed a sensual smile, "or insecurities. You see Bogheim, no matter if you are mortal or immortal, there will always be something greater than you to balance out the natural order of Life and Death. Nothing is given that can't be taken away, whether moments or eons after received. There will come a time where you will cease to exist and make room for another gift to be given a chance. This is not to say you will not return, but time spins differently for the spiritual realms than in the physical reality. 'Tis the balance of All."

Seeing the disbelief in his eyes growing, she sighed and whispered, "As for Death's sway over souls, it is a gravely growing concern for our Mother, one that has not gone unnoticed since the essence of Life has been drastically wavering."

She persisted gesturing her hand to Bog. Noticing her frustration, he hesitantly touched her translucent flesh. A breathtaking sensation ran through his body.

"Pure Immortality is driven by forces that involve the intertwining of the spirit and the particles of All. This is only allotted for the beings of the Divine Realm. Worldly immortality is a sheer mockery of the original concept and a pathetic consequence of living detached from elemental harmony."

Upon the liberation of her hand, he gasped. The ecstasy he felt was exhilarating. He wanted to feel the repeated spiritual release, and yearned to posses and control the sensation.

Draelia smiled with satisfaction and turned to walk several footfalls from him, his hunger tingling her backside. Glancing over her shoulder, she squinted her eyes and murmured darkly, "You had better be careful Bogheim, for what you are feeling in your heart right now is not purity, but a festering taint I have never felt before."

He looked down at his heaving chest, knowing she sensed how much the touch had affected his body. *Damn.* Averting his gaze, he was ashamed of what he had been feeling.

"If Light and Dark cannot become balanced once again, there will come a day when Death will feast on every living and non-living thing, destroying Life as you or I know it. This is not a struggle to defeat evil, it is a struggle to unify the two most important aspects Life holds dearest, and to keep her from becoming the ultimate weapon of Death."

With the last word, the fireflies dispersed, each going in separate directions until all, but one, was consumed by the darkness of the forest. Feeling defeated, he sat back against a tree trunk with an arm resting on his bent knee, his hands clasped together. Watching the last firefly lazily flicker about and finally fade into the distance, he knew there was no need to call out to her, no need to ask any more questions. He knew what he felt after she held and released his hand was a glimpse of something more powerful than he could ever hope to control. It was a concept he exposes himself to briefly when he inhales the dust of his feathers, or when he allows his rage to devour his emotions. Shame and disgust rose into his mind as a hidden anger and resentment boiled under his skin. Clenching his fists, sparks of violet radiated in the dark as he stared into the pitch black of the night.

The time seemed to drag on like the heat during a long summer's day. Bog sat weak eyed and sick against the wall. The giant guards had

continued to abuse him each time he moved a muscle. It had become a game to them. If he flinched, or they caught him blinking, they would take turns punching or kicking him until they drew new blood. Whichever drew blood the quickest would take a shot of amber liquid, laughing all the while about how each bone was going to be ripped from his body. Finally, a call came from above the small inlet in which they were all surrounded. Covered in mud, filth, and blood, he was lifted by the wood beam and settled on the shoulders of the two, biggest guards. Holding on as best as he could, his feet drug the ground. Exhausted and dazed, he did not have the strength to fight back. Ascending a brief flight of steps, they reached the ground level of the castle. He could barely see his surroundings from the amount of dried blood crusting around his eyes. He sensed they were taking him to the Great Hall by the sound of massive doors opening. Then, once in the Great Hall, he knew the destination. The guards had mentioned taking him to the outer bailey. He figured this was where they would torture him to death, or possibly be sacrificed.

*Mora.* The name sounded sweetly innocent when echoed in his head, and possibly, the only reason he had any will left to live. *What became of her after I was poisoned?* The enemy had infiltrated the one alliance he was familiar. *How could I have not seen this coming with the growing unrest in the northern Fire Country?*

Bothered by the questions running through his mind, he closed his eyes tight. Behind his fatigued eyelids, he could see a kaleidoscope of dancing colors and shapes, imprints of abstractions from the outside world. He imagined if he could keep his eyes closed, then death would come quick and painless. There would be no anticipation of the suffering yet to come, if luck were on his side. *Then, I will be in the clutches of Death.* The thought terrified him immensely.

Channeling his senses, Bog could smell the subtle, sweet fragrance of the pomegranate trees intertwined with the increasing sour odor of the surrounding bodies. A vague hint of burning embers scathed his nose and the wet aroma of rain charged a flood of memories from his youth into his recollection. In the distance, he could hear the faint sound of thunder rumbling. A flash of lightning imprinted against his kaleidoscopic lids. The sound of metal weapons clanked against the guards' chainmail. If he listened very carefully, he could hear whisperings about 'a female', 'the archer', and 'somewhere in the fortress'. A slight leap of relief resided in his heart. He hoped the references meant Mora had escaped and sought help. Knowing she could possibly live gave him a reason to stay calm and collective in this dire moment.

Finally feeling like his arms would rip from the sockets, the giant guards threw him to his knees. He could feel the sudden sensation of muddied, wet ground sopping through his breeches, to his flesh, and the grate of rock against bone. Still, without opening his eyes, he stayed on the ground, awaiting the arrival of Death. It seemed as though eternity had come and gone by the time he began to hear rhythmic footfall against the pebbles, stopping close enough for him to hear breathing. Nevertheless, he did not open his eyes.

"So, this is the wretch that murdered one of our guards in the dungeon?" the voice sneered.

Bog's lips curled in triumph.

"Aye," replied a menacing voice which sounded very much like nails scraping against metal.

"And this is the *beast* who arrived with the cunt?" the new guest inquired brashly.

His ears perked once he heard the newcomer utter a disgusting reference to Mora's presence. Also, anger rose from his stomach at the emphasis of 'beast'. He lifted his head, struggling to open his eyes. Before him, against the darkness and the faint glow of the flames surrounding the perimeter of the ward, stood a tall, brooding figure with eyes of piercing blue. *Didac.* The name resonated throughout his whole body in terror. *It cannot be.*

Although it took everything he possessed to remain motionless, he decided to speak. "What have you done with her?" he asked unflinchingly through gritted teeth.

"Ah, it speaks!" Didac lifted his head in malicious laughter toward the surrounding guards.

"Answer the fucking question," Bog demanded sternly, his eyes unwavering, blood spewing from his mouth.

"Bravery will get you no where in your current circumstance," Didac retorted with vehemence. "Your bitch seeks council with another being, someone more capable than you to protect her before I finally get my hands around her delicate neck." Clinching his fists, he smirked coldly. "Fortunately, she has a soft spot for cowards. She will seek out the bait and come running to your rescue, and you will watch her wither before your eyes…slowly." His eyes glowed bright in the heavy darkness. "*He* will be here soon. *He* has been so longingly wanting to see her in the flesh again."

Bog knew in an instant of whom he spoke. *Ekklips*. It had been foretold since his youth, and beyond, the two were inseparable in spirit. His countless efforts in searching for information about the purpose of creating a separate entity of Light had led him to the conclusion Dark had become her other half, an opposing ideal to enhance the deeper meaning of Life. The Trinitas were All, a production of balance, an established concept of hope. However, after the Fall, Ekklips wanted to possess the secrets of Life within Light's mind. Bog could sense it every time he saw her struggle. He clawed and grasped at her weaknesses, only concerned for His own growing empowerment as Dark and Death. He bowed his head in defeat. He could not watch the events unfold.

"Ah, I see." Didac smiled maliciously. "It knows, and yet it can do nothing to save neither itself, nor *her*. What joy this will bring me." He knelt in front of Bog and whispered in his ear, "I will make you an offer. Succumb to your madness and rage, and you can have the flesh of any creatural you wish for an eternity. I will even convince *Him* of your fortitude and indispensable value, allowing you to live more freely than you have ever in your worthless, bird shit life. You will only need to do one task."

Pausing briefly, Bog could feel the imminent danger in Didac's words. Beads of sweat serpentined down his brow, neck, back, and chest. Angrily, he spat, "And what the fuck would that be?"

Didac crouched lower to his ear and said in a low growl, "Give me your wings."

His head jerked up. Staring straight into Didac's eyes, he scowled. Despite how much he hated his wings, he would never allow this monster to possess them. "Piss off," he muttered, spitting into Didac's face.

In fury, Didac reared back and struck him across the mouth. Used to the punishment, he could taste the blood gathering from the fresh wound, the warmth running, once again, down his chin. He began to laugh in a steady, maniacal rumble.

"Piece of shit. Not even worthy enough to kill you myself," Didac hissed. He turned and trudged into the shadow.

Bog spit blood onto the ground. "Godsdamn bastard," he muttered and closed his eyes once more to the kaleidoscope of colors and shapes.

# An Unlikely Backbone

Mora fluttered her eyes, straining from the bright patches of sunlight through the canopy of trees. The air was warm, too warm for the cloak she was wrapped inside. Struggling to free her arm, she rubbed her head and sat up with difficulty, one arm at a time, until she propped herself against both hands, taking in glimpses of her blurry surroundings. Gasping, a piercing in her ribs shocked her body. As she laid back down, the pain seared.

"Keep lying back childling, I'll get ya fixed up in no time," a deep, gurgling, female voice murmured from above her head.

She was too worn to crane her neck. She merely laid there, closing her eyes, feeling the cloak being pushed away from her stomach. Startled by the ripping sound of her linens, a severely cold cloth was placed on her side. She jerked in reaction to the sudden temperature change.

"Stay still lovely. With yer fractured bones, rest is yer only ally."

"Comfort alludes my body," she spoke through gritted teeth.

"There is no argument. Ye will rest, or ye will be rendered forever useless in yer stubborn state."

She closed her eyes. The voice was harsh, but it sounded concerned. Judging from the slightly visible hands, the female was old and frail. Her foot made a brushing sound as it drug across the ground. After moments of unrest, she allowed herself to relax again, falling aimlessly into another deep slumber.

## The Keeper

Tossing and turning, Mora opened her eyes to the surrounding darkness. Tiny pinpoints of light freckled the indigo blanket above, brightly burning with a past unknown. She was lying on her back in a field of high grass. The tips of the grass were glowing, waving delicately in intervals with the cool breeze. Sitting upright, the grass caressed her cheek sensually, whispered sweetly, and energized her soul. Slowly standing to her feet, she realized there was no pain, no agony; she merely felt alive. Tenderly touching the tips of the glowing grass with her fingertips, a curious spark of energy and power tingled across her flesh. It felt rejuvenating. The breeze rustled her untamed curls as the never-ending specks of light bewildered and twinkled in her eyes. Astonished, she lifted her arms to welcome the source of power she could feel within the place.

*This is harmony.*

Spinning wildly around in a circle, letting the cool breeze ripple against the tiny, fine hairs of her body, she allowed herself to become completely unrestrained. Fortified, she realized what peace was comprised - a complete calm of both body and mind. There was nothing to fear. Gracious for the unexpected change in her dreams, she happily observed a beam of light fall from the sky merely a few paces from her feet. Then, she watched as a form comprised of light appeared, cloaked in sheer, sparkling purple. *Nephani.*

*Mora,* the voice echoed sweetly.

Although she could not see the expression Nephani possessed, she knew it would be smiling. *Aye,* she answered.

*Now that you have faced a darkness, do you have a better understanding about your truth and purpose?*

She replied truthfully, *Not completely.*

*You may see this as an attempt to sway your mind, but it is not so. You were not created by Life in your current, physical form. However, because life is governed by specific doctrines, you posses free will, an obstacle Dark did not wager, given His vanity. Your uninhibited nature is an empyrean weapon against Life and is meant to be unleashed in time.*

## The Keeper

She stuttered aloud, "But...," and tampered away. Despite the inability to see Nephani's face, she could still sense the condescending undertones in the words, a disappointment she had felt a multitude of times throughout her life from her mother, whom had also used the phrase 'empyrean weapon'.

*Mora, do you not listen to the words in which those around you speak? Take heed, but be leery of your dreams.*

*Isn't this a dream?*

*Nay, you are actually here in a type of physical form. Now, you must leave this place. A growing disturbance is tampering with your journey.*

*What?* Before she could comprehend the warning, it felt like a rope jerked her body and mind through an abysmal, tight tunnel.

Upon instantly waking, Mora vomited onto the forest floor. As if emerging from a distant memory, she knew not of how she succumbed to her physical body, but the pull had been too great to fight. She awoke with a shock, a shiver, and the drenching sweat pooling behind the small of her back. Feeling anxious, the morning chill made her skin feel clammy; however, it was welcomed against her face. Running her hands down her braid, her curls tangled in her fingers and dried blood matted several strands to her cheek. Glimpsing at her hands, it appeared like her smallest finger had been set, a throbbing pain twinging in the muscle. Shallow cuts had been cleaned, covered by a sticky salve.

A yearning fluttered in her chest. There was nothing more she wanted than to be back in the field of endless, tiny lights, bathing in the soft glow of the grass, and feeling the sensual breeze on her face. She awkwardly sat upright and rubbed her cheeks, peeling the stiff pieces of hair from her skin. Thankfully, there was little pain in her side, but she pressed a hand to her ribs to test the bones. Satisfied, she observed her surroundings and realized she was lying in a large, hollow log covered in moss. The forest was thick, and the tree trunks were a blood red, adorned with fiery orange and yellow leaves. Much of the lush vegetation above the blue-green moss was a mixture of warm colors.

*The fusion of hues is breathtaking.*

Noticing she was only in her tight breeches and her breasts covered by orange leaves the length of her forearm, she kept her arm across her chest and stepped out on the opposite side in which she had purged. Stumbling a bit, she attempted to balance herself with the help of a tree trunk while shaking the tingling sensation out of her feet. Cringing as she stepped, she hobbled over to a tree trough trickling of fresh water. Drinking a handful of crisp, sweet tasting water, she splashed her face and washed off the dried blood.

"It's nearly time you woke," a low, clear voice startled her from beyond the trough. Remmi was crouched cross-armed nearby.

Almost tripping over the protruding roots, Mora held the orange leaves stronger against her breasts. "Whatever do you mean?" she asked timidly.

"You have been asleep for six days." He had been sharpening arrow tips with a small knife before he saw Mora emerge from the hollow log. Standing up, he stretched and traipsed over to the trough.

"Six days!" She gawked.

"Aye, Abin and I already determined you would not awaken from your comatose state, but Bog insisted we give you more time." He snickered.

"I merely closed my eyes! It was only moments that I dreamt."

"Whether it was moments or moons, you babbled like a babe on its mother's tit as you slept."

While she thought it a relief to see him smile, no matter how crudely it looked, a painful thought ran through her mind. "Where *is* Bog?" she inquired hesitantly.

"At first, we imagined worse off than you, but he has been annoyingly alert since the second night you were sleeping. Not one time did he leave your side until last night, claiming he should be the one to tend to your wounds. Abin commanded he sleep." Throwing her a fresh tunic and a pair of moss colored breeches, he turned his back. "Those are from a local family with a young male."

She shot him a disturbingly angry glare.

Remmi rumbled with brief laughter. "Anyway, he protested the entire time. Bog, that is, not the youth."

Lifting an eyebrow, she began to meticulously clean under the orange leaves with great thoroughness. Hastily, she pulled the tunic over her head. To her annoyance, it was still a little big. *At least it is smaller than Abin's tunic.* Lifting her eyes slightly, she tore down her breeches and quickly took care of her personal areas quickly before nearly toppling back into the moss green ones. *At least they are soft.*

Satisfied she was covered, she stretched again and stepped over next to Remmi. "Where is he now?"

He looked her up and down. "Most likely asleep," he spoke frankly. Finally, he realized her concern. "If you need a larger area of water, there is an actual stream nearby."

Mora nearly elbowed the smirk from his smug face, but knew it would not be taken well. "Thanks," she replied in frustration.

Without waiting for a response, she begrudgingly walked in the direction he had pointed. At the sound of running water, her breath stopped immediately, a spark of fear searing in her blood. She knew it was not Didac, but the thought of his hideous form was still potent on her mind. At the sight of the gurgling stream, she took a deep breath and stepped in the shallow, cold water. After several moments of feeling grounded, she decided it would be nice to wash out her hair. Carefully unbraiding her hair despite the heavily matted folds, she ran her fingers stiffly through the sticky curls. Stepping out of the stream, she laid down on her back on a bed of dark blue moss. Adjusting her hair, she let the stream run sweetly over it, submerging the thick locks from the nape of her neck to her scalp. Combing back the hair on her forehead with her fingers, she closed her eyes at the serenity of the colorful forest around, ears immersed in the caged sounds of water.

Upon opening her eyes, she stared up at the canopy of the trees. They were a brilliant array of reds, yellows, and oranges with faint splotches of light grazing the tips. Lifting her head slightly to turn her neck, she could hear birds flying in and out of the leaves, frantically, but happily, chasing one another amongst the new day. *What it would be like to be a bird,* she thought, *flying high into the trees and sky, soaring on the wind, free to go wherever a whim takes you.*

Suddenly, she felt as though she would never be free of the

turmoils of this strange, new life. Straining to recall all the confusion and fear that had piled deep in her gut, she became extremely flustered and yelled, "How am I not mortal!"

"The same way every other immortal is created, lass" the brash voice startled her serenity, "by pissing off the gods and making sweet love to another immortal."

Abin came strolling down through the brittle leaves toward where she was lying in the moss. She pulled her hair from the stream, and with the excessive amount of water dripping down her back, grabbed it by the fistfuls and wrung it out. "Pissing off the gods? What does that bloody mean?"

Lingering on her question, he finally answered, "I am not entirely sure. But legends state, long ago, there were no mortals, only immortals. Three *superior* ones to be exact. These three created seven, primordial, immortal beings to do their bidding. What they took naught into consideration, was the conceptualization of desire. When tempted, it was eventually the beginning of Chaos. Destruction was birthed. In the end, all seven were banished and started breeding, creating various races of immortals and mortals. It's much more complicated than that, but you get the idea." He offered her a flask, but she refused. "It is merely what I have been taught my entire life, but not necessarily what I believe."

Even though his story made no sense to her, she nodded curtly. "Are you immortal?" she asked.

"I'd be damned if I was! Nay, I'm a full blooded mortal, destructible at any point, willing to swear by me mother's tit that I would welcome Death if he stood in front of me right now." He plopped down next to her, arms propped on his knees. "However, lass, I'm as indestructible as they come, I am. I do get to live a bit longer than them other fuckers, I suppose. Although, I care naught for any of the stories."

"Can you tell me anything more about *me*?"

"Nay. But what do you need to know that you don't already know somewhere deep inside that bloody mind of yours?"

"I had a dream. Except, it said I wasn't really in a dream…I was actually *there*." She combed her fingers through her hair, tugging through the tangles to smooth out the chaos in her wet curls. "And then it spoke of my truth."

## The Keeper

"You're concerned because you don't know exactly who you are in the entire scheme of All? Welcome to the clan of the fucking clueless."

Mora thoughtfully nodded her head. "Aye," she whispered.

"Did you ever think your entire existence is of your own choosing? That despite the bullshit you have been told, He has no more bearing on the final acceptance of your own identity than yourself?"

She smirked. "Bog would agree with you."

He grunted. "That'd be the first."

Thinking back on her life, she sighed. *I have no reason to feel swayed by another's decision about my life. My mother merely molded me for an entire spectrum of circumstances, and for that, I can finally be grateful. However, there is Him. He is enigmatic and magnificent, and He has the ability to make me helplessly succumb to His mind games.*

A tingle rolled up her thighs. *For an unknown reason, His presence feels like an ancient script written deep inside my bones. I feel a connection to something unlike any other I have experienced, despite my severe lack of connection outside my upbringing. An excitement develops deep within me at certain fleeting moments like the sudden appearance of a butterfly that is just out of reach. It is almost enough to make me want to summon Him to where I am, or close my eyes and see His face.* She shook her head. *Nevertheless, I also loathe Him, and am scared of His power over my emotions.* Finally, she peered at Abin, her face twisted in uncertainty.

"Aye, lass," he spoke, "I can see Him in your eyes right now. His essence lurks in every corner of your mind."

She had known him a very short amount of time, but since he had saved her life more than once, she felt a simple connection of gratitude and trust. Desperate, she pleaded, "Help me Abin, I don't want to feel this way."

"Are you certain?" he cocked his chin and grinned wryly. "Unfortunately, *I* can do nothing. You must find your own path, create your own fortuitous narrative." He stood up, offered his hand, and she took it graciously.

For only a moment, she glanced into his dark brown eyes. Filled with sorrow, hints of pity emerged from the corners as the feeling of self-loathing overtook her mind. For the first time since her mother disappeared, her heart longed for something more. It was not exactly love or acceptance, but peace and…*identity*.

# Root Extract #6

As Mora and Abin reached the top of a knoll amongst the blood red trunked trees, she was overwhelmed. *Bog.* Her heart fluttered.

"You're alive!" Bog exclaimed. He threw his arms around her waist, lifting her high, twisting in a circle.

She smiled, returning the embrace. He was the closest thing she had to someone who cared about her well-being. She fought back tears.

"You didn't bloody well think I would leave you alone with these two characters, did you?" She cocked her head toward Abin, and saw Remmi making his way along the trees.

He smiled his humored, dimpled grin. "I told them you were not dead. The bastards wanted to leave you amongst the hollow log."

Seeing Abin grimace, she delightedly replied, "Thank the gods I had someone looking out for me."

Abin mumbled from behind, "You'd think twice about thanking the bloody gods...," but the rest dwindled as Remmi joined them.

Unhindered by his musings, she looked at Bog's shoulder. "Is it healing properly?" Her eyes studied the rest of the cuts and bruises, and added in concern, "You're covered." When she touched a large bruise on his ribs and then along the incisions across his chest and abdomen, he flinched. Aghast, she choked on the words, "They flailed you?"

He shrugged. "Aye. Anyway, it's about as well as expected. After the beating those giants put me through, I'm lucky my shoulder wound didn't split all the way through to my legs." Rubbing his side, he grinned and said, "I've always healed quickly."

Seeing her glance at his shoulder, he stuttered, "Aye, well, except from poisons concocted from Death."

She smiled nervously. She had never seen him so elated and free spirited.

The sun had come up fully when she decided to wander around the tiny village they perched above. Needing to clear her head, she demanded to go alone. After several grumblings, Remmi insisted she don an oversized cloak to completely conceal herself. Promising she would return before long, she walked down the narrow, dirt pathway watching childlings run to and fro, one side to the next. The tiny village was nestled deep amongst the crimson trees, causing an eerie radiance. The canopy of thick orange and yellow leaves created a soft darkness with only intermittent splotches of sunlight twinkling on the green and blue moss growing patchily on the rooftops. It was the picturesque autumn she had imagined before leaving the sanctuary. The premature winter weather had baffled her beyond comprehension, but seeing it was not the same in the Fire Country comforted her greatly. She hoped to not see snow any time soon.

An old widow bustled outside, hanging her garments on a line alongside her cottage while a younger female washed in a nearby basin. The smell of delicious pastries wafted through the closest window causing her stomach to growl miserably. The twang of a blacksmith anvil echoed, steadily hammering the weapons Abin had given him from the Floating Fortress. Peeking through the doorway, she could see a lad, not much older than ten, fervently working the bellows, his feet raising off the ground every time he heaved it down and then allowed it to fill with air again. The sizzling of cold water on metal gave a satisfying hum. She briefly wondered if it was the lad's clothes she wore.

The further she meandered, the more sparse the structures became, creating a strange, surreal feeling of abandonment. Most appeared deserted with natural growth devouring each surface - the roof, the walls, the windows, similar to the dwellings along the main street of the Floating Fortress in which had been evacuated. *I wonder if these are the ones who escaped?* The thought was plausible considering how overgrown and tattered the village appeared.

Then, in the distance, a short way along the outskirts of the narrowing path, she saw an elderly female hobbling toward a massive, drooping, willow tree. The female paused, leered at her surroundings, pushed back the branches, and disappeared inside. Despite Remmi's words, '*Don't talk or make eye contact with anyone in the village*,' curiosity peeked her interest and she walked to the edge of the willow tree. A feeling of familiarity turned in her stomach. The last tree she sheltered under was her first experience with Ekklips and the faeries. They were liminal spaces, connecting realms and instigating dreams. Taking a deep breath, she hunched and peered through the low hanging branches.

Mora called out, "Excuse me?"

There was no answer.

Crouching closer inside, she saw a mound. Windowless, there sat a single, wooden door. Protruding from the top of the severely round mound was a cylindrical chimney creating smoke rings high into the canopied tree top. Bending a little lower, she knocked on the door. A latch sounded and a crack appeared, followed by a thin strip of warm light. The pungent smell of spices wafted, causing her nose to tickle.

The old hag peeked a soft, gray eye through the crack. "May I help you?" she snuffed.

"You are the old one who helped heal me, were you not?" she asked politely.

"I suppose I assisted a minor amount. What do you want?"

A hint of spite resonated through her voice, but she overlooked it as the sign of her tiresome old age. "I wanted to thank you. May I come in and speak with you?"

"I'm terribly busy pumpkin. Some other time. Run along now."

Reluctant, yet courteously, Mora forced out, "Oh, well, forgive the intrusion. Thank you again." Her shoulders sank, but as she turned to walk away from the door, a sigh resonated from the opening and the door squealed.

"Quickly. I don't have but a few moments to spare."

Satisfied, Mora's lip curled and she twisted toward the door. Inside, the mound was uniquely homely. There was a fire nestled in a stone niche with a cauldron boiling enthusiastically. A thin strip of iron lay across the top, smoking a miniature bird. Right of the fireplace, a bed stuffed of hay was nestled comfortably into another niche and was covered with a rough, gray patched, woolen blanket. A short legged table, built for one, with a matching stool pulled underneath was placed comfortably in front of the fire. There were several other little necessity items placed against the walls, but the one thing that caught her attention was the copious amount of filled bottles and plants strewn across a bench near the opposite wall. On the wooden surface there was a scrying bowl, a mortar and pestle, and a black mirror. It looked like each was in the process of being used.

She gazed over to the old hag and asked, "You are a witch?"

"I prefer the term healer around these parts." She grumbled, barely glancing up from her task of tying and hanging herbs.

Mora walked a little closer to the objects, barely reaching her fingers out to touch them when she heard a hiss.

"No one touches save the Maker!"

She recoiled her hand. "I apologize. Curiosity became me. I have never seen anything like these tools with my own eyes. I have just read about them in books. My mother taught me the very basics of healing and extractions, both for medicinal and culinary purposes."

Peering at the label on the bottle next to the mortar and pestle, it read *Root Extract #6*. It was a curious name for a substance. However, she was suddenly captivated by a subtle movement in the bowl. The black water began to swirl and ripple gently without external coaxing. Entranced, she took another step closer to the bench, careful not to touch the tools. A dreadful pull grasped strongly onto her mind. In anguish, she threw her hands around her head. Astonishingly, a series of distinct images appeared within the center of the churning liquid. First, she saw the back of a figure manically bellowing at the stern of a ship, water violently splintering through wood as easily as ripping parchment. Then, a creatural shot through the chest with six arrows, still fighting a distant foe. Recognition struck horror when she saw his piercing ,white-blue eyes. Facing Remmi, her stomach lurched when she saw *Him*, Ekklips, holding her key in His hand. He was laughing profusely, brandishing a bloodied sword.

She reached a hand over her chest, feeling the familiar outline of the key. A wave of relief sent her spiraling as the next image appeared. The glint of curly, blond hair swiftly ran through the darkness, blood pouring from holes in his back. When he turned to look behind, Mora gasped. The brilliant, bright, violet eyes were being swallowed by a malevolent, black haze. A jolt of lightning struck and an overwhelming burst of thunder made her stumble. Finally, she was standing on a severe cliff surrounded by crashing waves, wind and rain whipping maliciously to encase her body while a deep, throaty laughter barreled through the darkness. A blood curdling scream tore from her own throat while blood ran from her eyes like tears.

She gasped in horror, nearly fainting from the images. Feeling herself falling without the ability to grasp onto anything, the old hag, with surprising agility, grabbed the stool from beneath the table and slid it across the floor. Landing with a thump on the stool, Mora nodded meekly in gratitude. Holding a hand over the tightness in her chest, she took several deep breaths, unable to rid her mind of the strange images.

With a wad of chewing plant stuffed in her cheek, the old hag spit into a dried gourd. "The spirits do not speak to every one childling. What did you behold?" She started fanning Mora with the piece of parchment she had been inscribing on earlier.

Mora stared into the floor, repeating the images in her mind, rocking back and forth, but only one concept resonated in her thoughts. "Death," she whispered.

The hag grunted and hobbled over to the bench, concocting a drink. She placed it in Mora's hand, assisting her until it reached her mouth. "Drink. This will help you relax and bring you at peace with the projections."

Because her mouth had suddenly run dry, she drank the whole cup in a single swig. The liquid was bitter and her stomach nearly rejected it. She coughed and gagged. Lapping her tongue at the unwanted taste, she scrunched her face and sputtered, "Shit, what is this?"

"Aged ale. Family recipe. Enjoy."

When the old hag snickered, Mora could see her rotting and somewhat vacant teeth. However, before she limped back to the table, a flash of malice darted passed her gray eyes. A strange feeling of alarm rumbled in her gut, but she wanted answers. Therefore, she proceeded to ask about the events. "Why did I see the images?" Blinking her eyes a few times against a quick onset of lightheadedness, she felt her body begin to sway.

"I sense you are not of this world, pumpkin. You seem to have knowledge that far exceeds any of us. My question to you is, why are you surprised you saw them?"

Mora hiccuped. "Well, it is not a daily occurrence for me to foresee possible death and turmoil!" She giggled, swaying a bit on her stool. "Are they truths?" she slurred.

Shifting her eyes, the old hag growled, a slight hint of disappointment radiating in her words, "You must leave now. You have seen too much."

Forcing Mora from the stool with an abnormal strength, the hag shoved her out the door.

"Go straight, you will reach your companions shortly."

"But," Mora interrupted, sensing she was perturbed. "I wasn't done asking you questions." Stumbling back to the door, she hiccuped again.

"You need not ask questions. You already possess the answers." She slammed the door in Mora's face.

Stumbling, Mora blearily glanced about. "The direction has alluded my recollection!" Grumbling, she tripped through the willow branches and wandered toward the subtle lights of the village. Unfortunately, in spite of her best efforts to subdue the sloshy feeling in her stomach, it leapt and she purged against her control. Wincing at the aftertaste of the reemerging, aged ale, she stumbled to her feet, wiped her mouth with the back of her hand, and continued staggering along the dirt pathway. It was beginning to become dark and she could hardly see beyond the flame of lit street torches. Although, before heading into the encompassing light of the village, she peered back at the willow and squinted her eyes. Through the last bit of darkness, she saw a tall, cloaked figure emerge from the willow tree.

*Odd*, she thought hazily, *it doesn't hobble like the old hag, and there was certainly no other company when I was in the mound. Hmph.* She staggered and purged again. *I've got to stop taking drinks from strangers.*

After the second purge, she decided to call out to Bog. *He will come*, she persisted to think. "Bog!" she shouted, "Bog!"

In her stupor, she noticed she was drawing too much unwanted attention and shushed herself. *Obviously, his ears are beyond reach.*

The distance to the clearing felt like she had tread for an eternity when she finally reached the top of the knoll. *Why do we have to be so bloody far away?* She huffed and puffed.

Finally, bending over and placing her hands on her knees, she surveyed the area. The only element visible was the roaring fire, highlighting the sullen faces of Remmi and Abin conversing back and forth. Bog was sitting a little further away, staring blankly at the fire.

"Salve t'!" she slurred, hiccuped, and waved her arms.

Shocked, Bog stood up immediately with a very concerned look on his face.

Remmi and Abin watched her curiously.

Then, Abin slapped his knee and a boisterous laugh emerged. "She's drunk!"

"Drunk?" Bog repeated in a worried voice. "Mora, where did you partake in drink?"

"Oh, someth old witch in a willow tree gave it to me. Toldeth me it would maketh me feel better," she paused and threw her arms up, "and she was *righth*!"

Tripping close to the fire, Bog caught her arm and helped her sit down on a log. As she swayed, he propped her closer to his body.

Remmi glanced angrily at Abin and passed Mora a leather flask. "Here, drink this of its entirety. I told you to remain discreet."

She tilted the flask and proceeded to drink, water running down her chin. "Thank you, I waseth parched!" Giggling, she swayed on the log.

"I think I like her better this way, not a care in the world!" Abin laughed. Rubbing his neatly trimmed beard, he asked, "So, lass, who was this witch who gave you the spirits?"

With her ever-present, intoxicated grin, she eagerly glanced from Bog to Abin to Remmi. "The one who mendeth my wounds when I woketh the first time in the foreseth," she sputtered.

Abin, Remmi, and Bog all gawked at one another.

"The one who mended your wounds?" Remmi repeated. "We had no one approach you the entire time you slept. We told you Bog cleaned and fixed your wounds." He crouched in front of Mora and inspected her eyes. "We were not aware you woke before this morning." Smelling her breath, he balked before examining her fingernails.

Uncomfortably, she leaned away from Remmi and muttered, "Aye, she saideth she was a healereth."

Immediately, he glanced at Abin as a cloud of uncertainty settled on the company.

Bog shifted nervously, his shadow towering in between her and the flames. *She is placing the -eth on her words again.*

Placing a hand on Remmi's shoulder as he continued to stare in her direction, Abin inquired, "Where did you say this witch lived?"

There was a condescending tone in his voice Mora didn't care for, so she smirked, "In the willoweth tree on the far sideth of the village. Why do you looketh so sullen?" She playfully hit Bog on the thigh and sputtered, "How did you refereth to it Bog? A gorp?" Laughing, she suddenly purged over the log.

"Golp," he corrected in agitation. Wiping her mouth with the cloak, she swayed heavily on the log before he steadied her again.

"Bog, remain with Mora. We need to inquire about this *witch,*" Abin said gruffly as they hustled off toward the village.

"Whateth is their problemeth?" She giggled.

He looked at her with an unsettling seriousness and replied, "I do not know Mora, but it does not bode well." Then, he asked, "Are you hungry?"

"Are you completely jes*th*ing? Of course! I have not eaten a sthcrap all day. Or…" she held a finger to her mouth in contemplation, "… sixeth days!"

"No wonder you are in this state," he muttered, rolling his eyes in annoyance, "again."

She ate like a ferocious animal and wanted more after the first helping. He gave her the rest of the rabbit and a few of the fresh fruits and vegetables grown in the village. They were delicious. She could not remember the last time she ate a decent helping. Washing the rest of the scraps with the remaining bit of water, she finally relaxed and gazed at the fire, waiting for the return of Abin and Remmi.

The flames were brilliant, even more colorful since she observed their detail thoroughly. The small sparks emerging from the fire bounced and danced on the ground, making little popping sounds as they landed. The smoke billowed from the flames in droves, pushing each previous cloud out of the way as it climbed higher. Then, figures seemed to appear in the smoke before dissipating through the canopy. As she watched the life and death of the reoccurring images, she felt her eyes becoming increasingly heavy. All of a sudden, a strong arm wrapped a blanket around her shoulders.

Immediately, her head fell onto Bog's lap and her breathing became steady. Staying very still, he positioned his arms on the logs and listened to the sounds of night. The familiar feeling of Lychinus crept into his memory. Bending his free leg, he placed his elbow onto his knee and propped his head on his hand. He was angry at himself he had not insisted harder she be accompanied, or he should have at least stayed close behind. However, it would betray her trust, unraveling the thin threads he was desperately trying to weave into something more significant. *If I destroy her trust, then I loose All.*

Glancing down at Mora, he tucked a loose curl behind her ear. A tiny spark kissed his fingertips. She was very young and naive in the world, but he knew who she could become and that was both terrifying and humbling. Slightly curling his lip, he also thought about her stubbornness and passion, qualities he admired in her acceptance of the circumstances which would have potentially destroyed anyone else. Leaning his head back to peer beyond the canopy of the crimson trees, he saw the outline of a hawk fly peacefully overhead. *If only I had enjoyed flying as much.* Adjusting his wings without disturbing her position, he decided to settle his thoughts and close his eyes.

Although he thought it was only a brief moment, it was not until the fire died down he wearily began to hear footsteps echo in his subconscious. He opened one eye in time to see Remmi trudge up the path, followed by a disgruntled Abin. They both appeared distraught. Setting their equipment down on the ground, they slumped on the dirt and leaned against the nearest log.

"Did you locate her?" Bog inquired quietly.

Mora stirred.

Fixed upon their faces was a mixture of disappointment and worry. Remmi was the first to speak, his voice terribly sullen, "We found the mound beneath the willow tree. The residence has not been occupied in a long time. The ashes on the fireplace were not fresh and the door appeared to have been barred for many moons. There were cobwebs surrounding the handle and inside the corners of the room."

Sleepily, Mora rubbed her eyes. She had awoken when she heard the weapons dropped by the fire. Flustered, she held her head tight and sat up very slowly with the minimal aid of Bog. She grumbled, "How can that be? I left not too long before I came here."

Then, the images commenced to fluctuate in her mind. The whirling made her stomach churn as if she would purge again, but she choked it down by sipping on another flask of water Bog apparently had propped against her side while she was sleeping. She gasped for air, sputtering, "Wait! There was someone leaving the willow tree when I glanced back from the village. It was not the hobbling hag, but a tall, cloaked figure."

Abin continued his hard gaze inquisitively. "We think whomever it was may have tried to poison you - both the first time you woke, and then earlier."

Scrunching her nose, she whispered, "Poison? How do you figure?"

"We found this on the table." Remmi pulled out the bottle labeled *Root Extract #6.*

"I did notice."

"By the smell, it contains hints of Nightshade, or Belladonna, a female poison of choice. However, it also embodies several undertones of foul scents I cannot quite place." He placed it up to his nose. "Death's poison. I could smell a faint trace on your breath. It was highly masked with whatever ale you drank, concentrated enough to kill you swiftly, if you were any *regular* immortal." Then, he added, "Or on contact, if you were mortal."

The way he peered at her made her suspect he wanted to inquire further about her origins. Therefore, she changed the subject. "You spoke of how Alidyah concocted an 'unimaginative' female's weapon. You were referring to this particular extract?" Mora eyed Abin and pointed toward the bottle.

"Ah, aye, you remember." Abin grunted and rubbed the back of his neck.

Remmi glared at Abin, but he shot a look of pity in return.

"She deserves the right to know." He repositioned himself and folded his arms behind his head. "While an entirely different mixture from Death's poison, the idea behind it is the same. You see lass, I had been away from the castle for several months during a recent excursion to the east. I entrusted Remmi with the affairs and the protection of my partner, Alidyah. However, I received an urgent, coded message from the castle during the very last stretch of my return. When I arrived to the Staggering Stones, I was not greeted by my partner, but Remmi, who immediately disguised me. We ventured concealed across the stones and through the underground of the fortress."

Mora glanced from Remmi to Abin, but not before he caught a hint of her suspicion. He grinned, "I trust Remmi. Therefore, I knew the urgency was dealing with a life or death situation."

Remmi rubbed his face and turned away from the fire.

Bog watched closely as his blue eyes grew significantly far away, the white rim appearing more prominent.

"As we safely made it under the castle walls, he began informing me of the recent events. The Volant guards had spotted two travelers entering in the Fire Country, a Borgorian and a petite female. Immediately, under orders, they proceeded to the castle to inform the Queen. In the midst of their journey, they were mercilessly attacked, and only one guard was able to free himself. Severely injured, the survivor flew in haste."

Taking a swig of his flask, he offered the contents to the others. After each declined, he shrugged and continued, "Before he passed, he informed the Queen of the news from the Fire Country and of the unknown attackers. They had been sure the attackers were from the northwest and concluded the fortress had already been infiltrated. Worried, Remmi sent guards to each station surrounding the Floating Fortress in the hopes of defending the Queen."

Feeling the emotions threatening to emerge, he cleared his throat before his voice became too strained. "During his morning rounds, Remmi came across the body of the Queen's handmaid. Thereupon alarmed, he hastily ran to the Queen's chambers. To his surprise, he found the Queen, sewing in her usual spot by the window. Pardoning himself, he informed her of his tragic discovery. Strangely, she did not appear distraught about the news. Instead, she jerked, the needle accidentally pricking her finger. Brushing it off with a serene smile, Remmi noticed the smear was not blood, but black as soot. Excusing himself, he sent notice right away. Fortunately, he sent two servants, one with the real message and one with a counterfeit. Sending the fraudulent by the normal means, the young guard was immediately slain outside the gates. Concealed, the other lad traveled by an alternate route while the distraction was executed.

"Once upon hearing the news, I only had a short period to grieve for my murdered partner before fabricating plans to reveal whatever evil had befallen. Remmi coaxed a secret from a kitchen maid who overheard one of the guards give orders to retrieve Nightshade from one of the local village dealers. Because I was the only superior standing in the way, I assumed the poison was for me upon my return. Remmi paid the maid a handsome fee to be the one delivering the poisoned wine to me personally in my bedchamber."

Patting Remmi on the shoulder to bring him back to the present, Abin nodded his appreciation before turning his eyes back to Mora. "Therefore, Remmi discreetly made my return known through an elaborate story and concluded I was not feeling well enough for company. Carefully, I stuck my fingertip into the wine, barely enough to sedate me until discovered. Then, I spread a wee bit upon my lip, being careful not to rub any more in my mouth."

Mora interjected, "But you appeared dead."

"Aye, I had been traveling for many moons, living off berries and small animals, a fasting tactic I use during my extensive trips to disguise my identity. I hadn't eaten in two days before that evening. I also used a bit of chalk on my darker skin for a more pale complexion." A fleeting sense of pride hummed before he sighed, "Unfortunately, I have now realized the evil that had taken over Alidyah's body was only a replication of his creation. After witnessing the transformation into a dragon, I am convinced it is the only explanation. I'm certain Didac killed her, along with her handmaiden, but the body must have been more thoroughly disposed."

She saw a small tear run down his cheek.

He paused for a time, wiping away the single tear. "I loved her greatly. She was more than anything I could have ever dreamed."

### The Keeper

A long stretch of uncomfortable silence overtook the camp. As the fire began to dwindle, mixed emotions played in Mora's head and she could not think of any words to speak comfort at the time. However, before too long, she heard the deep, clear voice of Remmi start singing a hauntingly melodious tune. It was soft and the words were barely distinguishable, but she listened, entranced in the sweet serenity. Fluttering on the edge of sleep again, her head still pounding from the remnants of poisoned drink, she swayed to and fro with the tune of the lullaby. Finally, laying a head on Bog's shoulder, who had been uncomfortably silent since their return, she held firmly on the precipice of her dreams.

When she finally let herself slide into the chasm of slumber, she heard His voice whisper, *O'curem y'teruo. We will meet again.*

# On the Edge of Jealousy

 The mist was covering the ground, damp and in droves of thickness lapping at her bare feet. It was night. Mora walked through the trees watching fireflies coveting the land with their enchanting light speckled language, dancing and weaving in a sacred flow. *How did I get here? Am I still asleep?*

Walking to the edge of the grove, she paused. Startled, she took a couple steps back from an abrupt drop off, the black abyss below vast and heavy. Lingering her eyes in the distance, she strained to recognize her surroundings. As if the fireflies floated into the sky, stars began to appear, one by one, until the entire darkness was full of pinpointed lights. A shooting star traveled past her eyes and disappeared as quickly. The moon rose, massive and white against the night sky. The longing to touch each star lingered and tugged heavily in her heart. Holding her hand high, she closed her palm around the clusters as if she had the ability to embrace them. Disappointment settled when none lingered in her grasp.

A sweet vibration sent a sinful chill up her spine and she felt an alluring, seductive presence. Without turning around, she breathed, "What are you doing here?"

"You were expecting me."

The deep growl of His voice made her chest flutter.

"It has been too long."

When she spun gently on her heel, her hair falling softly in coiled droves over her shoulder, she saw Ekklips standing only a hand's length from her body. Hatefully, she gazed into the eyes of black ice, the depths of the mysterious void staring back. "I want nothing to do with you."

He moved closer, the coaxingly wry grin growing wider, while His dark indigo hair fell loosely over His forehead. He leaned in, His breath on her neck. "You know not of what you speak. You and I are intertwined in each other. You have merely lost your way." Gently, He kissed her neck. "Come back to me, Solora."

"Please stop." She slid away carefully, trying not to meander near the cliff. "You...or your monsters, have been constantly attempting to kill me."

Running a hand through His hair before hooking them behind His back, He shrugged and responded, "Kill you? Nay. Never kill you. My apologies if you have thought such. My...followers have such a vicious thirst for blood. It is an unfortunate burden in the confinement of your creatural body. However, death does not suit you, my light." He smiled, but it did not reach His eyes. "I only wish to possess your soul again."

"I'm not a godsdamn possession," Mora spoke angrily through gritted teeth. "Why do you claim my flesh? Who was I *before*? I want to know from your own lips."

He held out His hand and sighed. "Solora, do you not remember the beginning?" Encompassing her waist with His arms, He smelled her hair and caressed her skin with His lips. Floating His fingers down her arm, He could feel the heat rising in her flesh and growled hungrily.

Leading her in a slow sway around the firefly grass, He spoke in a soft manner, "From the beginning, you, *cuthos*, are Light, the Sun Goddess, Illumination, *Enlightenment*. We've created worlds together and we've watched them die together. We were the *Trinitas*: Life, Light, and Dark," He sneered, "until *He* wanted All."

She could feel tension in His grip, but the heady, darkly exotic scent of His skin was intoxicating. The aroma smelled of deep forest pine, the spice of oak cherry rum, and the coolness of night. Dipping her back in a graceful arch, blood rushed to her head as she felt His lips graze her shift covered nipples, progressing to her neck as He sensually lifted her against His body.

Although they were embraced in a sweet, rhythmic motion, Ekklips continued, the spite in his voice increasing, "I forbade it, and I

*344*

fought for my," He paused, "*our*, place in All. Without our help, He could not have created All. You and I, we were the balance of Life. But, I countered Him alone, unwilling to place you in the crossfire of our feud, until necessary. After He persisted to overshadow me out of my rightful place, I sought vengeance. I pleaded for you to see Him for the egotistical tyrant He had become."

She felt His hand drop lower on her back, making the lustful heat between their bodies intensify. When she tilted her head to look in His face, she saw Him staring hungrily down at her, the longing gaze penetrating the wall of uncertainty she had been building. Upon closer inspection, she could see subtle, gold flecks shimmering against the obsidian background of His eyes.

"I promised you freedom, and you followed me, leaving Him behind. However, He had been quicker than I, and once you stepped outside the Divine Realm, you were banished to become Chaos, unable to grasp your True Being. You see, as Light, He had entrusted you with His knowledge and secrets of All. You were known as The Keeper, the keybearer. He forbade it to be released into the world alongside my Being. He had grown to distrust my True Nature. And I…His."

Again, she felt His hand slide lower, hugging her curves, circling His thumb on her hip. Becoming overwhelmingly flustered, she took a deep breath as His other hand interlaced with hers and the sway became more of a dance. Her breasts pressed firmly against His black, linen shirt, while His lips lingered on her forehead. Her ears became filled with a harmonious tune, as if the wind were humming in synchronicity with their movements. She wondered if He was creating the tune.

After a moment, Ekklips snarled with anger and amusement. "You became enraged with Him; and I, Dark, used your inhibited spirit of Chaos against Him. You and I planned to destroy the worlds together, plotting immortal against immortal, until each consumed one another through greed, envy, and power. There would be nothing left of the original creations!" He glanced up at the night sky and grunted. "He was furious. Life was loosing control without our balance. Therefore, through His life altering sacrifice, He was able to curse me as Death, creating the first race of mortals. That moment, He took something of tremendous value from me, and I have vowed to reclaim it once again. Therefore, I built my kingdom opposite His, and, ironically, my initial transformation became His balance. Ultimately, it will also become His destruction. Life versus Death."

She contemplated His words momentarily, unable to comprehend the factual nature. If the truth, she had no recollection of an existence beyond her own with her mother. This being claimed to be ageless, the primal concept of immortality, and her the same, an equal and her balance. Feeling His grip strengthen on her hand, He released her waist and twirled her around beneath His seductive gaze.

"Those who are mortal or immortal, eventually come to me. Mortals beg for another chance, the rebirth of their soul. Immortals beg to be rid of living for eternity. However, much of the eternally damned I have used for my own personal gain." He sniggered. "I've heard some refer to them as my...Legion of Monsters."

Running His fingers down her cheek, He relished in the softness of her flesh. "Devastation increased as I commenced to manipulate the darkness on the land, creating shadows in my image, and intertwining it with my new position as God of Death and you, a harbinger of destruction and spirit of Chaos. However, I yearned to aid you back into your transformation as the Goddess of Light. Although you may not believe such, I do not yearn to become the absolute embodiment of Death, as Dark is my True Being, but it is slowly eating me alive. I need Light.

"One day, I was informed of the pleas of your unfortunate mother's soul. Already spiteful of her banishment, I convinced her I would bring her salvation if she would allow me to use her body as my vessel. You see, as a Primordial Being, she was still part of our primitive creations. There were seven we created beneath us and all were exiled in Life's fit of rage and jealousy. Because He was envious of my sway and enraged at the betrayal, He ultimately sentenced all seven to a type of death, which entailed a complete separation from the Divine Realm. Unfortunately, thus far, I have merely found three of the seven Primordial Beings who walk the land. Meridan, or Sila, as was her divine name, was the first of the seven to tread the soils of Atlastova, neither able to fully live, nor fully die. After spending centuries attempting to reincarnate your True Being, I finally decided to create life using my own power. I informed her I could unify your spirit within her womb, manifesting the embodiment of

## The Keeper

Enlightenment. Desperate for release, she relented."

Mora tensed at the mention of her mother, someone she thought she knew, but really knew nothing about. *Sila?* Tipping her head to look at the expression on His flawless face, she could see the fire in His eyes intensify.

He pressed her hips against Him, squeezing the curve of her hip. His deep voice resonated in His chest, "You, Solora, with the knowledge you possess, we can fulfill our promise to one another and birth a superior breed of beings and worlds unimaginably magnificent in everything pleasurable." Kissing her neck, He growled, "Yet, we have a hindrance. I did not foresee the creatural development of a conscious in your flesh, the innate sense to view the world as right and wrong, good and evil. I fear He tampered with your formation because the bitch, Sila, had the audacity to plead for forgiveness, bartering the creation I had instilled within her womb! Using a formidable, nearly untraceable magic, and His graces, she sheltered you from me until she became weaker, or merely gave up protecting you. Tell me, what do you plan to do with yourself once you have reached The Gateway?"

She pushed away. "The Gateway?" She suddenly felt weak and powerless. *Where have I heard of the place?* She raced through all her memories, but the concept eluded her grasp every twist and turn.

He smirked, closing in the distance once again. "Ah, I see. Along with your complete lack of knowledge in who you really are, and who you were before, you know not of where you are venturing. How do you expect to fulfill a deed in which you have no familiarity with at all? Has He revealed himself to you? Nay! He is weak, hiding Himself from All. Here I stand offering you an eternity of power and pleasure! Together, we can create life in our *own* image!" He took her in His arms and kissed her wildly.

After a moment, she sunk into Him, their tongues entangling passionately. A heat flickered in her core as she moved her hands to His shoulders. He grabbed her thighs and lifted her off the ground. She locked her legs around His waist and her hands moved their grip onto the back of His neck. He ravaged her flesh, swirling His tongue along her jawline and down her neck as she tilted her head back in pleasure. She moaned. The sudden forbidden sensation cascaded down her spine and into her core.

*The Keeper*

Guiding her hips rhythmically on the hardness between their forms, Ekklips groaned throatily. He dropped to His knees and laid her in the tall grass. He continued to kiss down her collarbone, hovering over her nipples, hard through the translucent shift. Rubbing them softly with His fingers, He lowered Himself to her center. Lifting the hem of her shift around her hips, He kissed around her inner thighs. Mora arched her back and grasped onto His loose hair. Kissing her intimately, His tongue began to dance hungrily against her wet, sensitive skin.

She gasped, never feeling anything like it before. Lifting her hips, she pulsated in rhythm with His tongue. The sensation was overwhelming, her skin tingled in ripples and her soul felt like it was on fire. He played at the entrance with His fingers before He thrust them deep inside, watching her bow in response. An insatiable need for release forced her body to move in sync with His fingers. An intoxicating, lustful build escalated until she began to feel her core light a euphoric match, sending her toppling over the edge of pleasure.

He growled in thirst of her essence, taking in the sight before He climbed back over her trembling body. "A ship stuck in the midst of a storm without a captain," He whispered tauntingly. "Let me in Solora."

Suddenly ashamed, she turned her head and pushed her way to her feet. Straightening the matted, sheer cloth, she fondled her braid as angry tears threatened and burned behind her eyes.

On His knees, Ekklips pushed His hair away from His forehead and rose to His feet. Walking over to her, He stroked her cheek with affection, but His stale voice threatened, "Your *friends* will not survive. No one will survive. The only reason you are not truly dead in this form, Solora, is because you and I belong together. I will find a way to release your True Being."

She scowled at Him with a cold look, pushing His hand away from her cheek. Backing away, she snarled, "This is not real. You are not truly here. Get out of my mind!"

Choosing to ignore her plea, His voice smoothed out, "When you were born in this flesh, Life's knowledge was restored in you. How? I'm not entirely sure. I cannot risk taking it away. But I promise you this, I will be next to you every step of the way, taking what is mine and what is most dear to you. I need not remind you I am a part of *you*. There is no way of destroying me, I am Death. If attempted, you will dismantle yourself and All combined. If you fail, Life will fail, and I will be there watching when you can't climb any higher." He smiled sourly and peered over the edge.

Still attempting to even her breathing from the pleasurable encounter, Mora straightened herself against the shadow He cast in the moonlight. "You are so confident of your power over me, over the worlds. You think because you tread in a tangible form upon the land, you own each and every thing. I may not know who *He* is, but I can guarantee you have less power than you realize over All."

"Tangible? A very curious term to describe my existence, indeed." Flashing His debonair smile, a loose hair waved slightly in the breeze as He replied casually, "Solora, you see, it is not whether I currently have the power to bend every knee to my bidding, it is that the power is rapidly growing. Because of the line of consciousness to distinguish between what is considered good and bad is teetering on disaster and destruction, my influence is growing exponentially. Your glorious form of Chaos aided it so many eons ago. Balance is becoming a game of extremes, nearly non-existent. Therefore, whether I remain in the shadows, or in the form of your closest and dearest friend, my plans will be essentially fulfilled by Life's choice to include freewill into the creation of All. During my descension as Death, the irony has unfolded to my advantage.

"Though, pushing the limits and recognizing how much you can get away with is all a part of mortal nature. They have divided themselves on various grounds in the name of religion and spirituality, their stance on morality, and establishing dominance in the name of progress and prosperity. I see and feel it festering through All like a voracious plague because they fear what happens after death. They find pleasure in playing gods, killing and controlling in the name of their own egotistical doctrines. The immortals, on the opposite side, are easier to convince. They see it as their 'divine' right to rule themselves without the tangible aid of gods. But because Life insisted on limiting their abilities, they became spiteful and are not difficult to manipulate over the theoretical ledge of truth."

She could see He had become lost in His own words, the growing distance lingering in His eyes. Unsure if she was in a dream, or in another plane of existence like she was with Nephani, she was leery about how she would escape His presence. Therefore, she needed to keep Him adrift of her true intentions. Inquisitively, she asked, "But if what you speak is true, and the Trinitas was the sincerest and primal beginning, how can one convince All that Life is dominant?"

Glancing briefly out of the corner of His eyes, He grinned wryly. "You are beginning to comprehend our dilemma. The more you realize who you are Solora, the greater you will understand the injustice of His tyranny and what we must do to make sure He never accumulates superior power over the entirety of All!"

Her mind raced through the few possibilities of escape at the edge of the cliff. Finally, she locked His gaze and slyly stepped toward Him, placing her hands on His chest. "And if I do realize, in all entirety, who you say I am, will we not have the power to confront Him with this... conundrum?"

"Comprehension resonates in your smile, but eludes the severity of your situation." He slid His arm around her waist and spun her around to face the abyss. Lowering to her ear, He whispered, "Do you remember our bond, Solora? I can hear the echoes of your intentions."

Realization sent a wave of fire ripping through her body as His grip on her waist tightened. She could not sway His stature. He pressed her back firmly against His chest as a hand moved to encompass her breast. Shaking, her breathing became shallow.

Leaning down to kiss her neck, He could taste her fear. Bittersweetly, He said, "I am not your enemy." With the last word, He released her over the ledge, turned, and walked away.

# Sun Shadow

Mora gasped for air and awoke to a thick mist surrounding the camp. Her body shook violently as she attempted to stand up straight. *It was a dream.* Walking silently past Bog as he snored gruffly on his side, head propped on his arm, she grabbed her knapsack. Stepping over Abin while he slept sitting upright against the log, she glanced around to find Remmi was absent from sight. Heading to the stream she had laid in the morning before, she knew she would have to bathe quickly because the morning was exceptionally drafty and a stinging chill penetrated her clothes. However, she felt a desperate need to wash away the events of the dream and the memory of Ekklips inside her flesh.

Reluctant to feel the icy cold bite of the water, she reassured herself by the time the sun rose fully, the Fire Country would be more pleasant. Because the seasons were unfamiliar to her outside her own knowledge of the sanctuary, she had stopped trying to keep track of the variations in temperature anymore. However, she was relieved there was already a slight twinge of warmth in the breeze.

The mist was low lying and the trees were still black in the dawn. She replayed the words Ekklips had spoken. Although, everything was nearly impossible to grasp upon, already fleeting into obscurity as many dreams do. She could not understand how she could be anything more than a mortal creatural, much less immortal, a Goddess, or Chaos. It sounded ridiculous, but she could find no logical answers to the series of events in which had occurred thus far on her journey. *Where the bloody curse of the gods am I supposed to go anyway?* She had never seen, nor heard of Life, but the mention of The Gateway still plagued her memory. Not to mention, there was a haunting conclusion to His words, *'I am not your enemy'*.

Continuing the highly vegetated trail to the babbling water, she peered up and down the stream. A deeper pool of water was desired to immerse her overwhelming thoughts and cleanse her body of all the discord. She told herself, *Traveling a little further won't hurt.* Glancing over her shoulder, she memorized the surrounding area and then proceeded to trudge upstream until stumbling upon a clear pool of water in the midst of a circlet of trees. Modestly, she looked around before removing the garments Remmi had supplied for her from the village. Laying them neatly on a rock, she submerged herself completely into the cool water and let out a long, deep breath. Bumps rolled up her skin, but she did not mind due to the fire lingering on her flesh. Strangely, the abnormal assurance of knowing she could drown and no one would hear enticed dark thoughts to fill her mind. However, the indelible recollection of the prophetical words that All hung in the balance of her actions, required she needn't be so rash and cruel. The slight feeling Ekklips would not be happy to greet her, despite His words about her coming willingly as a Goddess, played acidly around in her thoughts. With a slight smirk, she lowered into the water until it embraced her neckline. A relaxing lull sent a shiver up her spine.

Scrupulously cleansing her hair, she laid back and floated calmly, imagining what the top of the trees looked like from the sky with their brilliant orange and yellow leaves. The nonsense about supernatural vendettas alluded her sympathies. *Is it too much to ask to be left alone, to sleep in the silence?* Death exerted a viable outlet to her sorrows, to her broken heartedness, and to her abandonment.

Upon feeling the gravity of her thoughts, she completely submerged herself into the pool. However, this time, she held her breath until the last second, the last edge to suffocation, until she could stand it no longer. Throwing herself through the ceiling of water, she gasped for air, the overwhelming satisfaction exploding in her lungs. *Death by drowning would never be my first choice. I cannot willing choose to void the air I breathe or intentionally remove the dependence.* Sighing, she figured the demise by her own hand would not only be selfish, but it would feed her

*The Keeper*
directly into Ekklips' hands. She did not want this burden.

Taking the lavender scented soap from her knapsack she took from one of the washbasins in Lychinus, the enamoring scent filled her nostrils as she scrubbed it deeply through her hair with her fingernails. The sensation was as nearly gratifying as breathing. Then, she lathered her skin with a cleansing contentment, her flesh exuding its appreciation through bouts of shivers and tingles. When she reached the sensitive spot between her legs, she inhaled sharply as the lingering pleasure from her dream made her body jerk. Despite her reaction to His behavior in her dream, the sole thought of Ekklips enticed her to continue. Repeating the same, circular motion, she grasped onto the nearest fallen branch for support. The soap vigorously played on her center as she closed her eyes and tilted her head back. The piercingly black ice eyes radiated against the back of her eyelids, possessing a tinge of triumph at her actions. She held fervently onto the image as she released a pulsating wave of fulfillment. Gasping, she vigorously wiped her face and quickly placed the soap back in its beeswax wrap. After stuffing it into the knapsack, she climbing out of the pool, trembling from head to toe. Her entire body was flushed and her legs felt a little weak, but she balanced herself on the log. A glimpse of movement several trees in the distance startled her, and she froze.

"Who goes there?" she called out nervously.

*Nothing.*

The movement ceased and faltered no more. Hurriedly, she grasped her tunic and breeches, wrestling them over her body as the droplets of water caused the fabric to stick to her flesh. Grabbing the bone comb from her knapsack, she fought with the tangled curls before braiding her hair to the side. Then, in haste, she finished her ritual by tying her belt and sandals. As she walked back along the stream, she periodically glanced back toward the pool of water, but could see no one in sight.

By the time she reached the top of the knoll, the sun had broken through the treetops, casting splotchy bits of sparkling light over the forest floor. She could hear an argument erupting between Bog and Abin. Bog, a head taller than Abin, flung his arms in the air with frustration, his face almost the color of the tree trunks. Abin, smoking a pipe and shirtless, stood fuming with his hands on his hips. Curiously, she studied his chestnut brown skin. Tattooed in black across his front was the same, three-swirled patterns from the outside gate of the Floating Fortress. One was directly in the center of his chest, while two were beneath the pectoral muscles, one on each side of the ribs. When he turned around, the disturbing image of the eye was centered between his shoulder blades. Running down his spine were a series of sigils. However, she could not make sense of the language from her vantage point. She wandered closer, snapping a twig.

Bog whirled around, his violet eyes nearly glowing. "Sunshine! You're alive!" He embraced her with great fervor. *Shit, she smells amazing.*

"You spoke those words last time I walked up from the stream." She smirked and returned the hug, patting him on the back reassuringly.

Anxiously, he ran a hand through his hair and upturned the corner of his lip. "My apologies, but after the events that have occurred as of late, I do not hold my breath you will be here, nor alive, when I wake."

"How macabre of you." She laughed. Although, she had similar feelings as of recently.

Sardonically, Abin snorted from over her shoulder, throwing a tunic over his head. Then, he proceeded to walk around, picking up the few belongings strewn around the ashes of last night's fire.

"Where is Remmi?" she cocked her head and inquired.

"He had second duty," he spoke lethargically, but continued gathering items together. "Not that he ever seems to sleep. He should be back soon. He tends to be discrete about his whereabouts. Sneaky son of a bitch." He tossed a bag at Mora. "Help me pack."

Grudgingly, she grunted when the bag hit her in the stomach. Briefly peering at Bog, she bent down reluctantly to pick up a few items.

He smirked at her expression. "I'll be back." He heard her scoff before heading toward the stream to relieve and clean himself. He was also grateful for a way to distance himself from Abin.

Before she could protest, she finally caught sight of Remmi trudging up the hill. He nodded toward Bog as they passed each other. Tilting her head, she felt a wave of heat soak her cheeks because he had come from the direction of the pool. When he glanced in her direction, she immediately dropped her eyes and continued packing.

"Notice anything of interest, Rem?" Abin patted him on the shoulder.

## The Keeper

"Nothing save an unusually pleasurable sunrise."

She peered up to see him smirking before turning his eyes to Abin. She knew her entire body turned the same shade as the surrounding tree trunks at that point. *Curse of the gods, he bleeding saw me.*

Bog meandered down to the clear pool. Stripping off his breeches and boots, he stepped languidly into the coolness, fully submersing himself. With a groan of satisfaction, he began to wash with the refreshing water. Normally, he didn't like to go long without fully bathing, but circumstances were dire and the availability had been scarce since he located Mora. *Except in Lychinus,* he thought with a frown. The morning breeze rustled his wings. Stretching backward, arms raised, his spine made several, synchronized, popping noises before he emerged from the pool and took another pair of black breeches from his satchel. Rummaging around the village, they had been able to procure several necessary items to continue their journey northeast. Holding them to his waist, he knew they would be too short, but he could stuff them into the top of his boots, thoroughly securing them with his laces. Before he was able to pull the breeches over his other leg, a firefly danced in front of his face. Nearly tripping over the leg hole, he managed to tug them over the wetness before the fireflies accumulated into a familiar form. Although the light wasn't as vivid as their previous encounter, and her expression wasn't as enjoyably pleasant, he knew who she was: *Draelia.*

Fully forming into the outline of a female being, Draelia spoke in a soft, but urgent, tone, "Bog. I must speak to you before you leave the forest. There is unrest on your journey northeast. While injured, Didac has acquired forces outside of the Mortal Realm, forces which are being commissioned to stop Mora from reaching Borgoria."

"What kind of unrest?" He stepped closer to her, hoping she would touch his arm so he could feel the exhilaration of power once again. However, this time, she touched his cheek. An emotion of agony accompanied the caress, followed by pity.

"I'm so very sorry. I cannot give you the answers you want. For I am here without permission. I hope this dire warning will be enough to guide you to be wary."

He held her hand against his cheek, his gaze locked on her sultry, leaf green eyes. *Green eyes.* Then, he shook his head when Mora's face

**355**

lingered in his mind and took a step back.

Draelia closed the gap, stood on her tiptoes, and gently grazed Bog's lips with her own. "Bogheim, what you feel for her is only fleeting. There will come a time when she must choose and you will be forced to part ways. He will never allow her to be with another."

He shuddered at the thought.

Lingering her finger on his lips, she lowered and whispered sadly, "Don't let your anger cloud your judgment. You are strong and you are brave. Protect what you must until it is no longer needed and walk away. If you continue to follow, she will be the death of you. Take heed."

The fireflies burst into a lingering glow, dissipating into the depths of the forest. Standing for a moment more, watching the last disappear, he closed his eyes. Draelia's sweetness lingered on his lips. *Brave? Strong? I have not been referred to as either except by the wind. And the wind is fleeting.*

Opening his eyes, he glanced to the top of the hill where he met Remmi's uncomfortable gaze. He nodded shallowly before he proceeded to lace his boots over the unfortunately short breeches. When he looked up once more, Remmi was gone. Groaning, he grabbed his satchel and trudged back up the hill.

Mora watched Remmi closely out of the corner of her eyes. Out of her present company, he was the most mysterious. He was not emotionally readable and struggled with interactions, save for Abin. If he wrestled with inner daemons, the battle appeared to play repeatedly inside his mind, constantly distracting him from reality. She never knew how to approach him, even after he saved her life. Although, she hadn't technically had a moment alone with him since he found her in the chambers with the black, liquid monster.

He was always clad in a deep indigo tunic with black breeches and boots. Though, the most unusual piece of garb he wore constantly were the matching, deep indigo gloves covering his hands. The only flesh visible was his neck and face. Rivaling Bog in stature, his severe, blue eyes were so light, they almost always seemed to glow, sometimes appearing white. His hair, while it was loose when she first noticed him on the ledge, had been crudely pulled back on the sides, away from his face. Several strands still fell messily over his forehead, covering the scar. He loomed a formidable force and she willingly kept her distance. Notably, however, she would trust him to save her life...*again.*

Abin was a different sorts. She deduced he was gruff and unyielding in battle, never afraid to leave a warrior behind, but had a hidden tenderness, especially when he spoke of his late partner, Alidyah. His brawn overtook his brain, while his masculinity was as important as the sun itself. He was unable to venture into a conversation without showing off his unequivocal knowledge of the current circumstances. A warrior by birth, he needed to be the dominant figure, a leader. Whether his opponents were one to a thousand, or a thousand to one, he would swear by his malehood he would defeat each and every with one flash of his blade. He certainly brought humor to a dying world of extremities. If there were notorious gods, she humored at the thought they would be as humble as Abin.

Smirking to herself, she saw Remmi flash a serious glance in her direction. *Can he hear my thoughts? Surely not.*

Bog meandered back to the clearing. Remmi and Abin were ready with their belongings and Mora was resting on a log, rummaging through her knapsack. A few more spotty bits of sunlight had peeked through the trees. Briefly glancing at Remmi, he felt it odd how he had leered earlier. Nevertheless, he reminded himself, *I'm not fond of our found drifters, but the extra protection will be acceptable.* Flashing a smile at Mora, he offered his hand and was instantly relieved when she accepted. A slight spark made him wince, but he held her hand tight as he lifted her to her feet.

Bending low, he whispered in her ear, "How are you feeling?" The scent of lavender on her flesh created a strange pounding in his chest.

She smiled sweetly, but still felt ashamed of the previous night's dream and from her own hands this morning. "Thank you for your concern, Bog. My head still beats against my forehead aggressively, but it's been slower since I ate more and drank copious amounts of water." She placed her hand on his arm in reassurance and grinned. Slinging her bow and quiver over her shoulder, she bent down to retrieve her belongings.

He upturned his lip to convince her he understood. When she lifted her hand, he could still feel the tingle lingering on his arm as the hauntingly prophetical words from Draelia echoed in his mind - '*if you continue to follow, she will be the death of you*'. As if reacting to his thoughts, a large hawk rustled and cawed from the canopy. It had startled everyone, but as his heartbeat steadied, he thought, *I'm already dead then.*

"Here, Sunshine, I snatched this for you from the village leather-smith." He handed her a leather harness and belt with a new scabbard attached, her dagger already sheathed.

Her eyes widened. "Bog! It's perfect!" The corner of her lip curved as she gave him an unconvinced glare. "You *snatched* it?"

He ran his hand through his hair. "I bartered him to fashion it while you were sleeping. I brought him the dagger for measurement."

The wry, damn dimple appeared as she felt tears welling. "Thank you, Bog. I will always cherish this gift." She fastened it around her shoulders and waist, the twisted metal loop securing the leather straps.

"The twisted metal was created by the young, blacksmith apprentice. He said it was the first time he ever succeeded making a complete circle." Bog smiled widely.

Mora hugged him again. This time, she did it so tightly, she could feel every muscle in his stomach tense.

Unamused, Remmi watched them. Then, he cleared his throat and said, "We must be going. Bog, can I speak with you for a moment?"

Shooting a strange glance in his direction, Bog left Mora and walked to the edge of the camp with Remmi. "Aye?"

Surveying the trees, Remmi pushed the hair out of his eyes. "What did she say to you?"

Bog raised a skeptical eyebrow. "Mora? Nothing much as of late. She says her head is pounding after the poison."

With a curve of his lip, Remmi shook his head, unamused. "Nay. Don't act like you are oblivious." Facing Bog with an austere look, he said, "The tree nymph."

Shocked, Bog wiped the sweat from his brow and nervously laughed. "Who are you to ask me?"

Patting him on the shoulder, Remmi answered clearly, "More

inclined than you will ever know. But, mate, I will not force answers from you," he turned slightly and started walking back toward Abin, "yet."

Bog's chest twisted disagreeably, but he spoke over his shoulder, "She said there was unrest heading northeast toward Borgoria. Didac has managed a great deal of control for Mora's capture."

Pausing, Remmi gave a nod of satisfaction. "Aye, we will adjust accordingly. It would do you *a great deal* to stay unemotionally detached, Bog of Borgoria."

A bit of anger engulfed Bog's being after Remmi left him standing on the edge of the camp. *Who the* fuck *does he believe he is?* Balling his fists tight, he turned around and proceeded back toward Mora. A cool breeze rustled the feathers on his wings, a hint from the wind for him to quell the rage festering deep inside.

After clearing the area of their belongings, Mora, Bog, Remmi, and Abin commenced moving northeast. The vegetation of the land began to drastically change. It became a stark contrast to the blood red forest they had traveled amongst for many days. The land was hilly, with endless oceans of undulating, soft grass. The blue sky calmed their journey overhead and the night was as uneventful as the days. The moon had been waning, causing the nights to be increasingly darker. Passing sluggishly across the sky, the clouds billowed magnificently like puffy, white castles. These lands reminded Mora of the stretch of fields before the Staggering Stones.

As they trudged through the green seas of grass, Bog spoke of his land often. "Borgoria lies northeast of the Fire Country, split by the Nymian Sea and through the veil," he would begin, "where beauty meets magnificence. It is a sight like no other." Cocking his head in remembrance of his home, he would sigh. "I miss the scenery terribly."

"Oh, shut the fuck up," Abin would respond.

Undeterred, he would continue, "The lands of Borgoria are unrivaled. My mother and grandmother made it so."

"Mummy issues?" Abin would jest.

*359*

Bog would make a lewd gesture in return.

Mora tried to hide her amusement, but Bog would always flash her an unamused glance.

Remmi remained neutral.

Their journey advanced until the new moon. The fluctuation of the land eventually proving difficult. Her leather soles were beginning to wear and her body ached. From afar, they might appear a band of gypsies heaving along, parched from the sun, and tired from the exhaustion of a night cut short by the annoying habit of Remmi's inability to sleep much longer than several lengths of time.

*If he slept at all,* she thought.

One morning, he splashed out the fire and began moving around the camp.

She groaned.

Bog huffed.

Abin whined and grumbled, "Bloody curse of the gods! Why can't you wait until the morning light?"

Remmi grunted in return, but continued eliminating the dying fire.

Stumbling to his feet, Bog aided Mora in gathering herself before she asked for a moment to get ready for the day's journey. Obliging, he would relieve himself away from the company and pursue to survey the horizon.

Several days into the journey, she began to feel lightheaded, weary, and in desperate need of water. The grasslands were an unyielding torture. The more parched she became, the more she wanted to lick the dew off the blades of grass at first light. Her head ached and the air dried her throat. She could not advance any further or her body would ultimately fail. Praying for sustenance, or water, proved a disappointment. There was no stream, no cool breeze. The heat was sweltering, not the sensual, cool kiss of autumn she had felt the last morning in the sanctuary.

Suddenly, she began to laugh hysterically, fell to the ground, and laid on her back to stare at the blue sky.

## The Keeper

"Pick her up," Abin said sullenly to Bog. "We can each carry her until the sun sets."

"I need water...rest!" She stumbled to her feet and lunged at Abin.

Bog grabbed her by the waist, clinging her close to his chest. "Mora, it's the heat. Calm down."

Abin deliriously guffawed, "She is a female! There is a weakness to the sex."

"Fuck you!" she screamed over Bog's shoulder.

Remmi turned around and placed a hand on Abin's arm, "Abin, Bog is correct, it's the heat talking. Calm down." He nodded at Bog. "We will stop soon. Then, she can receive a decent night's sleep and rise tomorrow, ready for her journey."

"Gods forsaken each of us." Abin pulled his sack on his shoulder and trudged passed the company with an angry gait.

Out of nowhere, the ground commenced to vibrate. Mora felt the pressure would push her further toward the sky until she realized it was not her imagination. Shielding her eyes in the sun, she could see movement in the distance. It was fast approaching and monstrous in force.

"Quickly! Shield the female!" Abin yelled.

Entranced and irritated, she pushed Abin aside, stumbling toward the approaching caravan. Soon upon the band was a monument of horses, stout and glorious. They were wild creatures with lustrous manes blowing in the wind and a stature unlike any animal she had ever laid eyes on. Bog, Remmi, and Abin stood armed behind her, none advancing toward the horses. Then, she took a step toward them. In front was a beautiful mare, magnificently groomed and well-mannered. It was a majestic build of pure white. The mane was flawless, save for a thin streak of black. The eyes were a beautiful obsidian with flecks of gold, echoing with the great mysteries of the past.

She stroked the nuzzle. *Is this a* wild *horse?* She looked deep into the horse's eyes and whispered, "I will call you Sun Shadow."

Abin came forward, a hint of concern in his voice, "Lass, these horses are wild, far be it their demeanor to not kill you mid-ride."

"Nay," she whispered, entranced at the horse, "these are ethereal horses." Running her fingers between Sun Shadow's eyes, a symbol of the moon appeared between its brow. Abruptly, she glanced down at the crescent shaped birthmark on her wrist, enamored at the similarity. "They are a blessing and will be at our command 'til death."

She was bewildered by Sun Shadow. Gazing into the horse's eyes, she felt an intense connection as it stared back. It was as if their souls were intertwined. Proceeding to walk slowly around the magnificent creature, she ran her hand along the side of its muscular body. The enormous strength inside was exhilarating, coaxing a return in her will to live. Pausing midsection, but keeping her hand fixed, Sun Shadow knelt down on one knee, as if bowing. She gathered a handful of the mane in her hands and mounted the taut shoulders. When Sun Shadow returned to standing, she felt like a warrior high above the battlefield. Gleaming at her companions, they returned her look with reverence. A sense of purpose recoiled into her soul and a surge of exhilaration resonated deep within her body.

"Be no longer discouraged! Choose your wild and ride with me," she commanded her company with a bout of dignity.

A sense of confusion reflected back at her; save Remmi, who half smiled at the gesture.

Bog held a hand over his eyes to block the sun as he looked up at Mora. "Do you even know how to ride?"

It was a fair question, as she had never actually ridden a horse before, but something familiar hummed deep in her soul, like the act was second nature. "I feel...right," she replied, trying to keep the confidence she exerted in her voice moments before.

Studying each of her companions as they mounted the horse of their choosing, Abin sat upon the chestnut brown stallion, lightly spotted with hints of white on the sides, the eyes a rich blue color. Bog sat upon a gray steed, less majestic in size, but well suited for him, the eyes a hue of deep mauve. Then, she looked toward Remmi. He graced a higher horse than herself. The horse was pure black from its mane to its hooves, the color almost a deep indigo in the sunlight. She was amazed in its superiority, but its eyes caused her to gasp. They shared the very same, piercing, blue hue as Remmi's own. It appeared he and the stallion had been fashioned for one another. Clad in all bluish-black, the rider was one with the horse.

### The Keeper

She jerked her head away when he lifted his own. *There is something unusual about him,* but she knew not what.

Clearing her throat, she spoke confidently, "We must ride quickly to the Nymian Sea, each to their own accord. Lest they become a hindrance to the pack, the other horses will follow as protection." She knew not where each of the phrases she spoke manifested, but she knew it must be concise. Swiftly, she kicked the horse into a full-speed gallop.

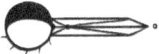

"They are near. You must make haste. Use whatever force necessary," a grim voice growled from the shadowed face.

"Aye, it has begun," a heavier voice replied.

# 'Ura-Ca

The trek over the grasslands was long, but the horses proved their worth as the wind blew strong during their gallop. It was a welcomed feeling as the air became even more sticky and hot. Upon departing the forest in the wide open terrain of the Fire Country, Mora had shed her cloak. However, even the linen tunic presently worn clung to her drenched skin. Tearing the sleeves away to her shoulders, she wiped her brow with the excess cloth. Still wearing the sandals laced over her breeches, the sweat proved uncomfortable sliding around her foot. Her braid trailed fiercely as they rode, loosening several curls from around her face. Regardless, sighing in pure ecstasy, she leaned her head back and closed her eyes. Sun Shadow knew the way.

Bog had taken the lead, knowing the journey to Borgoria better than the rest. He loved riding. He preferred it to flying. Hating his wings for the majority of his life, he chose to remain on the ground most of the time, unless he was forced. As a borgling, his mother knew of his uneasiness with flying. Therefore, when she could get away from his father, Gornya, she would take him to the stables, where she would let him choose his favorite horse. It was always the same one, a smaller pony with a sadness in its hazy, mauve eyes. There was something about the pony he both loved and pitied. The smallest in the stables, its dull gray coat was the least shiny, not as taken care of as the other stallions and mares.

His mother never questioned his choice of horse. They would ride for half a day, or until the sun set. Sometimes, on special days when his father was absent from Borgoria, they would take a picnic, spending the entire day riding and exploring. When he finally outgrew the pony, he would still visit until it died in a stable fire. Like his mother, he could not save the pony. For many moons, he would mourn the pony because it reminded him of the days with his mother.

His heart beat fiercely in his chest, partially from the impact of riding, but the majority because the remembrance of his mother always made emotions resurface he had spent a lifetime repressing. In turn, it would fuel his rage. Wiping the single tear escaping from his eye, he clenched his teeth and seethed to himself, *I will not fucking cry.* Furiously, he kicked his heels to spur the horse faster.

Mora could see nothing but the endless, tall reeds of swaying grass. Settled between Bog and Abin, with Remmi bringing up the rear, she was positive it was because he was watching and waiting. Bog sat tall on his horse. She could tell he knew how to ride well, but curiously wondered why he hated flying so much. He rarely talked about himself, so the question never surfaced long enough to get answered. His wings were no hinderance while he rode. In fact, oddly, it seemed to help him gain more speed.

Turning her head to glance at Abin, she did not think she would see anything different than him sitting strong, neck veins bulging from the matching chestnut skin of both rider and horse. His curly, black hair whipped fiercely behind and his dark brown eyes were serious and alert.

Finally, she briefly watched Remmi. He carried the look of how she thought a god would ride…*if they rode horses*. The idea made her smirk. He had pulled back all his hair to reveal his chiseled jawline and his eyes seemed both distant and ever-seeing. A hard grimace stretched across his face. As he held the reins with one, strong hand, the other remained rested on the hilt of his sword. Before she could turn her head to look forward, Sun Shadow reared abruptly on its mighty hind legs, whinnying in loud alarm. Nearly loosing her grip on the mane, she grasped on tighter. The other horses followed to a halt, each raising on their hind legs in response.

"What is it?" She rubbed Sun Shadow's mane gently as the horse backed up slightly. With growing apprehension, she glanced about, sweat dripping down her forehead. She could see nothing but the green and tan sea of grass.

Abin took action, riding to settle his horse in front of Mora, and spoke in authority, "Bloody show yourselves!"

As he suspected, one by one, with skin the color of molasses, half-naked males rose out of the tall grass holding spears and bows. Their bodies were painted the golden-green hue of the grass and their brown hair was braided long behind their backs, shaved on the sides. "Fall back Mora," he hissed.

Bog rode to the other side as Remmi took the rear. She was surrounded by the three beings she trusted the most, but a sudden fear of the camouflaged creaturals made her shudder.

After several moments of silence, Abin furrowed his brow and grimaced, "Take me to Ura-Ca," he commanded, his voice dark and deep.

Briefly taken aback, she watched as one of the males threw a rope around each of the horse's neck and commenced to lead them on foot.

With a low tone, Bog ridiculed, "What the curse of the gods is happening, Abin?"

"Control yourself bird-beast." Abin shot him an unnerving look. "Unless you want your malehood hanging on the next spear, I suggest you shut your damn mouth and let me do the talking."

Mora quietly peered around the band of painted males. The number grew in shocking amounts, each one covered in the same, neutral paint. Remmi was the only one who appeared unaltered by their sudden presence. He rode calmly, his stern eyes fixated ahead. When she looked at Bog, his face was retched with anger and annoyance. She trusted Abin, much to Bog's chagrin. *If we are still in the Fire Country, then Abin will handle the issue,* she tried to convince herself.

Glancing back in the direction they had been traveling, she sniggered. After the frightening ordeal at the Floating Fortress, she had begun to feel more alive than she had ever felt before. An energy jostled her senses and emotions like a fire beginning to kindle in the core of her soul. In spite of the uncertainty surrounding the new strangers, she began to hope the feeling would steadily grow. She could not imagine allowing the feeling to fade. It would create an agonizing hollowness.

They were being led at a slower pace, but at a surprisingly even stride for horse versus creatural. However, by the placement of the sun, they were traveling southeast. She knew this added to Bog's frustration.

## The Keeper

Her thoughts were interrupted by rolling bouts of hunger in her stomach, while weariness tugged behind her eyes. Although thankful for Sun Shadow, she felt the increasing numbness in her lower extremities would render her legs completely useless by the time they reached their destination. When she attempted to fondle her knapsack at her side, a pinch on her skin made her jump and whip her head around. A being walking behind her horse had jolted his spear tip at her hand. Apparently, she assumed, he saw her action as threatening. She cupped her hand to observe the wound, but the spear had merely nicked the skin, drawing only a small amount of blood.

Stubbornly, she made an action toward the assailant. Pointing toward her mouth, she said, "Food."

He continued to look ahead.

In anger, she grunted and turned to Abin, "Can you tell them we need food. I know it's beginning to affect *my* strength to ride."

Unaffected, he glanced back at Mora. "They understand you perfectly. They just do not give a shit." He sardonically chuckled.

She did not find his response amusing. Suddenly, a male on the other side of her tossed a leather pouch onto her lap. Out of shock, she jumped. However, she caught it before it fell off the opposite side. Surprised, she peered at him over the rim as she eagerly drank. After she took a few sips, she wiped her mouth and tossed it back. "Thank you." He simply nodded, but she sensed a hint of snide mockery when she saw him lift the side of his lip.

By sun down, she could see hints of light in the distance. As they progressed closer, the light of the fires began to multiply and expand tremendously. The source was not torches, but gigantic columns. Illuminated in the middle of the bleak terrain, each column was made of a light green stone with enormous bronze bowls filled with blue fire blazing at the top.

From a distance, it seemed as though there was no city to pair along with the columns, but the closer they progressed, she realized the city was not above the ground at all. On the edge of the cliff, they peered down into a vast crater of winding rock staircases and stone buildings. Built into the walls of the rock like massive, dirt spiderwebs, various stairways lead to a multitude of dwellings. The hustle and bustle could be compared to the interior of an anthill. The staircases were endless, eventually disappearing on the perimeter of neatly lined structures paralleling a main road. At the edge, with what little sunlight was left, the road bled into an unusually large area. It was expansive enough to be seen with the naked eye. She presumed it was a courtyard, the center of the vast, stone city. Within the center of the presumed courtyard rose a gigantic, round tower. Its tall, phallic shape gave her an uneasy feeling. She averted her gaze back to the columns.

The somber wailing of a horn resounded from outside the confines of the city as the painted beings continued to lead the horses down the stone stairway at the end. As they descended, the craftsmanship, while bland, possessed an impressive magnitude and sturdiness despite the inevitable erosion of stone. As the steps began to veer off from the side of the cliff, digressing into the main city, she noticed each structure they passed was nonetheless attached to the steps in some fashion. Whomever constructed the city never entirely chiseled through the stone. She would have felt tense with such a tremendous weight on the pathway if it were not for the solid rock underneath.

The males continued leading the horses into the streets of the city while naked childlings, not painted green, ran to and fro in front of the oncoming caravan. Females hustled around trying to move them quickly out of the way. They giggled merrily, intentionally avoiding the grasping hands. Mora saw a male shove one out of his way, making the wee being fall brutally against the stone wall. He began to wail as his mother ran over and swept him into her arms. It was unclear to her whether it was deliberate harshness or he was attempting to save the childling from being trampled. Either way, she began to worry about their descension into the cliff-fortified city.

Each female wore an extremely loose linen draped over their hips, breasts and torso exposed. It flowed, stopping around mid-calf. The linen donned a high slit, open on both sides of the legs. Their feet were bare. With skin much darker than her own, she thought it must be common in the Fire Country because it was closer to the chestnut brown skin of Abin. Observing a female close to her horse, she could see various, bronze flecks shimmering in her wide, brown eyes, glinting in the setting sun. Her hair was pulled high on top of her head, full of dark auburn-brown curls. Mora

## The Keeper

nodded to the female as she rode past, blushing at her beautiful stare. Then, she saw her eyes fearfully dart to the following company. At that point, she grabbed her childling, running into the nearest door. Mora glanced behind her and saw Bog watching the creaturals with a stern, vexing expression. Finally, his eyes locked with her own. Sadness and pain loomed, but he quickly looked away.

*That is odd.*

Riding further into the city, she glimpsed at the high, surrounding cliffs. They stretched long passed her view of the encompassing grasslands, but she could still see the tall, fiery columns at the top. The sun had descended behind the side of the wall the closer they advanced to the central tower. Torches were being lit by males chained to the metal poles lining the street. The sky above danced with a haunting mixture of dark blues and deep oranges. Amongst the approaching blanket of darkness, there was a calming appearance of tiny stars. The air had become cooler, but terribly stifled with the dust, and smelled slightly of sulfur. The phallic tower loomed even more intimidating, its eminence the apparent foundation of the city.

She presumed this was where the tribe was taking them, to whom Abin had called: *Ura-Ca.*

"Off," a bland voice instructed.

She glanced around. There was a short, squat male next to Abin's horse, gesturing him to accompany him on the ground. Another male forced her to hastily dismount, while Bog and Remmi did so willingly.

"What are you going to do with the horses?" she inquired desperately, reluctantly slipping off the side of Sun Shadow.

The heavy, green painted male merely stared blankly at her and led the horses away to the outside of the surrounding common area. She saw one of the painted beings speak to Remmi about the horses and he nodded. Curious, she walked over to where he stood and asked quietly, "What did he say?"

Remmi, while glaring at Abin and the one who had instructed the dismount, replied stoically, "They are taking them to their stables."

She looked suspiciously at Abin. "Does he know this tribe?" Suddenly, she saw his eyes dart around the tribe and knew it was not the time, nor place, to speak about the matter.

## The Keeper

Abin beckoned, but at the same time, the sound of drums resonated from inside the phallic tower. He whipped around. Appearing from the wall of the tower was a receding piece of stone. It was being pulled backward from the inside. Once it revealed a relatively thick indentation, another loud crack echoed and the piece was pulled apart from the middle. The two, separate, stone blocks gradually disappeared inside the wall. The drums grew louder as the hole opened.

Emerging from deep inside the phallic tower were half naked, thick drummers, a line of three opposite each other. They were not painted green like the accompanying tribe, but wore short, brown linens, belted at the waist, covering their genitals. Each was bald. In the middle of the drummers, three males came forth. The one in the front was a small being dressed in a long, brown cloak, with no body part visible below his collarbone. He was bald and had a white beard extending halfway down to his waist. The next creatural was a taller figure, also dressed in a brown cloak, belted at the waist, but atop his head were cropped, auburn-brown curls, with a long braid swaying behind. The last one to appear was a grotesquely massive individual, as round as he was tall. His hairline was receding, but it was still pulled back tightly in a dark brown and silver braid. He wore a long tunic of white. On top of the tunic, he donned a sleeveless, golden silk in which flowed openly.

Mora tried hard not to smirk at the expression on his face. She could feel the overwhelming sense of arrogance mixed with superiority. As he stepped, his jowls would shake like coagulated milk curds. She counted at least three rolls under his perfectly rounded chin. His beady eyes were hawk-like, much like his nose mimicked a beak. Because his appearance and demeanor were much like Master Verquan, she shuddered. The drums ceased when he took his place in front of the tribe, the other two, cloaked creaturals flanking on either side.

He squinted his eyes. "Abin," he scornfully spat.

# Phallic Assailant

Bog despised the feral creaturals. He had heard stories about the Ura tribe from bards who played for his mother long ago. They were a brutal, hedonistic brood who enjoyed the suffering of others, whether it be 'friend' or enemy. No Borgorian ever allowed the Ura to live when happening upon them; and here he was, at the mercy of the Ura. The males did not show their fear of a Borgorian, only the females as he rode passed.

*Damn Abin for allowing the savages to lead them like cattle to their own territory.*

He peered at Mora as she watched the procession feed from the tower. She was amused by the situation, he could see it, but she knew not of what the Ura were capable of executing. *If only there was a way to talk to her without suspicion,* he thought. *But at this point, there are already too many Ura.* They were surrounded. He shifted his stance and listened to Abin speak with this immensely massive individual.

"Ura-Ca," Abin nodded in amusement, "it has been a while. How are you bloody doing?" He gestured at his physique. "I see you must be treating yourself well."

Ura-Ca squinted his eyes at Abin. "Why do you pass through our lands? You...and your band of misfits." He laughed to the cloaked beings and they mimicked. Surveying the crowd until his eyes settled on Bog, his expression soured. "And you are in the company of a Borgorian. What do I owe this pleasure?" He hobbled nastily forward until he was peering up at

Bog's averted gaze.

Abin glanced sideways at Bog, repositioning his stance in Ura-Ca's sight. "He will do you no harm. His tongue may be sharp, but his blade is not. And, as you are well aware, the Fire Country is under the jurisdiction of the Coutarians."

Bog's blood boiled. He wanted to close his hands around Abin's throat, or better, strangle the fat fuck in whose breath he could feel on his chest. Though, he held his tongue and his actions.

"Immortality is wasted on the weak." Ura-Ca shook his head. "Come, Abin," he placed a hand on Abin's back, "we must speak." Peering maliciously at Bog, his stomach shook as he stepped back around toward the tower.

Ura-Ca began walking to the entrance of the tower, followed by his minions, and then Abin, Remmi, Mora, and Bog. Half of the green painted males followed as the rest dispersed into the streets. The males walked in a militaristic procession on either side of Ura-Ca. As he reached each of the drummers, they turned on a heel, and began drumming steadily in his rhythmic footfall. Once inside, the door into the tower closed with a mighty, thunderous, land trembling noise. A multitude of nearly naked beings pushed the stones back into place, each chained to the next one. The sound of clanking metal echoed in the dim light of the circular chamber as they walked, settling themselves back against the wall once the doorway was sealed.

"Prisoners," a whisper sounded next to Bog. Inconspicuously, he shifted his eyes, confused. It was the male who had offered water to Mora.

*Prisoners? Shit Abin,* he thought to himself, though he nodded politely.

After they entered the tower, a guard at the door barred their advancement. "Weapons," he commanded, pointing to an open chest to the inside left of the door.

Abin balked. "You must be jesting."

Ura-Ca turned around, a sly grin across his face. "One can never be too careful these days Abin, with the *chaos* ensuing." Darkly, he murmured, "And if you have no ill intentions against my kin, you will not be in need of your weapons."

Abin snarled when Ura-Ca turned back around to continue

through the tower. Dropping his swords into the chest, he stepped forward, blocked once again by the guard.

"Boots," the guard pointed.

"You want my damn boots? Ura-Ca doesn't provide quality necessities?" he replied sarcastically.

Unamused, the guard stood his ground.

Grunting, Abin pulled a knife from his boot, flashed it tauntingly in the guard's face and mumbled, "Satisfied, Ura-shit?"

Bog dropped a sword in next. Abin had provided him with the weapon from the village blacksmith in the crimson forest. While the metal held no comparison to Aloria's saber, he appreciated the well-crafted piece.

Reluctantly, Mora placed her bow and quiver in carefully. The shifty eyes followed the drop. Then, she unsheathed her dagger. *I'm not removing my bloody belt.*

Lastly, Remmi sauntered up, tossed his sword, along with his bow and quiver, into the chest and shoved past the guard. When the guard began to retort, he turned around and the guard immediately silenced.

Walking back a few steps, she discreetly watched him spin around, a luminosity in his eyes fading. *Curious,* she thought.

The tower was musty, vaguely lit, and damp. It smelled of sweat and soured ale. The space was huge and empty, appearing hostile and unlivable. Much of the original stone was jutting out along the floor, most big enough to see amidst the dark, but others only noticeable without warning. She tripped over a couple, holding back a few surprise jolts when she felt the stone pierce her skin.

They were led into a smaller chamber with a square, stone table in the middle. The chairs were hard, cold, immovable stones jutting from the ground. Ura-Ca sat at the head of the far end and gestured for everyone to take their seat. He saved the seat closest to his right hand for Abin. When everyone was settled, in the dim light of the chamber, he started to speak boisterously.

"Welcome to my table. I assume you have had a considerable journey and I would like to extend the invitation to partake in my hospitality for the night." He motioned to the nearest maleservant closest to the door.

Bog heard shackles dragging on the stone.

## The Keeper

"I am sure my cooks can scrounge up some ample servings for you all. Now, Abin, tell me of your journey. I have heard murmurings of your unfortunate events leading to the downfall of the Floating Fortress."

Abin replied gruffly, "Your false empathy does not readily surprise me. You were always envious." He cut his eyes viciously at Ura-Ca. "However, since it seems I have no choice but to acknowledge the events as of late, I am sure you will get a damn good laugh of my hapless circumstances."

Ura-Ca made an annoying clicking noise with his tongue. "Shame on you, Abin, after I welcome you to my table. Let us forget our aberrations and be civil about it, will you? With the Coutarian stronghold obliterated, I fear your authority does not hold as much sway over the Fire Country as it once did."

Abin remained stoic.

Ura-Ca's eyes lurked dangerously around the table and then settled on Mora. "A female on your journey? That is unlucky. Is she your whore, or does she actually have a purpose for being amongst a band of males other than to spread her legs?"

Bog saw Mora nearly hurdle from her seat, the rage in her eyes screaming.

Remmi, calm and collectively, unobtrusively grabbed her arm and held her down in the seat.

It still caught Ura-Ca's attention.

"Ah, she is feisty. Clean the bitch and she would make a fine jewel in my collection."

His disgusting eyes cut into Mora and she scowled. *I will cut each fat fucking chin off your godsdamn head!* she screamed in silence.

Bog shifted uneasily in his seat. He could feel the heat radiating from her skin.

Abin glanced at her briefly and then to Bog.

Sensing Abin was trying to caution them both without speaking in front of Ura-Ca, he placed a hand on Mora's shaking leg. Immediately, he felt a spark and the tension melt from her thigh.

"I am sure every female would leap for the opportunity to vigorously climb all over your layers," Abin cleared his throat, "but as she is in my possession, I do not wish to share my toys." He slightly curled the side of his lip, "And, as I recall, you prefer the company of younger *phallic musings.*"

Ura-Ca's thunderous laughter made Mora jump. A terrible chill tore through her when his beady eyes stared in her direction.

Curious, he averted back to Abin. "Your possession? Therefore, she is your *cun'ta*?" He peered harder as if accessing the truthfulness of the claim.

Bog could feel the tension between the two rising rapidly. He squeezed a little, hoping it would help her calm down. Finally, Ura-Ca spoke as the maleservants brought forth several bowls filled with a sour smelling soup.

"I see. Then you wouldn't mind showing me how much she means to you."

Bog felt his stomach lurch as the bowl was set in front of him on the table. Unfortunately, his action did not go unnoticed.

Ura-Ca jerked his head toward Bog and sneered, "The Borgorian feels our food is not worthy of his kind." His eyes squinted with malice. "Unless you feel like being forced to partake in my hospitality, perhaps we can convince you in another way of how delighted we are that you are amongst us."

Bog shuddered at the thought. Hesitantly, he picked up the bowl, placed it to his lips, and swallowed the foul tasting liquid. *Nasty tasting godsdamn shit.*

Somewhat satisfied, Ura-Ca turned back to Abin, his thought process unhindered. "Are you up to the task?"

Abin thought for a moment, a hand on his chin. "What are you suggesting?"

"A game," Ura-Ca said slyly. "If you win, you may take the whore and be on your way. If I win, she will be mine."

"I am not a damn trophy!" Mora screeched. All the eyes around the chamber turned toward her without a sound.

She did not cower at the attention either, leaving Bog to speculate she did not sense the gravity of the situation. He removed his hand. Discreetly, from the corner of his eye, he saw the servant, whom had spoken to him earlier, slip unnoticed from the room.

From the head of the table, Ura-Ca stood on his feet, knuckles hammering on the table. "Your cunt proves differently!" he roared.

Bog winced at the remark. This ruler was ferocious and he knew the game meant life or death.

Right away, Abin stood erect, rubbing his beard. "I accept."

With that, Ura-Ca calmed down, sitting heavily into his chair.

Bog glanced over to Mora and saw her staring infuriatingly at Abin.

"Well done," Ura-Ca hummed. "I am quite unaroused for the night and do not feel up to any more conversation. The festivities will come to a halt until the morrow." He stood and walked closer to Mora. "Until then, she will stay in my company." He snatched her arm and flung her out of her seat. She landed hard, her knees scraping into the stone.

Bog bolted to his feet and shouted angrily, "Keep your fat, filthy hands off of her!" and began to step around his chair.

Abin and Remmi grabbed Bog as he attempted to lunge for Mora.

Ura-Ca laughed gruffly. "I feel there may be more to this whore than you have divulged, Abin. You may have to watch your bird beast. His cock might have already been stuffing *your* bird!" His boisterous laughter echoed throughout the chamber. Then, he became serious.

He stepped closer to Bog, his rolls of flesh bouncing wildly at the slightest movement. Still holding Mora tightly by the arm, he looked up at his face with a scowl. When Ura-Ca opened his mouth to speak, the foulest of breath tinged his nostrils, sending a wave of bile up his throat.

"I suggest, *Borgorian,* if you wish to keep your pathetic life for the time being, you shut your godsdamn mouth."

Through gritted teeth, Bog responded, "You can't fucking kill *me.*"

"*I* don't have to," Ura-Ca sneered. With the threat, he roughly dragged Mora out of the chamber, leaving the others behind.

Bog shoved Abin and Remmi away as he attempted to control his anger. "And you just let him fucking take her!" he spurted while pacing back and forth.

"Calm down you bloody idiot!" Abin pointed toward the door. "*That* being can tear you limb from limb despite whether he can actually kill you or not! And you try to stand up to him in his own dwelling?"

"It was more than you did!" Bog yelled back.

Remmi stood between them. "Both of you need to calm down. We have visitors."

Bog and Abin glanced around at the same time to see two, cloaked figures hobble into the room.

"Master Abin," the leanest figure spoke blandly, "you and your friends will need to follow us to your quarters."

Bog's chest heaved fiercely as Abin pushed passed. Remmi patted him on the back before following in Abin's footsteps. The cloaked Ura led them through a dark passage and into a small room at the end of the hallway. The area was no bigger than a horse's stall. He had to duck his head before proceeding through the doorway. Once the three entered the room, they heard a cell door shut behind them.

Abin turned on his heel and shook the bars. "What the fuck is this?"

The short, cloaked being replied, "This will be your quarters for tonight. Ura-Ca has surpassed his hospitality and wished for you to reflect on your behavior in his presence."

He hit the bars violently. A vibration resonated throughout the area. "You had to be forceful," he hissed, pointing at Bog. "You couldn't have shut your godsdamn mouth like I had advised! Now we are going to soak in someone else's filth for the night." He leaned against the bars.

Remmi sat down silently in the corner of the cell, his arms resting on his bent knees.

"What will he do to her?" Bog managed to sputter in spite of his rage.

"Nothing." Abin spat. "He merely used it as a ploy. Did you not hear he prefers his dalliances to be of a more phallic gender. But he knows something is awry and he will do whatever he needs to find out whom he possesses."

"And the games?" Bog inquired, his indignation quelled momentarily.

"Hand to hand combat," Abin sullenly replied.

"With Ura-Ca?" Bog sat down opposite Remmi and waited for an answer. It was not Abin who spoke, but Remmi.

"Nay. A ruler of his mind does not set himself amidst the fight." He studied the ground, staring hard into the stone. "He will use his maleservants and it will solely be for his viewing pleasure. What's done is done, we will all battle to the death, regardless of immortality. We know not what he has concealed." He glanced hard at Abin.

Abin turned away from the bars and sunk down to the ground.

"And if *we* die, what will happen to Mora?" Bog inquired hesitantly.

"She will be given to the males to be raped and used until *she* dies," Abin answered bitterly.

"But..." Bog began, but bit his tongue. He did not want to continue arguing about whom he felt Mora to be, regardless of whether Abin agreed. The acts would continue until she took her own life, for no mortal could take it.

The wings on his back began to ache against the hard stone. Silence filled the small room, and before long, Abin had drifted off to sleep in a sitting position, his head flung back. Remmi never seemed to sleep, but his glazed over, blue-white eyes told Bog his mind was not in this present moment. Finally, he settled himself down further onto the stone, laying his head on a section of his wing to create a barrier between his face and the floor.

His mind began to wander. *Who is the Ura who spoke to me earlier? Why did he slip out of the chamber? Would they be able to escape this cruel city without one of them being killed or enslaved?*

As sleep became heavy on his eyelids, he attempted to call out to Draelia, or any spirit of the land, who may be listening. He silently hoped the wind would answer. However, all he felt was a cold, sinking feeling in the pit of his stomach. He had survived the dungeons of the Floating Fortress, being held captive by a malevolent immortal. Naively, he held hope of escaping the cursed place they currently occupied. As he began to think about the fight, he contemplated how Abin could survive. Abin was mortal and clearly frightened of these beings, despite his tough exterior. Bog knew not why, nor cared to inquire any further into his personal dealings. While he did not hold high regard for Abin, he admitted to himself they had one thing in common: their desire to keep Mora alive.

He lifted his eyes slightly again toward Remmi. He was confounded at his mysterious demeanor. He was like a shadow, following and waiting. Remmi's abrupt comments irritated him and he knew the being contained secrets deeper than any knife could cut. Worst of all, Remmi reminded him of Didac with his hauntingly penetrating, bright blue eyes.

As time passed, neither his fears, nor hopes, could coax his eyelids to remain open any longer. Finally, as the heaviness consumed his lids, he blinked and succumbed to a deep sleep as an image of Mora's face outlined his mind.

# A Lullaby

Mora attempted to loosen Ura-Ca's grip on her arm once he began to drag her up three flights of stairs. Higher and higher they climbed the phallic tower without a word mumbled. Finally, he flung her into a chamber lit by a roaring fire. He clapped his hands and a couple of maleservants fled to his side.

"See to it she is properly bathed and dressed. She smells of female sweat. It is making my stomach lurch."

As one of the maleservants took her by the arm, she saw Ura-Ca survey the male up and down approvingly. Heavily, he trudged over to the fire and plopped down in a enormous, stone chair with an unnecessarily high back. Pouring a glass of wine, he took a big swig, reached a hand to the other maleservant, and guided him to his knees.

Grateful she was taken behind a wall panel, concealing the hedonistic act taking place in front of the fire, her eyes followed the wisps of heat swirling high above the rim of a gold plated tub and out a slitted window. As the male began to take off her clothes, she resisted, tugging in return as he attempted to take it above her breasts. He stood up straight in front of her and she inhaled slightly, noticing it was the one who had given her the water on the journey. Halting her reaction, he placed a finger to her lips and stubbornly continued to remove her garments. When she was completely naked, he motioned for her to step in the hot water. Tiny bumps rose on her skin in satisfaction. Awkwardly embarrassed by the company, she faltered while attempting to shield herself from his obvious line of sight. However, he commenced to softly apply herbal lotions to her skin, mixing the water fervently until bubbles began to appear. It smelled of honey and sandalwood. Unnervingly, his hands fondled areas of her body, jolting at the sensations she had explored earlier in the forest. She knew it was not in the way he desired, but it made her wary all the same. This was duty, and the male was not interested in her femininity.

After he was done, he assisted her from the water and patted her dry with a fresh cloth. Brushing the tangles from her hair, he twisted it down her back and tied it with a cord. Grabbing a beige cloth from the small chair next to the tub, he placed it over her head and belted it right below her breasts with the leather Bog had gifted her from the village. The slits on the sides were extremely high, exposing much of her legs. Once she was dressed, he led her into the chamber where Ura-Ca had moved to a bed and was having another maleservant massage his grotesquely large hands and feet. The body of the smaller male was sprawled across his flesh, kneading with both his elbows and knees. He was naked, and she abashedly averted her gaze from the aroused phallus folding into Ura-Ca's rolls of flesh.

Nonchalantly peering over to Mora, Ura-Ca nodded in approval and grunted, "Come and sit." He gestured to a stone chair in front of the fire and offered a glass of wine.

She hesitated.

His chin jiggled as he smirked. "If you are afraid of my desires, trust me *cun'ta*, the female physique does not tickle my fancy." He petted the maleservant's chest, licking his lips as he glanced at his erection.

She strutted over to the chair, poised and refined.

"Now, what is your name?"

Gazing absently into the fire, the recollection of her brief time in the chamber at the Floating Fortress flashed through her mind. A chill shuddered her body. She had watched Bog sit in front of the fire while she laid in bed. He had been poisoned with the wine they had been supplied.

Ura-Ca inquired if she was cold, but she shook her head. "Mora. My name is Mora."

He waved the maleservant away, stood, and walked back over to the chair, his hands crossed down passed his stomach. He stared at her intently. "That is a curious name in the Fire Country." He cleared his throat, "Enlighten me, Mora, with your infatuation to travel with my *dear friend*, Abin?"

Nervously, she coughed in her hand. "I find him...intriguing," she replied sweetly. "He delights me in ways I have never experienced." She reminisced on Abin's claim about their coital relationship. She decided to play off the notion.

He rubbed his chin. "Delights you?"

"Aye. He is quick witted and brash, but gentle." The thought made her tongue sour. Abin was certainly not her idea of viable affection.

He slanted his eyes as a malicious grimace grew on his face. "I do agree Abin's masculinity is," he paused, "desirable. What about the Borgorian?"

The idea sent chills all the way down to her toes. She wanted nothing more than to protect Bog as he had done for her throughout their time together. "He is nothing but a friend, a *brotherly* companion. He is very protective."

He snapped his fingers and a different, slender maleservant traipsed naked to where he sat. Motioning to his lap, the maleservant sat down on his thick thigh. He began to kiss and suck on Ura-Ca's neck rolls. Unaffected, he gurgled, "Where are you bound?"

She thought quickly about the question. She did not know the lands well enough to conjure a decent lie. She sighed, "Unfortunately, we were headed toward to the land of Borgoria. You see, I lost my mother a season ago and, per chance, I stumbled upon my Borgorian companion on his way to his homeland. I knew not of the lands and he agreed to provide me with food and shelter once we reached Borgoria. Being jaded as I am, I agreed, for I had no one else to turn to after my mother passed." She watched uncomfortably as Ura-Ca began to fondle himself while the maleservant groped his neck.

Choking back her nerves, she continued, "Shortly after we crossed the border to the Fire Country, our stops became more frequent from sheer exhaustion. We happened upon the hospitalities of Abin and his... companion." She glanced around the room. She noticed the only other living being in the room was the male from the journey, the one whom had helped her bathe. When her eyes met back to Ura-Ca, she smiled sweetly. "Abin and I were instantly attracted to each other, and after the unfortunate events of the Floating Fortress, we turned to each other for solace."

"How fortunate you are to be in such deliciously *masculine* company." He steadily lowered the maleservant to his knees, holding his head between the folds of his thighs.

She sensed a lack of assurance in his voice. Then, her heart beat heavily at the uninhibited sexual act transpiring in front of her eyes. It was not entirely the same act she glimpsed before the bath; however, she had never witnessed such explicitness, let alone desired to experience anything similar. She managed a strangled breath. "Aye. I believed it to be a smooth journey through the Fire Country until your painted males bombarded us in the tall grasses."

"You cannot trust anyone anymore. We feel it our duty to patrol the grasslands of the Fire Country, despite our unfortunate long term quarrel with the Coutarian family." He adjusted his folds in the chair as his dalliance rearranged his mouth and grip. "However, times are cruel, and we must look to our own kind for assurance in safety. How unfortunate you are to have no other family but yourself. Were you not sired?"

Apprehension began to tighten her chest. She glanced toward the fire, attempting to avert her gaze from the unsavory act as the maleservant began to choke. The heat was beginning to become unbearable. "I know nothing of my...*father*, but am told he was a kind, mortal creatural." She did not want Ura-Ca to see through her lies, but it was becoming clear he knew the situation she was witnessing was making her uncomfortable. "He died when I was yet in my mother's womb."

"I see," he replied with speculation.

She could sense the hint of dissatisfaction in his voice, but he did not pursue the topic any further and took a gulp of his wine, yawning as he removed it from his lips. Then, she saw him look boldly upon her chest. Peering down, she noticed the key had been exposed.

His eyes widened in greed. "How lovely! Where does it lead?"

She felt her skin prickle and shifted in her chair to tilt her body away from his hungry gaze. "It was a gift from my mother. She had a beautifully carved, wooden chest she would keep next to her bed. Just before she passed, she destroyed the chest and gave me the key to remember her by."

"I want it," he growled as he grabbed the maleservant's hair by the handful.

"Pardon me?" she inquired, flustered.

"Give it to me. I simply adore keys. They hold a sense of mystery and allurement. I cannot see one without possessing it." He reached recklessly toward the necklace with his free hand, nearly smothering the maleservant with his massive rolls.

She pushed away. "My apologies, but this key is the last remnant of my mother. You cannot have it."

Ura-Ca peered eerily at her and spoke low, "I always get what I want." He snapped his fingers and another maleservant walked silently over to Mora. "You move and I will command him to break your neck."

Her head was held steady between firm hands. She did not dare move impulsively. Staring wide eyed at Ura-Ca, she took a deep breath to calm her nerves. Disgruntled, he shoved the maleservant off his cock and hobbled over. When he bent down, level with her face, she could smell the foul stench of his breath and see the rolls of flesh flopping against more chafed skin. Disgusting and horridly hideous, she turned her eyes away from his glare. Attempting to hold back tears, she kept her breathing even. He grabbed the key and yanked it from her neck. She gave a short yelp when she felt the pinch of the chain cut into her flesh. He backed away with the key tightly clutched in his hand and sat back down. Continuously averting her gaze, a tear escaped her eye and slid down her cheek.

He yawned again. "I am fatigued. Sing to me as I lie down." He shifted his enormous physique from the chair and stumbled to the bed. Snapping his fat fingers, the young maleservant laid down in front. He shifted, situating himself into the backside of the youth, his body appearing like a mountain of flesh consuming the smaller being into the rolling hills of his body.

When the maleservant shuddered, Mora flinched. Reluctant, but befuddled, she could not remember any lullabies her mother had ever sung to her as a childling. She thought harder. Finally, she remembered Remmi had sung a lullaby around the fire the night before they set out across the Fire Country.

Taking her silence as an offense, Ura-Ca yelled sleepily at her, "Hurry bitch! I want to hear you sing!"

She peered around the chamber, the other maleservant scarce after

## The Keeper

Ura-Ca snapped the necklace from around her neck. Timidly, she began to recollect the lullaby.

Singing too softly, Ura-Ca roared, "I can't hear you cunt!"

She raised her voice, singing the notes as similarly to Remmi as she could remember. The words were not clear, but her lyrical memory was magnificent. The winds around the tower tossed against the outside stone wall as her voice carried. She could feel a chill hit her skin and listened to the wailing as it flowed through the slitted windows of the chamber. She continued to sing. A mysterious feeling melted into her flesh causing her veins to burn. Ura-Ca had commenced to snore, but the winds from the outside echoed louder throughout the space. She wondered how he could not hear the increasing wail.

Becoming entranced, she stood and walked to the fire. The orange and blue flames roared with popping embers, sizzling onto the cold floor. She was mesmerized, but continued to hum. Her heart was racing and her body was not controlled by her own mind, but by a force outside her ability to grasp. When she stood a hand's length from the fiery hot flames, in which only a moment ago felt too hot to be near, she slowly lifted her arm into the fire. Amazed and baffled, her hand emerged unscathed, neither feeling hot, nor burned. When she finally reached the last line of the lullaby, upon humming the last note, the fire ceased. Shaking, she gazed hesitantly around the room, turning slightly on her heel. It was dark and cold. She could barely make out the outline of the bed on which Ura-Ca slept. The windows provided slits of contrast to the black chamber, but contained no visible stars. Nervously, she tried to take a few steps in the direction of the chairs. Her chest heaved and her breath was short. She no longer felt the force of overwhelming empowerment, but instead, she was vulnerable and frightened. An image of His liquid, black eyes flashed through her mind.

*You called me?* a voice startled Mora.

She whimpered, "Who's there?"

*You tremble, but you know,* the sultry, deep voice replied.

*Leave this place. I do not want you here,* her thoughts hissed.

*You know what you speak is not true. You have summoned me and I have responded. Do not speak maliciously, for I only yearn to be near you once more, to feel your spirit weave through mine.*

### The Keeper

She moved cautiously around the room.

*Face your true self,* Ekklips purred, *succumb to the power deep inside, free the Chaos within.* His words bounced throughout the chamber.

The winds grew heavy, bending around each corner of the tower. It screamed hauntingly within the narrow corridors, winding and twisting. As it raced faster into the chambers, singing against the metal bars of the doors, a stirring awoke a dangerous spirit. A hand, once dressed in black, seized the iron bars. Maliciously, the tower shook.

Mora jerked around when the tower quaked. A shadow appeared and then faded into the darkness. A force of wind knocked her down onto the cold, stone floor. Around her, mysterious sparks pulsated from the cracks like cage bars.

*You cannot run from me Solora! We posses a connection deeper than Life itself. I am you and you are me. There is no escaping what is and always will be!*

*Stop!* she screamed from her core. *You shall not control me!*

As she leaned back with her hands behind her on the rough stones, she felt the ground quiver from beneath her fingers. Her fingertips began to suck in sparks of light, the sensation pleasurably burning her veins. A power possessed her mind and her eyes became an ominous, glowing green. A blue circle of light appeared around her body and radiated around the room in a brilliant eruption of energy. This magnificent source of power was not completely her own. However, she could feel the essential vitality feeding off her spirit. Suddenly, a burst illuminated in the chamber like a bolt of lightning. She could feel the anger and malevolence hoisted out of the chamber and into the bleakness outside.

Then, it suddenly ceased. She sat there in silence, squinting into the dark chamber, cold and breathless, as the heavy Ura snored in the bed.

She peered at her fingers and then focused on her hands. *What did I just experience?*

Looking around the chamber, there was no visible sign of Ekklips. *I never actually saw His face, merely heard His voice.*

Presently, all she could hear was the howling of the wind outside. The sound of a latch resonated off the walls and she saw a figure walking to where she sat on the floor. She neither felt threatened, nor surprised, to see the face of the maleservant whom had bathed her earlier. He helped her to her feet, holding her steady as he led her to a chair. Lighting a candle, he poured her a glass of sweet wine and sat down across from her on the cushion.

Anxiously, she glanced at the bed. "Are you not afraid he will wake?"

The male shook his head. "I placed a heavy sedative into his wine earlier. He will not wake until morning."

She eyed him over her glass. "Who are you?"

"I am Dierdan," he replied, staring awestruck into her eyes. "And you," he pointed at her, "you are not of this world."

She did not know how to respond to his accusation. She had not known when Bog had said something similar, nor when Katheryn had alluded to the idea either. For she had been told many things since her journey began and it was something she could not fully grasp. "There have been speculations," she merely responded and then stared into the flame of the candle. "What will happen to my friends?"

He sighed. "They will be put to death. And whether or not Abin wins the games, will determine your fate."

She felt her breath catch in her throat. Clearing it, she stuttered, "I suppose by your unusual kindness, you're willing to help me?"

He looked from the bed, to the door, and said sullenly, "I was captured by Ura-Ca himself, commanded as a slave and punished to do things I would not otherwise have chosen. He has taken my life away."

"What will happen?" she asked, a sudden hopelessness invading her emotions. His gaze was deep and menacing, full of anguish and grief. He did not resemble the Ura. His eyes were of a dark blue, his flesh the color of burnt wood. His hair was cropped in Ura fashion, but it was textured and braided in small sections down his back. Around his neck there was a golden, metal band with little chains connected to his earlobes and nostrils. She was curious where he originated.

"I know not what events may arise, but the skies were stained with blood at dusk. Death is close at hand."

When he touched her hand, his skin was hot and callused.

"You must find the Light, or your life, and those of this world, will become meaningless and servile to the ominous grasp of turmoil, eating away at the flesh in a ceaseless struggle for spiritual recognition and acceptance. Judgment hath no mercy for the unjust and cruel, for this leaves the soul stricken with disease and decay. You must aid to balance Dark. If order is not established again, Chaos will emerge stronger."

"You speak as though there is already war and destruction upon the lands," she replied in exhaustion. *Chaos. Ekklips had spoken that name.*

"It is not the war and destruction of the lands I refer. The winds are changing. The sun no longer rises with freewill, it is a slave to the darkness, bound by the shackles of a menacing foe."

"Foe? You speak in riddles." She watched his ill-fated expression.

"A serpent lurks in the shadows, waiting to strike the iron when it is hot." His dark blue eyes glanced gloomily out the window.

A cold chill ran down her spine. She shook from the sudden gust of wind.

"The time is nigh. No one can stop it, as no one can resist its grasp." There was a pause. Dierdan brought his gaze back to Mora, attempting to portray a comforting smile on his face.

"Why do you speak of these premonitions to me?" she replied softly.

"Because you bear the mark of the Dark one."

Taken aback, she balked at the inclination. "The mark? Now I am convinced you are mad." She leaned back in her chair, utterly disappointed.

He quickly grabbed her hand.

She tried jerking it away, but his grip was too strong. He held her wrist tight, exposing the crescent moon birthmark. She grunted and spat, "Let me go! I've had it my entire life!"

"Ekklips," he whispered low.

Mora stopped writhing immediately and gazed horror stricken at

Dierdan. "How do you know that name?" she whispered. The only other one to say the name aloud was her mother's spirit.

Dierdan grinned suspiciously, followed by a low rumble of thunder.

# The Arena

With great strain, Bog's eyes crept open, adjusting to the faint light shining from down the corridor through the bars. He yawned, rubbed his eyes, and peered at Abin, still snoring at the opposite end. Then, he looked at Remmi, who was squatting with his back against the bars of the cell, wide awake, staring at the ground, chin settled on his clasped hands. He stood wearily, stretched, and popped his spine several times. Rubbing his lower back, he walked near the bars. He looked to his left and then to his right before leaning his arms outside the cell, propping himself adjacent to the metal. He began to wonder about the events of the day and how Mora fared during the night in the presence of Ura-Ca.

Feeling restless, he slowly started to recall a vague dream he had during the night concerning Mora. In the dream, she had been consumed with fire, but it did not burn her flesh, nor was it excruciatingly hot, but she had a seductive smile plastered on her face. Then, as she stepped closer to his, she took his hands. He felt a similar sensation when Draelia had touched him in the forest, and didn't want to let go. However, there was an obsessive difference. It sparked a fire within his own soul, awakening something intense inside. Passionately, she had placed her lips to his own. Although it had been a dream, he had never experienced the stirring desire which roared in the depths of his core when Mora's lips touched his - neither with Draelia, nor Katheryn. He seized her vehemently, embracing her naked, burning body until she began to slowly pull away. His yearning for her reached out desperately. Confused, he stood there, cold and weakened by the lack of her presence and touch. Gradually, she began to recede into the encroaching darkness. Without warning, a series of hands commenced to reach around her body. Several pairs lifted her high above cloaked figures, laying her upon the intertwining arms as if on a pyre. In a desperate attempt to reach for her, he found he could not move his feet. Hopelessness screamed inside his chest, tightening until he felt the constraint would consume him completely. Finally, the darkness swallowed her whole.

Immediately, another figure sauntered into his vision, a male clad in a black, belted tunic, and breeches. His face was concealed by a black mask, save for a mesmerizingly sinful grin, similar to how Mora had smiled only moments ago. His stature was impressive to his own. The dark one stopped when He was eye to eye with Bog. His eyes were captivating and sultry, as though filled with a mystical void. His indigo-black hair fell loosely over the mask, appearing to be made of melted coal. Bog could hear his heart thumping in his ears. The dark one held a hand to his cheek, running His thumb across Bog's lower lip. Then, He leaned in, kissing him as passionately as Mora had done. Unable to control his own limbs, he embraced the being as another awakening filled his soul. However, this time, it was deliciously cavernous and captivating, attempting to pull him over the ledge of the void.

Withdrawing, the dark one said nothing, but revealed a very long, thin knife from behind His back. Disoriented and afraid, Bog tried to move away, but he was still grounded. Placing the tip of the blade to Bog's bare chest as it heaved and dripped with sweat, He pressed firmly against his flesh. Bog began to feel an intense searing from the tip as it carved deep lines into his skin. Despite his previous sensation, the agony was nearly too much. Torturously, the ritualistic carving persisted with excruciating force as he yelled in unbearable pain.

At last, He removed the sharp tip of the blade from Bog's chest. Trembling, he glanced down. There was no blood, only a symbol burning a bright, molten red, as if he had been branded with a hot iron. He had never seen anything similar, but it continued to sear like it was on fire, causing him to twitch with intermittent pain and sending intense pangs pulsating throughout his body. From the angle he examined the wound, he saw a circle, part crescent moon and part sun, with three lines descending into the point of a dagger. An opaque semicircle was flush against the bottom of the circle. Angular lines connected the two outside lines at another opaque, small circle beneath. Then, the lines diverged toward the outside corners before all three became the point of the blade. At the very bottom, a small, vacant circle floated outside the point.

A seductive, growling voice caressed his ear, "You know who I am."

The hair on the back of his neck stood on end. When Bog lifted his head, the being had faded into the invading mist. Lethargically, at that point in the dream, he had begun to wake from the heavy slumber. Bog had not immediately remembered the dream when he opened his eyes. Alas, as he stood against the bars, he felt a slight twinge on his chest where the mark had been carved. He rubbed his skin softly and peered down, but he could not see anything. Shaking his head, his thoughts wandered back to Mora.

Suddenly, a faint pounding vibrated through the corridor. It resonated louder until it was trembling the ground. Abin popped up immediately, rubbed his eyes, and grabbed the iron bars. "The bloody drums," he hissed.

"From where do they originate?" Bog replied, glancing down at Remmi who had not moved from the crouching position next to the bars. "Does he sleep?" He motioned his head quietly.

Abin glanced down and shoved Remmi, causing him to unclasp his hands in order to catch himself. "He's lost in thought or meditating. Regardless, he does it often. I guess you can call it sleeping with his damn eyes open."

Remmi adjusted his boot and spoke in a gruff tone, "The drums are coming from the courtyard, signaling the commencement of the games."

"We are all in for a treat today bird-beast." Abin struck Bog on the shoulder. He trudged heavy footed to the back of the cell and leaned against the wall, his face half concealed in the shadows.

"We?" Bog stuttered, turning to face Abin. "What the curse of the gods do I have anything to do with the Ura?"

"You're going to be a main attraction!" Abin sputtered. "Your antics in the room gave Ura-Ca enough ammunition to fuel a whole arsenal of entertainment!" He spat into the dirt.

"Me? What about you? I thought you were the one who voluntarily agreed to fight for our *freedom?*" Bog gawked, fists clenched.

Remmi abrasively stood in between Abin and Bog.

"Listen, bird dick," Abin hissed as he advanced closer, glaring at Bog, "these mortals are dangerous! There is no mercy, no fear, and no compassion toward each other, much less outsiders. Blood will be shed today. Whether it is our own, or one of the tribe, Ura-Ca will continue to send as many warriors into the game as he sees fit."

Bog recognized a hint of fear flash across Abin's eyes, but his gaze still lingered maliciously on his own. However, before he could retort, the sound of metal clanked in the corridor. Footsteps were drawing near the cell. In hesitation, he backed away until he was shoulder to shoulder with Abin. An extremely large male walked in front of the bars wearing a metal collar around his rolling neck, securely attached to shackles on his wrists. He was bald, with one good eye and disgustingly raised scars brandishing his face from top to bottom. The only garb he wore was a loin cloth, barely covering his massive thighs and phallic bulge. He donned metal rings through his nose, ears, and nipples. Dragging behind him were three sets of shackles, rusted and sharp.

Tossing them through the bars, he grumbled, "Put dem on. Ya," he pointed his grubby finger at Bog, "er at de end."

Bog's eyes widened in fear. Without hesitation, he reached discreetly behind his back and plucked a feather from his wing. *Godsdamn the Ura.* He held his closed hand to his mouth and blew into the small hole made by his thumb and forefinger. A tiny flash of light barely illuminated through his fingers and he inhaled. Pretending to rub his nose, he felt the power starting to surge through his veins.

Remmi side eyed Bog. He could smell the faintest scent of burnt feather.

Then, void of argument, Abin, Remmi, and Bog clicked each cuff on their wrists and ankles, the chains attached to the other by a heavy lock. The massively disfigured male commenced to open the iron gate and retrieved a whip from the back of his loin cloth.

"Walk," he bellowed as he pointed to the right.

Awkwardly, they began to walk down the corridor. Bog nearly tripped from the unsynchronized rhythm of Remmi's footsteps as they tugged on his ankles. The steady beat of drums was escalating as they walked down a slanted hall toward a lighted gateway. Abin stopped at the iron barred door. The Ura slave clomped past them, shoving them to the wall as his massive body squeezed through.

"Open de gate!" he barked. The gate began to reluctantly give way to the bright glare of the sun. "Move!"

A crack of the whip sounded as Bog felt a sharp pang hit him on the shoulder. The feeling only made him more irate.

Once outside, he surveyed his surroundings. Glaring up, he could see a crowd of Ura cheering in what appeared to be an arena carved further into the ground. The arena expanded in a semi-circle around the tower. It was not as extremely deep as it was wide, but no empty seat was visible. The crowd flooded the top of the grounds also, overlooking the arena, pushing and shoving for a view. Opposite the crowd, jutting from the phallic stone tower, was an extended covered balcony. Ura-Ca sat in the center of the balcony with rolls of skin tumbling over the stone chair like layers of dough being squeezed through a grate.

Before averting his eyes, Bog's nerves struck a chord when he noticed the chain around Ura-Ca's neck. It was Mora's key, barely visible in the crease. He gritted his teeth, his veins beginning to protrude from his neck. Continuing to survey the balcony, he paused when he recognized Mora, her sullen eyes downcast. She was dressed in a garnet dress, her hair tied back with a gold ribbon weaving through a bun at the nape of her neck. A chain encompassed her throat like an animal on a leash. The male who had spoken to him initially in the room with Ura-Ca, was standing next to Mora, holding the chain connected to her neck. This enraged him further. A line of thirteen naked maleservants lined the back of the balcony behind Ura-Ca, while another one lazily draped over his beefy thighs, bigger than the servant was round. Ura-Ca's face gleamed with pride and exhilaration.

*Disgusting fuck*, Bog grimaced. *What has he done to her?*

Then, the memory of his dream flooded his sensations, causing his stomach to flutter. He blinked, rubbed his nose, and moved along the sand at the progression of Abin. All of a sudden, another crack of the whip, and Bog felt the sharp pain again between his wings. Fueling the flames of his anger, he clenched his jaw, plotting the pain he would cause the being holding the chain when the moment arose. The grotesquely large slave commanded them to turn and face Ura-Ca. They came to a halt and turned. Leaning his head back as the thrum of power danced through his body, Bog stared into the bright blue sky. A red streak of cloud stretched across sky, expanding beyond the entire arena. He had never seen such a strange sight. He lowered his head back down to view of the balcony. Amusingly, Ura-Ca was struggling to emerge from his chair, nearly knocking the maleservant over the balcony edge. Finally, after a couple other servants aided him, he plodded to the edge and smirked.

"Enjoy your stay, Abin?" He laughed cynically.

Abin returned the laugh and replied jovially, "Slept like a wee babe!"

Ura-Ca huffed at his comment. Unamused, he groaned, "As you know, I am quite fickle with my rules. It will be spectacular to see how agile you have become in your older age, you old shit. Remember the battles of the Isles long ago? Where each opponent threw himself into your blade when they noticed your advance?" He grinned maliciously and cleared his throat, "That will not be today. Because, as you well know, the brutality of the ages have changed, and I will not rest until justice is served. I have grown bored of petty battles. Your time has come, Abin, and I will be the one laughing as your head rolls across the sands. It will be a nice addition to my wall."

Abin shuffled, shackled hands crossed in front, and menacingly gazed up at Ura-Ca. "Do what you want you vengeful rat, but leave these two out of your antics." He flicked his head toward Remmi and Bog.

Ura-Ca laughed and shook his head. "Denied! You and your blue eyed friend will be my appetizers." His eyes narrowed on Bog. "Your Borgorian, with his glowing, violet eyes, will be my finale."

When Ura-Ca spoke about glowing eyes, Remmi glared hard at Bog, realizing what he had done.

Ura-Ca waved his wrists and said gutturally, "You will be provided your weapon of choice, but, be as it may, there is no threat of strength that compares to the stature of my slaves."

Unshackling their wrists and ankles, the massive being shoved

*The Keeper*

Bog over to the wall, keeping a spear at his neck. "Move en er neck will be slice't wide open," he spat harshly.

Bog watched carefully as a gate clattered open in the stone and two maleservants walked forth with a variety of weaponry.

"Choose your weapon," Ura-Ca guffawed while ravishing the meat off of a large bone. Pieces of spit and gristle showered from the balcony.

Remmi shuffled over to retrieve an axe.

Confidently, Abin walked stoutly up to the weapons, and without words, pulled out two, roughly cut steel swords. Rubbing them against each other, he spat on to the ground. "Oi! Who wants to ride my cocks of steel first, eh?" He bellowed with maniacal laughter. "I don't suppose you would be the first to *come* my way." His mocking voice echoed around the arena, directed at Ura-Ca.

"Fuck you." Ura-Ca spat onto the dust in front of Abin.

"That was my only offer you fat bastard." He pranced his arrogance around the stands, riling up the crowd of blood thirsty Ura. "Show me your best match." He bowed derisively.

Ura-Ca held up a hand and replied coldly, "As you wish."

Abin lifted his swords higher, yelled, and beat his chest hard. The sound of a chain rattled loudly from the iron gate at the far end of the arena. Much to Bog's surprise, Abin turned and laughed as a colossal figure loomed out of the gate. Like the maleservant who was guarding him, this slave was bald, with scars rippling across his bronzed flesh. However, through his nose was a small bone, and where his left eye would have been, there was a shallow ditch. Around his neck, wrists, and ankles were fiercely sharp spiked collars. Barely covering his genitals was a flapping piece of linen, leaving nothing to the imagination as his ass was bare. Quickly glancing at Abin, he saw an abnormally large smile grow across his face while Remmi remained stoic nearby, axe at the ready.

The hideous giant sneered.

"We meet again Ca-Dul," Abin taunted, swaying back and forth with his swords. "See any tits lately? Besides your own, that is," he snidely quipped.

The giant called Ca-Dul spit a wad of disgusting bile onto the dirt. "Don't 'ave to see 'em to fuck 'em."

## The Keeper

Abin shook his head sarcastically. "Even the most desperate whore wouldn't sit on your lap, you ugly son of a bitch!"

At the roar of the crowd, Ca-Dul became angrier. Bog lifted his head toward the balcony, the power in his veins nearly insatiable. Ura-Ca's face was full of blood thirst and ecstasy. Mora continued to stare absently down into the arena, seemingly unperturbed by the unfolding events. In horror, he turned back in time to see Ca-Dul charging Abin. With a swift jump, he dodged the mighty blow of Ca-Dul's mace, only to be caught by the backlash of his hand. He flew a few steps back as the crowd cheered. Remmi took the opportunity to advance on Ca-Dul, slicing his axe across his juicy thigh.

Ca-Dul wailed.

Abin spun into a forceful blow using the hilt of his sword and sent the mace swinging around Ca-Dul's head. Then, using the blade of his sword, he slashed at Ca-Dul, creating a nasty slice into the hanging flesh below his armpit. Blood spilled from the wound. Distracted, he swung his mace vigorously at Abin's head while Remmi slid through his mangled legs, effortlessly rose to his feet, and swung the axe so hard onto Ca-Dul's shoulder, it lopped off the arm.

Ca-Dul roared.

Abin wiped the splattered blood from his face as the giant charged, swinging the mace wildly with his other arm. Without cowering, he continued to fight fiercely, each blow greater than the last. Remmi joined. Both beings struck harder and faster. Abin ducked to avoid the mace, but was clipped by Ca-Dul's wrist blade. A trickle of blood appeared from a wound across his shoulder.

A quick glance at Ura-Ca, and Bog could see the mixture of suspension and uncertainty dawning across his face. The fight continued with blood splattering in puddles across the sand. Each component's hatred continued fueling them in unyielding energy. Ca-Dul stumbled close to the wall. Taking the opportunity, Remmi ran up the wall, swung around, and struck a blow onto the back of Ca-Dul's thick neck. The axe stuck deep in his meaty flesh. He landed, crouching low to the ground as Ca-Dul desperately swung his mace, hitting Abin when he turned. Losing his footing, Abin fell to the sand. One of the swords flung from his grip.

With Abin down, and Remmi without a weapon, Bog snapped.

*397*

Snatching the spear from the maleservant's grasp, he rammed it into his bulging stomach. The crowd cheered. Alarmed, Ura-Ca jolted to the edge of the balcony. Bog ripped the spear from the stomach as a long trail of intestines followed suit, slithering onto the sand. Every face in the crowd was beaming. Bloodlust in his eyes, Bog sprinted madly toward Ca-Dul.

Ura-Ca screamed, "The Borgorian! Seize the bird bastard!"

A dozen or more guards streaked through the gate and across the sands of the arena toward them. Bog's heart beat faster as he hustled toward Ca-Dul. Leaping high, he pulled his arm back and threw the spear straight through the giant's chest. The impact made Ca-Dul tumble to the ground, nearly crushing Abin. Abin seized the opportunity to scramble across the dirt for his other sword as guards advanced. Remmi had already retrieved the axe from the back of Ca-Dul's neck and swung at the nearest guard, slicing him in two. Both Abin and Remmi cut down more than seven guards before they saw more emerge from the gate.

Bog had cleared the body of Ca-Dul with ease. Then, crushing the head of an approaching guard between his hands, took the corpse's axe and sliced through Ca-Dul's neck, severing the head. Dragging it through the sand, he tossed it onto the ground below the balcony. The violet of his eyes became an immensely thin, luminescent ring around his enlarged pupils. With wings and body blood-stained, he smiled wryly at Ura-Ca.

Ura-Ca wailed, "You godsdamn sky scum! You will pay for that!"

He smirked. "I think not." He sprinted across the sand and jumped high off the heads of the progressing guards. Landing hard on the ledge of the balcony, the stones broke with a resounding *crack!* beneath his boots.

# Unknown Counterfeit

Mora watched the folds of Ura-Ca fall back over the stone chair as Bog landed directly in front of him on the balcony. The one other time she had seen his eyes illuminating with a brilliant violet which nearly engulfed his stark black pupils, was when he fought the Hawkend. This time, she could see the veins of his arms, chest, and neck pulsating underneath his skin. His breathing was heavy, and the heat of his rage radiated in waves at Ura-Ca.

"Bog," she said breathlessly.

At the sound of her voice, he jerked his head in her direction, and snarled at the cloaked servant holding the chain attached to her neck. Standing erect, he stepped heavily off the ledge.

*Dierdan.* She could see the hatred in Bog's eyes. Hearing Dierdan shuffle his feet behind her, she barred her hands against Bog's chest. "Nay. Not him."

He stopped, the touch of her hand sparked his flesh and ignited the memory of his dream. He caressed his fingers along her cheek. "I'm sorry," he groaned.

Dierdan squinted at Bog.

Ura-Ca, struggling to his feet, yelled, "Kill him! I want his wings mounted on my wall!"

Maleservants threw themselves at Bog without heeding the weapon he held tight in his grasp. Whipping the axe around his body, he swung at the nearest attacker. Slicing through the chest, Mora winced as blood splashed on her face. Dierdan pulled her backward before he swung again, his feathers tickling her cheeks. This time, he split open the servant's skull. One by one, he slaughtered each being that advanced. Fearfully, she watched the chaos unfold. His pure white wings were splattered with blood, the one black feather gradually blending in with the deep crimson.

Dierdan pulled her closer to his chest. His mere presence entranced her, engulfing every emotion she once willingly possessed. Since their discussion, he had made her feel overwhelmingly calm and emotionally trusting. She had expressed her concerns openly, but it felt like he could read her mind. Peering over her shoulder, she could see the deep-set, dark blue eyes staring harshly at Bog. He must have felt her gaze upon him, for he lowered his head to look into her face.

Then, it happened all at once. Dierdan bowed his head humbly to Mora, his face deepening in the shadows. With a swift jerk, he released the metal collar around her neck, wound the chain in his hands, and encompassed it forcefully around the nearest guard's neck. Kicking him in the small of his back, the maleservant flew frontwards over the rail. Bracing his foot on the railing, he held hard and the chain tightened, hanging the body from the balcony. She grabbed a sword from a fallen servant before Bog spun around, nearly slicing her arm open with his axe. She blocked him with the sword.

Heaving, his eyes widened in realization. "Damn, Mora!" He could feel the color drain from his face at the thought of what he could have done to her with the axe. Then, he spun on his heel, shielding her once again with his wings. His attention turned back to Ura-Ca, poorly concealed behind the stone chair.

With all eyes on the figure hanging from the balcony, Abin seized the opportunity to duck below an oblivious guard, slicing his ankles. Swiftly, he stood behind two more guards and thrust his swords into the backs of both. Procuring an opening, Remmi followed suit, fiercely breaking the necks of three more guards. Abin jumped up to the nearest wall and climbed toward the balcony. Once he sprung over the railing, he froze. Like the Floating Fortress, foreboding eyes met his own from the servant holding the chains, but only briefly, as the ghost of a memory from the past haunted his mind. Blinking, the image disappeared, as had the apparition. Shaking his head in disbelief, he fiercely began to fight once more.

Mora hastily peered back at Bog's looming body over a flailing Ura-Ca, his arm fat flapping wildly, smacking the stone chair like a fish out of water. Abruptly, his deathly stare caught her breath. He wobbled around the other side of the chair, reaching his stumpy hands forward to grab her neck. As she ducked, she heard his loose jowls slap together above her head. He whipped around as Bog yelled.

"Ura-Ca!"

"What do you bloody want sky scum?"

"That is not yours." He shot out a hand, grabbed Ura-Ca by the neck, and raised his axe.

"Bog!" Abin's raspy, gruff voice interjected over the chaos, "He is mine!"

Bog snapped the chain off Ura-Ca's fat neck and tossed it to Mora. Through gritted teeth, he muttered, "You're lucky it's not me tearing you limb from godsdamn limb you fat, pathetic fuck." Elbowing Ura-Ca in the face, blood spilled from his mouth.

Spitting, Ura-Ca smiled a disgustingly bloody, toothless grin. "I know who she is and your wings won't save you from *Him*."

Hearing those words made his eyes flare. He clenched his jaw hard and, like a predator, growled at Abin, "If you don't bloody kill him now, I will."

Abin smirked at Bog. "With pleasure." Standing behind Ura-Ca, he held the two swords crossed in the front of the numerous rolls on his neck. Lowering to his ear, he whispered, "Regardless of my own eminent mortality, I will get off at the fact I slit your fucking throat."

Ura-Ca's cackle turned into a bloody gurgle as Abin framed his knee into his spine and intentionally slid both swords through the layers of fatty flesh.

Mora saw the massive head fall backward, dangling, still attached to the spine of his neck. Disgusted, she purged when she saw the head lean toward her with the gruesome, bloody grin still plastered to his face.

Remmi seized her hand and yelled, "The columns!"

Dodging the lunges of the increasing guards and the massacred bodies of maleservants, she managed to reach the side of the balcony with Remmi. Lifting the red dress above her knees, she followed him over the broken railing onto a small ledge. He slid down a thin column from the top of the balcony. Motioning her to follow, a sudden pain jerked her head back before she bent down to scramble onto the column. A guard had grasped firmly onto the bun of hair, nearly scalping her clean. Struggling against his force, she clawed at his chest like a feral animal, digging her nails into his skin, creating troughs of blood. Raising his sword high into the air, she took a deep breath, readying for a painful blow. Suddenly, a blade violently burst through the guard's chest, a breadth away from securing a home within her breast. Blood splattered onto her neck and chin. Feeling the guard's grip fall from her hair, she immediately grasped for the rail to secure her nerves. As the body of the guard toppled over the ledge, Dierdan appeared, a hood covering his head, blood soaking through his robes.

He commanded brashly and tossed her leather harness and belt, "Slide!"

She caught her effects in confusion. Then, slinging it over her arm, she screamed back, a hand outstretched in his direction, "Come with me!"

"You will see me again, but not today."

A strange lighting flickered over his features. She thought she saw a completely different face than she stared into the previous night. *Strange*, she thought.

"I will hold the guards off!" He commenced fighting as he pushed her toward the column.

Forced to take hold of the column, she slid down to the sands of the arena. Chaos had overthrown the grounds as well. To get out alive would be a miracle. Females and childlings were screaming, running manically to avoid being a fatality of the carnage. Jerking her into the shadows of the wall, Remmi led them around the side of the tower to the steps ascending the stands. Tired of lifting her dress, she paused, bent down, and ripped the fabric to her knees.

Bog followed, leaping off the balcony and into the sands of the arena, his axe tearing through the onslaught of bodies from outside the tower. Abin threw beings from the balcony, each more violently maimed than its predecessor.

In front, Remmi barreled up the steps, fighting and flinging the adversaries off the stone. The ones that landed on the stone forced Mora to jump over them carefully without falling herself. Finally, she grabbed another weapon, a smaller sword, from a lifeless hand.

Abin joined Bog in the arena, plowing their way through the massacre toward Remmi and Mora. Already on the top of the stands, Remmi turned to sprint to the front of the tower. However, darting toward what appeared as an ambush, he grabbed Mora's hand and tore swiftly into a blind doorway. Pulling her powerfully into the opening and pushing her into a corner, he covered her with his body. Only moments passed before he gazed over his shoulder, clear of the oncoming mob. Without delay, he hoisted her to her feet and began running once more down a long corridor.

"Do you know where you are headed?" she frantically whispered.

"Do you not trust me?" he retorted.

She peered over her shoulder as he lead her further into the dim lit hallways of Ura-Ca's phallic fortress. Reaching a door to the side of the massive front, stone entrance, he struck its handle continuously with the hilt of his sword. Sparks flew as metal kissed metal, until it gave way, clanking to the stone floor. He threw himself against the door and sunlight pierced their eyes once again. The echo of swords and fighting bounced off the exterior walls of the fortress.

"Wait!" she cried, pointing at the chest.

He threw open the lid and grabbed his bow and quiver, Abin's swords, and Bog's sword. Mora tossed the small, Ura weapon to the side, quickly sheathed her dagger, and slung her quiver over her shoulder, bow in hand.

Now in the courtyard, a maleservant took notice of them and charged in their direction. She strung an arrow, releasing it directly into his chest, sending him flying backward in a burst of flames into the sand. A sudden movement caught her unprepared and another guard jabbed her in the ribcage with the tip of his spear before she whipped out of reach. She keeled over, holding her side. Before he flung the spear a second time, he dropped to his knees with two swords protruding from his chest. Abin flung his hand out to Mora. Immediately, she grabbed it, pulling herself up in time to see Bog fling another guard with his bare hands against the jagged rocks of the stone fortress, the body hanging limply from the sharp rock through his back.

### The Keeper

"Run!" Abin screamed as a herd of guards emerged from the tower's front gate. Like a stampede, the city was against the four of them.

"The stairs!" Remmi yelled as he continued to fight off the horde of oncoming assailants.

Abin pushed Mora into Bog. "Take her! I will follow!" With that, he leapt to the side, disappearing across the stone houses.

Without questioning where he was going, Bog saw Mora was injured and scooped her into his arms. Sensing she was in pain and exhausted, he pulled her closer to his chest while she clung tightly to her bow, chin tucked away from the debris. Running behind Remmi, dust was becoming an obstacle as the number of feet increased. It was difficult to see the direction in which they sought, but they kept darting through the onslaught.

Abin ran quickly to the stables, knowing it would be easier to successfully ascend the stairs on horseback. To his good fortune, the horses were saddled as if they were going to be ridden soon. He unlatched each stall before untying the horses. However, a movement from the corner of his eye made him duck behind the chestnut brown horse. Watching a hooded figure suspiciously step over to Mora's horse, the figure cut a section of the mane and tucked it into his cloak.

Before retreating, he peered up as if sensing someone was watching. As he lifted his head, a stretch of sunlight transformed his dark blue eyes into a deep brown, the color of wet leather. Then, he was gone. Abin rubbed his eyes, the uncertainty escalating his nerves.

Grabbing the satchels hanging on the stable doors, he pulled himself onto the chestnut steed, kicked his heels, and spat, "Yah!"

Still clutching Mora closely against his chest, Bog hurried behind Remmi, dodging a fury of stones falling from the cliffside. "The walls are beginning to cave in! We're not going to bloody make it before we are buried alive!" he yelled.

Suddenly, the ground started trembling closer to their progression through the stone village. Glancing over his shoulder, four horses appeared from the dust. Abin was at the forefront, riding his magnificent, matching steed. At his side galloped Sun Shadow, gallant and dominating. The gray horse halted abruptly at Bog's side. Swiftly placing Mora on the front of the saddle, he hauled himself behind her, cradling her between his arms. Holding both the axe and the rein in one hand, he kicked his horse into full speed. Sun Shadow followed close behind, blocking potential threats. Then, running alongside his stallion, in one fluid motion, Remmi grabbed the reins, swinging himself onto the saddle, bringing up the rear. Twisting and turning through the crumbling stone walls of the city, the horses rode faster than the wind.

Lightly treading footsteps betrayed the blood sodden ground.

"Where is she?" a calm, dark voice resonated in the shadows.

"She looks to the Lands of Borgoria," the approaching being said with a mischievous smile across his face.

"And the key?" the shadow asked.

The other choked back a cough and muttered, "She still possesses it."

"Why this unfortunate change of events?" the disappointment cut sharply through the words like a knife.

"The Borgorian snatched it from Ura-Ca's neck. His eyes illuminated a malicious violet and his strength was unfathomable." Angry, he punched the tower wall, creating a hole in the stone. "I could not stop him, nor her, without exposing myself. However, I did catch a glimpse of possible recognition upon Abin's face."

"Do not dwell on your past transgressions. What was your purpose for summoning me here amongst this filth?" an annoyance resonating in the reply.

The other chuckled gruffly. "I saw her soul, her intentions, and she unknowingly allowed my presence to embark across her mind as I offered her a trustworthy façade. She seeks answers and is intrigued by His nature. She is becoming less vulnerable and appears on the brink of knowledge." He lowered his voice, "But there is something else I sensed before I entered the chamber."

"Oh?" the shadow replied, intrigued.

"There's another force at work, and it was stronger than I have ever felt." He held up the strand of Sun Shadow's mane and added, "It also resonates in the horses."

The shadow sniffed the clipping. "Excellent, save for the unfortunate key mishap," the shadow sniggered, "I do love strong opponents." Bright blue eyes materialized ominously in the shadow. "Ready your monsters to cross the sea. You have been provided a task, see it is done swiftly and efficiently."

"See it done," he replied as he watched the figure disappear.

Galloping up the narrow staircase, guards on horses joined the maleservants on foot, all swiftly in pursuit. Bog watched the odd, red streak banding across the sky grow wider, menacingly covering the city. Clouds within the streak swirled rapidly and the wind whipped with fury.

"Faster!" Abin commanded behind, forcing his horse onward.

Stunned by the abnormal sight of the clouds, Bog lashed his horse faster, holding Mora tighter with one arm. Vaguely peering at the sky, she saw the winds become twisting tunnels of cloud. Loud cracks echoed across the lands. The ferocity of the wind tunnels broke and began to suck away the stone houses in blood red spirals of chaos. Several encircled the phallic fortress of Ura-Ca before hurdling the structure across the gorge as if picking up a pebble and tossing it across a meadow.

Holding her bleeding side, she squirmed closer to Bog, melting into the security of his body. The feral wind tunnels hit the bottom of the staircase. The once immovable, sturdy stones gave way, tossing the oncoming Ura and horses flippantly into the shattered abyss of rock and sand. Screams reverberated through the tunneling sound of torrential wind.

The closer they drew to the top of the gorge, the twisting clouds became more savage. Dust and stone shards intermittently hit her face. Squinting her eyes, she felt a sharp piece bust the same eyebrow Marwen had sewn. She closed her eye as the warmth trickled down her face.

All of a sudden, she heard an enormous sound of breaking rock in front of them. Peering out of one eye, she saw the top of the staircase beginning to detach itself from the surrounding land. "We will never make it!" she screamed.

Abin watched as the chasm widened. Determined, he beat the chestnut steed as hard as he could. With one final push, he clasped on tightly as his horse leapt. Bog's horse followed suit, Sun Shadow leaping almost as an extension. Noticing the horses barely clearing the void, Remmi barreled his stallion to the right, jumped onto a falling rock, and cleared the slanted wall.

Barreling through the tall columns at the entrance of Ura, the horses fought against the wind sucking tunnels attempting to pull them back into their wild embrace. Then, after allowing enough distance, they slowed. Trotting nervously around, they watched the wind tunnels take hold of the final piece of the city. Within moments, the clouds vanished as if nothing had ever happened and the air went stale. In front of their eyes lay a waste of detritus, stone, and dirt. The great stone city of Ura became extinct.

# 'Unrest

Abin somberly surveyed the land. The sun was past midday. While he didn't think there would be much threat considering the complete demise of another city, he wanted to make sure they weren't deterred any further to Borgoria. With the unrest escalating in the Fire Country, they needed to ride as close to the border as possible. Halting in between Remmi and Bog, he pointed east. "We need to ride as far east as we can before nightfall. From there, we can stay close to the bordered tip of the Halo Mountains and Nymian Sea."

"What are the Halo Mountains?" Mora sleepily inquired. Ever since the previous night, she had felt her head was lost in its own sea of strange, apathetic feelings. The haze had consumed her like a drug, but as she was slowly coming out of her cloudiness, she couldn't easily put together the pieces which had occurred in Ura's chamber.

Bog replied, "The thin mountain range bordering the most southern part of the Nymian Sea. Despite their name, they are a place of treacherous climates and deathly terrains. Nothing living usually dwells within the mountains." He could feel the power surge dwindling in his blood, his heart beating slower, and his veins no longer abnormally protruding.

"You said...*living*?" Choking back the bile rising in her throat after the agony in her ribs started pulsating harder, she shifted herself on his horse, realizing how close her body actually had pressed against his own.

"Aye," he sighed, "legend is the mountains are home to many of

Death's various monsters. The mountain range eventually slopes into the sea. Many ships who have attempted to venture through the pass are met with underwater peaks that will tear their ships in two. If there are survivors, they do not last long in the waters. Deep, dark creatures and monsters feast when ships tread."

She felt his grip loosen on her stomach. Remmi's clear, even voice spoke this time, startling her from her stupor.

"Not all of the beings residing in the Halo Mountains are of Death's creation." He stared stoically over the forsaken rubble of Ura-Ca's domain. "And I agree with Abin."

Abin grunted, "That's elusive." Then, he grinned wider than Mora had ever seen. "That's the first time you have admitted that out loud!"

Remmi smirked.

All the while, Bog's uncertainty with Remmi resurfaced. Not only did he not say much, but when he did, it was condescending, or seemed to have a hidden agenda. Either way, he left a bad taste in his mouth. He didn't trust him and hoped they weren't going to regret his company. Feeling Mora shiver, he leaned over and asked, "How are you?"

Her teeth began to chatter and she said feverishly, "I'm…I'm… cold."

He pushed her hair from her face and tucked it behind her ear, "Your skin is burning."

Abin kicked his horse into a full gallop and yelled over his shoulder, "Let's ride with haste. While her immortality will not let her die by the hands of a godsdamn Ura guard, we need to progress before we loose sunlight."

Taken aback by the brash response, Bog shook his head, feeling the waning effects of his power fully leaving his body. He wiped the sweat from his forehead and tightened his grip on her waist. He desperately wanted to help take her pain away, but he couldn't let her know what made him feel painless. "Hold on, Sunshine," he whispered in her ear as he heeled his horse into a gallop.

Watching him closely, Remmi followed behind.

As the sun began to linger over the horizon, Mora wiped more of the dried blood away from her eyes. In the distance, she could see massive peaks jutting out of the land like the jagged bottom teeth of a giant.

Curiously, she could feel a connection to Sun Shadow as the horse galloped closely to Bog's own the whole time they rode across the Fire Country. Abin led the way the entire ride, while Remmi brought up the rear. Shifting with the movement of Bog's body was hard, but she was grateful he held her securely. She knew she could not have ridden successfully. Her body greatly wavered with the jolting of the horse's movements, but she managed without too much pain.

Finally, as the bright orb of the sun lingered above the horizon, Abin slowed down and trotted to a stop. Observing the mountains in the distance, he leapt off his horse. "We'll stop here for the night. It's too flat for an ambush, and it's close enough to the Halo no one will be brave enough to venture in proximity of the mountains."

Remmi dismounted and led his horse next to Abin. "It's too warm for a fire, but if I can locate sustenance, be prepared to sweat." Leaving his horse, he sifted through the tall grass.

Dismounting his own horse, Bog helped Mora to the ground. The red of her gown made it hard to tell how much her wound had bleed through the fabric. A tap on his back, and he turned to see Abin standing behind him, holding his effects.

He grinned. "Maybe you'll find something useful in these." With that, he started clearing an area in the tall grass.

Nodding his head, Bog took the sacks and bent down to rummage through them, grateful Abin had the sense to grab them before departing the stables. Lifting his head, he smirked, "You're not going to like this Sunshine."

She rolled her eyes. "What?" He held up the transparent liquid bottle, an herb, a needle, and thread. When he wiggled it, she laughed in delirium, holding her stomach as she bent over.

"What are you two laughing about over there?" Abin yelled.

Peering gaily at her, Bog was happy to see her smile again. Still crouched, he responded over his shoulder, "Nothing really. It just seems that between us two, we could have already stitched a small tunic."

She lifted what remained of her garment to see the stab wound. "It's more deep than wide," she muttered.

Standing, he put his hands on her cheeks, heat radiating significantly from her flesh. "But you are still with fever. We need to take

**410**

care of this immediately." He pointed at her eyebrow. "At least this isn't as deep. Wasn't that where you were stitched when I found you?"

Sullenly, but managing a faint smile, she nodded and inquired, "Was it not that *I* found you?"

He smirked. "Technicality."

She followed him over to the clearing Abin had created amongst the grass. He was sitting down on the ground and had already pulled out a small pipe from his pocket. She watched him compact an herb down into the tiny hole. "Where in the curse of the gods were you hiding that?"

He smiled wryly. "I never leave home without it." Retrieving a piece of metal and flint from his other pocket, he lit a piece of thick grass and held it to the herb in his pipe. Puffing smoke from the corner of his mouth, he inhaled, held the smoke, and then exhaled heavily.

Before he put out the grass, Bog halted him, "Wait! I need that." Abin handed him the piece of lit grass and he sterilized the needle. "I'm going to need you to lay down."

Abin chuckled, "Aye, you will." He leaned back on his elbows and grinned. "You're not going to offer her a drink first?"

Kneeling next to Mora, Bog paused and squinted at Abin.

Abin winked as he pulled out his whetstone and began sharping his sword.

Bog turned back to Mora. "Would you like a drink?" Offering her the bottle, he uncorked the stopper.

Upturning the side of her lip, she bowed her head. "I graciously accept your offer before you stick me with your needle."

Abin guffawed so loud it could be heard for miles.

Bog sat back and propped his arm on his bent knee. Rubbing his hand on his chin, he glared at her and grumbled, "Thanks."

Giggling, she tipped the bottle, held the liquid to her lips, and took a couple hard gulps, shaking her head rapidly when she finished. Handing it back to him, she grinned and whispered, "I know better. I rode against you since the ruins." She laid back down on the grass.

*Shit.* He flushed. Positioning himself on his knees next to Mora, he poured the clear liquid on the wound and wiped around it with the cloth scraps she had hoarded in her knapsack. She flinched as he cleaned her wound. Finally, he took a deep inhale and said, "Hold still."

## The Keeper

From behind, with a thick cloud of smoke leaving his lips, Abin yelled, "Not the best start!"

Trying to ignore Abin, he saw Mora smirk. *At least she finally trusts me.* He thread the needle and braced himself against her side. Carefully, he stuck the needle in her flesh and felt her tense. Continuing, he stitched one after another. After about nine stitches, he cut the thread and sat back. Blotting the drips of blood from the new stitching with the soaked scrap, he helped her sit up. He handed her the soaked rag for her to clean her eyebrow.

While she examined the wound, he placed everything back into the knapsack and sat back on his elbows. Feeling a nudge on his arm, Abin offered him the pipe. Inhaling deeply, he held the smoke in for a moment before letting it billow from his lips. Feeling it begin to take the edge off of his nerves, he tried to pass it back.

Abin shook his head and laid back with his hands behind his head, looking at the changing hues of the sunset. "Keep it for now. Seems you need it more than I, mate."

Bog inhaled once again and watched Mora brush her hair off her face. "You need to wrap it." He motioned at the area of the wound with the pipe.

She shrugged. "It'll be fine for right now." Shivering, she pulled her knees carefully to her chest. "I am cold."

Concerned, he replied, "You still have a fever." Scooting closer, he put his arm around her shoulders.

With heavy lidded eyes, she teetered between wake and sleep. Finally, laying her head down on his lap, she fell off the edge into her waking world of dreams.

Exhaling, he laid back on his hands and watched the sky saunter through the intensely vibrant colors of dusk.

Mora woke to the dark blue eyes across from her kneeling on the stone floor. *Ekklips*, the figure had whispered. Gawking, she could not believe her ears. No one had spoken His name to her except for her mother's spirit, and currently, she was face to face with an Ura slave. As if she were back in Ura-Ca's chambers, the conversation continued.

"I was traveling through the Fire County years ago when I was kidnapped and enslaved by the Ura. My clan are of the Cau'o'tas tribe, sky readers."

Gazing into Dierdan's mesmerizing eyes, a lump caught in her throat. *Cau'o'tas? That is the tribe of Adeline and Nema.*

The memory of her time in the Realm of Immortals was brief, but it made her heart ache to remember Dresden's hearty laugh and see Marwen's heavily jolly smile, a pipe hanging out of the side of both their mouths, the smell of honey filling her nose. Adeline had been kind and Nema had helped her escape from Ekklips' advance. Curiously, Dierdan's eyes reminded her of Adeline and...*Alidyah.*

Nodding her head, she whispered, "I have heard of the Cau'o'tas tribe."

His eyes lit up. "You have?"

"Aye," she replied calmly, "They aided in my escape from...," she paused.

"Ekklips?" he finished for her, placing his hand on her own.

A loud snort came from Ura-Ca. She had no idea how the thin maleservant didn't get smothered to death. Then, she wondered if Dierdan had been used the same way. A tinge of sorrow fluttered in her chest. Finally, she shook her head in agreement. "It was my first time in the Realm of Immortals. I'm still not exactly sure how I came to be there. However, Ekklips exposed himself to me, attempting to lure me into His web of lies."

"I'm sorry to hear that. Death can be particularly cruel when He doesn't get his way. His wrath is unyielding. It was witnessed after the battle between the Glodians and Cau'o'tas. He was exceptionally cruel to the chief for attempting to deceive Him." Dierdan upturned his lip. "When Ura-Ca found out about my bloodline, my ranking grew overnight. Who doesn't want an immortal on their side when they are afraid of their own mortality?" A darkness danced through the haze of his eyes and he corrected, "At least thinking they are on your side."

Feeling a compelling calmness with him, she thought back on the story Adeline had spoken before Ekklips appeared. An unexpected question pulled her mind back to the room. "I beg your pardon?"

"Does He come to you often?" He inched closer so both hands were resting on Mora's palms.

Cocking her head to the side, she nodded absently. "Aye, He comes to me more in my dreams."

"Are you afraid of Him?"

Entranced, she shifted her weight. "I...I...haven't really been afraid as I am...uncomfortably intrigued?" She scrunched her face. "If that makes sense."

"How so?"

Stuttering, she attempted to gather all of her thoughts together from her encounters with Ekklips, but her mind was becoming hazy. "He's...he's forceful, but not in a way that frightens me. It's in a way of trying to control me, which enrages me. He's also quick to anger and has very little empathy for both mortals and immortals alike." Clearing her throat, a heat rose in her core. "But He's seductively magnificent and alluring."

Her cheeks reddened. Somewhere in the shadowed corners of her mind, in a voice not unlike her own, a warning pleaded desperately for her to stop revealing so much about herself. However, she couldn't. As much as she tried, she choked on the words, "He says He loves me. He says I'm His and He is mine. That...He is not my enemy."

"Was He here before I entered?"

"Well, aye...and, not. I mean...I heard Him, but I never *saw* Him, merely a shadow." Glancing down at his hands covering her own, she thought she saw thin, black lines pulsating like veins under his skin. "And then there were the blue flashes of light."

"Blue flashes of light?"

"Aye, from the cracks in the stone floor. They are what drove His voice away."

"Mora?" He leaned down to look deeper into her eyes. "Have you seen Ekklips in His actual, *physical* form or merely in shadow form?"

Her answer was lost as the stone floor faded into the night sky, full of moving constellations and phenomenal cloud structures, churning with spheres and other celestial objects. Colored lightning flashed through the puffs of smoke-like masses. Stars twinkled brightly against the darkness in a number too vast to count.

*Am I floating?*

The figure of Dierdan and Ura-Ca's chamber had disappeared, leaving her alone amongst the boundless stars. Standing gracefully, she took a hesitant step. A gold light illuminated under her foot, just like it had done in Lychinus. Filled with reverence, Mora walked amidst the twinkling lights. Within reach, she cupped her hand and scooped a star into her palm, placing her other hand over it in a dome, as if it would float away like a firefly. Peeking between the small hole above her thumb, the star began to glow brighter, attaching its tendrils of light to her flesh. It tickled her palms like insect feelers and she giggled. The top of her hand showed veins of light pulsating beneath her skin, into her arms, and through the rest of her naked body.

"Gloriously breathtaking," Ekklips' deeply seductive voice rumbled around the night sky. "The Goddess in her truest form, a beacon of light in the darkest of places."

Sliding His hands around her waist, she shivered. Releasing her hands, the star jolted from her grasp and floated back to its position.

He growled as He pressed against her back, moving His hand between her breasts and onto her chest. Lowering His lips to her ear, He groaned, "Why did you push me away?"

She closed her eyes and leaned her head against His shoulder. Drunk with the intoxicating scent of His presence and the infinite night sky, she replied, "I know not of what you speak." Lifting her arm over her head, she slid her fingertips across the nape of His neck, her fingers teasing through His hair.

"Don't lie, it leaves a bad taste on my tongue." Spinning her delicately around, He kissed her lips. "And the only taste I want on my tongue is your truth."

Heat shot through her body like lightning and settled in her very core. "What do I taste like?" Her head was cloudy and her thoughts were scattering quickly like leaves in the wind.

Grinning slyly, Ekklips moved His hands further down her back, embracing her curves. "Like the creamy melting hues of the sun at dusk, wet, cold raindrops penetrating through the summer heat, flurries of white, fluffy snowflakes cascading in the dead of a winter night..." He lifted her

*415*

chin and passionately kissed her again, "dewdrops dancing upon spring flowers at sunrise, and the first fire during a cool night in autumn."

Gazing into His intoxicating, dark eyes, she stood on her tiptoes and tauntingly whispered, "You're not really here."

Gritting His teeth, Ekklips snarled, "I'm always here."

Upon His words, she began falling freely through the night sky. The stars became a blur of lights streaking upward at an increasingly rapid rate, transforming into white bars, caging her into a tunnel of blinding light. Closing her eyes, her stomach dropped and her heart fluttered.

*Shadows. I'm dreaming.*

Mora jolted into a sitting position. Her chest was heaving. Sweat made her skin clammy and wet as a slight breeze stroked her cheek. Startled, she saw the blue-white eyes of Remmi staring at her from across the small clearing Abin created. He was sitting as still as stone, one arm propped on his bent knee, the other leg angled underneath. His face was eerily illuminated by the subtle glow of a fire.

"Welcome back." Holding out a stick with a descent amount of meat dripping of juices and smelling wonderfully delicious, he inquired, "Hungry?"

Wearily, she nodded her head. She was famished. When she took the stick, her stomach growled from the potent scent of cooked, hearty meat, and a tinge of sweetness. Biting into the tenderness made her salivate harder. Peering suspiciously at him, she took another rich bite, the meat practically falling apart on contact with her tongue.

A slight grin lined his face and he nodded his head. "It's yours. I have more."

With permission granted, she ravished the meat, feeling it appease the cramps in her stomach from lack of proper sustenance. Tearing the last pieces of meat off the small bones, she greedily licked her fingers. He offered her a leather pouch. When she upturned it on her lips, desperate for the cold sensation of water, she was met by a bitter, burning liquid. Coughing heavily, she felt Bog stir at her side.

A brief chuckle of amusement emerged from Remmi's mouth and he shrugged. "Apologies. That is all I have. It's Abin's."

"Thanks," she muttered and handed the leather pouch back, not interested in the after effects of heavy drink. An uncomfortable silence followed. She didn't know how long it would be before sunrise, but she would feel very awkward to be awake with him staring in her general direction.

Running a hand through the loose hair falling around his face, he asked, "Sleep well?"

*Damn, he's a being of little words.* She didn't necessarily feel like making small talk, but didn't want to be rude. "Aye." She gave him a little grin. "Satisfyingly dreamless." The last thing she wanted was for him to inquire about her dreams.

He squinted his eyes. "Right," he replied solemnly, twirling a piece of long grass in his gloved fingers. "You can get more sleep if you want. There's some time before sunrise."

It was Mora's opportunity to escape the awkward situation, but she was curious. "Don't you sleep?"

"How do you know I wasn't before you woke?" he murmured and peered at her beneath his eyelids.

*Elusive answers. He's a bloody wall.* Pursing her lips, she sighed and replied, "Right. Well, thank you for the food. It was…"

"Satisfyingly delicious?" he finished with his eyebrow raised.

At that moment, trying to look unperturbed, she knew he suspected she was lying about the dreamless sleep. She watched him toss the long grass into the flames, glimpse at her as he stood, and walk to the edge of the clearing, blending into the night sky. Abin startled her from her thoughts as he snorted and mumbled something unrecognizable about *breasts* before turning over. Shaking her head, she laid down on her side next to Bog and stared into the shadows of the flames dancing off the tall grass as it swayed gently in the breeze. Before she drifted to sleep, she felt the heavy arm of Bog fall over her hip when he rolled over. Instead of panicking, the security made her relax. Closing her eyes, she drifted back into an actual, satisfyingly dreamless sleep.

# The Nymian Sea

Bog peered sleepily through one eye. The sun was gradually lightening the indigo sky. A few stars still twinkled softly. He was lying flush against Mora's back, one arm thrown over her waist. His desire to stay in the position was more tempting than he thought he could handle. Therefore, when she shifted her hips, he knew he would be greatly embarrassed to have her wake to his cravings. Carefully, he rolled over, removed his arm, and sat up, adjusting himself in a less obvious position. Abin was still snoring and Remmi was nowhere to be seen. Therefore, he decided it was good time to relieve himself and find food.

Walking a little ways from the clearing, he squinted his eyes toward the Halo Mountains. A dark cloud appeared to float above them, similar to the one he saw in the distance when he stood on the canopy in Lychinus. This made him feel uneasy. Scanning the rest of the terrain, he finally saw Remmi. He was standing in the huddle of horses, as if they were having a dialogue and didn't want anyone listening. Every now and then one of the horses appeared to nod their head. Then, he would pet the horse lovingly. Tenderness was not a trait Bog believed him to possess. He was mysterious, elusive, quiet, strong, and condescending. He had not seen him bathe, eat, or sleep since he and Abin joined their journey, a favor he did not ask of the two males, but they have now assumed. He turned away and trudged back to where Mora slept.

With discretion, Remmi watched Bog walk back to the clearing.

Placing an exposed hand on each one of the muscular necks, concealed from view, faint blue rings of light pulsed and disappeared. Then, he placed his glove back on his hand and proceeded toward the camp.

Bog sat down next to Mora's sleeping figure again and noticed there were skewers of meat stuck in the ground, hovering over dying, black embers. His stomach rumbled with anger.

"Eat," Remmi spoke over Bog's shoulder.

Whipping his head around, he grumbled, "Sneaking up on someone doesn't always turn out well."

"Neither does watching them from a distance," Remmi countered as he stepped over to where Abin was sleeping.

Eyeing Remmi, Bog lifted to grab a skewer and sat back down. It smelled delicious, and he was exceptionally hungry. Pulling the meat off the bone, it practically melted in his mouth. *He may be an ass, but he knows how to cook meat.* Satisfied, he ate the slightly sweet meat and licked his fingers. At that moment, Mora stirred next to his side. He smiled when her eyes fluttered open. "Good morning, Sunshine."

Propping herself on her elbows, she looked around the clearing and then back at Bog. Returning the grin, still in a sleepy haze, she asked, "Are we getting ready to ride?" She desperately wanted to mount Sun Shadow again and feel the wind in her hair.

"Aye, if you're well enough to ride alone." He motioned to her wound.

When she curled up, the wound ached, but she didn't want to show how it still hurt. Lifting her torn gown above the stitches, she peered down. There was a little more dried blood around the outside and a bit of swollen redness where the stitches were sewn. She pressed around the warm, tender skin, flinching slightly.

"We should clean it a little more before wrapping it securely. I don't want it to open while you ride."

Feeling a bit sickened, she nodded. "Agreed." Once Bog stood and turned around to retrieve the knapsack, she winced as she laid back down.

Popping the cork off the liquid, he murmured, "We need more when we get to Loralimira." Crouching down, with another of her cloth scraps, he poured the clear liquid over the wound, dabbing around gently.

"Loralimira?" She grimaced when the liquid bubbled and he wiped the last of the dried blood.

"My home. The capital city of Borgoria." Helping her sit, he leaned back on his ankles. "Do you want me to wrap it for you?"

"Let me change into another tunic. I think I have one more decent piece of garment from Katheryn." At the mention of her name, she saw him cringe. "And I'm dying to put breeches back on."

Running his fingers through his loose curls before placing his hands on his knees to stand, he offered a hand. "Are you hungry?"

"Nay, thank you." She accepted his help and when she looked down at her red gown, there were rips and blood all over it. She began to laugh. "I look like..."

"Shit," Abin chimed in with a sleep-filled, raspy voice.

"She looks better than you, old fuck." Remmi tossed a bag onto his lap.

"Nobody is denying that," he grumbled, stretching and yawning.

Mora hadn't laughed heartily in so long, she couldn't stop. She guffawed hysterically until her belly hurt. "I'm sorry...," she snorted, "I'm sorry," she continued, trying to suck in her breath, "I...it's...hold on." She held up a finger and breathed in deeply. "I haven't laughed like that in a long time."

Bog enjoyed watching her laugh, he wished she would do it more often. *It brightens her face.*

"Lass has gone mad if you ask me." Abin smirked and turned away to relieve himself.

"All the better to deal with you," Remmi retorted, rolling his eyes.

She gasped, covered her eyes, and began laughing once again. Bog spread his wings in front of her, and for that she was thankful, but giggling, she stuttered, "I'll be back."

He glanced over his shoulder and spoke apologetically, "Sorry, there is no water around to wash. We'll rest briefly when we get to the water's edge before continuing to the docks." Watching her leave, he retracted his wings, realizing it was the first time he had done so without it hurting after plummeting from the treetop. Rubbing the wound from the Hawkend, he discovered it was fully healed.

"Bog!" Abin's voice shook him from his thoughts.

Shocked, he responded, "That's the second time you've actually called me by my name."

Abin made a puffing sound with his lips. "I started with bird-beast. Anyway, don't get used to it. We're going to ride hard today, do you think she can make it to the docks on the northeast end of the border?"

He grimaced, but replied confidently, "Aye. I'm sure she will be fine. She's stronger than you give her credit."

Remmi nodded in agreement. "I agree with Bog. Mora will able to ride swiftly. Sun Shadow will secure her arrival if she wavers."

"You act like you can read the minds of those damned, wild horses," Abin said cynically.

Remmi grunted.

When Mora returned, she was dressed in a black tunic, falling mid-thigh, with black breeches. She had traded her sandals for her boots, and had fastened the leather belt Bog had given her around her waist. Instead of the messy, low bun coiled at the nape of her neck, she had it braided from the top of her scalp to the small of her back. The wispy curls framing her face fluttered in the breeze.

Abin walked up with his mouth full of meat and said while chewing, "Black suits you lass."

Bog cut his eyes toward Abin. The black did compliment her, but that is what upset him the most. Abin was completely oblivious to his scowl.

Mora flushed and snickered. "Don't start acting too nice, Abin, it doesn't suit you. By the way, what does *cun'ta* mean?"

Waving the skewer at her playfully, he swallowed a large bite and raspingly said, "I knew I'd end up not merely tolerating your company. It's not a sweet sentiment if that's what you're seeking. Its closest interpretation is *loose female.*" Offering his leather pouch, he added, "Would you care for some?"

"Very endearing." Shaking her head, she balked a little. "I know what's in there."

He smiled heartily and shrugged his shoulders. "More for me!" The liquid dripped down his black beard.

Bog groaned.

Securing her harness, she threw her quiver and bow over her

shoulders and sheathed her dagger. She watched Bog flip an axe around in his hand. "Are you going to keep that?"

"Why not? It's a sturdy piece and light enough to carry along with this sword."

"Light?" She scrunched her nose.

"It's obviously not Ura made. It must have been a spoil of war." He squinted at the side of the blade. Wiping the dried blood off in the grass, his eyes widened. "This is the symbol of the Cau'o'tas tribe. How in the curse of the gods did Ura-Ca come to possess this?"

Abin tread over to Bog. "Let me see."

He held the symbol side up for him to see it clearly. "Wasn't Alidyah part of the Cau'o'tas tribe?"

"Aye," Abin responded. Lost in thought, he walked away. He ran a hand through his hair and vigorously rubbed his face. The eyes in the stable had been haunting him, but he couldn't figure out why. However, the symbol of the Cau'o'tas tribe amongst the Ura concerned him gravely.

All the while, Remmi had walked the horses over to the clearing. "Are you ready to ride?" he asked stoically.

With tremendous enthusiasm, Mora ducked beside Bog and over to Sun Shadow. Rubbing the nose, she whispered, "Did you miss me?" Sun Shadow nuzzled her cheek. A spark of energy thrummed through her body, rejuvenating her senses.

Standing next to the horse, with the exception of the black streak in the mane, she starkly contrasted the pure white mare. Unsure of why, a flare of anger rose in Bog's chest. *Fuck Ekklips.* Then, a realization made him rage more. *The seductive being in my dream was...Him.* He shuddered at the image of His onyx eyes staring from beneath the mask. He had witnessed the God of Dark.

Catching Remmi's eyes, he averted his gaze quickly as he strapped the axe onto his belt opposite his sword. With the handle pointing toward the ground, blade facing the backside, he mounted his gray steed. The last thing he wanted was to have the axe placed precariously in his belt loop. He ran a hand through the horse's mane and it responded with a frisky gait. Leaning down to the horse, he whispered, "I'm going to name you Alorian."

"Befitting the horse of a Borgorian," Remmi responded as he

stepped his horse beside Bog's. "She would be honored." Bowing his head, he trotted on.

Burrowing his eyes into Remmi's back, Bog stepped Alorian closer to Sun Shadow. "Comfortable?"

Mora smiled sweetly, "Bog, you really don't have to be so concerned about me. You had a worse injury than I." Touching the Hawkend scar, she said in surprise, "It's healed well, and awfully quick for being ripped open a few more times because of your foolishness. You can hardly see it."

A sly grin broke his previous anger and he looked down at her fingers on his chest.

"What's this?" She traced her finger on the left side of his chest, right below his collarbone.

He glanced down, but he couldn't see anything. However, a slight burning sensation felt like she was carving into his skin with her fingernail. "I don't see anything," he replied with apprehension.

Flattening her hand against his skin, she smirked, "You're heart is beating exceptionally fast. Are *you* fit to ride?"

He knew his entire face was flushed; he could feel it rising. He steadied Alorian as the horse fidgeted, stuttering, "Aye…nervous about going home." He attempted to don a convincing grin.

She eyed him skeptically and grunted.

"When you two are finished with your pathetically dull banter, we need to begin if we're going to get to the docks before nightfall."

Abin, who had been uncharacteristically quiet since seeing the symbol, spat and stuffed a wad of herbed grass into the side his cheek. She thought it looked a lot like the chewing herb Marwen had stuffed into her cheek. Not wanting to remember her time in the Realm of Immortals, she heeled Sun Shadow into a full, furious gallop.

Galloping across the tall, grassy terrain of the Fire Country, Abin led, followed by Mora, Bog, and then Remmi. A sudden urge to extend her arms outward, letting the wind rush over every part of her body, grasped tautly onto her heart. Tears of joy streamed down her face. The freedom of riding made her feel like she had the power to do anything. Sun Shadow energetically stepped in line with Abin's steed, but she knew if she wanted, they could outrun his horse.

## The Keeper

She chuckled to herself. *I could outrun both Abin's and Bog's horses.* Briefly glimpsing back at Remmi, she thought, *I do not believe I can outrun his horse though. He seems abnormally formidable.*

They rode at full gallop until Abin could see the Halo Mountains looming uncomfortably tall in the distance. The smell of the salt air was delightfully refreshing from the filth and decay they had all experienced recently. Veering to the left before they rode too close to the mountains, he dropped in pace with Mora. Leaning in the saddle, he yelled, "We'll stop at the water's edge briefly, then ride until nightfall. We don't want to stay too long this close to the waters of the Nymian Sea!"

She nodded as more loose hair whipped in her face.

Bog thought it was curious the black cloud he had seen this morning looming over the Halo was no longer there. *Had it merely been another illusion?* He hastened Alorian's stride. The closer they rode to the edge of the sea, the harder his heart beat inside his chest. While he wanted to see Aloria, he knew the reunion wouldn't be as welcoming from others.

Rapidly, Sun Shadow galloped toward the Nymian Sea. Mora lifted her hands again toward the skies in pure exuberance. Over the seas of everlasting grass, she felt a change in the wind. As she looked down, she could see a sea of calm, bluish black waters beckoning. The white capped waves rolled sensually across the top of the glassy surface. As they rode closer, the massive Halo Mountains were bigger than any mountains she had ever seen, or read about, in her mother's books. They were slate black and appeared to have jutted forcefully through the water, elevating to a tip of unrivaled severity. Ferocious waves were hammering against the sides, pounding so loudly, she could hear it vibrating in her ears. The sides of stone looked slick, and from between each of the mountains, enormous waterfalls dived into the depths of the black, churning waves of water. The Halo expanded further than the eye could see, never wavering as a giant wall of deadly sharp teeth.

Finally, they reached the edge of the Fire Country. Abin jumped off his horse. Putting a hand to his forehead to block the sun, he sauntered to the edge of a small hill overlooking a very narrow, sandy area.

She followed suit. There was something different about standing at the edge of the bank she couldn't quite grasp. *I wonder if it's because of the Halo Mountains?* She scanned the horizon. The stark line between the sea and the horizon was pristine. There were no ships, no waves, no ripples. Although, there was a serenity from gazing at the sea she had never experienced before. Closing her eyes, she took a deep breath of the salty air, filling her lungs with the freshness, and her mind with the memory. Bog and Remmi trudged up next to where she and Abin were standing.

"We have very little time before they sense our presence," Remmi spoke sternly.

Awakened from her peace, she gawked, "Who?"

"The sea nymphs," Bog stoically replied. "This close to the Halo, they are vicious, deadly beings. Legend has it they were once the most beautiful of sea nymphs with their brilliant scaled tails, shimmering with every hue of dusk and dawn. They had hair of deep mahogany, skin ranging from the most pure shades of ivory to the deepest desires of ebony, and eyes of sparkling silver and gold.

"The sea was their territory from east to west, north to south. Venturing into the depths of the Nymian Sea, Queen Kalvi fell in love with a creature of the deep who promised her an eternity of power. No one knows who this creature was, but the Queen accepted. After, her entire kingdom became ruthless and hungry for anything containing a pinch of light. Their outward, nor inward, beauty, was no longer."

Mora studied his features when he spoke. She could tell he had a passion for expressing the knowledge he had researched over the years; and while it drove her mad in the beginning, she began to enjoy the stories he told. "That's sad," she responded.

"Completely." His gaze never wavered. "This is why we ride to the docks by nightfall. Sailor's tales have told of hideous, merciless sea nymphs morphing from the water in the forms of females, seducing those who venture close to the sea's edge."

It occurred to her she didn't know how old he actually was in relation to her mere five and twenty years. Though he appeared to be around the same amount of years, she now had her doubts. Clearing her throat, and hoping it wasn't inappropriate, she meekly asked, "How old are you?"

He was caught off guard from the question. His own immortality had never actually made him think about how the years passed when he was a borgling, and even less as a grown Borgorian. He understood her curiosity, but was not prepared to answer. Shuffling his feet, he replied with an uncertainty in his voice, "I think around one hundred and seventy-five?" He scrunched his nose at the shock...*or horror?*...on her face.

"You *think*?" she exclaimed. "How the fuck do you *think* you know how old you are?"

Cautiously, he replied, "I stopped counting after one hundred."

"Godsdamn bird beast! You're almost as old as myself, theoretically speaking of course." Abin laughed.

Looking bewildered between Abin and Bog, she guffawed, "What does *theoretically speaking* mean?"

"Borgorians, immortals in general, age differently than mortals." Bog groaned.

"But, you said *I'm* immortal? And I haven't been around one hundred and seventy-five name days!"

"You're...different...," he began to say before Remmi intervened.

"Enough," Remmi commanded, "this ridiculous conversation is deterring our journey to the docks. Clean up and get back on your damn horses."

Abin, Mora, and Bog gawked at Remmi.

Bog cut his eyes at Mora and asked, "Do you want me to walk you down to the edge of the water to clean?" His eyes pleaded for her to acquiesce.

Uncomfortable from Remmi's sudden outburst, she looked at him shiftily and answered, "Aye, thanks."

Leaving Abin behind with Remmi, they began traipsing down to the water's edge. She reached the shore, quickly removed her boots, and stuck her toe in the lapping water. It was cold, but refreshing. While she knew she couldn't drink it, she was relieved to clean off. However, before she did anything, she eyed Bog, questioning, "How am I supposed to rinse?" She hoped he understood the underlying concern.

"I can turn around and spread out my wings. It no longer hurts," he replied.

Satisfied, she nodded her head and agreed, "That will be fine. Thank you."

When he turned around and spread his wings, she began to take off her breeches and tunic. Setting her belt on the rocky sand and unbraiding her hair, she stepped into the cold ocean. Dropping to her knees, in spite of the saltiness of the water and overwhelming coolness making her skin pimple, it was a refreshing sensation.

"That was an odd response, was it not?" she asked him as she removed bits of dried blood and thoroughly cleaned her wound.

He shifted and spoke to the side so she could hear him, "Aye. I'm not sure why he became terribly brash."

Hastening the cleaning and rinsing of her hair, she stood and squeezed the water out before placing her arms in various positions to traipse over to the shore. "He's very jaded."

He peered behind, seeing her emerge from the water made his blood boil. *Fuck*. He quickly turned his head. "I agree. I'm not entirely sure of his relationship to Abin either."

She jested, "Lovers?"

He couldn't help but keel over laughing until he heard her yell.

"Bog!"

Still sniggering, he stood up straight and stuttered, "My apologies. It's just…the idea is hilariously ridiculous. I would actually feel bad for Abin. Could you not imagine the tension?"

"It would be most brutal!" She furtively grinned as she shook as much water off as she could before lightly patting the rest with the tunic. After she finally had secured her belt, she said, "I'm decent."

He retracted his wings and turned around. "My turn?"

She giggled, running her fingers through the tangles of her hair. "Most certainly. I'll turn around."

He hastily removed his boots and breeches, ran, and dove into the water.

Curious, she peeked around as his head surfaced. "What the curse of the gods are you doing?" She laughed.

"Swimming?" Tilting his head, he stood up, the water reaching right below his naval. Rubbing a hand over his face, he flung the loose hair out of his eyes.

She put a hand to her mouth to subdue her snicker and turned her head back around. "Bog. Seriously? You're naked."

"And?" he replied honestly. "I didn't stand up completely out of curtesy for you, but I see nothing wrong with nakedness." He trudged heavily out of the water, dabbed the excess off his body, and pulled his breeches on one soppy leg at a time.

"It doesn't make you uncomfortable?"

"Why should it?"

She couldn't answer the question. She had never thought of why she was embarrassed. However, knowing he was much older, and most likely more experienced, than herself, made her blush. "I don't know. I guess it's because I haven't lived as long as you?" A sudden whisper in her ear made her jump.

"It's a number." He chuckled.

She whipped around and hit him on the arm. "You're an ass," she quipped.

"Possibly," he shrugged, "but you, Sunshine, are a prude."

"Fuck you!" She reached to pound her fists playfully against his chest, but he clasped her wrists and a shock kissed her skin. For a moment, her eyes met his own. When he looked at her in that way, his eyes illuminated like the violets after a summer's rain, the words Marwen had spoken. Her breathing quickened. She had never been intentionally this close to an actual physical male. Ekklips had always pressed against her in her dreams, but it was not real. Lately, she also questioned whether He was actually in the Realm of Immortals, or if it had been the shadow Dierdan had spoken about. Her face was heated and her body began to feel like it did in her dreams. A desire was awakening.

Bog's heart beat ferociously. He looked into her forest green eyes. *What the fuck am I thinking?* Holding her wrists, he desperately wanted to kiss her succulent, rose-pink lips. However, looking down, he knew she was as nervous as he was, her chest was heaving against his stomach. Never had he felt what he did with Mora. He wanted to hide her, save her from this life altering task. Nevertheless, deep down, he knew Ekklips wanted control of her, a balance he could never acquire himself. But...*I think I love her.*

"Bog!" the sound of Remmi's voice severely bit into his conscious and he dropped her wrists.

"Let's ride," he commanded gruffly.

He could see the intensity of Remmi's eyes from where he stood on the rocky sand with Mora. Closing his eyes as her hands slid down his chest, he laced his boots over his breeches and trudged up the hill toward the horses. The rage he had kept at bay clawed violently inside.

As he passed, Remmi grabbed his arm and murmured in his ear, "I told you to stay unemotionally detached."

"Don't touch me," he snarled and slung off his hand as he passed, finished buckling his belt, and leapt onto his horse, Alorian. The urge to grab a feather from his wing was tempting. *But I won't for her sake.*

Mora followed Bog, unsure of what she was feeling. *I thought him just a friend.*

As they began to ride, Remmi scowled over his shoulder at the eyes emerging from the sea's edge.

The sun sank below the Halo Mountains behind them. The rocky crags were silhouetted against the brilliance of the sunset. The reds, oranges, and yellows made the sky appear like they were on fire. The last rays of the sun beamed from behind the darkness of the massively jutting stones. Bog looked back, only to be met by the unsettling image of Remmi. The malice he held for him deepened every time he spoke to him directly. He never trusted him, but his loathing grew beyond the desire to ever try. Suddenly, a torch in the distance caught his attention.

As they encroached on the source of minimal light, Abin slowed down to a steady gait. His company followed. Cautiously, they approached a dock, the sun almost completely behind the Halo. He noticed a large ship, wading on the subtle waves. "Oi!" he called.

A limp sailor stood up behind a barrel close to the ramp. "Who calls?"

He responded with authority, "Abin of the Fire Country. Who questions?"

To Mora's surprise, the sailor who questioned could not be more than fifteen name days, shivering with the chill in the air, but attempting to sound older. "The servant of the Captain," he said as he sullenly bowed his head at Abin's presence.

"Lad, tell the Captain we seek passage to Loralimira." He

dismounted his horse.

The lad paused, wide-eyed.

"Make haste you little shit!" Abin barked.

"Aye!" He limped quickly over the ramp onto the ship's deck.

She felt the abnormal twinge of air she had experienced when she rode closer to the sea previously. Watching Bog dismount, she quietly asked, "What's the strange feeling surrounding this place?"

Confused, he replied, "What do you mean?"

"I merely get this sense we are bordering on the unknown," she said uncomfortably.

For a moment, he was baffled at what she was feeling, until he realized she had never consciously been aware of the transitions between realms. "The veil. You are feeling the essence of the veil. Regular mortals would only see a normal body of water in front of them, but the veil masks the two realms, mortal and immortal. You entered it when you approached Lychinus."

She wrinkled her nose. "The veil? I thought Abin was mortal?"

Standing almost level with her chest next to the horse, Bog didn't have to tilt his head much to look her square in the eyes. "By now, you do realize Abin is not a *normal* mortal."

The possibility Abin was strangely more than what he looked from the outside had crossed her mind. However, it wasn't until Bog pointed it out she really began to think about Abin's curious demeanor. She rolled her eyes in frustration. When he walked away, she dismounted Sun Shadow.

Bog and Abin were standing side by side, waiting on the arrival of the young servant. Finally, frazzled, the lad hobbled over the plank of wood.

Taking one look at Bog, his eyes went wide with surprise. "Oi, curse of the gods! Hold on." He turned on his heel and limped back over the plank. This time, he didn't take as long to reappear. A large, burly creatural followed behind.

"'Em th' Cap'n of this ship and I hers we 'ave a Borgorian wantin' a safe passage t' Loralimira?" his low, raspy voice sounded entertained. "Whys ya wantin' a passage t' yer homelands son when ya could jus' fly?"

The Captain was sun scorched with long, silver, unkempt, braided hair and a thick beard twisted down the front. His eyes were each a different color, one was a light blue with a harrowing scar slashed over it, and the other was hazel. Only one appeared to move. His teeth were terribly stained yellow and he wore an overcoat of brown with black trousers. A burly, hairy chest peeked through the top of his stained, linen tunic and was covered in the same, matching, silver strands.

Properly, Bog replied, "I am Bogheim of the House of Gornya. I journey with my companions, who, as you can very well see, cannot fly."

"Aye, weel, I assume yer pay hansomly for yer voyage as I see yer 'er travelin' with a female. An' ems bad luck." He motioned to Mora and adjusted his breeches. "'n there not be many female folk beside th' sea nymphs and 'ccasional kitchen whore who cross th' waters."

Clearing his throat and glancing at Mora, Bog nodded his head. "Aye, as soon as you dock in Loralimira *safely*, you will be rewarded by my own hand." He wanted to make sure the Captain understood the emphasis on the word safely.

"Aye. Yer won' any trouble on th' Queen Kalvi!" The Captain gestured toward his ship.

She scrunched her nose. "Queen Kalvi?" Looking at Bog, she inquired, "Isn't that the name of the sea nymph you spoke about earlier?"

The Captain responded before he could speak. "Mos' proper m' lass! It's a'node t' her majesty 'n retu'n of safe passage. It's th' fastest ship on 'em there waters!" He rubbed his rounded belly and rocked on his toes.

"Of course," she replied and nodded.

"An yer Lord Abin of ther Fire Country, sorry ta her' 'bout yer Fortress. Damn shame."

Abin spat into the water and cut his eyes at the Captain. "Word gets around quickly. Tell me, are you able to sail soon?"

"If yer Borgorian frien' her' pays extreh." His stained tooth grin grew and he motioned at Bog.

Bog grunted.

"Can our horses come aboard?" she added nervously.

"Fer double! We got sum stable lads 'n need of sum extreh work," he gaily replied, winking at Mora.

Before Bog argued, he saw the desperation in her eyes. "Agreed," he sighed.

"Thank you," she whispered.

Bog and Abin shook the Captain's burly hand.

"What are we waiting on!" Abin slapped the shoulder of the Captain.

Finally, Remmi dismounted his horse and walked over to Abin's side. The Captain looked him up and down with a perplexed expression. He nodded his head in acknowledgment, but his face showed no emotion.

Raising an eyebrow, the Captain, still unsure about Remmi's appearance, gestured toward the plank leading to the ship's deck. "All aboard!"

Clearly apprehensive, the horses bustled. Mora continued to stroke the side of Sun Shadow's neck. "Don't worry, lovely," she whispered to Sun Shadow, "I will be down there with you most of the time. The trip should not be long." The horse tossed its head in acknowledgment of the promise.

The hobbling servant lad led the horses into the ship on a bottom plank. Abin led the way along the top plank. She followed. It was not more than half her length in width and completely void of railing. Nervously peering down toward the water below, she noticed glimmers of light teal twinkling. It was a school of miniature fish, hardly visible save the occasional glance of sheen and shadow on the surface of the water. They brought a smile to her face. Once on the deck, she immediately scuttled over to the opposite railing and gazed out on the vast pastel sea, mirroring the brilliant sky. She breathed in deeply as the mixture of salt and fresh air swam in her nostrils.

Bog walked up beside her and placed his elbows on the rail, also taking in a large breath of salt air. "Magnificent, is it not?" His dimpled smile illuminated his shockingly violet eyes.

"It is so." She grinned back and then surveyed the sea as far as her vision would reach. The sea seemed calm, completely void of waves, but she could faintly hear the sound of rushing water. "Bog, what is the sound of rushing water I hear? And why did I just now hear it?"

"That would be the sound of the Nymia Towers. They are the only passage into the city of Loralimira. It is where the House of Gornya centers. The Nymia Towers are curtains of water expanding from the Nymian Sea to the clouds. They are so grand, you can still hear them more than half a day away. They are a significant part of the Borgorian Legends. They say, when Aloria and Borheim settled with the lands, now known as Borgoria, they required protection from Borheim's tribe. Because Aloria was once the mother of the skies, she commanded the clouds to pull the water from the seas to remain until the last generation ceases to exist. The curtains have endured the test of time many ages before, but those stories would take several moons, if not lifetimes, to speak about." He gazed out on the sea, lost in a memory of another lifetime too distant to touch.

Remmi and Abin approached the rail.

"We must receive cabin assignments or else be stuck on the lowest deck of the ship, soaked in animal shit." Abin's eye widened as a wench bustled by holding a tray full of ale. "The Captain was not wrong!" He proceeded to follow hungrily.

"Did he always act like this?" she inquired to Remmi. "And I thought females were bad luck?"

"He has always been as blunt as the broad side of a hoof, but he has become more lonely since Alidyah was murdered." He turned around and placed his elbows on the railing. "Captain said they were bad luck, but he didn't say they weren't allowed."

They glimpsed at Abin in time to see the wench slap him hard in the face. He smiled, winked, and continued to follow.

She could not help but snicker. "He is certainly a brute, but he would die for whom he considered kin regardless of the method." Peering at Remmi, realizing it was the most she had heard him reference something personal, she decided to ask, "And you? You appear to laugh in the face of fear."

He gazed at the sea, absently whittling at the side of the ship with a small knife. "I do not fear Death because death does not come easily for me." He turned around and propped against on the rail. "When you let fear overtake your emotions, you loose judgment, and when you loose judgment, you loose defense."

"But keeping your guard up means you fear the constant threat of dire circumstances?"

Shrugging his shoulders, he kept his eyes on the other side of the ship. "I don't keep my guard up. I have merely trained my impulse emotions to be strong enough to endure even the most excruciating of circumstances. Therefore, I am surprised by nothing."

Excited, she continued, "You said death does not come easily to you. I suppose you are immortal?"

"Aye, you can say that."

Inquisitively, she jerked her head sideways, sputtering, "What do you mean?"

"You may know someday." Pushing himself off the railing, he started walking toward a cabin door. Midway, he turned and tossed her the small knife, blade tucked into the slit on the side of the tang.

Squinting at an inscription across the surface, she read: *VAL RESURGIMUS*. Puzzled by the phrase, she pulled the blade open, looking for other inscriptions, but there were none. Glimpsing toward where he had been standing, she saw he had already ventured into the cabins. Placing it inside her boot, she turned to see if Bog was anywhere in sight. Not seeing him on deck, she trudged across the ship. Finally, she saw him emerging from a door.

"I have our cabin assignment," he said, scratching his head.

She pointed to the bow of the ship and he responded with an eager nod of his head. She grimaced at the thought of sharing a cabin with anyone else. Reluctantly, she climbed the stairs toward the wheel of the ship. From where she stood, she could see torches being lit against the oncoming night by various crew members. Several of the crew were Borgorians, like Bog. However, their wings not nearly as impressive, and much dirtier. Others were foreign individuals with dark, sunburned skin and black hair tied down their backs, well below their waist. The facial features were sharp, with many possessing a sort of roughly skewed beard. One crew mate, she observed, had a similarly twisted beard hanging in the front of his chest as the braid did his back. Multiple members had tattooed images of ships, sea monsters, or inscriptions on their flesh.

Bog joined her after talking to a couple of the crew mates.

She glanced at the parchment he handed her moments before. "We're bunk mates. But who is Zebrolan?"

"The mate assigning, and trust me, he was in no mood to argue, informed me we were only allowed three to a room, and one of the assigned must be a crew member."

She surveyed the deck for Abin and Remmi and asked, "I wonder if they were able to get a room together?"

He shrugged his shoulders. "Who knows? Abin was set on the kitchen wench. I am most certain he will not care where he sleeps, as long as she gives him some better sea legs."

She guffawed at the thought, and yet detested the image.

"Yer might wan'a tell yer frien' that 'em wenches are on a firs' come firs' serve basis, if yer know wha' I mean," the Captain's voice boomed from the bottom of the staircase.

They reacted by leaning over the rail.

"No need t' frighten' ya lass. This here's me ship an' yer on me bow."

"I apologize, Captain…" Bog responded, but paused.

"Lox, is tha name!"

"Captain Lox," he acknowledged, "we were admiring the view." The Captain was a large figure, but he stood about a half a head shorter than Bog. "Sorry for our intrusion."

"No harm done." Captain Lox smiled, revealing his yellow teeth, a few missing from the sides.

Inquisitively, she asked, "Where are you from, Captain?" She took notice of Bog cutting his eyes in her direction.

"I'm from th' south." He appeared to look past the sea. "Ja Velco, home of the Velcians."

"Part of your crew, they are Velcians, too?"

The Captain nodded.

She watched the handful of members starting to pull down on the halyard. The mainsail was so enormous, it nearly took a third of the crew to get it started until the wind caught on.

Captain Lox continued, "Aye. 'Em came wit' me ov'r the Nymian Sea 'til the Borgorians captur'd ar' boat an we agreed t' ferry to th' shores an' forth 'n return for food 'n shelter 'n Loralimira. Th' Borgorians don't take too nicely t' our kin'." He spat a large wad of chewed grass into a silver cup strung to his leather belt. "I keeps 'em straights, I do! 'Em mates can b' a rough crowd. Tha's why yer friend migh' wan'a stay away from 'em wenches. The' can be a damn territorial lot!" He laughed heartily.

She had a thought. "Can you point out Zebrolan? We are going to be bunk mates and we're curious whether he is Borgorian or Velcian?"

"Zebrolan's a new mate. He's par' of th' Velcian escapees that joined 'r crew recently. I thin' ye will find him 'n th' galley." He chuckled and added, "Ye don' wan'a piss him off! Yer b' eatin' yer arm by th' en'da th' trip!"

Watching the mainsail wiggle, he shouted jovially, "On now, scuttle 'way, let me get t' me wheel!" Slightly pushing his way to the wheel, he took hold and began shouting commands to the hands on deck.

Walking over to the laddered steps, Mora caught a glimpse of Remmi near the bow of the ship with Abin. Bog followed her against the deckhands shoving their way across the deck, attempting to get everything tied down. In stature, some of the Velcians surpassed Bog by half a head. Their physique was impressively proportionate to their stature. Glimpsing harder, each had been tattooed on their necks as well, underneath their ear. It was a symbol, number, or letter. A few of the Velcians, who had no clothing covering their chest, also had long scars protruding from the flesh on their backs. She had never seen such a scar. Unlike their Captain, the Velcian crew were not too friendly. Scowls possessed their faces. However, to her observation, the Borgorian crew did not appear to be working nearly as hard as the Velcian. Their tasks were more menial, such as giving commands or sweeping the deck.

Arriving to the bow of the ship, she could faintly hear Abin and Remmi muttering amongst themselves by the railing. "Ahoy!" she finally shouted after they had taken no notice of the oncoming company.

Abin groaned over his shoulder. "Pardon our ignorance, we were just discussing the journey." A pipe hung from his lips and the sweet herb he carried with him wafted into the air. "Do you know where we are headed?"

Bog answered, "To the House of Gornya."

Dully, he eyed him, and then looked back at Mora. He cleared his throat, "Do you know what you plan on accomplishing passed that point?"

She glanced from Abin to Remmi, feeling the icy cold realization she knew nothing of what lay beyond Borgoria. She had been blindly following, merely assuming she would possess the answers the further they traveled. She could not reassure herself, or any of her company, much more than the name of the destination Bog had repeated from the beginning. Then, she remembered something Ekklips had spoken about and said confidently, "I journey to The Gateway."

Remmi stared bluntly at Mora, his piercing eyes never wavering from her direction.

Abin choked on smoke, coughed, and sputtered, "The Gateway? You speak of myth! You spoke as if unsure of your journey and then you pipe in about *The Gateway*? You know not of what you believe yourself! There is no godsdamn reality in The Gateway. Speak, Rem! Tell the lass she is mad, is she not?"

Remmi broke his gaze from Mora and glanced out upon the sea. Clearing his throat, he replied, "I have heard rumors which may prove The Gateway is not a falsehood."

Irritated, Abin guffawed, "Now you're raving mad!" and began to walk away, "I won't stand for this nonsense."

Remmi shrugged and muttered, "Let us part to the stables and receive what is left of our belongings before thieves begin to wander around the lower decks tonight."

Bog rubbed the back of his neck. *Fuck. The Gateway?* Subtly, the breeze rustled his feathers and his chest started to sear. *Where did she hear about that?*

# Deception and Revelation

They could smell the stables on the lowest deck from midway down the ship. It was dark, save for sporadically positioned, bulbed lanterns lining the wall, appearing as though floating in the hallway. Upon closer glance, the bulbs were set in the wall, lit with candles, the smoke escaping through small holes cut in a semi-circle near the top of the glass. Mora assumed the candles were secured within the wood for fear of lighting the ship on fire if there was a storm at sea.

She followed closely behind Remmi. Bog had decided to stay at the entrance of the corridor to keep watch. Reaching the door of the lower deck stables, Sun Shadow's white mane was faintly visible amongst the dark exterior. She quickly ran to the mare and brushed back the mane.

"How are you holding out?" The horse merely shook its head back and forth. "My apologies you have been subjected to the lowest ranks of the ship. We will arrive by tomorrow, hopefully before midday."

She lifted the sheet Remmi had placed over Sun Shadow's back to conceal her wrapped bow and quiver. They did not want to attract attention to the gold weapon while amongst the ship's thieves, lucky it had not drawn attention in Ura. Unlatching the packaged weapon, she tucked it securely under her arm.

"Mora, we must depart, the night will be upon us soon and I loathe the idea of being amongst the outcasts at that hour." Remmi unlatched his bow and quiver from beneath his horse's cloth and slung it upon his back.

"You do not fear they will become suspicious of your weapon?" She inquired, lifting an eyebrow.

"They dare not ask," he grumbled. Illuminated by an unseen force, a fire gleamed in his blue-white eyes.

"If you insist," she answered hesitantly. Pulling the cloth further over Sun Shadow's neck and kissing the muzzle, she whispered, "I will come again soon."

His pace was absurdly quick as they climbed each story of the ship. As they closed in on the doorway, she could hear Bog muttering to himself about how he was out of his mind to be drawing more attention to their presence with the appearance of the weapon.

"Remmi, where is the location of your cabin?" she asked as he leapt the last several stairs two at a time.

"Across the corridor from your own." He did not slow his pace upon answering.

"What luck," Bog mumbled under his breath. Mora gave him an annoyed glance.

"Your luck indeed," Remmi retorted.

Bog grumbled.

Once they reached the upper cabins, the closest to the main deck, Remmi turned around. "I am going to find Abin. You must settle in for the night."

She began to protest, but Bog pulled her toward their cabin and spoke flatly, "Don't argue with him, it's not worth it. His intentions are not to protect you much more than he can hold a smile. You shall not waste your breath."

"I disagree," she hoarsely replied, "I believe he has better intentions than you realize."

"Right," he said dryly.

When they entered the cabin, they noticed it had already been preoccupied by the third bunk mate. He was in the corner of the room, sitting on the lowest bunk reading. He peered up immediately when they stumbled in the door. Mora thought it was unusual he was fully clothed with a loosely fitted tunic and breeches. With slightly softer features, his eyes were a dark brown, set in a fuller face. There was no obvious signs of stubble. When he stood, he was no taller than Bog and had a slender frame, very unlike the other Velcians on deck. Observing closer, the symbol tattooed beneath his ear was slightly smudged from the obvious perspiration.

When he spoke, the voice sounded immensely strained, "Zebrolan." He merely nodded and sat back down.

Mora introduced the both of them, "Mora and Bog." Discreetly, she laid her pack in the corner of the room next to an inlaid bed. Signaling to Bog, he stepped close and she whispered, "Go retrieve food from the galley, we have had no sustenance tonight."

There was a slight glance from Zebrolan when he began to question her request, but she peered in his disconcerting eyes. "Please?" she begged.

Leering in Zebrolan's direction, he unwillingly left the cabin, ducking as he went through the doorframe.

"Your disguise is flawed," she muttered quietly.

Quickly, Zebrolan stood up and trudged intimidatingly over to her, looking down into her face with rage. "Blasphemous!" the voice forced a deep-toned response.

"You are *no* male," she spoke clearer this time.

"How dare you!"

As a hand was raised in her direction, it came down on the wood of a small table with a *thump!* Mora flinched at the sound.

The female shook her head and uttered on the verge of tears, "How did you know?"

Her eyes were desperate and the tone in her voice was shaking slightly. "Female intuition?" Mora shrugged and said cautiously, "And your tattoo is smearing. I knew you must be disguising your identity."

"Damn you!" She jerked around and began pacing back and forth. "If you know, someone is sure to discover!"

"Calm yourself," Mora tried to gesture her condolences, "I'm not here to reveal you to anyone."

"You know what mine being a female means?" Her eyes were full of fear. "Being a stole away is punishable by flogging, but a female…" she stuttered desperately, "stole away is punishable by death!" There was sweat dripping down her neck.

"Needless to say, I am not here to reveal you," Mora reassured. "I merely stated an observation. I know not much about the lands outside my own and they have slowly become more severe the further I travel. I wanted to help you realize your disguise will fail you soon."

"Who are you?" she inquired.

Mora sat lazily down on the lower bunk and briefly glanced at what the female was reading, *The Legend of the Sun Goddess*. The title sounded familiar. Clearing her throat, she said, "Mora. I am from no where, I come from no one. I am merely Mora." With a tension in her voice, she continued to watch the figure pace and asked, "Who are you?"

She paused immediately and spun on her heel. Tugging at her braid, she said timidly, "I am Zalana, princess of Ja Velco."

Despite her modest demeanor, Zalana's eyes appeared stormy and full of hatred. "Princess?" the word stumbled from Mora's tongue. "Are you not unquestionably missing in your country?"

Zalana straightened. "I faked my own death."

"You…" she choked on the words, "…faked your own death?" The revelation was no less than shocking, and terribly strange. "May I inquire the details?"

"A sacrifice had to be made, and for love, my handmaiden died for my will to live." She stared behind Mora as if she was trying to remember the lost love. Rubbing her neck, she choked, "Disfigured, she was unrecognizable. I escaped on the next ship to Borgoria."

Mora knew not how to react. At a loss for words, she asked breathlessly, "Why?"

"Because I was to be married off to a formidable being with whom I did not love. His family had murdered a couple of my own brothers in war and, as we were graced with a time of peace, wanted to bestow his offering upon my father."

Her accent was heavy, but Mora could follow the story fairly well.

"He asked for my hand in exchange for a truce between our kingdoms, but I knew his true intentions were to succeed the throne and take what was unrightfully his." A tear ran down her face. "I told my beautiful Carisun, my companion from when I was a childling, and she devised the plan. I begged for her to not think of such things, but she knew it was the only way for me to be free." Blotting her tears, trying to return from her pain, she stuttered, "It…is for her I live, and I will make my way to Terrae Soliste, even if it kills me."

Mora thought for a moment of the place Zalana had spoken. She had never heard of *The Land of the Sun.* Therefore, she inquired about her journey further, "Why are you working for the ship?"

"I cannot venture alone," Zalana retorted, exasperated. "I must earn my wages to join a caravan." She wiped the sweat from her brow. "And the only way is by portraying myself as a male."

Mora remembered the symbol below the ears of the Velcians. "What are the numbers?"

"They are a branding, a male ritual. In Ja Velco, when a male youth comes of age, he is released in a pit of pantherios. They are awful, immensely strong, and brutal creatures with thick, black and white fur. They are able to tear your flesh like parchment with a swipe of their razor sharp, hand length claws. If the male survives the pit for four days, he is pulled from the pit and branded, both on the neck and the back. The neck is a number, to keep track of each male who survived the pit. The scars on their backs are a symbol of strength and power, called Utinoomo. My symbol was that of my eldest brother who was killed against Jukino, the monster with whom I was to be wed."

She touched the ink upon her neck. "The ink was branded to last a least a year. Instead, it has barely reached seven, full moons." Raising her arms up to the ceiling, she cursed.

"What is the number?"

"5053," Zalana spoke with her head down.

Mora picked up the book in which she was reading. "Who is the Sun Goddess?"

Zalana took the book into her hands, holding it to her chest. "Carisun gave this to me before she died. She told me the answers I seek lie within the book." With a thin lipped grin, she tossed it back on the bed. "I have read the book at least four times and nothing has appeared to console me in my agony. Yet, *The Legend of the Sun Goddess* is about Solora, one of the three breaths of All. There was Dark, Light, and Life. With all three, existence became. Theoretically, all three were thought to be equal. However, Life sought to be the most powerful, deeming Dark and Light as His protectors in order to sustain existence. *The Legend of Sun*

## The Keeper

*Goddess* is about retaining ultimate knowledge, the highest form of Enlightenment, and the concealment of Life's secrets. After His exile, out of jealousy, Dark, by tempting His balance - the Sun Goddess, unleashed Chaos. Life became harsh, envious, and unyielding after Dark extinguished Light. He damned Dark to become Death and freewill became an alienable concept of the mortal mind about their own existence, battling with the ideas of destiny or fate."

Snickering, she continued, waving her hand, "It's all very foolish, I know. It is only a story written by an immortal being in Ja Velco, but Carisun found wisdom in it. Therefore, I must continue her legacy by finding solace in the frivolities of folklore until I can join her spirit again someday, frolicking together in a timeless state of never-ending youth."

Gathering her thoughts, Mora asked, "Did Carisun leave any further notes about your reading?"

Zalana winced. "Nay, save for the margins."

Picking the book back off the bed, she thumbed through the pages. There were certainly a number of notes in the margins. One phrase specifically stood out to her, *val resurgimus.* She read further, curiously noting that on every other page, there was a circled word. Glancing up at Zalana, she inquired, "Have you written down the circled words on each page?"

She nodded and pointed to a page sticking out of the side. "The parchment at the end of the book. A few pages have been torn from near the end of the book, so I know not if there was more to read."

Mora pulled out the parchment and starting reading aloud:

> *"The Trinitas did not create immortals for empyrean authority. We are on the cusp of the Fall, the destruction of divinity and the annihilation of All. Because Dark yearned for the ability to create life, the Goddess, Solora, was incarnated from Her spirit of Chaos - not in Life's image, but in Dark's. However, Life's omnipotent presence intravenously flowed into Her veins through a Primordial vessel. Caged in flesh and bone, His ultimate knowledge will be restored in Her mind, remaining untouchable by mortal and immortals alike -*

**443**

## The Keeper

*even Dark cannot relish grasping the knowledge through Her creatural embodiment. Although She will be limited in Her divine connection, Light will nourish and prevail in enlightenment when She accepts and embraces Her True Being.*

*Be cautious, for Light does not walk the lands alone. For in the prophecy, Light incarnate will be tempted by Dark, but fueled by Life. When She stands before The Gateway, Light will have the choice between Death and Life. Weary, it will be no easy decision. For, as Dark continues His attempts to extinguish Life, His pleasures will excite and ignite Light, causing Her vitality to burn with lustful intensity. But, like a candle in the wind, Her flame will struggle to support Her True Being and Her residual desires will once again fuel the energy of Chaos. While it is uncertain what will become of All if She embraces Death, by choosing Life, She will extricate superior knowledge. Hence, if She succeeds, the connection between Dark and Death will become severed. If this comes to fruition, another, through a heinous sacrifice, will be forced to wear the heaviness of Death's mantle, the weight of All nearly incomprehensible.*

*Follow the Light, my love, for She will lead you through the darkness. Do not falter, nor leave Light to be smothered by Dark. Life cannot flourish alone. Without the Light, He is progressively weakening. If you allow Light to fail, Dark's transformation will be complete, oppress the lands, and infinite Chaos will ensue, exploiting Life as an eternal damnation of agony and defeat. Do not feel forlorn. Seek solace in knowing my spirit resides around you, in your very core. You are not..."*

She looked away from the parchment and into the eyes of Bog. He had entered the room quietly. Once she noticed his presence, Zalana immediately stood up in defense.

**444**

"Stop!" Mora shouted, "He will not hurt you."

Zalana backed away from her stance. "But he now knows my identity," she spoke in a soft, angry tone.

His eyes widened and he gawked. "A female?"

Mora nodded slightly. "I will explain later." Her eyes quickly moved toward Zalana. "Tell me, what is the language of the last words, *val resurgimus.*"

However, it was not Zalana's voice in which spoke when her mouth opened, it was Bog's, "It is the primitive language of Life, forsaken upon the exile of Dark, and adapted by Death."

Apprehensive, Mora glanced at Bog. He merely stood there, tray in hand, staring blankly into her eyes. After she took a few moments to contemplate, she said in a barely audible tone, "I must have fresh air." Absently laying the book back down on the bed, she pushed past Bog and made her way to the door.

Glaring at Zalana, he grabbed Mora's arm and whispered, "Mora, please don't."

Shaking off his grip, she proceeded through the door without acknowledging he had spoken.

445

# Nymia Towers

Mora stepped breathlessly out of the door onto the main deck and rubbed her eyes. She didn't know how long she had been down in the lower stables with Sun Shadow, but the night was heavy upon them and there was a thick silence encompassing the deck. The first thing she noticed was Remmi standing against the stars beside the rail, humming the enchanting lullaby under his breath as it was swept away on the breeze. Then, she saw Abin, passed out against the railing, snoring loudly as the ship sailed on the calm waters. It was cold, more so than it had been the past previous nights in the Fire Country.

The sea breeze tickled the loose hair around her ears. Pulling her cloak tighter over her shoulders, she glimpsed at the stars. Brilliant pinpoints of light careened down through the sky, visible to the naked eye, and flaunting their gloriousness on the black surface of the sea. The stars' presence appeared omnipotent, and yet ephemeral with the slightest, more dominating light in their presence. She knew they never actually disappeared, merely transitioned and evolved. She sighed and continued to languidly walk toward the railing.

Not looking in her direction, the humming stopped as Remmi spoke in a low, monotonous tone, "Why are you above deck?"

"I could not sleep," she answered. The last thing she wanted was to reveal she had been below, alone. A snort from Abin startled her as she advanced.

"You should not be here. It is a dangerous place for a female to be alone at night," he replied with a clear, calm voice.

"I am not alone, you are here." She half grinned.

"You know me very little, and yet you trust I will remain loyal to your cause."

She stepped next to him and set her arms on the smooth wood. The water looked like a black mirror, reflecting the unfathomable expansion of the night sky. Water lapped against the side of the boat and silently rippled away. "How is it the sea is so incredibly calm?" she inquired.

"This is no ordinary sea. It is a sea manipulated by an immortal being, it has no say in its behavior."

Eyeing him from the corner of her eyes, she asked, "Will it still be controlled by immortality if the immortal ceases to exist?"

"Why do you believe this immortal will cease to exist?" Haughtily, he glanced in her direction, the look of disconcertment obvious in her expression.

Lifting her shoulders, she said, "I'm not entirely sure *I* really *exist* anymore."

"That's a deep assumption," he replied gruffly, a slight snigger to his tone, "very existential."

She peered at Abin. "What happened to him?" She could see a dark, satin spot of blood on his linen and a dried stream of burgundy running from his lips.

"He was humping some wench when a Velcian became too jealous and overbearing. I arrived in time to see the Velcian throw a punch at Abin and smash him against a glass wardrobe filled with dishes. He was merely scraped, but he was fortunately drunk at the time and completely unfazed by the blow. I bargained with the Velcian. As I left, he smacked the wench twice in the face before bending her over the table."

"That is terrible! Why did you not stop him?" She was appalled and disgusted by his lack of empathy for the female, regardless of her chosen profession.

"Tell me, what would you have had me do? Kill him?" Impudence glazed over his eyes.

She blinked and retorted, "Nay, but at least remove her from the room!"

Uninterested in furthering the conversation, he hissed, "The wench chose her occupation. Who am I to interfere?"

"Who *are* you?" she balked in disapproval.

"I am nobody." Not wanting to further the conversation, he turned around and began to hum again.

"That says nothing," she barked angrily. "I demand to know who you are! I know it was you in the woods when I emerged from the pool."

He suppressed a laugh and replied, "And what an unusually pale sunrise I encountered."

She scoffed, "You sound like Abin."

"I am a male being. You need to learn to listen as much as you question." He spat into the sea. "You cannot expect me to explain who I am when you neither know who you are, nor know where you are going." Stretching, he turned his back to the rail, his bow slung low to his side.

"You are a bastard. I know that to be true." Mora acknowledged the comment was harsh, but she was not in a compassionate mood.

"More than you realize," he replied.

At his words, she felt a shrinking in the pit of her stomach, but she did not feel the need to apologize. Again, Abin snorted. She leaned further over the railing of the ship. In the distance, she could still hear the faint sound of the water towers and wondered how close they were to them. The idea of grandiose waterfalls in the middle of the ocean baffled, yet excited her senses. Glancing around the deck, she realized how very little movement there was amongst the crew members. Many appeared to have retired to their bunks or passed out in similar positions as Abin.

Still feeling pity at Remmi's response, she inquired, "Have you been here before?"

"I have been every where multiple times."

"How did you come to the Floating Fortress?"

"Let's merely speak of it as repaying a debt." He briefly glanced at her before he rubbed his face and added, "I made it my home."

The comment caught her off guard, but she did not pursue any more information surrounding the topic. She simply moved on. "Do we go near the water towers?"

"We pass through the middle of them in order to reach the port of Loralimira."

"Pass through the middle?" she repeated in disbelief. "There will be curtains of water surrounding the sides of the ship? How expansive is the passageway? And what happens if we try to go through the curtains of water?" With a growing anxiety, she wanted to continue to ask questions, but she heard a whistle.

On the crow's nest, she saw a Velcian waving a torch frantically, shouting to the deck below to survey the horizon behind the ship. Mora and Remmi immediately ran to the stern and gazed out in the distance. The slight shadow of another ship was contrasted with the slivered moon, blotting out a handful of distant stars. From their vantage point, the ship appeared to be at a disadvantage, but the shadow grew larger at an alarming rate until, by her account, it was no more than an estimated twenty ship lengths behind.

Concerned, she asked Remmi, "Who do you suppose it is?"

"Any idea eludes me, but I do not have a good feeling considering their speed at this point in the night." He peered at her through the darkness, his bright blue eyes illuminating in the flickering torchlight. "You will need to gather your bow immediately, but keep it concealed. I will awaken Abin."

She rapidly tumbled through the awakening crew until she reached the cabin door and started to sprint down the corridor. She flung herself into her assigned room. On opposite sides, Bog and Zalana were picking at the food he had brought earlier, not conversing, nor acknowledging each other's presence.

"Another ship," she panted heavily, "coming quickly, gaining on us at an unprecedented speed."

Zalana was already equipping herself when she heard the words 'another ship'.

Bog finished scarfing down the food before standing up and securing his weapons. Talking with his mouth full, he sputtered, "Did you see who it was?"

"Nay, it is too dark. They could be much closer than when I left." She grabbed her cloth containing her bow and quiver, holding it painfully close to her body.

"They could be from Ja Velco and have found out my trickery!" Zalana buckled her belt around her waist, a magnificently jeweled hilt peeking through the leather. She caught Mora staring. "My brother's sword. I stole it from my father's treasures, hoping I could replace it with a convincing fake. He must have recognized the deceit and sent soldiers."

By the time they left the cabin, Mora could hear yelling on the upper deck and a hoard of footsteps running around frantically. Once aloft, she could see the other vessel only a ship's length behind with a mast of black, torn sails. Immediately, she peered up at Captain Lox who was giving commands to ready the cannons, the catapult, and the archers. From the bow, a floor door was opened and more crew emerged hoisting a cannon out of the hold. Once the door was closed, they secured the board with heavy line on the stern of the ship. Other cannons had already been prepared and secured on deck, while a dangerous more waited in the shadows below, mid-ship. Males with large bows, Velcian and Borgorian alike, lined the deck at the ready.

The pirate ship was abaft. The sea was unnervingly quiet. Zalana had lined herself in the midst of two Borgorians, her stature seemingly more impressive. What the Captain would do in the event of a siege, Mora knew not, but chaos was following her like a starved wolven. She shuddered at the thought. Remaining in the shadows of the bow, she unwrapped her bow and quiver. The torches had been extinguished, but the gold glinted off the weapon from the light of the stars in spite of the surrounding darkness. She hoisted it on her back immediately and threw her cloak over before anyone caught sight of the metallic glint.

The vessel had slowed its advancement upon the side of the ship. She squinted in an attempt to see movement upon the deck, but she could see no one. The wheel was deserted and the sails flapped around in the slight breeze. The ongoing silence was unsettling. Her heartbeat thudded loudly in her ears and the crew anxiously shuffled their feet. Then, out of the silence, someone yelled *fire!* from the stern of the ship and heads turned aft to see a trail of flames advancing on the top of the water toward the adjacent ship.

Abin yelled, "Turn the ship starboard!" Running toward Captain Lox, he shouted, "Death's fire!"

The ship turned slightly starboard as an explosion roared through the darkness. The last thing Mora saw was Abin flying across the deck from the blast of the ship. Muffled sounds baffled her senses as she laid face down on the deck. Painfully, she pushed up on her hands and surveyed the damage, the ringing in her ears creating an aching pressure behind her eyes. She could see movement, but she felt like cloth had been stuffed violently into her ears. Eventually, she pulled herself to her feet, widened her mouth in desperate attempt to correct the sound, grasped onto the nearest object to balance, and adjusted her bow. Finally, after her ears popped, her eyes adjusted to the chaos of crew mates running back and forth in a panic while trying to assist the fallen. There were bodies and pieces of ship on fire. The screams penetrated the black night in waves of hysteria.

In horror, she saw large figures leap from the opposing ship. With many lying face down and lifeless on the boards, she attempted to sift through the bodies searching for Bog, Remmi, Abin, or even Zalana. However, another explosion sent her hands over her head as she hit the deck a second time. Shaking, she lifted herself from the wet planks as the acrid smoke filled her nostrils, stifling her breath. Sounds pounded as if there was padding stuffed in her ears again. Gravely, she peered through the dissipating smoke and saw Remmi standing by the railing of the ship, the blue of his eyes burning almost white and his severely scarred hands latching on tightly to the wood. She strained her eyes.

*He is without his gloves.*

The winds ripped with unparalleled savageness around the ships while the waters vehemently crashed against the sides, sending her staggering back amidst the pandemonium. She could still hear nothing but muffled screams and moans. The clouds above were spinning and lightning flashed brightly through the thick, black night. Gaining her footing, she pushed fervently through the mayhem toward the rail. Finally, she saw Abin, keeping the advance of enemies away from where Remmi stood motionless against the fire. Through the haze of smoke and bodies, she saw a blue light pulsing beneath his hands. Familiarity made her arm hair stand on end. It reverberated through the wood of the ship and, within moments, the death fires were extinguished. She saw him gasp. Then, without hesitation, he released the rail, slipped his gloves back on, and proceeded to fight with his sword.

In awe and distracted from what she just witnessed, she stumbled when a large body crashed into her shoulder, sending her flailing against another being. Ducking as a sword flung over her head, she thrust her dagger into the side of her assailant before a boot rammed behind her knees. Buckling to the blood soaked wood, she tucked and rolled beneath the legs of a Velcian crew member. When she stood, she saw Remmi staring in her direction. The bright, white light of his eyes had already faded. Before she could run over to where he and Abin were fighting, a hand wrapped her arm and she turned to see the mangled face of a mutant from the other ship. To her horror, blood dripped from an empty eye socket, over a hideously broken nose, and onto the peaks of two rows of razor sharp teeth. As she attempted to lift her dagger, a shower of blood spewed on her face as the head of the monster slid crudely off its shoulders.

"What the curse of the gods happened?" Bog barked through the madness as he pushed the body to the side, bloodied axe in hand.

Wiping the blood off her face, she sputtered, "I don't know! Remmi did something to the fire!"

As they continued dodging bodies, some lifeless and others stunned, she glanced over her shoulder to see Captain Lox stumbling to his feet to examine the state of his ship. Looking at the sails, the explosion had not done much damage to the larger sails, and, because of Remmi, the rest of Death's fire had been extinguished.

Captain Lox commanded, "All 'vailable hands 'n deck, throw th' lifeless to the'r watery graves 'n make sure 'em catapults 'r still at th' ready! I have a feelin' 'em will be back t' collect me ship, 'n I aren't handin' 'em me beauty!"

Immediately, she saw the crew mates start tossing bodies over board. Inspecting the cannons, four of the six were still standing, the ones below deck were possibly in similar condition. The catapult showed minimal damage, and there were at least half of the archers still capable of fighting. The pirate ship had been a bit smaller than Captain Lox's ship, and had exploded at about two ship lengths away from the Queen Kalvi. The wind slowly pushed the ship away from the fire wreckage. However, something caught her eye. Another ship was quickly advancing. This time, she could see much more movement amongst the lit torches.

As she turned to shout to Captain Lox, another magnificent sight stole her breath: the Nymia Towers. The curtains of water extended from the surface of the sea to as far as her eyes could reach toward the sky. Amidst the curtains, she could see streaks of light glistening. It looked like the lighted tunnel from her dream. It was breathtaking, and yet, a fear became apparent. *If we enter the Nymia Towers with the other ship, the waters may claim both, drowning all of us to a watery grave.* Like the increasing horror of the idea, the sound of rushing water was crescendoing.

She yelled out to Captain Lox, "It had been a ruse! Another ship! In the distance! It's advancing rapidly, and this one is inhabited with more than a few enemies!" She pointed back across the black sea.

Unfortunately, Captain Lox could not hear her, but a nearby Velcian did, and he ran to the Captain, pointing toward the ship.

Captain Lox trudged to his position behind the helm and whistled a command to hurry the tasks.

She ran to the Captain. "Are we going to continue to enter the Nymia Towers?"

"Aye! 'ey will give us 'r best defense. If th're is one thin' I know best, it's th' 'nds 'n outs of 'em towers!"

A cold wind whipped and an unusual rippling appeared in the waves. Wide-eyed, she looked nervously at Bog. "Do the seas get rough?"

"Never. The seas of Borgoria have never given harm to any traveler of pure intent," he responded as he glanced down at the sea. It commenced to lap with more force against the boat. "Until now…it seems."

The ship was only a few boat lengths behind and Mora could see a storm brewing overhead. She overheard Captain Lox command the limping servant lad to fetch any abled body to come take a bow. Adjusting her quiver, she knew it would aid in the fight if she could merely use it. *The circumstances are dire.* Searching for Remmi, she saw he was applying pressure to the side of Abin. Stubbornly, Abin would push him away. Briskly walking toward them, she noticed the archers were already commencing to line the rail. Then, she spied Zalana, standing tall between a Borgorian and a Velcian. Her face was stern and vengeful. Glimpsing at Mora, she nodded as a male would in the presence of any female.

"Ah! Lass! Alive and well, I see. Good for you," Abin slurred as he swigged a bottle of ale.

Disgusted, she looked at Remmi. "Where did he get that?"

He responded with a disgruntled shrug.

"Come off it! Drinking helps me feel brash, and ironically, a fucking good swordsman." He fingered his sword around like a stick. "Bring on 'em bastards, I'll slice each one's head off and stuff it in the next available ass!"

"Lovely," Bog grunted as he appeared. "Mora, the ship is almost upon us, we need to be prepared."

She could sense a tone of panic, but his composure was surprisingly calm. She acquiesced.

"Archers at th' ready!" Captain Lox yelled. "Dice th' catapult stones 'n ignite! Get ready crew!" His booming voice was barely audible against the roar of the Nymia Towers, in which were only a few ship-lengths in front.

In only moments they would enter and submerge into the inescapable walls of water. As the water began to push the ship from side to side, a gushing wave hit the bow of the ship, crashing hard enough to break the jib. Mora jolted toward the opposing ship, trying to see the occupants. To her horror, they were not creaturals, but hideous monsters. She could see the torches lighting their slimy faces and distorted, leathery skin, full of rings and bones. The archers took aim and released the first debris of arrows, showering down onto the opposing deck. Ducking beneath a barrel, she saw many fall.

Peering upward, she could see several forms standing on the opposite masts, ready to swing onto their ship. "Above!" she powerfully screamed with alarm.

At the helm, Captain Lox commanded to release the catapult and cannon balls as the gang from the masts swung down, violently hacking all onboard. She backed into a corner before pulling her first arrow from her quiver. Before she could string an arrow, a hand batted the bow down.

Remmi stood tall next to her and growled, "Not yet," and handed her a sword.

Disappointed, she emerged and began swinging at the nearest assailant. They came in a multitude of droves. She saw the catapult release another set of fiery stones. The sound of clanking swords was invariably overthrown by the onset of rushing water as they entered the Nymia Towers. The sea became wild, causing the fighters to loose their footing between the sporadic jolts of the ship. She could see Captain Lox fiercely reaching for the helm, jabbing at the monsters, but loosing hold of the wheel. The ship lurched and tilted close enough to the walls of water she could feel the droplets on her face. The Captain grabbed a hold of the wheel before it spun out of control. The ship continued to jerk violently against the waves while the enemy continued to flood onboard.

Without warning, the opposing vessel slammed with blunt force into the side of their ship. Once again, the ship tilted close the wall of water, but this time, it caught the side of the foremast. Many of the crew, including Mora, slid across the deck. Dangling halfway over the railing, she could feel the savage energy of swirling water. With her heart in her throat, she hoisted herself back onto the deck. Hearing a crack, she jerked her head and pounced out of the way as part of the mast came crashing down onto the wooden planks before being pulled into the water. Immediately, she cut the line attaching it to the ship.

The Captain straightened the ship to its normal position. Returning to her feet again, she attempted to move, but something caught hold to her hair and pulled her back into a slimy, foul body. It blocked her sword as she tried to turn around. With immense strength, it lifted her high by the neck as she kicked and screamed at the monster. Propping her feet against its foul flesh, she jerked her body backward at the very moment the point of a sword appeared through its chest. Its grip loosened and she fell roughly to the ground. In a flood of relief, she saw Zalana standing behind, drenched in a foul mess. Mora nodded frantically and retrieved her sword. Darting to the opposite railing, she gazed at the pirate ship. There were still a number of monsters and mutants, each waiting their turn to board. Straining to see the opposing helm, there was a body manning the wheel. It was the figure of a creatural male. Desperately, she tried to make out his face, however, his cloak covered his head.

*It is not Ekklips*, she assured herself, *I would have felt Him clearly by now.*

Again, the ship tilted toward the wall of water. This time, breaking a piece off the mainmast. She held onto the railing. When it returned to its position, she was nearly thrown overboard. Struggling to turn around, she managed to fight her way through the sea of bodies, both alive and dead. Peering up, she saw Abin at the bow, fighting against a number of monsters while holding his bottle of ale.

Breaking through, she screamed, "We need to take control of their ship!"

He flung himself to the railing. Eyeing the nearly abandoned helm, he smiled back at her and jumped onto a rope. "When I get over there, I will need you to release your arrow through the sails of the opposing ship."

"Are you mad? You will be on the ship! The fire will consume all!" she yelled back.

"These are immortal, Death's monsters. Do you not see how their numbers have not dwindled? They will continue to raid until each body is lying still. They have the darkness on their side! The fire will merely be a slight setback. Leave the rest to me!" He cut the rope and slung himself over the raging waters before landing onto the deck of the opposing ship.

Discretion was his ally, for the monsters had not seen his flight amongst their own. Mora continued to fight in between glimpses over at Abin. Viciously, the enemy advanced faster, but as she slew them, they fell, never to rise again. *How am I able to slay these monsters so effortlessly?* She felt powerful and completely invisible until a slash against her right, upper arm caused her to retract it in agonizing pain. Her sword fell to the ground. As she struggled to fight the searing wound, she keeled over to avoid any further hits. Terrified, she saw the grotesque mutant proceeding to finish what it started. Scrambling around, she desperately searched around for her sword. Next to her, part of the broken jib had flown into the ship. Stretching, she reached for the piece of sharp wood. As the figure retaliated, she stuck the heavy piece of the wood into its body, holding it forcefully in front of her own to keep space between her and the thrashing form. Opening her eyes after the jolt, she noticed its sword pointing toward her throat before it fell to the side. With all her might, she pushed the body to the side and took a deep breath. Quickly, she tore the bottom of her tunic and tied it over her wound, pulling it taut with her teeth. She grabbed her sword and stood.

Through the increasing hysteria, she looked about the ship. It was pure chaos and carnage, bodies lying everywhere on the deck. The darkness was growing exponentially. The once beautiful, reflective waters were torrential. When she fought her way to see Abin on the opposing ship, he was fighting the male she had seen at the helm. The raining mists of water made it hard to keep her eyes open. While it appeared to be an equal fight, Abin was starting to be pushed back toward the rail. She gasped for breath when she saw him trip, catching onto a loose rope dangling from a fallen mast. He quickly pulled himself up. Mercilessly, the cloaked figure lunged toward Abin. When the blow was countered, the enemy fell to his back and the hood exposed his face. Through the smoke, she nearly lost her footing, stumbling to get a better look. Abin stood frozen in front of the fallen figure.

Catching her breath, she flung herself onto the nearest ledge. It was the face of Dierdan. From where she stood, when she saw him, her stomach dropped. In a brief glitch, she thought the face became someone completely different. She knew Abin had seen it too; because, at that moment, he struck Dierdan, plunging his sword through his neck. Dierdan fell to the ground, lying motionless on the wooden planks of the ship as the face transformed into another, large and bald.

She screamed.

Abin wildly trudged over to the helm. His hair whipped around his face and his maniacal grin grew wider. With the Nymia Towers parallel with the ship, he fought the torrential wind and spray to grasp the wheel, holding it fiercely. Pushing his hair back, he searched for Mora. When he found her standing at the rail, a madness overcame his emotions. Raising his arm high, he forcefully jerked it down, signaling her to action.

Still in shock, but aware of his command, she resolutely strung an arrow from her quiver, undeterred by her slippery grip. Trembling, she focused on the sails of the opposing ship. Taking a deep breath, she released the arrow. A burst of flames flew from the tip, exploded into the sails, and created a burst of malevolent fire. The monsters writhed in the flames as they fell from the mast. A hoard flew to the railings of the Queen Kalvi, screaming in madness. Attempting to extinguish the flames, their attention suddenly turned to the unknown figure at the helm of their ship.

*Abin*, Mora whispered.

As though he could hear her, he voraciously held up the flask of ale, grinned wildly, and rapidly turned the wheel straight toward the wall of water. Her heart sank when she realized what he intended to do with the ship. She turned her attention to the advancing mob. Then, to her horror, noticed the body of the Dierdan was no longer lying on the ship's floor. When she looked back at Abin, a sudden flash illuminated a monstrous form looming behind his fading silhouette.

"Stop!" she screamed loudly over the railing as she saw, in what seemed like an eternity, the blazoned ship, piece by piece, being crushed into the wall of rushing water until Abin also… disappeared.

# Absynthe

Tears began to stream down Mora's face as the winds abruptly died down and the sea calmed. The clouds drifted apart to reveal a magnificent view of the stars above the alley of water walls. Stunned and unable to move, she stared longingly at the wall of water, hoping Abin would emerge. The saltiness of her tears mixed with the misting sea air. After a few more moments, she wiped her face and turned to the wreckage on the deck of the Queen Kalvi. The filthiness of bodies lying around the deck was gut wrenching, causing her to purge over the side of the ship. Feeling she had caused this chaos once again, a fear ran through her mind as she thought of Bog. Quickly, she began maneuvering through bodies, some quite dead, others were on the brink. Recognizing some of the faces from when she boarded, she started feeling sick again.

From behind a couple of barrels, she saw a pair of wings. Rushing over, disappointment stung when she realized the wings were not Bog's, but a cowardly Borgorian, trembling in the filth. Nervously glancing around, sweat streamed from her brow and down the back of her neck as her chest uncontrollably heaved. He was no where to be seen. Stumbling toward the cabins, covered with blood and sea mist, she heard voices. Quickening her pace, she pushed the door to her cabin open. A hand covered her mouth and the door was shoved shut.

As soon as she recognized the two beings in the room, she immediately stopped panicking. "What was the purpose for that?" she jeered when Bog's hand dropped.

"My apologies, but I had to make sure of your identity." Defeated, he sat down on the hay covered bed. His face and chest were blood splattered. The violent luminosity of his violet eyes was fading.

"What in the curse of the gods is going on here?" Zalana's voice echoed angrily from across the room.

His eyes toggled from Mora to Zalana, and then eventually back at Mora. He sighed and mumbled, "She saw you, the golden bow, and the golden arrow."

Mora had kept the cloth over the quiver and bow until right before Abin gave her the signal. Then, she had hastily covered it again, hoping to not have drawn much attention.

"She began screaming the Sun Goddess had appeared. I grabbed her before any more attention had been drawn and drug her into the cabin."

Zalana stepped toward Mora, a desperation apparent in her voice as she said, "Is it true? Are you of whom the prophecy speaks?"

She stared into Zalana's dark brown eyes. A sharp tinge of curiosity and power radiated from the tall, dark female. Remembering the bloody corpses on the deck, Abin's cynical wide grin, and the looming figure glowering behind him as the ship was obliterated in the Nymia Tower, a wave of madness came over her being. Fighting the sting of tears, she hissed sternly, "I am *nobody*."

"But I know what I saw! Carisun, my love, was right!" Zalana started frantically pacing across the room. "Tell me her death was not in vain!"

Mora glared at Bog, his eyes finally back to the beautiful violet she knew and trusted. However, a bitterness tore viciously in her stomach when she remembered the reason he had sought after her in the first place. Holding a finger in his direction, she snarled, "This is your doing. You are spreading lies! I am *no* Goddess! I am *Chaos!*"

As she screamed the words, she wrestled the lump in her throat and bolted from the room in shame. Running abaft, she burst through the door on the deck and breathed in the air. The stench of creatural flesh reeked all around. *The bards will sing of the carnage of Chaos on the Queen Kalvi.* Blindly, she trudged to the railing where she found Remmi standing silently, hands behind his back, and an empty stare toward the wall of water.

"He should not have done it," she choked back her threatening tears.

"He deemed what he thought necessary." His voice carried in the wind and barely surpassed the sound of the rushing towers of water. "Abin treated life as a game, a gamble, its entirety was about taking risks and testing how far he could tempt Death. He knew what he was doing," he paused, "but certainly not to be remembered...to be forgotten."

Thinking it was an unusual statement, she asked, "Why would he need to be forgotten?"

"If you knew, would you be less likely to forget him?"

He never looked in her direction. Pondering the thought, she could not discern the riddle. "I suppose not, but I can never forget him now. I watched him steer the ship into the curtain."

"It's not from you whom he wants to be forgotten." He continued to concentrate hard on the Nymia Towers.

*He is like stone again.* She didn't think it was a good time to inquire about the blue light pulsing from his hands earlier. She turned, but before she walked away, she said, "I saw the form of a dark-eyed figure transform from the Ura maleservant, Dierdan. He was the one at the helm."

Remmi nodded his head. "I know," he gravely replied.

She left to let him grieve the loss of his friend. However, she suddenly remembered the horses. Sprinting down the corridors, taking two or three steps at a time, her heart pounded hard in her chest. A few obstacles lay across her way, but she could smell the dung from the entrance of the lowest floor. Reaching the bottom, she cautiously waded through the darkness, traipsing through ankle-deep water. There was a slight sound of movement from smaller animals, but when she approached the corner of a stable door, she saw the four horses huddled together. Sun Shadow was in the very back, guarded by the other three. When she whistled, her horse broke free and heavily waded through the water. Laying her head on Sun Shadow's muzzle, she finally allowed her tears to roll down her cheeks. She had no words and the horse stood still while she cried.

After a while, Sun Shadow nudged her and she knew it was a way of informing her they would be fine. Rubbing her hands over her splotchy face, she wearily nodded. Sniffling and exhausted, she climbed back to the cabin. Shocked to see a hole in the door, she cautiously walked in and saw Zalana sitting with the book in her hand. Bog was absent. Without saying a word, she lunged into the inlaid bed and jerked the covers over her body. She adjusted the key stabbing underneath her armpit, pulled it out to glance at the symbols, and then tucked it safely back into the top of her tunic. *This burden is becoming heavier.* Cold with despair, and extinguishing the sounds and stench of the world around her, she fell back into the darkness of her mind, a place in which she was becoming to know very well.

*Are you restless?*
*Aye.*
*Are you weary?*
*Aye.*
*Are you sad?*
*Aye.*
*Are you angry?*
*Aye.*
*Then tell me, why are you waiting?*
*Waiting for what?*
*Death.*
*I don't want to die.*
*What have you to live for?*
*The ability to choose my own path.*
*You will die in the end.*
*So be it.*

Bog slammed his fist into the surface of the cabin door. The door cracked, leaving a large hole. Pulling the excess wood from his skin, he glanced over at Zalana. She was staring sharply at him from the shadow of the bunk. Grimacing, he opened the door and slammed it. *How dare she blame me for her misery!* Fists clenched, he stepped heavily onto the deck. Taking notice of Mora talking to Remmi at the railing, his body trembled with anger. Shaking, he turned to walk to the opposite side of the ship, concealing himself in the shadows. The crew mates who had survived were clearing the deck, throwing the bodies over the railing, and mopping the planks clean. Grasping tightly onto the rail, he peered into the calm, black sea. The Nymia Towers were glistening, seemingly an endless alley of water, but he knew what lay at the end of the towers: Loralimira.

Home.

He thought about how his sudden appearance, after the many years he had spent away, would be received. By most, not friendly. However, there was one he knew he could rely on to be elated at his return. It was the only reason he was returning home. The breeze tussled his feathers and he thought he heard a voice on the wind whisper, *Beware, caution, Death,* before another voice broke through the hush.

"Ah, Borgorian, 'tis nice t' see yer survive'," the heavy voice of Captain Lox resonated through the silence.

Even though he was enjoying the quiet, Bog sighed, "Aye." He didn't make eye contact with the Captain.

"Whe'r is y'or frien'?" Propping himself on the railing, the Captain crossed his arms and ankles.

"She is at the opposite side of the ship from ourselves," he muttered, still making no eye contact. Out of the corner of his eye, he saw the Captain shift his weight.

"Who is th' oth'r feller?"

"Another one of our company," his bitterness bit through the words.

"Aye, well, y'or frien', she is quite speci'l, ain't she?"

Bog jerked his gaze at the Captain immediately. *Fuck.*

Captain Lox leaned closer to him and whispered, "B' car'ful of th' crews, ther' 're criminal eyes all o'er. Din say ye weren' warned." Pushing himself off the railing, his heavy footsteps traipsed back to his cabin.

Thoughts jumbled in Bog's mind, clouding his ability to think clearly. He never considered how many crew mates saw Mora. The idea sent a sick feeling to his gut. Reluctantly, he peered back toward her in time to see her sprint to the hold. *I have no desire to be around anyone right now.* Glancing to his left, and then to his right, he saw the galley door flapping open. Immediately, he stepped in haste to the doorway and peeked inside. There was no one. He looked around for something to eat or drink. All the food crates were cracked and broken on the floor. However, a small, brown, leather flask was stuck between a pair of broken cabinet doors. Wrestling it out, he removed the secured cork and drank. Coughing, he rubbed the back of his hand on his mouth. It was awfully bitter with a herbal darkness, but it instantly sent a warmth throughout his entire body. Drinking more, his worries began to melt away. Stumbling out of the galley, he hugged the railing as he languidly walked to the front of the ship. Plopping down on a fallen part of the jib, he drank, upturning the flask until the last drop.

When it was gone, he threw the flask away from where he was sitting. However, there was a slight crashing sound behind. *That is odd.* Trying to focus on the moving sea, he began to hear footsteps. Irritated at the appearance of company, he ignored whomever was trudging around. To his annoyance, whomever it was stood unnervingly close to his back and breathed heavily upon his wings. The tiny, sheer hairs of his arms stood on end. *Something isn't right.* Hesitantly, he peered over his shoulder. To his terror, the grotesque mutant from the forest was standing behind him, a hideously distorted grin plastered to its face. Staggering to his feet, he backed away across the debris as it stepped closer.

"How did you find me?" Bog breathed deeply, his head swimming with malicious intent.

"I come to finish what I started," it huffed, the one good eye flaring.

He could feel his speech began to slur as he stuttered, "You...you were commanded not to touch me." Its body was an awkward blur, forcing him to close one eye to focus. Shaking his head, he stumbled aimlessly around on the detritus. "You...you were on the other ship!"

"Not entirely befuddled are we?" Its eye glowed a bright red-orange.

Wavering, he blinked, hoping it was merely the drink disturbing his head.

"I have been given special instructions, and you must not enter Loralimira."

Rubbing the sweat from his brow, he was taken aback. "Who has given you these commands?"

"Folly conversation was strictly forbidden." The mutant stepped further over the debris, its monstrous form advancing in wicked proximity.

He could sense the end of the ship behind his boots. Fervently, he squinted around the area. The detritus was thick, but there was a number of broken wood pieces and rope. *If only I can get my hands around something sharp.* However, he was having an even harder time focusing as his inebriation continued to cloud his judgment. *Damn the spirits!* Dangling around the edge, he heard the monster snickering.

It grumbled, "I was hoping to find you alone, but I didn't expect to find you intoxicated." It began to move again. Chortling, it gargled, "That was fortune."

He picked up a rough piece of broken wood at his feet and held it unsteadily, arms outstretched. It bellowed and snatched the piece from his hand, sending him stumbling backward. Blinking, he tried to focus on the disfigured body. Shimmering in the moonlight, he saw a shiny piece of broken metal to his left. Launching himself, he felt an abnormally forceful blow to the side of his face. The monster had swung, knocking him to the ground with its metal rod. He groaned. Spitting the warm blood from his mouth, he tried to focus once again on his surroundings. A hand jerked him by the arm, holding him in front of the cynical, mutilated face. In a pathetic attempt, he tried to swing, but he severely misjudged the distance and his fist never made contact. It thrust its leg maliciously upward, planting a knee into his stomach. He keeled over, cursed the pain, and purged some of the sour liquid. Again, the horrible laugh resonated.

The raspy voice sneered, "You're a pathetic excuse for a Borgorian."

*Can no one see what is taking place?* He tried to yell, but another fist impacted with his other cheek. Scrounging aimlessly, he scuttled across the floor blindly and purged again. The water droplets from the Towers pricked his face like razor sharp points and trickled down his flesh, the sensation almost painful.

Struggling to lift himself onto his hands and knees, another swift

*The Keeper*

kick into his side sent him rolling across the wood, dangerously close to the edge. Listening for the footsteps, he attempted to open his already swollen eyes. The water and blood stung fiercely, filling them with painful tears. Finally, he began dragging himself with growing difficulty across the deck. He heard a grunt and waited for another excruciating jab to his ribcage. However, as he reached to pull himself further, his hand grazed a sharp object, slicing his palm open. Without removing his hand, he painfully grasped it tighter, breathed heavily, and waited for the mangled figure to advance. It trudged closer to where he lay, still and silent, its sharp, brown toothy grin stretching across the taut skin of its face.

Listening carefully, despite the feeling of chaotic tumbling inside his head, he strained to hear the movement clearly above the roaring of the Towers. Then, hearing the close scraping of a boot, with all his dwindling strength, Bog rolled over and stabbed the object into its leg. Crying out in pain, it tried to grab its injured extremity, but stumbled backward. Catching sight of the glimmer of broken metal, he realized what he had found was a shard of the metal encasing of Death's fire from the other ship during the attack. He could feel the remnants of the fire running through his own veins from where he had seized it with his hand and sliced his flesh. The mutant continued to wail in pain, the essence of the fire obviously penetrating its body as well.

Bog maneuvered himself around to where he could grip a splintered, wooden beam. From a sitting position, with every last drop of strength, he swung the beam at its legs. Caught off guard, it stumbled over him and tripped without control over the debris until it teetered on the edge of the broken railing. Waving its arms in rapid circles, it lost its balance and toppled into the black water below. Frantically, he noticed he was lying amidst a tightening rope. Attempting to shimmy it off, but not being able to grab at a particular section because his eyes were seeing multiples, it snapped taut around his leg and drug him swiftly across the floor. Reaching for anything he could, his body suddenly wedged between a large piece of fallen mast dangling off the edge of the ship. The rope cinched tighter around his thigh. The weight of the hanging body sent searing pangs shooting through his leg. Cringing, he could feel the blood constricting from the knot. Without a sharp object, his leg was becoming numb from the overload of excruciating torture. The tension was accentuating the dizziness in his head. The Nymia Towers began to swirl in his eyes and the stars were melting into the black sky.

On the brink of despair, he felt someone grab his wrist tightly and dislodge him roughly from the broken beams. A snap, and the pressure from the rope released. A throbbing, yet satisfying, feeling exploded through his whole leg, causing it to tingle ferociously like thousands of minuscule needles fighting to escape his muscles. He felt broken, but his mind's numbness was increasing at a rapid rate. A hand rolled him over onto his back and a figure knelt down beside his body. Struggling to open one eye, all he could see through the darkness were the familiar, piercing, blue-white eyes. A sick feeling engrossed his whole body.

*Remmi.*

Remmi said nothing to Bog, but proceeded to settle him in a niche of fallen wood further away from the edge of the ship. *Godsdamn his ignorance.* Peering around, he removed his gloves. He inspected the wounds at Bog's sides, face, and hands. Then, he moved to his thigh.

Fading swiftly, the last image Bog witnessed was a strange, blue light pulsating through Remmi's ungloved fingers, but he could not focus directly. The sickening tumble of intoxication conquered his senses, and he faded into a restless stupor.

Remmi sat back, spat, and propped his arm onto his knee. He placed his gloves back on his hands and pushed his hair out of his face. Surveying the damage to the ship, he picked up the empty, leather flask and smelled the contents. Scrunching his nose, he recognized the liquid immediately. *I wonder how Bog attained such an illegal substance this close to Loralimira.* He stood up and tossed the flask into the black water below. With his arms crossed, he watched the recesses of the Towers disappear into the starry night. The surface of the water served as a mirror of the sky, creating the illusion they were floating through the vast cosmos.

A dim longing sparked in his chest. *It has begun.*

# *Loralimira*

The morning sun was bright against his eyelids. Bog squinted, reluctantly forcing his heavy lids to open. He was facing the sunrise. The brilliant colors accented the morning sky, while gulls flew over head. The sun was barely peeking over the edge of the horizon, the rich oranges lethargically transitioning from the saturated indigo. Yawning, he lifted his hands to rub his eyes, but felt a horrendous pain reverberate in his head. *Bloody curse of the gods.* He hesitantly peered down at his body, bruised and torn. There was a blood stained bandage around the palm of his left hand and one covering his midsection with small blotches of burgundy penetrating the cloth. Attempting to move his legs, his right thigh succumbed to a maddening agony.

Rolling over to his side, he tried to focus on where he was lying down. *What the fuck happened last night?* Putting pressure directly above his eyes with the base of his hands, the last thing he remembered was drinking the contents of the leather flask from the galley.

"Rough night?" A Velcian male inquired in a thick accent, appearing from around the wood niche.

"Aye," he mumbled and strained to sit upright. Propping against the wood, massaging the back of his neck, he inquired, "Are we docked?"

"Loralimira." He pointed and continued to pick up debris, tossing it into an unsettlingly massive pile.

Bog nodded and struggled to stand, steadying himself half way before he felt his stomach turn. He stumbled to the edge and purged savagely.

"Woul' ye like sum water, mate?" a familiar voice boomed from behind.

Holding his head from the sheer volume of Captain Lox's voice, he wiped his mouth and turned. Wearily, he nodded.

Captain Lox handed him a flask, but Bog hesitated.

He motioned for him to take it again and grumbled, "It's j'st water, mate."

He drank it savagely, rasping for breath.

"Damn, ye thin' yer were dyin'!" Captain Lox surveyed. "Wha' happened t' ye? Ye look like shit. Di' ye lass get careless?"

He shook his head, wincing at the pain. "Nay, but I am not quite sure what actually occurred." He squinted at the Captain.

Captain Lox considered this for a moment before speaking, "Ye look like ye got y'er hands on th' absynthe."

He glared in disdain. "Absynthe? What in the curse of the gods is that doing on the ship? It is illegal in Loralimira."

"Aye. But 'n all respects, ther' is quite th' coin fer th' black market drinks. An' an ol' Captain like me? I need th' extra sums." Shrugging his shoulders, he added, "Dunno what it'ere doin' above th' lower deck th'ou. Th' crates ar' not easily accessible."

Flashes of memory faded rapidly in and out of Bog's mind. He shook his head slightly, attempting to rattle them free. A jilt, a jab, the snap of a rope, the sounds echoed against the walls of the mind.

"Ye al'right?" the Captain asked, laying a heavy hand on his shoulder.

Sullenly grinning, with a slight nod, he replied, "I will be fine." Lethargically, he limped down the ladder and proceeded to the middle of the ship, but stopped to rest against the railing.

"Here, drink this as well," Remmi's clear voice appeared from behind.

Closing his eyes in frustration, he limped around, leaned back against the rail, and took the cup. "What happened to me last night?"

"What makes you think I know?" he responded stoically.

Bog snuffed. "When are you not lingering in the shadows, waiting?" Taking a swig of the substance, he balked. It tasted like dirt and grass splashed around with salt water. Gaining his composure, he continued, "Besides, I remember your face, right before I passed out."

Remmi curled his lip. "I know not what happened to you, but I do know that I heard a crashing sound coming from the end of the ship, and when I went to investigate, you were wedged between two pieces of wood." He moved to grab a piece of wood off the floor and throw it onto a pile of scraps. "Besides, after dislodging you, it was not a feat to realize, from the overwhelming odor, the activity you had partook in only moments prior. However, whatever was hanging from the other end of the rope will have a poor time escaping the Nymia Towers."

Bog glanced at him under his eyelids. "How do you know it wasn't worth trying to save?"

Lifting his shoulders, he muttered, "I don't. But whatever it was fucked you up worse than I think anyone on this ship would dare do to a Borgorian."

Annoyed, Bog drank the disgusting concoction and threw the cup aside. He gagged, but his head was already beginning to swim less. "Thanks," he murmured and limped away.

His injuries were hindering much activity, but he found solace in helping the crew mates remove detritus from the ship, a task in which had apparently lasted all night. *Thankfully, it didn't do more damage to the bilge.* He looked longingly in the direction of Loralimira. The sun had barely risen above the horizon, and while there was already a busy crowd bustling around the docks, the ship needed to be cleared before they ventured into the port of the city. However, the longer he worked, the quicker his strength came back. Irked by the bandage around his ribs, he carelessly removed the cloth and threw it in the pile of rubble. Examining the bruises and scrapes, a flash of a red-orange eye and a raspy gargle echoed in his mind, '*I have been given special instructions and you must not enter Loralimira.*'

*That is the second, clear warning*, he thought, biting his lip.

Mora rustled around on the hay filled sheets. The light faintly danced across the cabin through a thin slitted window. Crawling out of bed sluggishly, she was relieved for the dreamless sleep. The water basin had been filled and placed on the table in between the beds. Bog and Zalana were not present. Somberly, she washed her hands and face. Then, she tried to run her fingers through her stubborn hair before giving up and braiding her it down her back again. Then, she lifted her black tunic to examine her wound. It was sensitive, but the stitches were holding. While it looked terrible, it was not festering and strangely seemed to have already closed. *That's odd. I've never healed as quickly before.*

Picking up her knapsack, she retrieved the bow and quiver, already wrapped securely in the cloth. Opening the door, she walked down the shorter corridor and into the welcomed warmth of sunlight. The deck was being washed and scrubbed, all the bodies from the previous night had been disposed, and the debris was being consolidated into piles around the deck. The sea was calm. The pastel hues had returned vibrantly, transitioning softly from red orange, to orange, to yellow, and then to lavender. She leisurely surveyed the scenery, gasping when she beheld the most magnificent city. Climbing the steps of the stern, she shielded her eyes from the brilliant light and gazed upon walls of gorgeous, blue marble. Winding roads were occupied with growing amounts of carts, animals, and winged beings treading back and forth from the port to the city. Flocks of gulls were cawing and flying high above the docks, their white wings reflecting the radiance of the sun, much like the varied wings of the Borgorians.

Leaning off the side of the ship to gaze in the pastel, sky-reflecting waters, her eyes followed the colorful liquid flow to the bright, blue walls until it lapped against the stone. It was not shallow by any means, but it appeared to be, the bottom was visible. The clarity was shocking. Schools of sparkling, scaled fish swam spastically in groups, dodging floating traps and bilges of advancing boats. Occasionally, a bigger fish would swim close and the school of twinkling fish would maniacally disperse, only to come together further away. She smiled happily. She had never seen such a playful act.

Gazing at the water along the walls, she watched as elegantly winged Borgorians bustled. There were females beautifully draped in silks, bare chested males, and scarcely dressed borglings. All had various sized wings. Many of the younger Borgorians were playfully splashing along the slender stretch of shallow water on the outside of the wall and chasing the gulls. A long boardwalk extended into the Nymian Sea from a heavy stone and iron gate centered in the middle of the grandiose barrier of marble encompassing the city. The wall was a distinct separation between the port and the city, and the magnificent gate majestically opened to what she assumed was the unrivaled city of Loralimira.

There was a web of thinner docks connected to the main boardwalk. Carefully leaning further to peer at the docks, the horror of last night, mixed with the beauty of the day, felt surreal. Finally, she saw Bog helping to clear the debris off the ship and Remmi unloading cargo. She walked down the plank of wood connecting the ship to the exceptionally long boardwalk. Numerous leering stares from the Velcian crew followed her as she descended. Holding her belongings closer to her body, she quickened her pace, pushing her way through the hoard of workers toward Bog.

"Bog!" she called out, waving her hand while standing on her tiptoes.

Looking over the amassing crowd, once he caught sight of Mora, his eyes widened. Shoving through the distance between them, he shielded her presence with his body, glared around, and asked impatiently, "What in the curse of the gods are you doing?"

She furrowed her brows and tilted her head. "I awoke to neither you, nor Zalana, in the cabin." Oddly, his face had been more bruised and bloodied since she ran from the chamber after she wrongly accused him for her problems. For that, she felt ashamed. Remnants of dry blood were caked upon the side of his lip and both sides of his face showed slight swelling. "What happened to you?" a hint of concern evident in her words.

"You should not have been out of the cabin until Remmi or myself came to gather you." Eyeing the crew suspiciously, he whispered, "I wrote a note for you to stay discrete."

"I never saw a note," she replied.

"We've made better time than suspected and it causes me to think the essence of the sea sensed our urgency to arrive at Loralimira. However, there are also suspicions, talks of a supernatural appearance, and notions of blame. Unfortunately, your weapon of choice has been relayed amongst the crew." Pulling her into the shadows of a large piece of cargo on the dock, he lowered his voice, "Also, during the raid, a Velcian discovered Zalana's smeared tattoo, suspecting a stole away. The Captain is investigating the matter at this time."

Eyeing the deck in a panic, she asked, "Zalana? Where is she now?"

"She is with the horses on the lower deck, cloaked and ready to escort them with the cargo. Remmi is overseeing the transfer at present. We are hoping to divert suspicions if she can be concealed by the horses and movement of cargo."

"How?"

She searched around. He pointed at a ramp going down the side of the main dock and she realized the web of individual docks stemming from the main boardwalk had looked all one level from where she stood on the stern of the ship, but some of the docks were actually two or three-tiered to accommodate larger ships.

He continued with apprehension, "Because of the events last night, there has been an alert raised on the security of Loralimira. Precautions are currently being collected on all outsiders. Only the Elders of the House should know of your arrival and we must keep it that way. Wear this," he took a cloak off a nearby cart, "I bargained for it this morning. Be leery to show your face until we reach the House of Gornya. I will inform Remmi you are awake. We must hurry. Hand me your bow and quiver and stay in the shadows." He hustled back hastily through the crowd.

Nervously, she peered around at the crew from beneath the heavy hood. After a moment, she heard the sound of horses down on the lower dock. Inquisitively peering around the corner, she saw Abin's horse stand on its hind legs, batting its hooves at the crew trying to hold him down. Then, from the shadows, Remmi appeared to quell the chestnut steed. A sinking feeling in her stomach made the burning sensation behind her eyes reappear. Biting her lip to hold back the tears, she watched him speak to the crew. Nodding their heads, he took hold of the four horses. A peculiarly tall, cloaked figure appeared from behind the last two horses and disappeared like an apparition into the crowd.

*Zalana.* Mora proceeded down the ramp, her face concealed.

## The Keeper

Walking the horses through the multitude of creaturals, two in each hand, Remmi's features were solid and his eyes fierce. When he saw Mora approaching, he solemnly commanded, "Come."

Not looking at her directly when he passed, he proceeded up the ramp onto the long boardwalk toward the gate. Holding the side of the hood close to her cheek, she followed discreetly alongside the horses. Startled, she felt a hand grasp her shoulder and she jerked around to see Bog.

"Keep walking," he muttered as he quickened his step. "Once we get to the gates, they will be checking for weaponry. We will need to conceal your bow and quiver."

"How do you propose we go about that?" she asked quietly, her eyes ever surveilling the thick bustle of Borgorians, Velcians, and animals.

"The bow is currently concealed beneath Zalana's long gown she brought with her from home. She is taller and can step easily with it tucked underneath. They will not ask a female to remove her garments. The quiver is to be placed beneath Sun Shadow's saddle. I do hope word about a stole away has not reached the gates."

They found a shady area on the outer edge of the boardwalk to discretely maneuver her quiver under the saddle, concealing it so it appeared to be a sleeping pad. Remmi held the horses steady. Stepping back, Bog shrugged satisfactorily.

Remmi finished allowing the horses to feed before they continued down the docks. As they approached the abnormally massive gate, she realized the brilliant blue of the surrounding city wall were countless small tiles, each a various shade of blue. From afar, it appeared to be one color, but up close, the tiles radiated like the tiny scales of the fish she observed earlier. Because the sun had risen to mid-morning, the wall was beginning to mirror the vast, blue sky. Massive stone columns sectioned off equal parts of the wall. Pouring from the top middle of each section was a sparkling waterfall. They reminded her of the waterfalls cascading between each of the Halo Mountains, only Loralimira was bright and radiant, while the Halo were dark and brooding.

*Balance.*

Bog watched the gate closely. Four Borgorian guards were checking a cart full of fresh, exotic fruits. The search was thorough, revealing four swords underneath the fruit. The peasant in question said they were gifts to his sons, but the most intimidating of the Borgorians retorted the male was too nervous to be telling the truth and should prove otherwise to the House Guard if he wanted his weapons returned. Sullenly, the peasant turned to his reins and moved the cart onward.

*Godsdamn the guard.* Bog rubbed the sweat from the back of his neck.

"Halt," the Borgorian on his left commanded. "You sir, what is your business with the bow?" Glaring hard at Remmi, he spoke directly, "We are limiting all outsiders of their weaponry. There was an attack on one of our largest ships last night."

"I am aware. I was on board," he replied clear and cool. "If you feel you need me to surrender my bow, I will gladly give it to you."

The Borgorian was stunned at his offer. "Aye, right. That won't be necessary. You may keep it, and the sword, so long as they do not cause trouble."

He eyed Remmi curiously as if he didn't realize what he was saying. Finally, he gestured to Zalana and Mora, demanding, "Females, we need you to remove your cloaks."

Mora denoted a slight uneasiness in his voice, but before she could reply, Zalana stepped forward with a seductive gait.

"Sir, I wear nothing underneath. After the attack last night, my clothing was soiled. The cloak was the only clothing item I could find amidst the bodies of horribly slaughtered beings."

He squinted suspiciously and mumbled in a gruff tone, "Your accent, it is Velcian. There was word of a stole away on the ship. Females are already bad luck on ships, but no Velcian females are allow to cross the sea, it is treachery."

"Velcian?" she said slyly, her dark brown eyes burrowing into the guard. "You speak blasphemy Borgorian!" Holding her chin higher, she stood almost eye to eye with the guard. "I am no Velcian. I am from the Isle of Jei Vein, sister territory to Ja Velco, where our females are treated with more respect. My name is Carisun, if you desire specifics. My chosen profession is my business and I will wager you take pleasure in such acts yourself. Therefore, I demand you show me more respect before I curse your cock to be damned in unsavory, disease-ridden cunts for the

*The Keeper*

remainder of your pathetic existence."

Clearly threatened by the possibility Zalana could do such an act, he sized her up from top to bottom, making no further inquiries. He grunted and turned to Mora. "You are clearly no Velcian."

Offended, she opened her mouth to retort.

Immediately, Bog stepped in to speak, "My name is Bogheim, fourth son to Gornya. Let me pass before I proceed without your consent."

The stout Borgorian guard guffawed, followed by the others at the gate.

One spoke up, "Bog? That name is no longer spoken. Word is the Commander rejoiced when he was informed of his weakest son's death."

Fury grew in Bog's eyes, and in the midst of his rage, he grabbed the Borgorian's throat. He spat coldly into the guard's face, "Death? Do I look *dead* to you? How dare you laugh at me so!"

The other Borgorians were stupefied. Everything became quiet, save for the chatter of the gulls and the bustle further down the boardwalk. Then, a loud voice shouted from within the gate. Bog cringed at the sound of a voice he hadn't heard for many years. *Curse of the gods.*

"Enough," an authoritative Borgorian commanded as he traversed through the guards.

Bog threw the Borgorian to the ground and stood erect. "Korian," he said, gritting his teeth.

"The prodigal son returns. And not alone, I see." Malice radiated through his grin.

Korian was almost the same height as Bog, and his features were as strikingly beautiful. On face and body structure alone, Mora felt they could almost be a mirror image of each other. However, Korian's dark hair was cropped close to his head and his wings did not have the one, black feather amidst all the white, like Bog. Also, his eyes were light gray, not a luscious violet.

"Father will be ever so surprised," Korian said with a slight quivering upturn of his lip.

Clenching his fists, Bog stepped closer to Korian, and mumbled, "I'm sure he will, considering you were plausibly the one feeding him the lies I was dead." He shoved passed Korian.

Korian stood there solidly with an annoyed fix upon his face. "I see your anger hasn't changed a bit, *brother*."

Without pausing, Bog grunted, "Come, Mora."

In hesitation, she walked passed Korian. Half grinning, she took long strides to keep up with his quick pace. Once they climbed far enough along the streets, the gate no longer in sight, she marched next to Bog. Frustrated, she asked, "What was that all about?"

"Pardon?" he gruffly retorted.

"I have never seen you so blatantly malicious. Why are we here if you aren't welcomed by your own family?" At that point, she knew she had struck a chord.

He paused and glared straight in her eyes. "Damn you, Mora! I have done nothing to you to make you not trust me. I am no warrior like my brothers, or my father, but that does not mean I was not trained to be ruthless like one. However, I chose, and am *still* choosing, a different, fucking path to find knowledge. This is why you are here with me now!" Turning his back on her, he trekked onward to the highest level of the street.

He had never been outwardly irate with her since they had started traveling together. Slightly hurt, she fell in line with Sun Shadow, who was being led by Zalana, alongside Abin's horse. Remmi led the other two. Neither appeared phased by the incident, but the back of her neck tingled. She sensed someone was watching.

# The House of Gornya

The House of Gornya was an astonishing piece of architecture. The stone stairway was made of solid gray marble, glistening with pebble-sized, smooth diamonds set within the massive blocks. Widthwise, the stairs extended the entire façade, several hundred strides across in the shape of a semi-circular. The gigantic, blue walls of the city protruded from each side of the chateau. It was the epicenter of Loralimira, the highest point of the land. Billowing behind the House of Gornya was a rolling mist, shimmering in the sunlight, creating multiple rainbows floating high in the air. An energetic, meditative sound of rushing water poured into the inner walls of the city. As they advanced further, an ethereal sensation magnified. Sensual wisps of mist caressed the cheeks of all who climbed the grandiose steps.

Remmi tied the horses onto a nearby tree trunk.

At the top of the massive stairway, there were six, immaculately carved columns holding up the triangular roof of the portico. Elegant scenes encircled each column. The scenes were a procession, imparting a story from the bottom to the top. The narrative portrayed an expansive amount of emotions, battles, births, deaths, the sea, and the sky. Most all figures had graceful wings. On the top and bottom of each column was a scroll interlaced with dainty leaves of silver.

The diamond tiled floors of the portico extended the entire area of the stairway to a pair of stone and ironwork doors. The height of the doors surpassed Bog at least three times. The structure of the doors mirrored the design of the gate in which opened to the port. Like the columns, the doors were infused with a narrative. Through the narrative, arose a sense of glory and accomplishment, revealing the beauty of past generations. Each stone panel was sectioned off into eighteen squares, portraying a scene of utmost intricacy and detail, melded with iron. The square at eye level depicted a throne. Seated at the throne was a large bird-creatural, similar to Bog. It was a robed female, her features delicate and fair. To the front, stood a creatural. The being was neither kneeling, nor bowing, to the female Borgorian, but holding a shining orb.

Mora wondered what the orb symbolized.

Without hesitation, Bog took a deep breath and heaved the stone doors open to the Great Hall. On either side of the supreme foyer were six, different, chamber doors, each leading into a meeting room, a staircase, the dining hall, or a corridor. He had spent many years mapping the entire chateau and knew where every door lead. Settled between each door, a frosty, rectangular window was lit from the inside. The glass was wavering in thickness to give the effect of waterfall mist. The floor of the chamber was the same, diamond, tiled pattern as the portico. At the base of the Great Hall, opposite the entrance, loomed a dais with a throne nestled between two, tall columns. Wild, blue fire danced atop both.

"Welcome, Mora," a booming voice from the end of the foyer echoed throughout the Great Hall.

Straining her eyes, an abnormally sizable, female Borgorian sat on the throne. However, the voice could not have come from the source because she realized the being was made of marble. The regal statue was inlaid with lustrous, fire-amber stones around its neck and head. Carved hair was piled high on top of the head, adorned by flowers frozen in bloom. Furthermore, the eyes glistened wondrously with stones rivaling the glorious violet of Bog's eyes.

"Come closer to the throne so I may look upon you better," the bodiless, husky voice requested.

She glanced nervously at Bog. When he nodded grimly, she stepped closer to the statue. A shadow grew within the darkness behind. Once it took a step into the light, she was amazed at the resemblance to Korian. He was not a young Borgorian, and attempted to hide a small limp on the right side. There was a deep scar stretching from the top of his left shoulder, down across his right side. He was as tall as Bog, but his eyes were the matching, light gray color as Korian and his brown hair was cropped short. His presence was noble and severe.

"I am Gornya, Commander of the Borgorians."

Although the tension was as thick as mud, she answered politely, "I'm pleased to meet you."

A slight curl of his lip betrayed his skepticism. "Certainly," he murmured. Turning his attention to Bog, his face became emotionless. "Bog, my son, the whispers echoed of your death. I am...pleased to see you have returned. I presume you wish to gloat your intuition was correct?"

Rigidly, Bog retorted, "I do not gloat. My journey was not without strife, and many unforeseen circumstances have led to a number of difficult obstacles. That is for a later time though, I need to see Aloria."

Bowing his head somberly, Gornya acquiesced, "Very well. Let us proceed."

Gornya, joined by at least half a dozen, militaristic Borgorians, led the company into a smaller room at the east end of the Great Hall. The doorway led to a long corridor adorned with portraits of Borgorians. Some of the subjects were seated in their portraits, clothed regally and only shown from the chest up. Others were full length, with wildly provocative poses of subjects standing in suggestive, vicarious positions. Intertwined with the magnificent, natural scenery, some were scantily clad, while others were completely nude.

Mora blushed thinking about the conversation with Bog about nudity on the shore of the Nymian Sea. Slightly grinning, she focused her eyes in front, noticing the floor was covered with a soft, blue runner, contrasting the harsh, stone walls.

At the end, Gornya whispered a few unrecognizable syllables and a stone wall slide open. The room was fascinating. It was completely translucent, built with an exceptionally thick glass. If it were not because Gornya and Bog stepped through first, she would not have thought to enter. The intrinsically carved wooden table seated twenty-two chairs, ten on each side and one at both ends. She walked over to the far wall of the room, cautiously watching each step, feeling as though she was floating in the air. Gazing out into the intimidating scenery, she could see where the billowing mists rose. Below her, the waterfalls were majestic, ominous, and brooding. It appeared as though the water was falling violently off the edge of the world. The water was identical to the beautiful pastels of the sea and the sun reflected brilliantly off the surface. The mist was too thick to see the other side, or the bottom of the waterfalls. However, a land bridge stretched over the left side of the raging water, disappearing into the thick haze. Gulls twisted and turned, diving into the mist and emerging with sustenance. She touched the glass wall, running her finger along the curve of the waterfalls and around the gigantic cratered basin.

Bog stepped beside her and quietly asked, "Brilliant, isn't it?"

"Stunning couldn't even cover the description," she quietly replied. "Where do the waterfalls originate and where do they flow?"

"The water is supplied by the Nymian Sea. They flow along the rough terrain of the caves underneath the city of Loralimira and feed out along the Halo Mountain range."

She gawked. "Caves?"

"Aye, an endless web of caves bordering and diving beneath one of the most vast, northern ocean." He grinned reluctantly at her, hoping she had forgiven his earlier behavior. He loved seeing her smile.

She touched his arm, eagerness in her voice, "Can you show me the caves?"

There was a slight sense of electricity in her touch. The warmth of her hand on his arm made his heart beat faster. Rubbing the back of his neck, he hesitated. "I'm not sure. They aren't extremely safe."

She grinned slyly. "As if that has stopped us in the past." Peering behind them, she lowered her voice in excitement and whispered, "And where are the golps?"

Cutting his eyes playfully, he said, "They stay mainly in the shadows, completing the most unsavory tasks left by the Borgorian servants."

She turned her lip down in pity. "Poor creatures."

He chuckled at her reaction and gestured for her to take a chair opposite from Gornya, leaving the end vacant between them. He sat on her right, and next to him, sat Zalana. As usual, Remmi stood alert near the outside wall in the shadows.

Gornya spoke first, "You seek answers? We will provide as many answers as we are capable."

His face was not unkind, but he had a hard stare, stern and reflective. Mora glanced at each Borgorian sitting sporadically around the table, staring back at her like she was a childling in need of comfort. "Aye, I seek answers. I want to further examine a claim and why I am being hunted like a stag before the winter comes."

A callous smirk glowered upon Gornya's face. "We are all being hunted my *linas'ta*, immortal or mortal. Death still comes for us immortals, but it's usually for a gain, a balance needing to be weighed or a debt needing to be paid. What do you think yours will gain?"

Bog sourly intervened, "I will not allow you to question Mora until she is here."

Gornya sighed. "Bogheim, you have such little faith in your own kind. Has your heart been so burdened by your lack of conformity you disregard any trust in our company?"

"My existence never flourished through my Borgorian bloodline. My only loyalty is to the lands," he fought back his anger, "and my mother."

Gornya sneered. "Let us not discuss this any further," he rose with a tinge of caution in his voice. "She rests in peace."

Bog snapped, "She was murdered! You know it to be true!" His hands were fisted on the table, his knuckles white.

Taken aback at this revelation, Mora placed a hand on his thigh and the tension in his body released slightly.

"How dare you speak to me like that in front of the council!" Gornya's face was ravaged with fury. "I have every right to exile you from this land!" Raising himself gradually from his chair, his hissed, "You still haven't learned your place and I will gladly remind you of it if you choose to continue down this path." Then, realizing his outburst, he composed himself, lowered back down, and once again sat tall against his seat.

Bog never wavered. Glaring the entire time at his father, he knew Aloria would never allow his exile. *Bastard.*

The stone doorway slid open and an older, winged female gracefully walked to the end chair between Mora and Gornya. Her stature matched the militaristic males of the council and her skin glistened in the sunlight like all the Borgorians. Her eyes were a radiant violet, comparable to Bog's. She held herself in dignity and grandeur. *Aloria.* She stared. She had never seen such ancient beauty. Her hair mirrored the coif of the statue, riddled with delicate flowers, reminiscent of the light, pastel hues of the Nymian Sea at sunrise. Her silver, silk dress rustled as she took her place at the table, steadily peering about the silent room.

Finally, Aloria's gaze met Bog's and she smiled pleasantly. "I am elated to see you have returned. I never doubted your purpose."

He solemnly nodded.

Then, she grinned sweetly at Mora. "I see you have successfully found for whom you sought?"

Bowing his head in reverence, he replied, "Aye. This is Mora." When Aloria spoke, it was like silk spilling from her words.

"You seek answers Bog could not provide? I know you have endured a lifetime's worth of struggles in just a few moon phases."

Her demeanor was gentle. Mora felt calm in her presence.

"I do apologize you encountered such undeniable frustrations and will do the best I can to provide you with as many answers as you want to inquire. I am Aloria and these," she gestured to the room of Borgorians, "are my kin."

Mora gawked for a moment. At last, she gathered her thoughts, "Aloria? The mother of the skies? The first Messenger?"

Bog watched Aloria smile warmly at Mora. *When she smiles, it feels genuine. She is ethereal. It makes me remember the way my mother would smile and my soul would sing. The peace it radiated was like seeing the calm sea at sunrise, smelling the crisp, salty air, feeling the cool breeze on my cheek, and hearing the awakening of the natural world.* A tear threatened to emerge, but he held his breath. I will not allow Gornya to see my weakness. She raised her hand, motioning for the rest of the council to remove themselves from the transparent room. All, save for Gornya, left the room quietly.

"I see you have already been informed of our legend." She placed her hand on Mora's own. "Aye, Mora, I am Aloria. My immortality has allowed me to stay in the confines of my flesh until the time I am released by the Bidding. After thousands of years, I am no stranger to the nuances of evolution. I believe it has been more of a blessing, than a curse, to have observed the events shaping the worlds for better, or worse. I am weary though, and weep thinking about how my kin will transition once I am gone."

Bog inhaled sharply, remembering the words of Draelia. *Gone?* His chest tightened at the mere possibility those words could implicate. Delicately, Aloria laid her hands on the table. Her skin was scarred as if she had been burnt, but her fingers were still long and graceful.

Sighing, she moved the stone chair to the side and asked, "May I search your soul?"

In awe of the exquisite being, Mora timidly nodded. She obediently knelt down in front of Aloria's silken robes.

Gently, Aloria placed her graceful hands on Mora's cheeks, caressing her thumbs under her eyes and then over her eyebrows. Staring deeply into her forest green eyes, she said, "I will need you to clear your mind of all past transgressions." Then, she closed her eyes and started humming a soft tune.

Mora closed her eyes as well and took a deep breath. Attempting to clear her mind, the tune rang strangely familiar. However, when she began feeling the soft massage of Aloria's fingertips on her temples, her mind was no longer her own. After a time, her hands fell away. When she opened her eyes, she could see her trembling, tears filling her eyes.

Aloria whispered, "*Val resurgimus.*"

Bog felt Zalana shift uncomfortably next to his elbow. Peering at Remmi, his form remained a statue.

Mora rose to her feet and sat down on the chair, fixated upon Aloria's illustrious glow. "I don't understand."

"I have seen your soul. It is you. I never thought it possible after the exile." She placed a hand on Mora's hand. "You see, once He released you, sorrow flooded the Divine Realm. Souls were left empty because Light had been extinguished."

"Who is He and why did He release me?" She was saddened by Aloria's paled expression.

"Vitalis. You had become the embodiment of Chaos, completely eclipsed by Dark."

Mora's heart began to flutter at the thought of Ekklips. Her dreams had become unnaturally absent of His presence since they traveled over the Nymian Sea. *Why is He quiet?* It was both unnerving and devastating. She had become torn from her hatred of His purpose and need for control over her physical and mental self, but her love for Him increased through the emerging existence of an ancient and unyielding bond. Ekklips had been torturing her very mind for access to an identity she knew nothing about in declaration of this undying love. He had done unspeakable things. *But haven't I?* It did not go unnoticed something terrible happened each place they traveled, two of which no longer existed in the Mortal Realm. Chaos followed in her wake. The weight of her guilt was exponentially growing.

Peering at the bottomless falls, she thought the mountains of mist had begun to swell thicker from the depths. Aloria's soft voice pulled her back from the tragedy of her thoughts.

"Your love for Dark could not bear the exile of Him any longer. Life wept the day you adhered to Dark's will. He knew it would come, the night would prevail. You see, Life can't exist without balance. Therefore, before you were banished, Life, or as we referred to Him, Vitalis, kept the essence in which made you Light, but at a devastatingly sacrificial cost. Death was then merged with Dark's being, creating mortality, and a new balance of Life. The mortal races which emerged at the beginning were the most brutal and ferocious. Therefore, Vitalis would glance solemnly upon the world He created through His vengeance. Ekklips used your uninhibited essence, Chaos, to fuel the destruction. The retaliation against Vitalis grew cruel." Aloria paused.

Mora felt the tension growing in the room, but couldn't reason why, or from whom it emitted the most. No one seemed to be breathing, as if every word Aloria spoke was their next breath.

Inhaling deeply, she continued, "Out of desperation for your True Being, Ekklips persuaded you to take on a creatural form, hoping it would ignite the link of enlightenment between you and Vitalis. Of course, this was done by using your mother, Sila, one of the seven, primitive energies, three of which possessed female characteristics, three of male characteristics, and one of both, all created by the Trinitas. Successfully, Ekklips was able to create life. The essence of Vitalis quickly intervened, promising your mother's soul the eternity she had forsaken in exchange for her loyalty to Him, and only Him. Agreeing, she used what magic she had acquired throughout her life on the land, along with His aid, to shelter her and the babe outside of Ekklips' view. That is, until the day your awakening Light summoned the Dark."

Contemplating this for a moment, Mora scrunched her face. "If you claim I am Light, I never summoned Dark. At least not intentionally?"

"It is not your fault, my young one. Immortal or mortal, your soul cannot live without the dark, as it cannot live in the dark without the light. To truly live, you must recognize and accept both the light and dark."

"And Vitalis allowed this to happen?" Mora inquired.

"Unfortunately, I know not of what happened to Vitalis' True Being. Ever since Light was banished and He made the sacrifice, He became weakened with grief and betrayal. I, unfortunately, gave up my direct relationship with Him for love. Now, I only search souls for answers to their connection to Life."

Wearily, Aloria stood, bowed her head in reverence, and began to leave the room. "I am fatigued. I must lie down."

"May I inquire something before you retire?" Mora asked politely.

"Aye, my young one," Aloria acquiesced and elegantly turned around.

"My name day, does it hold any significance?"

"Certainly," she grinned, "the Winter Solstice. You are the Light in the darkest day of the year."

Gornya, with his hands crossed over his chest, peered beneath his heavily suspicious eyes at Bog, Remmi, Zalana, and Mora before rising to his feet. "It seems your intuitions were correct, Bogheim." Clearing his throat, he motioned to an abnormally petite, female Borgorian standing by the door. "I'm sure you and your guests are famished and weary from your journey. Hepshig will be happy to escort you to the dining hall and then show you to your accommodations." He bowed slightly and moved away from the table, pausing briefly to shrug his shoulders before continuing out the door.

"Would you allow me to see you to your accommodations before you head to the dining hall?" Hepshig asked.

Bog, who had risen when Aloria rose from her chair, was gazing out the walls. The tone in which Gornya had spoken was unnerving. His father had never been at a loss for words or condescending comments. *What did my father hear from Aloria that created the ominously looming cloud of suspicion?*

Realizing Bog wasn't paying attention, Mora nodded with a half grin at Hepshig and replied, "We would greatly appreciate your services." Placing a hand on his arm, she squeezed. "Bog?"

"Mhm?" he replied absently. Then, he felt the heat of her hand igniting his core. "Aye? Oh, certainly."

Three commenced to follow the small Borgorian, Hepshig, through the corridor leading back to the Great Hall. One stayed back to peer through the glass at the side of the transparent room. A disturbance in the falls shook the land, resonating deep within the vast darkness of the abyss. Inside the billowing mists appeared a blue streak of lightning. A web of blue light dispersed into the depths, striking into the heart of the falls like a serpent thrashing rapidly against the deceiving walls of liquid confinement.

# Through the Oculus

Bog glanced around the familiar chambers of his old room. Memories flooded in front of his eyes. The smell of fresh, pastel, Alorian flowers on the mantle above the fireplace were lodged in his throat. It was an aroma that brought back almost a couple hundred years of memory. The scent was light and sweet like the sunset on the Summer Solstice, but with a tinge of heavy sadness, reminding him of the first frost. Youthful, past apparitions ran across the room, lads with small wings, one of violet eyes and the rest gray. Wooden swords cracked, characters were created, and story time was acted out alongside their mother in front of the roaring fire. Then, grown, past ghosts entered, radiating heavy emotions of anger, hatred, and malice, an expanding chasm dividing the future. Tears were wept, arguments were unresolved, and pain carved unseen wounds deeper.

Throwing his satchel on the table, he shook himself from the intoxicating smell. He and Remmi were sharing the quarters during their time on the grounds as the majority of the rooms were being occupied by many of the guard. Bog loathed the idea, suspicious of Remmi's ulterior intentions and always disturbed by his overwhelming silence in the shadows. Unfortunately, his own presence in Loralimira was rapidly leaving an excruciatingly foul taste in his mouth. This was due, in part, to Korian and his father. However, there was another looming energy which had befallen, lurking in the halls and penetrating the walls. He sensed it seeping into his subconscious the moment he walked through the gates. It

## The Keeper

was one of the reasons he had become irrationally angry with Mora.

*If only I could obtain the answers I seek and leave immediately.*
He knew it was easier said, than done. Aloria's face appeared in his mind's eye. He could not leave her again, she had become a mother to him; and he could see a strange frailty sinking into her flesh. In frustration, he rubbed his hands on his cheeks and interlaced his fingers on top of his head. Turning around, he saw Remmi at the fireplace, using a fire iron to poke the wood, irritating the flames. His sullen face was glowing in the firelight.

Clearing his throat and grabbing a handful of flowers, he muttered, "I must go for a walk."

"Do as you may," Remmi responded, never turning his head in acknowledgement.

Shrugging his shoulders, Bog exited the chamber without hesitation. It had been long past since he had walked the corridors of the chateau. The most vivid memories were agonizingly tormenting, but it was because he had spent most of his years battling the physical daemons of his blood. There was only one place he wanted to visit, and he began feeling guilty too many years had passed since he had been back. Proceeding through the Great Hall, he turned right on the portico and slipped through an iron door nestled behind an ancient, twisting, Yew tree.

On the other side of the wall, a lush garden grew. Flowers of all colors and various fruit trees bloomed most of the year. Despite being further north, the climate was temperate. The islands of Borgoria were their own liminal spaces scattered along the northern Nymia Sea at the edge of The Mist. He supposed it had something to do with Aloria, but was never told for certain. He thought back on her haunting words, '*I am weary though, and weep thinking about how my kin will transition once I am gone*'.

His stomach tied in knots. *Gone?* He still couldn't fathom how those words could hold truth. A hawk cried overhead, the sound muffled by the roaring falls. He shivered and proceeded to the edge of the garden where one could overlook the majestic waterfalls. The House of Gornya was beset on the most glorious waterfalls in the known worlds. It was considered the end of the lands, the furthest point to venture northeast. Also, the most dangerous wonder because of the impenetrable wall of mists that lay beyond. No one who entered The Mist lived. Therefore, there

*The Keeper*
was only legend filling the minds and cascading from the tongues of the oldest immortal. Those sentenced to death at the House of Gornya were thrown off the east side of the chateau, through the opposite, iron door, and into the roaring waters. It was a similar demise as those released over the Staggering Stones.

Bog shivered at such an excruciating ending.

Traipsing up the path of the garden he had known so well as a borgling, he could feel the water droplets accumulating heavily on his flesh and wings. When he reached the railless edge, he slowed to a careful saunter. In front of him was a white, two columned mausoleum built between lusciously full, Chaste trees, the violet blooms softly blowing in the breeze. Engraved on the door was:

*Solienne Houndstead*
*Beloved Mother and Wife*
*May the Light give you peace.*
*Forevermore.*

He despised the inscription. He knew the truth behind her death. A tear rolled down his face as he put a hand on the stone, placing the Alorians onto the cold marble at his feet. "Why did you leave me?" he whispered somberly. Wiping the tears from his face, the wind rustled his hair and feathers.

"I never left you," a gentle voice surrounded him softly.

Startled, he jerked his head around in all directions. "Reveal yourself."

"You may not see me, my love, but I am always watching you," the mystical voice replied.

Another breeze caressed his cheek. "Mother?" he stuttered. He stood motionless with a heaving chest and sweaty palms.

"Aye, Bogheim, only in voice. My time is short and I must speak in haste. I am here to inform you there is treacherous work around you. Please, with urgency, go to the cellars of the chateau. You will find a box with your birth name inscribed upon it. There, you will find answers in which you have sought."

Almost immediately, her voice began to fade. "Mother!" He

called out, grasping onto the air. "Do not leave me! I do not seek answers more than I seek your presence!" Gripping his hair tightly, he screamed, "Please!", and fell to his knees at the steps of the mausoleum. *Three warnings.*

Silence, save for the belligerent waters of the falls, encompassed his being. Feeling once again forsaken, his heart beat harshly in his chest as if it would explode at any given moment. Lugging his body to his feet, he trudged heavy-footed to the edge of the garden. Despite the sickening feeling of being crushed by the weight of the waterfall, the urge to jump rushed through his veins. *Godsdamn Life and Death!*

He was startled by a sudden rustling of the hawk bolting through the trees. Clenching his fists, he yelled until his chest hurt, his veins popping from his neck. However, like the hawk's cry, the waters drowned out his voice.

Finally, exhausted and angry, he hung his head in defeat. His mother's use of the word urgency meant nothing to him at this time. He ached and felt an immense disappointment rushing like wildfire through his veins. Feeling heavy, he spun on his heel to return to his chambers until he felt the restless tension he was being watched. Surveying the windows, he spotted a pair of curtains three floors above the gardens slightly open in the middle. A dark shadow abruptly disappeared, leaving the curtains rustling. *That is strange.* Disturbed, he leered for a moment longer before shaking his head and departing.

The sun was below the horizon line, casting rays of light across the sky. Peering one more time toward his mother's mausoleum, he shut and latched the iron door. When he reached his old chambers, he saw Remmi standing in the same position in which he had been when Bog left. *At least it couldn't have been Remmi who was spying through the curtains.* Though it relieved him a bit, he couldn't help but feel the increasing uneasiness festering deeper. Disgruntled, he sighed and shook his head before flinging himself onto the bed and immediately drifting into a deep slumber.

## The Keeper

Mora was restless in her chamber. It was smaller than the one at the Floating Fortress, but it was warm with the roaring fire. Although the air had been temperate since entering Loralimira, she still reached for a cloak on the end of her bed before picking up a candelabra and deciding to briefly explore the chateau. The sky was not yet dark, but the light was fading fast. The window overlooked the west side of the falls. Peering out over the majestic waters was becoming unsettling. Mists concealed most of the falls below the initial drop of torrential water. When she squinted her eyes toward where the horizon would be, the mists were so heavy, she couldn't see the horizon line. Peering below on the grounds around the chateau, she saw a grove of trees with amber blooms. Protruding from the grove over the falls was a wooden platform. Her stomach churned when she thought what it would be like to stand over such unfathomable power.

Stepping back inside, she lit the candelabra and slowly pushed her door open. An awfully high-pitch, creaking sound echoed down the hallway. Once in the corridor, she proceeded past several chamber doors until she reached a circular room with various exits. Each door appeared identical. In between each doorway was a marble statue of a Borgorian with grand wings. Proud and unyielding expressions graced the faces of the statues, but their eyes were stained with sadness and longing. There were seven statues and seven doors. Carved onto the stone block of each statue was a particular word: *Forthimus. Amora. Misricorpia. Fithals. Yustyt'. Stide'*. She decided to proceed through the doorway next to *Lybratys* - Balance.

She wandered to the top of a stone staircase intricately wrapped around a tall tower on the far, eastern side of the fortress. The sound of the rushing waterfalls reverberated from the grand, arched windows aligning the stone wall. Stopping for a moment to look over the mighty, rushing water beneath her, she touched the thick ivy accumulating on the outside walls and took a deep breath of fresh air. Before she turned to ascend further, a figure in the darkening courtyard below caught her attention. She stared heavily at the gardens until her eyes got weary, unable to recognize the being. *They cannot be Borgorian, I see no wings*. Uneasily, she turned and commenced up the staircase, gently trailing her fingers along the cold stone wall as she ascended.

Once reaching the top, she saw a huge contraption in the center of the room. She walked around the object, feeling the cool, gold, outer shell and turning various knobs. Glimpsing into the small, glass holes, she could see the darkening sky clearly.

"It's a telescope."

Mora jumped backward. There were no windows in the dome save the large oculus in the ceiling. Fervently glancing around, she said, "Pardon?"

"I did not mean to frighten you, my young one. I come here at sunset every night to gaze upon the luminous stars."

She searched through the fading light of the room. Finally, she noticed Aloria sitting gracefully in a dark, wooden, rocking chair with a tall back supporting her majestic wings.

"My apologies," Mora replied and bowed reverently, "I did not mean to disturb you." She backed away toward the entrance.

"Do not be so quick to make your regards before you know whether or not you are welcomed," Aloria spoke with authority and stood. "I would be honored with your company. Come." She elegantly, yet meekly, gestured to the telescope.

Mora shyly returned to join Aloria.

"Please." Aloria held her fingers on a small, circular, metal opening attached to the base.

Cautiously, Mora crept closer and placed her eye in line with the opening as Aloria adjusted various knobs. She gasped. It was breathtaking. The light had quickly succumbed to the darkening sky in waves like an ocean's layered depths. Amidst the blanket of waning blues and purples were a multitude of pinpointed lights. As she gazed, she realized she could see various stars more clearly than others. One cluster of stars appeared to have a lingering dust cloud around them, discoloring the twinkling light to make them appear different shades of red and orange. At another angle, she could see a larger mass, one with rings and three lights close in proximity. Astounded, her stomach leapt as she saw a streak of light shoot across her line of vision, faster than she could catch her breath. Excited and enthralled, she continued to peer through the glass as more became clearer with the dying light.

"Magnificent, is it not?" Aloria inquired.

Mora stepped back, forgetting she was not alone. Realizing her rudeness, she bowed her head in reverence to Aloria. "It is breathtaking, like nothing I have ever laid eyes upon." Her blood began to boil with passion. "You have brought the stars closer."

"It is not I who built what you see before you," Aloria spoke, placing her hand upon the cool, gold metal. "In fact, it is a fairly new addition to our kind, only half a century prior. Its maker is none other than Gornya's son."

Mora glanced at her curiously. "Korian?"

Aloria smiled, but her sweet response was tinged with pity. "My, do you think so little of his abilities? Nay, it is his twin brother."

Bewildered, Mora sputtered, "Bog?" She had not realized they were twins. Of course, Bog had relayed very little information about his past to her in their brief travels together.

Aloria's laugh was delicate. "Aye, none other. He was never the fighter, although strong and brave. He was always his mother's borgling, more intelligent than any of his kind." She adjusted herself as she held onto the telescope. "The Borgorian race was gleaned to be warriors, fighters against seen and unseen enemies. My Borheim was exceptionally proud of the race we created together. He believed our kin would become superior and rule the northern hemisphere with an iron, yet passionate and just, fist.

"Our superiority came with a price, though. What we once believed an impenetrable force of immortal beings, became heavily ladened with a shrouded weakness. Greed and jealously ran through the blood of our descendants; and a storm, greater than we had ever foreseen, penetrated our work. Chaos. The land became stained with darkness, spreading through the hearts of those true to the Borgorian line. An upheaval arose, along with a massacre of the sacred blood. Those true to the purity of the race fought bravely and valiantly. In the end, the impurity was subdued, but my love, Borheim, did not return." A tear ran down her cheek.

Mora became uncomfortable, but her curiosity had been aroused. "The Borgorians, are you not immortal? How is it he did not return?"

Aloria smiled. "Ah, my dear, immortality is a form of trickery. For while we are blessed with an extensively longer life than any mortal can fathom, it can be cut short by another immortal of equal or greater force than thyself."

*494*

## The Keeper

Seeing the confusion on Mora's face, she continued, "Let me paint you a picture. Imagine your life is a beautiful diamond, the hardest element found in nature. It seems lovely and lustrous from the outside, but on the inside it is hard, brittle, and cold. Diamonds, like worldly immortality, are still a part of the natural world. It is likely to chip or crack along our line of weakness. However, to fully destroy the diamond, one must use another diamond, or search for a harder element, to penetrate the outer layer and destroy it."

"You said, '*worldly immortality*'. Are there various aspects?" Mora replied.

"Certainly. Hallowed immortality is only for the Elysian spirits. Divine immortality is the most superior of all. The latter is consecrated by the Trinitas."

"The Trinitas?" Mora responded. She had heard the term a few times throughout her journey, but the concept was still foreign. "And are you not considered an Elysian spirit?"

"In the form of three. Various beliefs refer to it as one whole, which is considered monotheistic; others, it is multiple, or polytheistic." Aloria peered deep into Mora's eyes. "In the most ancient of days, star gazers relied on the heavens to foretell their futures. Magnificent stones were erected to impress the highest of immortals. Sacrificial gifts were presented to each god and goddess, most of which possessed opposing concepts of morality and hedonism. Every clan, every group, every being, preferred their personal favorite god or goddess depending on their spiritual needs, or lack thereof."

Fingering the telescope's eye piece, she continued solemnly, "However, I am an Elysian spirit and, to my knowledge, the oldest Immortal walking amongst All. Once my light is extinguished, my purpose will pass to another. My soul will rest beyond the Divine Realm. That, my young one, is why I have endured these numerous eons of time."

Mora fiddled with her fingers. Without glancing up, she mumbled, "Bog does not believe in destiny or fate." Lifting her eyes, she saw the corners of Aloria's mouth curl in amusement. "And fully comprehending your words eludes me. Why do you speak as if gloom and death have already overcome your body?"

"Because they have, my lovely. I have long since been a victim of

*495*

Death and Dark myself. Dark has lurked within the shadows, hopeful I may depart willingly at His proposal. However, I have remained faithful to the trueness of my nature. I know not how I will release myself into the soul exhilarating state I have yearned for all of my years on this land, but I know it will come soon. It is as it should be."

Her eyes gazed longingly toward the stars. "You see, Mora, Ekklips was never evil. He was merely your balance, your equal. Together, with Life, you created worlds that needed and worshipped all three of you in various forms. Dark, nor Death, is the equivalent of evil. For evil is a part of life, a component of All, and occurs in the light as well as the dark. You must understand Death has always been a part of Life; but since the sacrifice, immortals have suffered from the destitute of harmony, a separation from utopian synchronicity, and a reincarnation of unyielding judgment. Life created worldly Death out of spite, and the thirst for revenge has tainted His True Being, a cataclysm in which is causing an insurmountable discord throughout All. Jealousy broke the Trinitas, and Dark was not the only sole initiator.

"Everyone, mortal and immortal, have both light and dark, each balancing the other. Without embracing your darkest side, you cannot fully embrace the lightest. Ekklips' followers merely became the scourge of All because He has been gradually transforming into the ultimate embodiment of Death, while still desperately clinging to Dark. He's attempting to create an interpretation of life in His wake without the balance of light. He is continuously plotting His vengeance against the one who wanted more control, and it has severely weakened His True Being as well. You, young one, have been caught in the crossfire of deceit."

"How do I embrace who I was...," Mora paused and considered her words, "...who I am?"

"Only you can discover your True Being, Mora." She gently rubbed Mora's cheek. She could feel the heat radiating below the surface. "Now, you must realize the company in which you keep."

However, before she could speak any further, a guard approached the tower, a grave expression upon his face. Aloria's grin was forced, but she placed a hand on Mora's wrist and held her voice low, "I do hope we speak again. But if not, remember knowledge extends beyond the tangible; and balance must be created in order to sustain Life. Both are as much internal as they are external. Be leery. Be strong. Be true to yourself."

Regally, she turned, but not before pausing a moment longer to linger on a thought. Tilting her head sideways, she spoke quietly, "Bog has an outstanding and unrivaled intelligence, one full of comprehending the most mystical of concepts. But even the most brilliant can have trouble balancing and maintaining the shadows of their mind." Upon her words, she floated passed the guard without looking back.

Mora knew deep inside those would be the last words she would hear Aloria utter.

In the darkness of the courtyard, facing toward the rushing falls, stood a shadow. A tall figure emerged from an archway under the tallest tower and sauntered into the amber-flowered trees, holding a tightly wrapped bundle.

"Were you discovered?" the shadow inquired in a low, monotonous tone.

"Nay," replied the other holding the bundle, "else my presence would be impossible."

"Excellent, and the key?" The shadow reached for the bundle. When it was retracted, there was a low snarl.

While there a was slight hesitation in the reply, the tall figure mumbled, "I have not gotten close enough to handle the matter, but it was closer than your pathetic attempts. He will be more than pleased with my offering. Where will you take it?"

The shadow grunted. With a forceful grab, he took possession of the bundle. "That is none of your fucking concern. It was not in our agreement to discuss the details of our bargain."

With a strong hint of disconcertedness resonating in the question, the tall figure inquired, "And where is my restitution?"

The shadow pulled out a tiny bag wrapped with a red string. "As agreed." Tossing it onto the stone walkway of the courtyard, the shadow turned and added, "She will be expecting it," as his form dissipated into the falls.

### The Keeper

The tall figure snatched the pouch and stood motionless, watching the shadow disappear, bundle in hand. A gust of wind from the falls revealed a faint glint of gold in the dark.

# Death's Kiss

Standing by the open window, she placed a soft, frail hand on the stone. It was a hand she no longer recognized, a hand that had possessed enough power to create an entire nation of beings, a hand in which had held the love of her life until Death pried him from her embrace. *Did Life forsaken me because I erected structures and grand cathedrals in the name of Light with the hope one day the Goddess would return to Her rightful place amongst the Divine Realm? I had been His Divine Messenger after all, until...*

"He never deserved your devotion," a voice whispered. "You kept hidden your intentions long enough to see them through."

"And yet, you're the one who hides in the shadows," Aloria responded gravely.

"I am the Shadow Leader and I have no qualms wielding it to my favor in times of necessity."

She saw the candle flicker out in the absence of wind, but then relight. "A pathetic tactic to gain the attention of a young female who knows not exactly who she was, is, or could be."

The shadows growled and wrapped around the room. "You worship Light, but don't give Solora credit."

"She is more Chaos, than Light, because of you," she chided.

"I didn't have much to work with during the early stage, but it will be corrected in time. She will be free to choose Her own vengeance against Him. Anyway," He chuckled, "we had a deal."

Her chest pounded. She knew she was not permitted to aid in the journey Mora took, although she wanted to intervene desperately, to save her from herself and the choice she would eventually have to make. However, her heart was also heavy because she didn't want to leave Bog, her only daughter's son whom she loved like her own. He did not know the dark past which possessed her to make such a deal with Ekklips, and hoped he never would.

Straightening her shoulders, she held her chin high, eyes still never wavering from The Mist beyond the waterfalls. It was a sight, a reminder, she had forced herself to gaze upon from her bedroom window every morning and every night for nearly two centuries. Clasping her hands in front of her silver shift, her violet eyes flashed in the dying light of the candle.

"How will you do it?"

"I will do nothing."

Inhaling deeply, realization prickled her skin and she shuddered. Though it may have sounded like a question to anyone else, she said in a strong voice, "Tonight."

Without answering, the candlelight sizzled and the room was embraced in complete shadow. A cold prick upon her cheek sent a chill down her spine. She knew she had just accepted Death's Kiss.

"Guards! Guards!"

Bog could hear the alarmed shouting down the hallway. A rush of hesitancy belittled his veins, causing his heart to skip a beat. He looked toward the open window. Dawn had peeked on the horizon, but the room was still dark. He rose from his bed, naked from the warmth of the fire and the anger which left beads of sweat dripping from his furrowed brow. Lighting a candle, he pulled his breeches on and peered over to where Remmi stood at the window.

*Bastard never sleeps*, he groaned.

Then, he vaguely started remembering the event which unfolded the evening prior with his mother's voice. It had been the third warning against his presence in Loralimira. Shrugging in unbelief of the sincerity, he had felt afraid it was a ruse to invade his thoughts and distract him from his purpose, playing on his vulnerabilities. Cracking the door open, he listened for the sound of footsteps. A familiar, menacing clank of weapons echoed against the smooth, stone walls from below. Quietly, he descended the stairs, keeping out of sight as he neared the bottom. When he rounded the doorway, he could see a hoard of guards pacing around in the Great Hall. Gornya, his father, was standing on the altar steps donning his customary, stern, facial expression. Bog had grown to know it well. Korian, his twin brother, was always next to their father, constantly hanging on his every word. He was nodding consistently to everything Gornya was speaking. While he never saw the likeness between himself and his twin brother, everyone else had said they looked similarly enough to be mistaken.

Beginning to wonder what the military fuss was about, he listened closely to the rambling of the military guards, but he could not recognize specifics. A surge of confidence ran up his spine and he decided to confront his father. Knowing he would not be pleased with the confrontation in front of his guard, Bog smirked with a tinge of satisfaction. Standing straighter and matting his wings, he stepped out of the doorway. As he approached the group of Borgorians huddled around his father and brother, a rush of whispers emerged. He suddenly felt less confident. However, he could not run away like he did as a borgling, embarrassed by his lack of respect as a son of Gornya. Without cowering, he came face to face with his father, a bold move in any situation where his father was partaking in military jargon. Unfortunately, though, he suddenly had the sensation the circumstances were different this time as the stern glower upon his father's natural façade faded into a pained expression of foreboding.

"What is the cause of alarm? Why must you assemble in the earliest morning light?" he inquired.

Running a hand through his beard, Gornya cleared his throat. Bog thought he was going to speak, but he merely laid a hand on his shoulder and pushed his way through the guards. A sick, twisted feeling was entrapped in his stomach. The only other time he had ever been carefully handled by his father was when his mother was murdered. He had been nearly eight when his mother died, leaving him alone to be raised by his brooding father, and less favored by his brothers. Korian was his only surviving brother.

His heart raced as he yelled after his father, "What in the curse of the gods is going on!" Anticipation and anxiety were growing internally at a sickening rate.

Gornya stopped, turned around, and stared heatedly into his eyes. He spoke in an uncharacteristically gentle manner, "It's Aloria. An unknown attempted to murder her last night. Currently, she has become comatose, barely alive, appearing to be in a deep slumber."

Shock. Desperation. Anger. Malicious emotions toiled with his whole self. Bog could not believe what his ears had just heard. He stood motionless, staring at his father in disbelief. After several moments, he gathered his thoughts and retorted, "How the fuck would it be attempted? By whom? Where does she lay?"

Gornya could sense Bog's rage. *Like a sleeping dragon.* Clearing his throat, he responded stoically, "We must remain calm, for the assassin could be anyone around the castle. The walls have ears. Therefore, we must be discrete. It's not the first time Death's assailants have penetrated these walls."

For the first time in his life, his father sounded sensible, caring. However, his mind burned and raced uncontrollably. "How can you just stand there and do nothing?" He gawked. "Do you have witnesses?"

Gornya cleared his throat, "We have a serving wench who swears she saw a short, cloaked figure hobbling the hallways around midnight. Unfortunately, for the lass, she was the last to see Aloria awake. Therefore, we can only assume the poisoning was by her hands. There are traces of a potent poison referred to as Death's Bloom, which was laced with another bitter scent we cannot identify, found in the kitchens amongst pieces of cut, red string."

Eerily, he and Mora both had consumed a heavy dose of potent poison in the Fire Country, each at a different time. Rubbing his hands together, he guffawed, "You cannot kill an innocent being without evidence."

"There is not much to be done at this time. We had to take measures. We know not if she acted alone. She had to be made an example."

"An example?" he sneered.

"Aye, she was dropped into the waters this morning. Not terribly long before you proceeded into the Great Hall." Gornya stepped sullenly to Bog, face to face. "My apologies," he murmured. Patting a hand on his shoulder, he returned to the huddle on the altar.

Desperate and disgusted, Bog stole away into the closest door. Beating his fists against the stone wall until blood trickled down his knuckles, he cursed his life. *Now, I know nothing keeping me bound to Borgoria.* Aloria was his single, living mentor, a mother figure who loved and nurtured his future and knowledge. A deep, dark yell escaped his throat. Tearing at his flesh, he could feel the torment of his mind burrowing in his skull. He wiped his violet eyes and began to stumble his way up the corridor, hastening his stride to the upper, right wing of the chateau in the direction of her quarters. Wiping another tear away from his face as he neared her chambers, he noticed the guards were stationed outside the doorway. When he stepped into sight, they blocked the entrance.

"No one advances unless Gornya orders otherwise."

"Move the fuck out of my way you insidious imps! I am the son of Gornya. I have the authority to throw you into the waters, if I so please." He did not cower at their brute. He was too consumed with anger to allow any to stand in his way of a proper mourning.

The guards glanced at each other and stepped away from the door. He pushed his way past the spears. Opening the door carefully, he could feel the coolness of the morning on his face. The window was ajar and silk, lavender curtains slowly swayed in the breeze. Next to the bed, the slight glow of candlelight illuminated the dim room. Reverently bowing his head, he quietly shut the door. Purposefully not surveying the room, he walked to the end of the bed. With reluctance, he raised his head and followed the luxurious sheets until he saw her face. Asleep, Aloria did not appear to be the towering, supreme, immortal ruler of the Borgorians. She had always been a proud, but caring, adopted mother since his own mother had passed. She had taught him everything he knew about the world and the living entities who shared in their journey. She had been the one who taught him about the otherworldly secrets yet to be discovered, prompting him to expand his ability to believe in circumstances other than what he could see before his own eyes. It was by her encouragement which lead him to seeking Mora.

Bog quietly walked to the side of the bed, watching Aloria's eyes, internally hoping they would open slightly enough for him to properly thank her and say good bye. Touching her fingers, he could feel the frailness overcoming her flesh and bone. Her life was barely pulsating and her skin was no longer warm. He wondered how such a superior immortal could become lifeless in a short amount of time. *And if she knew*, the thought flitted in his mind. He leaned his head closer, almost touching her nose, to listen to the barely visible puff of air emerging from her mouth. It was extremely intermittent. Too afraid someone may mistaken her as dead, he quickly devised a plan to encase her body until he could further examine the cause.

Grabbing a piece of parchment from a nearby table, he jostled it until an envelope fell onto the floor. The seal had been broken. However, focusing on the crest, the symbol was recognizable. The wax was green and the emblem was a leaf, filigreed with gold. Holding it under the candlelight, he inspected it further. Curious, he grabbed a small, wooden chair and set it next to the bedside. Opening the letter, it read:

*My dearest Aloria,*

*As you may have known, the light is fading rapidly. Life is faltering, swiftly loosing His grip on All as soil lacks a strongly rooted tree. Balance is teetering on fallibility. The prevalent arousal of Dark's Death is dominating Life through an escalating, constant, phallic battle of superiority. Without the sun, the moon cannot shine in darkness, leaving the dark to prevail over each and every soul. This, in turn, is breaking the harmony in which Life depends upon. Our kind cannot continue to thrive in our state without the moon to light our way. I beg for your guidance, for none know the ways of Life as you. I have included a number of maps that have been charted by our finest faeries. They reveal the most recent movements of the lands in comparison to the skies. I pray this letter finds you in capacity to speak further about these pressing matters.*

*May the Goddess be with you,*
*Katheryn*

*Katheryn?* A repulsion prickled his skin. Retrieving the map from behind the letter, Bog saw magnificent, intricately drawn constellations on one side of the parchment, and when he flipped it over, there was a map of Atlastova with primarily Mortal Realm locations. It was torn, many of the lands incomplete, and the edges frayed. *Why would they draw a map of the land on one side and the skies on the other? Why not just use another piece of parchment? How recent did Katheryn write to Aloria?* He wondered if it was before she met Mora. Contemplating the drawings, he flipped from one side to the other until he heard the faint sound of heavy footfall outside the door. He immediately tucked the parchments into his boot.

The door opened slightly. He could see the large wings of his brother poking through the crack. He grunted. Korian barged into the room after speaking with the guards. His face was expressionless, his eyes loathing.

Bog and his twin brother had nothing in common, save for the womb they had shared nearly two hundred name days ago. Korian had always boasted of his 'glorious emergence' from the womb only moments before Bog. Their father immediately took to his dominant son, leaving his wife to birth the other without him as he carried Korian through the halls, rejoicing of a grand heir. It was Aloria who received Bog, placing him to suckle immediately at his mother's tit; unlike Korian, who had no emotional attachment to their mother. If it weren't for Aloria's patience and love, Gornya would have sent Bog away immediately after Solienne's passing. In spite of the criticism and hate, Aloria stood firm for Bog. Unfortunately, as he glanced down at her dying body, and then to Korian, he knew he was no longer safe in Loralimira.

"Mourning brother?" Korian smirked. "The old hag was older

than the land itself. She needed to move aside for someone more qualified."

Bog's veins began to pump fiercely. "Withdraw Korian. You cared nothing for her in life, so why show your face at all? Depart this chamber and leave me to burden with the details." He did not hold back his hateful spite. "For all we know, it was you who attempted the murder." Peering sullenly from beneath his brow, he turned his back to Korian.

Korian hissed, "Hold your tongue, bastard! How dare you address me in that way. I, who will lead the Borgorians alongside father, will not stand for your blasphemy!"

Turning back around, Bog stared maliciously at Korian. He watched him attempt to raise his hand, but it stopped when he did not cower at his threat.

Korian started to chuckle. "Ah, I see. Your frail attempt at bravery will not last. You will leave this room feeling scared again and run to the bitch you have stashed away, claiming she is mightier than Aloria."

Brushing off the snideness, Bog stepped silently around the bed. "I will not leave this godsdamn house without placing her in a proper encasing. I will commission it myself," he said sullenly. "For what little mercy you retained at the death of my own mother, grant me the right to have responsibility over Aloria's resting place."

Korian lashed out, "Your mother? She was just as much my mother as your own! All the years she lived, she merely felt sorry for you, the black sheep, the anomaly to the Borgorian race! You practically suckled her tit until she died! She always adored me and awed in my greatness. You were nothing, but a burden. Your feebleness killed her in the end, your constant neediness and inability to live like a real, fucking Borgorian!" This time, he knocked over the chair as the hatred burned in his eyes.

Storming to the door, he jerked his head around. Bitterly, he seethed, "Do what you will with the sack of bones, but you will never show your face here again after tomorrow night." He slammed the door when he left.

Bog rubbed his face and peered at the bed. Out of frustration, he groaned. Thinking about the spitefulness of his brother, he trusted the speculation Korian was the one who attempted to rid the house of Aloria. *It would mean he made a deal with Death.* He tucked the thought into the back of his mind and picked up another parchment. *If I only have until tomorrow night, I must be quick.* He leaned down to kiss Aloria's cold forehead before exiting the chamber.

Darting down the hall, he turned the corner and ran into Zalana. "My apologies," he breathed heavily, placing a hand on her arm to check if she was fine.

"Oh, nay, my apologies!" she said matting down her cloak. "It was certainly my fault. I was not paying attention to where I was going." Flashing a sweet smile at him, it pleased her to see him blush. "Where might you be heading in such a hurry?"

He stuttered, "Well…tragically…Aloria is rapidly dying and I am hurrying to place together an encasement for her body, so as to preserve what is left before she fades away."

She gasped, "How awful!", and placed her hand against her mouth. "I regret to hear such daunting news. Can I be of service? I am especially good with my hands."

He thought for a moment. He did need to complete the encasement before tomorrow evening and extra help should be welcomed without hesitation. Regardless, he was reluctant to accept her assistance with such a delicate matter. Therefore, he responded out of politeness, secretly hoping she would find it horribly dull. "I would appreciate the help. If you would care to assist, I am heading to the cellars of the house. I will be sifting through centuries of grim and dust, collecting wood and glass to bring to my workshop."

*Cellars.* The thought hounded his subconscious. Then, the voice of his mother resonated with the warning of treachery and retrieving a box.

Zalana nodded. "Certainly." She cleared her throat, "If I may meet you down there, I have some business to attend first."

Wide-eyed, he stuttered, "Aye…well, I will…be off then." Briskly, he walked away, only to glance behind to see if she was watching. However, she had already disappeared down the corridor in which he had emerged. *That's peculiar.* Shaking his head to clear his thoughts, he continued advancing to the lowest floor of the chateau.

Descending toward the cellars, he stumbled on a golp cleaning the waste buckets, its beady eyes watching him suspiciously from a dark corner as he crossed the cold stone. Upon making eye contact, the golp slid further in the shadows, sneering. Although he had never thought twice about their purpose in the chateau, Mora's pitiful reaction to their servitude caused him great discomfort. *Despite my own abuse, have I been too privileged to realize the detrimental circumstances in which these creatures exist?* He had been taught to hate them, standing idle while watching their foul treatment at the hands of the Borgorians. *Would my mother have ever treated them as such?* He shook his head, disgusted at his own ruthful prejudice.

Once in the vast cellars of the house, he began swiftly searching for useful tools and materials he could use in order to build the encasement. He began pulling away old, dusty linen coverings from large, wooden panels which had allowed the dining hall tables to be extended. He examined the wood. Due to the various cracks and subtle signs of mold, it would most likely not keep for an extended period of time. He continued searching. Further and further he delved, uncovering trunks full of stored dining silver and candle wax, various linens and wool, old furniture and books, and eerie, timeworn portraits of Borgorians of a by-gone era he only recognized by name, several whom had been excommunicated from the race through disagreeable political acts.

Finally lighting a candle, Bog climbed past the boxes into a more secluded part of the cellar. Cobwebs and dust filled the air, making it harder to see. Once in the farthest corner, his light shone on a small box buried underneath over two centuries worth of dust, and two tarnished silver candlesticks. The memory of his mother's voice echoed, *a box with your true name inscribed upon it.* Setting the candle down carefully, he knelt, removed the candlesticks to pick up the box, and blew the excess dust off. This made him sneeze forcefully. He fanned the floating remnants away from his face.

The box was made of dark wood with filigreed, iron hinges. It smelled ancient, but he knew it could not be anymore than two centuries. There was a clear coating protecting it from water and other elements. Rubbing off the rest of the dust, his heart nearly stopped. Carved in delicate script on top was his birth name, Bogheim. He grimaced slightly. He had never been fond of his name. The shortened version made him sound like a desolate wetland. Nevertheless, it was the name his mother had given him at birth, and he respected it. She wanted it to correlate with

Aloria's husband, Borheim, undoubtedly with Aloria's blessing. Wiping the emerging tears, he opened the creaky lid.

On the inside, he found a gown made of white silk the size of his forearm. Two, small slits in the back were wide enough for three fingers. *My burden.* Next, he retrieved a miniature cloth doll, unrecognizable by the amount of holes and filth covering the body; however, it had wings, one with a black spot. Slightly grinning, he remembered when his mother made the pitiful creature. He would hug it tightly through the nights after she died to comfort his night terrors and tears. During the day, Korian would taunt and tease him about it, sometimes hiding the doll for many nights until their father got tired of hearing them yell. He rubbed the violet, buttoned eyes with his large thumb.

Pulling out one treasure at a time, he realized it was a collection solely of his youth memorabilia his mother must have collected before she died. At the bottom, there was a folded parchment. As he turned it over, he noticed the same symbol from Katheryn's letter, to Aloria, he had stuffed in his boot. It was still sealed. He slid his finger underneath the crest. Breaking it easily, he unfolded the letter and read:

*Bogheim, my love,*

*If you are reading this letter, then I am no longer amongst these lands. In the occurrence I had to leave you, I have written this letter for safe keeping until you came of age. You, my little bird, possess the ancient blood. The birth of you and your twin brother, Korian, were not sanctified within the confines of a proper, Borgorian matrimony. You both share my blood, but in my womb, you and Korian were planted from two, different seeds.*

*During birth, Korian was posterior first. After long hours of labour, I could not push any longer. You, my strong one, saved my life. The midwife spoke, when Korian at last appeared, your hand was on the top of his head, helping guide him forth. I know you are meant for greatness, whether it requires physical strength or mental endurance, your life is blessed by the power of the old ones.*

*Do not fear being unlike Korian's father, Gornya, for it is not his blood that dominates your veins. Your blood feeds off of the connection with Aloria, knowledge and a lust for answers, and the Other, physical and mental fortitude, a primordial strength in a direct connection to the vitality of All.*

*Follow the light, but do not trust easily. If you come across a hindrance, climb high or dig deep, but never loose sight of your own heart.*

*My Beloved, I am always with you.*

A shock of disbelief shuddered through his entire body. *My blood father is not Gornya?* Without hesitation, he retrieved the letter he had found in Aloria's chamber. Folding it alongside the letter from his mother, he stuck it back into his boot and tied his laces tighter. *How could I have not received this before now?* He had so many questions, but even fewer answers. A sudden crash startled him from beyond his thoughts and he jerked his head around to see Zalana peering out from behind a couple boards of wood.

"How long have you been down here?" Bog boldly inquired.

"I apologize. I did not mean to startle you. I have not been here for terribly long, but I noticed you were reading. I chose to wait until the opportune moment. It appeared intimate." She feigned a timid smile, bowing her head briefly.

Her glimpse at his boot did not go unnoticed. Clearing his throat, he replied, "Aye, it was nothing."

He closed the chest and placed it back in the corner. Moving around some of the items, he could feel her eyes baring into his backside as he passed her, still examining the possible materials for Aloria's encasement. Oddly, her presence made him leery as it had never done before.

She followed quietly behind.

Peering over his shoulder in her direction, he pointed to a stack of sturdy, thick boards. "I'm going to use the thick boards. I think I saw a few, used sheets of glass closer to the door. Could you retrieve them?" She had moved so close, he could feel the warmth of her body. Suddenly, her hand caressed his left wing.

"Such beautiful wings," she spoke softly, "more radiant than any of your kin."

He turned and glared at Zalana. He had never noticed the severity of her dark brown eyes. They appeared nearly black.

"Can I have one of your feathers?" She grinned sweetly, her big eyes fluttering.

He slightly gawked, disgusted at the proposal. Stumbling back, he turning his wings away from her hand. "I appreciate your compliment. However, they are as much a part of me as the hairs on my head. To pull them ajar would be an unnecessary moment of irritation. I prefer to let them be."

Clearly disappointed, her intentions became apparent. She moved a hand to his chest. She was a tall creatural, only half a head shorter than himself. As he slowly backed into a pile of old linens, she nearly stumbled into his lap.

"I have admired you greatly since I laid eyes on you on board the ship," she purred seductively.

He could smell the sweet lavender of her hair from a recent washing, but there was a slight, putrid scent wafting against his nose like a foul aftertaste. Recognition danced through his memory, but he could not pinpoint where he had smelled it before. He pushed her away carefully, but assertively. "I…I must begin the encasement," he stuttered. At the moment he spoke, he thought he saw a brief spark of madness in the depths of her eyes. However, as quickly as it appeared, it was extinguished.

She smiled and backed away. "I understand," she replied in a coy manner. "I am terribly embarrassed."

*Right.* Then, Bog forced out the words, "Do not be, it is I who is embarrassed. A beautiful being at my disposal and my mind is preoccupied with work." He cleared his throat again and scratched his neck nervously.

## The Keeper

"Charm has never been my forte." While he had not been void of affection for another, he did not actively seek it like his brother had done on a regular basis. *Then, there was the instance with Katheryn.* He shook his head, grabbed the large pieces of thick wood, and walked back through the room to where he saw the glass.

She cut her eyes in his direction.

Before she could speak, they heard a muffled voice, "Bog?"

Without hesitation, he yelled back, "Aye!" Disapproval donned over Zalana's face as he smiled anxiously.

Mora opened the very creaky door. Curiously, he wondered, *how in the curse of the gods did Zalana come through the door without making a sound?* Lifting the boards over his head, he peered up, and his eyes met Mora's reddened ones, enhancing the rich green of her eyes. He noticed she had changed from her black tunic to an evergreen one, cinched at the waist with the belt he had gifted her for her sheath. She wore form-fitting, brown breeches and cleaned boots. Falling over her shoulder, the mass of curls had been washed and left to dry naturally. *I've never seen her hair like that.* His heart fluttered.

"I have heard the news," she spoke fretfully, glancing toward Zalana, and then back at Bog. "What are you doing down in the cellars?"

Immediately, he propped the wood against the wall and stepped back to grab the long sheets of glass, hauling them over the rubble. "I am building an encasement to place Aloria in promptly. I fear Korian may hold true to his words and have me exiled by tomorrow night. Zalana offered her services." He placed the glass alongside the wood. There was an awkward silence. Glancing at Mora, he suspected she could see the anxiety in his grin.

Uncomfortably, she moved to help him with his task, asking with reticence, "Where do you want to transfer the glass?"

Surprised by her question, he placed his hands on his hips, his breathing unsteady. "In my workshop, up the stairs and to the left of the Great Hall."

She nodded. Half grinning at Zalana, she awkwardly picked up a sheet of the glass.

Zalana stood still, eyeing the activity of the room until she nodded and took leave without a word. Silently, she ascended the staircase.

### The Keeper

He watched her eventually disappear from view. *That is awkward. Surely it isn't because I denied her affections.* Suddenly, he felt Mora's hand grab his arm, the magnitude of their touch becoming more intense. He turned around to see her wide-eyed, the glass propped against the wall once again.

"There is something more," she whispered, the desperate tone raising silent alarm.

He could feel her grip tightening.

"My bow and quiver," she paused, "they have been stolen."

A tinge of fear resonated on his skin. "Stolen?" Lifting his arms over his head, he interlaced his fingers behind his neck and reached into his mind. *Who would have known about the bow and quiver apart from their own company?* An unusual darkness encompassed the room. "You must leave me alone with my thoughts and go to Aloria's chamber. Stay with her. I must contemplate on this grave revelation while I work quickly to assure she will have a proper burial." Tucking her hair behind her ear, he tried to sound reassuring and confident, "We'll find them, Sunshine."

With the affectionate touch of his fingers brushing her ear, Mora didn't know how to respond, but she nodded and half grinned before ascending the stairs, two at a time.

He watched her leave the room before he sighed and felt for the folded parchments he placed in his boot. Satisfied, he inhaled as the lingering lavender scent faded. Then, he picked up the sheets of glass and started ascending toward his workshop.

# Desperation

*A cloaked figure moved in the snow-filled darkness. The full moon rose in a cloud of gray and indigo mist. It was bitterly cold. The trees were a black silhouette against the brightness of the all-seeing orb. The cloaked figure moved with authority, treading heavily over the thick snow. On his hand was a wide, silver ring, laden with an unfamiliar crest and violet gems. It glistened in the moonlight, contrasting brightly against the blackness of the cloak.*

Bog awoke with a gasp and a radiating heat lingering in a clammy sweat over his flesh. *What have I just dreamt?* He could only remember the last part of the imagery, but it felt tangible. Shaking his head, he peered around the room. He was in his workshop. A cumbersome piece of work laid on the table behind. It was the glass encasement. He had become weary of the tedious work, drifting to slumber as he drafted the final piece. Standing up, he stretched his back, the cracking of his spine sending a rush of relief through his stiff bones. Rubbing his eyes, he proceeded to examine the encasement. He had worked through the rest of the previous day and all night without interruption. It was complete. The glass intricately covered each side of the encasement, with wood softening the corners. He ran his hand along the smooth glass, reluctant to proceed to Aloria's chamber. However, he knew he must make haste or Gornya may do something with her body without informing him first.

Leaving the room, he walked into the dark hallway. Faintly lit candles atop twisted sconces helped to not overpower the haziness of his drowsy eyes, but it was still difficult to see at this time of the morning. The

## The Keeper

House of Gornya appeared to be asleep. However, he knew the servants would be already awake in the kitchens and underbelly of the chateau to prepare for the day. His breath caught in his throat at the thought that once Aloria succumbs to death, Gornya will hold a council for the future of Loralimira before holding a proper funeral. Although, none of it made sense in his mind. *How did the oldest immortal walking the lands of both the immortal and mortal realms nearly cease to exist only hours after my return? Is it because I did not heed the warnings? And even so, she had sensed it was impending as she spoke to Mora in the meeting room.*

His stomach twisted in knots when he reached her chamber doors. Slowly, he opened the door, expecting to see Mora, but the room was cold and void of anyone else. He cautiously stepped over to the bed, his eyes fixated upon the near-death body of Aloria. The unwelcome voice of Korian echoed in his head, *'Do what you will with the sack of bones, but you will never show your face here again after tomorrow night'*. He leaned closer, examining her face to inspect the sullen emptiness soaking her skin. *She doesn't have long.*

Carefully placing his arms underneath her frail body, he lifted her as though a feather from the ground. As he progressed into the corridor, it had become abnormally frigid, nearly cutting into his warm skin. When he reached his workshop, he stopped harshly in his tracks. Leaning against the encasement was a shadowed figure. He could feel his chest heaving as the air constricted, the tension slicing through the heaviness of the room.

"Who are you?" he breathed in alarm.

"You know who I am," the seductive voice growled.

Bog blinked. The shadow figure manifested into the one entity he never wanted to come face to face with outside of his own imagination.

Ekklips' hand caressed the glass encasement. "Such fine craftsmanship." As a sly smile widened across His face, He tilted His head. "I am here to remove your burden."

Bog glanced down at the figure of Aloria and sputtered, "She is no burden."

Ekklips' onyx eyes glazed with intensity. "You cannot stop it. She is mine now."

A lump stuck in Bog's throat. "You can't. She is the original Messenger of the Gods, and she will return."

Ekklips' grin was as cold and dark as the night of the Winter Solstice. He snarled, "You know not of what you speak. I am *one of the Gods.*" He stepped over the window and peered over the falls. "Regardless, there are secrets your feeble mind cannot comprehend. Vitalis has grown weak. Life without purpose is not worth living and becomes the property of Death. I plan to keep it that way until He surrenders. He can't hide from me forever. I will always find what I seek. Such as I found Solora."

Bog placed Aloria into the encasement, shuddered at His reference to Mora, and turned to face Ekklips. "She is not yours to take." Upon the words, he knew not if he were speaking about Mora or Aloria.

Ekklips smirked. "I take what I want."

The wind's howl lightly kissed Bog's skin as a tear ran mournfully down his face. "What do you want?"

Sauntering to him, Ekklips stared fiercely into his violet eyes. Taking His finger, He began tracing along his chest, directly over his heart. A burning sensation made him flinch and his eyes widened as a molten shape began to appear. *It's the symbol from my dream.*

Ekklips leaned closer and purred low into his ear, "Aye, my valuable gambit."

A spark of realization struck a chord in his memory. *The woods. The hideous monster.*

Breathing on Bog's neck, He ran a thumb over his lower lip and whispered, "I know where the Goddess' weapon is located."

# The Departure

 Mora rubbed her eyes. The past day had been terribly long. Aloria's chamber was cold and the stars still occupied the hint of dawn. The chaise she slept on was not entirely comfortable, but her concerns for Bog caused her the most discomfort. They had risen greatly throughout the night. He was unhappy and unusually agitated. She knew his main emotion spawned from the sudden deterioration of Aloria, but a cloud had settled over the land, an ominous, menacing presence.

She pulled on her heavy, wool cloak and decided to leave the chamber to take care of her personal business. She would return after dawn to Aloria's chamber. Remembering the night's folly, she was pleasantly surprised at Ekklips' absence. Her sleep had remained dreamless since before she boarded the Queen Kalvi. However, a sudden pang of regret made her shudder with uncertainty at the events in which had unfolded only the day before. Recognition of Aloria's ultimate downfall made her heart sink. Yet, she felt more remorse toward Bog than her own sullen emotion. She wanted to try and comfort him, wherever he may be, after she readied herself.

Her chamber had been adjacent to Zalana's. Therefore, she peeked into the room before she walked to her own. A figure lay soundly within a heap of linens on the mattress. Satisfied, she tiptoed through her door, carefully closing it without making a sound. Pouring the cold water into the basin, she splashed her face and rubbed it vigorously. Seeing her reflection in the thin glass above, she decided to braid her hair to the side. Finishing her personal business, she sat on the end of her made bed and contemplated the previous interaction between herself and Zalana. Zalana's behavior in the cellars had been peculiar, considering the circumstances in which had transpired the night before. Bog appeared to be uncomfortable when she arrived, but shortly after, Zalana left without offering to help any further. She tugged at her braid. *Then again, Remmi has remained completely obsolete since our arrival.* She knew not where he bided his time during the day, only observing glimpses of him throughout her own exploration of the expansive chateau. Although, it had been before she discovered her weapon was missing and Bog sent her to Aloria's chamber.

Seeing the dawn awakening, Mora quietly traipsed through the heavy, wooden door into the drafty corridor. Pulling her cloak closer to her body, she proceeded down the hallway toward Aloria's chamber. When she reached the door, she noticed it had been opened. Hurrying inside, she saw the body was gone. Her heart started pounding frantically. Quickly, she hurried to Bog's workshop. Only faint, hazy flames lit the way since the candles had been covered by translucent, violet glass bulbs. They projected an eerie light. *Is it in mourning?*

Vaguely, she could see a subtle glow at the end of the corridor and wondered if he tried to sleep. She had begun worrying about his sanity after watching his interactions with Gornya and Korian since entering Loralimira. *Now that Aloria is gone, what will he do?*

She crept upon the ajar door into his workshop. It was not huge, but the piles of books, wood, and other tools made it appear cramped. A chandelier of candles hung from the ceiling, an obvious Bog-made convenience. Then, she caught her breath when she saw the encasement. Aloria's body had already been placed carefully inside and the glass was sealed shut by thick wood. A smokey vapor leisurely filled the box.

"We must proceed to the caves," Bog gruffly spoke amidst the chaotic rubble.

She glanced around a wall. He sat at an enormous, wooden desk, twiddling with a carved statue of a bird, his cheeks flushed. "Have you not slept all night?"

"I shut my eyes for a moment," he replied grimly without glancing toward her direction.

## The Keeper

"The caves? What leads you to believe we must venture there? You said they were dangerous when I suggested it." She crept closer to the desk.

"Because, I have reason to believe your weapon is down there." Discreetly, he rubbed the burning sensation on the left side of his chest.

*Has he already begun to take Aloria's decline excruciatingly hard?* She asked with reluctance, "What gave you this notion?"

After the silence stretched thin without his response, she shrugged, "If you believe we must, I will follow you."

He nodded slightly, a torment churning inside, but he fervently continued to whittle at the bird.

She tilted her head. His mannerism alarmed her, causing her to wonder what had made him so terribly jaded. He violently carved out the bird's eye until all that was left was a deep hole. The figure looked misshapen and pitiful. "When must we depart?" she finally asked with hesitance.

"At this very moment," he muttered. Rubbing his face, he continued to avert her gaze. His guilt would escalate if he looked into her eyes.

"Make haste now? The light has barely begun to show above the horizon." She glanced at him quizzically.

"Aye, all, save for the high guards and servants in the kitchen, will still be slumbering or readying themselves in their chambers. It will be to our advantage." He placed his tools down. "I have spoken to Remmi. He is aware of the plan and has been making progress himself."

"And Zalana?" She watched his weary hands nervously fidgeting through his hair. *He still hasn't made eye contact.*

"Remmi will partner with her. He has been given specific instructions on our departure. We must trust no one if we are to make it to the caves before midday." Standing, he began pulling books off the shelves.

"Will you not sway to your exhaustion?" She looked around the wall to Aloria's encasing. The older skin appeared sunken in and pasty, not the once radiant creatural she had spoken with only a couple nights before. Between her hands, clasped between her breasts, was a bouquet of exotic flowers. The flowers were a deep violet color with a trim of silver. The pistols were also a radiant silver nestled in petals, encompassing them like a cup. The stems of the flowers donned tiny thorns.

She glanced at Bog. "The flowers, what are they?"

"Alorians," he replied without turning. "Legend speaks of a massive garden, hundreds of acres of Alorians gracing the fields amongst the first walls of Borgoria. The variety of color changes with the seasons. They were grown by Aloria herself. The elders say she placed a drop of her blood on a strand of her hair and buried it deep in the land. She blessed it each day, giving the ground water from the liquid accumulated from the mists of the Falls.

"One day, a sprout grew from the dirt. It was so radiant, the clans named it after her, Aloria. They continue to speak of how the Alorians begun the foundations of Borgoria today - the multitude of sturdy walls, the gorgeous stonework, and the waterfalls. The waters surrounding Loralimira, and the broken islands of Borgoria, are the tears she has shed for the ones lost." Finally, he shifted to peer at Mora.

Shocked, she stared into his vibrant, violet eyes as if they had been strangers. A distance burrowed deep and radiated an intensity she had only seen a few times, but this time they weren't glowing. Despite, a strange knot still tangled in her stomach, similar to the one she felt on the sands of the Nymian Sea when he emerged from the waters. There was never denying how magnificent he was as an immortal being, but she had not considered him more than a friend throughout their time together. However, since the day on the shore, her heart leapt when he looked at her that way. *The same way it does when he calls me Sunshine.*

Blushing, she asked in a puzzled tone, "Why are you staring at me like that?"

He shook his head. "No particular reason." He smiled with caution, the dimple peeking through. "I was just lost in thought."

She nodded slightly and said, "Certainly. I fancy I must go gather my things." She moved to exit the room.

He grabbed her arm gently as a spark of heat shocked his hand. He scrunched his face, knowing she also felt it. "Be furtive, Sunshine. No one must know of our departure."

A shiver ran down her spine when his hand touched her arm and a familiar spark kissed her skin lightly. She flushed, knowing he could see how red her cheeks had become at his touch. "I understand," she agreed and hastily left the workshop.

Walking down the corridor, Mora felt a sense of reluctance. A feeling of apprehension overcame her body. There was a surreal movement within the air she was not fond of, nor did she know where it was radiating. Once she reached her door, she peered around at her surroundings before entering. Cautiously, she turned the wooden latch and stepped lightly. Shedding her cloak, which had been a gift left for her in the chamber upon her arrival, she quickly secured a harness and her belt before fastening her traveling cloak over her shoulders.

When she reached for her knapsack, a slight breeze blew in from the window, sounding of whispers. She paused briefly in alarm and listened with silent intent. When everything stayed quiet, she swiftly stepped back through the door. However, a slight movement in the corner of the corridor startled her enough to cause her to jump backward. Heavy, muffled footsteps shuffled close and resonated in her ears as loud as her beating heart. The crystal blue eyes of Remmi illuminated. Words choked in her throat, but Remmi shook his head and flashed the hard, smooth piece of metal from the sword he held at the ready. She closed her hand on the cold hilt of her sheathed dagger. He nodded to her, moved back into the shadows at the entrance of Zalana's side door, and disappeared. Disconcertingly, she turned on her heel and paced back through the surrounding bleakness, set upon finding Bog with urgency.

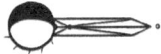

*What lie ahead for them both? Have I chosen the right path?*
Trying to snap himself out of the haze in which surrounded his thoughts, Bog quickly grabbed his satchel sitting on a nearby chair. He threw the parchments and maps in which he had been studying from the cellars carelessly into the bag, feeling the trickle of sweat running down his face. Blotting the back of his neck with a nearby cloth, he walked up to Aloria's encasement. He not dare open it. He had lit one of her feathers and placed it inside the glass. He hoped it would stimulate her heart to beat longer to find Life. The flowers were enough to preserve what little dignity

## The Keeper

Ekklips was allowing. The sun was rising quickly. He and Mora must hurriedly venture to the caves, or else he would loose everything he held most dear. He had a plan, but feared the outcome.

Moving to pull a single page from his desk, something fell off, shattering at its immediate impact on the stone floor. The noise was startling. Kneeling down on the ground, he peered closer at the glass shards. Lying peacefully amongst each little shard was a pinch of sand. Buried in the sand was a piece of parchment. He carefully picked up the tiny piece and began to open the intricately folded design. Inside, there was a handwritten inscription. Holding it under a magnifying glass, he arranged the inscription in his head. Finally, it translated from the old tongue:

> *You cannot escape Time. Time is continual. It neither has a beginning, nor an end. Time existed before the flesh, Time will exist after. For even though it is infinite, does not mean it forgoes its purpose. Sound does not fail to exist when there are no ears to listen. He who fails to recognize the divine power of Time will reap the consequences of Death without Life. He who succeeds in recognizing the authority of Time will sow the opportunities of Life with Death, and Life beyond Death. Although, like the wind, Time is a fleeting essence; but embrace it, and you will hold the energy of the infinite.*

He contemplated on the message for a moment. *Time.* He had never given much thought to the concept of time and its significance before and after death. He merely knew immortality reeked with indignation at the mention of time, for time was a wasteful subject. *What is time? Who is Time?*

He carefully folded the piece of parchment, anxious the concept would prove to be an ironic hindrance to his purpose. To stop and reflect on time would be a waste of his time at the moment. Mora would be on her way to the side of the chateau before himself if he did not follow through on his purpose. Therefore, carefully avoiding the sharp, glass shards, he stepped around the broken object and reached for the low burning candle on the desk. Securing the Cau'o'tas axe he acquired from the Ura territory onto his belt, he laid a hand on Aloria's encasing before he stepped to the door. Watching for movement within the corridor, he eventually stepped into the drafty darkness. The only visibility provided was from the light emitted by the flames inside the bulbs of violet, bouncing off the wall an arm's length in front of his path. The burn on his chest commenced to tingle slightly. Not knowing if Ekklips' presence had been completely tangible, or a projected figure from his lack of proper sleep, he could feel the shadows mocking him as he passed.

# In the Shadows

Staying in the shadows, Bog traipsed cautiously into the entry way of the chateau's lower, outside corridor. He knew there would be limited sentry on the exterior of the back wall between the east and west gardens because of the falls. Only a few footsteps on the pathway, and a poor being would slip into the rushing waters of the turbulent tides. Sentry were placed high above to monitor the side if ever someone tried, but over the thousands of years in the chateau, there had only been two attempts on the cliffs. Both, of which, had been very unsuccessful.

Dawn was already waking the world. He could see a sentry above, knowing in moments he would be relieved and another would step onto the stone precipice. Bog had extinguished his candle some footfalls before the arches. However, faint steps could be heard from behind. He tucked himself into a long niche in the corner and waited. A cloaked figure approached. He could tell by the stature who was concealed underneath. Quietly, as not to startle her, he slid from the niche. Mora still leapt silently away from where he emerged, but did not scream. He nodded in reassurance to her and she gestured the same. Together, they crept from the entry, onto the stone pathway at the lower side toward the falls.

Remaining close to the wall, he could feel his heart pounding against his chest and loudly in his ears. It was vibrating his body so fiercely, he would be surprised if Mora could not feel it also. Once on the pathway, there was no turning back. The falls roared loudly and the force of the waters could be felt on his body only a few steps back. The water droplets began to penetrate his breeches and accumulate on his face. Glancing back at Mora, he saw she kept her eyes turned down toward her feet, watching each careful footfall. The small, stone pathway was narrow and long. According to his calculations, they would make it to the caves before noon day, in spite of their descent into the encroaching darkness.

Wiping the water from his eyes, the path in front of them became narrower and the stones were more saturated. *I knew this path would not be easy.* Carefully, he stepped, scooting each foot a little further across the broken stones. He held his breath and grasped her hand tightly. He could feel the exchange of tension within her warm palms. Straining, he glanced further down. There were a few gaps in between stepping stones. However, the leftover planks remained large enough for two beings to rest before advancing. Stepping high, he slowly moved forward. As his boot came down, a rock broke from beneath his heel. Stumbling, he quickly adjusted his footing. The blood quickly drained from his face and he backed against the wall, nearly succumbing to the fright of falling...*and failing.* His wings would not even be of use due to the overwhelming weight of water.

Her fingernails cut deep into his skin. Prying them away in order to adjust himself on the ledge, he flinched as they retracted from his flesh. Finally composed, he peered into her eyes and pulled her quickly to his chest. Mortified the whole side would give way, they both froze. Then, without wasting anymore time, he gathered himself once more to step onto the next, protruding stone. The act began to feel familiar, as it was similar to their advancement of the Staggering Stones. He continued to pull she swiftly toward him, grasping her body hard against his own each time. At last, they reached the last platform of stone and he forced her first onto the continuing pathway. Stepping harshly from the end of the trail, he felt the stone give way and crash into the heavy cliffs below. Although he breathed a sigh of relief, he could not force himself to glance back at the gaping hole. The possibility of glimpsing the unforgivable destruction lying below their feet was unfathomable.

They continued to trek lightly on the stones, their bodies guarded against the shadow of the great wall. Bog could see the sloping of the gigantic staircase leading into the west garden of the chateau. He knew they were reaching a point in which they would have limited concealment.

## The Keeper

Glancing up, he could see a sentry pacing back and forth on the edge of the staircase high above. Breathing deeply, he continued to crouch low beneath the sloping shadow of the wall. As they crept closer to the last, several steps, he listened for movement.

As a borgling, he would climb down the opposite, less concealed pathway and hide against the wall, listening for his father's encroaching footsteps. Once his father approached, Bog would hold his breath and close his eyes, hoping if he could not see his father, his father would not be able to see him either. *A borgling's fantasy*, he scolded. For his father would stand at the edge of the step, high and mighty, and glare over the ledge. Blindly, Bog would feel a large hand grasp the nape of his neck, hoist him to eye level, and hold his body high in the air, dangling his feet over the falls. Gornya would proceed to threaten to drop him into the roaring waters of the falls if Bog continued to defy his authority. Cowering back to the chateau, Bog would be forced to work the prisons of Loralimira as punishment. He had always dreamed of running away. However, as he became of age, his father grew tired of the sight of him and allowed him to stay concealed in the shadows of the libraries and his studies, unless it was on the days he was forced to partake in combative training. On those days, Gornya found pleasure it the acts of malice and hatred between Bog and Korian.

He sneered.

Fortunately, Bog knew the grounds. He had created maps of the cliffs and pathways around the falls. Just beyond the staircase, toward the water, was another narrow trail. He had never actually ventured into the caves, though. Therefore, while he knew not where they ultimately led, he did know all the entrances around the House of Gornya. He would stand on the edge of the waterfalls watching birds and bats fly from behind the rushing waters. The path they tread should lead away from the abyss of the main falls and into an underground river.

*The most difficult part will be remaining shrouded from the bottom of the staircase, to the beginning of the narrow path.* Cautiously, he stood higher against the wall, peering over the side. Movement was his only ally. When he saw a sentry turn to pace in the opposite direction, he quickly retracted his head. Breathing deeply, he glanced over at Mora. Solemnly, she peered from beneath the hood of her cloak, her trustful eyes

## The Keeper

a piercing green. His stomach tumbled. *I will not deliver her to the hands of Death.* Listening carefully, he hoped to catch the brief sound of the sentry's fading footfall. Eventually the slow shuffle appeared to dwindle. Peering back over the edge of the wall, he could vaguely distinguish the back of the sentry. Seizing the opportunity, he grabbed Mora's hand and pulled her passed the bottom of the garden staircase silently.

Their brief exposure caused no alarm. When they reached the beginning of the descending passage, he kept a heavy grasp on her hand, leading her far enough down the cliff so as not to be seen by the returning guard. He felt the rushing water rumbling the ground beneath his boots. Just beyond the ledge of the next descending staircase were the mighty falls of crushing waters. *We must be careful, the ground is wet and slippery,* he pleaded in his mind. *If I were to loose my footing, Mora will follow, hopelessly lost in what lay beneath.* As the wind whipped his curly, blond hair, he descended further, clutching the side for any object to take hold. Breathing deep, he knew not how long they would tread this course, but he knew by the looming darkness of the caves, their descent would rapidly become more difficult.

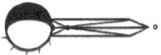

Mora could feel the heavy water droplets prick her skin like little needles. Her thoughts had consumed her since she left the room, barely noticing what was occurring around her, and aimlessly allowing Bog to guide her along the trails. Her mind echoed more loudly than the majestic falls which were slowly devouring their descent. However, the force of the falls was almost too overwhelming as she hugged the wet stones. *Does Bog know where he is going? Or is he as lost as I, faltered by the darkness that is consuming us both?*

After what felt like an eternity behind the falls, he turned to her and held up a hand. She saw his arm disappear into a niche in the stone. Without hesitation, he walked into the dank and dark alcove. He had only advanced about fifteen paces when she could make out the abstract shape of his form returning. Fighting the water falling into her eyes, she realized he had tried to speak to her through the deafening roar. She looked him desperately in the eyes and shook her head in confusion, shrugging her shoulders.

He yelled louder, "We will post here for the time being! We do not need to be hindered by fatigue as we enter the caves! We are nearly to the bottom! Eventually, we will not be able to distinguish between day or night!"

She acquiesced and followed him into the cavity of stone. The rest would be highly welcomed after the previous, troubled night, her eyes already feeling heavy from the exertion and lack of restful sleep in Aloria's chamber. The stone floor was wet with puddles accumulating sporadically throughout the alcove. Bog pointed at the wall. Blindly, she felt her way in his direction. He guided her hands to another small, tight crevice, barely big enough for a body to fit comfortably. She felt him boost her into the nook. *Where will he rest?* She could not discern where he turned to go, but her eyes fluttered with a heavy weariness, Unbeknownst to her senses, she drifted into the abyss of an agitated slumber.

After what seemed only a brief moment of time, she surprisingly opened her eyes. However, it was difficult to determine since her surroundings were in complete darkness. Nestled in the crevice, she began to hear a faint drip of water commence from behind her head. Reaching her arm in the direction of the drip, she realized the wall was absent. An undeniable curiosity festered in her mind. She began to scoot her body further into the crevice until her leg dropped out of the other side. Knowing not what lay upon the edge, she suddenly felt a calming sense of affirmation no harm would come. Her feet aimlessly reached for a floor. Finally, her boots hit the hard stone and she shimmied herself down from the crevice.

Turning around, tiny pinpoints of light began to appear in a circular wave of motion around the room. The chamber was very small in diameter. The furthest pinpoint of light across from where she stood seemed only two body lengths, but she knew it could be a trick of the eye and dared not move. Subconsciously, a sensation warned she should take no further steps to discover the accuracy of her theory. Frozen against the wall, she watched as more lights filled the chamber. Because it looked like the night sky, it both calmed and elated her soul. A brilliant array of hues illuminated: reds, violets, greens, blues, gold, and silver. She carefully turned to look closer at the wall to her side. Radiant crystals roughly stuck out from the dull stone. She attempted to remove one, but it was tightly wedged between others. Smiling at the gorgeous array of gems, the beauty was overwhelming and it caused her chest to flutter.

"Do you believe in your dreams?" a voice echoed off the walls of the chamber.

Startled, she straightened her back, pushing further against the wall. "I do not know," she responded timidly.

"Do they appear tangible? Or merely conceptual?" the bodiless voice spoke again.

She thought for a moment. While she neither felt threatened, nor alarmed, she responded reluctantly, "A mixture, I suppose." She continued to peer around the dimly lit chamber for the source of the voice. "They are ambiguous. I feel I am a part of a horrendously perplexing labyrinth of emotional and mental states. A puppet, if you will, caught on a string; controlled not only by one, but by whomever takes the strings at the current moment in time. I am beginning to feel I know not what is real anymore."

"Could they not both be real?" the voice spoke without much inflection. "Are you not able to touch the walls around you? Do you not feel the draft on your skin?"

"Aye, but there have also been times in which my body has not been removed from whence it slumbers," she stuttered, shifting her feet, "as though a waking dream inside my subconscious. Tell me, who inquires?"

"Friends," the voice replied.

"I have been told to be leery of even those closest to me. Why must I treat a faceless voice any differently?" She waited for an answer, but it took several moments.

"You cannot," the voice strongly confirmed. "However, if we were your enemy, you would have been dead the moment you stepped foot into the chamber. Witness."

Upon the last word, a bulb of light ignited in the middle of the chamber at Mora's eye level. She gazed at it with curiosity, watching it turn around and around slowly, giving off no heat. It dropped, and with it, her gaze followed. She could feel her stomach lurch into her chest as she watched the ball of light drop rapidly down a long shaft, the edge only a foot's length from the toe of her boots. Lightheaded, she did not continue to watch it fall aimlessly beneath the blanket of darkness. Clutching tighter to the wall behind, she swallowed a bulk of cold air, keeping the bile in her throat from rising any further. Then, she remembered the sensation she had when she entered the chamber telling her to go no further, for she would not be harmed.

"Frightened you may be, but harmed, you are not."

She was able to coax her shaky voice from of her mouth, "And with whom do I have the pleasure of thanking for this dubious gesture?"

There was a slow rumble of laughter. "Dear one, we have had the pleasure of speaking before. Do you not remember your feeble attempt to converse in the woods before tripping over your own two feet?"

She was not amused by the voice's sardonic implications toward her clumsiness, but a memory sparked deep within her mind, *the Guardians?*

"Aye," the voice responded to the words not spoken aloud, "you summoned us."

"There are more than your own here?" she inquired.

"There are four of us, and four of us have spoken."

She shook her head. "But you sound as if you are one."

"We are one in spirit," the Guardians' voices resonated around the chamber.

"How did I summon you?" she pleaded. "Apparently, this is not the first time I have unknowingly summoned something. How do I control it if I do not know the various means in which I communicate to the world around me? Much less that which is in my mind?"

"You need to learn to control your mind, knowing it has the potential to become a world of its own entirety if you allow it. Your journey is not an easy task. It is about listening and learning. For each time you can become stronger in this world, the more prepared you will be as you become engulfed in the other. Do not tread lightly on the gaining of knowledge, for it will ultimately accumulate into tasks which cannot be easily solved."

"For whom do you serve?" she asked reverently.

"We serve the Shadow King," the voice answered.

"Can I speak with them?"

"The time is not right," the voice seemed to be gradually fading. "If that is all you inquire, we will take our leave, for we do not desire to meddle with the delicate webs of worldly affairs too often."

"Wait! I am not sure of the path I must take from here," she shouted and slunk her shoulders in defeat.

"You will decide and choose. No one, but you, can choose. Be leery, you are not here by the innocence of chance." The voice disappeared into the darkness, and with it, the pinpointed lights of crystals in the chamber. The sound of the rushing falls echoed again off the cave walls.

Turning around, she wondered how she would pull herself up to the crevice in which she had emerged. Cautiously, she reached as high as she could, grabbing onto a handful of rock. Lifting herself with control, she continued reaching up to the nook's ledge. Unexpectedly, the stone her foot had been positioned gave way and she dangled in the darkness. Hardly able to hold on, she knew she could not risk letting go, for the ledge above the shaft was not wide. She yelled despite the roaring falls and struggled hastily to gain her footing. Her hand grew tired and her head grew light. She could feel her fingertips starting to tingle, as if someone were poking her with small needles a thousand times over. But as she felt her grip loosen, a hand grabbed her wrist. Slowly, she could feel the spark between the grip tightening around her flesh.

*Bog*, she thought as her heart skipped.

Crawling through the crack with Bog's guidance, she fell into his strong arms on the other side. Setting her down on her feet, he towered before her with a faint light from a lantern on his face, a pack slung low on his hip.

He furrowed his eyebrows, curious as to where she had been. Reluctantly letting go of her hand, he decided it would not be the time or place to inquire. Therefore, he turned to silently make his way toward the front of the niche.

"Bog?" She called out, surprised he did not ask her where she had been. Also curious as to where he had gone after helping her into the crevice, she began to wonder what burden was weighing most heavily on his shoulders. He had been acting very uncharacteristic since they departed for the falls.

## The Keeper

He peered back through the mist swirling around the lantern light. "Aye?"

"Have you heard of the Guardians?"

He paused for a moment. He knew of whom she referred. They had specifically spoken to him in the woods about protecting The Keeper, and then possibly again on the Queen Kalvi with a warning he did not heed before he was attacked by the hideous monster. Then, he thought about the Whispering Wind. Nevertheless, he had become irritated with bodiless spirits demanding his attention and speaking in unfinished, elusive details.

Nodding, he asked, "Why? Have you had an experience?"

She thoughtfully nodded her head, thinking about her previous interaction.

He stepped closer. "What did they say?"

She squinted through the drops accumulating on her eyelashes. "They told me I summoned them, that I need to learn to control my mind and become more receptive to knowledge. But they said they work for the Shadow King and," she scrunched her nose, "I am not here by the innocence of chance."

Contemplating the words for a moment, Bog grunted and anxiously ran a hand through his wet hair before turning around and continuing the descent.

*Odd,* she thought. Frustrated at the distance he was exhibiting, she followed him from the niche and continued descended behind the ravaging falls.

# Approaching Darkness

An ominous presence engrossed both their minds. The caves were bitterly cold and dark. Bog stepped down the last few stones, feeling his way through what appeared little depressions alternating through each crevice like bottomless black holes. The lantern's light was almost swallowed by the abysmal surroundings. The cave itself looked as if it was a void. He dared not think of what lay in the corners of the cold, lifeless rock.

"Are you ready?" he asked in a clear, deep voice.

"Aye," she responded quietly.

Mora had been consciously attempting to bar her mind from anything but her own thoughts. However, it burned deeply as if someone had set a fire raging out of control. Trying to hinder its growth, she could feel Ekklips fighting against her, fiercely prying at the door of her mind. Overwhelming dread of failure and death filled her thoughts, growing greater with every moment that passed.

"Stay close," he grumbled.

She knew he was right, but fear and resentment toward her task was always at the forefront of her mind. Smiling lightly, they entered into a limitless cavern. Knowing not what lie ahead was the most daunting part of her continuous thoughts. They were constantly replaying the events which led them to venture beneath the northernmost part of one of the largest oceans. Since Lychinus, she had only known peace for a brief part of their journey. Bog had felt positive she was the one he searched for, but she

**The Keeper**

began to doubt his certainty. Chaos had followed her everywhere since departing from the sanctuary where she had lived a melancholy life with her mother. Ekklips, like Bog, had attempted to convince her of a divinity she had little belief was the truth. She believed her entire existence had became a deliriously meaningless pantomime, a farce for the entertainment of cruel deities, and a pathetic excuse of life with dire consequences. Many had already died, cities had fallen, and the answers she had been given were far from pragmatic. Aloria had given her a lovely story, but highly questioned the certainty she was presently anything but...*Mora, daughter of Meridan.* Then, there was Bog's sudden, hostile demeanor. It unnerved her the most because he had been the one anchor she trusted to hold her down, tolerate her skepticism, make her smile despite the circumstance, comfort her fallibilities, and merely be there for her when she needed. She had never had a friend outside her mother, but she had never doubted the stability of their friendship.

*Until...now. Did I place too much blind trust in him and not in my own ability to survive?*

The light they carried was small compared to the malevolence and magnitude of the cavern walls. The reflection did not extend nearly enough to reveal but a few paces ahead, and the stones were exceptionally slippery. Every step had to be full of caution. In spite of her feelings about his behavior, she followed his every step exactly.

*The mountain terrain has been a long, hard road, yet does not compare to the path that lay in front of us now,* she huffed. *Step by step seems to bring us further into the depths of disparity than I could have ever been able to imagine.* A feeling of hopelessness descended upon her conscious. *Where has Nephani gone?* She had not heard it since after she wept on the lower deck of the Queen Kalvi next to the comforting muzzle of Sun Shadow.

She sighed, *Sun Shadow.* Tears burned her eyes.

Then, she remembered Nephani's voice had once spoken of two choices. Regardless, what resonated the deepest was when it said, *Your inhibited nature is a weapon against Life, and is meant to be unleashed in time.* She shuddered.

Suddenly, Bog caught her arm. Forcing her out of her wandering state, she glimpsed at him through the darkness, fear magnifying in his

534

face. He shoved her body against the side of the cave wall, pressing his own to her and extending his wings. Remembering he had used his wings to conceal her before, she listened carefully. Out of the abyss, she could hear footsteps. They were brisk and heavy, with a sense of urgency.

He pressed deeper and whispered in her ear, "Be still."

His breath was warm and his voice bounced around in her head like a faint drumming. Her skin was covered in tiny bumps. The air was heavy and constricting. They were intimately close. She could feel the warmth of his skin through her tunic as if lightning were radiating between their bodies, her chest rising and falling against his exposed skin. A growl vibrated in her mind, but she knew it had not come from Bog.

The low sound of Bog's breath quickened. Appearing out of the depths, he could see the illumination of several, small pinpoints of light, hastening in speed.

A voice broke through the silence, "What do you think he wants us to do when we get there?"

"Kill 'em all He says," was spoken by a second, rougher voice.

"But how we 'posed to do that? They's got that thing with them."

Illuminated by the little flecks of light, the figures arose from the darkness. The light was attached to their ears, blazing as if the skin was on fire at the point. The tips were several lengths longer than the tops of their heads. The faces of the monsters were disgustingly distorted and twisted. Their eyes were completely black with horrible white slits. With crooked mouths full of sharp teeth, saliva dripped freely down their chins. Attached to their heads, were grotesquely wide rings of skin posing as a neck. Their bodies, though covered by armor, were just as mangled, reflecting a slimy film which created a disturbing squishy noise as they tread heavily across the sharp stones.

"That 'thing' won't hold up for long if they don't knows we comin'. We take the base out and we's can go on ours way. If they come after us, we's will kill 'em all." The rougher voice laughed.

Shifting her hands onto Bog's chest, Mora looked into his wet face, his violet eyes stern with a flicker of nervousness. The skin over his heart was scalding, much warmer than the rest of his flesh, and she had wondered why since she had felt it on the Nymian coast. Drops of water trickled down his cheeks and lips, making him faintly glisten more than his flesh already did. As if she had no control, she moved her hand closer to his neck and sensed a tension tighten in his muscles. The hand encompassing her waist pulled her closer against his body, the other on the cave wall brushed her hip. Gazing into his eyes, she could feel the growing closeness of their faces.

Bog closed his eyes, feeling the heat radiating from her proximity excite his senses. The flesh over his heart seared as she lightly moved her hand over his chest, her fingertips brushing against his neck. He was desperately trying not to move and take her into his arms. *Fuck. If I don't move soon, she will realize my intentions.* Leaning over, he fought the urge to kiss her wet, pink lips. A flame ripped through his veins and tightened in his neck. He had never wanted anything more in his entire life. However, he knew the consequences.

Darting his gaze toward the monsters, he saw them disappear and immediately retracted his wings. Realizing how close their faces had come, his lips grazed her own when he murmured, "We must make haste, Sunshine." Moving away from her body, his hand slid over her waist, the desire to linger almost too much for him to bear. His fingers stalled only a moment before he grinned and ran them through his hair.

Her body ached for his closeness, his presence becoming a comfort to her flesh. Since standing on the shore of the Nymian Sea, his touch had excited her senses. The sensation was like what she experienced in her dreams with Ekklips; but it was real with Bog and their connection was electrifying.

Calming the fluttering in her chest, she asked, "What were they and do you suppose they are speaking about heading to Loralimira?"

"Grogans, the most heartless of all Ekklips' monsters; if you can say as much. The sentry will not allow them to exit the caves." He grunted and struck the lantern again. Adjusting himself, he clenched his jaw, grabbed her hand, and continued further into the darkness.

Her eyes widened as he guided her along. *That is the first time Bog said Ekklips' name.* Apprehensive, she shut it away for the moment. "Why are they considered such?"

"They will tear the shit out of the living to shreds in mere blinks. The lights on their ears are not only used for light, it is a source of venom. When in battle, they will head butt, or ram with their heads, stabbing their prey with the tips. Within moments, it will paralyze. After their prey is lying helpless on the ground, they will use their teeth to finish their...deed. They are merciless. To stand against one without knowledge of what they are is pure foolishness. Their only weakness is to stab the bubble behind their ears, releasing the venom, and cutting off the lobes. Otherwise, you stand no fucking chance."

"What if someone were paralyzed by the venom and they were able to escape still? Will the effects wear off?"

"That I cannot answer. I have never known anyone to survive a wound inflicted by a Grogan." He held her arm as she stepped over the rocky terrain.

Shaken a bit, she asked, "For whom do you suppose they spoke? Do you presume they could actually leave the caves?"

"I know not. The darkness is His territory though, no matter where it is, and He has certainly sent a multitude of monsters to scope out what may approach the shadows." Looking at her, he added in a low tone, "But you know, He is not the only one within these caves who has the potential to sense and see things others cannot."

Frustrated, because she knew he would never understand, she sighed deeply. "Bog, you know it feels tangible, or a memory. When it is a part of my waking dreams, my body is a physical acting part of my mind. I have not been able to control what I see or what I sense. I don't even know if it's possible. If I sense anything while awake, it is only Ekklips whom I can feel. And I'm starting to feel like it is only when He wills it, as though a defense tactic against my knowledge of His plans."

Mora stared into the unknown. *Bog, along with the others, does not understand the turmoil I feel. As of recently, the two worlds have become intermingled, causing more confusion and uncertainty. It's as if I am skipping on slippery stones between dreams. Which one am I currently living in? Ekklips consumes my thoughts.* She felt for the key around her neck. *However, I know in the midst of my struggles, I have been able to keep my promise to Nephani safe. Curiously though, it does not appear around my neck in my dreams. The weight is lifted...and the anxiety with it.*

She glanced at Bog and smiled uncomfortably.

"It will come upon you when you least expect it, an answer out of the darkness will become enlightened. You have not yet trusted in your

## The Keeper

True Being. Once you realize why it must be you, you will become aware of the task at hand. For now, I trust in you. I will follow to the death." He watched her hand caress the key. *A burden in itself.*

Her heart sank. *Nay, I will not allow you to die at my expense.*

Although it was difficult to see his expression clearly, it was not merely the weight of the dark pushing upon his shoulders. While she could sense the heaviness in his movements and tone of voice, her own distress was increasing with each and every step through the uncertainty. The caves would test their mental strength, along with their physical, more than the journey they had traveled thus far.

Bog watched her face, wondering whether her trust in him was wavering. *I will walk into the flames with her, despite the outcome.* He shivered, not from cold, but from the thought of what awaited them. Then, he mumbled frankly, "Trust me, Sunshine."

They scurried further into the darkness like rats in a corner, the terrain becoming more tumultuous the further they climbed through the caves. There was not much light, save the lantern Bog held. His clumsy, large boots made it hard for him to climb over each developing rock quarry, but he tried not to show it.

Mora could feel the sharp edges tearing at the leather on the bottom of her boots. *Soon,* she thought, *there will be nothing left to guard my soles from the surface of the stones.*

Still, they kept moving.

Then, out of the darkness, there arose a murmuring. It resonated like a tiny song, hauntingly echoing off the cavern walls. She marveled at the appearance of a multitude of speckled lights floating above. Approaching closer to the lights, mesmerized by the intensity, she heard Bog gasp as he jerked her elbow. Catching her breath, she listened as a rock fell deep into a chasm, hitting stone for stone on the way down, and ending in a muffled splash. Trying to swallow the lump in her throat, she realized how mesmerized she had been when she squinted below. The tiny lights reflected enough of the cavern to reveal an illuminated ring at the top edge of a formidable abyss.

A quick glance, and she saw Bog kneeling to her left, clutching the large stones around him, examining the path around the void as his chest heaved in and out, his wings rustling from the drafty air. Her momentary lapse of judgment sent her shifting quickly to his side, but as she moved her body toward his direction, the multitude of lights ascended with a billowing force.

Immediately, he outstretched a hand toward her and yelled, "Don't move!"

As he rose to grasp her hand, the wind swept her forcefully off her feet. Her screams were silenced when her head fell against the edge of a stone. To his horror, her body hung unconsciously suspended over the enormous pit.

# Ever-burning Fire

Day had not yet broken. The night squeezed the sky tightly inside its darkest robe. Tiny stars glistened happily. Mora could feel her head aching. She rubbed her temples in pressured circles, hoping it would alleviate some of the pain. *But from what?* A distant memory lingered on her mind, heavy with a thirst to emerge, but hesitant to remove itself from its hibernation. She glanced behind, there was nothing. She glanced side to side, but there was still nothing. However, to the front, she saw a crooked flash of light streak maliciously through the air like grotesquely misshapen fingers, followed by the rumble of mighty drums.

Another.

The wind rustled her hair, pulling it behind her ear with the most gentlest of movements. The brief sensation of when her mother would push the hair back behind her ears when she was a childling, tugged at her heart. The tears would flow from her tiny eyes and her mother would say, '*Now my sweet, only the weak worry. But do not fear letting your eye water flow, for when you pass on, the collected waters will wash away your flesh to reveal the true beauty of your soul.*'

The wind continued to caress her hair and the drums persisted. After a moment passed, she began to see a silhouette, a silhouette of an enormous tree against a sliver of light lining the horizon. Unexpectedly, another crash pierced her ears as lightning streaked across the menacing dark, struck forcefully into the tree, and launched ferocious flames high into the contrasting sky. She gasped. Her feet were frozen to the ground, her eyes fixated upon the brilliance of the tendrils of fire. After a moment, she shaded her eyes from the intensity, watching the tree branches closely. There was no acrid rush of smoke. *They are not burning. Nothing is weakening.* The tree stood strong, resisting the urge to collapse under the fierce and whipping fire. Unconsciously, from somewhere deep inside her mind, she realized this was a battle ground for enlightenment. *Is this where they are always searching for me, communicating to me, reaching for me? Is this... The Gateway?* Her blood started boiling. She wanted to scream out, but held her tongue in fear of unwanted ears.

Then, a prickling feeling on the back of her neck told her she was not alone. Squinting around at the landscape, hoping for the familiar presence of Nephani, the air remained bleak and dark save for the oranges and yellows of the fire. Her eyes returned to the source of enormous curiosity, holding her hand level with her face as to deter the luminosity of the sight. Though she stood some distance away, she could feel the flames dancing off the sides of her hand, pulsating through the folds of her palm and fingers. The sensation was enjoyable, and she smiled as the rivers of light ran inside her flesh. For a pleasurable moment, her senses were elated and strengthening. Though, as quickly, and without warning, something happened. Fire whipped through her body like a serpent striking its prey. She felt torn into two beings. Recoiling her hand, she opened her shaky palm as a blue light emerged from her body. Slowly, the light parted from her flesh, stood up, and peered directly into her eyes.

Mora gasped at the reflection. While this had not been the first time she had peered into her own reflection as if it were an entirely different entity, the shock would never cease to make her uneasy, nervous, and not whole. Tucking her hair behind her ear, the reflection followed suit. The sensation was strange and foreign, but familiar, as if she could feel from both sides, yet she was still in her own body. It felt similar to when Nephani had shown her a possible outcome of her choice in the illumination and she saw her reflection with Ekklips. *Or is it a memory?* Regardless, the reflection, like the other, felt sensual and reckless, domineering and transformative, the epitome of strength and resilience. The alluring other self turned, and Mora followed, entranced. However, after walking a few steps, she hit a barrier, a transparent wall in her path.

## The Keeper

The reflection continued sauntering toward the tree, neither halting, nor turning around. She called out, but no sound emerged from her throat. She reached out toward the tree, but immediately retracted as the wall stung her hand, burning her flesh.

Desperate, she watched.

There, within the barrier, the reflection stood solemnly. The blue light illuminated from her body, glowing in brilliance against the tree. Every now and again, the flames would leap from the tree and spark against the blue light, sending a pulse echoing across the surface of the skin and vibrate the ground. Mora could also feel the excitement it provoked. It would prick against her flesh and burn through her luminous veins. Even though she struggled with the initial shocks, she began to yearn for more, an insatiable desire to fill her entire body. Tears fought their way into the corners of her eyes. The growing need for the fire was overwhelming. Then, out of the darkness, she saw a figure approaching, tall and brooding.

As if she floated outside her body, her sight became the eyes of her counterpart and she saw the other clearly. *Ekklips.* She smiled and He returned the gesture. There was a hunger in His eyes, similar to when she saw Him in the Land of Immortals. He was naked, exposing the three, black bands surrounding his forearm beneath His elbow. However, this time, a symbol was burned on the left side of His chest. It was a circle: half moon, half sun. Three lines emerged down, joining at a point, like the end of a sword. A tiny circle floated just beyond the tip. It was not a symbol she had ever seen, but this time, she didn't hesitate to admire His body. *He is flawless.*

Sensually, He took her hand, interlacing their fingers, and pulled her close. She could feel the warmth of His form pressed firmly against her own nakedness. The heat radiated through her body, but she could feel it mainly escalating between her legs, tips of her breasts, and exposed neck. The raw desire to join their flesh was riveting her senses. It was as if she needed Him as much as her body needed food and water.

Then, her heart shuddered. Instantly, as if pulled back by an invisible rope, she became her own flesh once again, standing outside the barrier. She could no longer feel His warmth, His touch, the way she thirsted for His being. Watching the two figures, the flames from the tree began to swallow the trunk, consuming its own core, bark by bark. Naked, they danced in the ever-growing fire, the tendrils whipping fiercely around without burning their essence. The blue light pulsed between the bodies.

Outside, Mora felt a touch upon her shoulder. Startled, her blood boiled. She became frightened. Hesitant, she slowly spun on her heel to reveal no one. Shocked, because it wasn't there before, was a contrasting field of stark white.

"Who is there?" she called out.

No one answered.

Surveying the land in length, and convinced there was no one there, she gazed longingly once again toward the burning tree. Closing her eyes, she focused on the memory of her body engulfed in His embrace. Suddenly, as though here desire was heard, she became the reflection again. Hunger burrowed into Ekklips' eyes, always black as melting onyx. He pulled her closer as His intentions rose. Kissing her gently on the lips, He caressed His hands down the side of her breasts to the small of her back.

He persisted, motivated by the faint wisps of breath escaping her lips as His hands traveled lower.

Passionately kissing Him in return, strengthening her grip on His neck, she felt the incessant need for more coaxing her desires.

He trailed His tongue down her neck while moving His hand between her thighs. He growled at the way her body buckled in His grasp and whispered sinfully in her ear, "Surrender to me, my love."

She arched her back as He reached inside. Wicked vibrations shook the tree, snapping its molten arms on their bodies. Deep inside, she could feel the emotion of the tree. It was angry, projecting a heaviness it had been forsaken. However, this only made her crave His touch with more ferocity. She moved her hips in rhythm with His fingers, His palm placing pressure at the apex of her lust. Sweat trickled down her neck and back from the heat building underneath her flesh. She wanted the moment to last forever. Fervently clinging onto His shoulders, she encouraged His essence.

"Tempting?" an intoxicatingly deep voice mumbled from behind. "Have you missed me, my Light?"

Taken back through the barrier, she whipped her head around, following the sound of the voice. *Nothing.*

From frustration of the bleak, infinite whiteness, or the burning lust within the barrier, she screamed, "What do you want from me?" Her fists curled tighter causing her fingernails to cut through her skin. When the blood hit the ground, it sizzled. Panting, her flesh burned heavy and the heat rose in her head. A dizziness floated behind her eyes.

*The Gateway*, a voice hummed silently.

She pounded her fists hard against the invisible wall. Rippling blue waves bounced around the transparent obstacle every time she beat it. She ignored the tremors of pain every time she made contact. When she knew it would not lessen, she pitifully stared at the tree. Her body was beneath Ekklips' magnificent energy. They were becoming one. She could feel Him sexually pulsating deep within her soul, holding tightly to her flesh as she gave in to His appetite. Then, she pushed her body onto His, her hands around His neck. She ground her hips harder onto His length, His hands holding her figure, guiding her to ride with insurmountable, savage intensity.

An eruption from the tree burst into the dark. It commenced to melt beneath the malicious fire, flooding the ground with lava, encompassing the two essences. Unfazed as the molten began to swallow them, Mora's reflection lifted her hips higher, impaling herself on Him repetitively until she succumbed to the passion between their bodies. Screaming in pleasure, the thin line of the horizon exploded.

Outside the barrier, Mora felt her flesh rip apart in a blissful emission of light.

Within moments of when her body became suspended above the abyss, Bog backed away from the edge. Taking a running start, he tore over the stone and leapt high when his boot hit the ledge of the gorge. Soaring through the air, he grabbed Mora's body, clutching it to his own as he descended onto the other side. When his boots landed on the stone, the cave violently shook beneath his feet. He held her unconscious body against his own to lessen the impact.

## The Keeper

Kneeling with her in his arms, he pushed her hair off her forehead and rattled her cheeks. "Mora! Mora! Wake!"

Her eyes barely opened before the blurred visions became realizations. Feeling like her head split in two, she fiercely sucked in her breath. She could not bear it, the throbbing was horrible. *Surely I have just died, and if not, I yearn to now.* The pain started absorbing through her skin.

"What happened?" she managed to sputter, rubbing her skull hard. She could feel the warmth of blood beneath her fingertips. Finally, Bog's face came into view. The lingering burst of pleasure subsided in her body, leaving only confusion and shame.

"Quickly!" He pleaded in desperation, "Rise to your feet, but stay low!"

There was vaguely any light, but she could gather the faint outlines of his body and the surrounding cavern. Squinting in the direction of what had been the multitude of speckled lights, a grotesquely enormous shadow emerged overhead. Dragon-like, she could see faint, translucent scales accumulating. Each scale was accompanied by a pinpoint of light. Though hard to see, the ripple of lights extended to five, tree-shaped limbs. On the end of each limb, there were two, deadly sharp claws plastered to the cave ceiling. The transparent head stuck out from the center with a mouth that contained hundreds of little sharp fangs, visible on its jaw. Catching her breath, the eyes were the most horrible. They were bright red, burning with twinkles of yellow and orange.

*To look into them,* she thought, *it can sense my soul, invade the depths, and search for a weakness to strike.*

The hideous, nearly transparent, reptilian monster roared as it sensed their presence.

Struck with terror, she glanced over at Bog's face and surveyed the surroundings. There was no obvious sign of an escape. Looking again at the monster, she saw it was starting to rapidly sway back and forth in anger.

*What are you?* She whispered in her mind, *What is your weakness?*

It jolted and jerked its head in her direction as if she had just spoken her thoughts aloud. She saw the faintest hint of satisfaction melt

**545**

over its light-exposed mouth.

*I have no weakness. I am everywhere and everything.*

Gasping, she sucked in the frigid, cavern air. *It cannot be!* At once, as though slapped in the face, she knew there was only one, viable choice. *The only way I am going to find what I seek,* she weighed, *is to give myself to this monster, to succumb to its grasp, and let it take me to where He is waiting.* She knew there were no more secrets. He knew where she stood. This was His darkness. He had shown her as much in her mind.

Commencing to step from her crouched position behind the stone, Bog grabbed her arm tightly, a jolt of heat shooting through both their bodies.

Immediately, she jerked her head toward him, gazed sorrowfully into his eyes, and whispered the best answer she could, "I must."

"Stop," he winced as a tear fell from his eye, "you don't have to do this. I can help you."

Her heart hurt, pounding with severity against her chest. The look in his eyes was desperate. She wanted to stay with him, to escape with him, to feel the spark between their bodies again, despite the strange vision she had just experienced with Ekklips. Struggling with her mind, the realization fluttered in her chest. She loved Bog, and he would fight fiercely, only to die for her to live. He would endure the torment of her journey to the very end, no matter how severe circumstances. The unfathomable idea tore not only her mind into pieces, but her soul as well. She could never allow him to put himself in that position. Furthermore, even deeper down, she knew Ekklips would not allow him, and she didn't want Bog to die, or suffer, on her behalf at the hands of Dark and Death. Feeling him grasp her hand tighter, the heat intensified.

*He understands*, she whispered to herself, *this cannot be the end...for either of us.*

A growing wind tore around their bodies as Bog stood, staunch against the harrowing forces. The feathers of his wings flapped wildly. His face became pained with the realization of her intentions. Pulling her body to his own against the torrential air being created by the lurking monster, their bodies became enveloped in a tunnel of wind. Placing a hand on the back of her neck, he yelled, "I will find you!"

Locking her lips against his own, time seemed to stand still as they embraced each other without restraint, the air suspending them in a stolen moment of passion. He felt her hands move up his chest and around his neck. He could feel she wanted his touch as much as he wanted her touch. He should have never questioned it, he should have known it before the moment he felt Dark approaching. The grasp she held on his heart could stop time and surpass immortality. Even collecting all the stars in the sky could never radiate more brilliantly than the love he felt for her being, her existence was eternally ingrained in his soul.

Unwillingly, she pulled away, tears streaming down her cheeks. "I know," was all she could respond as the wind wrenched her body away from his embrace until their fingertips released.

He yelled in anguish, the caverns trembling at his cry.

With the exception of its eyes, three floating orbs in the air penetrated its surroundings and fed off of Mora's energy. The form began to take shape, one piece at a time, and its translucence allowed the monster to disguise itself until it was ready to strike. It drank in her fear.

Stumbling when the ground shook, but not taking her eyes away, she stayed strong. *Here I am, you fucking beast. At your mercy.*

It appeared to smirk, snorting a raw laughter. *You are always at my mercy, and fortunate I have such patience to give you. Your pleasure endeared me a moment ago, strengthening my hold on your mind, exposing my grasp on your flesh as well. However, your fear is belittling my amusement. I must build upon it, for you will not see the winged one again. He, like you, will be mine.* A loud scream reverberated from its open mouth.

Bog's body was pressed harder onto the stone floor with the pressure of an unseen force. He was kneeling, unable to stand on his feet.

Floating high, against her own will, she was being dragged into its mouth. Horror spawned and she desperately tried to pull away, waving her arms to cut the stench of the mouth's foul breath. She hopelessly looked at Bog, watching him attempt to rise to his feet against the wind.

*It is no use,* she thought as she begin to cry, *I am trapped within its grasp.* She reached out her hand toward him in one last, somber farewell of defeat. "I love you," she whispered.

As the words penetrated his mind, he glimpsed toward her, the rage inside of his body building, fighting, festering. The tears falling from her eyes propelled his heart forward. He yelled again as he stumbled to his feet, the pressure pushing against his body with an immense force. The wall of air ripped his skin like a thousand knives, but he persisted. One footfall at a time, he barred his body against the wall until he stood firmly at the edge of the abyss. His flesh tightened, stretching so taut it revealed the muscles and veins beating fiercely in increasing fury. He reached out his hand, hoping to curl his fingers around her soft flesh.

Suddenly, Mora saw the violet of his eyes begin to glow with an intensity she had never beheld. *Nay, Bog. I will not let you die for me.* Painfully, she released her strength and tumbled through the air toward the open mouth of the monster, succumbing to Dark's embrace.

# Rovínstool

*Alone.*

A tear fell solemnly from Bog's eye, the violet glow fading. The air was empty all around him, and the cold, dampness began seeping through his warm skin, stinging his very bones.

A sinking feeling fell hard into the bottom of his stomach. Thoughts echoed rapidly through his head, but his mouth could not utter a word. He fell to his knees. A flash of memory haunted him, her lips against his own, the desperation in her eyes, her confession, the release of strength. Arguing in his mind, he clutched his head and gritted his teeth. *I should have tried harder to stop her! I should have kept her in my embrace! I can fight the darkness!*

Suddenly, rage rushed over his entire body, jerking his heart awry, shaking the feathers on his wings. "Fuck!" he yelled with his whole being, eventually keeling over from the lack of air. The cave's coldness made it harder to breathe and his voice echoed harshly off the unforgiving walls. He maliciously punched the floor beneath. The cavern shook, sending a shower of rocks tumbling to the ground.

"Ye won' get 'er back tha' way, mate."

He nearly jumped out of his skin at the sound of another voice breaking the impenetrable silence. Too petrified to respond, he listened. The sound of a low, howling wind hummed deep within the cave.

"Ye's afraid of me? Tha' would be th' firs'!" the voice resonated off the walls.

He glanced in all directions.

"Aye, com' on ye goon. Ye'll righ' ou' see who's be talkin' to yeh."

He rubbed his eyes, trying to adjust them further past the length of his arm when, from the left, there came a clicking sound. A flame lit up a squat, grotesquely white face puffing on an unnaturally twisted pipe. The light reached halfway down his body. However, it proved to be no large feat. He could see the little being was wearing a linen shirt covered by a dark green doublet, lined with beautiful, gold stitching. The buttons were crystals, twinkling from the light of the flame. He was sitting crossed-legged on a rock with plain, dull brown, woolen breeches, opposite the elegance of his doublet. His face was freshly shaven and ghostly. Sporting two, golden ear rings, one in each of his ears, Bog immediately thought of Guilderon. However, his eyes were a striking, brilliant sea green, appearing to be a glowing liquid from where Bog was kneeling. The raven color of his hair disappeared into the atmosphere around them both. As the small creatural sat there smiling, his grin extending from ear to ear, Bog grimaced at the sight of his brown, chewing grass, stained teeth.

"H-how long have you been there?" he asked hesitantly, standing with caution.

"Lon' a-nuff ti see tha' damn Luminoff carry off yer female." A billow of smoke sputtered from his mouth once he spoke, obstructing his face, and climbing higher into the bleakness above.

He stared at him for a moment, gawking at the thought of him watching all of the events in which merely unfolded. Before he could speak again, the little creatural spurted.

"Carry off yer tongue too? Com' off it! If I were goin' ta kill ye mate, I coul' of already. Weel, if yer wer't mortal."

Bog frowned in disbelief. "Pardon? Killed me already? You? What the curse of the gods is that supposed to mean? And she isn't my…" He realized how youthful he sounded, stopped, and rubbed the back of his neck.

The little male balked and squealed, "Could 'ave fooled me b' the way yer kiss'd her 'n th' wind tunnel!"

*Godsdamnit.* Allowing the corner of his mouth to show a casual smirk at the thought of Mora's lips on his own, he reputed, "She is my friend." His shoulders fell a bit knowing the words emerging from his mouth sounded completely foolish, especially because he knew she expressed the feelings he had bottled for so long.

The small creatural burst out with an utterly annoying laugh.

Bog wanted to cover his ears out of sheer embarrassment. *His laugh is a combination of a screaming banshee and a piglet*, he concluded.

"Ye coul'n even argue ag'nst that! Ye look'd like ye wan'ed t' fuck 'er."

The continuation of his annoying laugh nearly knocked him off the rock he was perched. Finally, the laughing ceased.

"Come," he grumbled as he hopped over into the abyss, wiping the tears of his laughter from his face.

Stunned, Bog stepped to the side of the cliff and peered over. The little creatural was sitting on a ledge, dangling his feet. Foolishly, he continued to climb down, rock by rock, until there was barely any light left. Bog decided he had nothing to loose and, reaching for a foothold, he traversed down into the abyss. Attempting to not glance below, he progressed blindly, feeling for the protruding rocks beneath, grasping tightly with his hands. Suddenly, a loose rock caused his right hand to slip and he missed an edge with his foot. Hanging by his dominant arm, he began to fervently search for another stone.

"Damn idiot, let go," a voice retorted.

He released the rock and landed on a bed of smooth stones. Embarrassed, he straightened himself and dusted off his hands.

"Th' name's Omnoy. Foll'w me." Rolling his eyes, he gestured Bog to follow. "Watch yer head," he mumbled sharply, but last minute, as Bog ran into a large rock protruding from the ceiling.

"Shit!" Rubbing his head in annoyance, he asked, "Where are we headed?"

"A quaint place I refer to as the curse of the gods, but others know it as *home*," Omnoy responded plainly.

Bog noticed a faint light in the distant canal. The trickling of water echoed throughout the walls and the slipperiness of the rocks became harder to balance. As they approached the dim light, he could see movement. Finally, stepping onto a cobbled street, there was a percolation of creaturals politely going about their business in an underground dwelling. In its visual entirety, most were significantly shorter than himself, but astutely taller than Omnoy. The streets were composed of multi-colored, smooth, river stones. Aligning the streets were tightly-packed, miniature, patched huts with an unusual glowing vegetation residing along the sides. Carts jangled to and from another section of the town, accessible by a stone bridge. Peering into the huts as they walked along the road, he noticed most only contained one room, stuffed with hay mattresses and a fire pit in the center, with an oculus directly above for the smoke.

"Ah, good ol' streets of Rovinstool," Omnoy shouted drearily, slapping a young female on the ass when she walked by with a basket of linens on her head. She merely made a quirky response and giggled.

"May I ask where you are leading?" Bog inquired unnervingly.

"Ye may, but I ma' not feel like respondin'." He snickered. "Fer a Borgorian, ye'r not much of a warrior."

He twisted his face. "What the curse of the gods is that supposed to mean?"

"Yer a fuckin bitch. Ye could'v dun more fer yer...*friend*. I saw how yer eyes glow'd." Omnoy spit into the dark water as they crossed over the bridge.

Bog rolled his eyes. "I was raised a warrior, but that is not the path I chose."

"Whether ya chose it or not, ye have let yer fear overthrow yer impulse t' react."

Bog hissed, "What do you know of being a warrior?"

"Nothin'. But I do kn'er what it's like t' no' be taken seriously, whether it's yer stature, or yer bloody brawn, ye will need t' suck it up an' take a piss with th' bullies once n' a while." Omnoy stopped in front of a tavern. "Her' we 're!"

Sarcastically, Bog mumbled, "Therefore, we drink our weight in ale and overthrow the Luminoff with all of our piss until the very last drop. Then, we will surrender to our intimidating burliness at the last shake of the serpent?"

Turning on his heel, Omnoy laughed and retorted, "Shakin' serpents might be yer thin' with th' Luminoff, but I simply wan'd a drink! Or two, or three, or," he strutted into the tavern. "Hoora'!" he shouted.

It was followed by a quick, "Hoora'!", and a raising of glasses.

## The Keeper

"Grab us a table, m'h dear."

Bog glanced around at the nearest serving wench. "I don't think she heard you."

"Yer suppose I was talkin' t' her?" Omnoy laughed gruffly, looked him up and down, and proceeded to the bar.

Bog muttered sullenly to himself after sitting down by a small window. The bar was smokey and the males were becoming highly belligerent. The only females within the tavern were the wenches and barmaids, each receiving numerous advances and phallic gestures as the males bellowed in laughter. The appearance of the dwarves were similar to that of Omnoy, save for the slight height difference. They all possessed the eerily translucent, alabaster skin and sea green eyes in which appeared to glow.

Omnoy approached the table and placed two ales on the surface, the foam sloshing over the rims of the cave-stone vessels. "Drink up, Borgorian!"

"Bog," Bog responded annoyingly.

"Eh?" Omnoy half smiled. "Stupid name. Drink up...*Bog*."

He banged his vessel onto the table before swiftly gulping his ale down. Bog was astonished. He picked up his drink and smelt the sourness. *It smells like piss.* Holding it to his lips, he balked at the first swig. Peering over his glass to Omnoy, he saw him staring with a mocking smile. Upturning the pint, he smashed it on the table after the last gulp and shook his head vigorously.

Omnoy's smile widened. "That'a mate! Two more ov'r h'r!" He gestured to the nearest wench.

She winked at Bog while he merely nodded his head in return. One by one, as the table began to fill up with empty glasses, they began partaking in one of the most deep conversations Bog had ever heard...or at least he thought. He was participating in the conversation vaguely, but was more interested in listening with great intent to Omnoy's story.

"An' then th' mouse caught up wit its tail, and ye kno' what he did?" Omnoy shouted while everyone got quiet. "Nothin'," he whispered in a slur.

The overwhelming *"oohs"* and *"ahs"* filling the room resonated in Bog's ears. The evening, or what he supposed would be evening,

*553*

continued the same way, each one ending with a gargle of nonsense and drink.

Then, as Bog became filled with liquid courage, he commenced the next conversation. With an angry cry, he held up his pint and roared, "He never wanted me as a son! My twin, Korian, was always the most treasured! If mother would not have been murdered when I was so young, she would have understood my love for knowledge and not war!" He hiccuped. "But to find out…he's not my actual father!"

There was a mixture of silence and dumb stares at first. Then, it was followed by an even louder amount of *"oohs"* and *"ahs"*.

This amused Bog. "Fuck Gornya!" he cried.

"Fuck Gornya!" cried the tavern in unison, smashing their vessels down on the tables in a cacophony of explosive bursts and a shower of ale.

As the night came to an end, Bog stumbled from the tavern singing and prancing carelessly down the streets with Omnoy, shouting songs about the despicable Grogans and the menacing Luminoff.

# In the Flesh

Silence.

Mora could not hear the rush of the wind when she gazed upon the monster's faint bulbs of light as it hovered above the jagged rocks of the cave. As if she were floating, the appearance of the rocky terrain, from what little light she could see from inside the monster's belly, was passing tumultuously beneath. It was lighting its way with its suspended eyes. The acrid stench of rotting corpses singed her nostrils. The disgusting smell was a hefty mixture of its own transparent innards and the warm aroma of saliva. It caused her to stomach to churn violently, threatening to surface within the vile prison.

Her back ached. She fingered around her arm, feeling a long gash on her left shoulder blade. It was not terribly deep or thin enough to bleed profusely, but when her fingers reached her shoulder, she felt a protruding object. Painfully pulling it from her flesh, she could see a faintly dying bulb of light, throbbing for life. Around the beam, not visible to her own eyes, the outline felt like a small fang.

She ran her finger around the outside and yelped, "Shit!", as her finger slid across the sharp, razor-like edge. Throwing it down forcefully, she stuck her bleeding finger into her mouth and started to think about Bog. Hoping he was faring better than herself, she thought about the way his kiss felt on her lips in order to help calm the horror of being trapped within the monster.

When she opened her eyes, a growing luminescence intensified in the distance of the cave. She started to hopefully wonder if it was daylight; however, deep inside, she knew it could not be so. The monster had traveled deeper into the cave, descending at times, and without ascension. It was growing colder, yet her flesh was burning. Her toes were starting to tingle and the hairs on her limbs were standing on end. The glow increased and she began to see the outline of a gigantic, looming structure. It was embraced by a subtle illumination, with the structure itself ominous, dark, and silhouetted by the eerie light behind. She stood, balancing herself on whatever her hand could grasp.

The fortress was built of three, enormous, conical structures. In the middle, the largest conical structure was flanked by the smaller two, creating the illusion of an ominous triangle from the front, with a severely pointed tip. A deadly, ginormous stalactite joined the tip, surrounded by what appeared to be thousands of hanging spears. The closer she flew, she saw the towers were connected by deteriorating rope bridges, dangling with sporadic failing cords and chains from end to end. Moving figures advanced on the bridges, sluggishly swaying back and forth as they walked across carrying quivers slung low on their slouching backs.

The beast started descending between the conical structures toward the center of the fortress. It swung gloomily halfway in front of a large, onyx door set in the middle structure. The hinges sparkled in the pinpointed lights of the monster, appearing as though made from black diamonds. However, the surface of the structures were not as smooth as she initially thought. The bulk mirrored the black stones of the cavern, rough and speckled with obsidian gemstones. Sections of dripping water trickled and glistened in the mysterious glow.

Without warning, it landed with a hard *thud!* and dispersed into the little flecks of lights. She fell through, landing hard onto the rough, stone surface. On her knees, face down with her hands underneath, she heard the doors give way to the sound of footsteps.

"My Light."

A cool, deep voice sent icy chills from the top of her head to the end of her toes. Shaking, she glanced up through strands of loose curls.

"There is no need to look highly dispirited my muse. We are lovers, a balance, intertwined in our True Beings. Under the name *Mora,* it has been accentuated through your mind. Presently, I feel you yearning for it more in the flesh as my eternal. My…" He smirked seductively, "Solora."

Running a hand through His indigo-black hair, it fell loosely back onto His forehead. He was dressed in a black, long-sleeved tunic, unbuttoned at the collar to reveal His chest, black breeches, and shin-high boots. Although He wore a strapped harness, He carried no obvious weapons.

Like a wave of smoke, her mind's eye started filling with emotions. The one radiating with the most intensity was the emotion in her waking dreams. At the moment of His appearance through the doors, His presence felt more real, more tangible, as though she could feel the invisible thread connecting them both pulsating through the stone and into her fingertips.

An animalistic pleasure reverberated in His throat. "Aye, you felt it, too," He taunted with a half grin.

She could feel fire shooting through her veins, choking the words she wanted to scream. She managed to spew, "You've only been an *illusion* until now?"

"Shadow, my love. Harmonious, is it not? My shadow does my bidding, manifesting where and when I deem fit. I knew you would eventually come to me. I could not waste my time attempting to convince your creatural self to see the true connection between us. Therefore, I had to find another way to show you without being physically present." He stepped closer, a coy grin appearing. "Do not fret, I experience all it does."

She shuddered thinking about everything she had felt from His *shadow*.

He bent down and whispered, "The taste has been lingering on my tongue since the first encounter." Lifting His chin, He ordered, "Arise, Solora, Goddess of Light! May your stay be *enlightening*." He raised His hands high, his laugh sinister. A prelude of minions began crowding in from every direction.

Offering His hand, she staggered to her feet. Briefly peering at the onyx doors behind Ekklips, she saw there were reliefs carved in rows of three, twelve on each door, twenty-four in total. Starting from the top, left relief, there was a male. The male stood in a garden facing another male. The being on the right was shrouded in an extravagant white, linen tunic, a belt of inlaid gold, and sparkling rays of light encircling his head. The other being donned a black, linen tunic, a belt of inlaid silver, and a swirling dark mass above his head. They were the balance of one another. In the hands of the dark figure was a swirling orb of tiny, white specks. To Mora's surprise, they were notably moving, circling around a bright, center mass. It appeared he was presenting the gift to the being standing before his eyes.

A pang of familiarity resonated in her core. The similarity to the Borgorian relief glorifying the House of Gornya was astonishingly haunting.

Then, as she panned through the relief blocks, she saw the two males with swords drawn, each bearing a pained expression. Between the two, illuminated swords was the swirling ball of mass. The males became engulfed by the masses of twinkling light while elysian beings engaged in warfare around them.

Studying further, the last relief was the most disturbing. The swirling mass was perpetually moving around the dark-clad figure's head, encircling his mind. The white clothed figure knelt with his back to the dark, whose sword was drawn, hovering it above his opponent in a dishonorable act of impaling the blade through the other's flesh. The sword would slice through the neck, past the shoulder blades, and into the heart. His light would be extinguished, existence left only to the dark and its inhabitants.

Every relief was cut as though seen in the physical life, with the exception of the figures. They were flat, without detail. The only color opposing the onyx was the white of the orb and the opposer's tunic, emphasizing the ending defeat was lucid to every observer. The ultimate possession of the orb went to the one left standing.

Whether it was the hope of defeat, or the war to come, Mora managed to realize the goal of this Being standing before her was to possess All. She focused her eyes gravely in His direction.

"You are fascinated by my work?" With a cunning curve of His lip, Ekklips pointed toward the onyx doors. "I'm rather fond of it myself. It gives hope of what is to come." His black ice eyes locked onto her own in that moment. "And it will come," He snarled, a darkness coating His voice.

She felt Him trying to unlatch her inner being, clutching onto whatever weakness He could find. She struggled, trying not to allow her focus to waiver. Then, she thought about Bog.

A low, droll laugh reverberated. "Aye, your *friend*. You don't know what he bargained for the information he sought." Ekklips held His hand to Mora's cheek. "In exchange for the dwindling life source of Aloria, he sought the whereabouts of your bow and quiver. I knew he would bring you here amongst the caves. This is why I stand before you at Tenebris."

Closing her eyes, a sensual fire burned beneath her flesh. *Nay. Bog would never sacrifice me to Ekklips.*

"Not to worry, my love. If any luck, he will choose a quick and painless death before my monsters procure their hands, or should I say claws, in his flesh." Running His fingers along her chin, a laughter grumbled from His throat.

Terrified, she pleaded, "Leave him alone!" Tears flooded from her eyes. "All you want is *me*. Now I have given myself to you, you should be focused on how you wish to possess *me*." Composing her emotions, she held His impenetrable gaze.

His laughter oscillated. The shrieks and wails from the foulest of monsters resonated in throngs of revelry. She winced, but forced herself to remain calm and strong.

"My Goddess, your pleas mean nothing to my Grogans or Grigoyles. They were made to hunt for the weak, to rip the flesh apart, sparing none left but bone. You see, they do not care what is proved on the outside, it is what is heard on the inside. Trust me, my muse, they have been ravenously hungry since you and your winged *friend* stepped into the caves. They could already taste the sweetness of his soul, his lack of warrior nature, and his abrupt alertness for things that move in the dark. They will be released on my command." He continued to stroke His fingers down her cheek and onto her jawline. "He proved to be a valuable gambit. Now, I will destroy him because he is a threat to *my cause*."

Her chest tightened.

A sharp grin widened across His cheeks. "Listen, be still, and you will hear them sharpening their fangs."

She waited as every thing became unnervingly silent. From beyond the fortress walls, she could hear the rising cacophony of clanking, singing of metal on metal. It was followed by a bold resonation, as if

someone, or something, was wielding a hammer onto the end of a sword…
or fangs.

*Clank, clank, clank…*

The overwhelming sound of metal dishes consumed the pounding sense of inebriation in his head. As Bog sat up in a small room filled with other snoring beings, his skull threatened to explode, fluctuating unbearably with the sound of restless movement. Stumbling to his feet, he braced a hand to the wall, steadying himself against the cold stones. Finally, his eyes adjusted to the undulating sea of darkness surrounding the room. Walking outside the hut for fresh air, the cold and damp stifled his lungs, hindering his breath. The atmosphere was the same level of heavy as it had been the night before. After relieving himself, he peered around at the strange vegetation. He took a closer look at several, tiny, rapidly moving beetles.

"Beetlelows," a voice murmured.

Bog jumped, grabbing his head as the pain shot through his skull at the impact of sudden movement.

Omnoy stood in the doorway, stretching. "Jumpy shit en't ya? I wouldn' get t' close if I were ye. If the' feel threatene't, they'll let out small puff'er gas, toxic enough t' paralyze th' largest of creaturals fer a good half'ta day."

Bog backed away slowly, hardly moving any other muscle except his legs until he was far enough away from the beetle. "Do you speak through experience?" he asked curtly.

"Oi, numerous times. It were a prank m'h peers use't' play on th' *runt.*" Omnoy started reminiscing and snickered, "But I retaliated, causin' sum t' become afraid of meh, others became m'h best mates."

Bog replied in curiosity, "What does it feel like?"

Omnoy laughed. "Ye can't move! Y'er looking straight up 'nto th' air while others prance around ye, mockingly, 'til someone kin'ly comes 'n picks ye up, layin' ya down out of the way 'til ye can move again. As yer limbs slowly begin teh work again, ye can feel a tinglin' sensation, like needles, pricklin' all over yer body."

Bog briefly contemplated about this concept, and then subtly grabbed a small jar sitting outside of the house. He laid it down on the ground and scooped up three beetlelows huddling in the dirt. Looking around for his sack, he noticed the beetlelows had already intoxicated the jar, defecated, and remained deathly still. He grabbed his satchel from the bench he had been lying on and stuffed the jar securely inside. Walking back outside, he stretched his arms over his head.

"Make sure ye wrap th' glass u'tightly," Omnoy insisted, peering at the sack while puffing on a pipe of sweet smelling grass. "Er else ye may get an unsuspected surprise before ye ever try an' use it on whatever poor soul gets tha experience wit' tha multitude of stench."

Bog huffed and grabbed the jar out of the sack, wrapping it tightly in an extra, torn linen Mora enjoyed hoarding. A tinge of guilt stuck in his throat as he tried to swallow. "Now, I need your help," he directed sternly at Omnoy.

Omnoy handed him the long stemmed pipe.

Placing it to his lips, Bog sucked in deeply. He coughed and handed it back. "Strong," he choked and thought Abin would have been pleased with the herb.

"Whisper grass!" Omnoy guffawed. "Only grows 'n th' underbelly of th' caves. Very rare, but buries th' burdens of th' soul." He puffed again, this time making rings of smoke. "Ye want t' know wher' th' Luminoff took yer female."

"I know to *whom* it took her, and it was never my intention for her to fall directly into His hands. I led her into the caves in the hopes we could locate a stolen item of vital importance. I was coaxed under false pretenses, thinking I could protect her from His grasp." Bog wandered over to the nearby bridge, placed his hands on his hips, and glanced over. "In my grief, I was gullible. But I will not leave the caves without her. Therefore, I need to know how to get there."

"An' what ye suppose ye will do when ye get th'er? Sterm th' fortress, retrieve th' female, an' defeat the Grigoyles before killin' Death himself?" Omnoy smirked.

Annoyed, Bog replied, "Alas, mockery." Then, he tilted his head. "How did you know Death was there?"

Omnoy shrugged. "'Tis not how me knew, 'tis how long me knew. An' it's be'n ages. For 'nother day."

Curious, Bog eyed Omnoy with suspicion before he continued, "I'm no fool. I know it is not I who can ultimately save Mora from His influence over her mind, but it is *I* who can die trying to help her fight against the dark forces at work." He could not see his reflection in the water. "You see, I believe she is part of a prophecy. I have spent years researching through the manuscripts my great-ancestors had left behind about the Sun Goddess, Solora, and her fall from the Divine Realm. My conclusions far exceed anything in the mortal world, and greatly surpass those of the immortal world."

Omnoy puffed more smoke rings.

Bog sighed and pushed his golden curls back from his eyes. "The tragedy revolves around three, superior beings: Life, Light, and Dark, known ultimately as the Trinitas. Light was possessed with Enlightenment and The Keeper of all secrets of Life. Dark was possessed with the concept of Rejuvenation, allowing the mind a place to rest. Dark, or Death as He is becoming, has been referred to as the Shadow Leader…or, Ekklips." He waited for a howl of laughter, but Omnoy sat on the side of the bridge, staring off into the dark water.

After several moments of silence, Omnoy spoke, "And ye believe yer friend is tha Sun Goddess 'n flesh?"

"I do," Bog replied, fidgeting with the divots of the stone wall next to the bridge.

"Then we mus' talk covertly. There 'er ears 'n which ye must not speak these ideas t' within this town." He hopped off the wall and began walking toward the tavern they belligerently stumbled away from the previous evening.

"Must you partake in more libations at this time?" Bog groaned.

"Come off it," Omnoy replied spitefully.

He followed Omnoy through the tavern door, ducking again as he turned left toward the bar. Surprisingly, there was still a large crowd, dallying away in sardonic gesture. One wench turned to see him and, once again, winked from across the room. A tinge of satisfaction swayed his thoughts. He blushed and continued to follow Omnoy.

In the storage chamber behind the bar there was a wall with a multitude of various ales. Beside the wall, buried in a corner full of cobwebs, were three, stacked crates. Omnoy began to move the rubble away from the wall before attempting to push all three crates out of the way. Bog stepped to the side and shoved the crates, revealing a small, drafty doorway.

Omnoy grunted.

Lighting a match on the wall, he grabbed a cobwebbed torch to the inside of the doorway and proceeded down a narrow staircase. Barely fitting through the door, much less the staircase, Bog tried to push his wings closer together. They still dragged the encompassing stone. Once to the bottom, Omnoy opened a heavy-latched door leading to the cellar of the tavern. Upon entering, Bog noticed stacks of rolled up parchment, compasses, and large books. The desk in the far, right corner of the cellar appeared to still be in use, but covered in years worth of dust. Writing tools were strewn upon the parchment. Books, opened with their flaps overlapping, formed a semi-circle around the outside.

Omnoy moved closer to the desk, dusting the pages and parchment off as he settled himself into an overly disproportionate chair. "Sit," he commanded without glancing up at Bog and pointing to a smaller chair on the opposing side of the table.

Without saying a word, Bog sat quietly and watched him study the parchment. After a time passed, he interjected, "I am quite bored."

Omnoy glanced up, took a few rolls of parchment from the side of the table, and tossed them at Bog. "Read," he demanded.

Bog twitched as he tried to avoid the tossed rolls. Picking one off the floor, he unrolled it and placed it on his lap. It appeared to be a type of map, full of unfamiliar symbols and words. "What is it I am supposed to read exactly?" he asked.

"Nothin'. I jus' want'd ye t' shut up," Omnoy spat rudely.

Resentfully, he looked back down at the map. Certain familiar words appeared to jump out of the map toward him: *Ornux, Loralimira, Floating Fortress, Niska, Hestios, Vitar, Qailuena*. However, as he stared harder, there was faint writing beneath the main ink with words that read: *Rovinstool, Kilvashire, Edenston, Lowenbrooke, Milkinburough, Faeriton, Glaverton.* He suddenly realized the faint ink showed the caves underneath the mainlands. He studied the numbers on the side of the map.

*Coordinates*, he thought.

He grabbed a piece of parchment and a quill from the table. First, he found the coordinates for Ornux and Faeriton. Then, he proceeded with Loralimira and Rovinstool, Niska and Lowenbrooke, Hestios and Edenston, Floating Fortress and Kilvashire, Vitar and Milkinburough. Finally, as he drug his finger across the map to write the next coordinates for Qailuena and Glaverton, a scribbled location caught his attention. An oddly disturbing sensation filled his chest when he muttered, "Tenebris Fortress: 50,53", under his breath.

Immediately, Bog felt a sense of recognition at the numbers, 5053. *Zalana*, the thought appeared in his mind, *had them drawn on her neck*. Experience had shown him coincidence was rare, if existed at all. He began staring at the numbers, trying hard to configure a connection.

"Ah, this map is worthless!"

He was startled from his concentration when Omnoy threw the map onto the ground. "Tha piece of shit mus' be her' somewhere!" He started shifting through another roll of parchments.

"Look at this one," Bog spoke abruptly, "it has coordinates of underground towns correlating with the above ground lands. These four cities are mortal realm locations, are they not?" He turned the map toward Omnoy and pointed to the familiar coordinates. "You are mortal. I felt the veil when I climbed down the shaft. Are all of the dwarven race mortal?"

"Aye," Omnoy grunted while examining the map, "t' both th' questions. As far as't I know. Me mum told me tales 'bout th' origins of our kin, bu' I dinna remember any tha' referred t'em as immortal."

"What about this," he squinted closer, "Tenebris Fortress? Is the fortress a part of the Mortal Realm?" Quickly, he retrieved the parchment Katheryn had sent to Aloria. He had hastily stuffed it in his boot. Flattening the parchment, he compared it to the large map. Squinting, he tried to decipher the connections. *Now, what did Katheryn try to conceal inside her maps?* He traced his finger along nine, different, oddly shaped trees, with another five shown as burned markings.

Gawking, Omnoy studied harder, moving his fingers along the coordinates. "Tis it! Th's was th' last record of 'is travels." His eyes glowed.

"Who?" Bog inquired.

## The Keeper

"M' fah," Omnoy replied, "before he left an' never returned. The Tenebris Fortress is where th' Luminoff will fly, 'tis th' center of what us northern dwarves call th' broken islands. Qailuena was th' furthest he travelled east tha' I knew." He scratched his beard. "Qailuena is th' northeastern island of th' Nymian Sea, further than Loralimira, partially inside th' edge of The Mist."

Still studying the parchment, Bog flipped his hand in dismissal and said absently, "I know Qailuena, as it is a part of Borgorian lands." However, he had not considered how much closer Qailuena was to The Mist than Loralimira.

Omnoy frowned. "It is said the Halo Mountains end on the shore of th' Qailuenian sands. They wer'said t'once b' th' most magnificent mountain range before par' were's swallowed by th' sea." Grunting, he moved his attention to where Bog was pointing. "In legend, Tenebris Fortress tis wher' Death accumulates th' most foul, mortal souls. It's run by a tall, dark skinned female with severe, brown eyes."

When Bog began to reply, he paused as a connection dawned quickly in his mind. The dark cloud he saw in the sky to the east of Lychinus, and then in the Fire Country, was toward the Halo Mountains. He caught a glimpse of the crudely scribbled numbers next to Tenebris on the parchment. Upside-down, they read *ESOS*, the fives represented the letter 'S' and the three an 'E'.

Gathering his thoughts quickly, he tried to remember what he had read long ago. *Esos was the divine name given to one of the seven Primordial Beings created by the Trinitas. Each of the seven immortals were cast out after the betrayal of Ekklips, the God of Dark. Out of spite toward Life, Dark began coaxing the primal ones with promises of eternal power if they allowed Him to use them as vessels in His plans. Meridan, to his knowledge, was the only one to accept. Regardless, vessel or not, there were others who bent their knee to the Shadow Leader. Tall, dark skin... severe, brown eyes.* He rubbed his face in the dim light. *Zalana is Esos!*

"Bog!" Omnoy snapped.

Bog shook his head in alertness.

"M'h fah was a cartographer, a map maker, an' traced out each coordinatin' city to a coordinatin' Mortal Realm dwarf community. Not all dwarves live beneath the lan', but we 'er considered '*ntro incolenthium*, or 'cavern dwellers'. O'course, I sense th' term began wit' 'bottom feeders,' but what th' gods do I know, right?" He peered up and snickered.

Losing interest when Bog did not smile, he cleared his throat and continued, "Tough skin. 'Nway, th's map will lead ya t' th' Tenebris Fortress, th'r ya will find yer female friend, 'n ya can piss on th' Luminoff. An as fer th' veil, I know no 'ther Rovinstool dwarf t'ave knowledge of it's existence, save me fah, me mum, and m'self."

Bog steadily raised his head while still peering at the map. "I will need a guide. Someone who knows the caves. Are there more entry points to the Realm of Immortals in the caves? You are obviously able to access the veil, despite being mortal."

Omnoy guffawed, "I don't charm m'h wenches through acts of bravery an' heroism, I prefer to use m'h head." He cocked his chin toward Bog. "Ah, but don' be fooled, it is not this head I 'm talkin' about." Pointing to his head on his shoulders, He laughed and winked. "Can't judge th' size by th' body of th' dwarf! Not all 'em dwarves know where t' look."

Frustrated, Bog retorted, "Ah! Come off it! You act entirely snide and cock-centered, but you're nothing but an ass who needs to drink off his self-loathing for a piece of dignity amongst other drunkards! Fuck the wench that made you feel like you were worth your weight in anything. You're coming with me. You have no choice."

Determined to locate Mora without wasting another moment, he shoved the maps, along with the letters from his boot, off the table, rolled them up, and began walking up the staircase. Suddenly, he heard an awful, ear piercing cry reverberate from the tavern upstairs. He froze solid in his tracks.

# Unexpected Energy

Ekklips held Mora's face gently in His hands. "My love, we are equals, you and I. At least, once you finally embrace your True Being." Looping His arm through hers, He started leading Her into the doors. "You have my sincere vow, this is not where we will reside. It's merely a station run by another I appointed."

Reluctantly, she stepped alongside Him, guards at her back. Before entering, she peered around behind the doors and caught her breath. She saw sunken faces, nearly bone, with hideous, blank stares leering through stringy, gray hair. Bog had referred to them as Skulkins. She had seen death too many times not to acknowledge their existence. Averting her gaze, she proceeded through a hallway lit by ruby red lighting, arm in arm with Ekklips, the God of Dark and Death. The torches dripped of red wax onto the cold floor, accumulating like puddles of blood beneath, seeping rancorously through the cracks in the stones. The walls smelled of death, a rancid stench which burned her nose and choked in her throat. It was only moments ago she was surrounded by a similar aroma in the Luminoff. She could not escape the scent, it had penetrated her flesh. She wanted to gag, feeling she could taste the putridness lingering on her tongue. Vaguely glancing around to distract her senses, carved into small niches along the wall, were grotesquely disfigured bodies, writhing in pain. Each silent expression cried out against an unstoppable force. Occasionally, the breeze would catch a drip from the torches and splash the red wax onto the statues, making them appear to bleed.

As Ekklips guided her further into the fortress, they reached an enormous chamber. The lighting was the identical, dim glow of ruby torches; however, the air was not as putrid. She removed her arm from her nose. Although it held the metallic tinge of blood, the air was bearable. More hideously suffering statues, erected like colossal columns, lined the chamber. The floor was sectioned off in thin walkways, crossing between crimson, linear pools. The main pathway led to a molten throne. Six walkways lined each side perpendicular to the main path, only connecting to form around the columns, and then proceeded to disappear into the walls. The walls were burning vibrantly with the ruby red flames of the torches, nearly reaching half the height of the columns. It was uncomfortably warm, but not scorching hot like she would have thought with the amount of fire surrounding the throne room. Increasing the macabre aura of the fortress, she was horrified to hear the faint screams of creaturals resonating from both sides of the chamber, beyond the walls.

"It's very good of you to join us," a familiar female voice resounded around the room.

Mora abruptly glanced toward the throne. It was positioned directly in front of the brilliantly burning, back wall of fire. However, because the dim glow cast a silhouette, she could not see who occupied the throne.

"Remove yourself before I extinguish you," Ekklips unhooked Mora's arm and mumbled angrily as He strolled mid-way up the steps.

"You're in a good mood," the voice snickered. "It is such a pleasure to see you again... Mora."

The figure casually sauntered down the steps, only pausing briefly next to Ekklips to whisper in His ear. His face became intense and He nodded. Mora observed the female was nearly as tall as Ekklips, and outwardly vivacious. Her skin was dark, the color of mahogany. Then, as she leaned into His ear, Mora gasped in undeniable astonishment. The brilliance of the fire lit her face and, with it, her severe, brown eyes.

Feigning hurt, Zalana pouted. "I thought you would be happy to see me."

As she traipsed down the rest of the steps, Ekklips continued to ascend, seating Himself on His throne. Disgruntled, He watched with His hand resting on His chin.

Desperately, Mora tried holding back the twisting emotions of rage and sorrow building inside her mind. Finally, she hissed, "What did you do to Remmi?"

"Ah, he was not enjoyable company," she sulked, walking around Mora with poise. "Completely void of any emotional feelings! After he apathetically resisted my advances, I had to get messy. If only he would have made it easy on himself and been a brute, it would have been a thoroughly pleasurable way to die! Possibly painless! Well, there might have been a small pinch."

Mora felt a pinch on her shoulder and winced. Sneering, she snapped her head at Zalana.

A slow, unamused grunt rumbled from Ekklips' throat.

Shaking with fury, she peered up at Him.

"Mora, that sneer does not flatter your beauty. I see you have met Zalana, or better known as Esos. She, like your mother, is one of the Primordial Beings. She, unlike your pathetic mother, is only loyal to me." He nodded at Zalana. "She handles the operations at Tenebris Fortress in my absence."

He motioned for Mora to proceed up the stairs. Ascending, she saw the unsavory details of the throne. It was made of bones and skulls, tangled with metal swords, axes, spears, and knives. The metal glistened with reflections of the red flames, making it appear like rolling lava.

"You seem overtly entranced by my decor. Like I said, it's not my permanent residence, but it is where I conduct my business with the most *increatural* of mortals. Also, it's easier to deal with the dead underground." Leisurely, Ekklips flipped His wrist toward the side. "Esos, leave us, I require to speak with Solora, alone."

Mora could feel the hatred Zalana projected burning through her skin. While she did not directly glance toward the traitor, she saw her walk casually through the fires out of the corner of her eye. Sweat trickled down her body. Several emotions overwhelmed her thoughts the moment she and Bog entered the caves, but she had not been prepared to stand at Death's door, nor bear the weight she had blindly trusted another. Zalana was a vile serpent who not only betrayed her, but their entire company. She felt the guilt of Remmi's death on her shoulders as much as she felt it when Abin steered the ship into the Nymia Towers. Even Remmi's immortality could not surpass a Primordial, no matter how strong and prepared he was as a warrior.

Sorrowfully, she thought, *Has it all been for naught?* The excruciatingly painful knowledge she should have never abandoned Bog weighed heavily on her conscious. *It is only a matter of time until he will succumb to the clutches of Death.*

"You appear apprehensive." Dignified, Ekklips stood and began to circle Mora, hands behind His back. "Is it because this is our first *physical* meeting, face to face, no shadows, no dreams, no other Realms?" He drug His fingers sensually down her arms. "Is it not delightful?"

Her chest was heaving as His fingertips seductively caressed the back of her neck and around her jaw. It tensed when she clenched her teeth.

"You are speechless," He growled. "I imagined this would be more terrifying to you, but I only sense anger, not fear." Scoffing, He said in a deep rumble, "Then again, your rage would only fuel my desire more than your fear. Feast around you, this fire burns not on fear alone, but on the hunger of all Creaturality, their desires, their lust, their greed. Creaturals, mortal and immortal alike, no longer turn the other cheek. They retaliate. They seek vengeance. An eye for an eye. The blood that runs through the walls, is the blood spilled for mortal gluttony, greed, envy, a thirst to be a god in their own pathetic Mortal Realm. They exert an overconfidence in their endeavors until they become another conquered soul at my door."

When He stepped closer to Mora, His exposed chest was eye level. The scent of His skin was intoxicating. The aroma of deep forest pine, the spice of dark rum, and the coolness of night always lingered any time He had been inside her mind. Closing her eyes, a spark of lightning pulsed through her veins at His ethereal presence.

Pulling her chin toward His onyx eyes, He whispered, "Do you remember, Solora, the feeling of our two spirits, standing before one another, and the harmonious unification of our souls? Light and Dark. We should have created life *together*. But instead, Vitalis ultimately claimed to be our superior, jealous of our bond." Sensually, He caressed His lips against her forehead, drinking in her essence. "Together, my Goddess, we can conquer Life, ruling as one to create our own world of superb beings, serving us as the sole Creators! Without our bond, this world will not survive, Life will not thrive. All is on the brink of eternal darkness, void of light and vitality."

Her senses heightened, rising with voracious fervor and clawing against her extremities for release. Inhaling deep, she opened her eyes and gazed into the endless night sky of His eyes.

Passionately, He added, "I do not want that, Solora. I yearn for the flame that has always fueled me for eternity. The longing is devouring my soul. Death is penetrating my True Being, tainting it beyond repair." Dropping her chin, He turned cold. "But I will do what needs to be done against the one who took it all away from me. You have the choice, and once you are on the brink of physical death, you will realize the offer must be taken. Or you, and All, will cease to exist freely without the shackles of Chaos pulling you down every step you take!"

She could see His rage, the whites of His eyes nearly swallowed completely. Although His tone was sensual, He spoke firmly, "Do you understand me?"

Reluctantly she nodded, but muttered, "Our immortality is the same."

Ekklips paused, pressed against her back, and wrapped His arms around her waist. "Aye, your True Being is one and the same with my own, but I created your flesh with what tools I had. I am not Life. With that, your immortality is weakened in this form." He lightly fingered the linen stings at her neck, revealing her chest. "Where is the key?"

His hand slipped through the slit in her tunic, gently cupping her breast. A hungry growl vibrated in His chest. Mora could feel it on her back. Rubbing the delicate flesh underneath her breast, He grazed His thumb lightly over her nipple. Out of pure instinct, her head laid back against His chest. The sensation was awakening her senses, hardening both their desires.

The key hung between her breasts. He could see it clearly, but He enjoyed the view of her in His grasp and savored the heavy breaths she took as His hand lingered on her warm flesh. After enjoying a few more moments, He squeezed her breast before running His hand back over the key. Unlatching it with His other hand, He freed the chain from her neck.

Kissing her skin lightly, He pulled her hips against Him with more aggression. "I have waited so long to feel your skin against my own. Experiencing your lust through my shadow taunted me, teased me, aroused me. Being inside your mind, your dreams, was glorious, and I yearn for more. I want us to relish in our True Beings together once again, physically and mentally. Although, it would be foolish of me not to admit my growing jealousy at your feelings toward the Borgorian. He is quite the specimen, a genuinely enticing being. You became quite taken, and I had to find out why for myself. My shadow came to him in a dream and I tasted his potential. And while I agree it is stimulating, its too dormant, too broken, too vengeful."

Mora scoffed.

Ekklips' lip curved. "Regardless, you are mine as I am yours. How shall we commence our journey together? I know you have thought about the consummation of our reunification. I have felt your growing fantasies."

Feeling the weight of the key released made her angrier. Despite the sensational intensity Ekklips made her feel, the coldness of His intentions burned deep. The desperate rage in Bog's violet eyes scorched her mind. Along with it, the sharp pang of shame and regret. The cataclysmic agony of being torn between who she was as Mora, and who she may be as Solora, was torturing her mind.

*Ekklips doesn't call me* Mora, *and He knows nothing about who I have become.* She glowered, "I have told you before, I will never surrender my body, nor mind, to you willingly."

He released a low laugh and turned her around. His stark eyes reflected the flames behind the throne, but the white was slowly regulating.

Taking a deep breath, He stared into her brave glare, searching for the Goddess He loved and desired. In creatural form, He pitied her unwillingness to accept the inevitable. Although she may see Him as a monster, He did not want to succumb to the temptation to force her into acceptance. He admired her strength and despised the thought of her relenting out of fear.

With sorrow, He replied, "Willingly? I pity your stubbornness." Gently, He held her cheek and softly kissed her lips. Tasting her essence, He ran His thumb over her swollen, bottom lip and grinned. He stepped backward, sat onto His throne, and twirled the keychain around His finger.

## The Keeper

"I will send for you when I am ready. Esos!"

Zalana appeared through the fire in a sheer, black dress, accentuating her cupped breasts. Her dark hair was braided in multiples down her back, woven with silver strands. "Aye, my liege?" She hovered over the side of the throne, her long, dangling earrings clanking the metal.

"Take Solora to my guest chamber to get cleaned up. Then, come back to me, we need to discuss some expanding issues near Tenebris," He muttered coolly while staring at Mora, showing no interest in Esos' desperate need for attention. Her neediness bothered Him greatly.

"As you wish, my Dark Lord," she replied pouting, a sneer of malice trickling across her face. Sauntering passed Ekklips, she rubbed a gentle hand across His cheek.

He balked away from her touch. Then, propped His chin back on his hand, lost in disappointment and thought.

Picking up a rope, Zalana tied it tightly around Mora's wrists, cutting into the skin. Leading her to the wall of fire in which she emerged, she cackled and spat, "I hope you don't mind a little singe."

"Oh, and Esos," Ekklips growled, His voice carrying across the chamber.

She paused and turned around reluctantly at the sound of His voice.

"I forbid you to mangle or attempt to kill her. Lay a spiteful hand on her, and your punishment will be worse than death. She is, and always will be, mine."

Zalana scoffed and pulled Mora tighter by the rope. "Come, bitch," she mumbled under her breath.

He watched Mora as she stepped inside the flames, knowing she would eventually come to crave it more. *You will realize who you are, even if I have to destroy the entire, godsdamn existence of life itself.*

Frightened at the approaching flames, Mora hesitated. Zalana tugged harder. The rope caused a small tear in her flesh. When the blood trickled onto the stone floor, it hissed and sizzled.

Ekklips closed His eyes. He could taste her power as the lingering spice of her blood coated His tongue. Irate she had been shielded from Him for too long, He resented the effects the time had on her ability to remember. She was the only way He could grasp His True Being.

Otherwise, Death would consume Him completely. He balled His fists tight and took a deep breath.

Mora closed her eyes as they stepped into the fire. At first, as the flames began to engulf her, she felt like the heat was melting away her skin. Then, it started to massage her skin in a way she had not expected. The warmth felt like a surge of energy pulsing through her veins, giving her a power she did not yet possess. Once the rest of her body was emerged, a cooling sensation embraced her, awakening another spark inside she had never explored before. Two, internal struggles grappled for triumph over the other. Her mind started to race and her blood fiercely boiled. Opening her eyes, sparks flooded into her vision, showing her images she had never seen. She saw a life once led, and another which was presently trapped beneath her flesh. Rejoicing in the sensation until she was forced from the fire, she yearned to return. She could feel the particles were lingering in the depths of her soul, gradually increasing like the coaxing of embers.

*I must find a way to feel the fuel of the flames again.*

Zalana whipped the rope around tautly, rubbing against Mora's bone. She did not speak, but her eyes betrayed it all. The iron door slammed, alerting Mora she was gone. Surveying the room, she was left with a single candle to light the chamber. It was small, but it had an unlit fireplace and a hay stuffed coverlet on the bed. Next to the bed was a tray of bread and cheese alongside a carafe of crimson wine. She picked up the bread and began nibbling. It was pleasantly soft and warm on her tongue. She had not eaten or drank anything since before she went to sleep in Aloria's chamber. Cutting a few slices of the cheese made her senses dance. It had been a while since she had reveled in the delightful, diverse taste of cheese. It was a treat when she was a childling. They had one goat, and it provided the milk to make other treats, but it died when she was fifteen name days. The familiar, creamy taste made her smile and yearn to be back in the sanctuary with her mother, a lifetime she knew would never come again. The thought caused her stomach twist in knots, and the excruciating sadness made it hard to swallow. Therefore, after washing down the bread and cheese with the woodsy, lusciously dark wine, she decided to lay down. Her body hurt, but, to her surprise, the gash from the fang was gone. Touching her back and rubbing her healed wrists, she thought, *Did the fire rejuvenate my skin?*

While the awareness from the flames had completely worn away, the struggles inside her mind had increased. She began to feel weak and hopeless. *Have I made the wrong decision? Should I give into Ekklips to experience the sensation I brushed in the flames for eternity?*

Thinking back, the episode had been the second time in her whole life she had felt alive, like waking a monstrous dragon whom had been sleeping for eons, ready to spread its wings and soar. She shivered. The first time, her heart squeezed, had been when Bog embraced her in the wind tunnel and kissed her passionately as the light wove through each of their flesh.

*I want to feel alive again.*

Mora pulled her knees in tightly to her chest underneath the woolen blanket and reached for the feeling once more. Miserably failing, she screamed out in anger. The sound echoed off the cold, hard, stone walls. All her energy, all her passion, ran from her body like the rushing, relentless falls of Loralimira. The memory of the events since entering the caves toiled and tore through her mind as though savage beasts hunting their prey. Her head was full of confusion, nearly too heavy to hold, and it projected louder than the Luminoff's cry against the walls of her skull. Ekklips' sentiments toward her was different from her dreams. *His apathy has always been disturbing...but is it a result of becoming Death as well as being Dark?* There was something about His eyes which caused her feel torn between the sincerity of His words and the intentions He had already made clear. Finally succumbing to her internal pleas for rest, she sighed and clutched her arms tighter around her legs as she drifted away into a deep, inexorable sleep.

# *Liberation*

The screams became louder. A high pitched ringing vibrated in Bog's ears. He stumbled down the stairs, attempting to steady himself onto a pile of books, but failing miserably when they tumbled down to the ground under his weight. He whipped his head around, gawking at Omnoy, who was wide eyed and terrified. His face had become pure alabaster, whiter than it was naturally. His facial expression was stunned with fear, his mouth taut.

Bog, still holding tightly to the map, pulled himself off the ground quickly and staggered back to the table. As he bumped into the corner, he clumsily pushed a small candle over on the rest of the maps with his massive wings, lighting up the floor in a blaze. Stuck in between the fire and the horrible screeching sound, he desperately attempted to think of where they could run. As the fire began to catch onto the wooden table, it licked the sides of the walls, whipping its tendrils toward where they stood. He grabbed Omnoy's arm, jerking him, petrified, against the outside wall.

*Amongst a cellar full of parchment and books, we will be charred in only a matter of moments.*

"What the fuck is that?" he yelled over the noise, pointing to the steps.

"Grigoyles," Omnoy responded instantly, still in shock.

"How can we escape?" Bog frantically asked, surveying their limited surroundings.

"I'd rather be burned 'en face 'em bloodthirsty monsters!" Omnoy replied, his teeth chattering roughly.

## The Keeper

"I would prefer neither!" Bog yelled. "Is there another way out?" Seeing Omnoy was going to be no help, he searched frantically through the flames. Finally, he spotted a medium-sized, rectangular window hiding behind a piled stack of books. "Help me move the books!"

He shoved Omnoy in the direction of the window. The fire hissed and cackled. Sparks spewed from the collection of books shut tightly by a metal lock in a neighboring dresser case. Bog cursed as the embers landed on his skin and wings.

Madly heaving the books aside in bulk, he peered at the length of the window. *It looks too small for me to squeeze through*, he thought, *but I have no other choice.*

The Grigoyles' scream escalated closer to the cellar door. He hoisted Omnoy through the window, questioning him frantically on what he observed.

"Ther' 'er droves of dwarves runnin' from th' tavern doors, many bloodied!"

"Help me through!" he demanded as he reached for Omnoy.

His foot stepped onto a small pile of books, just tall enough to hoist him a little more toward the window. He successfully pulled the top of his shoulders out before his wings caught on the edge of the frame. He could feel the fire lapping at his heels, tormenting his skin. *Godsdamn burden!* He sank back through the window after yelling to Omnoy to 'hold on'. Feeling like the pain he was experiencing at the moment could not be any worse, he ripped a handful of feathers from his right wing, gritting his teeth through the irritation. Stuffing them hastily into his satchel, he placed two in his fist, blew through the hole between his thumb and forefinger, and inhaled deeply as a few feathers turned to powder. A barbaric energy ripped through his skull. His pupils became enormous, but instead of being black, they were consumed with a bright, violet glow.

Jumping once more to the window, he shoved his arms onto the stone cold ground, pulled himself to his shoulders, heaved forcefully against his wings, and grunted in shock as he felt the crack of bone. The screaming became louder behind him and he knew the foul monsters were descending the stairs. With an enormous surge of raging power, he rammed his wings countless times into the top of the window while thrusting himself off the pile of books. Finally, he roared in agony as his wings ripped from his flesh, falling into the cellar fire below in a crackling crash of flames. Hysterically scrambling out the window, he rose to his feet and searched for Omnoy. Lightheaded, he stumbled.

Overwhelmed by fear, Omnoy stared in astonishment, the intensity of Bog's eyes was nearly blinding. All of a sudden, before he could speak, the flames exploded through the window, sending him and Bog both spiraling toward the river side. After several moments, he opened his eyes, the blur of fire and bodies were overflowing in frantic masses on the roads of Rovinstool, the sounds muffled from the explosion. He stumbled painfully to his feet and grasped his head. Out of impulse, seeing Bog lying face down on the bank and covered with blood, he struggled to roll his large frame into the water.

The shock of the cold water brought Bog back to consciousness as he gasped for air. Hysterically, he tried to peer at his surroundings, but all he could see was the blurring brightness and hear the menacing screams of disproportionate silhouettes around various, mangled bodies. Feeling a sharp, stabbing pain rip across his back, he writhed and yelled in torturous anguish. Feeling Omnoy's hands at his feet, he could vaguely see the dwarf through the darkness, pulling him down the river as he swam along with the current. Balling his fists against the tumultuous pressure, he passed out once again.

He knew not how long he laid unconscious before a frigid trickle of water stung his face. Fighting to open his eyes, he was lying on his stomach on the cave floor, water running underneath his chest, and his arms immobile above his head. Every part of his body was numb and in agonizing pain. Unable to lift his head, he could see Omnoy's feet near, crouching down beside his arm. Listening to the faint movement of water, there was no light save for a subtle glow radiating close from a miniature lantern.

"I can't feel my body," he groaned. A baleful thrumming echoed through his head, knocking against the inside of his eyes, above his eyebrows, and in the middle of his forehead.

"Ye've been 'xtremely injured, 'n I'm not sure how t' treat 'em wounds. 'his might sting a little."

He howled as a burning liquid trickled down his back. It was so intense, it made it hard to breathe. Rigidly gasping for breath, he attempted to stop twitching despite the sizzling sensation on the top of his back and around his shoulder blades.

"I mus' cease th' bleeding, or'll die soon. Ev'n ye immortals need yer blood, and yer have already lost a significant 'mount of th' shit. Her', place this between yer teeth." Omnoy cut a leather strap and shoved it in Bog's mouth. "Hold still."

His eyes rolled back in his head and he lost consciousness.

When Bog passed out again, Omnoy got to work. He grated the sharp edges of bone with a textured tool used for sanding wood. Attempting to make it as even as possible, he closed one eye and held up the lantern. Every once in a while, Bog's body would jolt, but the loss of blood kept him unconscious. Sterilizing a sewing needle, he looped a fishing wire through the eye right next to the light. Snapping it between his teeth, he proceeded to lace it roughly in and out of the ripped skin over the exposed bone. The excessive bleeding eventually subsided once he cauterized the wound, but it was still seeping through the stitching. Finally, after the painstaking procedure, he sat back against a stone, pulled out a flask, and took three, huge swigs. Coughing a bit and putting the back of his hand up to his lips, he leaned his head back and closed his eyes for a moment.

After a while, Bog became responsive, feeling severely lightheaded. Staggering to his hands and knees, swooning back and forth, he splashed water on his face. Attempting to crawl across the stone, his stomach lurched and he purged. This continued intermittently as he put pressure on his hands and the surge of immeasurable pain shocked his body. Eventually, he was able to twist his hips and sit on the edge of an underground river. He gradually became aware of his surroundings. The blurry figure of Omnoy stepped into his line of sight, holding a tiny, glass bottle to his lips. Bitter tasting, he coughed and gagged, trying not the purge again. However, he was severely parched from lack of water and welcomed the substance.

"Milk of th' poppy. It shoul' relieve th' pain," Omnoy murmured.

With his arm propped on his knee, Bog rubbed his eyes and forehead vigorously. "What the fuck happened?" he groaned. Adjusting his body, he could feel a tight bondage around his chest. He glanced down to see a thick, leather strap wrapped securely over a white linen cloth.

*The Keeper*

Omnoy's face turned grave. "Ye broke yer wings, striping 'em clean off yer back as ya emerged from th' window." He shuffled around, held up the lantern, and peered at Bog's back. "I did what I'd've for ye bone 'n skin. While ye wer' unconscious, I 'ttempted t' even out th' breakage."

Seeing the shock and disbelief in Bog's face, he rubbed a hand on the back of his neck and mumbled hesitantly, "I wen' back t' th' town t' seek ou' any supplies left."

Bog was bewildered. "You went back to the town? Where had they gone? Why have they not sought us out?"

"Because them Grigoyles smell fear. Once I pusht ye 'to th' water, it washt 'way 'er scent. Th' tavern, 'n a number of adjoining buildings, have been burnt t' th' ground. Th' whole town 'ppeared consumed 'n chaos. M' apologies." He suddenly changed his tune to sound more lighthearted. "Yer bones 'er peculiarly hollow, I n'ver seen such. 'n I have seen th' inside of bone, it's not lookin' as yers does."

Bog grunted, "My ancestors were part bird." Pausing, he thought for a moment. "At least, my mother's ancestors were. Our bones are hollow so we may take flight. I have very rarely flown. I always preferred the ground." He shrugged, still in disbelief he had no wings. "It is no loss to me now." He cupped his hands and splashed his face with the cold, cave water.

"I sewed th' skin 'round 'tas much as I coul'. I place' solidago 'n yer wounds, diminishin' developing infections. Bindin' th' wound, I wrapped 'em linens around yer chest, followed by a coat've leather, tying it as tightly as I coul'. I didn't place too much 'n th' water, th' poppy should ease the pain."

"Where did you learn this?" Bog struggled to ask as he adjusted his sitting position, the phantom placement of his wings still a heavy burden on his shoulder blades. The poppy was starting to settle in, the effects relieving some of the painful tension in his upper back. He gritted his teeth.

"Me mum," Omnoy said as he cleared his throat, "'fore she died. As an only dwarfling, she allowt me t' watch 'er experiments 'n heal th' dwarves of th' town. Her 'n me da were th' only ones who accepted m' *short* comings. They were normal height fer th' Antro Dwarves, but were

## The Keeper

proud o'me through 'n through. Me mum had a collection of herbs 'n plants she'd gathered on th' occasions she would travel outside th' caves. They still remain 'n th' shelves o'er at her work house, I merely gathered 'em when I went back t' th' town lookin' fer anything I could t' work 'n yer back."

Bog listened intently, but the intensity of cave sounds were reverberating off the claustrophobic walls. The dripping of water, the subtly howling breeze, and the flutter of an occasional bat was making it harder to concentrate. He shook his head. Remembering he inhaled a fair share of the powder, he could feel the effects mixing with the poppy. It was exceptionally heady.

Begrudgingly, Omnoy continued, "When me mum died, me fa became engulfed 'n 'is mapmakin'. It twas as if I didn' exist. After he disappear't, I made me living 'n th' tavern." He sat down beside Bog. Taking out a flask, he took a swig before holding it up to Bog's mouth.

Bog balked at the sour stench, but needed to ease his mind.

"That's it, drink up. Ye'll be fallin' back asleep 'ere shortly. I'll make sure 'em Grigoyles don' come back fer ye."

With a faint curl of his lip at the nice gesture, Bog drank again. However, as he imagined Omnoy facing the Grigoyles alone, the information he had studied about the monsters began to resurface. Unlike Grogans, they were a combination of a mortal male and parts of large animals. With a creatural upper body, the lower body was bull, hoofed and hairy. The neck, along with the forearm, all the way to the tip of their three fingered hands, was scaly. Long, sharp fingernails protruded from the fingertips like iron nails. With a split tongue, poisonous fangs dripped thirstily with venom every time the mouth opened wide. The eyes were pitch black, with an added center eye on the opposite side of their bald head. Various, reptilian, bone reconstruction patterns protruded from their skull. They had the strength to rip a heart from the chest of any living being with ease and dismember it mercilessly.

*Omnoy stood no chance.*

"'ere, I grabbe't this fer ye." Omnoy tossed him a couple of tunics, a cloak, and carefully placed an axe down on the stone. "Mighty light fer a stout weapon."

Bog smirked. "Aye, it fell into my possession in the Fire Country.

It is fashioned by the Cau'o'tas, the star readers from whence the prophecy first came into existence."

He examined the tunics in the faint, lantern light. From what he observed, they were exceptionally stitched. One was solid black, as well as the cloak, and, surprisingly, large enough to fit his stature. The other was dark green. Shocked, he gawked at Omnoy. "Where in the curse of the gods did you get these?"

Omnoy smiled slyly. "Ye think we dwarves jus' make er livin' down her'n these bloody caves, do ye? Many creaturals pay han'somely fer dwarf made garb, including ye Borgorians. However, ye didn' need 'em slitted ones no more."

He tossed Bog the satchel containing the maps he had thrown outside of the window before he climbed out, folded his hands behind his head, and pulled his pipe from his vest. Stuffing it with the mossy grass, he lit it with the lantern flame and puffed the smoke until it billowed, disappearing into the darkness.

The gesture was kind. Bog began feeling comfortable around Omnoy. He took the offered pipe and inhaled deeply. The smell reminded him of Abin, but the taste was earthy and damp. He looked inside the little bowl on the end.

"Cave moss," Omnoy said and pointed toward the pipe. "Ain't th' strongest w've got, but it's quick t' satisfy." Inhaling again when Bog handed it back, he slit his eyes and lowered his voice, "Tell m' Bog. How's ye eyes glow't like 'em little illuminated cave werls when ye broke through th' window? I saw't it a bit after th' Luminoff, but not like tha'."

Peering at Omnoy beneath his eyelids while he fondled the seam of the tunic, he replied, "Although I have an early memory of my mother doing a similar task, it's something I learned about my wings a century ago. It was completely by accident. I had been traveling the border of the Fire Country when lightning struck a tree. The brush caught fire and surrounded my camp. Before I took flight, which I rarely cared to do, part of my wing caught fire. When I inhaled, it triggered something in my mind, and I felt a strange surge of energy." Shrugging his shoulders, he stuffed the dark, green tunic inside the satchel. "Over the next ten years, I perfected the rush, but using my own kind of magic."

"Magic," Omnoy raised an eyebrow, "what kin' o' magic?"

## The Keeper

"Borgorians are naturally warm. However, I can ignite objects by blowing on them."

"Ye can breathe fire?" Omnoy gasped.

Rolling his eyes, Bog grumbled, "It's not like that. I have this constant feeling rumbling in the depths of my bones and it scorches my veins. It becomes fueled when I get angry or passionate, sometimes nearly uncontrollable. However, I learned my feathers were a way to channel a controlled version of the energy...or light a fire. Although, I don't expose the ability when I'm in the presence of others." He laughed uncomfortably and added, "I guess I'll have to adapt another way and find another use for my *talent*."

Pulling the black tunic over his head, he winced as the linen grazed over the bandaged stitching. The sensation felt odd. There were very few times in his life he chose to wear a tunic. The Borgorian tunics were laced at the back hem and were a hassle to deal with on a daily basis without a servant. Also, the cloaks always needed to have slits down the back to accommodate their wings. It was inconvenient. The tunic Omnoy had supplied him was of a finely woven fabric, obviously crafted for a larger race of creaturals. The sleeves were loose and tied at the wrist. While the collar fell open, it could also be laced tighter. When he shifted to pull it over his abdomen, his weight felt off. He didn't know when, or if, the hauntingly surreal sensation he still possessed wings would disappear. He wanted to move them, but the bone tingled and nothing happened.

Omnoy was lost in thought. Then, he grunted and fingered something from a leather pouch. "Well, 'til ye figure out how t' control th' power, I found 'em 'n yer pocket." He laid a pile of feathers on the stone in the lantern light.

Rubbing his hair off his forehead, Bog muttered, "Shit, I forgot I pulled them out before I decided to force myself out of the window." He picked up the one black feather and held it in front of his eyes. Maddeningly, he began laughing. It was a deep, genuine belly laugh, one he didn't allow himself to do often. However, his head was feeling unsteady, and the burden he had carried for almost two hundred years, was suddenly lifted. He felt liberated.

Omnoy smirked and then joined in with the laughter, nearly rolling across the cave floor into the stream.

### The Keeper

After a while, the laughter died down. They shared some of the meat and bread Omnoy had retrieved from the village. Then, he removed a small flute from his pocket. Placing the flute to his lips, he began playing a serene lullaby. To Bog's amazement, it sounded similar to a the song his mother had sung to him as a borgling. The lyrics had become lost to him, but the tune constantly replayed over in his head. He leaned down on his elbow after laying his cloak on the cold stone. Making sure to not put pressure on his back, he closed his eyes.

Bog's dreams were filled with fires and figures of the shadows. Enormous, scaly monsters with blood red eyes and razor sharp teeth slithered into the tavern, screaming his name through their hideously disfigured mouths, and followed by a horribly nasty, gurgling sound. One of the monsters opened its large snout, revealing four rows of teeth and an acrid stench of death on its breath. Another had feathers stuck to the side of its jaws, looking similar to his own. Stupefied, he turned around to glance at his wings. They were gone, and he could smell his own escalating fear. He tried to run, but the door was sealed tight. He tried to reach a window, but there was a obstacle blocking him from the outside street. He yelled and beat his fists against the barrier, sensing the rancid breath gradually heating the back of his neck.

Outside, the dwarves were laughing, pointing, and traipsing around the street as if spreading invisible wings and gawking. Amongst them were Omnoy, Remmi, Zalana, Abin, and finally, Mora. Mora was standing closest to the window, watching him with her big, green eyes. A sad tear rolled down her cheek as she touched the invisible wall with her hand. He placed his hand even with her own and cried out, but his pleas were muffled by the ear piercing screams.

Finally, he commenced to angrily beat the barrier again with his shoulder. The ground quaked and the air vibrated with rage. Switching between shoulders, he struck repetitively until he was swollen and bruised. In despair, he reared back for one more hit before the barrier abruptly shattered and everything began to be sucked into the lung constricting air.

### The Keeper

He attempted to draw in deep breaths, but he could not inhale enough. It was increasing rapidly and he suddenly couldn't breathe. It felt like he was drowning in a waterless abyss of darkness, helpless and weary.

All the bodies fell aimlessly into the void. Bog, Mora, and shards of glass were falling faster than everything else, a sensation of the encroaching ground quickly approaching. However, before they hit the unrelenting stone, he jerked his body upward, grabbed Mora's hand, and flew out of his dream and into the cave.

He woke in a sweat, gasping for air. As he inhaled the frigid, cavern air, he reminded himself, *I have no wings.* It took his heaving chest a moment to realize it was not fighting for air. Glancing around, there was neither Mora, the Grigoyles, nor anyone else save Omnoy, who was fast asleep against a rock, snoring heavily. He could feel his upper back again. He could open and close his arms with slightly more ease. He touched his shoulders, but all he could feel was the leather wrapped tightly around his chest beneath the tunic. The pain had lessened. Nearly beyond parched, he drank a flask of water in huge gulps. Then, taking in the smell of the icy air, he basked in his triumph.

Staggering, he rose to his feet. The balance was awkward without his wings and he nearly fell back against the ground. Nevertheless, he managed to steady himself and gradually removed his hands from the surrounding rocks. When he was fully erect, he twisted around at the waist. Stretching out his back muscles, he suddenly felt naked and exposed without his wings in his line of sight. However, a powerful sensation overtook his being. *The weight is lifted. I survived the ancestral castration of my oppressive, Borgorian, physical attribute.* He gracefully raised his arms, watching each go up without the heaviness of the wings. *I truly am who I was always meant to be,* his smile widened victoriously across his face, *and no longer burdened by the mistakes of generations passed. It's my liberation.*

585

# Three Mirrors

*Free*, was the last word Mora heard behind her darkened eyelids. Slumber had come heavy upon her after entering Tenebris. Her eyes were weary and full of sleep. She felt as though something was weighing her down, like an anchor on a ship. Blurred visions danced in front of her glazed eyes as she heard the clicking sound of metal on metal coming from the heavy, iron door. Intoxicated with sleep, she felt a cold hand grab her arm between the elbow and shoulder, jerking her to her feet as she swayed. A hand braced the back of her neck and forcefully pushed her face into a basin of frigid water. The shock awakened her senses and she gasped for air when her face emerged. Fighting against another plunge, she stared callously through the shadows, vaguely deciphering the outline of Zalana.

Zalana muttered in a mocking tone, "'*Clean her off. Dress her properly*'. Like I'm His fucking servant."

Maliciously, she tugged on the harness around Mora's shoulders, removed the straps and belt, and threw the holder against the stone wall with a *clank!* before coercing her to her knees. She soaked her hair with the pitcher of frigid water and combed through the tangled mess, grumbling the entire time about Ekklips. Then, stripping her of her tunic, she forced her into a shin-length, sleeveless, garnet gown, black, leather bracers on her forearms, and black laced sandals extending to a finger's length below her knees. On her neck, she clasped a low-hanging, drop necklace made of onyx with a garnet gem in the shape of a crescent moon in the center,

*The Keeper*

hanging right above the middle of her breasts. Outlining her eyes in pitch and brushing a rouge chalk on her cheeks, she finished by coating her lips with a shiny layer of crushed gem powder. Finally, she pushed her toward the door.

Stumbling through the darkness, Mora could hear Zalana's oppressive breathing on her neck. *Esos*, a voice echoed in her mind. Begrudgingly coming to her senses, her sluggish walk became more upright and aware as they traversed through a corridor of complete dark, into a hall lit by a morosely reddish light. The air gradually warmed her skin, prickling the cold away and poking her flesh like a multitude of needle points. Zalana had not spoken a word directly to her since Ekklips had commanded her to take Mora to the guest chamber. By her grip, she could sense her continued, insatiable rage at having to cater to her care in Tenebris.

As Zalana forcefully tugged her arm, she recognized the corridor from the earlier trip. She wondered longingly if she would step through the fire once more. A spark of hopefulness ran in her veins, awakening a sleeping urge. *Can she feel my desire? Or is her jealously and hatred for me barricading her heightened senses?* Closing in on the end of the corridor, she saw two guards. Both were hideously disfigured, half-naked bodies, reeking with blood and sweat.

"Open the doors you fucking pigs!" Zalana screeched and threw her free arm aside in a violent gesture, pinching Mora's flesh tighter.

The guards quickly slung open the iron doors the moment before she assertively tramped inside a circular room, dragging Mora behind. Once again, an outer pool of liquid encompassed the perimeter. Thin pathways led to a circular, stone slab in the center of the chamber. In the middle of the slab, loomed three, triangular mirrors, attached by an ornate, ironwork pyramid at the top. Zalana shoved her toward the center. Cautiously, Mora made sure not to step into the thin strips of bubbling liquid. As she carefully stepped closer to the mirrors, she felt a hand on the back of her neck and was suddenly thrust onto the unforgiving stone. Feeling the icy surface cut into her flesh, the blood trickled from her exposed knees, seeping into the pools nearby with a faint hiss.

Zalana snickered.

As though summoned by her bloodshed, Ekklips growled, "Ah,

my love."

Grabbing Mora by the hair, Zalana sneered and yanked her to her feet, continuing to push her the rest of the way to the mirrors. When they stood in front of one of the mirror panes, she pressed down on shoulders again, forcing her into a kneeling position.

Mora's breath caught at the impact of her wounded knees. The thought of her open wounds nearly made her faint with pain, but she would not reveal her discomfort. With her head down and her wet curls falling in front of her face, she could hear soft footsteps resonating around the chamber. Peering under her eyelids, she could see the sudden appearance of Ekklips standing behind her reflection. His face reveled with the cunning smile she had come to know well. His hair was pushed back from His face, save for one strand falling loosely around His eyes. The eerie glow of the chamber illuminated His flawless complexion. Every curve, from His cheekbones to His chin, was seductive. A simple, black, belted tunic fell below His hips. His breeches were loose and His feet were bare.

Mora lowered her chin, allowing her hair to cover her face again.

"Arise. Your reverence is flattering, but does not suit you," Ekklips said sardonically.

She did not budge, continuing to stare placidly down at the stone. It did not take long until a swift hand grabbed beneath her arms and, with immense strength, forced her to her feet.

"Stand up, bitch," Zalana spit in her ear. "Goddess or not, you will respect the Dark Lord."

"Esos, you flatter me, but she is my guest and the future Queen of my kingdom. I command you to treat her with respect or I will hold true to my earlier threat," He muttered solemnly as He stepped closer to Mora. "Pull her hair away from her face. I want to see her alluringly dark green eyes."

Mora heard Zalana hiss under her breath in defiance. Nevertheless, her mannerisms became oddly seductive, stroking her hands all the way down to the ends of her hair as though the allure would entice Ekklips. After securing the sides of her hair behind her head, she held her gaze in the mirror. All three stood within her sight, but she watched as Zalana stared longingly toward Ekklips. *She is in love with Him.*

"You are magnificent," He whispered sweetly, smiling at Mora, taking no obvious notice of Zalana. "I yearn for the day you finally grasp who you are." Finally, He turned His eyes to Zalana and commanded, "Leave us be."

Obviously scorned, she turned and left through the door in which they had emerged earlier.

With a debonair aura, Ekklips, hands clasped behind His back, walked up behind Mora. Kissing her on the neck, He groaned with the scent of her flesh. "What do you see?"

Before she could inquire the meaning, He placed His hands on her shoulders. He began to caress His fingertips behind her ear, down the back of her neck, over the curve of her lower back, and maneuvered His hands sensually over her hips. His eyes lingered on each area, thirsty for her returned touch. Pulling her hips closer to His body, He met her eyes in the mirror before conjuring a black iris in His fingers and tucking it securely behind her ear.

The rolling petals tickled her cheek and it suddenly sparked the memory of their first meeting in the tower with the magnificently enchanted ceiling. *Had it been a waking dream? My perception of what is real and what is not is becoming blurred, nearly indiscernible.*

To her astonishment, her eyes widened when she peered into her reflection and saw the curls of her hair suddenly become dry and smooth, revealing a shade of the beautiful, auburn brown she had only seen when her mother washed it with lavender. It was parted to the side of her face, divulging a metal diadem across her forehead, shining pristinely of emerald green. A golden torc, interlaced with ivy and blood root, graced her neck. A downward semicircle, resembling a gold sun with emerald rays, fell below her collarbone. Her garb hung in droves of pure white, lace linen down to her bare feet and was belted with a gold, braided rope around her waist to accentuate her breasts. A faint exposure of her arms, between her elbow and shoulder, donned a gold band of intertwined ivy leading to a tattooed sun on her shoulder. On her forearm, right beneath her elbow, the three, black rings she had seen on Ekklips' forearm, were visible.

Mora was stunned.

He whispered, "This is how I see you through my eyes."

Catching her breath, she fondled the necklace around her neck and replied breathlessly, "What do you want of me?"

## The Keeper

He dropped His hands from her body and the image in the mirror disappeared. "What do I want of you?" He solemnly mocked. "What do I want of you?"

His repetition sounded perturbed, sorrowful. It made her want to reach out to Him, but the thought of what He had done prevented her from showing Him sympathy.

"Look at me, Solora. Do you not realize who I am to you?" He ran a hand through His hair. "Why must I persistently hear your agonizing questions?"

She stared at Him through the mirror, His eyes reflecting the passion in His soul.

Angrily, He grunted, "Your naivety is tearing me asunder! Your connection to Life has become pathetically moronic. If this were not the only way, I would shun you for your stupidity." Passionately, He grabbed her arm and slung her around to where her body was pressed firmly to His own.

She gazed defiantly into His eyes.

"You will know me for who I was, am, and always will be to you!" The flames fiercely illuminated the moment His ardor escalated, creating an eerie glow on His face.

She pulled back. Tripping, she hit the mirror, cracking it under the blunt force of her body. Regaining her composure, she stood straight.

Ekklips began to pace impatiently.

A door opened and Zalana entered, "I heard the mirror break...," but before she could finish her sentence, Ekklips clapped His hands together and fire appeared on the edge of the circle, blocking the doorway. When she attempted to enter the fire, she yelled in agony and fell back through the door.

Breathing deeply, Mora began to feel the flames dance upon her clammy skin. As it had done previously, the rejuvenating sensation commenced to bury itself deep within her mind. She turned to the mirror and ran her finger across the cracked glass. A drop of blood ran down into her palm and she heard Ekklips take a deep breath.

*The scent*, she thought, *He can smell my blood.*

He stopped pacing and walked toward her with a hunger in His eyes. Taking her hand, He inspected the cut on her finger, closed His eyes, and placed it in His mouth, His tongue swirling over the wound.

Her chest tightened. She closed her eyes in response to the sinful feeling of His mouth consuming her flesh. When her finger slid from His mouth, she balked at the absence of a wound. She gazed into His sultry, greedy eyes. The urge to kiss Him escalated quickly, igniting a fire within her core. As if He read her thoughts, He leaned down and claimed her mouth. Although she could still taste the metallic, tanginess on His tongue, the effect created an inebriated headiness. The sensation was different from when Bog kissed her, or even when His shadow had kissed her in her dreams; Ekklips tasted dark and ancient, omnipotent and ethereal. When He slowly pulled away, His lips lingered on her own briefly before she felt she could breathe again.

Interlacing her fingers with His, she followed to the second mirror, watching her reflection the entire time. A sudden movement within the mirror caught her eye and she stopped. Ekklips stepped away. The image of Bog manifested next to her, followed by her mother on the other side.

Ekklips paused, hand at His mouth, and chortled callously. "Aye, the mirror of guilt and shame."

She pushed back the tears, hastily stepping around to the next mirror. When she stopped and stared at her reflection, a childling appeared. She quickly recognized her own, youthful reflection. Before she had time to grasp the meaning, the image faded. Through the haze, another form began to grow, as if advancing from a long corridor. When she beheld the figure clearly, a knot caught in the back of her throat. The bright, white-blue eyes were piercing, unsurpassed by any she had beheld. Remmi's imposing figure stood strong before her, his eyes penetrating as though he could see through the glass. As their eyes locked, his expression became pained and mournful. Baffled why he appeared in the mirror, she hesitantly turned to walk away, but Ekklips stepped behind and placed a hand on her shoulder.

"For whom possesses the mirror of qualm and regret?" Genuinely curious, He watched the image gradually fade before gazing at Mora. "Tell me his name."

"Do you not know all of whom roam the lands?" she replied as she watched Him touch the mirror. "For you to be blatantly oblivious to this being must infer your lack of omnipotence and knowledge."

Irate at her flawed statement, He turned on His heel, fire magnifying His black ice stare as the whites of His eyes began to recede. In a severe, cold voice, He clenched His jaw and seethed, "Never undermine me, Solora. I do possess all knowledge that is deservedly mine! How dare you to question my authority in All."

She spoke in spite of the pressure building in her mind, "Regardless, he is of no importance, a wanderer, a being I know nothing about. He is one of little words. And in that, it is the truth." She stared heatedly into the face of the Being with whom she had longed for, but, all the while, feared and hated. "I dare not lie in the face of my captor."

He frowned, never letting His gaze falter. "Captor? The only prison is your mind." He raised an eyebrow and ran His thumb along her jawline. He leaned closer to her face, gently hovering His lips over her own.

The magnetic charge of His proximity made Mora's heart leap from her chest. *His shadow has been nothing in comparison to the flesh.* He trailed His lips along her cheek and kissed her forehead, but she yearned for more. Opening her eyes, He released her body and stepped away from where she stood, clasping His arms once again behind His back.

She cleared her throat to find her voice, "What is the mirror in which I have seen my transformed reflection?"

Ekklips rubbed His lips before turning His forlorn gaze upon Mora. His eyes were stern and ominous. "You will remain blinded by the ignorance of your own cognitive understanding lest you accept your past."

Upon the last word, He abruptly walked through the fire at the edge of the circle while she stood frozen, aghast at His sudden change in demeanor. Tearing the black petals away from her ear and throwing them onto the stones, she cautiously stepped over to the broken mirror to observe the fractures in the glass. A drop of her blood had run halfway down the mirror and stopped. She heeded a shard on the stone floor next to the mirror, stepping around to avoid the sharp edges threatening to pierce her flesh through the sandals. She had not noticed the piece of fallen glass previously. The reflection of the fire on the mirrored glass made it difficult to notice the hole halfway down. Being careful not to cut her finger again, she retrieved the shard and lifted it slightly to peer inside the hole.

### The Keeper

Moving it around a bit to gauge the interior, she finally realized the back of the mirrors were also mirrored, and they reflected a multitude of pedestals. However, atop the center pedestal, there was a small, black orb. From the shard she held at the hole, subtle flames reflected off the smooth, glossy surface. Carefully, she snapped away another loose shard of glass adjacent from the hole to make a larger gap. With caution, she reached her arm inside the hole and fingered the orb until she was able to fold her hand around it. Clasping it tightly, she expelled the orb through the hole. Studying it in her grip, it appeared to be a solid sphere of onyx, but was not exceptionally heavy. Amongst the reflection of the burning light, it looked like there were clusters of stars glistening off the surface. The piece was breathtaking and unlike anything she had ever laid eyes on. She wondered how valuable the orb was to Ekklips and what He would do if He knew she discovered it.

Suddenly, footsteps startled her from the outside chamber. Immediately, she carefully set the orb on the stone behind the triad of mirrors, hoping it didn't roll away. Scuttling back around, the footsteps stopped and a door manifested in the flames.

Zalana appeared, her face malicious and full of hatred. "What are you doing?" she demanded.

Standing straight, but still a head and a half shorter than Zalana, Mora replied coldly, "I am merely waiting."

Languidly traipsing toward Mora with a sly smile plastered to her face, she reached behind and violently jerked her hair back so her chin was pointing up. "I have the right mind to torture you until you beg for death," she balked through gritted teeth. "You are not worthy of the trouble He is dealing with to keep you alive."

Mora spit into her face. "Kill me then, bitch."

Annoyed, Zalana wiped her face with her free hand and loosened the grip on Mora's hair with the intention of grabbing her around the throat. However, chuckling, she backed away slightly. "I'm not idiotic enough to know the effort would prove fruitless since your immortality won't allow it. But, do you think your tongue will intimidate me? Lest you think again, allow me to show you something." She had changed from her breast-exposing, sheer gown to a high collared, long-sleeve, lace gown in which hugged her voluptuous curves all the way down her form. The bodice was lined with garnet buttons, and as she unfastened them, her full bosom gradually spilled out.

Guilefully, Zalana pulled out a black, metal chain, retrieving a key from between her breasts. Swinging the key on the chain, she said in a provoking tone, "Recognize this?" A hearty laugh reverberated in her throat.

Mora grabbed her own chest, knowing it wasn't there, but still gasped, "Nay, it can't be! Ekklips took it!"

Zalana commenced to circle her with a taunting gait, persistently swinging the chain. "That is where you are wrong. I switched it the night they left you alone in the woods after the Floating Fortress. It provided me with the opportune moment to take it while you lay unconscious."

Mora gawked, but the memory was haunting. "The healer?" she whispered in disbelief.

"Aye, it was not an easy task. I had to be discrete. Bog was menacingly worried about you, and there was always the lurking eyes of *Remmi*." Zalana scowled. "However, I knew Didac had failed to obtain it in the Floating Fortress and Ekklips would be furious. I became curious for more information about you for my own benefit since the Dark Lord was becoming so terribly agitated."

She held the key tightly, her stare ice cold. "Then, there was the issue of physically holding the key, an obstacle I eventually rectified using your own blood after retaining it in the forest. Luckily, your naivety was also helpful, easily luring you into the old hag's dwelling and weakening you with the poison, a dosage your beloved acquaintance, Aloria, could not withstand. After seeing the images in the scrying bowl, I knew you would eventually be in His presence within the caves, my caves. Therefore, I schemed my way onto the Queen Kalvi to earn your trust before docking in Loralimira. Now, I can show Him my trophy."

Mora became overwhelmingly angry. Feeling for the fractured mirror behind her back, she stealthily broke a piece into her hand. Gripping the glass until it cut into her flesh, she concealed it close to her back as the blood trickled down her fingers.

Zalana's eyes solidly held Mora's gaze as she began to retreat, the key once again dangling around her neck. "And then there was the bow and..."

## The Keeper

Too enraged to let her continue, and before she could advance any further, Mora tightened her grip on the glass shard in her hand and thrust it into Zalana's side. A screech of pain and rage pierced her ears. As she staggered, Mora slung her arm around into Zalana's face, scratching deeply down the flesh of her cheek until her hand reached the necklace. Breaking the chain violently from her neck, Mora was blindsided by a force gripping her own neck. Squeezing tighter, her breathing became more constricted and she thrashed fervently. Before Zalana could wrap her other hand around her neck, Mora managed to thrust her heel down on Zalana's foot. When her grip loosened, she writhed free and quickly caught her breath while darting around the mirrors.

Hastening her stride, she grabbed the orb and pushed it down inside the front of her gown. Lunging toward the fire, she yelped as Zalana caught her leg and pulled her down to the unyielding, stone floor. Struggling, she grabbed onto the hem of Mora's gown with one hand as she held her bleeding side with the other. Black liquid hissed into the thinly pooled trenches leading to the mirrors. Mora kicked until Zalana lost her grip. Both scrambled to their feet. Trying to keep the key securely in her grip, Zalana lunged toward her, causing her hands to fumble with the chain and drop the key onto the stone. She could hear the delicate *tink!* of the key on the ground. Searching frantically, she rapidly avoided a couple of Zalana's advancements until she managed to lunge and grab her hair. Screeching, Mora ducked and twisted against the Zalana's tightening grasp, her scalp burning with the increasing pressure. Finally, Mora kicked Zalana on her wounded side and she keeled over in agony.

Without hesitation, Mora bounded to the wall of fire. It whipped and screamed in fury. She froze long enough to feel a hand grab her by the arm. Zalana tugged maliciously. Unwilling to stay in the chamber with her until Ekklips returned, Mora remembered the reaction Zalana had had to the particular flames. With her entire body, she twisted and grabbed a handful of her braided hair. She hatefully flung Zalana's head into the fire. As it consumed her face, she screamed in turmoil. Craning her neck back toward Mora, charred from the flames, she struggled to hold her restraint on Mora's arm. However, using all her strength against the pressure of Zalana's resistance, she returned her head into the scorching flames. After a few moments, Zalana wailed and loosened her grip on Mora, falling limply to the stone. Briefly glancing down at her horrifying appearance, she held a hand toward the perimeter of fire and paused with a brief thought.

Zalana glared at her and screamed, "You will not defeat Him!"

"I don't plan to defeat Him," Mora responded with vehemence.

Deciding to quickly scramble around the opposite side of the chamber to locate the key, she screamed in frustration. After an unsuccessful search, and afraid for her life, she decided to face the fire wall, and the possible repercussions for loosing the key. Steadily reaching her hand into the fire, the rejuvenating sensation imbued her skin with all-consuming power. Satisfied, she delved into the flames and opened her eyes. Feeling alive, she allowed the heat to infiltrate her mind and body, immersed in a burning waterfall of unrivaled euphoria. She reveled in the pleasure and energy she was beginning to possess. Emotions flooded her memory once more - a time of bliss, a time of indulgence, a time of intensity, a time of...vitality. She knew not where the emotions emerged, but knew they were her own. Reluctantly, she stepped out of the flames and into the outside of the chamber. Peering back through the heat, she could see Zalana attempting to pull herself across the floor. Alert and aware, she knew she did not have much time. She could feel Ekklips' realization she had walked through the flames, and He was livid.

*Does He know what I have taken as well?*

Scurrying through an unguarded door, she relied on her instincts to lead her through the corridor. Out of desperation, she felt herself begging, yearning, for guidance from Nephani. Even for minimal protection, she miserably wished she still wore her belted harness. She had secured the dagger Katheryn had gifted her when they departed Lychinus within the sheath. *A lifetime ago...*

Upon the longing for the dagger, the thought of the sheath caused her heart to skip a beat. Bog had specially commissioned the piece for her in the little, Fire Country village. The image of him engulfed her mind, ignited her yearning, and caused her thoughts to wonder what had become of him since she had left him alone at the edge of the chasm. Then, the longing was overtaken by the unwelcome, disturbing memory of Remmi's appearance within the mirror. She shuddered. Coaxing her feet to run, she ran, feeling as if she stopped, she would die.

Faltering into a small vestibule with two doorways, a rat scuttled across the rank floor. Her breath caught in her throat and she backed against the wall in disgust. *Please help me to find the way out!* she begged.

Silence.

*Can it be I was forsaken when I entered the presence of Ekklips?* She cried out in frustration, "For all that is within me, show me the way to the light!"

Back and forth she glanced at each of the doorways. Lurking out of the gradual silence possessing her mind came voices of failure. Her mother's voice was the loudest of them all:

> *Give up Mora, you will fail. You were never worthy of being born of my womb. You are nothing. Recognize the end is nye, surrender to Him, and live out your days with the penitence of the shame you deserve.*

She covered her ears in resentment, crouching down onto the wet, hard stone. "Stop!" she screamed, her voice echoing off the walls.

The voices ceased. When she opened her eyes and lifted her head, she saw the silhouette of a cloaked figure standing several paces away. Standing warily, her heart pounding loudly in her ears, she stared at the shadow. Uncomfortably, she shifted her feet. Without making a sound, the figure walked lightly to the left doorway and entered. It neither turned back, nor stopped. Therefore, without much hesitation, she followed the hooded figure. Down the dark and dank corridor, she kept her distance behind the stranger until her eyes could see nothing in front.

"Help," she whispered.

There was no reply.

She held her shaking hands in front of her, guiding her path along the wall. The air became thick and muggy, as if near a bog. Liquid began to rise further on her legs. Before long, she was wading in a cold, icy body of water. Placing her hand on the wall, she kept her bearings on the claustrophobic path. The lump in her throat made it hard for her to swallow and she breathed in deep as she stepped lightly, dragging her toes in anticipation of a drop-off. No longer could she see the hooded stranger in sight, nor could she hear anything but her own movement. In madness, she continued, pulled by her desperation to escape. Nearly swimming, she found herself wondering why she had felt drawn to follow the stranger. *Had it been hopelessness? Recklessness? Frustration?*

The water was now too deep for her to stand. She was holding herself up by constantly stroking her arms and kicking her feet. Finding a small ledge on the wall, she grasped on swiftly. *Where do I go from here?*

Checking on the orb flush between her sternum and gown, she listened to her surroundings. All she could distinguish, besides the calm strokes of her limbs against the surface, was the growing sound of rushing water. A slight tugging told her the current was flowing out of the stone, further down the tunnel. Fearing she had no other choice, she began letting the water sweep her in the direction of the flow.

Her teeth began to chatter and her skin numb. *It will eventually flow into a bigger part of the cavern,* she thought hopefully.

Unfortunately, the water started rushing heavier and more violently. She found herself tossing and turning in the force of the current. She had no control and held onto the orb through her gown as firmly as she could, fighting the brutality of the undertow. Taking her breath in strides, she was immersed into the frigid water more frequently. Rolling about, the force began to take a dire toll on her body. The stones were hard against her back and the ability to keep her head from hitting rocks was becoming nearly impossible.

*If there is no end soon, I will surely drown.*

Accelerating, Mora took one final immersion into the water before feeling the wave push heavily against her back, pinning her down until the current calmed. With all her energy, she pulled her body to the surface. Gasping for breath, she heaved vigorously, trying to recover the lost air. As she inhaled deeply, she commenced to survey her surroundings. Wary of what may lurk in the black waters of the deep cavern, she began aimlessly swimming. Occasionally reaching down to make sure the orb was secure in her gown, she would pause, listen, and then paddle further. Finally, after rubbing her eyes a few times from the haziness the water had projected in her sight, her eyes adjusted, and she peered up to what echoed the night sky, twinkling with stars.

Fortunately, at the same time, her toes touched a rock, then another, and another, until she was able to ascend from the frigid waters. Shaking uncontrollably, and without more clothing, she was forced to strip naked in order to ring out as much excess water as possible. Before she untied her belt, surprised by its durability, she carefully placed the orb down on the stones. She laid her clothing out upon the rocks next to the orb and gazed up at the stars. However, disappointment stung deeper in her bones than the chill of the encompassing air when she realized they were not stars. The dome-shaped cavern came into view, spotted with star-like pinpoints of light.

*What are they?*

A myriad of colorful, glowing objects hung intermittently between long, cone-shaped rocks jutting from the cavern ceiling. They provided a faint light to the cavern, but not enough to feel safe. Crouching down, she hugged her knees tightly and stared into the orb. The ceiling reflected off the smooth surface. Closely examining the pristine, glossy sphere, the orb was no larger than the size of the palm of her hand. However, the deeper she gazed into the orb, the more mesmerized she became, and wondered why it had been hidden behind the mirrors.

An image of Ekklips seeped into her mind. The way His face twisted with the last words He spoke gave her an uneasy feeling. Pensively, she ambled through the reflections she had seen in the mirror. She replayed the way her body possessed a glow next to Him, the hungry way He looked at her through His seductive gaze, and the way He whispered, *'this is how I see you through my eyes'*. Gradually, the sensation from the fire began to burn deep within her core. Faintly, as if a candle had been lit, a glow drew her eyes to the center of the orb.

An idea ignited in her mind. She began to concentrate harder on the sensation she felt in the fire until the whole orb filled with a magnificent illumination, lighting the entire cavern. It radiated a sensual heat, warmed her skin, and dug through the layers of bitter cold. Amazed, and caught off guard, she glimpsed down at her flesh and lost her concentration. Like a snuffed candle, the light extinguished, causing the dark to embrace her once again. A desperate yearning for the light sent a wave of disappointment through her mind. Reaching toward the orb, at first she retracted her hand away from the surface's heat, but then tried again. As her fingers caressed the surface, she picked it up and held it between her palms. Hesitantly, she brought the orb closer to her eyes. Firmly concentrating, the light commenced to flicker. Reaching into the depths of her mind, the light grew progressively brighter. Shapes and forms commenced to circle languidly inside the light like stars and clusters of clouds in the sky. Then, she thought about how Ekklips kissed her in the mirror chamber. In the core, a dark circle expanded in diameter, forcefully pushing its way into the light as though ripping through fabric. The orb started spinning in her hand, while an agonizingly ear-piercing sound echoed off the domed ceiling. The tiny, hanging, glowing objects hastily dispersed.

Attempting to cover her ears, the sound was egressing from the orb. Floating in the position in which she had held it, the orb was rotating at an unfathomable speed. Against the force exerted by the orb, she attempted to reach her hand through the curtain of tormenting echoes while shielding her exposed ears between her other hand and shoulder. However, all of a sudden, the black hole abruptly consumed the light, causing a great wave of energy to penetrate the surrounding air. A loud *crack!* ricocheted around the dome, sending her flailing backward and a few of the sharp, cone-shaped ceiling rocks crashing into the water.

Silence.

The orb fell to the cavern floor with a clinking sound. Naked and cold, Mora peeled her aching body from the boulder she had fallen against. Crawling aimlessly toward the direction of the orb, she felt her way through the thick, black veil, until her eyes gradually adjusted and her hand brushed her wet gown. Then, she lowered further to feel for the orb. It was not easy, but she finally touched the smooth, round surface with her fingers. Scooping up the orb, the surface was still warm to the touch and it gave off a slight, radiating energy that pulsated through her fingertips. Thinking clearer, she felt the orb was not merely an inanimate object; it was important to Him and possibly *alive*. It possessed an undeniable amount of power in which she did not know how to control.

*However, if I can just light a small amount, I can create enough heat to dry my gown and light my way.*

She mustered the courage to imagine the smallest extent of desired sensation on her skin. The orb commenced to glow faintly. Satisfied, she wrapped the gown around the orb. As if by magic, the heat seeped through the fabric, drying the material enough she could pull it over her head without sticking too much to her skin. Tying her belt and sandals, she held the orb high into the air. The light reflected off the majestic ceiling. Abnormally large, cone-shaped stalactites clustered on the ceiling, many sparkled as if soaked with water. *It mirrors the cave ceiling above Tenebris.* The glowing objects began to twinkle once more, disappearing every time the light would pass over. Listening carefully to the faint dripping of water onto the lake she had emerged, they echoed off the cavern walls like small drops of rain. Nostalgia lingered in the air. She missed being above - the fresh air, the smell of the trees and flowers, the sunlight. Everything down in the deep caverns felt void of life, succumbed by darkness.

Trekking across the slippery rocks by the water, Mora knew she couldn't return in the direction from which she came. *If I am to have any choice in my life, I need to start fighting harder.* Nonetheless, by being plunged into the depths of the underworld, an evolving sense of hopelessness and despair festered like an agitated wound. She was alone and knew not of what dangers lurked in the murky walls of the caves.

Opposite of where she emerged from the water, she walked over to the foreboding walls. Holding the orb higher to the leaking stones, she gasped as a hoard of miniature, black beetles scattered and hissed at the presence of the light. Reluctantly touching the rocks, she stepped precariously along the side, desperate for an opening. For a while, she paced back and forth, appraising each stone from the floor to as far as she could reach, but there was no sign of an outlet. Frustrated, she picked up a rock, beat it forcefully on the stone wall and wailed maniacally. The echoes bounced from wall to wall, filling the cavern with a mixture of profanities and high-pitched screams. On the verge of delirium, she abruptly caught sight of a swirling fog moving inside the orb. Amazed, she gazed at the juxtaposition of golds and bronzes dancing gracefully through the hand-sized storm.

A voice hissed, *such anger, such malice.*

"Get out of my head!" she screeched.

*Give it back,* snarled another.

She didn't know if the voices were reverberating in her head or seeping through the orb. In one last impetuous, raging attempt to silence them, she struck the orb against the stone wall with an unmatchable fury.

All at once, a spark of blinding light bolted from the impact and she stood gawking as the stone wall fell away in the shape of a tattered doorway.

# Release

The corridor was unlit. Every soul was asleep in the chateau save for the night guard at the gate. It mattered naught; dark, nor light, was an obstacle. The air was restless. Talk of magnifying land quakes had the entire city on the edge of hysteria. Information had been collected by means of one-sided bargaining and tactful coercion.

*Is it a skill to take pride in? Nay. I have never been proud of my accumulating Creaturality. But it is a necessity in time of war. Therefore, I must obtain as much information as I can before I depart.*

The land trembled softly as though in fear, shaking the loose stones onto the carpeted hallway. A faint light could be seen leading into the workshop. Hammers and mallets hung from rusting nails. An anvil leaned sturdily next to a fire pit, ashes and soot skewed over the roughly cut, metal scraps. Swords and axe heads of various sizes and sharpness were strewn all over the corners. Rustling in the breeze from the open window were parchments, maps of the chateau, and the specifications of underlying waterfalls. Around the corner, a glass encasement lay, accumulating water droplets from the mists as they careen down its outer shell. A smokey haze filled the inside, concealing most of the once strong body of the superior, immortal being. The effects of the feather helped to maintain the subtle rise and fall of her chest.

Taking off his gloves, he ran his exposed fingers over the glass encasement. Unlatching the top, the smoke billowed from beyond the box and into the air. Deeply inhaling, the effects of the feather filled his veins.

### The Keeper

The sensation was overwhelmingly heady, yet satisfactorily familiar. A time long forgotten resurfaced, and the need to return was remembered. Standing at the edge of memory, eyes closed, the tears of impending failure threatened to pour like the Falls of Loralimira, an emotion he had long concealed in the very depths of his mind.

Before he upended his purpose, a flash of blue light sent a spark throughout the failing body, exploding in an all-consuming light around the entire lands of Borgoria. The ground quivered beneath his feet.

*It is beginning.*

# The Curtain of Dreams

Bog and Omnoy tread on the edge of the bitterly cold, cavern water, descending further into the abysmal confinement of stone. The air grew heavier with their descent, stifling deep breaths as though a cloak covered their noses. It was not long until Omnoy halted, placed his pack on a boulder jutting out of the stream, and pulled out the map. Bog walked a bit further, listening to the increasing sound of rushing water. As he stepped around the bend in the stream, he spied a thin waterfall on his left, subtly illuminated with the light from his candle. It poured into the pool in which he stood. He waded closer, the depth of the water rising around his mid-calf. The current was not strong compared to his stature, but he could still feel a slight tug around his boots. Slightly, he lifted a hand to feel the rushing energy over his fingers. While his eyes were continuously adjusting to the variations of dark, he held the tiny, glowing candle to the surrounding stones, making sure not to allow the water to snuff out its light.

Omnoy had taken plenty of candles when he returned to the destroyed, dwarf town of Rovinstool. Because they didn't know how long they would be immersed in the black cloak of the underworld, they burned the candles until the wax was pooled around the last of the charred, dead wick. He had attempted to coax Bog into showing him how the magic, he claimed to posses, worked, but was sorely disappointed when Bog continued to refuse. Occasionally, they would be forced to veer off their predetermined path due to the sporadic appearance of Death's monsters traversing through the caves, hunting and scouting for threats to their foul, cavernous confines. The thought of Mora exposed to the wretched beasts kept his sanity from spiraling. He hoped they would locate her before Ekklips convinced her to join His cause for revenge against Life, permanently unleashing Chaos. He knew her stubbornness well, and while he believed she would not be swayed easily, he did not trust Ekklips to be merciful for long.

Bog watched the subtle light playfully bounce off the curtain of water at chest level. Within the glassy sheen of the surface stood his reflection. Had he not recently seen his reflection in the glass at his workshop, he would not have believed the mirrored image was himself. His black tunic and breeches bled into the background, creating a contrasting halo of blonde, curly hair. His bright, violet eyes shown more amethyst in the shadows and their attention moved to the empty space behind his body. Previously, his wings would have occupied the entire span of the waterfall, and more. Reaching his free hand behind his shoulder, onto the outline of leather beneath his tunic, he could still feel the faint sensation of their presence. While his mind needed time to process the absence, a faint hint of nostalgia settled over his thoughts. It was brief, but significantly potent, before he shook his head and grinned.

*You look like a damn idiot grinning at your own reflection.* He languidly turned around and trudged away from the waterfall.

His thoughts returned to Mora. *Mora. What will she think of my transformation?* He felt a pang of shame and remorse for not attempting to follow the Luminoff. *But it was her choice.* He had yearned for her being, and the moment he took a chance, she was captured. The feeling of her lips, her tongue, and her body next to his was wondrous and exhilarating. *I could live inside her mind and embrace forever.* Regardless, had she not left him, he would still possess his ancestral burden.

"Bog!"

Omnoy's voice broke through his frivolous thoughts.

"Bog, take a' look at this."

He tread heavily back toward where he left Omnoy. He loathed wading through the water, and knew Omnoy shared his sentiments because he had overheard him mumbling about it earlier. He squinted his eyes at the little dwarf and grumbled, "I feel like an oversized prune wading constantly. My bloody boots are becoming nearly unbearable to wear…and smell." Omnoy huffed, obviously annoyed.

"Ye kno'why we do. 'nless ye want th' damn daemons t' come back fer ye, we mus' keep yer scent away from the' dry lands."

Grudgingly, he nodded and mumbled inaudibly, "They'll start smelling my fucking boots soon enough." Stepping onto the dry stone for a moment, he leaned down and asked, "What is it?" Omnoy pointed to a section of the map he had overlooked earlier.

"Th' stream, it follows directly 'n t' th' backside of th' fortress."

"The back end?" he replied, confused.

"Aye, 'pparently, we looped 'round several bends back. Th' stream circumnavigates 'round th' fortress." He laughed, unamused. "Th' fact that we ar' headin' 'n a large circle shoul' make th' journey easier."

Bog huffed. "Where are we as of right now? How do we know it's the correct stream? There appears to be an endless amount of them in the caves."

Omnoy flipped the map. "I 'pose we'ar somewhere 'round this point," he replied pointing to an area unfamiliar to Bog. "We mus' travel east yet 'gain, t' reach th' middle brook. That 'ill lead us t' th' fortress."

"I see."

He heard a slight nervousness within Bog's voice and glanced at him underneath his thick eyebrows. "What do ya 'pose we ar' goin' t' do once we get t' th' fortress?"

He peered carefully at Omnoy, searching for answers he knew were not going to appear. He shook the water droplets from the waterfall out of his hair. "First, we need to find Mora. She is the most important task as of right now. She is the reason I am here."

"Ah, aye, th' friend. However, 'ave ye ever thought th're may b'nother way beside her?"

Shaking drops of hot wax from his thumb, an undesirable reminder he was holding the candle incorrectly, he paced back and forth, occasionally ducking his head from low-hanging rocks. Stunned at the implication, he stammered, "What are you suggesting? That we leave her in *His* godsdamn hands?"

Omnoy shrugged. "If she's who ye say she is, she should b' quite comfortable wit' Him."

His heart fell in his chest at the idea Mora would choose Ekklips and stood with his mouth agape. Finally, he hissed, "How dare you speak such!"

Again, Omnoy shrugged. "Yer obvious conviction fer 'his female 'tis incomparable. However, 'ave ye not considered th' possibilities of'ther routes t' yer salvation? Th' vast All tis more coveting of knowledge than we know. Don' ye imagine other potential paths?"

Still gawking, Bog rubbed his hands through his hair and clasped them behind his neck. Then, he spat angrily, "I'm not searching for fucking salvation."

"Then, I only s'pose it's out'a friendship wit th' added benefit of poss'bly bein' a bloody deity? Do ya believe she 'tis really th' Goddess of Light?" Omnoy questioned, waving his disproportionately large hands freely in gestures of grandeur.

*A multitude of years were spent on countless research for this particular knowledge and now I'm questioned about my conviction?* Bog was annoyed. "My knowledge is not only rendered in mere fondness, but facts studied over a century and half of continuous dedication to research. I do believe she is the Goddess in creatural form."

Omnoy absently waved his hand and puffed smoke from his pipe. "It seems t' me ya rely t' much on th' stories o'what *was,* then what *tis.* Is it freewill when All leans one way er'nother depending on yer own personal dedications n' ideals? Am I damned 'cause I chose not t' accept a pre-determined avenue 'n this wretched game of existence?" He shook his head. "'Tis not I who accepted this idea. If there were'll powerful beings controllin' shit, they 'ave 'em own problems. There's no further inclination t' mess 'n realm affairs."

Snickering, he added, "'nd I sure as fuck wouldn't have chos'n t' b'a dwarf if'n I had any say."

Bog clapped him on the shoulder. "While I read prophecies of Solora during my research, I personally don't believe in fate, or destiny, if that makes it easier for you to comprehend in my journey. At least, not in a *predetermined, taunt you until you heed to a sole purpose* definition. However, are you willing to accept the reason for venturing to the fortress in which we seek?"

Omnoy smirked and replied plainly, "I can respect tha' mate. Yer had me fooled. Yer've a decent head on 'em wingless shoulders."

Bog chuckled and stepped back into the wading waters.

"'nyway, this bein', this concept, does not claim t' be me salvation. I believe what me eyes 'n ears tell me t' believe. Legends 'ave venture't t' th' fortress, drawn maps, pictures. I know it's 'ere. Th' other nonsense is only food fer th' imagination."

Smiling at him, Bog felt he had an actual friend for the first time in his life, save Mora. *But I fell in love with her quicker than I will ever admit to anyone.*

Omnoy cleared his throat, "As I was sayin'. Th' stream will lead us t' yer fortress. Fortunately, we ar' far enough away from any cavern village th't no'ne should disturb, 'er traipse, through th' streams."

Bog nodded in acceptance. "Should we set up for the night…" he caught himself mid-thought, "well, er, to rest?"

Doubtful they should stay stagnate for too long, Omnoy peered at Bog. "If'n we mus'." He glanced around and added, "But we mus' no' stay long. Respectively, we ar'n dangerous territory. 'ere eyes everywhere."

Bog surveyed the surrounding area he could visibly see with the subtle, radial glow of the candle and agreed, "So be it."

They set up camp at the stream's edge. A surprising weariness tugged behind his eyes. He laid down on his cloak and quickly fell asleep.

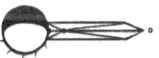

*In the mind, once held so dear,*
*A labyrinth of secrets all did fear.*

*Dreamers seek it amidst the allure of Night,*
*The renewed call it by the Light.*

*Behold how charismatic Life may be,*
*It is the most troubled of the Three.*

*For in its wake, Death lurks nearby,*
*Though the arousal of Light draws nye.*

### The Keeper

*In perfect harmony of Life's wake dost lay,*
*The unification of Light and Dark; come what may.*

*Whereas in seduction, betrayal lies deep,*
*Within Night's grasp, Light dost keep.*

*Life must struggle amidst the metal chains,*
*Proving the bond amid the lover's lain.*

*One entity may not prevail bereft the other,*
*But unite that which binds like childling and mother.*

*Deceit and beguile dost stroke the hand of Life,*
*Concealing the amorous blade of His knife...*

Bog gasped. Sweat poured from his body as his chest heaved with the weight of a thousand lifetimes. *The voice,* he contemplated, *it sounds strangely familiar, but I can't remember from whence I have heard the melody.*

He was confused. He had never had such a dream.

*What does it mean? A lifetime spent in one slumbering moment can be only a momentary lapse of mere thought in reality.*

His began to philosophize.

*For dreams are not of this world, nor are they a part of this reality. They are made up of a substance foreign to all of our physical senses.* Rapidly, his mind began to race, his eyelids fluttering, his chest pounding. *Do we glimpse into an allegorical reality? Can we possibly tread upon the delicate threads of knowledge to reach a more certain, enlightened parallel for which our understanding stretches beyond the furthest star of All?*

Overwhelmed by his sudden surge of contingent ideas, he sat up, rubbed his slightly stubbled chin, and placed his elbows on his knees.

## The Keeper

An unseen breeze blew and whispered, *What about Time?*

Somehow, he felt compelled to remember something ancient or forgotten, but he knew not what, or why. He glanced over at Omnoy sleeping heavily. Snoring a bit much for a comfortable continuation of slumber, Bog stood and stretched. It felt good not to feel the wet, cold water on his boots. He was beginning to shrivel more than he felt was healthy for his flesh. Strangely, he had a desirable sense of duty to explore his surroundings, as if an invisible thread was coaxing his mind beyond where he stood. He lit a candle and began to wander perpendicular to the stream.

Onward he stepped, feeling a compulsory pull to become completely immersed into the darkness. The stones were not easy to tread on, for they were rough and sharp, even through his boots. Occasionally, he would slip and feel the slight pinch of a rock against his flesh. Ignoring the pain, he trekked further over the slippery terrain. He slid over each variable surface, sometimes on all fours, adapting to the caves. Stealth, and his bodily movement modifications, made each individual awareness sink further into his flesh like a predator on the hunt. It was desirable and warm, and felt as though each element of nature was calling to not merely his physical senses, but his mental senses as well. For the first time in his life, he felt he could move and feel for himself. He listened to the steady tapping of water droplets onto the cave floor, sounding vaguely like light rain. The scent created a thirst in both the back of his throat and mind, one for sustenance, the other for knowledge.

As the way became more narrow on each side, he sensed the awakening of claustrophobia creep to the surface of his skin and wondered, *Should I turn back to where Omnoy sleeps?*

However, the stimulating thread of being alive dragged him further.

*Deceit and beguile dost stroke the hand of Life, concealing the amorous blade of his knife,* he repeated over in his head.

*Who was speaking to me?*

He knew the voice was like nothing he had ever heard when he was awake and alert. It sounded neither feminine, nor masculine, yet it was as sweet and lyrical, as it was forceful and domineering. It spoke with authority, but there was an underlying sadness. Then, he remembered what

## The Keeper

Mora had spoken of Nephani. She had been oppressed by the absence of the being since she had awoken from her slumber in the wooded country outside of the Floating Fortress.

*At least, that's the last time I knew.*

It was also how she had accumulated the key, a burden she had been forced to carry as the Keeper, or the keybearer. While he did not know the extensive purpose of the key, she had never outwardly expressed these feelings to him, but he could see it in her eyes. Strangely, the absence grew around the time they had been joined by the companionship of Remmi and Abin, whom he laid no trust. He leaned against a jutting rock and sat staring into the abysmal nothingness as the candle melted to halfway.

*Remmi.* He made Bog suspicious. He knew Mora was leery as well, but she trusted him slightly more than he did. He was certainly not of this world, and acted completely void of emotion, lost in a realm solely his own. This irked him tremendously. Escaping into the tunnels while Remmi stayed in Loralimira to keep an eye on Zalana, proved to be the most sensible plan at the time.

A distant voice in the back of his head whispered, *He might have been somewhat useful rescuing Mora from the Luminoff.*

He shook his head. "Fuck!" he yelled and hit the stone wall in front him, breaking off a large chunk of rock. Shocked, he looked at his unbloodied fist and then back to the wall. "How...?" he murmured.

Then, out of the dark, abysmal nothingness, he heard something. A significant vibration knocked him staggering against the wall. He looked in the direction of the sound, forgetting what had just occurred between his fist and the stone. Seeing a bright light flash in the distance, he lowered his arm and slunk toward the direction of the explosion. It had been a massive echo of sound. Frantically, he began to feel for a pathway, a crevice he could see through the stone wall. He knew there must be one, he had seen the flash of light illuminating the area. Groping, clawing, sliding his hands, he reached for one rock at a time. As he skimmed his hand across, one fell loose, rolling onto the ground. The sound of the falling stone resounded off the walls more than he expected, but he crouched closer to the floor, reaching his arms in multiple places across the rough surface.

Unexpectedly, Bog's hand fell through a hole in the bottom of the wall. He leaned down and tried to reach his arm further into the opening. To no prevail, he peered through the vent. Faintly, he could see a subtle light floating at the far end of an enormous, domed cavern, next to what appeared an ominous, underground lake. A figure was illuminated in the faint light. Unable to see the features clearly, it appeared female.

Squinting harder, pushing rocks aside to get a better view, he thought, *It can't be her, can it?*

His heart began to race at the thoughts invading his mind and clouding his judgment. Before he could muster enough energy to shout to whatever entity stood beyond distinction, from out of the surrounding emptiness, hammered a considerably heavy hand on his shoulder. It grabbed onto him and jerked him backward before he could think fast enough to struggle. Unable to turn his head, he flung his arms, catching onto the binding forearm muscles of his captor. A force jolted him against a stone, knocking the breath from his chest. Another blow hit him square across the jaw. He slid down the rough wall. Biting his tongue, the metallic taste of blood trickled from an open wound. Rubbing his jaw while unwanted colors danced in front of his vision, he squinted through the darkness.

A low series of mumbling voices filled his ears, and he realized he was surrounded. By the sound, he figured at least six beings, but where they were in relation to him, he could not tell. The voice from his assailant whispered something to another standing slightly behind where he sat. Heavy hands weighed down on his shoulders, keeping him from standing. With his elbows propped vicariously on his bent knees, he cursed his inattentiveness. *Damn.*

A moment later, a voice commanded in a clear, crisp tone, "Stand."

He stood slowly with the help of the being standing at his back, peered at his captor, and moaned begrudgingly to himself at his revelation. *If it were not for the one characteristic causing him to menacingly stand out in my mind, I would not have recognized the being.*

"Oi, what the fuck are you doing here?" he muttered, spitting blood.

The piercing, white-blue eyes squinted through the darkness. "Bog." Remmi struck a flint against the stone behind Bog's head, lit a soiled torch, and held it at eye level.

The sound of his name came blatant and stoic, he had not posed a question. Bog sighed in annoyance. "Unfortunately." He placed his hand on his jaw. "Godsdamnit. Why did you crack my bloody jaw, you ass?" he gurgled. This time, he spat intentionally toward Remmi's boots.

"It wasn't I," Remmi spoke blandly. He gestured to the figure behind. "Korian, help your brother get settled, we must move quickly."

Bog jerked his head around, glancing straight into his brother's stare of disbelief. A rage of madness danced through his veins, the ache to return the favor tingled in his fingertips. Though, on Remmi's orders, Korian grabbed him under the arm and vigorously began walking, followed by others.

# Pestilence

Astonished, Mora held the subtle glow of the orb at eye level and peered through the doorway, beholding a stunning sight. Brilliant, sparkling gems covered the walls and ceiling of the cave. Clustered between the precious stones were tiny mushrooms and cave moss, surrounded by little specks of dust. Although there was no external light, the multitude of colors beamed brightly, similar to the illuminated objects upon the domed ceiling of the cavern, twinkling like stars in the night sky. The passageway was breathtaking. Commencing ever so slightly to take a closer look at each, her eyes glistened with a magnificent variety of prismatic hues. Every now and then, as she walked further into the hollowness, she would side step massive, nearly translucent, formations jutting from the ground. There were no smooth protrusions; each had a number of different crystals extruding from the base to the tip. Everything was ethereal, pristine, and untainted.

The further she walked, the thicker and more damp the air became, stifling the ability to breathe in deeply. It was abnormally warm, resulting in a humid stickiness, matting her already damp hair onto her neck and cheeks. Her feet started sliding on the accumulating water droplets which splashed on the ground from the ceiling like delicate, spring rain. Following the twinkling of stone lights, in the distance, she began to hear a mild, roaring sound. Concentrating harder, the soft gleam of the orb increased its eerie glow. Although it marginally dampened the stellar radiance surrounding the cave, she could see her path better.

Continuing toward the growing thunder of water, she braced herself against the cavern wall until she saw another magnificent sight. Before her, stood a gigantic, underground waterfall. To look upward was to peer into an endless wall of water with no visible beginning to the majesty of the rapid thrashing of force. It reminded her of the Nymia Towers, otherworldly. She felt the mists floating onto her skin. They came to rest on her eyelashes like sparkling, minuscule snowflakes. Staggering closer, she rubbed the water away from her eyes and peered over the edge into a pool of black water. She held the orb with a steady grip in front of her face. Peculiarly, the waterfall was not crashing violently into the surrounding pool. The pool was hushed and unmoving. Dropping cautiously to her knees, she moved the light closer to the surface of the dark pool. The depths appeared to mirror the chasm she had stood with Bog, echoing a fear she would fall further beneath the awful caves into an abyss of uncertainty. If it had not been for the reflection staring back at her in the pristine, liquid surface, it would not have taken much to convince her the pool was merely a mirage. Peering back was a female of little recognition. *Have I become so unlike the being I once knew before this journey began? Or am I glimpsing into the shadow of who I am to become?*

Battered and bruised, her dark green eyes lingered on her features. Her lips were still as pink as pansies, despite the small patch of dried blood caked on the lower, right corner. Parts of her hair fell around her face, plastered to her cheeks, blending into the frightening smears of pitch running down her cheeks. Vigorously, she rubbed her flesh to remove the excesses of color Zalana painted on her face. She had seldom gazed upon her reflection, or given her physique any sort of consideration, but since the beginning of her journey, she had caught glimpses of her natural reflection a few times. When she stood in front of Ekklips' mirror, she had become aware of how He claimed to see her through His eyes. She saw none of it in the pool. While she was confident she was by no means unattractive, she felt merely awkward and unkempt most of the time. Like her mother had always told her, she was plain, nothing extraordinary. When she thought back on her mother's words, she wondered if she was referencing her external qualities or her internal qualities. Either way, she had yet to feel like she was anything, but ordinary.

*Except in the fire.* She had gazed upon what it would feel like if

## The Keeper

she were the being whom Bog, Ekklips, and Aloria believed she was underneath her creatural skin, in the very depths of her core.

*I want to feel the fire again.*

Frustrated, she threw a rock into the pool, hoping to break the unadulterated mirror. However, when the rock hit the water, it stopped abruptly. Tilting her head, Mora peered with growing curiosity at the slate. It had hit the bottom of the pool. Reaching for the rock, she retrieved it from its resting place, inspected it, and then threw it further into the center. It plopped on the glassy surface and created a series of ripples.

*Ripples,* Ekklips' voice undulated in her mind.

Quizzically, it landed on the bottom of the pool with half still protruding. Intrigued, she stood, quickly twisted her hair into a bun, and untied her sandals. Holding the orb in one hand, she placed a toe into the black water. The deceitful depth only rose to her ankles. Taking wary steps, she waded slowly toward the middle of the pool, the water level never changing. As she crept closer to the waterfall, the forceful aura of the water blew gusts of wind around her body. It felt as if it was wanting her to advance, but also cautioning her to keep her distance. The closer she stepped, the more a heavy mist of water droplets clung to her flesh and trickled down her cheeks. Her body started to feel laden with exhaustion. Finally, she stood face to face with the rushing water.

To her amazement, she realized the water was not flowing down, but upward. Reclining her head, she watched the water ascend into the starless night. Lifting a shaky hand into the liquid structure, almost instantly, a trickle of gold threads emitted from her fingertips and into the climbing rush. Her eyes followed the trail high into the darkness above. Like stars shooting across a moonless night, the gold threads began to eat away the darkness, appearing as though branches of a monumental tree.

She sighed. *It is as if I have opened an enchanting doorway to All.*

Closing her eyes, beneath her eyelids, she could see the infinite amount of magnificent stars clustered around colossal dust clouds. The imagery was similar to her waking dreams with Ekklips. The lights twinkled like diamonds. Hesitantly, she placed her other hand into the rushing water and felt the surge of energy accelerate. Opening her eyes, she saw the whole cavern commence to illuminate with the infinite expansion of golden strands, showering like gold rain. The beauty was radiantly breathtaking, nearly indescribable.

Then, inside the depths, behind the waterfall, another light grew. Expanding fast, she quickly removed her hands from the water when a sudden fear whipped through her senses. She took several steps back. The palm-sized light hastened through the bleakness of the water, followed by a projected vision on the liquid surface. Fire cascaded violently from the image, causing the waters to lash like ferocious, slimy tentacles into the open. Jumping further back, another vague image arose from the fire. Her heart leapt. It was the figure of Ekklips, but He was not staring in her direction. Another joined Him in the form of a slender, tall, dark-skinned female.

*Esos.*

A feeling unlike she had ever experienced festered under her skin. Throwing a hand over her stomach, she felt like she had just been bludgeoned. Their bodies came together with passionate moans of pleasure echoing around the cavern walls. As a spark of envy shook her body, Mora clenched her fists tighter. Out of rage, she grabbed the nearest rock and threw it as hard as she could at the vision of Ekklips and Esos. Then, when she screamed, it masked the echoes of lust beneath wallowing cries of tortured pain.

*Why am I feeling this way?* she thought to herself. *He means nothing to me!*

The gust of air brought her to her knees as she held herself panting, watching as the water consumed the fire and suddenly became calm. Overwhelmed, she sighed heavily. She did not know how to process the strange feelings the waterfall forced her to acknowledge after merely experiencing the ecstasy of splaying the golden threads upon the ceiling and marveling at the untouched beauty of All. However, before she could calm her mind, emerging from within the depths, was another body. The light outlined the form, illuminating it from behind. It was in the fetal position, arms wrapped over its head, hiding its face. Propped upon her knees an arm's length away from the ascension of water, she sat frozen, uncomfortably staring into the projection. Almost breaking from the surface, a horrifying hand extended toward her without hesitation. Falling backward, her heart almost burst from her chest. She watched on the border of tears as the body blindly flung its savage fists with malicious

**The Keeper**

intent against the wall, bound within the confines of the liquid prison.

*It is mortality.*

She whipped around, stricken by the intense sight of Nephani. She held her hands in front of her face, shielding her eyes. "Nephani?" her harrowed voice echoed throughout the cavern.

*Remove your hands. You need no filter to gaze upon light,* Nephani replied.

"I simply am not used to the sight of bright light. My eyes have yearned to look once again upon the sun, but I fear that dream is lost." Still squinting, she slowly lowered her arms. She could see the wispy drapes of the silken, purple garb swaying in the subtle breeze of the waterfall. "I thought you had abandoned me. I have felt nothing but suffrage at the loss of your guidance. Why have you forsaken me?"

*Forsaken you? You need not my continuous help. I am merely The Defender. I have been summoned.*

"Summoned? By whom have you been summoned?" Mora inquired, frustrated.

*By the Light,* Nephani replied. *You stand in the pool of antithesis. When you reached into the water, your light began to purify the ancient corruption controlling this intense and mighty force. Ekklips knows where you stand as well.*

She glanced back at the constantly rushing surface of the liquid structure. The form had disappeared, yet the water continued to ascend toward the abysmal ceiling. "Why did the ceiling give way to such a magnificently wondrous sight when I touched the waterfall?"

*Because even the smallest amount of Light can provide a pathway through the darkest of ways.* The hood of Nephani's cloak nodded solemnly. *The darker the night sky, the brighter the light of the stars.*

Inquisitively, she scrunched her nose and asked, "What do you mean about the *thing* being mortality?"

*You have stumbled upon a life force of Death. When Life imposed Dark to become Death, mortality was created. The water feeds upon the ground of mortals, soaking deep into the land, infiltrating the various sources of water in the Mortal Realm. With each passing generation, the waterfall grows more violent, filled with an epidemic of greed, power, lust, gluttony, selfishness, hate, and even as you witnessed, envy. It is a continuous cycle of impurity, sending forth the feces of generations past and impregnating the unborn with a closer link to despair and tribulation.*

"Is this Ekklips' only waterfall?"

There was a pause. *Return, Mora.*

She gawked and sputtered, "Return where? You didn't answer my question!"

*To Him,* Nephani replied without further explanation.

"Why should I return? I have escaped Him and you ask me to go back and sacrifice myself?" She stared belligerently at Nephani. "And..." she stiffened, the shame heating her face, "I have lost the key. I have failed as The Keeper."

*Yet, I would not ask you to return if I did not think it would benefit your journey.* Nephani's voice grew grave. *You are not The Keeper because you were entrusted with the key. You are The Keeper of enlightenment and knowledge, that is most vital. The key is not gone, merely lost. Don't let denial for what is, affect what could be.*

"But you cannot see the future! How am I to trust you? You have not provided me with the aid I have so yearned and pleaded for in desperation!" The shrill in her voice scratched her throat, bordering on insanity. "And what of The Gateway?"

A long silence ensued. She counted her breaths in an attempt to even them with the steady drops percolating from the hem of her tattered gown. Parasitic ideas spawned, attaching themselves relentlessly to her thoughts. They were as wicked and malicious, as they were frightening and selfish. A taste of chaos melted onto her tongue and slithered down her throat. The initial flavor was savory, heady, and luscious, like she imagined the first day of spring would taste if it were bottled with sprigs of mint. As she swallowed, she nearly gagged on the bitter aftertaste. It was putrid, vile, and exuded a potent tinge of decay. However, the thoughts were addicting, despite the repulsive result. Then, Nephani's robes changed direction from the slight breeze released by the waterfall.

*You must return. It is the sole way to reawaken. It is the only way to survive, to make sense of the suffering you have and will endure. Embrace the light within, only then will you understand.*

Nephani began to fade.

Forlorn and weighed down by the negative thoughts permeating her mind, Mora slashed at the robes as tears streamed rapidly down her face, arguing, "Reawaken what? You are foolish! Your words mean shit to me!" When she spat the last words, she fell to her knees and watched as the glowing form gradually disappeared.

In the fading light, she looked at her reflection in the water. Anguish and rage betook her as she clawed violently at the surface, her fingernails scratching against the slated floor of the pool. As the final light disappeared, she sat back on her heels, drenched, the blood from her fingertips running down her palms and forearms. Her chest heaved in and out, tears stung her eyes, and her voice started to falter amidst the aggressive screaming. In moments, the room began to swim in her mind and pain grew exponentially behind her eyes. She felt her head would burst from the pressure.

*Madness.*

She had been driven mad - mad by the darkness, mad by the loneliness, mad by the uncertainty. As if linked by unseen threads, she stumbled to her feet. Flesh had become a pestilence in her mind. She began desiring to rid herself of the pain and suffering she had been enduring since departing the sanctuary. Desolation buried its claws, reopening and festering a bygone wound which she had only been able to eradicate when she stepped into the fires at Tenebris. Without hope of ever feeling the vitality of the euphoric flames again, she would end it all.

Coaxing the conclusion in her mind, she growled, *I will return. Not because Nephani told me, but because I know the suffering He will inflict can repress the pain my mind no longer desires. They can call me weak. They can call me Death's whore. They can call me an abomination. I will look away. My soul will become unredeemable. I am no Goddess.*

She lifted the orb from where it laid beside her in the shallow pool and lit the fire inside. Holding it in front, she sought a way out. *I will not return the way I came, even if it means I must blow up another godsdamn wall.*

She waded to the outside of the pool. Tying her sandals, they weighed on her ankles like shackles. Sluggishly dragging her feet, she held the light up and noticed the edge of the pool circled behind the waterfall. A slight tug in her mind told her it was the correct path. Cautiously, she traversed along the side of the slippery rocks. The heavy misted water did not phase her, for her whole body was drenched, penetrating severely into her skin, causing her to become numb. Tucking her loose hair behind her ears, she walked further behind the waterfall until it revealed a small outlet, barely big enough for a full, grown being to fit comfortably. Folding her shoulders into her body, she squeezed through and progressed. Even though the rocks were slippery underneath her feet, it was the multitude of white, sharp rocks protruding from the walls that slashed and opened her flesh. It was a nuisance, but would not deter the labored steps she took toward Tenebris because the numbness was already consuming her mind like a hungry predator. The choice to end her suffering had clawed its fangs into her mind, burrowing deep enough to feed off any resilience she had left.

The light of the orb bounced off the glistening walls and her eyes twinkled with the kaleidoscope of warm lights. Every time she jerked her head left or right, the light followed her eyes. Eventually, the claustrophobic space became too much to handle and she laid down, defeated, on the merciless, unforgiving stone. Shivering from the growing mental weight of anxiety, the physical penetration of stifling, bitter air, and the emotional pressure of agonizing despair, she closed her eyes and covered her ears to impede the escalating voice of madness from consuming her entire being.

She knew not how long she laid frozen upon the rough, isolated terrain, but an image of Bog's damn dimple manifested behind her eyelids. Suddenly, it caused her heart to ache with such an excruciating pain, she screamed until her lungs felt they would burst from her chest. She became furious and it spurred her determination to be rid of the burdens she had accumulated in such a short amount of time. Sighing pitifully, she peeled herself away from the sharp rocks, the tips already becoming a part of her exposed flesh. She winced at the retraction, but it did not compare to the internal torture piercing her mind with its menacing claws. Faltering on the uneven stones, further and further she trudged.

As the obstacles of the tunnel became diluted, a sensual hum began to resonate and grow within the caves. Echoing off the walls into the depths of the claustrophobic chamber, it illuminated the corridors and hollows of her mind. He knew she sought Him. He knew she was surrendering herself to Him this time. *He knows I'm delivering myself willingly.* Pathetic, weak, undeserving, were a few of the words forming in her thoughts, characteristics she convinced herself were true.

The fires burned brighter in her mind and the pathway became easier, as if the land was opening for her passage. Whether they were internal, or external, voices echoed. They called, commanded, asked indecipherable phrases. She knew not determine what they wanted, but she was getting closer, close enough to catch the acrid scent of decay.

*I'm ready*, she repeated in her mind to coax her steps onward into the sanctification of darkness. She knew He would be waiting, watching for her to emerge onto the stone shelf of Tenebris.

# A Return

With spite, Bog trudged through the dark with an unwanted hand firmly gripped on his upper arm. He was feeling nauseous from the amount of blood he swallowed from the unnecessary blow to his jaw bone. Feeling like a prisoner, he roughly shrugged Korian's hand off. He had no idea where he was being led, but Remmi never glanced back in his direction. The rest of the soldiers were walking several foot falls away on both sides, just out of sight. Reluctantly, he turned his head slightly to glance behind. The grave facial expression on the Borgorian at his back was neither shocking, nor disconcerting, because the mutual feeling of disgust had festered deep enough to destroy any respect either had ever held for the other. Nevertheless, there was an obvious fear which lingered upon Korian's expression. Dismissing it as a projected weakness, Bog continued dragging along silently.

Swiftly, Remmi led them all into an archway of stones. Inside, the gems sparkled like stars. Each and every eye gawked at the surrounding glory of the chamber. The small band of Borgorians followed Remmi to a larger tent, set near the back wall. Patchy tents were crudely set-up, cramped like rows of linens hanging on a line. Satchels were scattered along the entrances as though they had been in the caves for a while.

Once inside, Remmi threw down his bow and poured water from a flask into a roughly fashioned mug. Handing it to Bog, he spoke toward the soldiers, "Leave us be. Save you, Korian."

## The Keeper

Bog could not stomach his brother's name, and watched as Korian crassly walked around to a boulder and perched stoically. His gray eyes were still fixated upon him, staring at him in a strange disbelief. He assumed it was mainly in awe of the absence of the great wings which once graced his back. As though reading his thoughts, he heard Remmi clear his throat.

"How have you come to eradicate your wings?"

Bog brushed the back of his neck and barely glanced in the direction of Korian before speaking, "It was by no choice of my own. I was cornered in a cellar against the Grigoyles. My only outlet - a medium-sized, thin window." He sighed in remembrance. "The torment was agonizing, nearly unbearable. I forced my body through, but in doing so, broke the wings from my back. If it were not for Omnoy, I would be dead." He rubbed his shoulder and took a seat opposite Remmi, holding his head between his knees.

"You have never been worthy of the bloodline," Korian sneered, "you are truly no Borgorian anymore."

Anger flooded into Bog so fiercely, he almost leapt at Korian before he was intercepted by Remmi.

"You must not seek vengeance on each other at this time. Sit and listen. This will require both of you: strength and intelligence."

His eyes still fixed upon Korian, Bog sat down silently, his chest heaving, forcing each breath.

Korian turned his back on Bog, rustling the wings on his back with pride. "I am only here on request from my father. I will not be held responsible for *his* death," he sneered and nodded his head toward Bog.

"No one is responsible for anyone else except themselves. However, we must fight as one in order to help Mora continue on her journey." Remmi propped himself against the rock, arms crossed.

Bog glared and said, "First, inform me on how you have come to be down here. Then, I may abide by your plan."

Remmi stoically peered at Bog and cleared his throat. "The morning you informed me of your venture with Mora, I had been watching the chateau. I knew the enemy was amongst the throngs of immortals hustling about. But, I knew only one who had the power to coax their way into the chambers of Aloria with foul intention."

## The Keeper

Bog jerked his head up in recognition of his own epiphany and interrupted, "Zalana."

Remmi, though curious of how Bog had deduced, nodded. "Aye. I watched and waited. There was nothing. I did not want her to know of your disappearance. Therefore, I asked her to accompany me to the stables where we could inspect the horses. She obliged. On our way down to the stables, she suggested we ride out near the falls to investigate the territory. I concurred." He shifted his weight. "After riding to the falls, we dismounted and commenced on foot. As expected, she ended up inquiring about your whereabouts. I suggested you and Mora were still in the chateau attending to Aloria's arrangements. Then, her face turned coy and she smirked at me as though her feminine wile would persuade me to reveal any more information."

Pushing off the wall, he grabbed the flask and took a swig. "'*I know they have left,*' she proceeded to say, '*I'm disappointed they didn't have enough faith in you to protect them.*' I merely watched her steps. '*You know who I am?*' she asked me."

Quenching the growing irritation in his throat from talking, he took another sip and sat down across from Bog. "I nodded my head in response to her question. Swiftly, she advanced upon me. However, from beyond the brush, Sun Shadow bucked into her path, kicking her to the ground. I leapt upon the horse and held my sword at her throat. '*Run,*' I told her, '*run swiftly. Tell Him we are coming.*' And with that, she scoured away."

Restlessly, he twisted the leather strap on the flask. There was an uncomfortable stirring within him which had started to fester since they descended into the caves. "That is when I turned my attention to the chateau. I requested a conference with your father, convinced him of my intentions, and asked him for a decent troupe. The Borgorians had to be willing to die, because Death was the ultimate opponent. The details were not important at the time being. He acquiesced without any question as to your own whereabouts. The next morning, I led them into the caves, not expecting to find you *alone* in the darkness."

Bog shifted uncomfortably and summarized what had happened in the caves since the morning they left the chateau. Then, he mumbled, "I saw her."

## The Keeper

Surprised, Remmi turned his eyes in disbelief. "Where?"

"Before Korian hit me in the bloody jaw," he sneered at his brother. "She was in the cavern, with a bright light source in her hand."

Remmi contemplated this for a moment. Then, he whistled to a hand full of troops outside the tent and commanded, "Go forth to the place where we retrieved Bog. See if you can find any trace of the female."

The tallest bowed his head and hastily left the tent with two others in tow.

"And Omnoy? Where is he?" Bog inquired fretfully.

"Who?"

"The dwarf whom accompanied me." He watched Remmi pause briefly in confusion.

"I know nothing of him, but I will inquire into his whereabouts when they return." Remmi continued about his business.

Korian remained in the shadows, listening.

After a while, lost in his own thoughts, Bog inquired, "What are we to do?"

"We must march upon Tenebris, destroying everything in our path," Remmi responded briskly. The back of his neck tingled at an unknown force. He glanced out of the tent after the slight disturbance and immediately closed the curtain. Grunting, he added, "I fear He will find her sooner than us, if He has not already. Her mind is too weak right now."

Clearing his throat, he briefly searched through a small bundle of parchments. "He will find her, or since you saw her alone, she will return to Him; either way, we must release her from the confines of His grasp by any means possible. Bog, this is where you will be useful. If we can find her in time, you must convince her that her journey lies forth, away from the company, and away from the caves. Lead her to venture east. She will listen to you." He glanced back at Korian. "Korian and I will lead the Borgorians against the monsters of this underworld. Dark, I imagine, will be close at hand the entire time until she runs. But hopefully by the time He notices she has escaped, she will be free of the caves. If she complies to your command to go east, she will emerge amongst a section of the Halo Mountains."

Bog wondered for only a moment how Remmi knew this information before asking, "How do you expect to defeat Death?"

Remmi smiled wryly. "I don't. One day perhaps, but that day is not today, as it is not tomorrow, yet the opportunity will arise, and with it, those opposed to His tyrannical nature. Until then, we are to hold them back until Mora escapes. Then, I suspect it will be every Borgorian for themself. Those who survive will be forever changed. Those who don't survive may be used to further Dark's gambit. Either way, there will be a significant amount of casualties."

Bog could feel the tension rise. He saw Korian's look of discomfort. Deep down, he cared not to see his brother's face, but he dare not wish to see him used as a pawn for Ekklips either.

Remmi continued, "However, there is another task of distraction, and if you are willing, I believe you can follow through until she escapes to follow Ekklips like a bitch in heat."

He glowered and hatefully responded, "Esos," as he fingered the black feather in his pocket. His violet eyes flickered at the thought of justified revenge.

# Surrender

The endless void transitioned from the heavy cloak of dark to the faint, haunting glow Mora had arrived previously from inside the Luminoff. Barely scraping through the last of the stone corridor, she saw Tenebris once more, its looming, severely triangular presence taunting her every step. The fetid scent wafted into her nose, causing her to balk slightly before the loud, vicious cries of the Grigoyles and Grogans bombarded her ears, distracting her from the undesired stench of the Fortress. Without hesitation, she trudged to the mighty doors and stood frozen. Noticing more details of the structure, she looked up to see hideous gargoyles perched sporadically on jutting stones. They seemed to laugh in mockery at her arrival. Before her impulse to run again, a click resounded, and the door opened. Ekklips emerged, followed by a ragged and burnt, but healing, Esos, and a monstrous form holding a spiked mallet.

Mora adjusted her stance, stood strong, and stared harshly into the eyes of Ekklips, waiting for Him to speak first.

"I knew you would return," He opened seductively. "I believe you have something of mine."

She saw Esos smirk from behind Ekklips. Holding her hands behind her back, she fondled the smooth orb she had tucked safely inside her tattered gown before exiting the claustrophobic tunnel she had traversed. He slightly nodded His head and, from behind where she stood, marched a couple of His grotesquely shaped minions. She never removed her eyes from His own. "That would be impossible. It was destroyed when

I caused an explosion."

"I do admire your boldness. However, considering your return, I believe you lust for something more." Suspiciously, He looked her up and down. He knew she was lying. "And I must say, I would not have needed to send my shadow to coax your return," He licked His lips, "Solora."

She grunted. "I neither returned for my own salvation, nor your thirst for my mind. I am here upon tranquility."

Ekklips snickered. "Ah, my love, you will not find that here! It does not bode well to expect mercy from me, neither should you count on it being tranquil. However, your failed escape only proves we can never be eternally separated for long. You will always yearn for my True Being."

"It is not you I desire to escape."

Her eyes resonated with a meticulous glare and He was intrigued. Lifting an eyebrow, He gestured for her to continue.

"You see, I have lived in my own personal damnation for long enough. I yearn to release myself of this anguish." Then, she cruelly whispered, "By your hand I live, and by your hand I die. I thought it only fitting it should be you who accepts my request. I no longer wish to be a pawn in anyone's game."

Ekklips stepped closer.

Agony ran through her mind as she saw the slight glisten of the false key in the firelight dangling around His neck, a taunting reminder she had failed to keep it safe. The only hope she held for redemption was that Esos believed she found the key in the chamber; all the while, praying it will remain lost forever in the fires.

He placed His hands on her shoulders, leaned over, and kissed her cheek softly, whispering back, "You will not die, my love." Next, placing a hand upon her cheek, He kissed her forehead, considering her abnormal request. "It will be a tumultuous coercion. I do fiercely desire to release you from Life's grasp and into my own. But, as you know, Life controls immortality. At least, He did. In the end, I fear we would be back to where we began, with the release of Chaos. And while I yearn for the revival of Light, I can exist with Chaos by my side. Either way, I will have an essence of you, my Light."

She thought she saw the slightest hint of sympathy glisten in the corners of His eyes. It was the first time she believed He was capable of emotion. Her stomach tumbled. *Is this really what I want?*

As He pulled His head away, He sighed woefully, "But if you are willing to try, I cannot help but acquiesce. I do not believe you will receive the desired outcome you expect."

With a trembling voice, she said meekly, "And what do you think I expect?"

"Peace...silence...release...concepts demolished when Life forced mortality upon All. I will loathe seeing my future Queen suffer so." He applied force upon her shoulders, causing her to kneel in front of the Fortress.

Closing her eyes, she lowered her head. When she did, she heard the sound of a blade pulled from its sheath. The clean sound revealed the sword's bite. Becoming unnerved by the position she had allowed herself to be placed, Mora began to hum Remmi's haunting lullaby. The cold metal kissed the nape of her neck. She could feel the hard, rhythmic beating of her heart, while her blood rushed like fire through her veins, her sweat undulating toward her breasts as she took deep, meditative breaths. A dream, *or was it a premonition?*, in which she had continuously replayed over and over in her mind, coaxed her memory. She recited it verbatim in the hope she could interpret its meaning before she died.

*Is this it? Please purge me of my sins and forgive me of my relentless attempts to carry this burden alone. I am no hero. I am no sorceress. I am no savior. I am merely Mora, daughter of Meridan. For thousands of centuries, Creaturality has yearned to possess the knowledge I hold, while millions have died to capture a glimpse of the mystery behind my eyes. I fear I have nothing left. Greed, denial, and temptation have betrayed my trustful nature. I am alone in my quest until the day my mind is released from this prison of flesh.*

Focusing harder, she exasperated the words until her head ached and her heart became almost too heavy to contain. *What do the words mean?* After moments of taunting silence, her senses became painfully aware of Ekklips' hesitation. The acrid smell of death no longer burned her nose, the screech of grinding metal no longer pierced her ears, the open sores upon her flesh no longer hurt. She truly believed she was freeing herself, and those she loved, from following her into the clutches of Death.

She knew the risks associated with dying. Nephani had been intermittent, a source which had never really given her the concrete guidance she needed, desired, and wanted. Her trust merely came from uncertainty and helplessness. It was possible the madness had festered in her mind, strengthening its grip since the waterfall, but she felt this would be the only way to achieve the peace she sought, removing the shackles binding her to a divine identity she held no desire to claim. However torn she had become about the allegations of who she was before as Light, and then ultimately as Chaos, if she were truly Solora, the Sun Goddess, then she would rejoin Life beyond her creatural flesh. If she was just another immortal, her soul would still be controlled by Life, allowing her to be reconnected with her mother. The idea brought her a slight comfort. Either way, she did not believe Ekklips' words about how Chaos would ensue upon her demise. Regretfully, she believed chaos had followed her thus far because of His insatiable hunger, and would not cease until she walked the lands no more. While everything held an exponential amount of ambivalence, she did not want to be the cause of further death and destruction.

Mora's focus left her alone with the lullaby, echoing off the chambers of her mind, leading no army of tears from her eyes. *The swipe of the blade will be quicker than falling asleep. I have endured the last of my pain.* Waiting in anticipation for the blade to come down, she began to hum louder.

The haunting lullaby resonated throughout Tenebris' walls and each eye turned to watch her last breath. Ekklips listened sweetly to the lullaby, closing His eyes briefly to inhale the scent of her flesh and listen to the rapid pulse of her heart. Leaning down once more, He spoke low, thus ensuring no other ear could hear His words, "Solora, my love, my Light, this is your last chance to escape the torture you will endure once this blade hits your skin."

He waited. At her stubborn silence, He stepped back and muttered, "Esos, if you will."

Panic arose in Mora's mind when she realized Ekklips did not intend to inflict the torture Himself. Her heart thudded like a savage, imprisoned beast inside her chest and her head pounded with an excruciating pressure behind her eyes. *If I am truly Solora, I cannot die at the hands of Esos! This is not what I planned!* Bile rose in her throat as she choked down the thought. His words, *tumultuous coercion*, began clear. He intended to allow Esos to torture her until she ceded to His requests. *How foolish of me!* Her heart tore asunder. *Now I will never be free of His grasp.*

Ekklips watched Esos lift her arms high into the air, the blade glistening with the fires surrounding Tenebris. As she thrust the pristine metal toward Mora's flesh, He silently assured Himself, *She will know.* Hungrily, He kept His stoic face fixed upon the tip of the blade.

A slight gasp of wind rose the hairs on the back of Mora's neck as the cold metal kissed her flesh. The absence of pain was alarming. Then, she heard the clanking of the sword falling onto the rock. Realizing the blade had merely scraped the side of her neck, she glanced up to see Ekklips standing to the side, arrow in His chest. Wide-eyed and confused, He was stumbling backward. Quickly, she turned her head in time to see the formidable form of Remmi emerge from amidst the surrounding flames, his white-blue eyes reflecting the belligerence of the fire, another arrow locked in place. A wondrous flash of blue light extinguished the fiercely whipping tendrils in one, brief swoop. At once, he was followed by a band of Borgorians. As the being on his right manifested, Mora gasped. Without wings, she did not know if it was truly who she desired, or if it were a trick of her eyes, but the gut-wrenching sight of him sent waves of heat through her body. With a fierce demeanor, he held his axe in one hand and a sword in the other, his violet eyes burning with rage.

*Bog.*

She whipped her head back to look at Ekklips. He was irate. She could sense His unyielding anger. He grabbed the arrow and pulled it from His chest. Blood flowed freely from the wound as she saw rivers of black veins slithering up His neck. His onyx eyes melted with an all-consuming darkness, no white visible, as He fixated them upon Remmi.

Suddenly, realization dawned in His gaze and He hissed at Mora, "I see." A smirk appeared. "Release the Grigoyles!" He yelled.

A great gust of wind arose and chains resounded against the Fortress walls. What appeared like gigantic, flying larva emerged from high over the ramparts. Their tails were serpent-like with twelve squirmy legs. Upon their backs, sat the nasty bodies of the Grigoyles. The snarling and gnashing of teeth reverberated throughout the menacing caverns. A series of arrows were released from the wall of Borgorians as the monsters settled in upon the ranks. Mora ducked as a body flew over her head. Flashing a glance at the face of the lifeless Borgorian, she recognized him as a guard from the House of Gornya and winced.

A commanding voice resonated amongst the army of winged Borgorians, "Look above!" The militaristic stature of Korian leapt off the ground and took flight, swords in hand.

When she caught a glimpse of where Korian had pointed, horror lurched in her stomach as she saw a multitude of Hawkends descending from the stone walls of Tenebris. A band of Borgorians followed Korian, several falling upon impact in a futile struggle against the birds of Death. She had no weapon and did not desire to be trampled by the oncoming slew of beings and monsters. Therefore, she scrambled to her feet and turned her body to run. Before she could get far, a hand grabbed her arm with such force, it made her slam into the chest of a much bigger being. At first, she thought it was Ekklips. However, when she lifted her arms to fight back, she stared into the face of Bog.

"Watch out!" he shouted while shielding her body in time to feel an arrow scrape against his shoulder. His axe struck the nearest monster, slicing the disfigured head off its mangled shoulders. "It's an improvement!" he roared before turning back to Mora.

She covered her face against the spew of blood. "I need a weapon!" she yelled, surveying the chaos she had created.

In a blur, a highly unbalanced battle had commenced, Borgorians against a legion of monsters. Blood spewed everywhere. It was carnage. Bog tugged her through the tumultuous field of fallen soldiers, fighting every opposition in their way. She ducked and dodged as blades and spikes flew harshly in her direction. She caught sight of Remmi successfully fighting off two, nasty Grogans with his sword, while Korian fought valiantly at his side. However, Ekklips and Esos were no where to be seen.

"Make haste!" he commanded over his shoulder.

Once hidden behind the enormous, stone walls, he released her hand and peered around the corner, axe at the ready. She stared at him, completely in shock of the form standing in front of her eyes. She had never seen him wear a tunic, his upper body had always been exposed, unless he donned his slitted cloak. The black of his garb contrasted with his shockingly blonde hair, nearly turning it silver.

He whipped around. "Are you hurt?" he gravely inquired.

"Shaken. That is all," she replied. "Where did you come from? And what has happened?" She reached behind his shoulder and touched where his wings would have been, through the tunic.

He winced. The spark between their touch excited him greatly, but he knew he could not show it. Alert, he glanced around the corner again. Pushing his golden, strewn curls out of his eyes, he sighed, "It is too much to speak of now. My mutilation is an exoneration of my ancestral history."

Stunned, she knew not what to say, but as he stood extremely close, she wanted to touch his flesh, feel his wounds, and lose herself in his embrace. The energy swirled fervently around their bodies, much like it had begun to do before the Luminoff carried her away. She yearned to increase it and never let it go.

Concealing her from the eye of every Borgorian and monster with his body, Bog's face turned grave and somber. "Please listen carefully. You must run, Mora. Leave this damned cave and continue your journey to The Gateway."

Taken aback, she stubbornly replied, "Not without you." She stared him fiercely in the eyes, her gaze relentless. "I refuse to continue on my own. It has driven me to madness. I wanted to die at the hands of Death. Without your knowledge, I am nothing." She touched him on the hand.

With her touch, his skin burned with desire. He wanted to run away with her, conceal her in his arms, and never let go. The proximity of her body was almost too overwhelming for his senses. Everything became heightened, but the awareness of the battle never wavered. He cursed Remmi in his mind. It was excruciating to dismiss her pleas. She was close enough for him to hold, but he had to push it aside with great difficulty. "It is not I who contains the knowledge of your reclamation of self. You must seek it for yourself. There are none stronger, nor more courageous than you, whether as Mora…" he paused and bit back the belligerent sorrow welling in his tone, "or Solora."

Running his knuckles down her tear stained cheek, he took a deep breath. "But note this," his brooding eyes reflected in amethyst as he spoke, "there is nothing innocent in the thirst for superior knowledge. I have always believed in you. You will prevail."

Confused, Mora squinted her eyes. "Then, you shall go with me."

Pushing a loose hair behind her ear, he spoke blatantly, "My companionship will only be a burden to your mission. You must run east."

She felt like he had ripped her heart from her chest with his bare hands and gripped it so tightly she could still feel the pressure in the empty cavity. Anger and sadness mixed together as she tried to understand why he would not leave. Reaching for his arm as he turned away, tears streaming aimlessly from her eyes, she cried, "Bog, please."

Not wanting to see her tears, in fear he would never be able to leave, he barely glimpsed over his shoulder and said without emotion, "I will always follow…Sunshine." He turned the corner to return to battle, his heart torn asunder, axe held high.

It was the hardest task he had to endure thus far. Even loosing his wings could not compare to the pain he was feeling. She had become his light and he knew he had fractured their bond by crassly releasing her into the unknown. Remmi had told him it would be difficult, and he resented him for that fact. He needed a distraction. Therefore, the lines on his face hardened. He knew who he sought, and he would show no mercy in his fight to distract her wickedness from pursuing Mora. He slung his axe into the chest of a mutilated, skull-exposed, Jun'gore. It clawed profusely while it melted to the stone, but he shoved his boot into its face and cracked the neck sideways. Surveying the multitude of bodies, he jolted toward the entrance of Tenebris. *If she isn't on the battlefield, she has fled into the cold stones of that damnable place.*

Before he entered the doors, he reached into his pocket and pulled out two feathers. Seeing one was white and the other black, he contemplated both for a moment. The overwhelming temptation to try the opposite was taunting him aggressively. It had been his first thought when Remmi had tasked him with hunting Esos. With guilt, he glanced briefly to where he had left Mora, but she could no longer be seen. Shaking his head to gain focus, he stuffed the black feather securely back into his pocket, held the white feather in his enclosed palm, blew lightly, and fiercely inhaled. When his violet eyes illuminated, he leapt over a fallen Borgorian and ran into the Fortress.

Maliciously, the thought of Esos as Zalana entered his mind. *The bitch hypnotized me, making me feel sorry for her*. He wished he had figured it out earlier. Zalana was a murderer, and once she was found, he would die trying to kill her with his bare hands, despite her immortal status. Running through the corridors of Tenebris, he kicked in doors, yelled her name, and slayed those who stood in his way with his axe. The battle had only begun to fall into the Fortress. Jun'gores, Kryptoads, and Druscans scurried to gather weapons as numerous Borgorians filled the chambers, raiding each and hunting for Death. Grogans and Grigoyles piled through obscure doors, stabbing victims with their illuminated ears and tearing through flesh with their fangs as if ripping thin parchment.

Bog's fury grew exceptionally, nearly overtaking him in a psychotic rage as he careened his axe through the multitude of bodies and throats. He felt impenetrable. He grabbed a Kryptoad by the throat and pointed the sharpened blade into the side of its neck. "Where is Esos?" he demanded.

The foul breath of the Kryptoad reeked in his nostrils between its hideous laughter and gurgling drops of blood. "You seek the cunt of Death," it spit into his face, "you will be greatly disappointed. No creatural eagerly seeks castration without already feeling the castration of his own demise."

In his rage, he sliced off the Kryptoad's arm and growled, "Where is she!"

It begun to guffaw horribly. "Seek Death and she will follow like a chastised bitch."

He rammed the blade through its chest and drug it down its body, exposing the inner workings of Death's monsters. *I've heard enough.*

The faster he ran, the louder his thoughts rang out clear and concise, *Reveal yourself bastard! I seek council with your whore!* With the plea, he smashed down a door leading to a circular chamber. Fires roared from the walls like waterfalls. Located in the middle of the chamber, there stood three mirrors in the shape of a pyramid. As he walked into the room, surveying the thin pathways of blood leading to a ring around the mirrors, the wall of fire closed over the entrance in which he had emerged. Slowly, he stepped over the ring and stood in front of a mirror, axe grasped firmly in his hand.

In one moment, he noted the broken glass lying on the stone in front of the mirror to his left and wondered if Mora had been brought to the chamber. As he approached another, a shape took form in front of his eyes. It was his own reflection, but he wore a dark, indigo tunic, each stitch threaded with silver. An emblem was intricately woven into the breast. It possessed an orb-tipped, vertical scepter overlapped by the face of a ferocious bear with violet gems inlaid for eyes. Upon his head, a silver crown of vines wove sensually through his golden curls. In the light of the flames, his hair sparkled and his skin had a supple sheen. His illuminated, violet eyes accented the dark tunic and mirrored the magnificence of the gems. When he touched his hair, his reflection did as well. As he ran his fingers along the threads of the crest, his reflection did as well.

*Who have I become in the mirror?*

He moved slightly to the right and saw a figure manifest behind his shoulder. The glaring, pitch black eyes were unmistakable. *Ekklips.* He jerked around, but no one was there. Turning back to the mirror, the image of Ekklips had vanished, and so had his transformation.

Cautiously, he walked around to the next mirror. Waiting, he soon saw the image of Mora appear. Her evergreen eyes were lovingly gazing out at him; her skin soft and clean. Her auburn-brown curls fell down around her breasts, framing her face softly. A timid smile graced her face. He reached up to touch the mirror and she did as well.

"I'm sorry," he whispered. Her lips reflected his own as he spoke.

From behind his left shoulder, another image appeared. *Aloria.* Her stature, almost as impressive as his own, still held an endless beauty after eons of time. However, he felt a tinge of cold when she placed a fragile hand onto his shoulder. A tear ran down both their faces. Reaching up to touch her hand, he was disconcerted when he merely felt the soft linen of his tunic. Peering back at Mora, her eyes became sorrowful. A bitter sting overcame his heart as he heard a putrid laughter echo within his mind. He wiped the tear from his cheek and moved away from the mirror.

## The Keeper

Reluctantly, he stepped in front of the last, broken mirror. It was his own reflection, his eyebrows furrowed, violet eyes glowing, and fists balled. However, the subtle image of his mother manifested. He gasped. It had been nearly two centuries since he saw her, but her beauty radiated with the glory he had remembered from so long ago.

"The mirrors never lie."

A dark, seductive voice appeared from beside Bog, but he neither glanced to the side, nor winced.

"I have seen your desires. I have seen your heart. I know your mind. I also spoke of how you would return to me."

A sensual hand grazed across his hip, but then disappeared. After a moment, a cackle resonated in his ears, causing the hair on his flesh to stand on end. A thick cloud billowed in his mind as he recognized the other acidic voice.

"I was hoping I would see you again."

Esos appeared. Her hands caressed his arms and chest, sending a repulsive wave across his flesh. She batted her seductive eyelashes as he stood idle. He would wait for the opportune moment to strike.

"How I admire an immortal with a scowl," she whispered while her slender fingertips continued to traipse around his body and down toward his core.

Filled with insatiable rage for the whore who attempted to send Aloria to her death, Bog raised his hands and ran his fingertips along her exposed skin. Turning around to face her, he flinched at the slightly charred, scabbed skin on her cheeks, but continued to lightly dance his fingers over the sheer fabric on her breasts. She moaned in delight. While he could sense her desire, his disgust escalated exponentially. Sensually, his hands traipsed softly over her peaked nipples and climbed to her neck. With a slight embrace, he encompassed her neck between his large palms. Willing himself to caress her throat with his thumbs, he slowly increased the pressure.

Esos gasped and gagged, struggling for air.

He began to lift her off the ground by her neck. Kicking him violently with her feet and clawing at his flesh with her fingernails, she was met with a wall of tense muscle and throbbing veins. He was consumed by his thirst for revenge. Maliciously, he slammed Esos' head into the mirror. With a thud, she landed hard onto the stone. He spit on her body as it convulsed.

"Magnificent," a voice spoke in delight.

Bog jerked his head toward Ekklips. The black-garbed male stood tall with His hands behind His back. The unforgettable eyes he had met in his workshop were derisive. As He approached him, a darkness vibrated, growled, and clawed deep in his core. Standing eye to eye with Ekklips, the skin over his heart burned.

Passionately, Ekklips' hand grazed Bog's neck and around his jawline before running a hand through his hair. With a firm grasp on his hair, He held his chin high and raked His teeth below Bog's ear, drawing blood. A delicious purr trembled upon His lips. "Finish the job." Loosening His grip, He stepped back to peer at the delectable being.

Bog peered down at Esos, who was rubbing her neck and sneering.

Nervously, she fixated her eyes on Ekklips, unsure of the words He had just spoke.

Amused, He grinned. "He is no ordinary immortal, Esos. I have tasted power. It seems I have overlooked a far greater weapon to my cause."

"I will never join you," Bog gritted through his teeth.

"You already have," Ekklips cut His eyes and replied slyly.

"Never!" Bog lunged toward Ekklips before He was already by his side with a hand around his throat. He began to feel like his veins were on fire. Sparks were shooting with ferocity throughout his body and he dropped to his knees, writhing in pain.

Ekklips bent down to Bog's ear and whispered, "Even you cannot overcome Dark and Death." Grasping his hair once more, He licked off small trickle of blood from his jaw and added, "I will find out from whence you came."

Pulling Bog to his feet, He kissed his lips before releasing his hair. He muttered, "I have business to attend." He shot a deadly look at Esos and then back to Bog. "Besides, the pathetic cunt attempted to deceive me, thinking she would gain favor. Clean up your mess once you are finished." With the last word, He vanished through the waterfall of fire.

Angrily, Bog turned to watch Esos prop herself against the mirror, blood running down her face from the protruding glass shards.

She cleared her throat and said through uncertainty, "I'm sure we can settle this in some other way."

He snorted, "You bitch, I came to avenge, not compromise."

Esos grinned wryly and hissed, "Oh, aye, the old bird." She stretched her neck, rolling it around. "I merely did you a favor. She would have not lasted much longer. She didn't want to last longer. I simply assisted her."

He could see her eyes glaring with lies. Attempting to lunge at Esos, he retracted as the burning sensation in his veins seared. "You tried to murder her. For all I know, she is dead as we speak." His furrowed eyebrows sunk lower over his eyes. He clenched his fists and snarled, "Just as you murdered the other innocent creaturals in Ja Velco."

Esos snapped and slung her hand at his face, clawing him across the cheek. "There is no innocence in power!"

His ears pricked. The words echoed in his mind, for they were similar to what he had spoken to Mora not long ago.

"Life, Himself, is no more innocent than a sadistic psychopath. Lest you think otherwise, Death speaks truth, no lies pertaining to salvation, nor redemption in knowledge. With Death will come Enlightenment. For no one, nor nothing, can resist Death."

Feeling the fresh blood dripping down his cheek, he countered, "If Death is so powerful, why is there still Life? Do you merely believe one outweighs the other? Death cannot control Life, as Dark cannot control Light! Your foolish ideals will not poison my mind. I believe the Light will rightfully restore its place amongst the darkness and create balance."

He scowled at Esos, and, despite the burn, stepped firmly against her body. "Weakness of the flesh will never dominate the strength of the mind. For once the flesh is eaten away by the maggots of the land, the mind journeys through space and time, never ceasing to be amazed at its endless potential. However, balance needs to be met, and without Light, the mind cannot contain harmony with the Trinitas. Dark has only gained His knowledge through eons of imbalance in nature, and it leans in His favor. Although…" he paused and scowled at her, "He is becoming more Death, than Dark. You and I both know this to be true. Regardless, Knowledge and Enlightenment will be restored, whether I am dead or alive. I will make sure Mora illuminates All with her rightful place, separate from Ekklips."

She cackled and spat, "You cannot ensure it if you are *dead*!"

Stepping closer to Esos' face, her body secure between his and the mirror, he stared intensely into her dark brown eyes. He snarled, "Tell me, where are the bow and quiver?"

She laughed heartily and spit into his face. "Let your accusations fly! You will never lay eyes upon them, as you will never touch your feeble minded whore again!" Her teeth were stained with black blood as she sinisterly chortled, "You cannot defeat me, my immortality outranks your own feeble bloodline."

While staring eye to eye with a distracted Esos, he thrust a knife into her ribs. Grabbing her by the neck with his other hand, he pushed it further into her flesh. Forcefully, he yanked out the blade. She screamed in agony before resuming her laughter. Her laugh only fueled his rage. He thrust it into the back of her neck and was satisfied when her laughter turned to horror.

Wide eyed, Esos screamed, "It can't be!" A tear of black ran down her face until an emptiness consumed her eyes.

"You know nothing of my bloodline," Bog growled, letting her lifeless body fall to the stone floor, blood pooling around her head like a black halo. As he turned to leave, he paused, knelt, and fingered a couple of black petals gradually becoming contaminated with Esos' blood. Clutching one in his hand, he growled and bolted out the door.

Mora had waited for Bog to glance back toward her, but he leapt precariously into the battlefield. Alone again, she watched silently from the shadows. Borgorians, and the damned monsters alike, were slaughtered heedlessly on the stone walkway, arrows bellowing out of the air, swords and axes tearing flesh apart without restraint.

She knew she did not have long to decide what to do. *Should I run east as Bog instructed?*

A fallen Borgorian laid dead several footsteps from where she remained covert. His slitted cloak had been thrust over his head as he lay lifeless on his stomach. She crept closer to the body, outstretched her arms toward the cloak, and harshly wriggled the soiled material free of the body. Revealing a dagger, she also stealthily drug it into the shadows, placing it in her flimsy, string belt. The cloak was too large. However, it covered her perfectly from head to toe, leaving nothing exposed.

Staying close to the shadowed walls, she stepped with caution behind the rocks next to the Fortress. Keeping a watchful eye on the battle, she saw Korian fighting three Kryptoads. Each left its mark on his skin, but he never relented. Then, she surveyed for Remmi. Before she could find him, a voice reverberated loudly over the battlefield. All eyes glared toward Tenebris. Standing tall on the ledge over the mighty doors, was Ekklips. From where she stood, she could see His prominent scowl. His magnificent presence made even the most gruesome monster cower. The damned kneeled at His voice; the Borgorians stood frozen in their strides.

"Listen you godsdamn fools!" He bellowed. "Your bravery has been noted, but your foolishness is most prevalent. You cannot defeat Death! For whom do you fight? The female?" A horrible laugh echoed over the carnage. "Even now she abandons you in the time of need. But find her, and I will reward you with mercy beyond what you deserve!"

Disgusted, but nervous, she pulled the hood further over her eyes, turning to progress into the darkness. However, she gasped in horror when she saw a madly disfigured Grogan standing in her path. His teeth were dripping with saliva, rotten and black, and its glowing ears pulsated. It grabbed her by the throat with intimidating strength and lifted her high into the air. Wriggling for breath and kicking her feet ferociously against its mangled body, she felt defenseless. She desperately tried to slide her hand between its claws and her neck while attempting to grab her blade. It squeezed harder and bared its teeth in satisfaction. Suddenly, through her desolation, she felt a release and tumbled onto the ground as the top half of the Grogan slid onto the cold stone.

Remmi's white-blue eyes loomed against the Fortress and he hissed, "Your disguise is fallible. You must vanish inevitably."

"Where do I go if I know not where I am going?" she pleaded and glanced at the towering figure pacing on the top of the Fortress, hands clasped tightly behind His back.

## The Keeper

"You must run east and never look back." A bright blue light pushed her to the side as he leapt at three Kryptoads lunging over the rocks.

Nearly stumbling to her knees, she stood up and peered into the ever-looming darkness. Without immediately heeding to his words, she glanced at the Fortress. Ekklips was glaring in their direction. Panicked, she watched Remmi fall to his knee with an arrow straight through his chest. Another arrow pierced his stomach, followed by a third. Still gallantly swinging at his opponents, he never faltered.

"Run!" he sneered angrily.

She glanced back toward Tenebris. Ekklips had vanished. Not lingering any longer, she ran swiftly, tears stinging her face as the cave became icier, more desolate. The sounds of fighting and hollering echoed from behind her ears, spurring her further into the cave's menacing and dark embrace. Relinquishing the burdensome weight of the cloak, she glimpsed at her arm and saw fresh blood accumulating from the Kryptoad's strike. Numb from the cold and desperation, she could not feel the sting.

A slight shutter vibrated in the cloth fold of her tunic against her spine. Pausing momentarily, she reached a hand to the small of her back, fondled her gown, and retrieved the orb from inside the material. It had significant value to Ekklips, but she knew not why. *I must keep this close, keep it safe, and not allow Him to access the essence it holds. Nephani will know what to do.* Lighting it faintly with the thought of sunlight, she ran aimlessly through the darkness in the direction Remmi had pointed.

# Deliverance

*He's furious.*

Mora could feel it enveloping her, smothering her, weaving her in its spider-like tendrils to coax her into its intricate web. Occasionally stumbling on a jagged rock or a loose stone, her tread was consistent. She could not fully see where she was going, save for the faint circle of light from the orb, but she was being swiftly pulled to ascend by an invisible force. The horrible clash of swords and deathly screams could no longer be heard. While Bog had made the choice to disappear amidst the chaos and fighting, the thought of him made a tear trickle down her face. Swiping a quick hand over her cheek, Ekklips was rapidly advancing. She knew not how, nor how fast, but her mind was trembling with His rage. Holding the orb up to the wound on her arm, it was still bleeding, dripping onto the rocks as she passed. Worried He could smell the potency of her blood, she frantically looked around. *An outlet must be around here somewhere, Bog told me to run east and I trust him.*

Instinctively, she knew there was an outlet on the side of the caves. A familiar awareness danced in her subconscious, a strange feeling she could feel the pull of the moon, hear the twinkle of the stars, and smell the salt of the sea. Grounding her feet on the stones, she sensed a faint tremble of waves and heard the sound of water splashing fiercely against majestic rocks. The consciousness was growing stronger as she ascended the stone wall.

As she climbed a long ledge, grasping for protruding rocks to strengthen her hold, she slipped on water, loosing her footing. With her

*The Keeper*

breath caught in her throat, she regained her grip and pulled herself over the edge. Scraping her knees, she dropped the orb, accidentally extinguishing her connection with the light. It clanked on the stone, rolled, and stopped. With fervor, she scrambled around aimlessly, wading her hands through the shallow puddles as she progressed forward on her calloused and skinned knees. The sharp edges were grinding into her flesh against the bone. Silently, she screamed in frustration. *It has to be here! I heard it fall and stop on the rocks.* With force, she pushed her loose hairs out of her face and felt the surge of desperation escalate. The surface of the stone vibrated, increasing the longer she crawled. She reluctantly outstretched her hand every couple of spaces to feel for the cave wall, hoping to not hit her head against the stone.

Ekklips was advancing. As if she could feel His rage, her skin began to warm and prickle. Wiping sweat from her forehead, her heartbeat pounded behind her eyes and she started feeling nauseous.

*Give it back*, He hissed.

Feeling as though his words punched her in the stomach, she responded belligerently, *Come and retrieve it.* With a passion, she threatened to destroy the orb if He dared to force it from her hand.

*You don't know what you possess*, He responded with a dark tone, hinting of madness.

Then, she froze and realized she was directly communicating with Him through her mind. She had not noticed in her anger, but something had changed drastically when she entered His Fortress and stolen the orb. *This is dangerous*, she thought.

He growled deeply, *More than you will ever comprehend. You can't control it.*

*Fuck.* Immediately, she closed her thoughts, knowing she would need to learn how to intentionally shut Him out of her mind.

Even more frantically she searched for the orb, the rocks tearing cuts deeper into her palms and knees. *Tink!* She hit the orb with her fingertips. Extending her arm, she fondled the slick surface of the orb, grabbed it, and jumped to her feet. She couldn't illuminate it without opening her thoughts, but she was desperate. This time, a clear image of the crescent moon appeared in her mind and the orb emitted a subtle glow.

Ekklips chuckled.

### The Keeper

She glanced over her shoulder. Rapidly, she commenced to climb the ascending stones. Carefully, as to not drop the orb again, she saw a slight discoloration in the rocks above her head. Desperate for the freedom of the caves, she fingered the odd stone. *A hole!* Stretching her neck, she could smell the salty sea and hear the waves crashing. Clamoring out onto a thin ledge, her stomach twisted at the sight in front of her eyes. She was standing on a hardly visible stone protruding above a black sea. The sliver of moonlight revealed the white crests of torrential waves pounding against the surrounding rocks like the fists of angry giants. Glancing to her left, and then right, she concluded either way sang with utter death, but she had to try. Peering around her shoulder, she saw the vague outline of a swaying, rickety bridge connected to an obtrusively massive silhouette looming behind.

The cliff shook with enough violence, its clear intentions were to swallow her beneath the watery abyss. Taking a deep breath, she stepped warily to the entrance of the swinging bridge. Grasping the roughly cut, wooden stumps with both hands, she stepped onto the precarious planks, secured by rattling chains. The wind began to blow harder as she advanced over the relentless tendrils of water splashing through the cracks. Holding onto the chained rail, she forced herself through the wall of wind. She had the suspicion her presence was not welcomed, as though something was voraciously attempting to prevent her from crossing. The tattered soles of her sandals slipped across the splintered wood. She cried out in pain as a thin piece of wood cut through the sensitive flesh on the bottom of her foot. Catching herself on the chains, she continued across, limping slightly from the pressure. The wind whipped the water painfully on her face, stinging like needles. She was soaked to the bone. Tears stung her eyes and her body struggled for the strength she needed to escape. As if the orb would dissipate into the swirling mist, she clung it closer to her breasts.

In a pitiful whisper, she thought, *How will I escape?*

*You can't,* His voice responded plainly.

Steadying herself on the last plank, she held the light of the orb out in front of her, noticing a narrow path. She ascended the bumpy trail in agony, placing more pressure on her good foot. The increasing cold numbed her face as the mountain continued to shake intensely with the force of ten thousand giants beating their mangled fists against the stone.

### The Keeper

The salty spray of the sea stuck to her lips and her scratchy throat yearned for fresh water.

"Solora!" Ekklips yelled from behind.

Her heart skipped a beat in her chest and she stumbled on the path. He was on the mountain. Hastening her pace, she hobbled onto snow, the icy surface crunching under her bloodied and calloused soles. Whimpering as the intense temperature shocked her senses, she willed herself to persist through the tumultuous pain. The moon lingered above, faintly taunting the never-ending ascent. Then, in the distance, sporadic flashes of lightning rode vehemently across the sky, followed by a low rumble of thunder. Unanticipatedly, she halted, circling her arms to catch her balance. A cliff materialized at her feet. She could go no further. Gasping, she clutched her chest for breath, the orb pulsating in her palm. Hopeless, exhausted, and completely alone, she peered out over the black sea into the growing storm.

*I've failed. I have been selfish. I sought answers to questions, but never intently listened to the response. I was careless and spiteful, abandoned by my mother to survive a journey I never anticipated. I am hurt, I am stubborn, and I am in denial. Bog is more than a friend, but I didn't trust him enough to help me fight. Remmi and Abin have died for my escape. Zalana,* disgust trampled her stomach, *a heinous traitor. I'm lost and alone.*

"You're not alone," replied His sultry voice.

*He is here.* His footsteps became crisp behind her, His boots languidly crunching on the snow. Appalled with her circumstances, Mora turned around to face His silhouette.

He slowed down. "Don't be foolish. Did you really think you could disappear successfully in complete darkness?"

His beautiful smile radiated through the black night. It took her breath away.

"I am Dark, as you are Light, Solora."

"It matters not anymore. I stand on the cliff above the sea, on the precipice of despair, on the edge of failure." She looked Him straight in the eyes, knowing if she showed any fear, He would grasp onto it and hold tightly.

"Aye, you chose the path you would take." His grin was haunting.

"You've never trusted me enough to show you the light inside. Give me the orb and I will reveal the hallowed truth that lies dormant in the most concealed shadows of your mind." He held out a hand, aware she may make another rash decision if He attempted to move closer.

She sighed, fondling the smooth surface. With an absent grin, she held the orb in front of her eyes as the light made the snow glisten. "I have been foolish. I know my choices led me to this ledge. I threw those I admired and loved the most into danger." The orb's core flickered like a flame. "And you, you are allowing Death to become your soul's identity. True love is being replaced by power and manipulation."

Ekklips stood still as ice, but unaffected by the cold. His black hair whipped in the wind. "That may be, but I know who I am and whence I came." He grimaced. "I was here in the beginning and I will be here in the end."

When He took another step, the distant thunder rolled. She backed a little closer toward the ledge as a couple of rocks crumbled beneath her heel.

He stopped. "It wasn't *I* who chose to become Death. Life created the concept of Death. Life *was* Death. It was He who sacrificed part of His True Being out of spite and jealousy to form the concept the worlds know as death. It hasn't diminished His detestation for me. His accusations of my treachery have made me the monster you see standing in front of your eyes. His hatred fuels my vengeance, His jealously ignites my desire, and His impulsiveness strengthens my power. His sacrifice has made Him vulnerable. I seek to strike Him at His weakest." Seething at the thought of Life, He took another, slight step toward her, holding His hands up to caution her movement.

Feeling the muscles in her back and shoulders tighten, the shooting rigidity down her legs nearly made her knees buckle. Scrunching her face, she forced the question, "Who, or what is, Life?"

Her head pounded in rhythm with the giant waves, causing the tension to increase significantly behind her eyes and into her temples. Mustering what little strength she had left, she stood straighter. For the first time, she noticed an uncertainty flash across Ekklips' eyes, but it was masked immediately.

"For a millennia He has failed to intervene directly in All, but I feel Him, like wakening from a restless slumber. When He reveals Himself to me, there will be war." He balled His fists and hatefully spat, "But He cares nothing for you! The moment you chose to join me, Chaos manifested. He sees you as nothing else. Life has been made hard and ruthless. You will not create balance without me, Solora. Life will continue to wither away, devoured by my all-consuming darkness. Light will follow if you don't embrace your True Being. You will eventually be Chaos. Forevermore."

Lightning cracked diagonally across the black sky, caressing its bony fingers across the water, illuminating His perfect features and wild eyes. Thunder followed, vibrating the ground. A few more rocks tumbled from beneath her heels. She clenched her teeth. "And you will forever be Death. Always at war with Life. You will deteriorate your True Being once you embrace the ruthless inevitably Death holds, despite your claim as Dark."

Unable to hold back the tears any longer, she wanted to fight for what she believed to be right. "I'm not afraid of the dark, Ekklips. A wise being once told me your True Being is not evil, for one can't have Light without the Dark, and one can't have ultimate balance with Life if one doesn't embrace both. I'm finally willing to search within myself to find the light, desperate to discover from whence I came."

Ekklips stood silent, wondering if this was the moment He had waited so long to witness, to feel.

Opening her mind, she searched for answers. Finally, she closed her eyes and whispered, "I will discover why I am known as Light and what it means to be *Cuthos*. I can't do it at the constant threat of Dark and Death. Ekklips, you are embracing a path I am not willing to follow."

When she opened her eyes, He felt a surge of power for the first time in her soul. He gazed wondrously as her green eyes illuminated with passion. "Solora," He growled hungrily, "I…"

The lightning exploded overhead, the thunder booming and rumbling in unison with His voice. Even though her voice quivered, she spoke with conviction, "With whatever power I may possess in this moment, it is, and always will be, mine."

Flashes of her life raced through her mind at the speed of light, from the moment she was born, to the present. The faces included that of her mother, Marwen, Dresden, Adeline, Katheryn, Guilderon, Abin, Remmi, and Aloria. Bog, wingless and powerful, was the last image to flash. His eyes, like violets after a summer's rain, made her heart leap wildly against her chest. Any harder, it would break her ribs. However, his magnificent eyes had also suddenly possessed a dark secret, one she knew she may never discover. Outstretching her arms, tears overflowed from her doleful eyes. She clasped her hands together over the orb. The storm was now upon them, the lightning illuminating the surrounding area as the thunder shook in rhythm with the drumming waves. She could see Ekklips' features clearly, a lustful hunger transfixed on His face. With each streak of lightning, He crept closer.

Aware of her proximity to the ledge, Mora stepped as close as she could, holding the orb high above her head. Another storm bellowed and raged inside the orb, mirroring the tempestuous atmosphere. While a blustery wind encompassed her body, a faint pinpoint of light floated down from the abyssal sky. *Snow.* As if the world stood frozen, she lowered the orb and held out her palm. The delicate design landed sweetly into her hand. She looked close at the uniquely shaped snowflake. Its continual radiance melted into her flesh, leaving a faint glow beneath her skin. Her veins turned to illuminated rivers of light, twisting and turning through her body. Her hair vigorously lashed around her face, swirling with the surrounding vortex. She briefly glanced over her shoulder into the abyssal sea of black. Her heartbeat quickened and her blood commenced to boil. Warmth trickled freely from her open wounds. As her blood fell to the accumulating snow, she heard a faint sizzle. Turning around once again in the direction of Ekklips, the tunnel of light ceased and she stared bravely into the void of His eyes.

"Don't," He sneered and lunged. Hitting a wall of wind, the rage inside exploded. Suddenly, the whites of His eyes were completely swallowed by the dark as rivers of black veins surfaced from beneath His flesh. With arms thrown wide, He cried, "Solora!"

Sinfully smiling, her eyes flickering a radiant green, Mora held her arms wide open and released herself into the abyss.

# Epilogue

 In a forsaken country, a city forgotten from all time and thought, an old figure stood at a window overlooking the castle tower walls, overgrown with ivy and vine.

"Here is your drink, Papa." A young female set down a tray next to the old one.

"Ah, thank you Aiy'Anna. Will you please pour me a chalice of the wine?" With eyes as still as stone, he waved his hand to the side.

"Aye, Papa."

The young one, called Aiy'Anna, curtsied beside him, head lowered in reverence. She unstopped the wine bottle and poured a full chalice of sweet red. Placing it in his hand, she waited for him to speak further.

The old one put the chalice to his lips and his thin grin lit up his face. Nodding his head, he spoke gently, "Suitable. I must say, you are an exceptional young *dali*. Come, search the world with me." He gestured a winkled hand toward Aiy'Anna.

She stepped to the window and rested her hand on the back of the chair.

"Do you sense that youngling?" His nose was high in the air, a mysterious scent catching his curiosity. "My eyes may be void of sight, but my mind's eye has not faded with time."

She peered into his absent eyes and moved her soft hand to his shoulder. "What is it, Papa?"

"The light, *dali*, it has gone dim like my sight. I cannot sense its presence against my skin, but I can smell a change. What is it you see?"

"Dark Papa, the sun has set."

Pure carnage. The ground was riddled with bodies, both Borgorian and Death's monsters alike. Languidly, he walked amongst the bodies, pushing them over with his boots. A movement out of the corner of his eye caught his attention. He turned his head in the direction of the disturbance. A grin flashed upon his face and he jumped hastily over, offering his hand.

"It's about time you made it back, you bastard." His white-blue eyes blinked carelessly, trying to focus on the weathered face.

Then, casting a disconcerting look down at his own chest, he realized the arrows were still precariously protruding. He grabbed an arrow and pulled it carefully from his flesh. He winced. *It still hurts, no matter how many times it happens.* Grimacing, he pulled another, and then another, until they were all gathered on the ground next to him, six in total.

Rubbing his chest, he muttered, "It's becoming harder each time."

Gruffly, a hand patted him on the back. "I am truly sorry, mate. I tried to make it back in time. I was stalled. The fucker jumped ship right before the Falls, and I had little time to disappear before we hit the water." He shifted his weight and glanced around the grounds. "Where is she?"

Sighing, Remmi quickly scanned the Fortress. "I commanded Bog to release her in the hopes she would escape, but I fear it is too late." His eyes met the weary, dark brown of the other. Speaking plainly, he huffed, "We must make haste and find Bog, there is a great, unforeseen disturbance."

Moaning, Abin huffed, "The bloody bird dick?"

Pulling his gloves back over his scarred hands, Remmi peered beneath his eyelids. "Aye, if you only knew."

# About the Author

Brittany Dixon is a mother of two, wonderful childlings, artist, writer, and illustrator with a passion to whimsically traverse the world of imagination, creativity, and diversity in an ever-changing world of digital footprints and inescapable attention-seeking platforms. Her love for nature, mushrooms, Medieval Celtic and Norse mythology, collecting odd trinkets, and amassing unique jewelry helps her to fashion a fantastical world, exploring how the melange of humankind shapes our surroundings, beliefs, spirituality, and perception of purpose.

One day, she hopes to be a bestselling, fantasy author, children's book illustrator, and amass her own foraging farm where she can enjoy the company of a variety of fungi. Meanwhile, she hides in her own liminal space of enchantment to turn her dreams into reality. Whether she's entertaining herself with painting, jewelry making, reading, writing, traveling, crocheting, or merely sitting outside to watch the brilliant kaleidoscopic turn of each season, she delights in expanding and seeking new ways to express herself; while also enthusiastically encouraging her childlings to join her on her adventures.

@writersheroine